A TREASURY OF
GREAT HISTORICAL NOVELS

A
TREASURY
OF
Great
Historical
Novels

SELECTED BY THE EDITORS OF
READER'S DIGEST CONDENSED BOOKS

The Reader's Digest Association, Inc.
Pleasantville, New York
Cape Town, Hong Kong, London,
Montreal, Sydney

THE FOXES OF HARROW

A CONDENSATION OF THE NOVEL BY
Frank Yerby

ILLUSTRATED BY BEN WOHLBERG

When the Irishman Stephen Fox arrived in New Orleans in 1825, he was nothing but a penniless gambler with a fantastic dream and the iron determination to make it come true. With his uncanny skill at cards he amassed a fortune and built Harrow, the most magnificent plantation in all Louisiana. But the grandeur of the Old South was not to last. As the nation plunged headlong into the tumultuous conflict of civil war, the Fox family of the great house of Harrow began to show signs of coming strife.

The Foxes of Harrow was the first of many best-sellers for prize-winning author Frank Yerby. Others include *The Golden Hawk*, *Pride's Castle* and *The Dahomean*.

Contents

ABOUT FIFTEEN MILES above New Orleans the river goes very slowly. It has broadened out there until it is almost a sea and the water is yellow with the mud of half a continent. Where the sun strikes it, it is golden.

At night the water talks with dark voices. It goes whispering down the Natchez Trace, past Ormand until it reaches the old d'Estrehan place, and flows by that singing. But when it passes Harrow, it is silent. Men say that it is because the river is so broad here that you cannot hear the sound of the waters. But it is as broad by Ormand and d'Estrehan.

Yet before Harrow in the night it is silent.

It is better to see Harrow at night. The moonlight is kinder. The north wing has no roof and through the eyeless sockets of the windows the stars shine. Yet at night when the moon is full, Harrow is still magnificent. By day you can see that the white paint has peeled off and that all the doors are gone. But at night the moon brings back the white and the shadows hide the weeds between the flagstones. The Corinthian columns stand up slim and silver, the great veranda sweeps across the front, and the red flagstone swings in perfect curves through the weed-choked garden where once the cape jasmine grew, past the mud-filled birdbath and the broken crystal ball on the column to the smokehouse and the kitchen house and the sugar mill and the slave quarters.

You walk very fast over the flagstones and resist the impulse to whirl suddenly in your tracks and look back at Harrow. The lights are *not* on. The crystal and chandeliers are *not* ablaze. And there are no dancers in the great hall.

In the brick kitchen house it is dark. The great open fireplace, fourteen feet across, is silent and cold. But the small pots still stand on the trivets after eighty years, rust-covered but otherwise unchanged. And the ovens still stand on the hearth waiting for old Caleen to push them into the fire to bake her master's bread, humming softly under her breath.

It is no good to stay. So you come out of the kitchen house and walk very fast down the old wagon trail, until you come to the landing and untie the boat and yank the cord that starts the outboard coughing and barking and roar away downstream in the still water that is silent before Harrow. And you don't look back.

CHAPTER ONE

THE *PRAIRIE BELLE* came nuzzling up to the sandbar. The big side wheels slowed and the white boiling of the water stopped and the *Belle* came to a halt.

Stephen Fox fingered the single rich ruffle that stood out from his shirt front. His fingers caressed the pearl that gleamed like a bird's egg against the dark silk scarf wound about his throat. He put his hand into his pocket and came out with the golden snuffbox. Then he put it back again. To take snuff under these circumstances would have been a gesture, and Stephen despised gestures. For the same reason he kept his tall gray hat firmly on his head, although convention demanded that he at least salute the ladies.

"All right, Mr. Fox," the captain said. "Up with you."

Stephen stepped onto the single oaken plank that had been placed between the vessel and the sandbar. He strode along it very solidly, keeping every trace of jauntiness out of his step. That would have shown something—defiance, perhaps; some indication that what they were doing to him mattered. As he walked down the plank there was not the slightest sign in his bearing that the *Prairie Belle* existed or that the men and women lining her decks were alive.

A little murmur started among the passengers. Then someone said it aloud and another and another until they were all shouting it at the tall, slim man with the burnished copper hair who was standing on the muddy finger that lay one hundred yards from the left bank of the Mississippi.

"Cheat! Sharper! Card shark!"

The captain sighed a little and nodded to the second officer. "All right, Mr. Anthony," he said.

The bells jangled. Two great clouds billowed up from the high twin stacks and the great side wheels turned over once, twice, then took up their steady beat, the water boiling white beneath them. The plank was lifted and the *Belle* stood out for midchannel, heading southward toward New Orleans.

The captain spat into the yellow water. "A scoundrel, Mr. Anthony," he said. "A black-hearted scoundrel—but still . . ."

The second officer nodded. "But still a man," he said. "Very much a man—eh, Captain?"

STEPHEN FOX GAZED upstream. He had only two choices, and one of them he rejected at once. That was to swim ashore and make his way southward through the bayou country afoot. The second was more reasonable: he could stay where he was and take the chance of hailing some passing river craft and making his way to New Orleans in comparative comfort. His brows gathered into a frown as he gazed over the surface of the water.

In that year, 1825, there were still only a few steamboats plying the Mississippi, but there were hundreds of flatboats drifting south, and even a lonely keelboat or two. Stephen took out the golden snuffbox and poured out a pinch of brown dust on the back of his hand. He sniffed briefly up each nostril. The water talked darkly in the night, but he didn't listen. He walked back and forth, remembering London, Paris, Vienna, New York.

"A long trail," he said aloud. "But this time the trail ends—for good. No more wandering. It's the broad lands for me." He threw back his head and laughed. "Fine chance of that," he said, his clear baritone carrying out over the water. "A Dublin guttersnipe can't become one of the landed gentry—not even in this mad new land . . ."

He stiffened suddenly, listening. A sound came, far off and faint. "Hullo! Hullo therrre!"

Stephen lifted up his head and cupped his hand. "Hullo!" he called. "Hullo!"

"Where are you?"

"Here to your right—on the bar! For God's sake, man, make haste." A lantern glowed faintly from the river. Then the black bulk of a flatboat was looming up through the darkness and a strong smell came rolling in over the water.

"A pig boat! By Our Lady!" But Stephen knew he could not afford to be choosy.

A huge man with a patch over one eye was standing in the curving bow of the flatboat holding the lantern. By the saints, Stephen thought, a face like that would chase all the devils out of hell.

The flatboat touched the bar now and hung there, grinding. "Well, if this don't beat all," the lantern bearer said. "A gentleman, no less—all got up in top hat and fancy waistcoat. Who might you be, me fine lad?"

"I'm Stephen Fox and I'm plagued cold and hungrier than a grizzly. May I come aboard?"

"Now, that depends. First I think you better explain what you be doin' in the middle of the river."

"Well," Stephen said, "as one Irishman to another, I am a gambler. But aboard the *Prairie Belle* there were tinhorn sports who bore their losses badly. They complained to the captain, and here I am. Now may I come aboard?"

"Here's me hand. Up with you, me lad!"

Stephen scrambled aboard. The smell from the hogs was formidable, but no worse than that from the various members of the crew who came crowding around to examine him. He turned to the one-eyed giant who wore the red turkey feather in his hat indicating he had knocked down, gouged, bitten and spiked into unconsciousness half a hundred fierce flatboatmen. "A word with ye, Captain?"

The captain nodded his massive head. He was a huge man, all muscle. The two of them walked back toward the stern of the craft, past the hog pens, past the great oaken keg of Monongahela rye whiskey with the tin cup chained to it.

Stephen's hand swept up to his throat with a lightninglike

movement. When it came away, the golden setting at the top of the stickpin gleamed empty; the big pearl was gone. "Now, Captain," he said, "in my money belt there are thirty gold dollars. They are yours, and this golden snuffbox. Deliver me to New Orleans and ye get my coat and waistcoat and this hat."

The captain laughed. "Keep your duds," he said. "The box I will take, but I offer you this pewter one of mine in its stead. A man should not be without his snuff."

Stephen put out his hand and the captain took it. "Now if ye have something that a man might eat . . ."

"Right you are. Louie!" A hulk of a man whose spine curved over into a bow came into the glow of the lantern. "Fetch some grub for Mr. Fox." Louie shuffled off into the darkness and came back with a moldy cheese, a jug of whiskey, a loaf of stonelike hardness and a huge case knife.

Stephen scraped away as much of the mold as he could see by the flickering light of the lantern, and cut off a slice.

"Me name's Mike Farrel," the captain said. He brought out a battered cob pipe and lit it with flint and steel. "For forty years I've worked the river. The sights I've seen, lad, you wouldn't believe them. But all that is going now."

"Why?" Stephen asked.

"The steamboat. When it came, the river died. Afore then . . . the river was the place for men. Why, the ears I've seen chewed off and the eyes gouged out . . ." He sighed deeply. " 'Tis a good life," he said. "I don't regret it. But it could be that I'm aheadin' for the salvage docks. A man don't last forever."

"Ye're not old," Stephen told him. "I see ye still wear the red feather. It means ye're the champion of the river."

"Yes. I've held it nigh onto eight years." He sighed. "Me father brung me over from Ireland afore I could walk, and the two of us, we licked the river. Only it don't stay licked. It got the old man finally. It'll get me too someday. You know how it goes?"

Stephen did know, but he sensed also that the big man wanted an audience. Mike Farrel seemed intelligent and he was strong as a bull, a friend well worth making. "No," Stephen said kindly. "Tell me."

"You gets a consignment. Then you picks up a flatboat and ships on a crew. First you must knock their thick skulls together to let them know who's boss. Then you come driftin' down the river, avoidin' the shoals and the sandbars. Come night, be it fair, you keeps on. Foul, you ties up at some town and seeks out the bullies from the other flats and keels. Then you thrashes them one at a time."

"Always?" Stephen demanded.

"Always. 'Tain't safe for you or the crew till you prove your mettle. When you finally gets where you're goin', you sells the consignment and stays roarin' drunk for two weeks. Then you goes back and does it again. A fine life, if cutthroats don't get to you while you're passin' through." Mike picked up the jug of Monongahela whiskey that the flatboatman called Nongela, and drank deeply. He stood up. "Well, I'll see after me bullies now. See you later, Mr. Fox."

Stephen stretched out on the rough oaken planks and put his gray hat over his eyes. The little waves slapped against the sides of the flatboat as Stephen slipped down the river toward New Orleans, wrapped in a bright dream of broad acres and a huge white house set down among the oaks, not far from the water.

WHEN HE AWOKE, the sun was high in the heavens. The crew were lounging about, feeding the pigs and taking turns drinking the throat-searing whiskey. Their hairy, gigantically muscled chests were burned brown as teak. Seeing Stephen, they laughed.

"Have some Nongela," one of them called. "It's good for a fine gent like you!"

"Ain't he the swell, I ask you?" cried another.

"Maybe I should get him a little dirty?"

Mike Farrel raised a paw like a grizzly's. "Hush, me lads!" he said. "Mr. Fox is my guest and a paying one at that. If one of you touches so much as one red hair on his fine young head, I will cut out your liver and make you eat it!"

"I think," Stephen said clearly, "I'll go aft among the pigs. I find them better company."

"I theenk," a big Canadian half-breed said, "I theenk I keel heem now."

Stephen turned slowly and put his hand inside his coat. When it came out, a little double-barreled derringer lay loosely in his palm. The half-breed halted suddenly.

The rest of the crew broke into a roar of laughter. "Go on," someone said. "That little thing can't shoot!"

"Sometime I do it," the half-breed said. "Sometime I do it for sure!"

Stephen put the pistol back in his pocket and looked out over the broadening river. He turned to the captain. "How far?" he asked.

"Be there tomorrow," Mike said. "Afore noon, if all goes well."

That day they had more of the stone bread and rotten cheese. As an extra treat Mike ordered Louie to prepare some bacon. Stephen threw his overboard when the others were not looking.

The hours went by like the river, slowly. Then, as the creaking, clumsy ark drew nearer New Orleans, something very like a fever ran from man to man. The card games on the deck stopped and one by one the crew stood up and began to look downriver, not saying anything.

"Nawleans," Mike said to Stephen. "It's the wickedest city in the whole blame country. But once you've tied up along Tchoupitoulas Road, you'll always come back. That you will."

"I don't aim to leave," Stephen said. "A place of my own, that's what I want. A plantation. A big one."

"You aim high, don't you? Still, it is in my mind that you'll get whatever you go after. And when you do . . ."

"Yes?" Stephen said, smiling.

"A glass and a bed for old Mike Farrel when he comes ashore. Your promise, lad?"

"My hand on it," Stephen said.

"Good. Tomorrow we dock. A good night to you, Mr. Fox."

Nobody slept that night. The voices of the crew rose, quarrelsome, boasting. Then the sun was up all at once without warning and the city grew from a smudge on the bank to a cluster of tumbledown buildings. The crew was working the great oars now, angling the clumsy flatboat in toward the landing at Tchoupitoulas Road.

There were miles upon miles of flatboats tied up in rows so that they hid the banks. Then, miraculously, there was a hole, and the steersmen were sliding the flatboat in, the whole crew laughing and shouting at the top of their voices.

"There's a place that a man can get lodging hereabouts?" Stephen asked Mike Farrel.

"Aye—for about six cents you can get a bed, not too clean, all the whiskey you can drink and a wench to keep your back warm. But," Mike added, "you better not close an eye. For such

15

boots and such a waistcoat, they'd murder Our Lady herself."

Stephen looked at Mike. "I think I'll chance it for tonight. Tomorrow I'll start the long climb to repair my fortune."

"Well—come along with you then," said Mike.

The two of them walked across the flatboats until they came ashore. The urchins looked with openmouthed wonder at Stephen's fine dress, and the prostitutes sauntered out and clutched him boldly by the arm. He shrugged them off and walked on with Mike between the filthy, tumbledown buildings until they came to the Protestant Cemetery at Cypress and South Liberty streets.

"It is here that I take leave of you," Mike said. "If you have need of me, leave word at the Rest for Weary Boatmen. And, for the love of God, be careful!"

Stephen put out his hand. "It has been a pleasure," he said. "Don't worry about me, Mike. I can take care of myself."

"Aye—that I believe. But keep your pistol handy!"

Watching the big man roll away, Stephen felt suddenly very lonely. He went first to a dive called the Sure Enuff. He took a table, ordered wine and watched the play. The games were faro and roulette. In two minutes Stephen saw that the player had no chance at all. The wheels were fixed. Stephen paid the few cents that the watered wine cost and moved on. No, he told himself, ye must not play. 'Tis a beginning ye wish to make—not an end.

Then at last it was night. Stephen entered the cleanest-looking hostel he could find. "A room," he said to the bedraggled harridan who sat behind the bar. "How much?"

"A room he says!" she cackled. "A bed ye can have—the best in the house. But a room—think ye this is the Hotel d'Orleans?"

"I want privacy," Stephen said.

"I can give ye the grand bed with curtains for two bits."

"All right. Let's see it."

He walked behind the old woman through a large hall with twenty-five or thirty beds rowed off, so that every available inch of space was taken. About half the beds were filled, the occupants snoring lustily. In the center was a huge canopied bed of carved mahogany. Curtains hung down from the sides of it, drawn aside with cords. When they were dropped, his privacy would be complete.

Stephen gave the woman two bit pieces, the last coins in his pocket except for a few coppers. When she was gone, he sat down on the bed and drew off his boots and one of his stockings. His great toe was an angry red. He bent down and removed the big pearl from between it and his second toe. "Ye're my last hope," he said gently.

He lay back and sighed. A moment later he was asleep.

TOWARD MORNING the sound of voices woke Stephen. He groaned and propped his head up on one elbow, looking out through a slit in the curtains.

"So," a tall young man was saying as he yanked a pretty girl against his chest, "you hide the best ones, you old witch!"

"Maw!" the girl squealed. "Mama!"

"For her," the old woman said flatly, "it'll be two dollars extra—in advance!"

An older man, standing nearby, dug deep into his pockets and came out with a bill.

"Here's a dixie," he said, extending the New Orleans–printed ten-dollar note that was lettered in French with the word *dix* inscribed in the corners instead of the figure ten. Then he turned to the tall man. "Now, Hank," he said, taking out a wicked clasp knife, "just pass me over that little gal."

"I'll be double damned and pickled in brine 'fore I will."

Stephen sat on the edge of the bed and drew on his boots. Then he stood up, put the gray hat on his head and hung his coat, waistcoat and the dark silk scarf over one arm. He walked across the room, past the young man, who was hammering at his rival's head with a post broken from a corner of the four-poster bed, and with the other was making blue lightning with his slashing blade. As Stephen went out the door, the crash of breaking furniture and the screams of the women echoed in his ears.

Outside, in the street, he moved off slowly until the sounds were left behind him in the darkness. He smiled wryly. "A trifle strenuous, this town," he said.

It was still hours until morning, and Stephen stood on a street corner looking in all directions. Irresolutely, his fingers touched the handle of the derringer. By all the saints, he thought, just one thing more, just one, and I'll know I'm mad!

"Help!" a voice answered him like an echo, speaking urgently in French. "Help me!"

Stephen opened his mouth and let the laughter rocket skyward.

"I asked for it, by God," he roared.

"If you please," the voice went on.

"Where are ye?"

"Here, behind this wall. I've been robbed!"

Stephen put his hands on the wall and raised himself to the top. A young man was crouched on the other side, shivering in a shirt and silken underwear.

"Now I've seen everything!" Stephen declared.

The other said, "You speak French, do you not?"

"Not if I can help it. French sits uncommonly hard on an Irishman's tongue. *Mais, si vous désirez . . .*"

"But you sound like a Parisian!"

"That's where I learned it," Stephen said. "Now, I think we'd better do something about your trousers."

"Yes, but what?"

Stephen's slim fingers caressed his chin. "Is there a place near here where gentlemen drink heartily?"

"But of a certainty! Still, I don't see—"

"Listen, Mr. . . . whatever ye're called—"

"Le Blanc—André Le Blanc."

"Mr. Le Blanc, I don't have a sou. Neither, it appears, do ye. I intend, therefore, to bow to circumstance and—borrow a pair of trousers for ye."

"Monsieur, you don't mean . . ."

"The name is Fox—Stephen Fox. And we're only borrowing the trousers. Come along with ye now!"

André moved behind him in an odd half-cringing position. They turned a corner. Across the street yellow light was rolling out of the low windows of a two-story frame building richly ornamented with iron scrollwork.

"*Là,*" André said. "There!"

Even as they watched, several shadowy figures came out of the door. They were swaying a bit on their feet. André looked up at Stephen.

"Too many," said Stephen. "One man alone, and much, much drunker."

They waited. The slate-gray fog began to pale into morning. André shifted his weight nervously from one foot to the other.

"Now!" Stephen said suddenly. "Now!"

A fat man was staggering out of the door, singing to himself.

"A hand over his mouth," Stephen whispered, "and don't let go, even if he bites."

The two of them moved rapidly through the mist. When they were close, André's hand shot out and Stephen put his knee into the small of the singer's back and swept both his hands backward.

"Quick," he said to André. "His scarf!" André whipped it off with his free hand and gagged the victim. Stephen bound his wrists with his own scarf. Then they laid him gently upon the ground and removed his trousers. They both laughed.

Stephen ran his hands expertly through the fat man's pockets. He came up with a purse and several letters. "Name is Metoyer," he said, "and he lives on Poydras Street. Remember that when we go to abduct his wife and daughter."

"Give him back the letters," André said. "Now, how do I look?"

"Like a prince of the blood. But off with ye, we still have to bludgeon that old widow near the Ramparts."

"Shall I untie him?" André whispered.

"No. Let the police find him. He'll probably describe us as two of the most fiendish footpads that ever desecrated the city. A good day to ye, sir!" he added loudly. "I trust ye will sleep most comfortably!" The two of them moved off, arm in arm, leaving their clear laughter floating on the fog.

"We'll go to my home," André said. "First we'll breakfast, then we'll sleep an hour or two. Afterward I'll show you the town."

They turned down a number of twisted, ill-paved streets. Stagnant water stood in the gutters, and a smell rose up and struck Stephen in the face. He saw the bloated carcass of a dog floating in the cypress-lined gutter.

"By Our Lady!" he swore. "This is the filthiest hole! Don't the authorities ever—"

"No," André said. "And when it is hot, the people die like flies."

They walked along in silence. The sun was up and the morning mist had melted away. The streets were narrow, mere lanes, unpaved except for stretches of cobblestone, broken and irregular. The houses, Stephen saw, came down to the very edge of the sidewalks, and lacked walks or verandas. Most of them, however, had overhanging balconies called *galleries*, richly ornamented with wrought iron. André's house was larger and finer than any of the others. The massive oaken door opened directly onto the street. Inside, it was cool and dark, and even before his eyes had grown accustomed to the gloom, Stephen knew that it was magnificently furnished.

André's manservant took their hats and cloaks.

"Good morning, Monsieur André," he said. "Your father—"

"Is displeased. Papa is nearly always displeased," André said to Stephen. "I sleep in the daytime and prowl at night; that displeases him. I loathe planting. At La Place des Rivières—that's our plantation—I die of boredom. That displeases Papa. I won't get married. That doesn't displease Papa—it infuriates him." He turned to the servant. "Ti Demon, we'll have our coffee in the courtyard. And brandy. Come, Stephen—you don't mind if I call you that? It seems I've known you so long."

"Not at all," Stephen said.

Magnificent cut-glass chandeliers tinkled softly as they passed through the rooms to the courtyard, which was paved with blue-gray flagstones. Flowering oleanders grew in large jars and there were ferns suspended from the windows overlooking the yard.

André laced his coffee liberally with liquor, but Stephen drank his brandy first. Then as the warm feeling began to swim in slow circles in his head, he gulped the coffee quickly.

"Now we will sleep," André said. "All day if you like."

"Excuse me, Monsieur André," Ti Demon said. "But today is the celebration for the gran' general, the Marquis de Lafayette."

"Is it today? Well, we mustn't miss that, Stephen. Everybody will turn out. You'll see more of the gentry of New Orleans than ordinarily you could meet in a year." He stifled a yawn with the back of his hand. "Ti Demon, show Monsieur Fox to the guest chamber. Then I have an errand for you to run."

"Ye're sending back the trousers?" Stephen asked.

"But certainly." He put out his hand. "Sleep well, my friend. Ti Demon will awaken us before the parades start."

Stephen followed the lean figure of the black man through a maze of rooms and up sweeping flights of stairs. Then Ti Demon opened a door and stood aside. Stephen went in.

The chamber was richly decorated and in the center stood a massive canopied bed. Ti Demon crossed the room and adjusted the cover.

"Monsieur wants something?"

"Nothing now, thank ye. When ye wake me, some hot water for a bath, and a razor."

Ti Demon bowed silently out of the room. This was it, Stephen thought. To live like this—graciously, with leisure to cultivate taste and to indulge every pleasure. Leave the work for the blacks. Breed a new generation of aristocrats. New Orleans had it all over Philadelphia, which he had called home since he had come to America. That had been four years ago, when he had just turned twenty-one. Since then he had filled out, broadened. He knew what he wanted now: freedom for himself and his sons; mastery over this earth; a dynasty of men who could stride this American soil unafraid, never needing to cheat and lie and steal.

He pillowed his head upon his arm and slept.

As ANDRE AND STEPHEN MOVED slowly through the crowds, heads turned in their direction. There were not many men so tall as Stephen, and his coppery red hair was like a beacon among the dark Creoles. It was surprising, too, to see an American on so friendly terms with an aristocratic young Creole. The older Frenchmen shook their heads sadly, and spoke of it as one more evidence of the degeneration of modern youth. The American section of New Orleans was growing like a weed, crowding the lordly Creoles back into the old square, the original boundaries of the city. And the Frenchmen had had many sad experiences with the fierce flatboatmen, who fought with knives or fists, but never with a rapier.

"We might as well rest," André said. "The *Natchez*, carrying Lafayette from Mobile, won't be here for hours."

"All right," Stephen agreed. "I could do with a glass. What about that café yonder?"

"Heavens no! That's the Café des Améliorations."

"So? They have wine, don't they?"

"You don't understand, Stephen. The men that go there are old. They have old-fashioned ways. They see no reason why Louisiana should not still be a part of France. And perhaps they hate the devil himself no worse than they do an American."

"I could say I am not an American," Stephen said slowly. "After all, I've been here only four years. But I'm in no mood for quarreling. We'll go elsewhere."

"Good. I suggest La Bourse de Maspero."

"Maspero's it is then. Carry on, lad."

They used their elbows to make a way through the mass of people in the square, but they made little progress.

"It's not worth it," Stephen declared. "I vote we take our refreshments from the roadside like the others."

André shrugged and the two of them moved through the crowd to the place where a dark little Greek in an enormous crimson fez was selling oysters in the half shell and ginger beer and sherbet. When they came away, they felt full and vastly pleased with themselves. "*Estomac mulâtre!*" an old Negro woman called out as they passed. "Belly of mulatto! Come and eat!"

"Are ye cannibals too in this country?" Stephen asked.

"One moment," André said, turning to the old woman. "*Tante!* Give me eight pieces of mulatto's belly!" He gave her a coin. The old woman put her hand inside the basket and came out with eight small round cakes, smelling of spices, still hot from the oven. "Here," André said to Stephen. "Four for me and four for you. Our mulattoes have delicious bellies, do they not?"

"What a name to give gingercake! Now I know ye French are crazy!"

"Perhaps. But there is another of our products—look!"

Stephen turned. A group of young girls dressed in bright colors was slipping through the throng like gayly chattering songbirds. They carried no parasols, and their lovely young faces were bared to the sun. Strangest of all, they wore the bright tignons of the slaves on their heads instead of the bonnets of the Creole ladies.

"They're dressed like blacks," Stephen said.

"They're quadroons. Their fathers and grandfathers—"

"Were white. While their mothers were like the one who sold us mulatto's belly. I don't see how ye Frenchmen do it, André."

"You haven't been here long. You'll acquire your own pretty little *placée* before many moons, I'll wager."

"Never," Stephen said flatly. "Never."

The crowd jostled them along the Place d'Armes. There was the sound of a cannon booming, and all the people surged forward at once.

"That's it!" André said. "The *Natchez* has docked!"

Stephen let his eye wander over the throng to where the coaches, barouches, landaus, phaetons and cabriolets waited. There the women were dressed in watered silk and India muslin; there the

little bunches of curls bobbed over each shell-like ear as they smiled and talked, while their beribboned parasols nodded deliciously.

"They're coming," André said. "There's Lafayette! That's Mayor de Roffenac with him, and Joseph Duplantier . . ."

But Stephen wasn't looking. A saucy little green-and-gold landaulette had come flashing up to the square, drawn by two spanking bays. Stephen's eyes swept past the horses and coachman. "Who," he demanded, "is *that?*"

André turned. "You have an eye for beauty," he said. "Those are the Arceneaux sisters. In my opinion, the two loveliest girls in New Orleans."

"I didn't ask ye about both of them. That one—with hair like night cascading out of God's own heaven, unlighted by a star— that one. The girl I'm going to marry!"

"Not so fast, my friend. Her name is Odalie. And every man of wealth and distinction in New Orleans has already asked for her hand. I would suggest that you try someone a trifle less difficult— say the Crown Princess of England."

"Hang your suggestions! Ye're going to present me—now!"

"I'm sorry, my dear friend, but that is quite impossible. Here, in this public square, it would be the height of impoliteness. I'm not at all sure Odalie wouldn't cut me dead for even associating with a *mauvais* Kaintock."

"I'm not from Kentucky!" Stephen snapped.

"To a Creole," André said gently, "all Americans are from Kentucky—and they're all bad. And let's be frank, my good Stephen. You're penniless and something of an adventurer. At the moment, your chances with Mademoiselle Odalie Arceneaux are exactly nil. I'd say wait. Fatten your purse, distinguish yourself somehow. Then—who knows? Truly many have failed; but they were none of them like you."

"Ye're right, lad," Stephen said. "I'll go slowly. But I'll wager ye a thousand dollars that I'll marry the girl!"

"Done!" André said. They shook hands, and André turned back to the square where the eloquent Bernard de Marigny was describing the valiant aid that Lafayette, the great soldier of France, had brought to the infant Republic of which Louisiana was now a part.

Stephen studied Odalie with half-closed eyes. She seemed to be completely captured by the most eloquent spokesman of New France. But the pink of her clear, shell-like earlobes deepened. The color mounted to her face. Still Stephen stared.

André turned to him. "For my part," he whispered, "you've chosen the poorer one. The younger sister, Aurore, is more beautiful. You don't see it at first, nobody does. She is so much softer and sweeter. Odalie, with her imperious ways, overshadows Aurore; but the beauty is there—and it's from the heart."

The speaking was done now, and Stephen and André made their way through the multicolored throng. As they passed the Arceneaux landaulette, André lifted his hat. Stephen bowed. Odalie nodded stiffly, but Aurore both inclined her head and smiled so that the soft brown cluster of curls waved about her ears.

Stephen and André turned and walked toward André's house. Ahead, the street narrowed, the overhanging galleries almost meeting, so that the light was dim. Suddenly Stephen halted. Before him, a diminutive shop window was jutting out halfway across the banquette. In it were displayed rings, pins, pendants, ornamented dueling pistols and snuffboxes galore. Stephen's eye wandered upward to the sign, *Mont-de-piété*, which swung on a green shingle in letters of tarnished gold.

"André," he said, "would ye mind proceeding without me? I'll join ye in half an hour."

"Yes," André said. "I mind very much. You're my guest."

"I have things to do, lad, and plans to make—some of them not fit for your young eyes. I'll join ye within the hour—truly."

André bowed a little, very stiffly. "I'll leave you. Pawn your back teeth if you like!"

Stephen stood a moment looking after his new friend's retreating back, then turned into the pawnbroker's. It was close and the air had a musty smell. The pawnbroker was a fat little man, swart and oily of skin, wearing the huge powdered wig of the last century.

"M'sieur wants something?" the broker began.

"For this pearl—how much?" Stephen loosened the spring-catch setting of the stickpin. The huge milky pearl caught the light and spun it into a rainbow.

"One hundred dollars," the pawnbroker said.

" 'Tis worth all of twenty thousand and ye know it."

"Cinq cent dollar?" the broker said hopefully. "Five hundred."

"One thousand," Stephen said. "And ye're not to sell it for thirty days. Agreed?"

"It is my life's blood," the pawnbroker wailed. "Perhaps M'sieur would take eight hundred . . ."

"One thousand in gold."

Stephen held the pearl higher. Now it was milky, now like snow; now it was seafoam breaking white on the crest of a long green wave; now it was moonmist riding the face of the river.

The broker waved one hand weakly in assent. "A thousand dollars," he mumbled, "in gold!"

Stephen took the little canvas sack, heavy with gold pieces, and strode from the shop, his fair brows knitting into a frown. "I'll have ye back," he muttered, "and soon!"

ANDRE WAS WAITING when Stephen returned, his dark face still and unsmiling. Stephen looked at him and grinned. "I meant no offense, André. What I had to do was painful, even to me. Ye'll forgive an old boor?"

"It's nothing," André said, taking the offered hand. "*Ma foi*, but you're a trying one!"

"And now ye really can help me," Stephen said. "I'll need rooms, and a tailor. And a manservant, if ye can purchase a good one."

"Your ship from the Indies has arrived, no doubt?"

"No," Stephen said slowly. "No, André, the voyage has just begun."

CHAPTER TWO

THE STREET SOUNDS drifted up through Stephen's window. He opened one eye lazily, blinking at the brilliant autumn sunlight, stretched out his legs luxuriously and yawned. A soft knocking came from the door.

"Come in," Stephen called; and Georges, his newly acquired manservant, crossed the room, his black face lit with a pleased smile. It was six months to the day since Stephen had stepped ashore from Mike Farrel's flatboat.

"Good morning, master," Georges said, putting the tray down on the bedside table. As usual, there were several kinds of meats, cooked *à la grillade*. Georges had also brought biscuits and steaming piles of *pain perdu*—slices of bread dipped in beaten eggs and milk and fried in deep fat.

While Stephen ate the huge breakfast, his mind was busy with a thousand schemes. So far, everything had gone well. Slowly, cautiously, he had begun to make his pile, utilizing the one skill he possessed. Certainly he had come to the right place; New Orleans was a gambler's paradise. Everyone played, and they played every known game. The Creoles liked vingt-et-un and écarté; the Americans played poker, faro, roulette, and the new game called craps, a name shortened from the contemptuous appellation *Johnny Crapaud* that they gave to all Frenchmen.

Stephen did not often play with the Creoles. When he did, the stakes were small, and he lost more often than he won. With them and with the more prominent Americans, he succeeded to some extent in creating the impression he wished to implant—that of a gentleman sportsman who played for love of the game. With others, however, the steamboat captains, commercial travelers, merchants and the raw German immigrants, Stephen could afford to be merciless. They were people of no import, their fates not likely to be noised abroad. So the stacks of silver dollars grew behind the lean fingers holding the fanned cards. The crisp green bank notes fluttered across the table through the blue haze of tobacco smoke. And Stephen pocketed them smiling, saying apologetically, " 'Tis the run of the cards. Better luck next time!"

He had redeemed his giant pearl from the pawnbroker, and Lagoaster, the celebrated quadroon tailor, had turned out for him several outfits, all of a quiet elegance that commanded respect. Yes, he had done well. His moves could become bolder.

Stephen finished his breakfast and Georges helped him dress. His mind was weighted with conflict. He'd gone into business with Tom Warren and was doing well. Now John Davis, one of the many white refugees who had escaped the murderous uprising of the blacks of Santo Domingo, was planning to build two palatial gaming houses, and Stephen had a chance to invest in the venture. Gambling, because of the Creole temperament, was a sure investment. Still, while the Creoles laughed and jested with gamblers, they did not invite them to their houses. And the Mademoiselles Arceneaux were Creoles . . .

THAT NIGHT STEPHEN attended the Théâtre d'Orléans, where he vainly scanned the boxes for a glimpse of Odalie. He even peered suspiciously at the *Loges Grilles*, the enclosed boxes that encircled the elevated parquet, although he knew full well they were reserved for people in mourning and pregnant women.

At the end of the first act he left, having made certain that neither of the Arceneaux sisters was present. In the street he took out his massive gold watch. He groaned aloud. Now there was barely time to reach the Café des Emigrés, where Hugo Waguespack awaited him. What a terrible player the huge German planter was! There was no pleasure in playing him and absolutely no risk. He turned his steps toward the café.

The German was waiting. The play went on for two hours, with Stephen winning constantly. He looked across the table at Hugo with revulsion. Six months of this now—six months of gazing across the tables of little smoky back rooms into stupid faces. However, the risks of testing his skill against an opponent of intelligence, discernment and taste were too great. He *had* to win. His whole future was at stake.

"Enough for tonight?" Stephen asked the German, whose face was florid, flushing to crimson below his flaxen hair.

"No!" Hugo growled. "Seven thousand you have already from me. If I thought . . ."

Stephen looked at him, his eyes as cold and blue as Hugo's own. "Ye bring your own deck. I've told ye I never cheat at cards, but if ye persist in disbelieving me . . ."

Hugo's little eyes wavered, half lost in his enormous face. "All right," he said. "One more round. My lands upriver, against all I've ever lost to you. A single hand and I'm done with you. Either way I'm done—win or lose."

Stephen shrugged. "Agreed," he said. "But ye may have a month to raise the money. After that I'll take the land. I want to be fair."

"You seem damned sure of winning," the German growled.

"I am," Stephen said. "Ye play badly." He put twenty bank notes upon the table, all one-thousand-dollar bills. Then he extended his pewter snuffbox, but Hugo waved it aside.

"That is a hideous thing," he said. "I wonder that you keep it."

"It's lucky," Stephen declared, his slim fingers caressing the pearl that gleamed softly at his throat. "I exchanged a gold one for it—and I've never regretted the swap. Cut for the deal?"

"No. You deal. I trust you that far."

The play went on, first one player turning a trick, then the other. When they had exhausted their hands, Hugo said, "All right, score it up."

The result was as Stephen had predicted. Hugo stood up, slamming the cards across the table.

"You aren't quarreling?" The two of them turned. André was standing in the doorway of the little back room of the café.

"No, monsieur," Hugo said. "We aren't quarreling. I don't quarrel. That is a sport for children. Good day, Monsieur Le Blanc and Monsieur Fox. Your servant!" Hugo walked past them out of the small room.

"I don't like that man," André said.

"Nor I," Stephen agreed. " 'Tis the last time. Tomorrow I'm quitting this for good. A few transactions at Maspero's, and then . . ."

"Mademoiselle Arceneaux? You haven't changed your mind about that, Stephen?"

"No. I saw her again yesterday in Chartres Street with that sister of hers. Ye know, André, she almost nodded. The sister, however, returned my salutation like an old friend. Too bad it isn't the other way around."

"If you'll condescend to leave this hole," André said, "I have a surprise for you. In fact, he's waiting for us now at La Bourse de Maspero: Vicomte Henri Marie Louis Pierre d'Arceneaux."

"The father?" Stephen's eyes were suddenly cold, intent on far distances. "Yes—that would be the way. A friendship with the old one. Yes. Ye're wise, André—and a very good friend."

"It is time, Stephen. You're becoming quite a figure in New Orleans. Many ladies of high birth have dropped discreet hints in my presence for information about your background."

"Including Odalie Arceneaux?"

"No. But tonight we're taking the first step."

They passed down the narrow streets under the oil lanterns swinging on heavy chains. At Maspero's a number of Creole and American gentlemen sat at the small tables, talking and laughing in the friendliest possible manner.

"Yes," André said, seeing Stephen's raised eyebrows, "the barriers are going. We are both learning it is better to get along."

André inclined his head. An old man sat alone at a table, pulling at a long-stemmed pipe of white clay. His face was as brown as an Indian's and his hair gleamed silver. Heavy white brows jutted imperiously over a nose like the blade of an axe. He wore a scarf of white silk, and his coat was of maroon, richly brocaded. André stopped before him and bowed.

"Monsieur le Vicomte," he said in French, "have I your permission to present my good friend, Etienne Reynard?"

The old man nodded a bit, his black eyes boring into Stephen's.

"I am called Fox, monsieur," Stephen said deliberately, "and my first name is Stephen. Your servant, Monsieur le Vicomte!"

The thin lips twisted into a grim smile. "You are right," he said in old French. "Make no apologies for your name. It is a good one. André thinks I'm an old ogre. That is why he translated it."

"And are ye an old ogre?" Stephen asked, smiling.

"Upon occasion. You speak French well, young man. André tells me you learned it in Paris. What were you doing there?"

"What does one usually do in Paris, monsieur? Gambling, wenching, anything to amuse oneself . . ."

Pierre Arceneaux threw back his head and laughed. "I have done the same thing when my father gave me the Grand Tour. For my education, you understand. I educated myself with every well-turned ankle on the Continent. I've heard it said that you're a gambler, Monsieur Fox."

"Ye heard rightly," Stephen said. " 'Tis a profession not without honor. But I am leaving it for good."

"Why?" the old man demanded. "I couldn't think of a more fascinating life."

"One grows older," Stephen said quietly. "And the blood cools. There are things a man wants: a home, a wife, children. Perhaps I aim too high, but the sort of girl I'd take to wife would not ordinarily marry a gambler. I am currently in business with a Mr. Warren, a sort of brokerage, sir."

"I see," the old man said. The black eyes regarded Stephen steadily, and something very like a smile played about the corners of the thin old mouth. "You don't mind advice, my son?"

"Not at all."

"Then look to the land. This of business—stocks, bonds, mortgages, holdings—is but little better than the cards. Get your roots in the earth and grow with it. When you've done that—with your looks and manners—there's not a house in Louisiana that will not welcome you. Now, Monsieur Gambler, what say you to a little game? You play écarté, do you not?"

"Yes," Stephen said.

André was conscious almost at once that Stephen was playing badly. When the game was over, he had lost a cool thousand to Monsieur Arceneaux, who was beaming and boasting of his skill. "We must play again soon," he said to Stephen. "I must give you a chance to recoup your losses."

"Very well." Stephen smiled. "Wednesday night, perhaps? Monsieur Maspero will hold the little room for us."

"Wednesday night it is. It was a pleasure, Monsieur Fox."

"The pleasure was mine, sir," Stephen said.

The old man touched his cane to the brim of his hat and strode through the doorway.

"Couldn't you have been a little less obvious?" André said. "An imbecile could play better écarté!"

"Next time I'll win a bit, but always allowing him to remain about three hundred ahead. I think my father-in-law is an agreeable old fellow, don't ye?"

"But you shouldn't have admitted being a gambler. Old Arceneaux will never sanction a connection now."

"We'll see, André. Who knows? I'm off to bed now—alone," he added, seeing André's mischievous grin. "Tomorrow, I want ye to come help me. I'm seeing Mr. Warren in Chartres Street at seven o'clock. Ye'll meet us there?"

"Seven o'clock—*mon Dieu!*"

"Nevertheless, I shall expect ye. *Au 'voir,* André."

"*Au 'voir.* Seven o'clock, upon my word!"

André wandered off, shaking his head.

THE SUN SLANTED low through Chartres Street as André stumbled along at half past seven in the morning. The mist had come in from the river, and under the galleries, where Stephen and Thomas Warren waited, the shadows were a cool blue.

"Ye're late," Stephen said sternly.

"Late? Impossible!" André said. "How can one be late before eleven? My God, what a head I have!"

"If you'll come in," Thomas Warren said, "coffee might help."

"A thousand thanks!" André said. "You are Monsieur Warren, no doubt?"

"Forgive me, André." Stephen smiled. "This is my friend and associate, Tom Warren, who is broker, factor, entrepreneur—in fact, all things to all men."

André took Warren's hand and looked up at him. Tom Warren was a big man, all of two hundred pounds and more than six feet tall. His hair was very black and his eyebrows grew straight across his nose, so that his small, rapidly shifting green-gray eyes were almost hidden by them. His voice had a hearty quality that, oddly, struck André as being carefully controlled.

They went through a doorway shaded by an overhead gallery. Inside, the room was furnished as an office. "My living quarters are above," Tom Warren said, going ahead of them up a stairway into rooms that were neatly, if plainly, furnished. "Delphine!" he called. "Is the coffee ready?"

A pretty mulatto girl came into the room bearing a tray with cups, saucers and twin silver pitchers, one with coffee and the other with scalding milk for café au lait.

"And now, Mr. Fox," Warren said, "perhaps you'll explain the reason for so early a visit."

"That land along the river next to the Waguespack place, Tom," Stephen said. "I want it."

"I've already purchased it for you, Mr. Fox. Fifteen hundred acres at twenty dollars an acre."

"Ye paid cash?"

"No. You could not spare that much cash, sir. I gave a note against the crop."

"I see. Now ye must purchase blacks for me. Good ones, well trained. I'm going to become a planter, Tom."

"Your friend Herr Waguespack plans to put the bulk of his slaves up for auction in order to raise money to prevent a foreclosure on his place. I think we'll be able to name our own price. By the way, you hold that note against Herr Waguespack, don't you, Mr. Fox?"

Stephen looked at him, his blue eyes very clear. "Ye're a fast man, Tom," he said slowly. "I've only held that note since last night."

"It's my business to know things fast," Tom Warren said. "I'll buy that note from you at any reasonable price."

"No," Stephen said. "No."

"Then foreclose! Waguespack is a good planter. With his already cultivated lands you could make that crop with ease."

"I gave him thirty days," Stephen said.

"In writing?"

"My word." Stephen's voice was very low, but the tone was unmistakable.

Warren's face flushed a dark red. "I see. Then we'd better proceed with the other things. You'll need machinery: crushers, vats, ploughs, scythes—"

"Get them. Give a note against the crop." He stood up.

"And *our* business?"

"I'm staying in it. I never desert a friend, Tom. Ye know that. Now, let us be off. I want André to see how our business works."

The three went down the stairs and out into the street.

"This is good news," André said, "tremendous news! I'll see that it reaches the right ears."

"No. When it is done, it will speak for itself. Until that time I pledge ye to silence. When Mademoiselle Arceneaux sees Harrow, her blood will thaw. Old man Arceneaux called me a gambler—well, this is it, the biggest game of all for the highest of stakes."

They were approaching the river now. The waters close to the shore were covered with flatboats, lying side by side.

"See the jug of Nongela tied to the pole in the center of that boat?" Tom pointed ahead. "That means they're open for business." He walked rapidly in the direction he had indicated.

As André and Stephen watched, several men, richly if not tastefully dressed, began to converge on the clumsy vessel. "Brokers," Stephen said. "They bid for the contents and the boats. But we always outbid them—if it is worth our while."

"You bid for flatboats?"

"Yes. Or rather Tom does. We break the boat up for lumber, and we market the cargo at public auctions, getting much more than we paid for it. I have that old pirate Mike Farrel holing up in Natchez. He sends word by the fastest packet of what boats passing there are bearing. When they get here, we are ready. Lately we have bought all the wheat we can lay our hands on."

"Why wheat?"

"One must have bread, mustn't one? I daresay, my good André, that every ounce of wheat that the steamboats don't bring in will soon be in our hands. When the millers start in to make the new batch of flour, they'll buy from us, at our price."

"And the price of bread will go up," André said half to himself. "And hungry children will go hungrier. You know, Stephen, you have the makings of a scoundrel in you."

"A man can't grow wealthy on a squeamish stomach, André. But here comes Tom back again."

"I closed it," Warren said, "for three thousand. It will be worth eight or ten when it hits the market. Shall I proceed with the machinery for the plantation?"

"Yes. When is the sale of Waguespack's blacks to take place?"

"One week from tomorrow. Now, if you don't mind, I'll take my leave of you gentlemen. I have a few errands to run. Good day, sirs." He lifted his hat politely and was gone, striding down the levee.

"A strange man, your Tom Warren," André said. "Yet he seems very devoted to your service."

"Tom is as good as gold," Stephen declared. "Now, what say ye to a long ride to Harrow—my new place. 'Tis all of fifteen miles. It sits on the river between d'Estrehan's and Waguespack's, and it's the most beautiful spot this side of paradise. By the way, did I tell ye I've bought a horse?"

"No. But then, you never tell me anything. Where is this steed of yours?"

"Being groomed at present. Prince Michael is a palomino from Texas. He has a coat of buff satin and a mane and tail of silver. I want to try him over a distance. Come with me on the ride."

AROUND NOON THAT same day André rode his horse to Stephen's place, where he was introduced to Prince Michael. He looked the palomino over critically before turning to Stephen with a smile. "Now I know you're a liar," he said. "You've sworn by all the saints in heaven that you dislike show. Yet you buy the showiest horse that ever these eyes have seen!"

"Perhaps the time has come for show," Stephen said. "Besides, he is a good horse, sound in wind and limb." Prince Michael whinnied and stretched out his long, graceful neck toward Stephen. "See? Already he knows me."

Soon they were off, trotting briskly along the river front, headed northward away from New Orleans. They rode in silence, admiring the great expanse of land on both sides of the water—thousands of acres of virgin land of almost unbelievable fertility, as yet untouched by axe or plow.

Then Stephen was reining Prince Michael to a stop. "This," he said, "is Harrow."

André looked out over the tangled woodland. Wild cane and palmetto stretched out for endless miles. In the center of the uncleared land was a grove of stately oaks trailing streamers of Spanish moss. Off to the south was a cypress grove.

"Lovely, isn't it?"

"Lovely?" André groaned. "It's impossible! It will take you three years to clear enough of it for even a small crop."

"Ye forget I'm not a Frenchman, André. I have no real aversion to hard work." He swung down from the saddle, knelt and dug his fingers into the black, rich earth. "The new Harrow," he said, "and such a place as the old one never was!"

"There was another Harrow?" André asked.

"Yes. 'Tis in Ireland not very far from Dublin." Stephen's blue eyes looked past André out over the face of the river. "A place of mist and cloud and a gypsy sun. Rains whispering to ye in the night, and the greenest sod ever granted to the hands of mortals . . ."

"You lived there and you loved it. Why did you leave?"

Stephen stood up and looked straight at André. "In the first place," he said, grinning wickedly, "I'm a bastard."

"I've often thought so." André laughed. "But go on."

"No, I mean truly. I was born out of wedlock. My mother never told me who my father was."

"That's nothing." André chuckled. "Old Arceneaux swears that my family and his and nearly every other of any account in Louisiana are descended from a band of female thieves and prostitutes who were brought from La Salpêtrière, a house of correction in Paris! But, you were going to tell me why you left."

"Had to," Stephen said. "I got possession of a certain article of value." His fingers strayed upward to the great pearl gleaming softly at his throat.

"You—you stole it?"

"No. I won it gaming. But my opponent was the son of a man highly placed in life. The pearl was his father's. I merely wouldn't give it back."

"Why not, Stephen? That would have been the simplest way."

"I don't know. There's an alchemy about the thing." Stephen was silent for a long time, watching the river. " 'Twas not its value that I wanted. I've lain in gutters with my belly caved in with hunger, holding the pearl in my fist when it would have brought me food. I've fought like all the devils in hell to keep it. I've never owned it, André; always it has owned me."

"You talk riddles, Stephen."

"No—truly. It was not to be sold. It must be worn. I think I always knew it could only be worn by a gentleman. I went up to Dublin, 'twas the best place to hide. I slept in the streets, and lived by begging and stealing. All the time, André, this was with me, driving the restlessness in so deep it can never come out. This seems mad?"

"Of course not. Please go on."

"After a half-year I apprenticed myself to a printer. I slept in a loft over the presses, and he allowed me to take up books to read by a stub inch or two of candle, after my fourteen hours of work."

"My God!" André said. "When did you sleep?"

"I didn't. Ye have no idea what a starved young mind can make a body do. I read all the classics, setting them up in fine type. Before I left, I could read the principal modern tongues and falter through the ancients. But, ye see, the printer had a daughter off in England at school. She came back, André."

"And that was the finish." André laughed.

"I read Horace to her. The Odes. But one day the old man found in her things a free translation from Sappho—inscribed in my own fine hand. 'Twas one of the more passionate fragments, and the printer concluded that perhaps his daughter knew the way to my dingy loft."

"And did she?"

Stephen looked at his friend, one eyebrow lifted mockingly. "The virtue of a woman, André—and her age—are never topics for discussion. In any case, I was impelled onto the wet cobblestones by a hobnailed boot against my rear. So I stowed away to England. My only connection there was a wine merchant in London. He taught me to play cards in order to win back the miserable wages he paid me. Under the circumstances, I had to learn to beat him at least some of the time. He used to journey to Italy, Austria and the South of France to obtain his wines. I went with him. He was quite fond of me. But in France the need for fine raiment grew upon me. The girls, ye see, were most affectionate. So I began to win regularly and he discharged me. 'Twas then I started my wanderings with nothing but the cards and my fingers' skill to sustain me. I wore the pearl in France for the first time, feeling as though I'd committed a sacrilege. But I brazened it out." He paused, frowning a little. "I'm still brazening it out."

"But when you have held your land," André asked, "will you then be able to wear your pearl in comfort?"

Stephen scooped up a handful of earth and let it run like water between his outstretched fingers. "In one year," he said, "I shall clear this land of debt. In the next I shall build me such a house as was never matched in the Old World or the New."

André looked at him long and searchingly. "Yes," he said at last. "Yes, I believe you. You cannot be stopped. You must drive forward, because you can't help it. It is a terrible thing, Stephen. Sometimes I pity you."

"Save your pity," Stephen said, rising. "Fools that we are, we brought no lunch. But I have an idea. We are not far from the lands of the gigantic Hugo. Let us presume upon his hospitality. For some good German cooking right now I'd endure even Hugo."

They turned their horses' heads again northward.

The tangled woodland dropped away abruptly and before them stretched cleared and cultivated fields. Every tillable inch of ground was laid out in precise, orderly rows.

"*Ma foi!*" André said. "That Waguespack is a planter."

But as they approached the house, all order disappeared. Debris littered the yard, and four flaxen-haired children, dressed in rags, played with the swine.

The door of the house swung open, teetering perilously on its one remaining hinge, and a buxom young woman came out, her eyes glancing every half-minute in the direction of the fields.

"Good day, gracious lady," Stephen said in German. "We are friends of your husband's, and we want to see him. But we have ridden many miles and are very hungry . . ."

At the sound of the *sehr hungrig*, the woman nodded rapidly.

Inside the house the furniture was falling to pieces, but the rooms were fairly clean. Frau Waguespack seated them at the big table and busied herself before the huge grate.

"In the house!" André exclaimed. "She cooks inside!"

"And what's wrong with that?"

"In the city, nothing. But on a plantation where there are no fire brigades—a kitchen house of brick at least one hundred yards away from the house. Remember that, Stephen, when you build."

Frau Waguespack was approaching the table, huge stacks of pancakes piled in steaming golden mounds on the thick china plates. She brought coffee and butter and a pitcher of syrup.

"Good," Stephen said after his first bite, then: "Very good, indeed! What are you called?"

"Minna—Minna Wagonsbeck."

"Wagonsbeck?" André echoed.

"That is Hugo's name," Stephen said. "Waguespack is Frenchified." He turned to Minna. "Thanks for your kindness. And now, if you will tell us where we may find your husband . . ."

Minna's blue eyes wavered. "Out there," she said. "In the southwest fields, but—do not to my husband say that you have been here. Please!"

"Do not worry—Minna," Stephen said to the girl, for she was scarcely more. "I'll say nothing!"

It was a short ride to the fields. As they rounded a cypress wood, a group of Negroes came into sight, digging furiously, laying the long stalks of cane end to end in the furrows. "Never," André declared, "have I seen blacks move that fast! I wonder . . ."

As if in answer they heard the singing whine of a lash, ending in a crack like a pistol shot. Another half-turn and they were upon him. Hugo Waguespack pulled up his nag savagely. "Good day, gentlemen. This is an unexpected honor!"

"Your blacks," Stephen said without ceremony. "I hear ye intend to sell them. I'll buy the lot—now."

"No, Monsieur Fox," Hugo said, smiling. "I fear your sentimentality. You'd spoil them to the man."

"My God!" André said. "He's beaten them all!"

"Only ten lashes apiece," Hugo said. "I'm humane, Monsieur Le Blanc. Besides, your friend should be pleased that I take such excellent care of lands so soon to become his."

André had got down from his horse and was bathing the face of an old Negro, who lay prostrate on the ground, with water another slave had brought from the spring.

Hugo climbed heavily from his horse. "One moment, monsieur," he said politely. Then, with slow deliberation, he kicked the old man in the ribs, not quite hard enough to break them.

"You're a dirty swine!" André said.

"Softly, monsieur," Hugo said calmly. "It would be very convenient if you provoked me into a duel, wouldn't it? You know that I have no skill with the rapier or with the *clochemarde*. And people would never know that you were killing me so that your friend, Monsieur Fox, could get hold of my land and my slaves."

André struck him then, hard across the face.

"André!" Stephen said.

"Don't worry," Hugo said calmly. "I will not give him the pleasure of killing me. Now, may I suggest that you gentlemen cease delaying me?"

"Swine!" André half wept.

"Come, André," Stephen said. "Come."

CHAPTER THREE

STEPHEN'S KNEES FELT stiff kneeling in the pew at Saint Louis Cathedral. The mass that Père Antoine was reciting seemed unusually long, and Stephen was having difficulty following it. Half a dozen times he rose late, and André, at his side, could not entirely repress a smile at his friend's flounderings.

Part of the trouble, André knew, was that Stephen had not been to confession or mass in six or eight years; but the overwhelming cause of his inattention was kneeling devoutly just across the aisle, her slim fingers busy with her rosary. Truly, André was forced to admit, Odalie was a beautiful creature.

Now André turned his head slightly to the left. Stephen was sitting tall in his seat, his blue eyes caressing Odalie. André stared recklessly. Yes! This time he'd caught her! The black eyes had shifted for the tiniest part of a second. The glances had crossed in midair like épées! Now again, thrust and parry. Beyond her, Aurore too was watching, and her young face, angelic in its sweetness, was shadowed by an indefinable expression.

When mass was over and the parishioners were filing out, Stephen said, "I'm afraid that the blessings of Mother Church are not for me. Never could my knees stand the kneeling."

"You're a thoroughgoing pagan, Stephen. I think your patron saint is Aphrodite."

"Ye were watching me, then?"

"And the Arceneaux. The glacier begins to melt. I'm going to lose that thousand. Look. Here come the two Graces now."

The carriage came abreast slowly, moving in a swarming tangle of vehicles. André and Stephen both removed their hats and bowed. Pierre Arceneaux saluted them gravely in return.

"Come here, gentlemen," the old man called. "I want you to meet my daughters. Odalie, Aurore—Monsieur Fox. You know André already."

Stephen bowed. "The hope of this honor," he said in perfect French, "has been the one thing sustaining my drab existence."

"Do you customarily go around staring at girls, sir?" Odalie asked boldly.

"Only when they're as beautiful as Mademoiselle," Stephen said. "Therefore I can truthfully say that I've never before stared at a woman."

"My daughters have no manners." Pierre chuckled. "They're just like me!"

"Please forgive her, Monsieur Fox," Aurore said softly. "She's had her way for so long that she forgets to be ladylike. Everybody spoils her—even I."

"How could they help it?" Stephen murmured. "But you, mademoiselle, does no one spoil you?"

"No one," Aurore said, and her voice was genuinely sad.

"An oversight that I shall attempt to remedy at my earliest opportunity," André declared. "Your permission to call upon Aurore, Monsieur Arceneaux?"

"Ask her. My girls have been reared very independently."

"May I, Aurore?"

"Of course, André. You've always been like a brother to me."

"I had imagined as much," André said sadly.

"And I, mademoiselle," Stephen asked Odalie. "Might I?"

"No. Later, perhaps. I shall have to know you much better."

"You're both welcome at my house anytime you choose to call," Arceneaux declared flatly.

"Thank you, sir," Stephen said quietly. "But ye'll forgive me if I don't avail myself of your courtesy until such time as I feel my welcome is unanimous. Good day, monsieur. Good day, ladies. Your servant!"

As SOON AS he and André reached the auction block the next afternoon, Stephen knew the bidding was lagging. The auctioneer kept mopping his forehead with a large cotton handkerchief and looking out with disgust at the tiny crowd before him.

"Gentlemen, please!" he shouted. "I have here a prime field hand, sound of wind and limb, capable of the hardest kind of labor!

I ask you to look him over, gentlemen. Now what am I bid?"

"One hundred dollars," Tom Warren said calmly.

"Do I hear another bid, gentlemen? Look at the muscles of his arms! Why, he could do anything, gentlemen, anything!"

"Right," a voice behind Stephen declared. "Even murder!"

Stephen and André both turned.

"I say," Stephen demanded. "What did ye mean by that?"

"The truth is, stranger, the whole shootin' match of them was brung in from Santo Domingo. They've seen other blacks kill white men and maybe they've kilt some themselves."

"I thought the importation of Saint Domingue blacks was forbidden," André declared.

"It is," the man said. "But they was smuggled in. That Waguespack were a smart one."

"You'd better stop Tom from buying them!" André said.

"No," Stephen said quietly. "No."

Tom Warren was walking forward now, approaching the auctioneer. "Mister," he said, "tell you what I'll do. I'll buy the entire lot off of you for five thousand."

"Five thousand! Are you crazy? Any three of them field hands there are worth that much!"

"Take it or leave it," Tom Warren said.

The auctioneer was looking imploringly from face to face. Every face stared back at him coldly, tight-lipped and grim. "All right," he said weakly. "I'll take it."

Suddenly André gripped Stephen's arm. "Look who's just arrived!" he whispered.

Stephen turned. In the square was the green-and-gold coach of the Arceneaux. Stephen walked over to the hitching rail where Prince Michael was tethered. He released him and swung into the saddle.

"Miss Arceneaux has looked down on me for the last time," Stephen said grimly to himself. "This time she is going to look up!" He reined Prince Michael in sharply so that the palomino danced sideways as he drew alongside the coach.

"Monsieur Fox," Pierre Arceneaux said, "don't tell me you're buying Negroes!"

Stephen saluted the two girls, then turned to the old man. "I've just bought the whole lot," he said.

"What," Odalie asked, "does a gambler need with blacks?"

"Perhaps to gamble with, mademoiselle," Stephen said. But Tom Warren was riding up.

"Pardon me, ladies," he said. "Shall I take the slaves out to your place, Mr. Fox?"

"Yes," Stephen said. "But let them rest today. Hugo didn't treat them any too kindly. They'll need time to recover."

"As you say, sir. Good day, ladies. Good day, sirs."

The long line of Negroes filed past to the carts waiting across the square. As they passed, an old woman suddenly broke from the line and ran up to Stephen breathlessly. "Master," she cried. "Good master. You good man, the good God bless you!"

"Thank ye, *tante*," Stephen said. "What are ye called?"

"Caleen," she said. "I will serve you well, master!"

"Very well, Tante Caleen. Run along now with the others."

"You have a way with Negroes," Pierre Arceneaux declared. "They'll work well for you."

Aurore had stretched out a slim hand and was gently stroking Prince Michael's satiny coat. "I don't think I've ever seen a horse quite that color."

"They're rare," Stephen said. "I'm glad ye like him."

"So," a heavy voice said, "the grand Monsieur Fox on his elegant horse conversing with elegant ladies!"

Stephen only half turned.

"Ye're drunk, Waguespack. I want no quarrel with ye."

"Yes, I'm drunk. I'm verree drunk, but I'm not a fool! Think you I don't know it was your Tom Warren who spread that lying rumor about my slaves being from Santo Domingo!"

"I know nothing of that!" Stephen said. "And I must trouble ye to remember that there are ladies here."

"Ladies?" Hugo mumbled. "Oh, yes, there are ladies in Louisiana, are there not? All beautiful and spirited. A trait no doubt inherited from their famed ancestors, the correction girls!"

Old Arceneaux's mouth came open with an explosive outrush of air. André, who was at that moment riding up, took off one of his gloves and reined in toward Hugo. He was about to challenge the German, but Stephen stopped him with a lifted hand.

"Very well, Hugo," he said wearily. "Ye win. I'll meet ye at any time and place ye see fit. My seconds will call on ye to arrange the details. *Au 'voir*."

"'Voir!" Hugo grunted. "You'll make a very pretty corpse."

"Monsieur Fox," Arceneaux roared, "I demand the honor of seconding you!"

"And I also," André said quietly.

"Thank ye, gentlemen," Stephen said, then to the girls, who were sitting breathless and round-eyed on the edge of their seats, "Your forgiveness, ladies. This episode was not of my choosing."

Aurore suddenly laid her hand on Stephen's arm. "Don't," she said. "Don't meet him!"

"Don't be silly," Odalie said. "He has to meet him now!"

"But he might be killed!"

"Then," Stephen murmured, looking at Odalie, "the world will have lost a gambler, a blackguard and an ogler of women." He swung Prince Michael in a circle and trotted off.

"I don't like this," André blurted. "I'll wager that Hugo will choose pistols. And the fat swine is a deadly shot, while Stephen . . ."

"Is a poor shot, André?" Aurore's voice was taut with concern.

"That's just it: I don't know. I never had occasion to find out, but it's desperately late to be discovering it. Shall I meet you within the hour, sir? It is a long ride to Waguespack's."

"Yes." Then, lowering his voice to a whisper, old Arceneaux bent toward André's ear: "Think you we can arrange for the small swords? I like that red-headed devil!"

WHEN ANDRE RETURNED to Stephen's rooms, it was after midnight.

"*Mon Dieu!*" he cried. "That swine Hugo insists upon pistols, Stephen, and we could not dissuade him!"

"Why did ye try? No harm can come to me. I'll pink him a bit— a ball through the arm, or perhaps the kneecap to give him an illustrious limp, and that will be . . . What is it, Georges?"

"A message, sir, from Monsieur Warren. He says to come quickly. Your warehouse is on fire."

Stephen was out of the bed in an instant, drawing on his trousers. "Saddle Prince Michael," he said to Georges.

The sky toward the river was an angry orange-red as the horses thundered through the dark streets, and Stephen and André could hear the brazen clangor of the bell in Saint Louis Cathedral warning the sleeping city. Then suddenly they burst into the full glare of the fire. There was a compact crowd of men near the front of the warehouse, and Stephen could see Tom Warren towering over all the rest.

Stephen reined Prince Michael in, dismounted and strode over to the little group.

"It was set, Mr. Fox," Warren said heavily. "Deliberately and maliciously set. This here black . . ."

Stephen followed the pointing finger downward. The Negro was stretched out dead at Tom Warren's feet. "Ye shot him?"

"Yes. He was coming from the warehouse, the torch in his hand."

"I gave ye credit for more head, Tom. Now we will never know who sent him."

"There were another one," one of the other men put in. "He run out just afore this one come out. I seen him."

"No," Tom Warren said coldly. "You're mistaken. There was only one."

"I coulda sworn—" the man began doubtfully.

" 'Tis of no importance," Stephen said. "The question is, who sent him?"

"I think," André said clearly, "that you need not be lenient with Waguespack tomorrow, Stephen."

"But we have no proof," Stephen said.

"Who else could it be?" Warren asked.

"Who else?" Stephen echoed, and turned his face toward the flames that were billowing upward, bloodying the sky.

UNDER THE OAKS of morning it was cool and green. The sun was struggling with the mist, and everything was touched with un-clarity, like figures in a dream landscape.

"You know the terms, gentlemen," Dr. Lefevre said. "You're to fire one shot each at the count of three. If neither of you is hit, you may reload and fire again, or you may choose the wiser course and consider yourselves satisfied. Are you ready?"

"Yes!" Hugo said. "Yes!"

"Yes," Stephen said very quietly.

"One!" Dr. Lefevre said; and Hugo jerked his pistol level, aiming carefully. Stephen left his dangling at his side.

Mon Dieu! André and Arceneaux said in the same breath. "Why doesn't he . . ."

"Two!" Stephen's pistol remained unmoved. Hugo pulled the hammer back with a click that to André seemed as loud as a shot.

"Thr—" Dr. Lefevre began, but the rest of the word was lost in the crack of Hugo's pistol. The whole world was suddenly a sick dizziness to André. When it cleared, Stephen was still standing there, swaying a little, but inch by inch, with deliberate, terrifying slowness, his pistol came level, pointing at Hugo.

Little beads of moisture began collecting on Hugo's forehead. Then his gigantic fatty body started trembling all over so that even Stephen, thirty yards away, could see it through the red curtain closing down over his left eye where Hugo's ball had laid open his scalp.

There were three things he could do, Stephen decided without haste. He could point the pistol skyward and spare Hugo with a grand gesture. Or he could fire his shot straight downward with abysmal contempt. Or he could deliberately miss Hugo, but by so little that the German would carry with him always, branded on his brain, the whistle of the passing ball.

So it was that at the exact moment when André, unable to contain himself longer, cried out, "For God's sake, man, fire!" Stephen, without seeming to take aim, pulled the trigger, pointing to the left far enough to miss Hugo as he now stood, but not far enough to miss the huge bulk as Hugo threw himself downward and to the left to avoid the anticipated path of the ball. Then the big man was hanging there; he opened his mouth to say something, but the blood gurgled up through his throat and he went over backward.

Dr. Lefevre knelt briefly. "I think, gentlemen," he said, "that the less said about this affair, the better—considering the unusual features of the occasion."

"What do ye mean?" Stephen asked coldly.

"The length of time between shots," the doctor said. "The abundant opportunity you had to spare this man's life—to wound him slightly, or to let him go free. I came to see a duel, not an execution!"

"Take that back!" André cried. "Or I'll demand satisfaction."

"Softly, André," Stephen said. "There has been enough bloodletting for one day. The good doctor is entitled to his opinion. And now, sir, if I may trouble ye to stanch this scratch, I have work to do."

MINNA WAGUESPACK SAT huddled before the fire, weeping. Outside, it was raining, a hard, steady downpour, and the ancient door groaned on its one remaining hinge until at last the wind slammed it shut. Then came the clap of the horses' hooves in the courtyard. Pray God he's not drunk, Minna thought.

But the footsteps were lighter than the heavy boots of Hugo, and a light, almost gentle knocking sounded on the door. "Who is it?" she called.

"Herr Fox," the clear baritone answered. "Let me come in!"

Minna sprang to the door. Stephen stood swaying in the doorway, his face drained of all color; the water streaming down the sodden bandage was tinged with crimson.

"*Ach Gott!*" Minna cried. "You're hurt!"

"A scratch," Stephen said. His eyes sought and held hers. "Your husband, Minna—is dead. I've killed him. There was a duel. I—I tried not to hit him, but he moved. If there is anything . . ."

But Minna was looking at him closely. "You're hurt. Sit while I make you some hot rum punch."

"But you don't understand, Minna. Hugo is dead. I've killed him! Don't you—don't you care?"

"Yes. Hugo I loved. Very much I loved him. But this thing I have expected for a long time. Always he was quarreling with the men. What happens, happens. For this thing, I am sorry. And most of all I am sorry that it had to be you."

"Minna," Stephen said, "ye can stay here. And the children, I'll send ye money for them as long as I live."

"You're good. . . . But no, it is too much. Pay for me and the children the passage to Philadelphia. I have an uncle there who wants me in his bakery. He long ago told me not to marry Hugo, but I was young, and a fool."

"Then I'll send a coach for ye," Stephen said, rising. In the doorway he paused. "I have your forgiveness, Minna?"

"Yes," she said. "Go with God!"

By the time Stephen got to Harrow, he was shaking with weakness and the chill. Tom Warren was waiting, surrounded by a huddle of wet, miserable Negroes, shivering in their ragged clothing. Warren pointed to a row of open-faced lean-tos. "That's the best I could do as yet, sir," he said.

" 'Twill have to do, Tom," Stephen said wearily. And then with a wry smile, "Which one is mine?"

"God forbid!" Warren declared. "You're coming back to town with me. Why, in your condition, it would mean your death!"

"I'll chance it, Tom," Stephen said. " 'Tis late, and there's much to be done. But I have a commission for ye. Hire a coach and bring it to Waguespack's place by eleven tomorrow morning. And book passage on a steamer for Minna and the children. Give them a thousand to tide them over. I'm paying them for the place."

"Seems to me that Waguespack's children are no concern of yours, Mr. Fox. After all, you held his note . . ."

"Please do as I ask," Stephen said sharply.

"All right, sir, but your debts now are upward of fifty thousand and your assets practically nil. I've held aside enough to pay for whatever machinery you'll need and added a bit of my own . . ."

"Thank ye, Tom. I shall not fail ye."

Tom Warren mounted his horse and turned in the direction of New Orleans. Stephen stood in the pouring rain and looked over his land; never in all his life had he seen a more dismal sight. From the Negroes around him came something like a moan.

"Get ye inside," he said harshly. "And warm yourselves!"

He bent his head and entered one of the lean-tos. A smoky fire struggled bravely with the damp wood. He laid his cloak upon the wet earth and stretched out beside the fire, his head throbbing and his stomach sick with hunger and weakness. From outside came a faint whimper. Looking out, he could see a mulatto girl and old Tante Caleen, shivering and soaked to the skin. This was the lean-to that had been built for them.

"Come in," he said. "Ye're no good to me dead of lung fever!"

Timidly the two of them came in past the fire. Then, without a word, the old woman went back out into the rain. She was gone almost a half hour, but when she came back, her arms were full of dry twigs she had dug out from under branches and roots.

In a little while she had the fire blazing merrily, so that Stephen could feel the stiffness and the cold stealing out of his limbs. He stretched himself out on his cloak and slept.

When he awakened, it was to find his head being bathed very gently with a warm, soothing liquid. Tante Caleen took a strip of cloth, torn from one of her petticoats, and bound up the wound, pressing an odd sort of leaf inside the bandage against Stephen's torn flesh. Stephen could feel it drawing out the inflammation and the fever. He felt stronger. "Thank ye, Caleen," he said. "Ye're the best of the lot!"

He looked out of the opening and saw that the rain had stopped; the sun was already up over the river. He got up and called all the Negroes together. "We must work hard," he said. "Nobody is to be beaten. Ye obey my orders promptly and all will go well. If not, I'll sell ye back to the Germans." Then he put Tante Caleen and the other women to work making corn bread. The children he sent to dig crayfish from their castlelike mounds near the river. Soon the slaves were crowded around a huge iron pot, blowing on their bread and scalding their fingers as they scooped up the crayfish.

Stephen sat on a fallen log, a little apart from his people, and Tante Caleen brought him his corn bread and crayfish. When the Negroes had eaten, Stephen stood up again. "Ye men," he said, "go to the wagons and get axes. Start in here, next to the river, and clear the land in squares."

Some of the Negroes nodded, but others looked blank, so Stephen repeated his orders in French. Then they filed away, toward the wagons and the ox carts, and stood there in line while a gigantic black passed out the axes and saws.

They've been well disciplined, Stephen decided. And that big one, he has the makings of a leader. "Ye there!" he called. "Come here!" The big Negro ambled over, looking down upon the white-bandaged head of his master. "What are ye called?" Stephen demanded.

"Achille, master," the Negro replied.

"Well, Achille, ye're captain here. When I'm away, ye're to see that the work goes forward. There must be no laziness and no shirking. Take these men and clear away the palmetto first."

"Thank you, master." Achille smiled. Then he turned fiercely to the others. "I'm the captain!" he growled. "You work good for me, yes!"

The others looked at him and grinned, but almost at once the air began to ring with the sound of the axes and scythes.

CHAPTER FOUR

RIDING OUT TO Harrow, early in the summer, André felt the sky was dropping down over his head. The heat came up from the road in shimmering waves, and the Spanish moss trailing from the oaks was bleached white and dry as hay. He wondered idly if Stephen was angry with him. Not since the day of the duel had they met. He shrugged his shoulders listlessly. He must chance Stephen's anger, that was all. The road was curving now, and this was the beginning of Harrow, though it was yet two miles to the grove in which Stephen intended that his manor house should stand.

Then at last the fields came into sight. André pulled up his horse with a gasp. Stephen had nearly half of the visible acreage cleared and under cultivation, and mounds of cordwood lay stacked high all the way down to a freshly built steamboat landing. Long rows of cabins made of slashed cypress board housed the slaves. Under the stately oaks André could see a rude oaken house, larger than the others, but just as crude.

He rode on past the house and out into the fields. There he saw that one of the workers was white, his hands and arms covered with freckles. *"Mon Dieu!"* André said. "So it's true!"

"André! I thought ye were sick or dead!"

"But no! Stephen, Stephen! *Ma foi*, how terrible you look!"

Stephen grinned, the great scar on his temple glowing scarlet, angling upward into his red hair. It gave him a curiously diabolical look. He pushed back his wide-brimmed straw hat. "What are they saying about me in New Orleans?" he asked.

"They no longer blame you for the duel," André said. "They have discovered you are mad. They say you live in a hovel, and work in the fields with the blacks."

"And for that I am considered mad?" Stephen laughed. "Listen, André, I owe more than seventy thousand dollars for the land and supplies. I have to pay it back."

"How? Does money grow on trees at Harrow?"

"No—but it comes from trees. Ye've seen my landing? And the cordwood? Practically every other steamboat on the river stops here for fuel. By the end of the summer I'll have sold seven thousand dollars' worth of wood. And the supply, my good André, is practically inexhaustible. But ye, where have ye been hiding?"

"The truth is, Stephen, I've been spending my time in vain pursuit of Aurore. Even Papa approves. In fact, everybody approves—except Aurore."

"Poor fellow," Stephen said. "Come, let us go up to the house for a drink. By the way, how is Odalie?"

"Rumor has linked her name to half a dozen beaux, but you know, Stephen, I think she's waiting for you. Why don't you take a day off and come in to see her?"

"Too busy," Stephen grunted. "Ye may tell Mademoiselle Odalie for me that if she wishes to see me, she knows the way to Harrow."

"I'll do just that"—André grinned—"if only for the pleasure of seeing her fly into a rage. But what on earth is that?" He pointed to a new red brick building some distance behind the house.

"The sugar house," Stephen said. " 'Tis waiting only for the machinery I've ordered. I'm having steam crushers, André. All the bigger planters are putting them in. But here we are—up with ye, lad. I'll have Georges bring us wine from the spring."

They sat in the bare-boarded room sipping cool wine. The lines about Stephen's eyes were deeper, and his whole face seemed older somehow, quieter and more certain, André thought.

"This year and the next, André—by then, I will have made it, or I will have failed. At the moment I'm not sure I care."

"You won't fail, Stephen. Whether what you'll win is worth the struggle, I don't know; but you won't fail." He rose and walked to the doorway. "I must be going now," he said. Then he paused, grinning wickedly. "I'll deliver that message."

ONE DAY FUSED with the next and Stephen lost all track of time. But the cane and cotton grew, and in the sugar house all the kettles and tanks had been set up and were ready.

Stephen worked in the fields alongside his slaves and wondered if André had delivered his message. All day and far into the night they picked the bursting pods of cotton, piling up the bales by the steamboat landing.

Then it was fall and almost time for harvesting the cane. Stephen rode through the fields next to the road. He was hatless, and his shirt was open halfway to the waist. The breeze from the river blew across his face and stirred his coppery hair. He pulled Prince Michael to a stop and looked out over the expanse of his fields. *His* fields! The cotton crop had brought in nineteen thousand dollars. And when the sugar was sold . . .

He stiffened suddenly, listening. From the roadway came the sound of hoofbeats. A horse was coming up the road, and as it neared, Stephen could see that the rider was riding sidesaddle on a sleek black mare, beautifully groomed. But Stephen was looking at the rider and his blue eyes were bright in his sun-whipped face. "Odalie!" he said.

"Yes, monsieur. The mountain is come to Mohammed."

"I'm flattered and honored," Stephen said.

"You needn't be. Perhaps I came to see the mad planter who holds one of the largest and richest plantations in Louisiana and yet lives in a shack."

Stephen was watching the sun touch the midnight masses of hair with golden highlights; the mockery passed by him unheard. "What if someone saw ye here like this?" he asked.

"But no one did, monsieur. Are you going to show me your place?"

"Yes," Stephen said. "This way, mademoiselle." They rode through the waving sea of cane toward the rude house in the grove. As they neared it, Odalie reined in her horse, looking from the rough planking to the smooth pink outlines of the sugar house. *"Mon Dieu!"* she said at last. "You *are* mad!"

They turned their horses toward the river. As they approached the road that paralleled it, Odalie stiffened suddenly. "I hear a coach," she said.

Stephen sat very still, listening. "Ye're right," he said. "Into that cypress grove there. Quickly!"

But just before they reached the trees, the coach rounded the bend in the road so that to its occupants the horses were clearly visible. Stephen and Odalie both leaned forward, urging the horses into a gallop.

"Sacred Mother of God!" Odalie whispered. "That was the Cloutiers' coach—and Aurore was in it! They're probably taking her out to their place."

"So now ye're compromised." Stephen grinned.

"My father will probably kill you," Odalie said. "Or worse still, he might insist upon your marrying me."

"Is that so terrible?" Stephen demanded.

"To live in these wilds—in a shack—with a madman? I'd hang myself first!"

Stephen touched Prince Michael lightly so that he moved in quickly with a dancing step. Odalie was so close he could smell the perfume in her hair. Abruptly he leaned down and kissed her, twisting his mouth cruelly against hers. He could feel the soft roundness of her breasts, and through them the quick fluttering of her pulse, like captive wings.

Her hands were against his chest, pushing hard. He released

her suddenly, seeing the light dancing in her black eyes and the corners of her mouth trembling.

"Ye will make a fine mistress for Harrow," he said. "Ye have spirit. I like that in my horses—and my women. *Au 'voir.*"

Odalie half rose from the saddle and swung her crop sideways with all her force. It caught Stephen high on the side of his face, crisscrossing the scar left by Hugo's bullet.

"Ye little witch!" Stephen said very softly as he watched the black mare swinging around the curve, out of sight.

TANTE CALEEN WAS waiting for Stephen when he rode in. "Master shouldn't ride through the brush," she said severely. "You now have a mark on your face!"

"Ye're a bossy old devil, Caleen," Stephen said. "I sometimes wonder if I own ye, or ye own me."

"We own each other," Tante Caleen said calmly. She lifted her face skyward and sniffed the air. "I smells wind," she said, "big wind. The grand tempest come from the islands."

Stephen eyed her narrowly. Tante Caleen's knowledge of the weather was positively uncanny.

"How long?" he asked.

"Two, three day, but she come!"

"Achille!" Stephen roared.

The big Negro came running through the cane, his eyes wide.

"Get the cane knives out. And the wagons! We're harvesting now."

"But, master, it is too soon—the stalks are not so high . . ."

"Do as I tell ye, Achille!"

In half an hour all the Negroes were busy working down the rows, the cane falling before them. The wagons hauled the cane to the sugar house, from whose tall chimney the black wood smoke was billowing.

Three days later the cane was all in, and almost to the minute the black clouds came massing in from over the Gulf. When the storm was done, the fields were flattened as if by the hand of a giant. Many planters were completely ruined. But when Stephen Fox walked out of the offices of the factors in New Orleans, his eyes were dancing in a face deliberately grave and still.

He had sold his crop for a little short of one hundred thousand dollars.

Aurore was sitting by one of the windows at the Arceneaux town house in Conti Street, watching the thin, miserable drizzle so characteristic of winter in New Orleans. Across the room Odalie was putting fresh sachets of vetiver in the armoire.

"Why don't you consent, Aurore?" Odalie asked. "André would make you a wonderful husband."

"You're right," Aurore said slowly. "Only—I don't love him."

Odalie's fingers toyed with the fine linen she was scenting.

"I see. There is someone else, perhaps?"

"Yes."

"Who?"

"That is my affair, my dear sister. It's no good, and nothing will come of it . . . ever. And you, Odalie. What about you?"

"I am growing old," Odalie said, as though she were talking to herself. "I'm twenty-two. All my friends have been married for ages."

"You've had hundreds of beaux," Aurore said.

"They—they bother me. I don't like being touched or kissed or fawned at. There's something—well, private here"—she touched her breast—"something inviolable. And men are such beasts!"

"I'm wondering," Aurore said softly, "just when you discovered that bestiality. Was it in the fall, perhaps?"

Odalie opened her mouth to say something, but Zerline, the maidservant of the Arceneaux, was coming into the room. "Monsieur André, Mademoiselle Aurore," she said.

André entered the room, his young face beaming. "Good day!" he exclaimed. "Ah, how happy I am to see you!"

"You seem in good spirits, André," Odalie said.

"I am. I've just come back from visiting Stephen at Harrow. The news there is good—very good."

"You mean to say that he is there now—in midwinter?" Aurore demanded. "Everybody—"

"—comes into town for the winter," André finished for her. "But not Stephen. He is clearing the land. By spring every inch of it will be ready for cultivation. And he is building a house—the grandest mansion that Louisiana has ever seen. I rode out with the architect, Monsieur Pouilly, today. The foundations are already laid. It is such a house as will shape generations of men."

"But he has no wife," Odalie said. "Where are these generations to come from, André?"

"Stephen will take a wife," André said softly, "and she'll be the girl of his choice, I'll wager you."

"But if it happens that this girl thinks otherwise?"

"The good God help her. For she'll be subjected to such a courtship as was never seen before on land or sea!"

"It seems to me," Aurore said quietly to her sister, "that you know a great deal about the state of mind of this mysterious fiancée of Monsieur Fox's."

"Oh, bother!" Odalie said, and walked away with great dignity through the doorway.

André looked after her. "Your sister seems to be of a divided mind," he said to Aurore.

"Yes. She loves him, I think. But she doesn't know it yet. And she's afraid—terribly afraid—of—of love itself."

"Why?"

"I don't know. Perhaps it's because she's so beautiful. It's given her a kind of mastery. Or perhaps she is really cold—frozen all the way through. I simply don't know."

"But you, my sweet," André said, "are you also afraid of love?"

"No, André, I'm not afraid."

"Then—Aurore—oh, Aurore!"

"No, André, no. I wish I did love you. God knows I should. You've been generous and patient and kind . . . but I just can't."

"I see," André said slowly. "There is someone else. My felicitations, Aurore, to this very fortunate man. Is the date set?"

"No, André, the date will never be set." Aurore laughed suddenly. "All your children shall call me Tante Aurore and laugh at the little dried-up old spinster whenever they hear her say, 'Once I was in love . . .'"

André's brown eyes were very dark in his handsome face. "You too!" he whispered, half to himself. "I think sometimes he is a devil—so easily does he do things like this—without caring—without even knowing." André's eyes came back from vast distances. "Your forgiveness, Aurore, for this and all my past intrusions. Good night. Adieu, Mademoiselle Arceneaux!"

"But, André, you'll call again. You're welcome any evening."

"To come and sit and look at you and torture myself? No, Aurore. This is the end. Good night, mademoiselle!" Then he was gone, striding through the doorway, his back very stiff and proud.

THROUGHOUT THE LONG winter the work went forward. The tall sailing vessels came riding into the harbor below the city, their holds bulging with goods. And always there were consignments for Stephen Fox, gentleman planter. Teak from the tropics for balustrades, hardwoods for flooring, rich darker woods for inlay patterns. Furniture turned out in the ancient shops of England and France, shaped by the hands of the finest craftsmen. Gigantic crystal chandeliers from Ghent, Antwerp and Brussels. Red flagstone from Spain. Tile from Morocco. Carpets from the looms of Holland, rugs from far-off Persia. Solid silver services with tracings of leaves and vines in gold. All this waited in the warehouses, while the walls of the great house grew.

André practically lived at Harrow, quarreling busily with Stephen over points in the design. "Classic Greek," he cried. "But still, that is no reason why you could not introduce a little ironwork on the galleries!"

"No," Stephen declared. "Nothing of Louisiana. 'Tis for myself I am building, André. Look ye, lad. Here a great gallery across the front, and around the two wings. And above it, another. Corinthian columns going straight through, supporting the roof. And from the upper gallery two great curving stairs of teak, so that one can alight from one's coach and go at once to the high porch, from whence ye can see the river."

"Good," André said. "It's good, I have to admit. Painted white, of course?"

"Yes. And with a roof of green tile. Forty rooms, André, and a long straight drive to the river road, with the branches of the oaks making a canopy. And here, at the gate, two forks, swinging in great curves up to the patio from two directions. There will be nothing like it in all the South, André."

"You're lucky, Stephen," André declared. "Everything you want you get. I sometimes wonder if there isn't truth in some of the stories they tell about you."

Stephen's left eyebrow rose mockingly. "And how do they explain my luck?" he said.

"Tante Caleen. Everyone knows she's a *mamaloi*, a sort of high priestess of voodoo. Through her you're said to have a direct connection with the devil."

Stephen leaned against a piece of the scaffolding and laughed until his face was wet with tears.

André joined in the laughter. "But you are lucky, Stephen," he said. "By the way, where is your old witch now?"

"In the fields, I'd say, talking to Achille."

"She seems fond of your number-one man. Odd, isn't it?"

"Not at all. Achille is her son. Neither of them has had a pleasant life. It seems Caleen came to New Orleans while she was yet a girl—many years before the insurrections that Tom Warren has credited her with having had a hand in fomenting."

"He is a queer one, your Tom Warren," André observed.

"So I am beginning to learn. There's no question of his fidelity to my interests, though some of his methods . . . But back to Tante Caleen. Achille's father was one of the leaders of the black revolt of ninety-five. Deuced odd name he had—Inch, Big Inch. They hanged him before the parish church at New Orleans."

"So Tom Warren isn't entirely wrong!"

"Not entirely. And Tante Caleen *is* unusual. I sometimes think that she only tolerates whites as mere children in the eyes of her ancient wisdom."

"Then she is a witch?"

"Rot. Come, there is still much to do."

BY THE SPRING of 1827 the great mansion of Harrow was substantially finished. From the first it had a majesty about it—a regal air of pride and lofty disdain. Try as they would, neither the Creoles nor the Americans could disregard it, and even their contemptuous title, "Fox's Lair," died when they saw the completed house standing in all the austere purity of the classic Grecian line.

Stephen had bought a gardener called Jupiter for the amazing sum of three thousand dollars. Whatever the old black touched grew and flourished. In the courtyard the pink, lavender and white crepe myrtles glowed softly; the red and white oleanders blazed. The yellowish-pink mimosa hung low over the crystal ball on the pedestal. There were cape jasmine, and the heavy waxen blossoms of magnolia; there were the cruel spines of the yucca with its crown of creamy flowers, roses with buds like blood drops, and lilies whiter than mountain snow.

When the sugar-making season began, Stephen prepared the invitations to the grand ball that was to mark the official opening of Harrow. André took up residence in rooms that Stephen had ordered perpetually reserved for him, and the two of them worked out to the last detail this formal assault upon New Orleans society.

"But suppose they refuse you, Stephen," André worried. "Suppose they don't come."

"They'll come," Stephen declared dryly.

So the invitations went out to the Marignys, the Cloutiers, the Lambres, the Prudhommes, the de Pontablas—and the Arceneaux. They went, too, to the Wilsons, the Claibornes, the Roberts, the Smiths and the Thompsons.

In the mornings Stephen and André, accompanied by their Negroes, rode into the bayou country to shoot waterfowl. At night they came back laden, and the birds were turned over to Tante Caleen to be hung in preparation for cooking.

For the messengers had returned triumphant.

"They are coming!" Georges crowed. "All the true gentlemen!"

"And the *grandes dames*, too," Ti Demon echoed.

Now Harrow was a gigantic madhouse. Tante Caleen presided over everything, regally ordering Stephen and André out of her way. For days Harrow resounded with the pounding of her mallet, hammering the cone-shaped loaves of hard sugar into powder fine enough to be used in the cakes and delicate pastries she was baking.

The smoke rose up straight from the great chimney of the kitchen house on the last day, only a few hours before the guests were due. Caleen supervised the cooks as they pushed the ovens with their hollowed-out tops filled with live coals into the great fireplace. In the smaller pots on the trivets the gravies, soups and gumbos simmered. Across the front of the fourteen-foot-wide fireplace, venison, wild hog and wild fowl turned on the spits, the rich juices dripping into pots set on the hearth below.

Outside the big house the strongest slaves were taking turns whirling huge cylinders in tubs of ice. These contained the ice cream that had been made by boiling whole vanilla beans in sweetened milk. Ruefully the men blew on their freezing palms, but Tante Caleen was everywhere, her tongue keener than any lash.

Inside, Stephen himself supervised the placing of the wines and liquors on the side table. Jupiter filled the costly urns and vases with flowers, and garlanded the magnificent curving staircase with pink ramblers and blood-colored garden roses for a full three flights of stairs.

The house servants were instructed and instructed again. Their livery was new from the skin out. Two little turbaned pages took their places on each side of the great tables, with their hands on the golden cords that moved the huge, swinging fans. And the butler, who could read, stood at the doorway to take the cards and call out the names of each entering guest. Now, at last, everything was still, waiting . . .

ANDRE AND STEPHEN dressed in the north wing with the assistance of Georges and Ti Demon. The ruffles on the white silk shirts stood out rigidly from the two broad chests, and the new dark cutaway coats had been brushed and brushed again. The waistcoats were cream, with embossed patterns of fleur de lis, and their boots had been polished until they reflected the light of every candle.

And now the valets brushed the glossy hair upon the imperious young heads, and smoothed the long sideburns. Truly, Stephen and André were striking foils for each other on this night, the dark, wonderfully handsome Creole setting off the lean, fair Irishman to unusual advantage.

"You're shaking," André observed as Stephen took a glass of wine from the hands of Georges.

"Of course," Stephen said. "I'm as jumpy as a filly. This means everything to me."

"Why? The people you've invited are insufferably stuffy. To go to all this trouble and expense . . ."

"For them? No, André. For one only. Afterward they may drown themselves in the Mississippi, but I will have Odalie." His hands stroked the great pearl. "I can wear this now," he said.

"Of course. But, Stephen, why are you seating me next to this Miss Rogers? I don't know her."

"Wait and see," Stephen said, smiling.

Ti Demon came running into the room at that moment, his big eyes popping from their sockets. "I see the coaches!" he cried.

"We'd better go down," André said.

"Right," Stephen agreed, and he finished the glass of wine in one gulp.

They walked to the stairway, which descended in a tremendous spiral. At this height, the magnificent crystal chandelier, blazing with hundreds of candles, was below them. Through its dazzling facets they could see the first arrivals.

Stephen moved down to the vast foyer to greet the guests. The men took his offered hand firmly, and the women simpered as he bowed low over their gloved fingers. Inside the ballroom the slave orchestra struck up a tune. Importantly, the butler bawled out the names. André stood a little apart, watching the show.

"Mr. and Mrs. Rogers!" the butler called. "And Miss Amelia Rogers!"

André leaned forward suddenly. And I accused him of having no heart, he thought. Then he moved toward the tall girl whose walk was the waving of a young willow in a spring wind, and whose silvery hair reflected the light of the candles like a halo. The face was kind, too, and heartbreakingly lovely. As he walked toward her, the blue eyes fixed upon his dark young face.

All the guests were in the great hall—except the Arceneaux. Stephen was glancing nervously toward the door. Then at last the butler was swelling out his chest importantly: "Monsieur le Vicomte Henri Marie Louis Pierre d'Arceneaux! And the Mademoiselles Aurore and Odalie Arceneaux!"

As the maidservant took away Odalie's wrap, something between a breath and a sigh rose from the lips of the men in the hall and hovered in the air like an echo. Her hair was not—as was the hair of every other woman in the place—parted in the middle and tortured into small bunches of curls above her ears; it simply fell in heavy midnight masses about her shoulders, over the gown of ancient French lace cut in extreme décolletage. And when Stephen bent wordlessly over her hand, she smiled, a slow, deep, triumphant smile implicit with the luxurious mastery of surrender.

The music had begun now, and the dancing. André touched Amelia's hand lightly, and swung into the swirling sweep of the waltz, lost forever, knowing it, and glorying in the knowledge.

"All my life," he whispered, "I've been waiting. Without knowing it, I've been waiting for you."

The blue eyes beneath the ash-blond brows looked calmly into the dark face that was as handsome as a young god's, and there was no coquetry in them, only pure candor and trust. "I'm very glad," she said clearly, "that you waited."

With amazing control, Stephen made the rounds of the young women, smiling at them, whispering flattering words into each ear. But when Odalie was his partner, the tall young man with the scarred face moved through the measures of the contredanse with a trancelike grace, and the eyes of Odalie never left his—never for an instant.

Then it was midnight and the guests were following Stephen into the great dining salon, where the gigantic tables of carved mahogany had been placed end to end. When everyone had been seated, the procession of servants bearing the turkey, goose, chicken, venison and wild hog began. On some of the side tables were the salads, salamis, gelatins and huge pyramids of iced cakes. Upon other tables the cold meats waited, and the snowy mounds of ice cream. The wines glowed richly in their cut-glass decanters. And for each lady there was a little basket of candied orange peel with sugared petals of rose, violet and orange blossoms.

Behind each chair the waiters moved like ghosts, seeing that no one of the beautiful crystal goblets went for an instant unfilled. And Stephen was bending toward Odalie, his pale blue eyes aglow. Looking at him, Odalie's hand trembled as with a sudden chill, so that she dropped her spoon.

"Ye're trembling," Stephen said. "Are ye cold?"

"No. I think I'm a little afraid."

"Of what? There's no one here who would harm ye."

"Not even you, monsieur?"

Stephen smiled wickedly. " 'Tis just possible I might," he said thoughtfully. "I have not yet had my revenge for that blow ye struck me . . ."

But the butler was bending over Stephen, whispering, "A man wants to see you, master. Outside on the terrace." Stephen made a gesture of extreme annoyance. "He said to show you—this." And in the butler's hand the golden snuffbox gleamed dully under the flickering candles.

Stephen rose at once. "A thousand pardons, mademoiselle. Ye'll excuse me?"

Outside on the gallery Stephen hesitated a moment. Then he saw the brief glow of redness as the big man standing at the foot of the curving stairway drew upon his pipe. "Mike!" he cried, and went bounding down the stairs.

"Aye, me little red-haired cockeroo!" Mike Farrel bellowed. "And 'tis thinkin' I was that you had forgotten an old friend!"

"Never," Stephen said. Then, with only the slightest hesitation, he added, "Come in and join the party."

Mike's big bass voice was curiously soft. "You be all man—and all Irish. You'd take me in amongst all those swells and let them know you associated with river scum, and mayhap lose even your fine lady? No, 'tis too much. I'll come again tomorrow." He turned away abruptly.

But Stephen caught him by the arm. "No! Ye're staying here tonight. Ye don't have to join the party if ye don't want to, but ye're staying. Come."

Then, taking Mike's big arm, Stephen led him up the stairs and through the doorway.

As they passed the hall, Stephen nodded curtly to a waiter. The black came at once to his master's side. "A bottle of whiskey," Stephen said, "up to the north wing rooms for this gentleman."

"I had me a black," Mike said suddenly. "He were a queer little fellow, always shakin' like a leaf and mutterin' to himself about some big fire and shootin' and burnin'. He were a runaway. They caught him up near Natchez, but nobody ever claimed him. Me money ran low, so I had to sell him."

"Tomorrow we'll ride into town and buy him back," Stephen said.

"Aye. Now go back to your guests. But don't forget that whiskey!"

When Stephen came back into the salon the whispers of the few guests who had seen Mike pass the open double doors stopped abruptly. Odalie looked at him inquiringly. "A relative of yours?" she asked mockingly.

"No," Stephen said softly. " 'Tis merely a river man who once saved my life, and one of the finest men to whom the good God ever gave breath." His eyes rested upon her warmly. "Ye're beautiful, Odalie," he said. "Much too beautiful."

It was just at that moment, when the crimson was mounting into Odalie's cheeks, that André lifted his eyes from the face of Amelia Rogers to where Aurore sat across from him. Her eyes were upon Stephen, watching his every move as he bent toward Odalie. And André was conscious of a feeling very like pain.

"André," Amelia whispered, "you were in love with that girl once, weren't you?"

"Yes," he said. "Yes I was. But time did not exist before tonight."

Afterward the music started again and the dancing lasted until dawn. Then the waiters brought the plates of gumbo and scalding cups of black coffee, and one by one the guests took their leave. Odalie lingered after the others.

"And if I call," Stephen was saying, "ye will receive me?"

"Yes," she said. "I shall always be at home—to you."

Waiting for her in the coach on the red flagstone drive, Aurore knotted her handkerchief into a ball; but even when Stephen bent low over Odalie's hand, she held back the tears that trembled under her eyelids.

CHAPTER SIX

THE MORNING AFTER the great ball Stephen, Mike Farrel and André rode down Stephen's alley of oaks toward the river road.

"Ye remember the dealer to whom ye sold your black?" Stephen asked Mike.

"Yes. And he be a fair one by all accounts. 'Taint likely he could've sold poor Josh yet anyways, he were so puny. But I never had trouble out of him."

"We'll have him back," Stephen said. "Never ye fear. Well, André, how did ye like the lean American female?"

André looked at Stephen and his eyes were very clear. "I'm eternally grateful to you." He smiled. "I'm going back to work, Stephen. I'm going to become a planter. After all, La Place des Rivières will be mine one day."

"Ye gods!" Stephen roared. "This is serious."

"I'm going to marry her, Stephen."

Stephen put out his hand to his friend. "Good," he said. "I'll give ye back that wager that ye've lost to me as a wedding present, and add something useful to boot. And what about Aurore, André?"

"I loved her," André said slowly, "and if she returned my affections—even a little—I should be greatly troubled. But she doesn't—so I guess my way is clear."

"I'm told 'tis the other filly of old Arceneaux you be plannin' to get spliced with," Mike said to Stephen.

"Ye're told! By Our Lady, Mike, ye've got an uncommonly large store of information about my affairs!"

"I take an interest." Mike grinned. "You're like a son to me, lad. I must see this gal someday soon, so as to make me mind up whether or no I'll give me consent. I want you happy, Stevie."

"Then put your foot down, Mike," André said suddenly, and his tone was only half jesting. "Don't let him do it!"

Stephen looked at him keenly. "Why don't you like Odalie, André?" he asked.

"I do like her. It's only that sometimes I think she has no heart."

"She has," Stephen said. "But 'tis frozen. I'll thaw it out for her, never ye fear."

After miles of riding, they came to the slave mart in the American section of New Orleans. The block was empty and deserted and the house behind it was closed. Stephen knocked smartly on the door with his crop.

After a moment a lean, tanned man pushed it open. "Good day, gentlemen," he said. "What can I do for you?"

"Ye have a black," Stephen said, "bought yesterday from this man. Have ye sold him yet?"

"No," the man said gravely. "And I doubt I can ever sell him. Why didn't you tell me he was crazy?"

"You didn't ask me." Mike grinned. "Anyways, we've come to buy him back."

"There's a little matter of the expense of feeding and lodging him," the slave trader began.

"I'll give ye fifty dollars above what ye paid for him," Stephen said. "Come, let us see him."

"Very well," the man said, and after a moment he was back, leading not one Negro but two. The first was small, ill formed and undernourished. He was trembling from head to foot, and great tears streaked his thin cheeks. "They'll send me back to Master Tom," Josh moaned. "And he'll kill me jes like he done Rad. Don't let them do it, Master Mike!"

"He's sick, poor devil," Stephen said.

"Beggin' your pardon, sir," the slave trader said. "But since you seem to be in the market for slaves, I thought maybe . . ."

Stephen looked at the second slave, a girl. "Hmmm," he said. "What think ye, André?"

"*Ma foi*, but she's beautiful!" André said.

She was tall, with a small rounded head on a long graceful neck. The hair was closely cropped, like a woolly skullcap, but her body was all grace, and her skin was black velvet. Stephen looked into the face with the small nose, almost as thin as a Caucasian's, and the slanted, half-closed eyes, smoldering yellow-brown under the heavy lids.

"All right," he said, "I'll buy her."

"Wait," the man said. "I got a reputation for square dealing. This gal is a livin' fiend. Got her off a ship straight from Africa."

"Give her to me, Stevie boy," Mike said with a grin, "and I'll have her tamed by mornin'."

"I don't doubt it," Stephen said. "But I was thinking of buying her for Achille. She has no physical defects?"

In answer, the trader seized her jaw and tried to force open her mouth. Instantly her lips bared her gleaming teeth; the man let out a yell. The pointed teeth had gone through his hand.

The men sprang forward. It took all three of them to force open her mouth and release the trader's hand. Then he lashed out with his foot, the kick catching her high on the thigh and sending her to the ground. She was up at once, nails and teeth bared, her eyes gleaming yellow like a leopard's.

"I'll give ye three hundred for her as she stands," Stephen said. "My man will call for them in the morning with a wagon."

"You're mad," André declared.

"I think not," Stephen said. "She can be tamed."

As the three of them were mounting their horses, Stephen turned to Mike. "Ye know, Mike," he said, "I think I'd better keep your Josh. He seems badly in need of care. I'll give ye another black in his stead and turn him over to Caleen for treatment."

"Awright!" Mike grinned, winking his one eye at André. "But keep your blacks. They're more trouble than they're worth. Just save a bed and a place at your board for old Mike, like we agreed."

"I haven't forgotten," Stephen said. "Now come, let's go down to Maspero's for dinner. Then we can discuss our plans for the evening."

They sat at one of the little tables eating steaming bouillabaisse. André's mind was busy and troubled. Would his father take kindly to his marriage to an American girl? Perhaps when he *saw* Amelia—but the old man was so confounded stubborn. "Tell me, Stephen," he asked suddenly, "how did you come to meet Colonel Rogers?"

"On the steamboats." Stephen chuckled. "He is the best poker player in the entire Mississippi valley. He used to beat me regularly—which is probably the reason he is so fond of me."

"He is fond of you? Then will you come with me to call upon the colonel?"

"Don't ye want to think this over, André?"

"I've got to have her, Stephen. You should understand that."

"I do," Stephen said gravely, rising from his seat. "Let us be off, then."

They rode northward to Saint Phillip Street, where Stephen reined Prince Michael in before an American Gothic house with huge verandas and oddly assorted spires and gables projecting from the roof. Stephen knocked boldly and soon the door flew open.

"Stephen!" the great voice roared. "Come in, my boy! Who is this blasted Frenchman you introduced my daughter to? She can talk of nothing else—and you know I cannot abide foreigners!"

"Permit me to present him," Stephen said. "This is André Le Blanc, a very blasted Frenchman at the moment."

"Good day, sir," André murmured politely.

"And this is Mike Farrel," Stephen said, "my biggest and best friend."

The colonel looked at André from under his thick, bushy eyebrows. "You're a man of substance, aren't you, Mr. Le Blanc?" he asked abruptly.

"My father's plantation is one of the largest in the state," André said stiffly.

"And I am right in assuming that the purpose of this visit is to gain my permission to pay court to my daughter?"

"Yes," André said, "it is."

"You're a friend of Stephen's," the old man said, half to himself. "That means a lot to me. You know, Stephen was the first honest gambler I ever met on the river." He turned abruptly to Stephen. "Well, lad, what do you say? I rather fancied *you* as a son-in-law."

"Suppose we let Amelia decide," Stephen said smoothly. "After all, 'tis she who will have to be troubled with a husband."

"Right," the colonel said, then, "Oh, 'Melia!"

Amelia came down the stairs and André stood up, frozen, all of his life caught up in his eyes.

"André!" she whispered, and Stephen thought he had never heard so much gladness in one voice. "Father—André—I—I see you've met," she finished lamely.

"It seems to be out of our hands," Stephen whispered loudly to the colonel. "What say ye to a hand of twenty-one? In the drawing room, of course, so we won't be drowned in sighs."

"All right," the colonel growled. "Mr. Le Blanc, tell your father that I'll call upon him next Friday afternoon. Come, Stephen, and you, Mr. Farrel."

Stephen bowed mockingly toward André and Amelia. "Bless ye, my children," he murmured, then followed the colonel and Mike through the doorway.

BACK AT HARROW, Stephen rode straight to the sugar house. There was this matter of a wife for Achille. Perhaps that wildcat—La Belle Sauvage—would do. Achille was now in his prime, a giant of a black, intelligent and capable of carrying out the most exacting task without supervision. 'Twould be well to preserve that strain.

The smoke came up from the big chimney, and inside the sugar house the slaves worked busily. Achille came forward, his white teeth gleaming against his sweat-glistening face.

"How goes it, Achille?" Stephen asked.

"Good—very good."

"Tomorrow I have an errand for ye. Go down to the small slave market in the American section of the city and bring back two new blacks I've bought. Take Henri and Gros Tom with ye. Ye'll need help with the wench. By the way, Achille, look her over well. She's intended for ye if she suits your fancy."

"Yes, sir," Achille said a little doubtfully.

"Ye're a confirmed woman hater, aren't ye, Achille?"

"They talk too much." Achille grinned. "Always they have the big mouth, yes?"

"Yes." Stephen laughed. "Well, keep the men at it. I must ride out to the south fields to see how the late harvesting goes."

Up at the big house Mike Farrel lay half asleep in the huge bed. Suzette, the mulatto girl who had shared the lean-to with Stephen and Tante Caleen on that first day at Harrow, was tiptoeing through the room, busily dusting the furniture. Mike raised up on one elbow.

The dark eyes widened in Suzette's soft yellow face. "Monsieur wants something, yes?"

"Yes," Mike declared. "A little closer so's I can whisper."

Suzette's warm red lips rounded into a little O of curiosity. She walked over quite near to where the big man lay. He smiled disarmingly, but his huge arm shot out suddenly with all the speed and power of a grizzly striking.

Suzette screamed—a high, edged sound, hanging on the air, and Mike clamped a hairy paw over her mouth. Suzette kicked with both feet and brought her long nails upward, raking across Mike's forehead and into his one good eye. Mike released her instantly, bellowing with pain. Then she was gone, and down the stairs. In the pantry she hurled herself upon Caleen, sobbing and fighting for breath. "Tante Caleen!" she wailed. "That big one, he—"

"Hush, chile," old Caleen whispered. "It been like that. Always it been like that. But he don't touch you, him. I fix him!"

The next Sunday Stephen dressed with unusual care. He and André were to visit the Arceneaux at their plantation, called Bellefont. André wanted to say a last farewell to Aurore. Stephen hoped to make a beginning with Odalie.

Georges worked over him busily, bringing out the new dark green coat, the pale wine-colored waistcoat and the crimson scarf. "When that lady see you now," Georges said, "she get up on Prince Michael behind you and come home with you tonight."

"Ye're an optimist, Georges," Stephen said dryly.

Outside, Achille waited with Prince Michael. The palomino had been curried and groomed until his coat shone like satin. Stephen swung into the saddle and looked down at Achille. "Ye've done a good job," he said. "How d'ye like the new wench?"

"She's wild, that one! But I tame her—she's something, her!"

"Then ye find her to your liking? Good." Stephen touched his riding crop to the brim of his hat and was off.

André was waiting for him at the fork of the road that led to his father's plantation. His young face was gloomy and there were lines of fatigue around his eyes.

"By Our Lady!" Stephen declared. "Ye have been working, haven't ye?"

"Yes," André said. "Dear Papa is pleased as punch with me."

"But how did the visit from Colonel Rogers affect him?"

"That was amazing! Papa took him all over the place, all the time deploring the enmity between the Creoles and the Americans. They parted the best of friends."

"Then your father approves of Amelia?"

"Last night he insisted upon accompanying me to call on her. And when he saw her . . . Well, Papa kissed her—a privilege I have yet to gain. The old devil!"

Soon they were turning into the big iron gates of Bellefont. The old groom was at the foot of the stairs, bowing grandly, and Stephen and André dismounted, throwing him the reins. They went up the stairs and into the big house, where another ancient Negro took their hats, cloaks and gloves. Then there was the light whisper of footsteps on the winding stairway, and Aurore came down into the hall.

"André!" she said. "And Monsieur Fox—how nice!"

André's face was scarlet under his tan, but Stephen bowed calmly over her hand with all the grace of a dancing master.

"But I thought you were angry with me, André," Aurore teased as she led the way into the drawing room. "I thought you swore never to call again."

"I—I came for a reason, Aurore."

"But, of course, my poor friend! The Mademoiselle Rogers is lovely. I trust you'll be very happy."

"Then you knew?"

"Yes, André—I and everyone else who was at Harrow that night. I have never seen a man so smitten! My congratulations, my friend—I wish you every happiness."

Stephen made a little gesture of impatience.

"Odalie will come down in a moment," Aurore whispered. "Come, André, we must leave them alone. Besides, I want to enjoy the little of your company that is left to me."

Stephen's hand went into his pocket and came out with the massive gold watch that wound with a key; but before he had time to open the case to look at it, Odalie came through the door. Stephen stood up and went forward to meet her, his eyes alight.

"Good day, monsieur," Odalie said. "I was beginning to wonder if you had forgotten your promise to call."

"Would ye have cared?" Stephen asked.

Odalie's black eyes widened. "Yes," she said. "I would have cared. Won't you sit down?"

Stephen sank into a great chair facing her. "Ye've changed since the days when ye hated me."

"I never hated you, Stephen."

"I'm glad. Ye cost me many troubled nights, Odalie."

Odalie smiled slowly. Watching the wine-red lips moving, Stephen knew that all the sun-blasted days in the fields, all the nights of sleepless scheming, all the work and waiting and worry would be an insignificance against the gaining of this woman.

"It pleases me to know that I meant more to you than—than a horse, perhaps," she said. "I was unaccustomed to being looked at appraisingly, like a slave girl."

"Yet there were many men who looked upon ye with humility and awe and worship—and ye married none of them."

"And I have not married you."

"No—not yet. But ye're going to. Ye know that, don't ye?"

"If you mean that for a proposal, my answer is—"

"Wait a bit, Odalie. Do not spoil things because of my boldness. There is too much between us now—far too much."

"But I see nothing between us—nothing at all."

Stephen looked at her and his face was still and unsmiling. Only his eyes were alive—moving like the strokes of an etcher's pen, short, swift and deft, limning her image as she was at that instant forever on his brain. His voice was very deep when he spoke. "There is Harrow."

"Harrow?"

"Yes. Always I've had the dream of it, but 'twas ye that shaped it into reality. When first I saw ye, in the Place d'Armes, the dream became an obsession, a means toward an end rather than an end in itself. Ye were the end, Odalie. Harrow was no longer important—it was the mistress of Harrow that mattered."

"You—you built Harrow—for me?"

"Yes, I could not have built it without ye—not as it is now. And until ye come, it will have no life."

"I—I don't know what to say . . . "

"Nothing yet. I shall be patient. But it must end thus. It must, Odalie." He stood up and she rose too, her eyes very wide and dark, searching his face. She laid a hand upon his arm. It trembled so that he felt it through his coat.

"I think," she said, "that never before was a woman so honored."

A little glint of mockery stole into Stephen's eyes. "Then why do ye tremble?"

"Because I am afraid. Other men I could turn aside, but not you, Stephen. You're so direct and simple, yet so endlessly complicated at the same time."

"Yet I am nothing to fear."

"I—I've made a sort of obsession of privacy, Stephen," she said, not looking at him. "I've enjoyed being—well, cool and aloof—it made me different somehow. And I think now that it provoked men into greater efforts. I've never liked being touched, not even by my father. While in marriage—to such a man as you . . ." Her eyes were suddenly bright with dismay. "*Ma foi!* What am I saying?"

Stephen's expression did not change. "Ye will find me patient," he murmured. "And very gentle." He bent over her hand, then strode through the door.

She was still standing there, looking after him, her face bathed in crimson, when Aurore came in. "What ails you?" the younger girl demanded.

"I said the most awful, unladylike things. Oh, Aurore!"

Aurore came up to her and put her arms around her waist. "Don't trouble yourself, my dear. He didn't seem to mind. You shall be mistress of Harrow—and that is something."

"Mistress of Harrow," Odalie repeated after her, and her voice was filled with something very like glory.

CHAPTER SEVEN

STEPHEN CLOSED THE huge ledger wearily. It was long past midnight and a new year had come in with the crying winter rains. Tomorrow—New Year's Day—he would ride into New Orleans and make the rounds of the great houses of the city bearing gifts to some of his closer friends, and he would stop at André's house and salute him and his bride of one week with foaming eggnog.

Stephen remembered the faces of the young couple at the ceremony. Never had he seen such tenderness upon the face of a man—it was almost reverence. And Amelia, lifting her face to her new husband to be kissed, had been as beautiful as an angel. Afterward the emptiness of Harrow had become unbearable.

Odalie must give him an answer. Clearly she loved him—she admitted it quite honestly. She let him kiss her—quick, brushing kisses, her hands always pushing against his chest in half-protest. Stephen was going mad with wanting her, watching her cool loveliness that even in his arms was just out of his reach. "By all the fruits of Tantalus," he said, "today it ends!"

As he went down the stairs from his study, his mind wandered over a number of people. How was Achille making out with La Belle Sauvage? That wild woman was becoming tamer under Caleen's wise old hands, but she was still a savage thing. And Josh, the feeble, half-mad Negro he had bought for Mike, was a wonderful fisherman, and his skill as a gardener was only less than Jupiter's own. Still he was always talking about "the big fire, down by the river when poor Rad got kilt." Not much sense to it, but there must be something behind it to make the poor black so afraid.

And Mike. The big river man stayed on at Harrow month after month, growing quarrelsome and staying sober for shorter and shorter periods. At least twice a week they would hear him roaring in his rooms, and find him threshing about convulsively in the throes of a drunken nightmare. Caleen, Mike swore, caused these black and vivid dreams.

Even now, as Stephen descended the stairs, Mike was coming out of his rooms, all his belongings slung in a bundle on his back.

"Where on earth are ye going?" Stephen demanded.

"Away from this devil-cursed, hag-ridden place of yours!"

"Softly, Mike," Stephen said. "What's troubling ye now?"

"That old black witch! There's a fire in the brush. Caleen set it! I followed her. And you know what she was doing? She had made up me image in clay—and she were stickin' pins in it!"

"Why should Tante Caleen want to harm ye?"

"Because she hates all whites—even you, Stephen. And because of the little yaller wench, Suzette."

"Suzette?"

"Yes. I tried several times to get her to bed down with me—just a wee bit of sport, Stephen. But she runs to Caleen, and the old devil starts in to save her from me—with her spells and curses and clay dolls!"

"This voodoo business will stop, Mike. I will see Caleen at once. I promised ye that Harrow would be another home to ye, and I shall need your help in the future. I've plans for both of us."

"What kind of plans?" Mike growled darkly.

"A steamboat line of my own—with ye as captain of my fastest packet. 'Twill be many years before I can do it, but when I do, I want to be able to put my hands on ye."

"That you will, me fine lad! But I think still I'll go up to Natchez until the old witch has forgotten this affair."

"As ye will," Stephen said. "But do not stay away too long. I shall take Caleen in hand this night!"

OUTSIDE IN THE OAK grove the rain was like needles of ice. Stephen walked rapidly, bending his head before the wind. After ten minutes of pushing through brush he came to a little clearing. Caleen was sitting in the middle of it, crouched before a flickering fire. Slowly, and with great ceremony, she was dismembering a doll of clay and tossing the pieces into the fire, crooning a weird dirgelike song. Another doll waited at her side. It was crudely done, but Stephen had no trouble recognizing La Belle Sauvage.

"Caleen!" he said sharply. "Ye would harm Mike Farrel with your witchery? And the girl, what mean ye to do to her?"

Caleen looked up at him, and there was no fear in her bloodshot, anciently wicked eyes. "I take care of Harrow and you, master. The girl, I only fix her so that she love my Achille. He crazy mad for her, him."

Stephen walked up to the fire and kicked it apart. "I've never had one of my people whipped," he said. "But by heaven, Caleen, if ye continue this witchcraft, I'll send ye up to the calaboose and order thirty lashes. Ye hear me now?"

Walking away, Stephen realized that Caleen's silence had a fine excess to it—just enough to hint at mockery. There was nothing anyone could do with Caleen—nothing at all.

Back at Harrow, he stripped off his wet garments and plunged between the icy sheets. Gradually he fell asleep, but he was troubled by swift, senseless dreams that swept through his mind in an endless train. It was as though icy fingers clutched his heart, and he let out a cry so sharp that it awakened him. He pulled the bell cord that summoned Georges. "Come, man, bring me my clothes," he said, "and hot buttered rum!"

Stephen drank the rum while he dressed. It warmed him all over and made him feel cheerful again. Then he ate a light breakfast and set out for New Orleans, accompanied by Georges. The Negro had huge saddlebags full of gifts slung across his nag. Stephen had decided he would dispatch Georges with presents and cards to houses he had no desire to visit. André he would visit himself, and after that, Odalie. He sent Georges on his way and turned Prince Michael toward the house of the Le Blancs.

Ti Demon opened the door. And then André came toward Stephen, both hands outstretched, the happiness on his face outshining the candles.

"It goes well with ye—this marriage business!" Stephen said.

"It is beyond all paradise!" André declared. "And I owe it all to you. She is the sweetest and the loveliest and the—"

"André! Who is it, dearest?"

"Stephen," André called back. "He's come to see whether you throw pots and pans at me yet."

"But of course I do," Amelia said as she came down the stairs. "Although my aim still isn't very good." She walked up to Stephen and gave him her slim white hand. "Thank you, Stephen," she said softly, "for all the happiness in the world."

Stephen laughed. "In a year I will see if ye are still grateful."

"Make it ten years," André said, "or fifty, and still you'll find me the happiest of mortals. But how goes it with you and Odalie, Stephen?"

Stephen shrugged expressively. "Have ye no eggnog for an old and tired man?" he said smoothly.

"Forgive our thoughtlessness, my friend," André said. "This way, please."

Sipping the foaming eggnog, Stephen was conscious of a feeling akin to pain. It wasn't envy—at least not malicious envy. Rather it was the bitterness of contrast. He who had worked and suffered had gained exactly nothing, while André's joy had been handed him on a silver platter. He put down his glass and stood up. "I go to call upon Odalie now. Tonight I have hopes . . ."

André put out his hand. "Every happiness, Stephen," he said. "You deserve it."

"Thank ye," Stephen said soberly. "A Happy New Year to ye both." He turned abruptly on his heel and marched toward the door.

THE CANDLES WERE ablaze in every window of the Arceneaux town house. Stephen followed the old butler into the salon, where a half-dozen Creole youths were clustered about Odalie and an equal number about Aurore. The great scar on the side of his face flared scarlet. All these oily little bounders!

But Odalie was coming forward to greet him, a smile of pleasure lighting her face. "Stephen," she said, "I thought you were never coming."

"I can see how bitterly ye missed me," Stephen observed dryly. "I wanted very badly to talk to ye alone."

"We'll go into the little room. You've come such a long way and I—I like talking to you alone."

"I was beginning to think I gave ye the horrors."

Odalie made an impish face at him and took his hand. As they approached the others, all the young men stood up. Stephen knew most of them, but one young man was distinctly strange— an uncommonly handsome lad with boldness written all over his finely chiseled face.

"You'll excuse me for a while, won't you, gentlemen?" Odalie asked. "There is a matter that Monsieur Fox and I must discuss."

"Oh, we were about to go anyway," they chorused politely.

But the strange lad lingered a moment after the others. He walked boldly up to Stephen. "You will pardon me, sir," he said, "but I have heard so much of you since my return. My name is Cloutier, Phillippe Cloutier."

Stephen shook hands with the young Creole. "I've heard tell of ye," he said. "Ye've been abroad?"

Phillippe Cloutier smiled. "I am the black sheep of my family," he admitted. "It is the reason for the long extension of my Grand Tour. But I trust I shall see more of you, sir."

"Dine with me at Harrow," Stephen invited. "I knew Paris well—there are many things I would like to ask ye about."

Phillippe made him a low bow, and bent for a moment over the hand of Odalie. Then he turned and followed the others.

Odalie opened the door into the smaller guest room.

"Odalie," Stephen said, "ye know what I want to ask ye."

"Stephen I . . . I don't know . . . it's all so strange . . ."

The candlelight danced like fire in his eyes. "Come here, Odalie."

The words were spoken very quietly. Odalie came over to him and he slipped his arm lightly, loosely, around her waist. "Ye're beautiful," he said. "Enough to drive a man to despair. But I have worked too long, and waited too long. I am not waiting longer." He bent his head down and locked his lips expertly against hers. At once her hands came up against his chest, pushing him gently away as always. But his arms tightened, and he drove his iron hand inward at the small of her back so that her body ground against his. Suddenly her lips softened and parted and the sweet young breath came sighing through. When he released her, she fell back, her black eyes as wide as the night, dancing suddenly with the diamond brightness of her tears. "Stephen," she whispered. "Stephen . . ."

"When?" he demanded sternly.

"In the spring," she said.

"The twenty-fifth of April," Stephen said softly. "The anniversary of the day that I first saw ye."

"Yes," she said. "Yes . . . Oh, Stephen . . ."

At once he held her again in his arms. Strange how strong they were, she found herself thinking, like bands of steel, for all his slimness. And again she lifted her face upward to meet his kiss. Then the thinking stopped altogether.

ON THE NIGHT of April 25, 1829, the Negroes watched and waited for the new yellow maple coach bringing their master back to Harrow—Stephen Fox and his bride. As the sleek brace of roans rounded the bend, Achille, standing on the levee, fired his ancient shotgun into the air. At the sound of the shot, cries and laughter burst forth, and the instant the coach stopped, it was surrounded.

Stephen got down and extended a hand into the darkened coach. The slaves held their breaths as the slim white arm stole out and took his gently. Odalie hesitated fearfully.

"Speak to them, my darling," Stephen whispered. "They've all come to see ye."

All Odalie could manage was a feeble, "Good evening, my

people," and the air was rent with a great gale of excited laughter and chatter. Then Stephen swept her up into his arms and marched with her through the cheering crowd up the sweeping flight of stairs and into the great hall of Harrow.

The field Negroes crowded near the door, all of them packed in a great semicircle around Harrow. All of them except one. In the shadows of the oaks La Belle Sauvage lingered, her great yellow-brown eyes glowing in her velvety black face. Achille saw her and moved toward her silently. Tonight was the night for nuptials for the good young master—why not for him?

"Slave!" she spat at him, and turned and walked away, swinging her hips like a queen.

The rage mounted in Achille's throat until it was brine and black bile and fire. He came up to her, caught her by the shoulder and spun her around to face him. "You my woman!" he said. "I your man!"

La Belle Sauvage looked at him and her full lips curled contemptuously. "You no man," she said flatly. "My tribesman no make slave. Even woman no make slave, kill self first."

"You slave just like me, you!" Achille cried.

"No slave," she taunted. "No work—no bow down. Sauvage still princess." Then she turned and walked away in the direction of the cabins. Achille walked along beside her, his brow furrowed with thought. She had no right to make him feel like a dog or a horse or any owned thing. Yet he must have her, with all her arrogant beauty.

They were passing his cabin now. Achille's little eyes narrowed. Then all at once he swept her up into his arms. She kicked out and tore the skin of his face into ribbons, but he shouldered his way into the cabin with her and kicked the door shut behind him.

UP AT HARROW, Stephen, in his dressing gown, fingered the long-stemmed goblet of wine. He could hear Odalie moving up and down behind the closed door, hear the soft rustling of her wedding garments as she removed them. This was maddening, this waiting. And when at last her voice came through the door, very high and frightened, he stood up so suddenly that the glass crashed to the floor; the wine left a stain like blood.

He pushed open the door gently. Her gown was of lace net and silk and her hair was all darkness against the candles. She stood there trembling and he could see great tears spilling over the long lashes, gleaming like diamond drops in the candle flame. "My God, but ye're beautiful!" he whispered.

"Oh, Stephen, I'm so afraid!" she wailed as he drew her to him.

"Don't be," he said. "Ye've nothing to fear." Then he bent and kissed her cold lips softly.

"Stephen!" she said. "You said you'd have patience! You promised, Stephen, you promised!" Then she struck out wildly with her fists, hard against his chest, his shoulders, his throat.

Something very like madness exploded in Stephen's brain. He jerked her to him so hard that the single cry, "Stephen!" broke in half upon her lips. Then, just as abruptly, the rage was gone and he released her. "Good night—Madame Fox," he said. Then he turned and was gone.

Odalie lay weeping across the great bed. She had intended to submit. She wanted to be a good wife—she wanted to give Stephen tall, manly sons with hair like foxfire—but this horror of being touched was too strong. After a time her sobs quieted. She stood up and crossed the room. At the door she hesitated—then at last she pushed it open.

The hallway was vast and dark; she trembled like a small woods creature crossing it. At last her hand came down upon the knob and she was twisting it, pushing the door open. "Stephen," she whispered.

He looked up from his long white pipe of Irish clay. "Yes?" he said, and his voice was gentle. "Yes, my dear?"

"I've come to be your wife," she said. "If you still want me . . ."

"Still want ye," he said. "Still want ye? Oh, all ye blessed saints in heaven!" She took a half-step forward and the next instant she was in his arms.

Afterward it was very quiet at Harrow. There was no sound except the quiet rustle of Stephen's breath as he lay sleeping, one arm around the shoulders of his bride. But Odalie's silken pillow was sodden with tears. This—this was marriage! This was how a man expressed tenderness and devotion. Then human beings *were* animals after all, despite all the lace and perfume and poetry. And there were years of this before her.

She raised herself up and looked down at Stephen's sleeping face in the moonlight. The scarred side was turned against the pillow, and his face was strong and beautiful in its manhood. "I love you, my husband," she whispered. "For you I'll be patient and submissive and try to comprehend." Then, very softly, she began to pray.

STEPHEN WAITED AT the foot of the stairs as Amelia and André alighted from their landau. It was still early in the summer and Amelia was cool in her dress of thin India muslin, despite the great ham-shaped sleeves and the numerous petticoats. Her face, under the big straw hat, was radiant. André, who had put on weight since his marriage, strutted about like a turkey cock, looking for the moment so much like old Le Blanc in one of his more expansive moods that Stephen laughed aloud. "So!" he exclaimed. "Already I am to become a godfather!"

"Stephen!" Amelia's face was stricken. "How did you know?"

"My apologies, Amelia. I didn't mean to be so indelicate. But look at him, will ye—what else could make him strut so? And your face, my dear—it has the look of the angels."

"You won't tell your wife?"

"Of course not! But come—she's been on pins all day waiting on ye two."

Odalie greeted them inside the house. Her dress of flowered chintz was cool and sweet, and her black hair was worn loose despite the fashion because Stephen liked it so. She extended both her hands to Amelia and the smile on her face was genuine. "I've been looking forward so to meeting you," she said, speaking English with only the faintest trace of an accent. "Of course, we did meet before—but there was such a crowd, and we had no chance to talk." She linked her arm through Amelia's and walked ahead of the men. "You're so beautiful," Odalie added warmly. "Stephen raves over you—and now I see why. Such hair! How I envy you!"

"It's like old straw," Amelia declared. "André often repeats what your husband said when first he saw you: 'Hair like midnight cascading from God's own heaven, unlighted by a star.' "

"Stephen said that? Strange he never told me. I'll remember it. Thank you very much, Madame Le Blanc."

"Please call me Amelia. I hope we're going to be friends."

"And you must call me Odalie. But here we are. Sit there across from me, so we can talk. It's been ages since I've talked to a woman other than the slaves."

"But your sister? She comes to see you often, doesn't she?"

Odalie's lovely face clouded. "No," she said. "No, she doesn't. In fact, she's visited us here only once. Of course, it is a long ride . . ."

They took their places at the table and the slaves brought the gleaming dishes. While they ate, Odalie kept up a running fire of small talk, but Stephen said scarcely a word. There was a little pool of silence in which the clinking of the knives and forks sounded too loudly.

André cleared his throat. "You've heard about Tom Warren?"

"No," Stephen said. "What about him?"

"He grows richer by the minute. It was rumored that he made a killing in wheat at first, but that couldn't be. All his wheat burned in that warehouse of yours, didn't it?"

"Yes," Stephen said. "It did."

"You don't see much of him, do you?"

"He hasn't been out to Harrow in nearly two years. I guess he's busy."

"But you do have many visitors, don't you?" Amelia asked.

"Quite a few. Young Cloutier is the most frequent. I think he'd like to relieve me of my wife," Stephen said wickedly.

"Must you say things like that?" Odalie snapped. "You'll have Amelia thinking—"

"That ye're the loveliest creature on earth and no man can resist ye? Why not, my dear? 'Tis true. By the way, André, I married my Achille off to that African wildcat—at last. She gives him not a moment's peace. She's either being terrifically affectionate or throwing him out on his ear! Poor fellow! At least he's never bored."

"And you, my dear," Odalie murmured. "Are you bored?"

"Of course not," Stephen declared stoutly. "How could I be?"

"I was merely wondering, darling. But come, Amelia, let's go up to my rooms and leave the men in peace."

After they had gone, Stephen turned to the sideboard.

"Well, Stephen," André asked, "how does it feel to have succeeded in all your aims?"

"I don't know, André," he said soberly, handing him a glass of port. "It takes getting used to—this marriage business."

André raised the glass of ruby-colored liquid. "Your health, my good friend—and your happiness."

Stephen raised his own glass. "To the coming heir of the Le Blancs," he said.

"Thank you, Stephen," André said. "It makes me feel old somehow—and curiously humble. Still—it is a wonderful thing."

"Aye," Stephen said, and his voice had such a huskiness to it that André turned and stared openly into his face. "Aye," Stephen said again very softly, " 'tis a wonderful thing, André, a very wonderful thing."

AFTER ANDRE AND Amelia had left Harrow, Stephen went up the stairs to his rooms to pick up his hat and gloves. As he gave one last look into the mirror, Odalie turned the gleaming brass knob and stood there in the doorway. "You're not going out again?" she asked. "It's so lonely here. Might I ask where you're going?"

"Ye might," Stephen said tartly. "Although it seems scarcely becoming of a wife to question her husband's doings. I go to the city—to be exact, to the gambling house of one John Davis. I shan't lose, if that's what's troubling ye."

"No—it's not that. It's just that I see so little of you."

"And that bothers ye?"

"Yes." She lifted her face up to his, moving very close to him so that he could smell the perfume in her hair. "I want to have a baby," she said, her voice quivering.

Stephen put down his hat and his gloves slowly, and took her by the shoulders, gently with both hands. "But ye hate my touching ye," he said. "In my arms ye tremble like a wild thing—frightened almost to death."

"I know—and of that I'm horribly ashamed, Stephen my husband. Perhaps I shall change. . . . I . . . I don't know. Only I want you to have your son, Stephen. However I am—however frightened and shy—I love you with all my heart."

"Holy Mother of God!" Stephen whispered and his arms were around her, holding her tight against him. Then effortlessly he swept her up into his arms. But afterward it was the same, with all the rigidity and trembling and cold tears. Stephen got up without a word and began to dress rapidly.

"Stephen!" The word was half a sob.

"Yes," he snarled. "Yes, I'm going!"

Then he strode from the room and his boots sounded clearly on the stairs going down.

CHAPTER EIGHT

DAY AFTER DAY the summer heat mounted. The sun rose over the fields of Harrow, white in a steel-white sky. The swamps began to dry up and sandbars showed through the waters of the Mississippi. Looking out of her window, Odalie could see the dwarfed stalks of cane standing up bare and brown in the naked fields.

Stephen was down there. She could see the gleam of his bright hair. He was working like mad, driving himself and the slaves to exhaustion in his efforts to save the crop. At night he would bathe and dress himself and ride away to New Orleans. Toward Odalie he was grave and exquisitely polite. But he had not come near her again.

Watching him now, Odalie could feel the pain lying upon her heart like a weight of lead. Such a man she had, and between them was this thing she seemed powerless to fight. All she could do was to kneel at her casement and look out at him and pray to the Virgin to send rain before the crop was ruined.

Suddenly the weakness and the nausea that she had noticed several times of a morning were upon her: this time far stronger. She took a tentative step, but she felt the floor coming up to meet her.

"Zerline!" she got out, but the maidservant she had brought from Bellefont was out of hearing. It was Caleen who came flying through the door to catch her in her arms.

"Easy, mistress," Caleen said. With one spidery black arm, she led her to the big bed. "I bring you something, yes."

"Thank you," Odalie whispered. "Oh, Caleen, I'm so sick!"

"It does that, yes. Great lady not like field woman. The master is ver' glad, him, I bet."

"I—I haven't told him. I wasn't sure."

"Well, you sure now!"

Caleen scurried from the room. Odalie sank back upon her bed, pressing both hands over her eyes. Then she heard footsteps on the stairs, pausing outside her door, approaching her bedside. "Caleen?" she whispered hoarsely.

"No," Stephen's vŏice came down to her. " 'Tis not Caleen. What ails ye, my dear? Shall I call Dr. Terrebonne for ye?"

"No, no—Caleen is taking care of me. Besides, I feel much better now—since you've come."

There was the scraping of a chair as he drew it up beside her bed. Then Caleen came in with steaming tea that smelled of mint. "Men," she said with mock severity, "always make trouble, yes. You go 'way from here, master! Already you done enough, you!"

Stephen turned to Odalie. "What on earth is she talking about?" he demanded. "Odalie! You don't mean . . ."

"Yes, my husband," Odalie said gently.

The chair went over backward with a crash, and Stephen was on his knees beside the bed, gathering her into his arms. Then Odalie nestled her head against his shoulder and loosed her tears.

"Why do ye cry?" he asked. " 'Tis a thing for joy and laughter."

"Because I'm happier than I can bear. Because you take me in your arms and do not turn away. And because there will be a son for Harrow."

"A son for Harrow," Stephen repeated after her. Not his son, not hers, but Harrow's—a son to be shaped by the house into the finely tempered image of a gentleman, who would grow with it until at last he became master of it. And so it would go, for generations. Harrow. This was it. Completion. Fulfillment.

He looked out the window to where the sun was scorching the earth with wave upon wave of heat.

"What is it, Stephen?" Odalie whispered.

" 'Tis only I'm thinking that if this heat does not abate soon, 'twill be a poor heritage that the lad will come into. Caleen! Ye're not to leave your mistress," Stephen said sternly. "She is not to exert herself in any way. Anything she wants, ye will get for her and promptly. I'm holding ye responsible, mind ye!"

He turned again to his wife. He bent and kissed her gently and Odalie realized suddenly with vast relief that there would be no more passion in his caresses—not for a long time now. She was conscious of a feeling of shame at her relief. It must be a boy, she decided. She must not fail him in that, too.

"I must ride into town," Stephen said, "to arrange a loan. The crop is a failure. Even if it rains now, it will still be a failure. I'll see Tom Warren. My credit is excellent hereabouts. Take care of yourself, my darling. Follow Caleen's suggestions. She's a wise one, for all that she's an old devil!" Again he bent and kissed her, then he turned and strode through the doorway.

STEPHEN RODE ALONG the highway with his head bent upon his chest. A son for Harrow. Now he must work even harder. The plantation must be put on a firm basis for all time so that his son would never want for anything. The Foxes would leave their mark on this New World. Having no ancestors, he told himself, I am become one. The thought pleased him.

He noticed a horseman bearing down upon him, sitting in the saddle like a centaur. That would be young Cloutier—nowhere in the state was there a better horseman.

As the two riders closed the gap between them, the young man's face lighted. "I was bound for Harrow," he said. "But now that I see you're not there . . ." He reined in his horse.

Stephen looked at Phillippe Cloutier. Truly the lad was a handsome devil. "My absence is no cause for ye to change your intent," he said. "Madame Fox will be glad to see ye. And anything that brings her happiness is not displeasing to me. Ride on, lad. Ye're always welcome at Harrow."

Phillippe lifted his hat and the clatter of the horse's hooves rang sharply upon the sunbaked road. Stephen dismissed him from his mind almost at once. Whatever Phillippe's intent might be, he was aeons from its accomplishment. There was this about Odalie—a husband of hers would never wear horns.

Later, winding through the streets of New Orleans, Stephen was struck by the desolation and squalor of the place. The thrifty, enterprising Americans produced most of the wealth of the city. Yet the Creole council persistently vetoed any appropriations to improve it; the streets remained unpaved, the wharves were rotting away. The stench of the drainage was enough to sicken a man. And the yellow fever killed hundreds yearly. The Creoles only shrugged. Yellow Jack was a "stranger's disease." They did not die of it. Used to the climate, habitually drinking wine instead of water, they lived calmly through epidemic after epidemic, while the raw Irish immigrants, the Germans, the English and the Americans were decimated. Damn the Creoles anyway!

Stephen rode on, holding a fine handkerchief to his nose. In the Vieux Carré conditions were only a trifle better. Here, to be sure, were paved streets, but they were so narrow that two coaches could not pass abreast.

Stephen turned into Chartres Street and stopped before an imposing edifice four stories tall and glistening in its newness.

Truly Tom Warren must have struck it rich. Well, he had done Tom favors in the past; 'twould not be amiss to ask one now.

He climbed down from Prince Michael and went through the doorway. One of the half-dozen clerks who were busy with their pens at the high desks scurried into an inner chamber to summon Tom Warren.

The big man appeared and stretched out his hand. "Stephen!" he said. " 'Tis good to see you again."

Stephen took the offered hand. He's put on flesh, he decided. Dresses better, too. And it's "Stephen" now. Always before it was "Mr. Fox." He followed Warren into the well-equipped inner office. "Ye've prospered," he said. "I'm very glad."

"Thank you," Tom said. "But to what do I owe the pleasure of this visit?"

"I need your help," Stephen said bluntly. "Cane needs water— lots of water—and ye know how this summer has been."

"Do I! How much do you need, Stephen?"

"Fifteen thousand. And I'll need it until next harvest."

Without a word, Tom Warren took up his pen and checkbook. Scarcely glancing at Stephen, he wrote rapidly. He sanded the check, dusted it off and passed it to Stephen.

The amount was thirty thousand dollars. "I asked ye for fifteen only," Stephen said.

"You shouldn't figure so closely, Stephen," Tom Warren observed. "I know the expense of running a place."

"And what are your rates?" Stephen asked.

"To you—none. And the date of repayment is left to your judgment. Take what time you will."

"Ye're a good friend, Tom," Stephen said. "But I shall repay ye at the next harvest—and with interest too. A thousand thanks for your kindness. Come visit us at Harrow."

"I'll try hard to come," Tom Warren said. "But do not hold it against me if I do not. It will be only because I'm infernally busy. My regards to Madame Fox. You're a lucky man, Stephen."

"Thank ye," Stephen said, and took his leave. Whatever might be said about the sharpness of Tom Warren's dealings, there was no denying that he had a heart.

There was really no reason to rush back to Harrow, Stephen decided as he left the bank after having deposited Tom's draft. Odalie was probably pleasantly occupied with Phillippe Cloutier. Why not drop in at Bellefont and lunch with old Arceneaux and Aurore? Stephen was genuinely fond of both his in-laws. Aurore, he reflected, was a lovely girl. Strange that she had not married. She'd had her share of beaux.

Aurore was standing on the broad gallery looking out over the drive as Stephen rode up to Bellefont. She came down the stairs to greet him, a tiny smile curving the corners of her mouth.

"My dear little sister," he said, bending over her hand, "I came especially to see ye. Would ye object to exchanging a pleasant word or two with your brother-in-law?"

"Not at all. In fact, I'm very glad to see you. It's nice that you're 'family' now, Stephen."

"Why?"

"Because I couldn't sit and talk with you without Father being here if you weren't. Would you like some coffee and cake?"

Following her into the house, Stephen was struck by her grace. She grows more like Odalie every day, he thought; the coloring is different—still, they are much alike. But Aurore was turning into the dining hall and the dim light edged her profile briefly. Stephen found himself reversing his judgment: there was only the family similarity; in all else Odalie and Aurore were different.

As they sat at the table Stephen looked at her over his steaming cup. The look was hard, intent. The small smile on Aurore's face wavered. And her eyes, meeting his, were utterly naked. She stood up suddenly.

"What is it, Aurore? What's troubling ye?" Stephen asked.

"Nothing—really, it's nothing, Stephen. The heat and all. You'll excuse me, won't you?"

"Not until I have your promise to visit us more often at Harrow. We've missed ye sadly."

"Oh, I'll come! Please now, Stephen. I really must lie down."

"Very well." Then a mischievous glint came into Stephen's eyes. "But first ye must salute me with a sisterly kiss, or else I shall not budge from this spot."

He stepped forward and caught both her hands at the wrists. He could feel her pulse pounding against the palms of his hands.

"No, Stephen." Her voice was very quiet. "You mustn't."

"And ye said I was 'family,'" Stephen mocked. Then he leaned forward suddenly. But she turned her head very rapidly so that his kiss brushed lightly across the corner of her mouth.

"That wasn't much of a kiss." He laughed. "But 'twill have to do for now. Good day, my dear sister." His bow was unnecessarily deep, and his laughter floated back after he had gone.

ODALIE SAT IN the *chambre-à-brin*—the little screened enclosure in a corner of the great gallery—talking to Phillippe Cloutier. It was necessary for her to have fresh air, but the fierce mosquitoes of the bayou country would have devoured her alive if she had not had the protection of the screening. Strange that Stephen had not yet returned, she thought.

Phillippe's heavy black brows came together in a frown. "You say you love him, this husband of yours, this foreigner—you could not love another man?"

"You, for instance? No, Phillippe, I couldn't. There is nowhere on this earth such a man as he."

"I'll prove you're mistaken!" Phillippe said. He bent forward suddenly and swept her into his arms. Then very slowly and with great deliberation he kissed her, hard upon the mouth. Odalie did not resist but she made no response—no response at all.

When he released her, she looked at him calmly. "I'm sorry you did that," she said. "Now I must ask you to go and never come back again."

"You're being unfair," he said. "Monstrously unfair."

"I shall miss you, Phillippe, and if I ever—by word or gesture— led you to think that I would permit such liberties, please forgive me, for it was not my intention. Good-by, Phillippe."

He bowed silently and went down the stairs.

THROUGHOUT THE FALL the heat continued. Had it not been for Tom Warren's loan, Stephen would have had to sell some of the land to meet his notes, but as it was, he was able to ride over into winter with a comfortable margin of security.

The heat was a great burden to Odalie. Delicate by nature, she continued to have sieges of nausea and fainting. Swollen ankles and knees kept her abed most of the day; and she was constantly in tears, fearing the permanent loss of her former litheness, storming at Stephen, swearing she hated him.

All this Stephen bore with great patience—especially after the heat had abated and the winter rains had set in. He knew that next year the crop would be good. Odalie would be occupied with the child, and she would therefore give him little trouble.

The winter went by slowly. Never, it seemed, would the icy rains cease. Stephen rode out to inspect his property, stopping at the slave cabins to see after the welfare of his people. One of the last cabins to be visited was that of Achille, proud now that his own black wife had become pregnant. Achille's cabin was scrupulously clean, and the big slave had made rude furniture for it, fashioned, as far as Stephen could see, in imitation of the furniture up at Harrow. La Belle Sauvage lay on the bed, moaning softly.

"How goes it with her?" Stephen asked.

"Bad, master. She suffers like a lady—it's not easy for her like field woman."

"Sauvage princess," the girl on the bed got out between moans. "No field woman, me! No slave!"

"Hush," Achille growled.

" 'Tis nothing, Achille," Stephen said. "They all want a bit of humoring when they're like that."

He looked up from the bed toward the rough stone mantel and noticed a carved wooden figurine. Some fetish or tribal god, Stephen decided. He walked over to it and picked it up in his hand. Held loosely in his palm, it seemed almost obscene. "What is this?" he demanded.

"Wanga!" Achille muttered uneasily. "Powerful Wanga!"

"Ye worship this monstrosity, Achille?"

"I am a Catholic," Achille declared. "Same as you, master. But she's still wild."

The great yellow-brown eyes glowed up at him. "Ye must not worship this thing," Stephen said calmly. "It has no power over ye. See, it burns like any other wood." He tossed it lightly into the fire. La Belle Sauvage sat straight up on her bed and made the cabin quiver with her screams. Strongly but gently Achille pressed her back upon the bed.

"She'll have a fit now," he said to Stephen. "Best that you go, master."

Wrapping his greatcoat about him, Stephen went out into the driving rain. As he approached the house, he saw a horse standing near the foot of the stairs. When he neared the top, the doors swung open and the warm yellow light poured out.

"Master," Georges's excited voice called. "You never guess—"

Then Ti Demon was shouldering Georges aside, his big white teeth gleaming in a huge grin. He extended a rain-soaked piece of paper to Stephen. Stephen opened it and read:

My dear Stephen:
It's a son and heir! He is beautiful beyond belief—with Amelia's hair and eyes and the set chin of the Le Blancs. I am taking the liberty of naming him Stephen, after you, my old one! We are eagerly awaiting your visit.

André

Stephen's pale eyes were very clear, and a little smile played about the corners of his mouth. André a father! He spun on his heel and marched in the direction of Odalie's room. "How are ye, my dear?" he asked as he crossed to the bed upon which she was lying.

"What do you care?" she stormed. "You got me like this! And now you stay away forever and care not if I die!"

"Softly, my dear," Stephen said. "Ye should not excite yourself so." He sat down beside the bed. "André and Amelia have their wish," he told her. "It is a son, called Stephen in my honor."

"Oh, Stephen, they can't! You mustn't let them! What on earth will we call *our* baby?"

"Holy saints! That I had forgotten."

"Stephen, would you mind very much if I called him Etienne? I know you don't like French names, but after all, the meaning is the same."

"Suppose it is a girl?" Stephen grinned. "What then, Odalie?"

"Oh, Stephen, no! It can't be! I'd die if it were only a girl!"

"Ye'll love and cherish it, whatever it is," he said gently. He kissed her and got to his feet. "Call it whatever ye like," he said softly, and crossed the room to the door.

THE SPRING CAME whispering in with rains that probed like warm fingers into the black earth. Already the cane was up, taller than it usually was by midsummer, and the cotton stalks clustered over mile after mile of fields. The river, swollen by the months of rainfall and the melting snows of the north, was growling a few scant feet below the top of the levee.

Now that it was almost time for her travail, Odalie found herself surprisingly well. Often of an evening she was driven into New

Orleans, where, heavily veiled, she would descend from the coach at a private side entrance of the Théâtre d'Orléans. She would be conducted up a hidden stairway to the *Loges Grilles*, and from behind the lattices that hid her from the public eye, she would enjoy the new series of light operas that had recently been introduced. Sitting beside her now, Stephen decided that *La Dame Blanche* was but an indifferent opera. Still, if it pleased Odalie . . . She caught his hand suddenly. Her grip was fierce, the fingers biting into his flesh. "Stephen," she whispered. He stood up, taking her arm. "Stephen—it's come—and we'd better hurry!"

"Dr. Terrebonne's but a few blocks beyond—"

"No. Harrow, Stephen—he must be born at Harrow!"

Stephen bent and swept her up into his arms. He went down the stairs to the waiting coach. "Harrow," he said to the coachman. "And be quick about it!" To a messenger he said, "Tell Dr. Terrebonne that we shall expect him at Harrow within the hour. Be off with ye now!"

All the way to Harrow, Odalie held Stephen's hand tightly. Never did she permit the slightest moan to escape her lips, but at times her grip tightened and a fine dew of perspiration filmed her brow. Stephen drew her head down upon his shoulder and tried to protect her from the jolting of the coach.

Then they were swinging up the alley of oaks before Harrow. Stephen leaped to the ground and reached for Odalie. She sank into his arms. He carried her up the stairs very fast, yet smoothly, to find old Caleen waiting at the top. "The water soon be to a boil. I take care of her now," she said.

"How the devil did ye know?" Stephen demanded.

"Caleen have ways," she said mysteriously. In truth, she had been watching from the belvedere and had seen the coach thundering up the river road. Only one thing, she knew, would make the master drive so fast with the young mistress aboard. But better he believe in her mystic powers.

An hour and a half later Dr. Terrebonne arrived. Stephen was hard put to conceal his impatience at the delay. But the fat little Creole was bustling with good humor. "You have whiskey?" he asked merrily. Stephen nodded. "Good. Go then and get splendidly drunk, but stay out of my way. I will need the assistance of a woman—with strong nerves."

Stephen inclined his head dumbly toward Caleen.

"Come," Dr. Terrebonne said. Then, smiling broadly, he added, "Perhaps I shall have need of a witch!"

Stephen stood outside the door of the bedchamber and waited, rigid as a statue. When, at last, the little doctor came out, his round, owlish face was grave. "I want you to dispatch a man to the house of my colleague, Lefevre. Tell him to take over my practice for tonight. I'm remaining here."

"It—it's that bad, Doctor?"

"She is not built for childbearing," he said softly. "She is too slim in the flanks and the child seems unusually large. If she survives this one, it must be the last. Remember that."

"If she survives—my God, do ye know what ye're saying?"

"Yes," the doctor said, "I know."

Throughout the night only Dr. Terrebonne slept, and he but at intervals. Odalie's agony was a fearsome thing. Watching her Stephen found almost unendurable. All through the next day and into the night the anguished labor continued.

Toward morning the exhausted little doctor was sleeping fitfully in his chamber in the north wing while outside the room Stephen paced up and down like a caged beast. Caleen watched by her mistress's side. Suddenly Odalie moaned softly and began writhing on the great bed. Caleen bent over her. There was no time to summon the doctor. What must be done must be done now—alone.

Fifteen minutes later Stephen's stride was arrested abruptly. From the chamber came a series of sharp slaps, then a lusty howling that filled even the great hall. Stephen hung over the brass knob, too weak to open the door.

Then the gigantic form of Achille was shouldering past him, his eyes glazed over, oblivious of everything. "Caleen!" he roared. "My baby—come, Caleen, come!"

Caleen's voice was like ice as she faced her son. "Get out of here, you!" she said very quietly. "Before you kills the young mistress! Your woman no die, and if she do, good! I comes when I can. Go, you!"

Achille stood trembling before his mother's wrath, great tears streaking his black face. Then, without a word, he turned and left the room. Stephen, white and shaking, was bending over the still form of his wife. "Is she," he quavered, "is she . . . ?"

"She be all right," Caleen said sternly.

When Dr. Terrebonne came to examine Odalie, Stephen waited outside. Afterward, the doctor's round face wore a look of astonishment. "Name your price for that old woman," he said to Stephen. "Never in all my years of practice . . ."

"There is not that much money in the world," Stephen said.

"You have a perfect son," the doctor went on. "You can see him now if you will."

"If I will!" Stephen growled. "Ye should try to stop me!"

As they entered the room, Caleen was holding the baby. Stephen bent over his son, sleeping peacefully in the old woman's arms.

"Black hair like his mother," Caleen declared. "But him got eyes blue like yours, master."

Stephen turned away from the child and knelt beside the bed.

"So," Odalie was whispering, "I didn't die after all. . . . The child—how is it, Stephen?"

"Perfect." Stephen smiled. "A son, as ye wished."

"May I hold my little 'Tienne? Where is he?"

Caleen bent and placed the sleeping child in Odalie's arms.

"How beautiful he is," she whispered. "He pleases you, my husband?"

"Beyond comprehension," Stephen said. "Now ye must rest. 'Tis a frightful siege ye've undergone." He bent and kissed her, lightly, upon the mouth. There was the taste of blood upon her lips, where she had bitten them through. "Stay with her, Caleen," Stephen ordered.

"Master permit I call Zerline? Mistress all right now. I want to see after the baby of Achille—my grandson. Maybe him die, yes, with no one there."

"My God," Stephen said, "I'd forgotten. Come, Caleen, I'll go with ye."

Hurrying down the road toward the slave cabins, Stephen could hear the booming of the river; the top of the levee was almost awash. Caleen was ahead of him, and he followed her into the cabin, holding his handkerchief against his nose to keep out the dark, fetid smells of birth. La Belle Sauvage lay upon the rude bed with an infant cradled in her arms. The child was bluish black, large and sound of limb, and Stephen could see it had something of its mother's striking dark beauty.

"A manchild," Sauvage whispered. "A warrior for his people!" She began to chant a wild, savage song to the baby.

Achille's face was split by a pleased grin. "All by herself she had him! She bit the cord through with them cat teeth. I tell you, master, she's something, that one!"

Stephen was examining the child. "He is a fine one, Belle," he said. "I want him trained as a manservant for my Etienne. He will be taught many things."

Caleen smiled slowly. But La Belle Sauvage was coming erect in the bed. "My child no slave!" she said. "Him prince—warrior prince! Him nobody servant, nobody slave!"

"Hush, girl!" Achille growled. "We do like he say!"

" 'Tis not so harsh a fate, Belle," Stephen said gently. "Here, let me hold him."

"No lay hands on him, no!" the girl screamed. Then, like a great cat, she sprang from the bed and dashed for the door. Achille sprang after her, and Stephen and Caleen followed. But they were no match for her lithe swiftness. Her slim body innocent of clothing, La Belle Sauvage ran straight for the river.

She went up the incline like a black panther, with catlike grace, the long ebony legs shooting out and the earth flowing backward under the slim feet. Still holding the child, she stood for a moment atop the levee, outlined sharply against the light, lifting the child high above her head. "Him warrior!" she chanted. "Him die, but him never be slave!"

Then Achille was upon her and Stephen was but a step behind. Together they snatched the crying infant from her arms. The girl fell back. Then with a cry, she whirled and threw herself out and down into the swirling water. It rose like dirty yellow wings as she went in, then it fell back, and the current howled like a living thing.

Achille thrust the child into Caleen's arms. But Stephen lunged and grasped the big man about the waist.

"Lemme go!" he cried. "She drown, her! She drown!"

"And so will ye!" Stephen said. "There's no saving her now."

Fifty yards downstream Sauvage's head broke water; then the swirling yellow torrent rode over her. The sound of the river pounded upon their eardrums.

They all went down the levee together. Achille's big hands hung loosely at his sides, and the tears streaked his black face.

Stephen put a hand upon his shoulder. "She was never the one for ye," he said. "I will get ye another—gentle and comely, better for ye and the baby."

Achille did not answer. He went on down the road to the cabins, his great body shaken with sobs.

And old Caleen held the baby, her ancient eyes veiled and crafty. Inch I will call him, she mused. After his grandfather. Never he be like Achille, but a man, him. His body they will enslave, yes, but never his mind and his heart. I will teach him.

She smiled slowly to herself.

CHAPTER NINE

THE YEAR 1831 was a good one throughout the bayou country. The great plantations grew and prospered. And of them none grew richer than Harrow. Stephen paid off his debt to Tom Warren and invested money in newer and finer machinery. He opened accounts with two of the largest banks in New Orleans, but the bulk of his profits he sent away to far-off Philadelphia. "For monetary affairs," he remarked to André, "give me a vinegary Yankee every time."

Little Etienne Fox, at the age of one year, was trying his first steps. All life at Harrow revolved around him. Odalie forgot Stephen existed in her preoccupation with the child; Aurore Arceneaux's visits increased, and old Pierre fairly lived at Harrow.

Etienne was a striking child. He had reached far back among his swarthy Mediterranean ancestors for the dark complexion and inky hair that curled in great masses above his forehead. But he had Stephen's eyes, their pale blueness set off by the darkness of his skin. He was a quiet child, little given to laughing. He seemed to live always in a world apart.

As soon as the babies could crawl, André and Stephen brought their two heirs together. Little Stephen Le Blanc was as fair as Etienne was dark, and the two of them made the same sort of pleasing contrast, in reverse, as their fathers had before them.

Amelia and Odalie, too, found themselves bound together by motherhood. On Odalie's part, the friendship was warm and genuine; she grew to depend upon the levelheaded judgment of this American girl and to admire and cultivate her ways. Amelia, however, recognized that her own feeling toward the beautiful Creole was one of sympathy more than friendship; she actually liked Aurore better than she did her cold, imperious sister. Half a glance sufficed to let her know what Aurore's trouble was, and her heart went out to the lovely young girl whose face held the sad sweetness of an angel. Soon Odalie was complaining that her sister spent more time at La Place des Rivières than at Harrow.

Thus matters rested when Mike Farrel chose to put in his appearance at the big plantation. "The trouble is," he said to Stephen, "that nobody wants an old flatboatman anymore. The packets can do the job almost as cheap and twice as fast. I've lived too long."

"Nonsense," Stephen told him. "Ye'll make as fine a steamboat captain as ever was seen upon the river. 'Tis high time we started upon that business anyway."

By the early spring of 1832 there was a fast new steamer upon the river, the *Creole Belle*. Mike avidly undertook the business of learning steam navigation. Doggedly he studied until the steamboatmen were forced to admit grudgingly that here was a formidable rival. On her first trip under Mike's full command, the *Creole Belle* came within minutes of breaking the upriver record to Cincinnati.

While in port, Mike continued to live at Harrow. No longer did he feel humiliated by Stephen's bounty. He was a person of importance now, a river captain, and he dressed and lived the role to the hilt. He felt freer than ever to indulge his fondness for good liquors and mulatto wenches.

"I won't have him here!" Odalie stormed. "He is a beast, this friend of yours! Why cannot he leave the girls alone? There are two near-white babies in the infirmary now, and some would say that these children are yours, Stephen."

Stephen stood up, his fair brows coming together over his nose. "That's enough," he said quietly. "If I choose to have Mike stay at Harrow, 'tis my affair, and, by all the saints, he stays!"

"Oh, you!" Odalie exploded, and marched from the room. She went up the stairs to her bedroom and picked up the sewing she had laid aside. Her head ached abominably. She pulled the bell cord. When Zerline came into the room, Odalie looked up with an expression of annoyance. "Must you be so slow?" she demanded.

"I'm sorry, mistress," the girl whispered.

Odalie could see the tears standing in her eyes. "You've put on weight," Odalie said, her black eyes narrowing. "And all of it about the waist too. Zerline . . ."

"Oh, mistress," the girl cried out.

"Who was it, Zerline? Come, girl, pull yourself together!"

"Him, mistress knows—him. Suzette, she runs—but I am not so fast as Suzette. One time I am too slow—and he is so strong, like a bear."

Odalie stood up slowly, the headache forgotten. "Go downstairs," she said softly. "Tell Caleen that you are to receive the best of everything. She is not to reproach you." Zerline looked at her mistress with eyes filled with tears of adoration. They went out the door together and down the stairs. Zerline hurried off to find Caleen, and Odalie went immediately to Stephen.

He was busy at the great ledger book, recording the sale of a thousand bales of cotton held over in his warehouse from last harvest.

"Stephen," Odalie said sternly, "I must ask you to have that man leave Harrow. When he goes so far as to violate my own personal maidservant, it seems to me high time to call a halt!"

"Mike did that?"

"Yes."

"I must warn him to confine his activities to Girod Street. This is not a thing to be tolerated. But he has a home here for life. I gave him my word."

"Either he goes," Odalie declared, "or I do!"

"It is up to ye." Stephen stood up, taking his hat and riding crop in his hand. "Adieu, my dear," he said. "I have work to do."

Odalie watched him striding away in the direction of the stables. Her face was still.

"Georges!" she called. Stephen's valet came out of the pantry. "Have the coach hitched. Get Caleen—and Zerline, too, at once!"

"Yes, mistress," Georges said, and his voice was frightened. Never had he seen the young mistress look like this. He scurried away to fetch the others.

Two hours later the yellow coach was rolling away toward New Orleans. In it were Odalie and little Etienne, Caleen, Zerline, and Jean, a manservant. Zerline was crying softly, but Odalie's face was pale and still. Old Caleen stared blankly out of the window.

Pierre Arceneaux had aged greatly in the last three years. As he greeted his elder daughter, his face was lined and grave. "I have no doubt that you know what you're doing," he said, "but any dissolution of the marriage contract grieves me. However, come in, child. You're always welcome."

Odalie walked into the house and went at once to her rooms on the second floor. Slowly the old man climbed the curving stairs, and in Odalie's room sank down upon the nearest chair. "What if I sent a messenger to Stephen asking him to come and discuss this difficulty?"

"No, Father. I'll never go back. What's done is done. If Stephen prefers his brute of a river captain to me—why then, let the two of them stay up at Harrow without me." She rose and crossed the room.

Down below, the alley was all but deserted. As Odalie watched, a wooden ox cart, piled high and covered with canvas, groaned through the narrow street. As it passed beneath her, the heavy stench rose and struck her in the face.

"That wagon—" Odalie said. "Father, am I mad, or is that a human leg I see sticking out from under the canvas?"

"You're quite sane," Pierre told her grimly. "They pass this way every day with the unclaimed dead stacked up like cordwood. The whole world seems to be dying, Odalie."

"But, Father, what on earth—why?"

"The fever again—and worse than ever before. . . . Still want to stay in New Orleans, Odalie?"

The tall girl faced her father. "I'll chance it," she said, and went on with her unpacking.

Throughout the summer and fall the deaths continued to mount. Odalie forbade Caleen to take little Etienne outside of the house even for air, and the boy fretted in the sweltering heat. At night no one slept, and Zerline, heavy with child, would toss upon her cot, her lips swollen and covered with blisters. There had been a headlong rush to leave the city. By October 25 only thirty-five thousand people were left out of New Orleans' normal population of more than eighty thousand souls. Still Odalie held on grimly.

On the night of October 28 Odalie was shaken awake by Caleen's horny old hand. "Mistress, come," she said. "Zerline is dying!"

Odalie ran down the dark hall in her nightdress. The mulatto girl was twisting on her cot, locked in convulsions.

"Tell Jean to ride for Dr. Terrebone," Odalie said. "Come, Caleen, we've work to do."

Caleen shook her head. "Too late," she said.

Dr. Terrebonne did not reach the house of Pierre Arceneaux until six o'clock the next morning. By that time Zerline had been dead almost eight hours. Odalie scarcely recognized the little doctor. His clothes hung loosely like bags from his once ample form, and his eyes, streaked with fiery red, peered out from great blue hollows. "You come too late," Odalie said.

"I know. I am always too late now. Merciful God! As if the fever were not enough . . ."

"Not enough? You mean there is something more?"

"Cholera. Madame," he said, "I can only suggest that you drive out of New Orleans—this instant—at a gallop. Good night, madame. I will have the death cart call for the remains."

"No!" Odalie said. "She will have a decent Christian burial."

"If Madame can find a priest. Most have died, ministering unto the sick. Perhaps Madame is willing to undertake the labor of grave digging with her own patrician hands."

He left with a curt bow, already hurrying to his next call. He's mad, Odalie thought.

Carefully she and Caleen wrapped the bloated figure of the girl in a winding sheet. Then they summoned Jean, and Jules, old Arceneaux's manservant, and had her lifted tenderly into the carriage. After arming the Negroes with spades, they set out for the burial ground.

As they passed through the deserted streets, they saw houses boarded up, and time and again Odalie had to turn her head to avoid the sight of sodden, shapeless bundles that had once been human beings lying amid the filth of a gutter.

They drove through the gates of the cemetery. Leaning out, Odalie could see the great open trenches into which the death carts were dumping their loads. She pointed to a clear spot and Jean and Jules went to work. When they were done, they laid the body gently in the earth, then waited bareheaded while their mistress said a prayer. At last they covered Zerline with the rich black earth and turned homeward.

When Odalie reached her father's house, she was met at the

door by a slave. "Mistress," the woman said, "the baby, him sick. Your papa sick, too. Maybe they die."

Without a word, Odalie went up the stairs two at a time. In his little bed Etienne twisted soundlessly, his naturally dark face flushed a deep mahogany red. Odalie put a hand to his hot forehead. Then she ran from the room toward her father's bedchamber.

The old man lay unconscious and shrunken upon his bed, his eyes wide and staring and his breath coming out in feeble puffs and whistles. Odalie saw that the look of death was already in his face. As she stood there, the proud old eyes opened suddenly. "Get Father Antoine," he whispered. "I have sins to confess— many sins. . . ." But there was no need to do anything but kneel beside his bed and say a prayer for his soul. Pierre Arceneaux was dead.

Dry-eyed, Odalie came out of the room to meet Caleen in the corridor. "I sent Jean for the doctor fast," the old woman said. "The baby is ver' sick!"

"Father," Odalie said, "Father. . . ." Then she bent her face against Caleen's shoulder and cried aloud—dry, racking sobs, utterly without tears. Caleen patted her gently upon the back.

When Jean returned an hour later, he and Jules started to work in the courtyard, tearing up the flagstones to make a grave for Pierre Arceneaux. Odalie had decided not to risk another trip to the graveyard. Holding the fever-racked body of little Etienne in her arms, she looked out of the window at the burning barrels of pitch and tar by which means the medical authorities sought to purify the air. The fires crackled fiercely, hurling flames higher than the houses. Now and again, from the distant parts of the city, a cannon boomed, meant to change the air currents and drive away the malignant vapors that were converting New Orleans into a city of the dead.

Odalie closed the window and sat down, sinking back into her chair, cradling the sick child to her breast. "Holy Mother of God," she prayed. "Holy, compassionate Mother of God . . ."

Then Caleen was leading a strange doctor into the room. "I am Dr. Lefevre," he announced a trifle pompously. "My colleague, Dr. Terrebonne, died this afternoon of the cholera. May I see the child, please."

Without a word, Odalie passed Etienne over to him. "It is not the cholera," he said, "for which you may be grateful. He has yellow fever. We may be able to pull him through."

He took from his bag a great array of small vials and powders. "Tisanes, cataplasms and purgatives," he announced. "We shall try them first. If he is not improved by morning, we will try a spoonful of croton oil with three drops of mercury. That should break the fever. Afterward, calcined magnesia, olive oil and juice of citron, alternated with—"

"But he is only a baby," Odalie whispered.

"You want him to live, don't you?" the doctor said sternly.

"Yes," Odalie said, "yes."

"Then do as I say. We cannot be certain even then. Much depends upon the patient." He smiled wryly. "I once saw Monsieur Fox fight a duel. He stood without moving, without even lifting his pistol, and allowed Monsieur Waguespack to fire at a perfectly stationary target. With the inheritance of such courage, this child should certainly survive. Good night, Madame Fox. I'll call again tomorrow."

Dr. Lefevre called daily at the Arceneaux mansion, but little 'Tienne got no better. Finally the doctor looked down upon the barely breathing child in whom the fever still mounted. "There is but one hope," he said. "Sometimes the fever is cooled by a diminution of the blood. We must bleed him."

"No!" Odalie cried. "No!"

"It is the only way, madame," the doctor said patiently.

"No!" Caleen screeched. She sprang forward and gathered little 'Tienne into her arms. "Mistress great fool!" she stormed. "We go back to Harrow, now! And I cure him! No great fool of a *docteur* kill my baby! Come now, mistress. Come!"

The doctor glared at the old woman, but Odalie followed her helplessly out of the room.

Caleen rode behind Odalie on the single ancient nag, the baby cradled in her arms. There were no longer any slaves to hitch and drive the carriage. Jules and Jean had died of the fever, along with most of the Arceneaux household.

Old Josh spied them from the levee, and dashed off to inform his master. So it was that when they turned up the oak alley that led to Harrow, Stephen was waiting.

"I have brought you back your son," Odalie said with great dignity, "so that he may die in the house of his father."

Stephen looked at the tiny bundle of skin and bones that should have been a healthy, prattling child of almost three years. "If he does," he said grimly, "God and Our Lady forgive ye, for I never shall!" Then he took Etienne in his arms and marched up the steps and into the house.

FOR THE NEXT four days old Caleen was in complete charge of everything. She stubbornly got drop after drop of orange juice, lemon juice and lime juice down the child's parched little throat. Precious ice was wrapped in thin cloths that were placed upon the boy's blazing forehead, as Caleen fought the temperature down and kept the slender thread of life from snapping.

On the morning of the fourth day Caleen's grandson, Little Inch, was standing by the crib, his bright eyes resting fearfully on the face of his little master. " 'Tienne die?" he asked.

Caleen bent forward suddenly. Etienne's body was wet from head to foot; but this time from his own sweat. And his forehead was cool to the touch. "No," the old woman said. " 'Tienne no die! He getting well, him!"

"Holy Blessed Mother of God!" Stephen whispered. "Odalie!"

Odalie came into the room, all color gone from her face. "Is he—is he . . ." she managed; but the child opened his eyes.

"Mo ganye faim," he whispered. *"Mo ganye faim."*

Odalie took a half-step forward and fell into Stephen's arms, weeping. Holding her close against him, he raised his eyebrows at Caleen. "What on earth is he saying?" he whispered.

"He say him hungry, in Gumbo French. He hear me talk and Little Inch. Now I go get him soup, me." She slipped from the room.

"Stephen," Odalie said, "Stephen . . ."

"He lives, Odalie. That's all that matters. And in the growing, he will need both a father and a mother. Ye can find it in your heart to tolerate an old boor for a little longer, can ye not?"

"Tolerate?" Odalie said. "Oh, Stephen—Stephen, why can't you understand?"

"I think I do," Stephen said. They went over to the crib and looked down. Etienne was sleeping like a tiny angel. Then they tiptoed from the room.

Mike Farrel called the next day from his rooms in the city to pay his respects. He stood before the mistress of Harrow, twisting

a big kerchief nervously in his powerful hands. "I come to ask your forgiveness, me lady," he said. "You have no use for the likes of me, I know. But if Stevie's wee one had died, I would have felt myself a murderer. You have me word I'll never trouble you again."

"You're welcome at Harrow," Odalie said softly. "I ask only that you leave the servants alone."

"Thank you, me lady," Mike said, and bowed himself out with great dignity.

BEFORE THE MIDDLE of winter Etienne was running around the house as vigorously as ever. Only he seemed to have retreated even further into his own private world, into which he permitted only the slightest glimpses. Inch was constantly at his side, but André brought little Stephen less and less frequently.

"They have brought forth a monster!" he confided to Amelia. "The last time 'Tienne wanted to play Spanish Inquisition, with our Stephen as the victim of torture. I tell you, the boy is mad!"

" 'Tis the aftereffects of the fever," Amelia said gently, cuddling their third child to her breast. "He will get over it."

CHAPTER TEN

LATE IN MARCH of 1836 Stephen met André at the fork of the river road, and the two of them rode to New Orleans. André was afire with enthusiasm.

"This means everything to us, Stephen," he said. "As soon as Texas wins her independence—and she will win it, never you fear—we must annex her! Don't you see, Stephen, out of Texas we can carve five slave-holding states."

"Aye," Stephen said grimly. "And 'tis a thing that troubles me: this race between us for more lands, more peoples, more votes. I have good friends in Philadelphia and New York. And now there is much bitterness because of this thing."

"Filthy money grubbers!" André said. "They dare to point at us in scorn because of slavery. Everybody knows that slavery is the natural order of things, ordained by God."

Stephen threw back his head and laughed aloud. "How I envy ye your Louisiana faculty for self-delusion! Slavery is a very convenient and pleasant system—for us. But I've often had qualms over the rightness of a system that permits me to sell a man as though he were a mule."

"Stephen! You talk like an abolitionist! But you may tell your Yankee friends that if they interfere, we shall leave them and continue on alone in our own way."

Stephen was no longer smiling. " 'Tis a terrible thing, this secession business. Can a hand declare itself independent of the body? I tell ye, André, that what we have here in America is something new in the world. 'Tis not a loose collection of sovereign states. This is a people's government—the truest republic the world has ever seen."

"Yes, but when a state sees its rights interfered with—"

"States have no rights! Only the people have rights. There must be conciliation between us. We must get along with each other. The Union must be preserved."

Stephen paused and looked out toward the river. "I've seen a goodly part of this land of ours, André," he said softly. "The vastness of it, the bigness of tree and hill, the sweep of plain, the might of its rivers. 'Tis a big land, André, for big men to carve out and build and conceive the shape of human destiny."

They rode on in silence. At last they were turning off Gravier Street into Magazine. They dismounted before the new three-story building and walked into a glass-covered courtyard.

"Banks Arcade," André said in a low voice. " 'Tis only three years old, but I'll wager that more expeditions have been organized here than in any other place in the city."

Stephen lifted a hand. An orator was reading from a document in the middle of the courtyard.

" 'I shall never surrender or retreat,' " the orator intoned. " 'If this call is neglected, I am determined to sustain myself as long as possible and die like a soldier who never forgets what is due his own honor and that of his country—*Victory or Death!* Signed, William Barret Travis, Lieutenant Colonel, Commanding.' That, gentlemen, was the last message from the Alamo. Colonel Travis died there, and Davy Crockett, and our own Jim Bowie!"

The roar of the crowd pulsated upon the air. Before it had entirely died, Phillippe Cloutier sprang to the rostrum. "I offer my services, sir," he said. "I will endeavor to raise a company of men and outfit them at my own expense!"

Other men of wealth and prominence followed Phillippe to the rostrum. In half an hour twelve companies had been started and one hundred and fifty thousand dollars had been pledged to the cause of the new Republic of Texas. Stephen and André had both signed notes for ten thousand dollars apiece.

By the end of May 1836 the rebellion of the people of Texas against Mexico was over. To cries of "Remember the Alamo!" an army commanded by Sam Houston had captured General Antonio López de Santa Anna. Texas was free. In September the Lone Star Republic took its place among the nations. Of the hundreds of Louisianians who had taken part in the revolt, the vast majority were back in New Orleans, boasting grandly of their exploits. Some, however, chose to remain in Texas. Among these was Phillippe Cloutier. Better the sweep of plains and the waters moving between him and Odalie; better a new life, in a new land.

IN JANUARY OF 1837 Stephen Fox was thirty-seven years old. The years had changed him little, except to add a fine network of lines at the corners of his eyes. His body was as lean as a rapier, and as full of deadly grace. He rode to the hunt, shot, fenced and gambled with the best. And more and more he became interested in politics. He stood for the city council and was elected.

Stephen's political activities were a cause for wonder: he was now the greatest landowner in the state, both because of the additions to Harrow and because of Bellefont, held in trust by him for his wife and her sister after the death of Pierre Arceneaux. Certainly he had no need to fatten his purse from the affairs of state; why, then, should he trouble himself?

"We are shaping a new life," he said to André as the two of them sat over *café noir* at Harrow. "And I would have a hand in it. Texas will come in, and after that, the Californias. This land will sweep from sea to sea—free men acting in just causes. 'Twill shake the earth, André."

"If only those money grubbers of New England would hush their pious nonsense! That's the main reason we must have Texas, Stephen. We've got to have more weight than they in Congress."

Stephen picked up his long-stemmed clay pipe. "Aye," he said grimly, "there's the danger. There's the rock on which the Union might split."

"Then let it! With our lands and our slaves we can be the wealthiest and most powerful nation on earth—without them!"

Stephen looked into the earnest face. "No, André. If it comes to that, 'tis we, not they, who will fall. In all the South we could not cast as many cannon as they could in one of their cities. We could never muster as many men. And behind us we would leave the brooding mass of blacks ready to spring the minute our backs are turned."

"We're better fighters," André declared hotly. "One gentleman is worth any ten merchants! We'd have allies—England, possibly France. And the blacks would never revolt—they're like children, lacking both the mind and the heart. Besides, they've been kindly treated and they love their masters."

"I don't know," Stephen said, but Odalie's voice, trembling with anger, interrupted him. "Stephen!"

Stephen got up wearily and André rose with him. "I must be going," André said as the two of them walked out into the great hall.

There Odalie met them and clutched Stephen's arm. "Come," she said to André. "I want you to see how my husband rears his son!"

They crossed the hall and stood outside the opened doorway. There, seated across the table from Little Inch, was the seven-year-old Etienne, cards fanned out in his little hand. Inch's black face was furrowed. "Deal me another one," he said.

Odalie was trembling with fury, but Stephen's face, watching his son, was gleeful.

"Pay up," Etienne said in French. "I've got a full house!"

But Little Inch smiled. "Gotcha, 'Tienne!" he said, reaching for the coins. "I got four of a kind!"

Etienne glared at the cards. Then with all his force he brought his fist down on Inch's fingers, smashing them against the table. The coins rolled over the floor. Little Inch howled. And before the three spectators could cross the room, Etienne had the little black boy down on the floor and was pounding him in the face with both fists.

Stephen dragged his son from the prostrated slave. " 'Tienne!" he roared. "Have ye taken leave of your senses? Get down and pick up the coins!" Sullenly Etienne obeyed. "Now give them to Inch, and up with ye to your room! By all the saints, I will not stomach a bad loser!"

"You see," Odalie cried, turning to André. "Not a word against the gambling! And 'Tienne must humble himself to a slave because of his father's peculiar conception of honor! Here, Inch," she said, "give me the money. Now go to Caleen and tell her how wicked you've been." Little Inch scurried from the room.

"Ye'll excuse us, my dear?" Stephen said.

Odalie nodded mutely. The two men walked toward the door.

"He is difficult," Stephen said. "His whole life is spent in plaguing me and his mother."

"Patience, Stephen," André said. "The boy will outgrow it. Too bad he's an only child. There's nothing like a crew of brothers and sisters to knock the devilry out of them."

"Ye should know, with five at La Place." Stephen laughed. "Next month is 'Tienne's birthday fête, André. Ye and Amelia must come and bring the brood—all of them. And now I must go up to my rooms in the north wing and rest for an hour. I've had no sleep these three nights."

André's eyebrows rose. The north wing was the bachelor quarters. The bridal chambers were in the south wing. "It's none of my affair," he said, "but how long have you slept in those rooms?"

"Since 'Tienne's birth," Stephen said gravely. "My wife's health has been delicate since the child."

"I see," André said; then to himself as he strode down the stairs, "Seven years, *ma foi!*"

THE MORNING OF Etienne's birthday dawned bright and clear and the crowds began to gather. There were plantation owners, traders and working men, for Stephen Fox's philosophy of democracy had become a thing very real to him, for which he was willing to brave the ill-concealed sneers of his fellow planters.

On the lawn before Harrow a great table had been spread. Etienne sat at the head of it, while Little Inch stood behind his master to fulfill his every wish. Inch did not smile now, despite the gaiety. He had learned his lesson well. When he had gone to Caleen with the story of his latest beating at the hands of Etienne, she had whispered to him softly, "Be clever like a swamp fox. 'Tienne tell you to do something, do it, too quick. We outsmart him. Learn to read and write. But keep your mouth shut. Grow up strong in the back like your *grand-père*, Big Inch, and smart in the head like me. Someday freedom come. 'Tienne wash your feet then!"

Etienne was showered with gifts and he received them with the bored disdain of a young prince. But when Stephen's gift was brought to him, he straightened up, his blue eyes alight. It was a pony, fully equipped with saddle and bridle. At once Etienne got down from his place; but Stephen lifted a warning hand.

"First ye must say a word of thanks to your guests," he said.

"A thousand thanks to you all," Etienne said rapidly in French. The American tradesmen looked at him blankly.

"Now in English," Stephen said.

"Thank—you—all—ver' much . . . *'Mericain cochons!*" A little titter of laughter ran through the Creole ranks. Here and there an American frowned.

" 'Tis ye who are a pig, my lad," Stephen said softly. "Now get ye to your room and await me!"

Stephen ordered the Negroes to bring wine, and afterward the adults retired to the great hall. The slave orchestra struck up a tune and there was dancing. But it was no use. Not even the wine could bring good feeling. One by one the guests made their excuses and left.

When all had gone, Stephen strode up the stairs to Etienne's room, but it was empty. Frowning, he went back down the stairs and out into the courtyard. He bent down, staring at the soft earth. The tracks were there, small and well shod, and they led off toward the cypress wood. Stephen followed, swearing softly under his breath.

Before he reached the clump of woods he heard the pony squealing in anguish. Then came the singing whine of a whip. Stephen ran forward. Just inside the screen of branches the pony was tethered, rearing and plunging like a wild thing. And beside him, Etienne lifted the whip.

Then Stephen was upon his son, tearing the whip from his hands. "Ye little beast!" he roared, and lifted the whip. Etienne stood without flinching, his pale eyes steady upon his father's face. Stephen lowered the whip slowly; then, with a quick motion, he broke it across his knee. Without another word, he turned and strode back toward Harrow.

Etienne stood looking after him, his blue eyes bleak in his dark face. "Father," he whispered. "Father."

Inside the house Stephen walked dully into his study. He paused to light a candle, then turned to the rows of leather-bound volumes that lined the walls. He stood there, frowning a moment, then stretched forth his hand. There was a little scurrying noise behind him, and he whirled. Little Inch stood there frozen.

"Inch!" Stephen said. "What the devil do ye here?"

"I—I was reading, master," Inch stammered.

"Reading?" Stephen said. "Who taught ye to read?"

"*Grand-mère* and 'Tienne, a little. Please . . ."

Stephen bent and picked up the open book from the floor. It was Molière, a bound volume of the plays.

"A black with a mind," Stephen said, half to himself. "Inch, listen to me. I like this, your knowledge. But when ye would have books, come to me and ask for them. There are many books that will cause only confusion in your mind. From now on there will be no lack of books, but they will be the right ones. Here, ponder over this one. When ye have finished it, I shall have a report from ye over its meaning. Ye may go now."

Inch smiled and scurried from the room, clutching the catechism Stephen had given him.

Stephen had turned again to his books when Georges entered and paused before his master. "Well," Stephen said, "what is it, Georges?"

"Monsieur André, sir, outside on the terrace."

Stephen made a little gesture of annoyance and put the book back in its place. When he reached the terrace, he saw the rotund figure of André Le Blanc pacing nervously back and forth. "André," Stephen said, "what ails ye, man?"

"I'm in trouble, Stephen, terrible trouble. The Second Bank of the United States—this morning it withdrew all its deposits from its fiscal agencies. Then later, the Bank of England contracted its credits. They're asking for gold, Stephen. And all my creditors are calling in their notes against La Place. By nightfall 'Melia and the children will no longer have a roof over their heads!"

"My God!" Stephen exclaimed. "I have no ready cash, André. My accounts were in the Second Bank, too. But I will give your creditors a lien against as much of Harrow as is necessary."

"No, Stephen, never in honor could I permit—"

"Silence! Ye know well I keep the bulk of my accounts in Philadelphia. I have enough to tide us both over."

"That is if the Philadelphia banks do not fail, Stephen. I understand this thing is nationwide."

The two of them went into the house, and Stephen ordered wine and sent Georges to fetch Odalie. When she came, Stephen went straight to the point. "There is a financial panic, my dear," he explained. "The currency is worthless, having no gold to back it up. André here is in a fair way to be ruined. Have I your consent to pledge outlying lands against André's outstanding debts?"

Odalie did not even hesitate. "Of course," she said. "We have more land than we'll ever need. Pledge Bellefont—I'm sure Aurore will be agreeable."

"Ye understand that we are in a bad way ourselves?"

"There are other things in the world besides money."

"Thank ye, my dear." He pulled on the bell cord and Georges appeared. "Pen and paper, Georges—and the sandbox."

When Georges returned, Stephen took up his pen and wrote:

> To whom it may concern: I, Stephen Fox, do hereby pledge and commit certain of my lands: the entire southern tract, lying nearest to New Orleans, and the plantation of Bellefont, as security against the debts of André Le Blanc of this parish, my friend and associate.
>
> Done by my own hand, at Harrow, May 13, 1837.

"We shall need witnesses," he said as he signed his name with a flourish. "We'd best ride into the city, André. Ye'll excuse us, my dear?"

Odalie nodded. Stephen and André stood up, but as Stephen waited for his hat, gloves and crop, a horseman came pounding up the oak alley at a full gallop. He leaped from his horse, flung the reins to the astonished Georges and ran up the stairs, two at a time.

"Tom!" Stephen said. "Tom Warren! So it took a panic to make ye visit Harrow!"

"I need money, Stephen," he said. "I'm in a hellish fix!"

"Softly, Tom," Stephen said. "So are we all."

"Not the kind I'm in. I—I speculated a bit with monies that were not actually mine. It will mean prison for me."

Silently Stephen extended the note he had just written. "I was coming in for ye to witness this," he said simply.

Warren's eyes ran rapidly over the page.

"So," he said, "you've tied up all your visible assets for this man. A fine friend you've proved yourself, Stephen Fox!"

"I'm sorry, Tom. Money I have not. But this talk of prison is nonsense. My word alone is enough to keep ye out."

Tom Warren looked from one to the other of them. "Give me the paper," he said at last. "I'll witness it."

When Warren had signed the paper, the three men went down the great stairs together and stood for a moment in talk. Then André swung his great bulk aboard his horse. As he started away, old Josh appeared, a string of fish glistening in his hand.

"Evenin', sir." Josh grinned, took off his battered hat and bowed. Then his mouth gaped open. "That's Master Tom!" he quavered. "That's the one who kilt poor Rad! He tried to kill me, too. Don' let him get me!"

Stephen turned to Tom Warren. "What's he talking about, Tom? He appears to know ye."

Tom Warren's little piglike eyes were shifting rapidly. "I never saw him before," he said. "I think he's mad."

"What's this all about, Josh? Speak up, man."

"Me'n' Rad moved all that wheat outa the warehouse by the river like he done tell us to. We took it 'cross town in the wagon. We musta gone back'n' forth a hundred times. After that he tell us to set the warehouse on fire, an' we done that too. An' when poor Rad come out—Master Ste—"

Stephen whirled, but the blast of the pistol leaped out between him and Josh. The old black staggered, clawing at his throat where the ball had gone through; then he went down in the dirt.

Very slowly Stephen started toward Tom. André sat paralyzed upon his horse, watching. Again Tom Warren lifted the pistol. "Easy, Stephen," he said. "I still have three shots."

"It matters not if ye have a hundred," Stephen said, and lunged forward all at once. The pistol made a mushroom of flame and smoke; and Stephen's fingers, as he fell, tore loose the buttons of Tom's waistcoat. Warren leveled the pistol at him as he lay there, but André was kicking his horse forward, unsheathing his sword as he came.

The big man whirled, firing as he turned, but André ducked low along the horse's neck and deftly ran the point of the sword through the wrist of Tom Warren's hand. Tom dropped the pistol and ran to drag himself up onto his horse.

111

André bent over Stephen, stanching the gaping wound the slug had torn low on Stephen's left side. It had gone completely through Stephen's lean body, too far to the side to puncture the internal organs, but he was bleeding frightfully.

Odalie had heard the shots and had come running out on the gallery. "Stephen!" she gasped. "Stephen!" Then she was cradling her husband's head in her arms and the two of them got him to the bedroom. Not until Caleen had taken full charge did Odalie slip quietly to the floor in a dead faint.

Caleen stepped over her without even a downward glance. There was the water to be heated, fresh cloths to be fetched, and herbs to be brewed against infection. She worked with light-ninglike rapidity, until at last the thick stream of blood stopped. "He be all right now, Monsieur André," she said.

André lifted Odalie from the floor. "Is he—is he . . ." she said.

"No," André answered. "He is not dead—in fact, he's going to get better." He stood up, and his round face was grim. "Now, if Madame will excuse me, I have work to do."

André rode straight to Maspero's, where he stood in the middle of the barroom and told his story. When he left, every man in the place filed silently out behind him, for there were not many there whom Stephen had not befriended in some way. They dispersed to their homes, to rejoin the procession later, armed with sabers, rapiers, fowling pieces and every sort of pistol made.

André rode alone to the riverbank. He went from den to den, where the fierce riverboatmen looked at him curiously, until finally at the Sure Enuff his quest was rewarded. There, in a faro game, half sunk into a drunken stupor, sat Mike Farrel.

"We have need of you at Harrow," André told him. "Tom Warren has shot Stephen without just cause."

Mike was on his feet in an instant. "Awright, lad," he growled. "Lead me to him!"

The moon rode in over the cypress trees and the road was silver. When André and Mike reached the edge of the bayou, they met a crowd of horsemen. The stillness of the night was broken only by the heavy breathing of winded horses and the occasional clink of a weapon.

The crowd milled about them in a semicircle. "We'd best dismount," André said. "It's no fit footing for horses. He was headed this way when I saw him last."

At once Mike took the lead, mumbling to himself. They scattered in a dozen different directions, so that their diverging lights danced like great fireflies in the dark woodland. Mike was bending close to the earth, the mumbling in his throat deeper, until it had the sound of a wild animal.

Then the ground was no longer firm under their feet, but a green ooze that sucked audibly with every step. The black waters of the bayou itself were ahead. Mike lifted his hand for silence. The sound came riding in over the bayou, far away and faint, but very clear. Someone was walking in the shallows. They raced along the bank, their feet sticking with every step in the mud, until at last they saw him, walking with his head down, holding his wounded wrist, around which a white cloth showed.

With a roar, Mike was in the water. Tom Warren turned, holding the pistol in his left hand. He fired, and the orange-yellow flame split the night open. Mike came on. Twice more Tom Warren fired, but Mike plunged on, shaking his massive head and roaring. Then his big hairy paws were gripping Tom's shoulders, and they went down into the bayou. The black water boiled, hiding the two men.

Then the boiling ceased. Mike stood up and walked slowly through the trailing waters. Heavily, he climbed the bank.

The men crowded around him. Leaning forward, André saw the bloodstains on his shirt front. "Let the bayou have him," Mike growled. He turned and started back the way they had come, the men following.

On the road again, Mike headed toward Harrow.

"You're hurt, Mike," André said, "badly hurt. You have need of a doctor!"

"First I'm gonna see after Stevie," Mike said.

Up at Harrow the lights blazed from every window. As André and Mike turned into the alley of oaks, a sleek black mare shot past them at a gallop. André saw that the rider was female, mounted sidesaddle, her long hair loose and blowing behind her. The woman drew her mount up before the great stairs, sawing at its mouth so savagely that it reared, almost unseating her. Grimly she fought for control of the excited animal.

But André had reached her now and was pulling on the reins with all his weight. Slowly the mare quieted. "Aurore!" André whispered.

"How is he, André?" she demanded. "Don't tell me he's . . . Oh, no, André! Don't tell me that!"

"Softly, Aurore," André said. "Your sister's husband is neither dead nor dying. Come, I'll take you inside."

Aurore smiled at him, but her eyes were bright with tears. "My sister's husband," she murmured. "Thank you, André. I needed reminding, didn't I?"

Silently André offered her his arm and they started up the stairs together. But behind them Mike Farrel hung half over the balustrade. Instantly André released Aurore and ran back down the stairs to the big man.

"I'm a trifle spent, me lad," Mike said.

André put one arm around the big man's waist, and together he and Aurore helped Mike up the stairs. When they were inside, André called slaves to carry Mike to his old rooms and ordered them to dress his wounds at once.

Then he and Aurore went to the master bedchamber. Outside the door Little Inch stood guard, his eyes red with weeping. Beside him 'Tienne sat, his blue eyes fixed cold and unmoving on the closed door. Gently André pushed it open. In the semi-darkness, Odalie was kneeling beside the bed, her whole body shaken with sobbing. Aurore's fingers were ice brands, biting into André's arm.

On the other side of the room Caleen's face was a grotesque African death mask. "He's worse," she said simply. "Doctor say him die soon." Aurore turned and buried her face against André's shoulder. "But doctor great fool," Caleen went on. "I make him better in one hour, me."

"Then for God's sake, do it!" Aurore cried.

"You leave the chamber—all you. Leave nobody here but me and master. Then I cure him."

"All right," André said. "But no witchcraft, Caleen!"

Caleen smiled blandly and bent down to lift the half-dazed form of Odalie from the floor. But André and Aurore raised Odalie between them, and the three of them went through the doorway.

When they had gone, Caleen crossed herself and bent over Stephen's still form. "Master," she crooned in a slow singsong voice. "You not happy—Caleen knows. But don't die. Easy to die, but hard to live, yes, when no joy in it. But you got strong, fine son. Live for him. Make him strong like you, brave like you. Cowards die. Brave men don't die; they live, yes!"

Over and over she talked to him, whispering, half singing the words. Then slowly the gray tide stole out of his cheeks and faint flushes of color stole in. While she talked, his breathing evened until something very like a smile played about the corner of his lips. Caleen tiptoed to the door and opened it. Odalie, Aurore and André trooped in and looked at Stephen. Then with a single motion they turned and faced Caleen.

"You old witch!" André said. "You blessed old witch!"

CHAPTER ELEVEN

IT WAS MANY weeks before Stephen could leave his bed. While he lay there, André ran both Harrow and La Place. Aurore moved into Harrow and assisted Odalie in the nursing of Stephen and Mike Farrel, who had three bullets in his gigantic chest. The big man was an easy patient, following Aurore's every move with worshipful eyes.

The crops that year were good, so that despite the unsettled condition of the country's finances, Harrow made money. André was able with the help of Stephen's note to obtain extensions from his creditors, and by fall La Place was paying off its debts. But the city recovered slowly from the panic and most of the banks remained closed.

By the time the great clouds of smoke were billowing up from the sugar house, Stephen was on his feet again, moving slowly, restlessly about the plantation like a pale ghost. His thinness was painful to behold. His eyes were deep and ringed with blue circles. But André was conscious of something else—a brittle bitterness that edged every word he spoke.

Throughout the winter Stephen continued to gain strength. By spring he was riding over his lands again, and he fairly lived on Royal Street in the palatial gaming houses. André watched him with growing concern. Something must be done about this, he decided, and soon.

"Stephen," he said one evening as they rode toward La Place, "how would you like to attend a ball?"

Stephen looked at him with a grimace of acute disgust.

"No ordinary ball," André said slyly. "Have you never heard of the *Bal du Cordon Bleu?*"

Stephen laughed. "So, ye propose to obtain me a mulatto wench? What a wickedness!"

"I propose to let you see them—that's all. Any objections?"

One corner of Stephen's mouth curved into a smile.

"No," he said, "no objections."

As ANDRE AND Stephen rode up to the Orleans Ballroom on a spring night early in 1838, it was ablaze with light, and the sound of music and laughing voices floated downward into the street. They paid the admission fee of two dollars apiece and went up the stairs into the ballroom. Gigantic crystal chandeliers swung low over the dance floor. In niches around the walls stood statues that would not have disgraced a hall at Versailles, and paintings that Stephen's practiced eye recognized at once as originals.

On the magnificent oak dance floor the young, and not so young, gentlemen of New Orleans were dancing. Half a glance told Stephen that almost everyone he knew was here; then his gaze traveled on to their partners.

"Lovely, aren't they?" André said.

Stephen stifled a yawn with the back of his hand.

"Of course they're pretty," he said. "But your mixed-strain wenches don't seem particularly remarkable to me. Those fat old yellow mothers of theirs seem to be watching them like hawks."

"You don't understand. For them the connections they make here are as honorable as marriage. Of course the mothers watch. They would object to an unwise connection as strenuously as would a white mother to an unwise marriage."

As André and Stephen circled the ballroom, the girls watched them from behind their fans. When they came abreast of the stairway, Stephen stopped, his slim fingers tightening on André's arm. "I think," he said slowly, "I think I see what ye mean!" A group of quadroon and octoroon girls was coming down the stairs. There was no need for André to ask which one Stephen meant.

She was taller by half a head than any of the others, and her skin was a light golden color. But it was her hair that made her stand out—a tawny mane of chestnut, lightening to pure gold in the highlights, with overtones of auburn that ran like flame through the waves whenever she tossed her head. As she neared

Stephen, he put out his hand and touched her arm. "Tonight," he said, "ye're dancing with me."

She turned toward him without speaking, and the heavy lids lifted to reveal eyes that were as cool and green as the sea. "You had better ask Madame my mother, monsieur," she said, her voice deep and rich.

Stephen looked her straight in the face. "To hell with Madame your mother," he said clearly. "Ye're dancing with me."

"And after tonight?" she said.

Stephen lashed her with his glance, letting his eyes wander over the décolleté gown. "Ye may call the tune," he said, "I'll play the fiddle."

He swung her away into the dance, gazing down into her face. She lifted it to his, until her lips were almost touching his throat. A perfume floated up from the chestnut-russet-golden hair; it was elusive, but subtly, insistently provocative.

Stephen took her arm and swept her out onto the gallery that overlooked the gardens. A thin sickle of a moon gleamed silver, with a great halo of white around it. He grasped her by both her soft, rounded shoulders and held her away from him at arm's length. The moonlight caught in her hair, in her sooty lashes. Stephen drew his breath in sharply. "Ye're lovely!" he said. "God, but ye're lovely!"

"Thank you, monsieur," she murmured, and he drew her to him. Her face was lifted to his, and the wine-red lips softened and parted. She rolled her head ever so slightly upon her neck so that her lips caressed his. Then madness flamed in Stephen's veins. His arms tightened ferociously about her slim waist until a little cry of pain was locked somewhere deep in her throat.

Abruptly he released her. "My dear," he said, "what is your name?"

"Désirée," she said. "Does monsieur like it?"

"Like it? 'Tis perfect. And now 'tis time I had a word with Madame your mother. If ye'll be so good as to conduct me . . ."

Désirée took his arm and the two of them went back into the ballroom. The girl led him to a tall, middle-aged quadroon sitting regally in one of the great chairs. At once Stephen saw where Désirée got her beauty.

"This gentleman wishes a word with you, *maman*," Désirée said.

Stephen hesitated, and seeing his perplexity, André crossed

117

the room and stood at his friend's side. "Permit me, madame," he said politely, "to present my friend, Monsieur Fox. Your name is, madame?"

"Hippolyte. Madame Hippolyte. Is Monsieur Fox of the plantation Harrow?"

"Aye," Stephen said. "How did ye know of Harrow?"

"Everyone knows of Harrow, monsieur."

Stephen cleared his throat. This was a new thing: this shameless willingness to sell a daughter into concubinage. There were many men they could marry. He knew quadroons, like the Lagoasters, who held great plantations and lived as richly among their slaves as any white. A girl like Désirée . . . any man . . . any man at all . . .

"I take it that Monsieur wishes to form a connection with my daughter," Madame Hippolyte said.

"Aye," Stephen said stiffly, "that is my intent."

"My daughter would be amply provided for?"

"Monsieur Fox is the richest man in Louisiana," André told her. "Désirée will live like a princess. You will, of course, accept some token of his esteem . . ."

"Not one cent," Madame Hippolyte said firmly. "But if Désirée wants him . . ." She looked at her daughter. Désirée nodded wordlessly. "Shall we discuss the terms, gentlemen?"

"Yes," Stephen said, "anything ye will."

"Monsieur will provide a house for my daughter down by the Ramparts in the old quarter. It will be richer and more beautiful than any other on the street, with a maidservant and a cook. He will see that she is suitably attired. He will visit her with discretion, so that no scandal will be attached to her name or his. And any children born of this connection he will fully provide for, educating them in the same style as whites. And, further, Monsieur is not to see Désirée until this house is completed."

Stephen's fair brows met over his nose, and the great scar flamed on the side of his forehead.

"Careful, Stephen," André whispered. "It's best to humor her."

"Very well," Stephen said. "Construction will begin tomorrow!" He touched Désirée's hand and swept her away in a waltz. She followed him effortlessly, gazing intently into his face.

"Why do ye watch me so?" Stephen demanded.

"Monsieur's eyes are very blue and his hair is like fire. I want to remember. It will be so long before I see you again. I will live for that."

" 'Twill be a great happiness having ye," Stephen said. Then, as she smiled at him, the great curving lashes closing over her eyes, he whispered, "Nay, more—'twill be a glory!"

When at last the *Bal du Cordon Bleu* was over, Stephen surrendered Désirée to her mother. Then he and André left the ballroom together.

André chuckled. "So you've taken on the *placée* you swore you'd never have! But you must be careful, Stephen. Odalie must never know."

"Odalie," Stephen said slowly. "Do you know, André, for the moment I'd forgotten her?"

"I don't doubt it. But she has no cause for complaint. You've treated her well, Stephen."

"Aye," Stephen said. " 'Twas a mistake—our marriage. But it cannot be undone now. I shall take whatever joy there is left for me in life and make the best of it. Come, lad, 'tis a long way yet."

WITHIN ONE MONTH the little white house by the Ramparts was finished. Stephen's hands were trembling as he dressed in his new clothing, far richer than any he had bought before. Outside his window the evening was purpling into night.

As Stephen quietly passed Odalie's room she came out and stood there staring at him. "How handsome you are," she said. "Where do you go?"

"To the city," Stephen said shortly.

"To the city—always to the city! Is there nothing I can do . . ."

"Aye, but there is," Stephen said. "And what it is ye know!"

The tears sparkled in Odalie's eyes. "Another child would cost me my life," she whispered. "You know that, Stephen. Still . . . if you wish . . ."

"No," he said gently. "Ye're right. Don't wait up for me, I shall be very late."

When Stephen reached Rampart Street, a light glowed softly in the little white house. As he raised the brass knocker, the door flew open, and that wonderfully rich, deep voice was whispering, "Come in, monsieur. I've been waiting for hours!"

Inside, Désirée put out both her hands to Stephen.

"Aye," he said. "Ye're as I remembered."

"And how was that, monsieur?"

"Unbelievable." His eyes strayed around the little house. Désirée had arranged it so that it was quietly, elegantly perfect. "Ye've done well," he said.

"I'm glad Monsieur likes it. Monsieur would have wine?"

"Yes," Stephen said. He sank down into the great chair. Désirée brought the sparkling ruby-colored liquid in a bell-shaped goblet. She leaned over the fiery mass of curls upon Stephen's head. Here and there was a strand of white at the temples. Slowly she stroked his forehead, and Stephen could feel the tension ease under her touch. He caught both her hands and drew them downward, turning at the same time and gazing upward into her face.

"Monsieur is unhappy," she whispered. "But this house was built only for joy."

"Ye are very wise, Désirée. How old are ye?"

"Sixteen," she said.

"Holy Mother of God!"

"That troubles you, monsieur? Don't let it. This wisdom, as you call it, is handed down from mother to daughter for generations. This is what I was born for."

Stephen sat very still, watching her move gracefully about the table, preparing the meal. He felt strangely at peace, savoring every moment as it passed. Silently she took her place across from him, the outlines of her face softened in the small flame-glow of the candles. She kept watching him, the sea-green eyes dancing under the long lashes.

"Ye're not eating," he said.

"I'm not hungry, monsieur."

Abruptly he pushed back his chair and stood up. "Come here," he said.

She came to him very simply, lifting her face to his.

IN THE WEEKS that followed, Stephen went almost nightly to Rampart Street. Odalie's eyes grew dark and ringed from watching for his return. Yet, never had life gone smoother at Harrow. Stephen was good-natured, smiling, impervious to her worst outbursts of temper. Not even Etienne could disturb him. At last the boy was beginning to follow his father around the plantation in silent companionship. And Etienne was learning English, slowly and haltingly, but entirely of his own free will.

Sitting at the great table awaiting Stephen at the evening meal, Odalie heard him coming through the hall, whistling to himself. Her hands tensed upon the edge of the table. He had no right to be so happy—so outrageously, completely happy. He crossed to where she sat, and bent to kiss her cheek. "Stephen," she began, "Friday night there is a ball at the City Exchange. I promised Amelia that we would come."

Friday night was the final *Grand Bal du Cordon Bleu*. "No," he said shortly. " 'Tis quite impossible!"

"Why, Stephen?" She leaned forward across the table. "Who is keeping you away from me?"

"About that, I would not inquire if I were ye," he said. Then he stood up, his dinner untasted. "Very well," he told her slowly. "We shall attend your ball!"

Odalie sat in dumb misery, watching him stride through the doorway.

On Rampart Street Stephen swung down from his horse and entered the house without knocking. Instantly a handsome young man sprang to his feet. Stephen inspected him coldly. The youth was fair of skin, with great masses of tawny chestnut hair curling thickly over his high white forehead. Stephen looked from him to Désirée, but the girl was smiling serenely. "Monsieur," she said, "this is my brother, Aupré. He has just returned from France."

"Your brother?" Stephen exclaimed. "But this one is white!"

The youth flushed and Désirée laughed, a clear, golden sound.

"Only I inherited the blood of the blacks," she said. "Aupré labors under no such disadvantage."

Stephen looked at the youth. Yes, the resemblance was there; even to the beauty of face and form. Stephen put out his hand. " 'Tis glad I am to meet ye, Aupré," he said.

The boy stood before him, as rigid as a statue, his hands limp at his sides. Stephen's fair brows flew together. "I offered ye my hand!" he thundered. Slowly, the boy put out his hand. Stephen took it, almost crushing it in his grip. Then with a sound very like a sob, Aupré whirled and was gone through the door.

"Did you have to humiliate him so, monsieur?" Désirée said. Her eyes were bright with tears. "He was debating whether or not to return to France. Now he will go, and I'll never see him again."

"What was it that upset him so?" Stephen asked.

"Put yourself in his place, monsieur. Suppose you returned to find your sister flown, unmarried, to the arms of a lover—and that lover a man of another race. What would you do?"

"Aye, I see. Such a one would not live one hour. But since ye think like this—why did ye not marry a man of your own race?"

Désirée's face showed disgust. "They are not men. You do not permit them to be. To live at all they have to fawn and bow. I am a woman, monsieur; I can only love a man—not a thing!"

"Holy blessed Mother of God," Stephen whispered.

"Forgive me, monsieur; I—I forgot my place."

"There's nothing to forgive," Stephen said. "I have no wish to hurt ye." He stopped, frowning. "Yet I'm afraid I must. Désirée, I cannot take ye to the ball Friday night."

The girl stepped backward and her face was stricken. Then instantly she was all composure. "As Monsieur wills," she murmured.

"No," Stephen said gently. "Such submissiveness ill becomes ye. Say what ye will."

"If I do not attend the ball," Désirée said, "tongues will wag. If I go alone, I shall be the laughingstock of the whole quarter. But . . . if Monsieur will condescend to leave the City Exchange and come to the Orleans Ballroom just for one dance . . ."

"I see," Stephen said gravely, but there was a laughing light in his pale eyes. "Ye're a lovely little witch!"

"I wish I were. Then I'd cast a spell so you'd never leave me. It is my nightmare that someday a night will fall without you in it. I try to think how it will be to live not hearing your voice or seeing your face. I can't—the thought itself is a kind of death."

Stephen put his arms around her. "Then why think so?" he asked. "Such a day may never come."

"Oh, but it will. There are oceans of blood between us," she said, sitting down in his lap, twining her arms about his neck. "But now you must make me happy."

"How?"

"By kissing me. Kiss me a thousand times. No—a million. Kiss me and never, never stop."

THE CITY EXCHANGE was an architectural triumph, with its magnificent ballrooms on the second floor and its awe-inspiring rotunda. And on Friday night most of the first families of New

Orleans were in full attendance. The music was superb, and outwardly at least the ball had an air of carefree gaiety. But as the evening wore on, the number of males present steadily decreased.

"The men," Odalie said to Amelia, "they're all going!"

"Those quadroons," Amelia snorted. "Don't tell me you've never heard of their balls?"

"*Ma foi!* You mean that the men are leaving these girls to disport themselves with black wenches?"

"Not black—quadroons, octoroons. And I'm quite sure they give their filthy balls deliberately on the same nights as ours to flaunt in our faces their power over the men."

"My Stephen would never do a thing like that," Odalie said.

"Perhaps not," Amelia declared. "But I'm wondering where Stephen is now—and André."

"I'll send Georges to the barroom," Odalie said, "to inquire after them."

Odalie and Amelia went out of the door on Royal Street and walked around to the stables. Georges was sprawled over the seat of the yellow coach, fast asleep.

"Go up into the bar," Odalie commanded, "and tell Mr. Fox I'd like to have a word with him."

Georges's eyes were big in his black face. Then he was off as fast as his legs could carry him. In a few minutes he was back. "The master isn't there," he said. "Perhaps he go back to the dance, yes."

"Georges," Odalie said, "call a cabriolet for us. Quickly now." Georges scurried off, his face gray with fright. Any way this ended, it would be bad.

At the Orleans Ballroom Stephen was dancing with Désirée. Her golden face was radiant. "I knew you'd come," she whispered. "I knew it!"

"One dance, remember," Stephen warned. "Only one!"

Désirée tilted her head back and swung up on tiptoe, whirling expertly so that her lips were like wine flames, inches from Stephen's mouth. "I love you, monsieur," she said, "so very, very much!"

"Time we were off, Stephen," André said, whirling past with a slim quadroon beauty in his arms.

But Désirée reached up and brushed Stephen's lips lightly with her own.

"To hell with that!" Stephen said. "I'm staying!"

Outside, in Orleans Street, Amelia and Odalie sat in the hired carriage for almost three hours. Then, abruptly, Amelia laid a hand on Odalie's arm. Stephen and André were coming down the stairs, laughing. They walked arm in arm toward their curtained cab.

"Drive on!" Odalie said furiously to the driver. The whip slashed down and the cabriolet moved off.

When they reached the Exchange, both Stephen and André found that their coaches were gone and they were faced with the necessity of hiring horses to get back to their plantations.

"Oh, my God!" André groaned. "What if they've found out? I only went to that accursed ball on your account, And by now 'Melia probably thinks I've got a yellow *placée* . . ."

"Then ye haven't?"

"Of course not! 'Melia is an angel! I've never even looked at another woman since we were married."

To their astonishment the first stable they tried was open. The Creole liveryman met them with an air of bland amusement. "I always stay open on those nights that the *Bal du Cordon Bleu* conflicts with a ball at the 'Change." He grinned. "There are always many who have need of my services."

So, after having paid exorbitant fees for their use, Stephen and André limped homeward on a couple of ancient splay-shanked nags that could not move above a slow walk.

CHAPTER TWELVE

ALONG THE EDGE of the bayou the fronds of the palmettos waved like giant hands, and the willows sighed, dripping their branches into the water. It was morning, so early that the mists had not yet left the bayou road, yet Aurore was already up, riding her chestnut mare toward Harrow.

It is a very great sin that I do, she thought bitterly. Father DuGois says the sins of the mind are no less than the sins of the body. But I cannot help loving him. It is a thing beyond my will. And this is the worst of it, this shameless riding out to see him so early that he will not have gone into the fields.

As she rode up the oak-canopied drive to Harrow, Georges came scurrying out to take the reins.

"Is your mistress up yet?" Aurore asked.

"Oh, yes, she's up. She's been up for hours."

That was odd, Aurore decided as she swung down from the horse. And the morning after a ball, too.

She crossed the great hall rapidly, her mind so preoccupied that she passed through the doorway and into the dining room before the voices arrested her.

Odalie was weeping. "So you've come home to me night after night with your lips still warm from the kisses of another woman! Filthy, disgusting beast! What under heaven could possess you to ride fifteen miles to visit a mulatto wench?"

"That ye could never understand," Stephen said dryly. " 'Twould be like describing the colors of a sunset to a blind man. And now, if ye've finished this senseless tirade, I have work to do." He made a half-turn, but Odalie laid a hand upon his arm.

"Never go to her again," she said. "Promise me, Stephen!"

Stephen's eyes were like blue glacier ice. Gently he disengaged her hand from his arm and turned to go.

"I shall have her whipped!" Odalie cried. "You know I can! It's the law, Stephen, it's the law."

Stephen turned back to face her. "Aye," he said quietly, " 'tis the law, all right. But if ye ever dare invoke it, ye know right well who will suffer."

"Stephen, you—you don't mean you would leave me for her—for a—"

"And why not? She is twice the woman, and thrice the wife that ye ever were." He spun on his heel so that his eyes met the stricken face of Aurore, who was still standing, as though frozen, in the doorway.

"No, Stephen," she whispered. "I cannot believe—not you."

"Thank ye for your trust," he said. "But 'tis true, Aurore. Good day to ye, ladies."

"Stay with me, Aurore," Odalie sobbed. "I need you."

Aurore crossed the room and folded her sister against her. Both of them wept.

NIGHT AFTER NIGHT Stephen rode away to the little house on Rampart Street. All his better judgment rebelled against this thing, but, for the first time in his life, he was powerless. 'Tis wrong, wrong, wrong! he would tell himself, and the next instant an image of Désirée would arise in his mind, and groaningly he would commit himself to damnation.

At Harrow Odalie grew thin and pale from days of scarcely touching food and nights of sleepless waiting. It was on one of these nights that Caleen came into the room.

"Well," Odalie snapped, "what do you want?"

"Only to help," Caleen said. "Somebody got to have sense 'round Harrow, so I have it, me; ain't nobody else got none."

"All right, Caleen, get to the point."

"I know a wise woman, a *mamaloi*. She can tell mistress what to do."

"One of those voodoo priestesses? Don't be ridiculous!"

The old woman drew herself up proudly to her full height. "Got to fight magic with magic: gris-gris with better gris-gris. We get the master back . . . tonight."

"Tonight? But, Caleen, it's raining like mad and it's late."

"You want him back?"

"All right, Caleen. Go get my things."

A half-hour later a small black coach rocked away from Harrow through the driving rain. Caleen sat beside her mistress, who was dressed in black and heavily veiled. Hours later, in New Orleans, they came to the quarter where the free Negroes lived. It was a dark, evil-smelling collection of ruined buildings.

Caleen ordered the coachman to stop. "Come," the old woman commanded. "I'll go in front, me."

Odalie stepped down into the inky road. They turned and twisted through a labyrinth of narrow lanes, covered ankle deep with mud and icy water. Suddenly Caleen stopped. "Here," she muttered, "here."

Odalie could feel a great trembling throughout her entire body. Caleen was knocking now, three times. The door swung open, and a rich, rolling bass called out in Gumbo French, "Who's there?"

"Tante Caleen. *Voodoo Magnian!*"

"*Voodoo Magnian,*" the voice repeated. "Enter!"

The two of them slipped into a hallway, and the door was shut behind them. There was no light, and the blackness seemed compounded of smoke and the smell of musk and oil. The man who had admitted them was a magnificent Negro, more than six feet tall. "Enter," he said again.

They went into a room illuminated by half a dozen flambeaux. When the smoke had ceased to sting Odalie's eyes, she could see a large, handsome mulatto woman seated on a rude throne. "Closer, my child," the woman said in perfect French. "Do not fear. What is it you desire of Selada?"

Odalie stood before her, her lips moving, but no sound came from them, no sound at all.

"It does not matter much," Selada said, her eyes resting for a moment on Odalie's heavy gold wedding band. "*Voodoo Magnian* will speak to me. Your husband, is it not so?"

Odalie nodded dumbly.

"I will help you. Hercule!" The magnificent black man appeared and bowed low before Selada. "Summon the others. We will dance *calinda*. We must make strong gris-gris for Madame."

Hercule was gone as silently as he came. Selada indicated that Odalie and Caleen should be seated. After a moment Hercule was back, followed by twenty-five or thirty Negroes of various ages and colors. Two men only a shade less perfectly developed than Hercule seated themselves before drums and began to beat them with the palms of their hands, a slow, steady African rhythm. Odalie could feel her breath coming quicker.

Selada made an imperceptible gesture and the beat changed. Faster it grew, faster, louder: low thunder on the dog-skin drums. A beautiful young quadroon girl placed a baked clay vase filled to the brim with tafia before each of the guests. They began to drink the cane rum, and Odalie, fearing to be different, sipped hers once, and again as the beat of the drums increased, then again and again until the ice water in her veins changed into warm wine and her patrician body was swaying with those of the others.

Selada waved a hand. Hercule sprang to his feet and tore off his clothes until he was naked except for a loincloth. Never had Odalie seen such a man. Then the quadroon girl jumped up. There was the sound of cloth tearing and she stood before Hercule clad only in a chemise. With her perfect legs spread wide apart, she began to undulate her body in a dance so sensual that Odalie could feel the pounding of her pulse in her throat. Hercule advanced toward the girl and matched her every movement.

Odalie could feel her own breath coming out in short, sharp gusts. Hercule was running his huge black hands over the girl's body like great black spiders on the creamy flesh. Then as they tightened, drawing her to him, Selada gave a signal and the drums crashed into silence. The girl hung limply in Hercule's mighty arms. He picked her up as lightly as a leaf and walked through the doorway into the dark.

"Enough!" Selada said, coming down from the throne, a glass vial in her hand. She gave it to Odalie. "A little in his wine or his coffee," she said. "But only a little. Too much might harm him."

Odalie was fumbling in her purse for money, but Selada raised a hand. "You may send it by Tante Caleen," she said. "One word more. Love is an art. For the woman it must be all giving, nothing held back. Remember that. If Madame could for once *want* Monsieur—instead of passively submitting—then Madame would learn that love is the most wonderful gift of God, in which fierceness and tenderness are so entwined that never can they be separated, nor pain from ecstasy! Good night, madame."

Caleen touched Odalie's arm and they went back through the doors, through the inky hallway, into the cold, rain-lanced night.

Was it, then, this withholding of self that drove men like Stephen to other women? Did he want a woman who matched mood for brutal mood as the yellow dancer had matched Hercule step for step in that wild dance? Odalie looked at Caleen. "Could a woman," she whispered, "*want* to do things like that?"

Caleen's eyes widened at the question. "Unless she do—until she do, she ain't no woman. Here's the coach. Mistress come."

ODALIE SAT BEFORE the mirror between the twin silver candlesticks. I am afraid, she told herself; but the image in the mirror looked back with serene unconcern. Caleen stood behind her, pinning the heavy masses of hair up on top of her mistress's head so that Odalie's neck and shoulders were bare. "Now, Mistress do what Caleen say."

Odalie's eyebrows rose, but she followed the old woman into the little chamber to the tiny slipper-shaped bathtub. Slowly Odalie took off her garments while Caleen brought forth a small gourd from the folds of her apron and spilled the violet-colored powder into the bath. Instantly it steamed up in a great cloud, and the whole room was filled with the perfume.

Odalie's black eyes widened. Never had she encountered a scent like this. It was not heavy and sweet, but elusive to the point that the senses were unsure of its existence. She stepped into the tub and sat down. Caleen knelt beside her and began to bathe her with a soft cloth, rubbing firmly. Afterward she let Odalie relax in the tub, leaning against the high back.

"Mistress get out now."

Obediently Odalie stood up, and Caleen wrapped her in the big towels. Even after she was dried, the perfume lingered. Then, clad in robe and slippers, she went back to the bedroom.

"Take off the robe," Caleen commanded. "Mistress drink this and lie down on the bed."

Odalie took the glass; it was a wine that gleamed like amber. Without question, without hesitation, she drank it down and sank back upon the bed. Then suddenly she could feel Caleen's cool hands moving over her body. She opened her mouth to protest, but the wine was curling warm within her and all her limbs were loosening. She sighed and turned her head aside.

Caleen dipped her fingers into an earthenware jug. They came out dripping. The thin oil had the same scent as the perfume. She rubbed it gently into the pores of her mistress's skin, working from head to heel over the entire lovely body. Then she massaged the flesh until Odalie glowed all over.

After a while Caleen leaned close to Odalie's ear.

"The master is a good man," she whispered. "But he a devil-saint with blood like fire. When he kiss like fire, kiss back like fire. You do this, he come back to you!" Then she was gone, like a gaunt black ghost, guttering the candles as she went.

Odalie got up like a sleepwalker and lit the candles. Her eyes peered back at her from the mirror, black and lightless, velvet soft. Sitting there nude, she began to brush down her hair. Leave it like this, she thought, he likes it loose, he likes . . .

Then she was picking up her clothes from the chair. A white dress with a bodice like a silver sheath, satiny skirts that billowed endlessly, the chemise, the numerous petticoats—every one of them held the faint, elusive scent of that perfume. At last she fastened the triple string of pearls, with the heavy golden catch, about her neck. She stood back, gazing at herself in the mirror. She smiled, feeling the warmth stealing slowly along the hidden surface of her flesh. Then she turned and left the room. "Pray God he has not gone," she whispered. "Pray God . . ."

She stood for a long time before his door. I did this once, she thought, and I failed. I must not fail him now; no, never again must I fail him. Then she twisted the doorknob.

Stephen was standing by the window, gazing out over his darkened acres. Slowly he turned, and his pale eyes widened. "Ye're very beautiful, my dear," he said. "Do ye know, I'd almost forgotten that?"

She did not answer, but stood there, both hands behind her, leaning against the doorknob. Stephen raised one eyebrow. "Ye wear your hair loose. And that dress. Is there a ball?"

"No, Stephen," she said, "there's no ball."

Stephen crossed to her and lifted her chin with one hand. "What is it, Odalie?" he asked gently. Then he stopped. The perfume came up from her hair, from her shoulders, from the deep vale between her breasts. That perfume—but was there a perfume? There must be—still, how beautiful Odalie is!

Then suddenly, unexpectedly, her arms were sweeping up and around his neck. Her body arched upward against his; her eyes closed, she sought his lips. Stephen was lost in amazement; then he kissed her achingly, softly, tenderly. Her mouth burned upon his, the lips slackening, parting. For another long moment Stephen was limp against her, then his arms tightened around the slim waist until her body ground against his. "I love you, my husband," she whispered, "so much I love you—so very much!"

Stephen swept her up into his arms and laid her gently upon his own narrow bed. Odalie's hands urgently drew him to her. He paused. "Those pearls," he said. She fumbled briefly at the catch. It wouldn't work. Then both of her hands swept up suddenly and caught at the triple strings; she drew them out and down until they broke, scattering over the bed, over the floor. There on the rug they picked up the candle glow: tiny blue-white mounds gleaming in the darkness . . .

In the morning it was the sun itself that awakened Stephen. It fell across his face through the open window. He lay quite still, blinking. There were little points of light, scattered wildly about on the floor. Stephen studied them carefully. Yes, there was no doubt about it, they were pearls; but how on earth . . . ?

His arm felt numb; there was a weight upon it. Slowly he turned his head, and his fair brows flew upward. There beside him Odalie slept. Stephen smiled, remembering. He looked out over the disordered room, half covered with the garments she had discarded. This was all planned, he decided, even down to that devilish perfume. I've been tricked, he told himself, but, by heaven, I like such trickery!

Gently he eased his arm out from under her head. Odalie came awake at once, and sat up beside him. "Good morning, Stephen," she said clearly.

"Good morning, my dear," he said with grave mockery. "Ye slept well, I trust?"

She looked up at him, her black eyes searching his. Then she saw the little laughing light dancing, far back in his eyes. She bent forward to be kissed, but stopped her face inches from his. Then, as if by a signal, they both exploded into laughter.

AFTERWARD LIFE WAS very good at Harrow. Stephen went no more to the little house by the Ramparts. And Odalie, although in her middle thirties, grew hourly more beautiful. It was during this period that the portrait of her that hangs in the great hall at Harrow was painted. To the day of his death the artist, Paul Dumaine *père*, spoke of it as his finest work.

"This change in ye, Odalie," Stephen said. "After all these years ye became what I dreamed ye were. Why, Odalie, why?"

"I don't know, Stephen," she said. "Truly I don't. I think when I saw I was losing you, I became a woman. Now I fear that sometimes I tire you with my ardor!"

" 'Tis a fatigue I like," he said. "I love ye."

"Stephen . . . how would you like another son? Or a daughter perhaps?"

Stephen frowned. "That—no. Dr. Terrebonne said 'twould be extremely dangerous."

Odalie smiled up at him, a slow, misty smile. "The—the chance must be taken, my husband," she said softly.

Stephen's pale eyes were suddenly fierce. "No," he said, half to himself. "Ye must be mistaken!"

"There is no doubt. Are you sorry, Stephen?"

"No—not sorry, frightened." He took her hands and looked down into her face a long, long time before he kissed her.

Unseen in the doorway, Aurore turned and went back down the great stairs and rode away, the tears bright and heavy on her lashes. As she veered away from Harrow, she was conscious of another horse, standing quietly in the cypress shade. She reined in, looking curiously at the rider, a very young girl dressed in a rich green riding habit.

Mon Dieu, she's lovely, Aurore thought. But something in the girl's pure golden coloring struck her. She rode in closer. "Who are you?" she demanded. "What are you doing here?"

The girl's eyes, beneath her dark lashes, were a cool green. When she smiled, little flakes of gold swam in their depths.

"My errand is perhaps the same as Mademoiselle's own—to see that which I cannot have."

"You—you were Stephen's mistress!" Aurore said.

The girl laughed, a dark, rich sound—like the echoes of a soft, golden gong. "Yes," she said. "And Mademoiselle?"

"Oh," Aurore cried, completely beside herself, "you—you baggage!" Then she brought the crop down across her horse's flank and thundered off, down the road.

The girl sat very quietly upon her horse looking after her. Then again she turned her face toward Harrow. It would be a long wait, she knew. Sighing, she half closed her eyes. At last she saw the big palomino angling out toward the fields. Instantly she tapped her rawboned stallion with her crop.

Stephen rode on in the morning sun, whistling a gay tune. But suddenly Prince Michael stopped short in his tracks and whinnied. Stephen turned. Almost at once he recognized the rider of the roan stallion. "Désirée!" he said aloud.

"Forgive me," she whispered, "I had to come." As she talked, her eyes were searching his face, moving very rapidly, her gaze caressing him.

"What is it that ye want?" Stephen said harshly.

"You. I want you to come back to me."

"Little Désirée," Stephen said more gently, "there are others with a better claim on me. I'm afraid 'tis quite impossible."

Désirée's hand tightened upon the reins. The deep-green eyes widened endlessly. Then, deliberately, she tossed her reins high upon the roan stallion's neck and raised her crop above her head.

"Désirée!" Stephen cried.

But she brought the crop down viciously. The stallion screamed—a high, thin sound—and lunged forward across the fields. Stephen bent low over Prince Michael's neck and urged him forward; but the old palomino was no match for the pain-maddened roan. Désirée lashed the stallion again and again, driving him onward, the reins flapping loosely about his neck.

Before her now was the canebrake, behind which, Stephen knew, was the millstream, dropping away a full fifteen feet below. Unless that horse was a jumper . . .

Then the roan was soaring up and out over the brake, as effortlessly as a great bird. Stephen saw the stallion's forelegs striking the opposite bank. For a brief second they held, then they doubled under him, and he rolled over and over, throwing Désirée clear. The stallion thrashed about and screamed like a woman in agony; but the crumpled little figure in the green riding habit was quite still.

Stephen jumped to the ground and slid down into water up to his thighs. He strode across to the horse, the little derringer he carried with him always ready in his hand. He fired just once, and the thrashing and the screaming stopped. Then he knelt down beside the girl.

"For me," she whispered. "You saved one for me? It has two barrels, hasn't it?"

"Holy Mother of God!"

"Please, monsieur. Inside I'm—all broken. Am I not more to you than a horse?" Stephen slipped his arms under the slight form of the girl, then he lifted her and started back toward Harrow. Désirée nestled her head against his chest and bit her lip to keep back her moans at every jolting step.

At last he was going up the great stairs into Harrow. When Stephen reached the top step, Odalie was there. She bent curiously over the still form in his arms. "Who is she?" she demanded. "What ails her?"

Stephen did not answer. He walked quietly past his wife into the great hall. Odalie kept pace behind him. Suddenly she leaned close. "Stephen," she whispered. "This is—this is— By the good God! You'd do a thing like this! You'd bring *her* here—into my house!"

"Hush," Stephen said. "She's dying." He laid her in a small chamber in the south wing and summoned Caleen to do what she could. Caleen examined the girl briefly, with all the native hatred the pure black has for the mixed breed glaring from her eyes. "She no die, her," the old woman grunted. "Only got three ribs busted, more's the pity!"

"Then do something for her," Stephen commanded.

"I no touch her. Have me whipped, but I no touch her!"

Stephen measured her with his glance. "Get Suzette," he said shortly. "Tell her to see that she wants for nothing."

For three weeks Désirée lay upon the little bed, and in all that time not one word passed between Stephen and Odalie. The mistress of Harrow locked herself in her room and refused to listen to any sort of explanation. Even Etienne and Little Inch were caught in the upheaval. Everywhere they went they were greeted with tears or gruff-voiced dismissals.

When Désirée was well enough to be moved, a small wagon, well oiled and loaded down with bedding, carried her away from Harrow. Odalie came out of her rooms to watch the departure.

"My dear," Stephen began.

"No, no!" Odalie cried. "There is nothing to be said! Go to her and leave me alone!"

Stephen's eyes spoke icy fire. "Thank ye," he said evenly. "Perhaps I will—at that."

CHAPTER THIRTEEN

DURING ALL THE months of Odalie's second pregnancy scarcely a word passed between her and Stephen. She rarely slept and only a few crusts of bread and countless cups of *café noir* passed between her lips. On several occasions Stephen swallowed his pride and went to her with explanations and apologies upon the tip of his tongue, only to be rebuffed before he could utter them. Finally he gave it up, and in pique and confusion and trouble of mind, he turned once more to Désirée.

Early in the summer, while she lay abed with her injuries, he visited her almost nightly and attended to her wants with tenderness. But after she was again upon her feet, his visits lessened. And when he did come, he talked to her gravely and kissed her with calm, paternal affection.

To Désirée this was maddening. "Am I a child?" she stormed. "Have I grown ugly? Why do you no longer love me, monsieur?"

"I've grown old, Désirée," he said. "And there is enough trouble already. I have a house—the greatest in the state—in which I am hated. I have a son, but he is strange and wild toward me. I have much wealth—but no happiness."

"Monsieur also has one thing more. Monsieur has me."

"And ye have broken your lovely body because of me, and brought down my life around my ears!"

Désirée knelt like a child at his feet. The tears sparkled upon the long curving lashes. "Better I should have died than to have hurt you," she whispered.

He bent down and kissed her gently, but her lips clung to his as lightly as a breath and her arms stole upward around his neck. "Never let me go," she cried. "Never, never, never!"

IT WAS LATE in the winter of 1839 when the time came for Odalie to be delivered of her child. Aurore came to stay at Harrow and Caleen was on duty day and night. Dr. Lefevre, too, took up residence at the great house. Stephen went no more to the city.

For Odalie was pitifully weak from long starvation, and her thin form was racked with unceasing anguish. "Frankly," Dr. Lefevre said to Aurore, "it is to be doubted that she will survive. There is no will to live. If only I knew what the trouble was . . ."

"I do," Aurore said grimly. "And, by heaven, I'm going to mend it, now!" She strode away from the doctor and crossed the hall to Stephen's study. She twisted the knob angrily and stepped into the room. There Stephen's bright head was bent over the desk, pillowed upon his arms, and she could see the empty cut-glass whiskey decanter.

Aurore snorted in disgust. Stephen lifted his head with a look of so great hurt and trouble upon his face that all Aurore's anger vanished as though it had never been. Always I could forgive him anything, she thought; even this . . .

"Stephen," she said gently. "Odalie is worse. There are—complications. You are the only one who can help her now."

Stephen smiled crookedly. "That I doubt," he said. "God and Our Lady, how she hates me!"

"You deserve it," Aurore declared. "But the fact is she loves you so much that it is chiefly of heartbreak that she is dying."

Stephen rose to his feet at once. "Dying!" he said. "Ye said she is dying?"

"Yes," Aurore said simply. "Please come to her, Stephen."

"Aye," Stephen said slowly. "Many times now I have tried; but one more time, or one million more times, would not be amiss now."

In the bedchamber Stephen bent over the twisting form of his wife. Aurore stood in the doorway, unnoticed.

"Odalie," Stephen said slowly, "when that girl came to Harrow, she came without my knowledge. I had broken with her long ago."

On the bed Odalie lay very still, looking up at her husband. "You—you do not lie to me?" she whispered.

"I never lie," Stephen said simply.

"And now, Stephen?" she whispered.

"And now I promise ye I shall never consort with her again."

Her lips widened pitifully into a smile, but her words were so low that Stephen had to bend his head to hear them. "Thank you, my husband," she said. "Now no more will I fear it—this business of dying."

"Ye aren't going to die," Stephen said. "Ye cannot!"

"I'm afraid I must, my husband," she said quite clearly.

Stephen gave a short cry and sank down beside her, burying his face in the covers. In the doorway Aurore wept.

FOUR NIGHTS LATER Odalie gave birth to a stillborn child—a daughter. She herself never regained consciousness, but died, very quietly, in her sleep.

Looking at Stephen, Aurore forgot to cry. Quietly she left the bedchamber and summoned Georges. "Collect the master's weapons," she said, "all of them, and bring them to me at once."

"Yes, mademoiselle, and I watch him—never I let him out of my sight."

Aurore went into the study and sat down. Her head ached abominably. There was so much to be done. The invitations to the funeral must be engraved and sent, a mausoleum built. She would need help. As she rose, she met Dr. Lefevre coming into the study. "I gave him a sleeping draft," he said. "He is resting very quietly now."

Aurore nodded dumbly and slipped out into the hall. Moved by a sudden impulse, she climbed the stairs to Stephen's chamber. He lay abed, still fully clothed. In sleep all the lines of his face were softened, and even the patches of white that were spreading above his temples did not detract from the strangely youthful cast of his features. A little cry came from his lips and his lean body thrashed briefly. Aurore drew back to the door; then she was running down the stairs, whispering to herself, over and over again, "God forgive me for my thoughts! Good Blessed God, forgive me!"

AMELIA AND ANDRE came before daybreak and took charge of everything. Etienne and Little Inch were sent to La Place. Mike Farrel appeared and dogged Stephen's steps like a huge shadow. "She were a cold, high-strung wench," he whispered to André, "but how Stevie loved her! I'm gonna keep me eye upon him."

And in the cypress grove near Harrow stonemasons were at work building the magnificent mausoleum, with twin stone angels guarding the door. Inside, there was a niche already reserved for Stephen; this fact was a source of great trouble to his friends.

André came out of Harrow late in the evening to find Stephen watching the almost finished work. "Stephen," he said, "my old one—you must not—it is a thing that happens to us all."

Stephen's blue eyes, as he gazed upon his friend, were very clear. "I shall do myself no violence," he said softly. "She would not wish it, and there is still the boy. But God knows 'twould be easier, André, than to live with my thoughts."

"Nonsense—" André began, but Stephen stopped him.

"I drove her to her death," he declared. "There is a kind of black madness in me." He fell silent, shaking his head. André, too, was still; he knew when a man should hold his tongue.

AFTER THE FUNERAL Harrow was a great, echoing tomb of silence. Stephen Fox sat for endless hours in his study gazing upon vacancy. But at last, upon an evening, he rode to the city. On Rampart Street, in the little white house, Désirée awaited him. As the big horse rounded the corner, she swayed dizzily, her hands tight upon the windowsill. I must tell him, she thought. He cannot leave me now—he cannot!

Then Stephen's knock was sounding from the door, twice repeated clearly. Désirée fought back a feeling of nausea and ran forward to open the door. She stood there a moment, swaying a little as she looked at him; then, very quietly, she said, "Come in, monsieur."

"Désirée," Stephen began, " 'tis a hard thing I must say to ye now."

The girl drew herself up proudly. "I know what you would say, monsieur," she said softly. "Your wife is dead. And before she died, she was grieved by this thing between us. So, in honor, you cannot continue with me longer."

"Aye," Stephen said grimly, "that is it."

"Very well. But there is this that I must say. . . ." Her eyes were very wide and bright with trembling tears. "When you go through that door, I shall die a little. And every day that you are gone from me I shall die a little more until I am all dead. And then I shall be happy, but never again until then."

"The house is yours," Stephen said. "And everything in it. I have arranged a settlement to be paid ye monthly as long as ye shall live. Is there anything more that ye want?"

"Only that which I cannot have," she whispered.

Stephen took a step toward her; then he stopped, turned swiftly and walked through the opened door. Désirée held her breath, listening to the sound of his footsteps. A sudden wave of weakness and nausea struck her and she went down upon her knees to the floor. I couldn't tell him, she thought; there was already too much anguish in his eyes. "It shall have red hair," she whispered, "this my son, and eyes like blue ice and a smile that is never quite a whole smile, but always has mockery in it. And I shall watch over him and cherish him and he shall be my life—my whole life." She turned away from the window and walked back into the darkened room.

Up at Harrow a stillness lay like a weight upon the whole land. The fields stretched out over the rim of the world and the cane grew tall. Then knives were brought out and the stalks fell before their bright flashes, but the Negroes did not sing as they worked.

It was upon such a day that Aurore Arceneaux came riding up to Harrow in her small carriage. All her belongings were packed in valises upon the top. "I've come to stay," she said simply. "Harrow needs a woman's hand, and it is no good that the boy goes motherless. You don't mind, do you, Stephen?"

"No," Stephen said, "I don't mind. But ye're still a young and lovely woman. There are those who might think ill of this."

"Let them. If there are any sinful ideas left in an old spinster of thirty-one years, it is time we had them out, don't you think?"

Stephen smiled, with almost a twinkle in his bleak eyes.

Going into the great hall, Aurore noticed dust upon the lower rungs of the furniture, the rugs neither beaten nor swept. When Caleen showed her to her rooms, Aurore turned to her. "Get Suzette and the other women, Tante," she said firmly. "We shall have a housecleaning here."

In a few hours the cut glass glistened, the silver sparkled and tablecloths glowed whitely in the gentle light.

Then Aurore found Etienne, dirty and unkempt, playing cards with Little Inch back of the stables. "Come with me, 'Tienne," she said gently. "And you too, Inch."

She led them upstairs to the little bathing chamber. Inch was sent for water and, under Aurore's direction, scrubbed his young master vigorously. Afterward the little black boy was sent away to bathe himself, and Aurore trimmed 'Tienne's great black mane of hair. Then, brushed and combed and dressed in new, fresh clothing, he stood before her for inspection. "Ah, now you look the gentleman!" she said. "Please go and bring me your books, 'Tienne."

The boy scampered away, adoration glowing in his pale blue eyes. When he returned, Aurore had him read to her. His education, she discovered, was sadly lacking. So, gently, she began to instruct him. She read him the stories dear to the heart of a boy: tales of the heroes of the old France and the new, deeds of chivalry and heroism, stories of noblesse oblige so precious to the aristocratic South. A gentleman, Etienne learned, had much greater responsibilities than an ordinary mortal. And soon he decided, with grave precocity, that there was no escaping his destiny.

So life went on at Harrow, and tongues began to wag in New Orleans.

One night Aurore lay awake listening to Stephen's footsteps in the great hall. Back and forth they went, but at one place they paused. Aurore knew that this was before Odalie's portrait, glowing with unearthly loveliness upon the wall. How many nights had she heard those footsteps?

But now, suddenly, frighteningly, there was prolonged silence. Aurore drew on her robe and stole out into the hall. There was no sound but the pounding of her heart. She went forward until she reached the picture. Before it, curled up in a big chair, Stephen slept. Exhaustion had finally done its work.

Aurore leaned close to study his face, illumined by the candles glowing softly in the silver candlesticks. The mouth, so stern and commanding when he was awake, in sleep was pitiful and lost like the lips of a child. She had an impulse to smother his face against her breasts and rock to and fro, crooning to him softly. "Do not grieve, my Stephen," she whispered. "Never in the world was she worth so much pain. Not she nor any woman."

Stephen half turned in his sleep and Aurore's face moved closer. Her lips touched his as lightly as a breath; but involuntarily they lingered, caressingly. Then, without opening his eyes, Stephen's lean arms stole upward, drawing her downward to him. She struggled briefly, and the pale blue eyes flew wide.

"Aurore!" He held her firmly in his arms, his eyes studying her face. "Ye kissed me," he said. "Why?"

"Let me go—please, Stephen, please!" she whispered.

"No," he said gravely. "No. I must understand this thing."

She buried her face against his chest so that her voice was muffled and thick with tears. "I love you," she said. "Always I've loved you—since that day in the Place d'Armes when Lafayette came and you stared and stared at Odalie until my heart broke in two. Whatever you did—your mockery, your mistress, your loving Odalie—I forgave you, Stephen. I lived only for the precious minutes when I should see you."

Stephen lay very still, but his arms did not move. "There is nothing left in me of love, Aurore," he said gently, "but 'tis certain I cannot live alone for long. Already I am unsure between the real and the dreamed. Perhaps in time I can learn again to feel as a man ought."

He stopped, gazing upward at the picture. "We shall be married at once," he said. "God knows that never before was a man so honored. I am simply and humbly grateful."

LATE IN THE morning of the following day the great yellow coach from Harrow rode up the long driveway of La Place des Rivières. Stephen was flawlessly attired in the very latest fashion. In the great knob of his cravat the big pearl stickpin gleamed softly. He extended his hand into the coach and helped Aurore down. Her face was pale with nervousness.

Amelia came down the stairs to meet them. "At last!" She laughed. "I was beginning to believe that you two would never again honor La Place."

"The honor is ours," Stephen said, "that still ye receive us. My dear Amelia, we come to seek your aid . . . for a wedding."

Amelia's coral lips formed a soft O, but she smiled at Aurore. "I'm glad," she said. "It's unconventional and will make a scandal, but it's the right thing—especially since you've lived up at Harrow all these months."

"Amelia!" Aurore's voice was stricken. "Surely you don't think that I—that we—"

"Of course not," Amelia said. "I know you too well, both of you. But there are others who don't."

The two women locked arms and started up the stairs. Stephen strode along beside them, looking from one to the other.

"At least ye don't think me a monster, Amelia," he remarked.

"You're too stupid to be a scoundrel, Stephen," Amelia mocked. "That you could have looked into Aurore's face all these years and not discovered how she worshiped you called for a stupendous amount of stupidity. Even André knew, and God knows he's not overly bright."

"Thus do American women speak of their husbands!" Stephen laughed. "Perhaps I've done well to escape them."

"Perhaps you have." Amelia smiled. "But then, perhaps you might have been agreeably surprised."

"As André was. I envy ye both your happiness."

"Soon you will have no cause to. It's made up of many things, Stephen—deep and abiding love, and mutual trust and respect. Tenderness too, and a certain sharing of sorrows. And sometimes you must laugh—without mockery—and at yourself."

"Ye're lecturing me?" Stephen growled in mock anger.

"Yes. Laughter is important. I shall never forget my poor André's face the morning after you took him to that filthy quadroon ball. He looked so pitiful that I couldn't keep from laughing, and there the matter ended."

Stephen threw back his head and laughed aloud. But Aurore's face was white and still. Amelia squeezed her arm.

"Forgive me," she whispered. "I do talk too much, don't I?"

"It's nothing," Aurore said. "Only I want to forget that he ever belonged to anyone else."

When André came in from the fields and was told the news, he fairly danced with glee. "So," he chortled, "at last, my old one, you begin to develop intelligence. When is it to be?"

"Tomorrow—with your aid."

"Then we'd best ride into New Orleans and make the arrangements. And I must have the honor of buying you your last bachelor dinner. Give me half an hour in which to dress."

THE NEXT EVENING the yellow coach drew up before the cathedral, and André and Amelia and Stephen and Aurore got out. To their vast astonishment, the stalls were filled with spectators.

"How on earth?" Aurore gasped.

"Negro grapevine," André said grimly.

The ceremony was brief, but Aurore's face was so transfixed with happiness that even those who had come to mock were stilled. The four of them left the church together, and the spectators filed out after them into the street.

"We shall go to the new town house," Stephen said. "It was to have been for Odalie but . . . it was never occupied. Afterward we will decide upon a honeymoon."

The wedding supper was a good one with much wine. Stephen urged the Le Blancs to remain overnight, but André declined with thanks, and he and Amelia started homeward in a hired carriage.

Then it was very still at Bonheur, as Odalie had christened the new house she did not live to enter. Stephen looked at his bride and hesitated. So much love was shining out of her clear hazel eyes that he was awed and humbled. At last he walked toward her. 'Tis better that it begins, he thought, our life together. Perhaps this will dispel the other.

Stephen bent and kissed her gently. She drew back. "No, no!" she whispered huskily. "Not like that! I'm no longer your sister."

"And how shall I kiss ye, my dearest?"

"Like this," she murmured. "Like this . . ."

A FEW DAYS later Stephen and Aurore engaged a stateroom aboard a packet bound upriver to New York via the new Erie Canal. Etienne became a member of André's household for the duration of the honeymoon, and set about a career of such extravagant misbehavior that his hosts were tempted to write Stephen to cut short his journey and come to their rescue.

For the rest of the summer the Foxes stayed at a fashionable hotel at Saratoga Springs, making, of course, trips into Philadelphia and New York. Slowly, to his own astonishment, Stephen was being forced to the realization that he was actually happy. He smiled often and freely. Aurore teased him, played with him, laughed at him and loved him with all her heart.

In the fall they returned to Harrow, and the great house came alive. There were endless parties and entertainments. And the gentry of New Orleans came: after all, one could not hold flouting convention against such a charming couple as the Foxes. There was one convention, however, that Aurore did not disregard. She waited almost two years, until the fall of 1841, before presenting Stephen with an eight-pound daughter, delivered without the slightest fuss or bother. They called the child Julie.

CHAPTER FOURTEEN

In May of 1853 Stephen Fox rode through the broad fields of Harrow on a tour of inspection. Etienne had been in France for almost three years now, studying in Paris. Behind Stephen, on a shaggy, fat Shetland pony, rode his daughter, Julie. Each time Stephen turned to look back at her, his hard blue eyes softened and warmed with pleasure.

At eleven, Julie was already a beauty. Her hair was a coppery gold, but her eyes were as black as Odalie's had been. Her face, however, had the shape and softness of her mother's, although there was a look of gentle mischief about her that came more, perhaps, from Stephen.

The plantation was producing almost triple its yield of ten or twelve years before. The cane grew up in the fields and the cloudless blue sky crowned the earth with a dome of sapphire. Stephen looked down upon his daughter and smiled. " 'Tis something, this land," he said.

"You know, Papa," Julie declared, accenting the second syllable of the word in the French fashion, "I think Harrow is the prettiest place in all the world!"

"Aye." Stephen smiled. "So it is. But 'twas not alone of Harrow that I spoke. I mean the whole land—all of it—Texas, California, and even the northern states."

"But the people in the North—they're so strange," she said. "And they hate us so."

"In that ye wrong the Northerners," Stephen said. "They don't hate us, Julie—'tis only slavery that they hate."

"Why?" the girl asked. "Stephen Le Blanc says it's a holy system ordained by God. Why should they hate it?"

"It goes a long way back, into the mentalities of the two regions. In the North the climate is cold. The blood flows briskly through the veins and work is a pleasure and labor is honorable. Therefore, no prejudice ever arose against a gentleman's working."

"But Stephen says there are no gentlemen in the North."

"Ye must not accept my godson's views without question," Stephen said, laughing. "The point is, Julie, that since slavery is unprofitable in the North, 'tis easy for Northerners to oppose it. Here in the South we find slavery to our profit, so we deify it. And that, too, is wrong."

"Why?"

"There is much that is wrong with slavery. Ye've never seen the wrongs, because we do not whip our slaves or separate families. But those things are done."

"Then it is wrong to hold slaves, Papa?"

"That I don't know. . . . But enough of this—we're wasting time."

They turned and headed back toward Harrow. As they trotted briskly up the oak alley and the house came into sight, gleaming white among the trees, Aurore waited on the gallery.

"Stephen," she called, "a letter just came from Etienne! He should be here within the week!"

"So," Stephen said. " 'Twill be good to have the lad back."

Together Stephen and Julie went into the great hall, where Caleen waited. So old now that she herself had forgotten her years, she had changed but little; she was thinner, and a little more stooped. All the Foxes confidently expected her to live forever. Now she was smiling, a wide, toothless smile.

"Ah, Caleen," Stephen said, "we will see our lads again. Ye had a message from Inch, of course?"

"Yes, sir," the old woman said. "He writes beautiful, like a white!"

"I'm not surprised," Stephen said. "The lad has a head."

Dinner went by rapidly, paced by Stephen's gently cynical talk. He poked fun at Aurore and Julie and the Le Blancs. "He has become a political fanatic, that André," he informed them. "A man grows weary of it. The crime of admitting California as a free state. The tardiness of carving up Texas to equal the northern electoral votes. When ye mention the District of Columbia, he foams at the mouth! He calls it a direct slap at the South that the capital of the nation should be free soil."

"Well," Aurore said, "isn't it?"

"Ye too? After all, my dearest, we've gained many advantages. The people will not permit slavery to be made legal all over the nation."

"Then what is the answer, Stephen—secession?"

Stephen frowned, and his silver-white brows knitted together. "That—no. The Union must be preserved."

"An unpopular notion nowadays, my husband. We don't need the North—and they do need us."

"That is typically southern, Aurore, and typically wrongheaded. They could continue to flourish if we perished tomorrow, while we cannot exist without the products of their industry."

"Then what must we do, Stephen?"

"Free the Negroes by gradual emancipation—and retain them upon the land under small wages and our patronage. We could control them as well as now, and remove at the same time the squeamish ethical questions that plague the North."

"That would be hypocrisy," Aurore said clearly.

"Admitted. But 'tis that or the North will destroy us." He rose from his place. "Forgive me," he said. "I must finish my tour. But one thing more. 'Tis the nation I love, not any one part of it. I would not see it rent asunder. Never upon earth has the poor man had such freedom; never has there been so much respect for the essential dignity of mankind. As long as it exists, men everywhere have hope."

"Even the blacks?" Aurore asked.

"Aye," Stephen said. "We shall find men with minds like Inch's among them, and in the end they will take their part in the nation." Then he was gone, striding through the great hall and out upon the gallery.

Stephen's face was frowning as he mounted his horse. The bitterness of the quarrel between the North and the South was growing hourly. How would it all end? His head ached at the thought as he rounded the curve that brought him in sight of the private burial ground of Harrow. Abruptly his hand tightened upon the reins, for there before him was a short, ugly horse with a long head and shaggy coat standing riderless in the road. This was a prairie horse—a mustang, a breed never seen in Louisiana.

An instant later his gaze came to rest upon the rider. A tall man with inky black hair was standing quietly before the tomb of Odalie. Stephen swung down from the palomino, one of the many descendants of the original Prince Michael, and approached him. When he was but a yard away the stranger turned. There was the passage of hard, slow years written in that face, and the savage erosion of wind and sun, but Stephen recognized it at once.

"Phillippe Cloutier!" he said. "So ye've come back."

"Yes," Phillippe said. "But years too late, I see."

"No rancor, Phillippe," Stephen said slowly. "I want no quarrel with ye."

"You'll have none," Phillippe said. "Forgive me my harshness. Seventeen years in Texas are no aid to good manners." Awkwardly he put out his hand. Stephen took it firmly.

"Why did ye come back?" he asked. "I've heard ye mentioned to succeed Houston. Ye made quite a place for yourself there."

"My family is gone, so I have returned to take over Rosemont. I couldn't bring myself to sell it. Besides, there is my daughter to think of."

"Ye have a daughter? Ye could not have been too troubled about Odalie to have taken upon yourself a wife."

"I took no wife," Phillippe said harshly. "Ceclie is a natural child. Her mother was a squatter's daughter—part Navaho and part Irish. Two very savage races," he added with a wicked grin.

Stephen laughed. "Then ye have trouble upon your hands," he said. "I don't envy ye, Phillippe."

"She is sixteen years of age now and difficult. That was another reason for returning to civilized territory. . . . I'll ride with you, Stephen, if I may. I need to be brought up to date on the affairs of New Orleans. Texas is like another world." He mounted the short prairie horse and the two of them rode toward the bayou road.

"We've had a time of it since ye left, Phillippe," Stephen said. "We've moved our business section from Chartres to Canal, we've grown to the fourth city in size in the country, we've been visited again by Old Hickory, and by your Sam Houston. Ye knew about our panic?"

"Did I? All the loans we were trying to float went haywire."

"Well, apart from the fact that the whole city nearly burned to the ground in 'forty-four, and was almost washed away in the flood of 'forty-nine—"

"But are we becoming civilized?" Phillippe interrupted. "New Orleans boasts of its culture, yet I don't see any signs of its overtaking Paris."

Stephen laughed. "Ye ask too much. We have established a National Art Gallery, and applauded a new singer—Jenny Lind—quite a nice voice. That old rogue P. T. Barnum brought her here, but aside from that, and perhaps the new custom of masking in street carnivals just before Lent that some young blades started in 'thirty-seven, we're about the same as before. . . . But come back up to the house. Aurore will be glad to see you."

Phillippe's black brows rose. "Aurore? What is she doing at Harrow?"

"My wife has every right to be at Harrow, don't ye think? Ye have no objections, I hope," Stephen said mockingly, "to this second marriage of mine?"

"Would be rather too late if I did," Phillippe declared. "But I must ask to be excused from your invitation at the present. Make my apologies to Madame Fox, won't you? I shall expect you both at Rosemont as soon as the place is put to rights. For that matter, I want you to come out before then. I fear the equipment at Rosemont is sadly out of date, and I need the advice of Louisiana's most successful planter."

Stephen took his hand and Phillippe rode away. Stephen looked after him with a puzzled frown. Texas had done something to Phillippe Cloutier. There was about him now a directness that was completely American, and a suggestion of well-controlled force. Stephen shrugged. After all, Phillippe's oddities were really no concern of his.

SEVERAL DAYS later the steamer *Le Cygne*, inward bound from France, dropped anchor in the harbor at New Orleans.

"New Orleans!" Paul Dumaine exclaimed to the three other men on the upper deck. "Father never grew tired of talking about it. There was only one other topic more frequently upon his tongue."

"And what was that, Paul?" Etienne Fox asked.

"Your mother. He kept two dozen paintings of her that he'd

done from memory after his return to France. But Father used to weep—quite literally, 'Tienne—at their inadequacy."

"There's one that he did from life," Etienne said. "It hangs at Harrow. You'll see it tonight."

"I know. Father calls it the crowning masterpiece of his career. Until I can equal it, he says, I am no painter."

"You'll never be able to touch that one—never!"

The other two men stood a little apart from Etienne and Paul. The face of one of them, a man older by perhaps ten years than any of the others, was somber. He wore the huge sloppy bow tie of Paris and a frock coat of glistening black broadcloth.

"What ails ye, Aupré?" Paul Dumaine said with a laugh. "You seem sorry to come back to your New Orleans."

Aupré pushed back his hat so that his chestnut curls caught the light. "I love New Orleans," he said huskily. "But I cannot live here. Someday I shall tell you why—both of you."

Etienne's hand went to the tiny S-shaped scar on his left cheek. "Perhaps Aupré has memories," he said. "Perhaps he has a past such as the one he accuses my father of."

"Forgive me for that, 'Tienne. But your father was such unparalleled material for a play . . ."

" 'Twas having it paraded before the audiences of the Comédie Française that I objected to."

"And your objection was overruled by Aupré's pointed arguments," Paul reminded him, chuckling.

Again Etienne touched the scar. "I was always a miserable swordsman," he said. "While Aupré here is the best. 'Twas a kindness that he didn't kill me."

Aupré smiled slowly. "I was tempted to. But I must confess to a sort of admiration for the Foxes. Let's forget all this, shall we, 'Tienne?"

" 'Tis forgotten and forgiven. You'll dine with us at Harrow tonight?"

"That, no," Aupré said abruptly. "I shall be damnably busy—settling Mother's estate and all—and I must leave again for France within a fortnight."

Etienne turned to the fourth man. He was a Negro with a face of polished ebony, but his dress and his bearing differed little from those of the three white men.

"Inch!" Etienne barked. "Is our baggage ready?"

"Yes, sir."

"Then go down and bring it up! Move faster, you scoundrel!"

Inch walked away, his pace but little accelerated by his master's commands.

"France ruined him," Etienne growled. "He stole away nights and studied at the Ecole de la Jurisprudence de Paris. Law, no less!"

"But if he had an aptitude for it—" Paul began.

"You Frenchmen! I grant you that Inch is damned intelligent, but he must be kept in his place."

Inch came back with the valises, and the four of them went down a ladder into the boat. When finally they stepped out upon the quay, Aupré bade them an abrupt farewell and disappeared into one of the streets leading away from the docks.

Etienne turned toward the river, where several vessels lay in a line. He noticed a sudden flurry of action; a group of men were rowing like mad toward the quay upon which he and Paul stood. When they reached it, they swarmed up the pilings like so many monkeys. As the last man passed, Etienne took hold of his arm.

"I say," he began, "what's the trouble out there?"

"It be Yellow Jack!"

"Yellow Jack?" Paul Dumaine echoed blankly.

"Yellow fever," Etienne explained. He turned to the seaman. "Are you sure?" he asked.

"We be the shore crew. 'Tis our job to tidy up them ships. An' I tell you, there ain't a ship amongst 'em free o' the taint."

"Hadn't you better report this to the city authorities?" Paul suggested.

"The city authorities!" the crewman snorted. "Helluva lot o' good that'd do!"

"He's right," Etienne said. "They wouldn't lift a finger. They never have."

On the drive out to Harrow Paul Dumaine was all eyes. "What a place in which to paint!" he cried over and over again. "Father should never have left—never!"

Then they were rolling up the alley of oaks before Harrow, and the great white house gleamed softly in the early afternoon sun.

"*Ma foi!*" Paul said. " 'Tienne, why didn't you tell me that in your own land you are a prince!"

Etienne looked at the house. "This is Harrow," he said softly. "Harrow . . ."

Paul got down first from the carriage. Then Etienne appeared, and Julie let out a squeal of pure delight and bounded down the steps three at a time, her parents close behind her. Stephen stood back and measured his son.

"Ye've changed," he said. "But 'tis for the better, I think. And your friend is . . . ?"

"Father, this is Paul Dumaine, son of the Paul Dumaine who painted Mother's picture. He's an artist, too."

"Welcome." Aurore smiled. "While you are here you must consider yourself a second son."

"Come into the house and have breakfast," Stephen said.

A moment later Paul stood before the picture hanging in the great hall, his eyes widening. "Could anyone have been as lovely as that?" he whispered.

"Actually, Paul," Stephen said, "Odalie was never so beautiful as Aurore here, but somehow she made everyone—including myself—think her the loveliest lady on earth. I think it was because she believed herself so. Faith is a wonderful thing."

They went into the dining hall. Presently the Negroes appeared with two steaming breakfasts, and the young men began to eat.

"Ye have a scar," Stephen said to Etienne. "Still following my bad example, son? With whom did ye fight?"

"It was in your behalf, Father," Etienne said. "Aupré d'Hippolyte wrote a play about you—a satire. 'Twas all the rage. Aupré is from New Orleans—strange that I never knew him before. Anyway, he is one of France's leading playwrights."

"Hmmm—d'Hippolyte. So he's an aristocrat now. But I must say ye've become quite democratic, 'Tienne—crossing swords with mulattoes."

"Mulattoes!"

"Aye."

Etienne was on his feet. "Inch! Inch!" he called. "Where the deuce is that black scoundrel!"

Inch, at the moment, was down in the kitchen, talking earnestly with old Caleen.

"It was wonderful, Grandmother," he said. "There the people care not if a man is black. I learned many things."

"Good." Tante Caleen beamed. "Now when the time come, you be ready, you! I can't fight. But you got weapons. I don't hate

151

the master and the mistress. They treat the Negroes good, yes. But it ain't right, Inch baby, it ain't right."

"Yes, Grandmother," Inch said. "I can't belong to 'Tienne like his horse! I'm made in the image of Almighty God and there is Godhood in me—there is. To me this paternalistic kindness of the Foxes is more cruel than whippings. I admit of inferiority to no one of any race! And one day, these pale ones will dance to our tune—"

"Inch!" Etienne's voice came floating through the corridor. "Where the devil are you!"

Inch stood very still, his clenched uplifted fist arrested in midair. Slowly he let it fall. "Coming, sir," he said.

Etienne's dark face was clouded with anger. "Inch," he said, "you will ride into the city for me. Find out where Aupré has gone. Don't let him see you, but when you've found him, report to me at once." He turned away muttering to himself, "The pompous, lying yellow hound!"

"So," Inch murmured under his breath, "you've found out, my good master. I could have told you this months ago. 'Tis a thing one senses—this kinship of the blood."

TWO NIGHTS LATER five horsemen sat very quietly upon their mounts at an intersection of Rampart Street. Three of them were great, muscular field hands bearing long staves in their black horny hands. The other two were Inch and Etienne Fox.

Inch looked at his master. I thank you, 'Tienne, he thought, for this show. If there is any one thing more despicable than a white, it is one of these yellow ones. He would leave his race, this Aupré. 'Twill be good to see him brought low!

Precisely at the same time as yesterday and the day before, Aupré passed the corner. Etienne nodded to his men. At once the big Negroes swarmed down from their nags, and Aupré looked up to find himself surrounded.

"What the deuce—" he began, but the biggest of the blacks struck him hard across the mouth with the stave. The slight octoroon went down in a crumpled heap in the mud.

"Help!" he screamed. "Help!" Then, seeing Etienne: "Help me, 'Tienne, for the love of God!"

Again Etienne nodded. The Negroes rained blows upon Aupré. The slender figure twisted silently upon the ground.

Etienne raised a hand. "Enough," he said quietly. The Negroes remounted their horses and the little cavalcade rounded the corner, out of sight.

Aupré lifted his bloody, broken face out of the stinking mud of the street. Then, groaning, inch by inch he drew himself erect. He stood swaying in the flickering light of the lanterns. There was no other sound in the street but the rasping of his breath and the racking sound of his sobs.

LATE IN AUGUST of 1853 Stephen Fox, Etienne and Paul Dumaine rode into New Orleans. Black clouds massed low over the bayou country and lances of rain slanted down at a sharp angle.

"Father," Etienne complained, "you should put your foot down! This charity might cost Mother her life."

"Aye," Stephen said grimly, "so I've told her, but she would go. The people need her, she says."

From the direction of the city came a deep-bellied booming, and clouds of inky smoke billowed upward into the air.

"What on earth—" Paul began.

"Cannon," Stephen told him. "And the smoke is from barrels of burning pitch. They tried the same remedies twenty-one years ago—when ye nearly died of the fever, 'Tienne. And in all that time, they've learned nothing. I hope ye have a strong stomach, Paul."

"Why?"

"The sights ye will see would sicken a he-goat! They've stopped trying to bury the dead. They simply dump them on the ground of the cemeteries and leave them there to rot."

"How many have died, Father?"

"Twelve thousand. Aurore tells me that the rate is two thousand a day. Aurore recovered from a childhood siege, so she fancies herself immune. Here, give me your handkerchiefs."

The two youths passed them over and Stephen drenched them in a rich perfume he had brought in a large vial. "Bind them over your mouths and nostrils," he commanded. "Even from this distance the stench is formidable."

They rode into the deserted streets of the dying city. Paul's horse shied with a mincing, dancing step and the young Frenchman leaned down to see what had frightened his mount. There in the street lay the naked body of a young woman. From her crumpled, twisted posture, it was evident she had been thrown from the window of an upper story.

"The death cart will pick her up," Stephen said. "In two or three days perhaps."

Down by the levee a gigantic warehouse had been converted into a hospital, and in this Aurore and old Caleen labored together with a dozen nuns and two or three other public-spirited women. Stephen and Etienne and Paul dismounted, and Stephen unslung the saddlebags in which he had brought wine and a few dainties to tempt Aurore's fading appetite, although he knew well that the entire store would find its way to the dying. In addition, he had brought a change of linen for his wife and a bag of tobacco for old Caleen.

Aurore's lovely matronly face was pale and thin, but she smiled bravely at her visitors. "I'm so glad you came," she said brightly. "Here, Stephen, help me turn this man over. I'm afraid he's getting bedsores."

Stephen looked at her wordlessly. Then firmly he heaved the fat old man up and over. Not even the perfumed handkerchiefs could keep down the stench. Paul reeled dizzily to the door and was sick upon the ground. Aurore looked after him anxiously. "He'll be all right," Stephen told her. "But ye—ye're coming home with me!"

"No, Stephen," she said gently, "my place is here. But I wish you'd take Caleen back. She performs daily miracles, attending blacks and whites alike. But she's too old . . ."

Caleen flatly refused to budge. And in the end they had to ride back to Harrow without either Caleen or Aurore.

THAT SUMMER OF 1853 was miserable at Harrow. There was little that Etienne could do to entertain Paul. Visiting, one of the chief pleasures of plantation life, was too dangerous. One never knew where one might run into a case of the fever. All assemblies were forbidden, putting an end to cockfighting, the theater, the opera and even gambling.

Paul, however, happily entered into the life at Harrow as though he had been born there. He painted portraits of everybody— Julie, Etienne, Stephen and even some of the Negroes. He wandered all over the plantation, even in the driving rains, making sodden little sketches from which he painted huge landscapes.

Stephen rode daily into the plague-stricken city, but nothing could induce Aurore to leave as long as there were sick to be aided, comforted, saved. And at her side there was always Caleen, moving like a gaunt black shadow. More than one young doctor listened carefully to Caleen when she explained her methods, and the number of cures in the warehouse increased steadily.

Finally in the late fall the rains abated and the fever left New Orleans. Only one thing marred the joy at Harrow. Two weeks after the epidemic had officially been declared over, a wagon rode slowly up the alley of oaks. In it were Aurore, a manservant and all that was mortal of old Caleen. Stephen looked down at the lean, covered figure. "How long?" he asked.

"This morning, Stephen," Aurore whispered. "It was not the fever. She died of old age and fatigue."

Stephen's face was stern and set. "She will lie in state at Harrow—not in a slave cabin. God knows 'twas as much her home as mine."

A few hours later, bathed and clothed, Caleen lay in the great hall at Harrow. Stephen was forced to keep her above ground for three days, while more than three thousand people, Negroes and whites alike, came to pay their last respects.

Inch stood tirelessly beside the bier, his black face unmoving. It was not until, at the final rites, he saw Aurore bury her head against Stephen's shoulder and weep aloud that he permitted the tears to slip silently down his smooth cheeks. "She gave her life for you," he muttered. "She—a thing that you owned like the mules that draw the cane wagons. This is a thing that must end—it must!"

He felt a soft hand on his arm. Turning, he looked into Julie's tear-wet face. "Don't cry, Inch," she said. "Caleen's in heaven now. God knows how good she was."

Inch looked at the lovely golden-haired girl. "I wonder," he said harshly, "if there, too, she is a slave!"

CHAPTER FIFTEEN

A MONTH LATER Etienne and Paul were riding upon the levee near the city. It was a bright November day, and the air was as warm as spring. A hundred yards down the levee they noticed a crowd surging around a figure on horseback. As they drew closer, they could see that it was a girl.

" 'Tienne, look!" Paul gasped. "She's riding astride like a man!"

As the two of them neared the group, the pedestrians made a lane for them. The girl sat very straight in the saddle. Her riding dress had been slashed to the waist, and under it she wore a pair of masculine riding breeches, which fitted snugly into the tops of slim riding boots. Her little hat was of the latest fashion, and her whole attire was indisputably expensive.

Paul was looking at the masses of black hair, drawn softly down upon her neck in a huge ball, and the deep brown eyes that were alight with an unholy glee.

But Etienne was talking to the short, ugly man in the battered stovepipe hat who was leading the girl's horse. "What's the trouble here, Officer?" he asked.

"This girl," the policeman said, "was making a scandal. I'm booking her for indecent display in public."

Etienne looked at the girl, then back at the policeman. "The lady," he said smoothly, "is—ah—a distant relative of mine. Perhaps your honor might be prevailed upon to release her—to my custody?" He pulled out a ten-dollar bill.

"Right you are, sir!" The policeman grinned and passed the reins over to Etienne.

"And now, cousin, if you will ride with us, we'll try to devise a suitable punishment for your high crimes and misdemeanors!"

The three of them broke away from the crowd in a spanking trot, and all the people laughed and cheered.

"Perhaps Mademoiselle would be so good as to tell us her name," Etienne suggested.

"Cloutier," the girl said, "Ceclie Cloutier."

"But I know the Cloutiers," Etienne said, speaking rapidly in French, "and they are none of them like you!"

"Speak English," the girl said sharply.

"You're a Cloutier," Etienne said in English. "And yet you don't speak French. How can that be?"

"My father speaks it. He tried to teach me, but I wouldn't learn. I don't like it. It's a womanish language!"

"Who is your father?"

"Phillippe Cloutier. We came from Texas. I wish I were back!"

"Perhaps," Etienne said, "I can change your mind." He reined in his horse so that the animal's flank was against Ceclie's booted leg, and he took her in his arms.

She gazed very quietly into his face. "If you kiss me," she said, "my father will kill you."

Etienne looked down at the inky masses of hair, the thin nostrils flared. A spirited filly, aren't you? he thought. But I'll break you if it takes all winter. " 'Twill be a sweet death," he said, and brushed her cheek with his lips. Then he kissed her hard upon the mouth.

"Cry, damn you!" he muttered, his lips moving on hers. "Beg me to release you! We'll see who's master here!"

But she made no sound. Etienne loosed his grip and sat back looking at her, his pale blue eyes blazing.

"My God!" Paul said. "What savagery!"

"You hurt me," Ceclie said very quietly. Then her full lips widened into a smile. "You're very like a Texan!"

"You don't want to slap my face?"

"I'm not one of your soft Louisiana women. I don't say what I don't mean or act as I don't feel. Besides, I liked it."

Again Etienne hauled at the reins.

"No," Ceclie said clearly. "Later, when we have more time, and"—looking at Paul—"no audience. Good-by Mr.—"

"Fox—Etienne Fox. When shall I see you again?"

"I'll arrange it. You live at Harrow, don't you?"

"Yes. How did you know?"

"My father speaks of yours with great admiration. Good-by, Etienne Fox—till we meet again!" She brought her riding crop down sharply against the mustang's flank and leaned forward over his neck like a jockey.

"Venerable saints!" Paul said. "The girl can ride!"

"I think," Etienne said, "that this will be more than I bargained for—yes, much more."

LATE IN DECEMBER Stephen Fox stood with Aurore just inside the great doors of Harrow and looked out over the desolate landscape. It was raining—the usual cold winter rain of the bayou country that had a way of penetrating to the very marrow of one's bones. "Stephen, look!" Aurore said, taking his arm. "That's not 'Tienne, is it?"

"No. 'Tis no horse of ours."

"Oh, Stephen, how shameless! It's a woman, and she sits astride."

The horsewoman had reached the foot of the great stairs, where, dismounting, she threw the reins to the shivering Negro who had come out at the sound of the hooves. Stephen and Aurore stepped out upon the broad gallery just as the girl reached the top stair.

"Good day, mademoiselle," Stephen said.

"Good day, sir—and madame," the girl said politely. "Is Mr. Etienne Fox in?"

"No," Aurore said sharply. "He isn't in. Who shall we tell him called?" Her eyes went to the riding dress that was split from waist to hem, and to the close-fitting riding breeches visible beneath it.

"My name is Ceclie Cloutier."

"Phillippe's daughter!" Aurore said. "But, my dear, you talk like an American!"

"I am an American," Ceclie said tartly. "Please tell Etienne I'm sorry I missed him." She turned and bounded down the stairs.

"Of all the brazen, shameless—" Aurore began.

Stephen looked at his wife with a frown. "Best of all in ye," he said slowly, "I like your unwillingness to censor. Please don't change now, Aurore."

Not five minutes later Etienne came up the stairs, his face as black as a thundercloud.

"Why so glum, lad," Stephen asked, laughing, "when you have the girls pursuing you to your very door? Well, one at least. A little black-haired creature with a bewitching western drawl—"

"Ceclie! Where is she? How long ago was it?"

"Not yet five minutes. But, 'Tienne—"

"See you later, Mother and Father, I'm off!"

Stephen and Aurore watched as Etienne mounted quickly and swung his palomino around the curved drive in a full gallop.

Ahead of him on the bayou road Etienne could see the miniature figure of Ceclie far in the distance. He slashed down savagely with the whip until the palomino was heaving and throwing flecks of foam backward into the driving wind. He gained steadily. At last Ceclie reined in and sat very quietly in the icy rain until he came up to her.

"Ceclie!" he said, sawing at the bit until the horse's mouth was streaked with crimson. "You wanted to see me?"

"I'm not sure I want to anymore. Any man who would abuse a horse—"

"Sacred name of a camel!" Etienne exploded. "You ride from

Rosemont to Harrow in a pouring rain, and when I do catch up with you, you talk about horses!"

"You want to know why I came? Father won't permit me to have callers at Rosemont, and I had to see you—that's all. I wanted to find out whether I still liked kissing you . . ."

Etienne bent down to her. Her hands moved caressingly over the back of his neck, the fingers working through the rain-wet curls.

"And do you?"

"Yes. Very much. I never kissed anyone before. I didn't think I'd like it. It's nice being in love with you, 'Tienne."

"Oh, my God!"

"You're sorry I love you, 'Tienne?"

"No—only your father won't permit you to have callers, and certainly you cannot continue to visit me at Harrow. 'Twould make a hideous scandal."

"I see. You care about that very much, don't you? The formalities and outward show. Perhaps you don't care very much about *me* after all."

Etienne's face darkened. He swung down from the horse. He lifted Ceclie down, holding her high in the air, then letting her slide slowly against him. Suddenly he kissed her, so hard that her lips bruised against her teeth. At last he released her and stepped back. "Convinced?" he asked.

"Yes. But don't kiss me again, 'Tienne. I'm afraid I couldn't bear it. In two years, when I'm eighteen, you can ask Father for my hand, or . . . we don't have to wait," she whispered. "Words before a priest won't make me any more yours than I am right now."

"Ceclie!" Etienne said. "I can't imagine life without you. But I'm sure of one thing— I shan't make a mistress of you. I will not shame you. I want to worship you, and the world to honor you."

"And in the meantime?"

"In the meantime, I suffer."

"*We* suffer," Ceclie corrected. "But I'm glad, 'Tienne. I do so want to be a lady. Father's tried hard to make me one."

"You are a lady," Etienne said, "a great lady. The mistress of Harrow can be no less. It's like being a queen, Ceclie."

"I know," she said. "It frightens me—that house. It has a life of its own. I'm not sure it wants me, 'Tienne."

"That is a mad idea, my darling. Have you it shall, and that's all there is to it."

THROUGH THE REST of the winter they met almost daily. Etienne grew thin and drawn riding out from Harrow in the eternal rains day after day, never daring to be with Ceclie where it was warm and dry.

"When you go," Ceclie told him, "I run up to my room and cry all night. Oh, 'Tienne, 'Tienne . . . "

"No," Etienne pleaded. "No."

"But I love you so much that all inside I hurt. Kiss me, 'Tienne, please, please kiss me until I go entirely out of my mind!"

She threw her arms about his neck. Etienne's hand swept up and broke her grip, then he flung himself into the saddle and thundered away down the muddy road.

When he reached Harrow he strode through the hall and up the stairs to Paul's room. Paul looked up from the picture he was painting, and his lips curled into a slow smile. "So," he said kindly, "it grows worse, my old one?"

"Much worse," Etienne groaned. "There is the necessity of doing something about Ceclie quickly or else I will die!"

"What you need is a safety valve—you know, like a steamboat. And I think I have one for you. Come around here." Etienne crossed the room until he could see the painting. He stopped short before it, as though arrested by an invisible wall.

"She does not exist," he whispered softly. "A woman so beautiful is but a figment of your disordered intelligence."

"She exists all right. And this painting does not even approach her loveliness. She's an octoroon, 'Tienne. She says she has thirty-one years, yet she looks like a girl. She allows me to paint her in the nude—as you see—yet she will not permit me to lay a finger upon her. But you have a way with women. You'll ride in with me tomorrow?"

Etienne was studying the picture. "Yes," he said slowly, "yes!"

Early in the afternoon Etienne and Paul turned their horses into Dauphine Street. Etienne's heavy black eyebrows rose. "She lives here?" he asked.

"She has a house on Rampart Street. But we are going to my studio. She comes there to pose. She permits no whites to visit her house."

"She permits! She is uncommonly high flown for an octoroon."

"She has no need for humility, 'Tienne. She is the loveliest woman I've ever seen. She has a trust fund set up for her by a former protector. In addition, she has a son being educated in New England. The money I pay her helps."

"This protector of hers made no provision for his offspring?"

"The break between them came while she was carrying the child, and she never told him. Women are queer creatures."

They dismounted in front of a typical house of the old quarter. As Paul searched through his pockets for the key, a voice floated down from the gallery. "It's not locked, monsieur. You're very forgetful."

Etienne backed out into the muddy street and gazed upward. The woman was leaning over the wrought-iron balustrade. Her hair was a tawny chestnut, and despite the thick overcast, Etienne could catch the gleam of golden highlights in it.

"*Ma foi!*" he whispered. "You didn't lie—did you, Paul!"

When they reached the landing, the voice came out again to greet them: "Come in, messieurs." It had a haunting, lingering quality.

She was standing in the middle of the room. In her maroon velvet riding dress she had the figure of a girl. Her fine brows rose, then the sooty lashes swept down over her great eyes. Green, Etienne decided, but a green I've never before seen.

"Désirée," Paul Dumaine was saying, "may I present my friend, Monsieur Etienne Fox?"

"Fox?" she said, and her voice sank deeper into her throat. "Fox? But yes, of course, Fox—those eyes . . ."

"What about my eyes?" Etienne demanded.

"They are very blue," Désirée murmured. "There are not many men with such eyes. They remind me of someone I knew long ago. But since you have company, Monsieur Dumaine, I had best be going."

"No," Etienne said. "Stay and sup with us."

As Désirée looked at him, little flakes of sea-gold caught the light of the candles and sparkled in her green eyes. "Very well," she said softly, "I will stay."

She sank down upon the divan and watched Etienne. He pulled up a chair and sat facing her, looking gravely into her eyes.

"And you're like someone else, too," he declared, "someone I know—but I cannot recall . . ."

"Perhaps you have met my brother, Aupré Hippolyte."

Etienne's black brows almost met over the bridge of his

nose. "Yes," he said, "I knew Aupré—well. Where is he now?"

"Gone back to France. Here he was set upon by footpads and beaten so badly that he almost died. I nursed him back to health and then I sent him away. I hope he is happy there."

"But these—assailants of his, didn't he recognize them?"

"He couldn't bear to talk about it, monsieur. I didn't urge him."

"Good," Etienne said. "You were very wise."

Paul busied himself with the preparation of supper, for he lived very simply without a servant of any kind. At once Désirée ran to help him spread the little table with cheese and brioche and steaming café au lait. Etienne watched the way her graceful hands moved, pouring the coffee. And that voice, so slow and soft and deep. It could steal into a man's veins and sear away his senses.

"Désirée," he said after they had eaten, "I should like to see you home. And afterward I want to visit you there."

"I'm sorry, monsieur," she murmured, "but that is quite impossible. For me the time has passed for arrangements of any sort. The days of the quadroon balls are over." She stood up. "Adieu, messieurs."

Etienne frowned. Then, very slowly, he got to his feet. "You're right," he said deliberately, "the days of the balls are over. But there is one thing you've forgotten, Désirée. I am a Louisiana white. I have never permitted my wishes to be gainsaid by one of your race—and I don't propose to begin now. This is your cloak?"

Désirée looked at him. The little golden flakes in her green eyes swam together and made a ring around the pupils. "Yes," she said. "Yes—that is my cloak."

Etienne slipped it around her shoulders. Then he took her arm and the two of them went out the door together.

STEPHEN FOX BROKE the seals on the letter that the rider had brought from New Orleans. Aurore looked up from her sewing.

"What is it, Stephen?"

"A letter from Mike Farrel. He is going to race the *Creole Belle* against the *Thomas Moore*—downriver from Saint Louis to New Orleans. And the stakes are already a hundred thousand dollars. 'Twill be his last voyage, he swears."

"When is this race to be, Stephen?"

"The twenty-seventh, he says. Why, that was yesterday! He should pass Harrow tomorrow morning early."

The heavy figure of old Jean-Jacques, the butler, hovered in the doorway.

"Yes?" Aurore said. "What is it, Jean-Jacques?"

"A young lady. She wants to see you."

Aurore turned to Stephen, her eyebrows rising. There was the clatter of booted feet in the hall, and then Ceclie Cloutier was leaning against the door frame, her young face completely devoid of color. "Where is he?" she said, the great tears making streaks down her pale cheeks. "You're keeping him from me! I know you are! I haven't seen him in three weeks."

"Won't you sit down, my dear?" Aurore said gently.

Stephen rose and pushed forward a chair.

"Now," he said kindly, "begin at the beginning, little Ceclie."

"I was raised in Texas," Ceclie said. Aurore looked at Stephen and saw him wince at the "raised." "I don't know how to do things right. I wanted to see 'Tienne, and Father said I was too young to receive company, so I came here to see him. Mostly we sat on horseback in the rain and talked and talked . . . "

Aurore looked at her sharply.

"Yes, I kissed him!" the girl said defiantly. "Anybody would want to kiss 'Tienne! But that was all. 'Tienne is a gentleman—a real gentleman. If I don't see him soon, I'm going to die." She buried her face in her hands and shook with sobs.

Aurore got up and crossed to where she sat. Gently she put her arms around the girl's shaking shoulders. "Ceclie," she said softly, "never did I forbid Etienne your company. And today my husband will ride out to Rosemont to ask your father to permit Etienne to call upon you properly."

"Oh, madame!" Ceclie cried. "Thank you!"

"It is nothing, my dear. Love can be a great burden. Now, as to Etienne's whereabouts—truthfully, I don't know. He stays away from Harrow for days at a time. Be patient. We shall have him out to Rosemont within the week."

"Thank you," Ceclie whispered. "Thank you so very much!" She got to her feet, took a step, and then pitched forward full length upon the floor.

Aurore sank down beside her. "Get water, Stephen," she said. "The poor child has fainted."

Stephen left the room and was back in a moment with a glass. He raised Ceclie's head and Aurore got a little of the water down her throat. The brown eyes fluttered and slowly came open.

Stephen gazed into Ceclie's face. "How long," he said, "has it been since ye've eaten, child?"

"Four days," Ceclie whispered. "How did you know?"

"I know the symptoms of starvation." He turned to Aurore. "Have the servants put her to bed. I'm riding out to Rosemont. Phillippe and I will have to have this out—and at once!"

It was very still at Harrow after he had gone. Ceclie lay abed sipping hot spiced brandy and milk. Her brown eyes rested upon Aurore with something near devotion shining out of them. "I wish I could be like you," she said. " 'Tienne is ashamed of me. He talks French so that it sounds like singing, but I can't understand a word he says. I know I'm not good enough for 'Tienne, but I love him so . . . "

"How would you like to come over here every morning and have lessons with Julie?" Aurore said. "I could teach you French and English grammar and needlework . . . "

"Oh, madame, could I?" Then Ceclie's face fell. "But Father would never permit it," she said.

"That remains to be seen. Now try to sleep until your father comes for you. It won't be long, if I know Phillippe."

When Phillippe Cloutier reached Harrow four hours later, Ceclie was sleeping soundly. The tall Creole stood beside the bed and looked down at the slight figure of his daughter. "Perhaps I have been harsh," he said, "but it was for her own good."

"Phillippe," Aurore began, "I have a request to make of you. I want you to let Ceclie come here daily to study with Julie. I'll see that she's properly chaperoned. Etienne will see her only at your house, and with your permission."

Phillippe frowned. "Very well," he said at last, looking down at Ceclie, who was sleeping like a small child.

"Don't awaken her, Phillippe. Let her rest the night."

"And stay yourself," Stephen said. "The *Creole Belle* will pass here in the morning in a race with the *Tom Moore*. 'Twill be a sight worth seeing."

Phillippe grinned. "For that I'd stay in Hades itself," he said. "A thousand on the *Thomas Moore*—even odds, Stephen?"

"Done! In fact, I'll give ye two to your one. There is no packet on the river that can catch the *Belle*."

"Now look what I've done!" Aurore wailed. "I asked Stephen

to bring you here, and you, Phillippe, start him gambling again!"

"Forgive me, Aurore. But a chance to shake down Stephen Fox is too good to miss."

THE NEXT MORNING, just around the bend above Harrow, the *Creole Belle* was laboring in the yellow-white swell boiling back from the paddle wheels of the *Thomas Moore*.

"Damn it!" Mike Farrel bellowed in the glass pilothouse. "Are all them men below asleep or dead? Here, you," he said to his pilot, "ride her in! I'll get up speed, I will. Afore I'll have Stevie watch me beaten, I'll bust her boilers!"

Then he was stamping down the stairs, as spry as a youth for all his seventy-odd years. "Juniper!" Mike roared. "What ails you? Can't you get up steam?"

The black fireman pointed a trembling finger at the pressure gauge. The needle was quivering on the brink of the red danger line.

"To hell with that!" Mike roared. "Get up steam!"

The crew turned frightened eyes toward the old captain. They started to heave the logs in, but at a snaillike pace. Instantly Mike descended upon them, roaring. A few well-placed kicks brought a noticeable acceleration.

Mike watched the gauge as streamers of orange-red flame escaped the edge of the firebox door. Slowly the needle climbed upward toward the red line. Mike pointed a hairy finger at the safety valve.

"Tie it," he said. "Tie it down, Juniper."

"But Master Mike!" Juniper wailed.

"Tie it, I says, or I'll flay you inch by inch."

Juniper approached the safety valve. But as he attempted to tie the release down, his hands trembled so that the cord fell to the floor. Calmly Mike picked it up and tied down the valve himself. "Now," he said to Juniper, "break out them bunches of fat lightwood."

"Please, Master Mike!" Juniper quavered. "You blows us all to hell and back!"

"Then," Mike said quietly, " 'twill be the fastest ride to hell that ever the devil seen! Get moving!"

Juniper moved off, driving the other blacks before him. A moment later they were back, carrying the fat, resinous lightwood that would burn like tinder.

The fire doors came open and the yellow flame shot out from them for a full two yards. Then the sweating Negroes hurled in the bunches of lightwood. Mike stood back, quietly watching the pressure gauge crawl up past the red mark, up, up, up. Satisfied, he turned again toward the stairs.

In the pilothouse, the pilot was clinging to the wheel, alternately cursing and praying. The *Creole Belle* rocked and quivered like a wild thing, and inch by slow inch she overtook the *Thomas Moore*.

On the levee of Stephen's plantation the Negroes were screaming at the top of their lungs. Shotguns crashed into the air. Great grease-soaked bonfires flamed all along the mound of earth.

On the belvedere Ceclie and Julie were hugging each other as the two boats rounded the bend, exactly abreast. Even as they watched, the *Creole Belle* drew ahead—white water showed between the packets and widened steadily.

Stephen turned triumphantly to Phillippe. "Ye see!" he crowed.

But Phillippe was leaning forward, his fingers bands of iron closing viselike upon Stephen's arm. His lips moved, but no sound came out of them, no sound at all. Frowning, Stephen turned again toward the river.

A long tongue of flame shot out of the bowels of the *Creole Belle* and rolled majestically across the face of the river. Then came the ear-shattering roar of the explosion. The flames soared straight up for two hundred feet, carrying bits of hulk wood and metal with them. Stephen could see the pilot hanging half out of one of the smashed windows, and the gigantic figure of old Mike hauling upon the wheel, swinging the *Belle's* bow inward, angling for a landing.

Now the *Belle* was a sheet of living flame, blazing from stem to stern, but slowly, persistently, old Mike fought her in toward the landing. Up ahead, the *Thomas Moore* was reversing her engines, trying vainly to come to the aid of her stricken rival.

And Stephen Fox was sprinting down the stairs. "Georges! Inch! Jean-Jacques!" he roared. "Flour! Every sack that ye can find!"

Phillippe and the girls were at his heels, and behind them came Aurore.

By the time they reached the landing, Mike had driven the bow of the *Creole Belle* into the soft mud and was holding her there with all his remaining power. The passengers and crew ran like living torches, hair and clothing aflame, to fall upon the muddy earth and roll there, twisting and screaming in pain.

Already the Negroes were busy beating at the flaming garments, stripping them from men and women alike, and rolling the naked, pitifully burned scarecrows that had once been human beings in the flour. Some had plunged blazing over the side, to sizzle in the boiling water at the *Belle*'s side and sink in the treacherous shoal currents. And up in the pilothouse Mike Farrel perished as he had lived—grandly!

Of those who got ashore, only five were living at the end of an hour. These were borne up to Harrow and laid tenderly in the great beds. Julie walked beside Inch and Jean-Jacques as they bore between them the slim figure of a lad of some seventeen years. By some odd chance, his face and hair were untouched, though the rest of his body was horribly burned. The face was as handsome as a young god's, and heavy locks of blond hair curled damply over his forehead. He made no sound, but fixed his great blue eyes upon Julie.

"Take him to my room," Julie whispered. "I will care for him there."

They laid him upon the bed, and Julie motioned for them to leave. Slowly, carefully, she cleansed away the flour and dirt from his blistered, blackened body. Then she washed him tenderly all over with sweet oil. From time to time the boy jerked violently and a ghost of a moan escaped his lips.

When she had finished, Julie stood up, her lips trembling, and, blushing furiously, drew up the sheet to cover his nakedness. "No!" he whispered. "No covers! I can't bear it!"

Julie drew the covers down and sat beside him.

"You—you're an angel," he got out. "I'm not dead yet—am I?"

"No," Julie said, "and you won't die! I won't let you!"

The boy's fair face twisted into a grimace oddly resembling a smile. "This—is—your—home?"

"Yes," Julie whispered. "Yes."

"You're so good," he muttered. "I don't understand . . ."

"What is it you don't understand?" Julie prompted.

"How—someone so beautiful—can live—upon wealth gained from the sweat of other men's faces." He drew himself half up, his voice growing stronger. "My father is Thomas Meredith—the abolitionist—we're from Boston. He says that it's a wicked system that uses— " He stopped, his breath gone.

"You mustn't exert yourself, really you mustn't!" Julie begged.

"—men like brutish beasts," young Meredith went on, as though he had not heard her. He looked at her, his blue eyes peering from under the tired lids. "What—is—your name?"

"Julie," the girl sobbed.

"You—are—so lovely," he whispered. "Julie. I like—that—name—Julie. I want to—die—saying it. Tell my father—and my brother that Dan . . . " He fell back, unconscious, upon the bed.

All through the day Julie watched beside him. He talked frequently, wildly—often to people who were not there. Toward night he awoke again. "Julie," he whispered, "it grows dark—very dark. Bring the—candles closer, Julie—I want to see—your face."

Julie turned and ran across the room. A moment later she was back, holding the silver candelabra close to her cheek. "See, Dan—see!" But there was no answer. Slowly, she bent down and placed the candelabra upon the floor. Then, pillowing her face upon her arms, she wept.

CHAPTER SIXTEEN

THE NEXT MORNING, after the Cloutiers had gone, Etienne Fox rode up to Harrow, morose and sullen. Plague take that wench! Not even the sophisticates of old France had so devilish many ways of eluding a man. A look—a gesture—a laugh—the worst was her harping upon the difference in their ages.

"Damnation!" he would roar. "You know well that there is but eight years between us!"

"So little?" she would murmur. "It seems more . . ."

There must be some way of bringing her to heel. He paused suddenly, sniffing at the air. Had something been burning here? Harrow? His heart contracted at the thought. But when he turned toward the steamboat landing, it was a smoldering ruin, and beyond it, in the river, lay the blackened hulk of a river packet.

As he rode up the alley of oaks, he saw a large group of Negroes digging a huge trench in the bare plot next to the family burial grounds. Beside them were rows of grotesque shapes wrapped in cloths. Etienne counted more than a hundred.

He turned his eyes toward the spot where his mother lay. There, not very far off, a cross of wood marked a fresh grave.

Someone of the family! He swung down from the horse and ran across the muddy earth. The words carved into the rude cross stopped him. *Michael Farrel*, they read. *Born*—then a blank space; *Died: June 3rd, 1854. Rest in Peace.*

Slowly Etienne remounted and rode silently up to the house. In the hallway Stephen met him.

" 'Tienne," Stephen began, "yesterday we had great need of ye. The *Creole Belle*—"

"I saw," Etienne said harshly.

"And the Cloutiers were here. Phillippe granted ye his permission to call upon his daughter."

"He did! That's grand, Father! I'll see her at once!"

" 'Tis time, I should think. Ye let three weeks elapse without seeing your little prairie flower at all."

"My absence was my own affair, Father."

"Ye need explain nothing, 'Tienne. But ye have no right to cause your mother anxiety."

Etienne looked at Stephen and one corner of his mouth curved into a wicked smile. "Please tender my dear aunt-mother my humblest apologies," he murmured, "and say that I was kept from home by the so far unsuccessful pursuit of an octoroon called Désirée."

Stephen's blue eyes took on an icy calm. " 'Tienne," he said, "this dalliance with Désirée is folly. It must stop, or else ye must seek a home elsewhere—and that is final." He turned on his heel and strode toward the stairs.

Then something like a light gleamed in Etienne's eyes; on his face was an expression of sudden realization.

"Father!"

Stephen turned.

"Yes, 'Tienne?" he said softly.

"Sixteen years ago, when I was eight, Désirée was already sixteen. She was very beautiful then, wasn't she, Father? So beautiful, in fact, that you wrecked Harrow and broke my mother's heart because of her! Désirée Hippolyte. Désirée of the tawny hair and haunting voice and the sea-green eyes. You recognize the portrait, Father?"

"Yes," Stephen said, "I recognize it."

Etienne threw back his head and hurled his laughter upward toward the high vaulted ceiling.

"There are many kinds of hell," Stephen said, half to himself. "I have created mine. I had hoped that ye would be wiser than your father, 'Tienne. 'Twas too much to be expected. Go as ye will, lad."

He turned with great dignity and went up the curving stairs, slowly, like a man very tired, and very old.

Etienne watched him, frowning. Then he ran to his room, calling out to Inch to bring fresh linen and draw water for his bath. There was no answer. It was old Jean-Jacques who came at last, trembling before Etienne's fury. "Inch isn't here," he quavered. "He told me to give you this."

Etienne took the letter and broke open the seals. " 'My good master,' " he read aloud, " 'when you receive this I shall be many miles away—on the road to freedom. You will say that you have treated me kindly: and so you have, apart from a few cuffs and kicks. But I have not the mentality of a slave. I don't want to be treated kindly like a valuable animal. I want to be treated like a man. Remembering my mother, who died rather than submit to servitude, and my grandmother, who longed all her life for freedom, I can do no more than to take this risk. I do not want your protection, nor the easy life at Harrow; I want nothing done *for* me, but many things done *by* me. In short, I want freedom, and I shall achieve it, with the help of God.' " It was signed, very simply: "Inch."

Etienne's eyes danced like arctic fire, but his voice was perfectly controlled when he turned to Jean-Jacques. "Draw water for my bath," he said, "and bring me pen and paper."

Twenty minutes later Etienne was sitting comfortably in his bath. "Write thus," he said to Jean-Jacques. " 'An advertisement: Run away from my plantation, Harrow, my manservant, Inch. He is coal black in color, dresses after the fashion of a white. Reads and writes an excellent hand. Will probably attempt to pass himself off as a freedman. Speaks English with a slight accent, and French with great fluency. Anyone notifying me of his whereabouts, or capturing and returning him to me at my plantation near New Orleans, will receive a liberal reward. Signed, Etienne Fox.' "

Three quarters of an hour later Etienne swung around the sweeping curves of the oak alley on one of the justly celebrated palominos that were known throughout the bayou country as the hallmark of Harrow. Despite many requests, Stephen Fox never sold one of them, nor put any stallion out to stud.

Etienne's eyes turned to the burial plot he was at that moment passing. Julie was kneeling upon a fresh-made grave a little apart from the common grave. On the other side of the road Stephen stood with bowed head beside the grave of Mike Farrel. Poor father, Etienne thought briefly . . . he has had his share of grief. 'Twas beastly unkind of me to taunt him so. Oh, well, there is time to make amends . . .

IN HIS STUDIO on Dauphine Street Paul Dumaine was putting the finishing touches on the painting of Désirée. She had posed lying upon a low couch covered with a panther's skin. The effect was splendidly barbaric. Yet Paul was vaguely dissatisfied. As he walked closer to the painting and picked up his brush, he was interrupted by a firm knock upon the door.

"Come in!" he called, but did not leave his place. I'll have to get that lock fixed someday soon, he thought.

As the inner door creaked open, Paul turned. Ceclie Cloutier stood in the doorway, smiling a little breathlessly.

"Come in, come in!" Paul said. "I'm more than honored!"

"Thank you," the girl said. "I want you to do me a favor, Mr. Dumaine. Will you paint a miniature of me . . . for Etienne, so that he can carry it with him always?"

"Well," Paul began, "I've never painted a miniature . . . but for you and 'Tienne . . . Besides, it is always the keenest pleasure to paint such a rare, lovely girl."

"You say nice things." She walked over to the easel and studied the painting of Désirée at length. "A woman sat here naked . . . and let you look at her?"

"Mademoiselle, that which I find beautiful, I paint: a sunset— or a woman. And I look upon one as impersonally as the other."

"No man," Ceclie said, "could be impersonal around a woman that beautiful." A mischievous little smile played around the corners of her mouth. "I wish I had a picture of me like that. I'd give it to 'Tienne!"

"And have him shoot me? No, thank you, mademoiselle! Now, if you'll turn your face a little to the right, we can begin."

His fingers flew over the paper, making his first rough pencil sketch. He worked diligently for a half-hour.

"Mademoiselle is tired?" he asked finally.

"A little. It's the smell of the paint, mostly. I think I'll go out upon the veranda and catch a breath."

Paul walked with her out upon the gallery and looked up and down the narrow street. Suddenly Ceclie took hold of his arm. "Look!" she said breathlessly. "Isn't that 'Tienne?"

"Yes," he said. "Yes it is."

"He didn't stop!" Ceclie whispered. "Why, Paul?"

"I don't know—" Paul began, but Ceclie was already flying out of the little studio.

"Mademoiselle!" Paul cried. "Wait! Don't follow him! Please!" But Ceclie's booted feet were clattering down the stairs.

Ceclie flung herself into the saddle and thundered down the street behind Etienne, but at the corner she pulled the mustang up abruptly. "No," she whispered, "I'll let him go wherever he's going . . . and then I'll know why he stays away from me so long."

She started out again, holding the vicious little beast to a walk. A block farther on, Etienne rounded the corner into Rampart Street. He dismounted and walked firmly to the door of the little house that sat flush with the street. Ceclie was so close she could hear his knocking.

The door opened, and a woman stood there, smiling. Ceclie's brown eyes widened. The woman of Paul's painting! She who had sat all day unclothed before a man's eyes . . . "No, 'Tienne," the girl whispered. "No!"

Ceclie yanked the mustang around in a tight semicircle. Slashing at his shaggy hide with all her force, it took her only minutes to cover the few blocks back to the studio. But when she ran inside, Paul was not there.

Ceclie stood staring at the painting of Désirée. Then her eyes fell upon the short flat-bladed knife that painters use to scrape off excess paint. She bent and pushed it through the painted figure at the exact spot where the heart would have been had it been alive. She drew it up and down, then across, and across again.

"Mademoiselle," Paul said softly.

She whirled, facing him.

"You realize," he said sadly, "that you have destroyed what to me was priceless. A thing I can never replace?"

"Yes," Ceclie said fiercely, "yes, I've ruined it! But I'll give

173

you another. Set up a canvas, Mr. Dumaine!" Already her fingers were busy with the buttons of her riding habit.

"No!" Paul said. "For God's sake, no!" But the jacket fell softly to the floor. Ceclie sat down, tugging at her boots.

"Ceclie," Paul said, "you don't know what you're doing!"

A long moment later Ceclie stood up, making no effort to cover herself. "Now," she said, "I'm as beautiful as she! Aren't I, Paul?"

Paul bent swiftly and lifted one of the largest of the prepared canvases that stood in a row against the wall. "Yes," he whispered. "Yes. Oh, yes!"

IN THE LITTLE house on Rampart Street Désirée stood very quietly facing Etienne. "I shan't come again," Etienne said harshly.

"I'm sorry," she said. "I've enjoyed your company."

"So much that you've driven me half mad!"

"About that I am more than sorry, but Monsieur asks the impossible."

"Why?" Etienne demanded.

Désirée's eyes were wide and grave as she looked at him. "Because I don't love you, monsieur. My body is not a thing to be given lightly. And then, I cannot help but make comparisons . . ."

"Between me and my father?" Etienne demanded.

"Yes."

"And in this comparison, I suffer?"

"Yes."

Etienne's blue eyes blazed in his dark face. "Yet I shall have you," he said. "Now!"

He caught her by both her arms and jerked her to him, tightening his hands around her waist. Désirée's face was still and unfrightened. He kissed her, fiercely. She made no struggle. Her body was utterly without response.

"Well," he growled, "aren't you going to beg for mercy!"

"No," she said. "If you have so little shame—"

"Shame!" Etienne said. "Shame!" Then he lifted her as lightly as if she were a leaf and strode into the bedroom. He tossed her upon her high, canopied bed. But she did not even open her eyes.

It was over in an incredibly brief time. Etienne sat up, his pale eyes somber. "Désirée," he whispered.

Slowly the green eyes opened. Her hands came up from under

the huge pillow—holding a knife with an eight-inch blade that gleamed in the dusk.

"Désirée!"

She sat up and looked at him. Then slowly her fingers loosened until the knife fell to the floor. "Go," she said in her husky voice.

"My God!" Etienne whispered.

"I've had that a long time," she said. "You see, monsieur, my brother never reached France. He died aboard ship from the internal injuries your Negroes gave him."

"Then why . . . why?"

"Because I couldn't. You were Stephen Fox all over again. So many times I planned it . . . if ever you touched me . . . if ever you mentioned my brother's name . . ."

"I see," Etienne said. Then very quickly he walked toward the door. In the doorway he looked back at her. She was still sitting there; not even her eyes had moved.

Etienne turned and went out into the street. He moved very slowly, like a man already old.

CHAPTER SEVENTEEN

WEEKS LATER Etienne rode toward New Orleans at a fast trot. Again Ceclie had refused to see him! This made six times in a row. Something was definitely wrong here. Well, damn it all, he wouldn't try anymore! She'd come to him on her hands and knees—or would she?

He stopped first at the sheriff's office, to inquire about Inch. As he expected, there was no news. The black appeared to have made good his escape.

Etienne rode aimlessly through the streets of the old quarter. Ahead of him was a group of young men, all talking and laughing at once. Etienne recognized them: they were Pierre Aucoin, Henri Lascals, Jean Sompayrac: but there were also Bob Norton, James Duckett and Walter McGarth. Today one thought little about whether a person was of American or Creole origin.

Young Norton ran out into the street and grasped the bridle. " 'Tienne," he roared, "join a bunch of good fellows!"

Smiling, Etienne dismounted.

"Walter, get someone to take care of this off-color nag while we take 'Tienne to catch up on his drinking," Norton said. He and Lascals locked arms with Etienne and they all went into the bar of the Saint Louis Hotel.

Henri Lascals pounded the bar. "Waiter!" he roared. "For this lackadaisical, erstwhile drunkard," he said, "*four* Sazeracs."

"Four!" Etienne said. "My God, Henri, two would kill a man!"

"You'll make a cheerful corpse."

A half-hour later they were all singing at the top of their lungs. Henri Lascals was admiring his own image in the mirror.

"You know, 'Tienne," he declared, "I am a very handsome lad. I should have my portrait painted. By the way, where is Paul? We haven't seen him in more than three weeks."

"Nor have I," Etienne said.

"Let's go up there," Bob Norton suggested. "They tell me he has gorgeous paintings . . . such women!"

"And all in complete *déshabillé*," Henri gloated.

Out on the banquette they marched along, swaying grandly. Suddenly Etienne felt Henri's hand upon his arm. "Look, 'Tienne," he said, "isn't that Paul riding away from us? We'll never see those paintings now!"

"Wait," Etienne said, "maybe we can see them. The lock on Paul's door doesn't work."

Etienne turned in toward the door of the studio. He put his weight against it and pushed. Slowly it groaned open and they all went up the stairs, laughing throatily in the darkness.

Inside the studio it was black as pitch, but Etienne walked straight to the candelabra and struck a match. The soft glow stole through the room and all the young men turned. Here were the landscapes—the river and the oaks of Harrow, the house itself; portraits of prominent people; studies of Negroes; and three nudes—all of Désirée, and all painted from memory in vain attempts to recapture the picture that Ceclie had destroyed.

In the middle of the studio Bob Norton stopped before a huge canvas draped with cloth. He lifted one corner and a slim white leg glowed softly before his eyes. He raised the cloth higher. " 'Tienne," he roared, "come help me get this cloth off!"

In the next instant half a dozen hands tugged the cover free. The veins at Etienne's temple throbbed visibly as behind him Bob Norton's voice softly whispered, "My God!"

The figure upon the canvas was reclining, and slow, spine-tingling invitation was painted into every line of it. Etienne had not realized that Ceclie was so beautiful; every curve of that perfect body sang from the canvas. His hand went into his pocket and came out with a jackknife. Slowly, carefully, he cut the painting from its frame and rolled it into a huge roll. "Let's go," he said.

One by one the others followed him down the creaking stairs and into the street.

IT WAS WELL after midnight when Etienne reached Rosemont. Twenty minutes of thunderous knocking at last brought out the butler, who stood blinking like a fat black owl.

"Awaken Miss Ceclie," Etienne snapped.

"Awright," the butler said. "But Master Phillippe be powerful mad!" He shuffled away, head bent toward the stairs.

Etienne paced up and down the hallway, holding the painting tightly in his hand. At the swift whisper of footsteps on the stair, he looked up to see Ceclie in her nightdress, her robe falling loosely about her shoulders.

"Well?" Ceclie said. "Well—what is it, 'Tienne?"

Wordlessly, Etienne unrolled the painting.

Ceclie looked at it; then her brown eyes raised to Etienne's face. "Yes, I posed for it. Beautiful, isn't it, 'Tienne?"

"You sat there like that and let a man look at you?"

"Yes."

"What else, Ceclie?" Etienne's voice was terribly quiet.

"Do you really want me to answer, 'Tienne?"

Etienne's pale eyes caught the candle flame like twin mirrors. His lips moved slowly, shaping the words: "You whore!"

"Yes," Ceclie said, "there is such a word for a woman. But what is there for a man, 'Tienne? How I loved you! But you went to another, and I was to sit patiently and wait. It never occurred to you that I could match anything that you did!"

Etienne stepped back away from her. Then he slapped her, hard across the face. She stood there, facing him, quivering all over like a willow sapling in a high wind.

"You have a weapon, monsieur?"

Etienne whirled. Phillippe Cloutier was standing in the doorway, clad in a dressing gown. His eyes searched the youth briefly. "I see that you have not," he said quietly. "Then we had best postpone this until morning. Is the Oaks agreeable to you?"

Etienne licked his dry lips. "Yes," he got out, "yes—quite."

Ceclie did not move. She was staring at her father. "You mustn't, Father! You can't kill 'Tienne! I won't let you! I don't care what he did to me. Look there upon the table. Look and see how well I deserved that slap. Go on, Father. Look!"

Phillippe stared at the painting spread out across the table. He looked at it for a long time, then stared at the painter's signature. "I see," he said at last. "You'll accept my apology, monsieur?"

"I—I forgot myself, sir," Etienne said. "I ask your forgiveness and Mademoiselle's. That was a hard thing to take."

"You know where this Dumaine lives?"

"Yes."

"Then you'll guide me there."

"Father," Ceclie whispered, "Father . . ."

"Go to your room, Ceclie. I'll attend to you later."

The sky was lightening a little when they reached New Orleans. They rode in silence to the studio. Then they dismounted and knocked at the door.

Paul's voice floated down the stairway. "Come in, messieurs," he said. "I've been expecting you."

Etienne and Phillippe stood in the doorway staring at the young painter. He was haggard, and his hair and clothing were in wild disarray. But his voice was calm. "Well," he said, "I take it that you have something to say to me."

"Louisiana has been kind to you, monsieur," Phillippe said. "I'm afraid we pay too much attention to this democratic rot to have so enriched the son of a penniless, worthless dauber!"

Paul shrugged wearily. "I had expected a challenge," he said. "But since it pleases Monsieur to provoke me into challenging him, very well. I'll meet you at any time and place you set." He smiled a little.

"The east bank of the river—ten miles below the city, this afternoon—about five—"

"Very well—and the weapons?"

"Knives," Phillippe said flatly.

"Very well," Paul said. "You'll provide me with seconds, 'Tienne? I really don't know anyone well enough . . ."

Etienne nodded, sickness spreading through him in cold waves. Damn Ceclie anyway! Damn her and Désirée and all women!

Riding away from the city with Phillippe, Etienne was silent. Paul was my friend, he thought; and, whatever happened, Ceclie started it.

Phillippe half turned in the saddle. "You seem troubled," he said gravely. "But I won't kill the boy. I'll just notch his nostrils and his ears. Then we'll see how he'll fare as a seducer!"

Etienne said nothing. He had a horrible fear that in another moment he was going to vomit there before Phillippe's eyes. But at last there was the fork where their roads separated.

"*Au revoir,* Etienne," Phillippe Cloutier said, "till five!"

"Till five," Etienne echoed. Then he galloped off in the direction of Harrow. For the first time in his adult life he felt the need for counsel. As he rounded the drive into the courtyard, he saw Stephen's big palomino coming toward him.

"So early, lad?" Stephen smiled.

"Father, there's going to be a duel . . ."

Stephen's white brows bristled. "Ye young fool!" he said. "The day for that sort of folly is gone forever. Who is it that ye're to fight?"

"Easy, Father. I'm not to fight. The quarrel is between Phillippe Cloutier and Paul. Paul . . . dishonored Ceclie . . ."

Stephen looked at his son.

"While ye were running pell-mell after Désirée, your Ceclie turned to other consolations. How little ye know of women, lad! Was that woman, beautiful as she is, worth this?"

"No. But what should I do now? Monsieur Cloutier had his choice of weapons . . . and he chose knives, Father."

"Holy Mother of God! When is this butchery to take place?"

"This afternoon . . . at five."

"Good. 'Tis thinking I am that I had better deal myself in. Paul is a fine lad. I won't have him slaughtered because ye were a fool and your Ceclie a spiteful minx. Go up to the house now, and try to rest."

AT HALF PAST FOUR Stephen and Etienne were already at the appointed place. At a quarter to five Paul Dumaine arrived with his seconds, Henri Lascals and Pierre Aucoin. Paul was perfectly composed, but his face was very white. Stephen took his arm and the two of them walked a little apart from the others. Etienne could see his father talking earnestly.

At two minutes of five Phillippe arrived with his seconds and the surgeon. Under his arm he carried a case. He dismounted, opened it and walked over to Paul. The great blades of the knives gleamed like silver in the sunlight. "Your choice, sir," he said.

"Wait," Stephen said. "The lad has a statement to make."

"This is none of your affair, Stephen Fox!" Phillippe declared.

"Aye, but I'm making it my affair. I'll not see the lad murdered! Hear him out, Phillippe."

Paul looked at Stephen, then at Etienne. He cleared his throat. "Gentlemen," he said, "this duel was occasioned by the accidental discovery of a painting that I made of Mademoiselle Cloutier. I want only to say that I painted the picture as a jest to plague my good friend Etienne Fox. It was done without Mademoiselle's knowledge or consent. She posed only for the head, thinking that I intended it for a miniature that she had promised Etienne as a gift. The figure was posed by an octoroon. I say this to clear Mademoiselle Cloutier's reputation of any hint of stain. As for myself, I do not attempt to justify my gross error. I place myself at Monsieur's pleasure."

"You lie!" Phillippe spat out.

"Softly, Phillippe," Stephen said. "If ye say that the lad lies, ye yourself impugn your daughter's honor."

Phillippe's face was mottled with rage. "You're a clever bastard, Fox!" he got out. He whirled on his heel and strode back to his waiting horse.

Paul turned to Stephen. "Thank you, sir," he said.

"Think nothing of it, lad. But if ye'll take my advice, I suggest that ye leave the state—at least until this blows over."

Paul Dumaine turned to Etienne. " 'Tienne," he began, and half extended his hand.

"There is nothing to be said between us, Paul," Etienne declared. "Ever!"

"Young fools!" Stephen snorted, and threw a lean leg across the palomino. Etienne mounted in his turn, but Paul stood very still, watching his friend. Stephen turned in the saddle and saluted the young painter gravely. Paul returned the gesture, his eyes fixed upon Etienne, who sat like a statue, staring out over the river. Stephen looked from one to the other of them; then he shrugged. "Come, lad," he said, and the two of them turned their horses' heads northward, toward New Orleans.

CHAPTER EIGHTEEN

Spring came late that year in the upper reaches of the Ohio valley. The river itself was still half choked with ice, and a thin, miserable drizzle whined down upon the snow-covered ground. On the south bank of the Ohio, not three hundred yards from the river, the farmhouse stood, shrouded in winter white.

Inside the house the logs blazed on the hearth. Beside it, the farmer dozed in a big rocker. His square gray beard fell gently on his ample bosom. His wife sat on the other chair, knitting; suddenly the needles were still, and the old woman leaned forward. "Silas!" she whispered.

He came awake at once, without even blinking. "Yes," he grunted. "Yes, Hope?"

"There's somebody outside . . . in the snow."

Silas got up and crossed the room, as silent as a cat, for all his great bulk. He drew on his sheepskin-lined jacket and a coonskin cap and took the ancient flintlock rifle down from the mantel. Then he strode out into the storm. He took a cautious step forward, then another. Something moved out there in the drifted snow. He turned and floundered toward the moving object. When he was close, he bent down.

It was a Negro clad only in a rude shirt and trousers, barefoot and shivering. The black lifted his trembling, cold gray face, and his lips moved briefly. "Liberty—" he whispered.

"—lies northward!" Silas said, completing the password of the Underground Railroad.

Then Silas bent and picked the Negro up, holding him like a babe in his giant arms. Hope opened the door to his muffled knock. She looked down at the frozen black face, and instantly her lean fingers flew to loosen the Negro's clothes. Silas set a small saucepan of water on the hearth to boil. Then he went to work chafing the thin wrists and arms, which were a purplish gray from the cold, with handfuls of snow. A few minutes later Hope took up the saucepan and poured the bubbling water into the earthenware teapot. "Lace it with rum," Silas said.

The big man lifted the black's head and the old woman poured tea down his throat. Almost at once they could see life flowing back into the near-frozen limbs. Silas took cold water and began to bathe the Negro's feet and hands, and his wife poured drink after drink of the rum tea down his throat.

At last the eyelids flickered open. "Thank you," he whispered. "Never did I believe that there were white people who . . ."

"Don't talk," Silas cautioned. "Save your strength."

"You'll rest here till you're better," the woman said kindly.

"No," the Negro said. "No! They're after me! You'll get in trouble."

"Nonsense, boy. What is your name?"

"Inch," the man whispered. "I am called Inch."

Two nights later a dinghy slipped between the lessening ice floes and pushed its way to the other side of the Ohio. Inch stepped ashore. He was warmly clad, and on his feet were good, stout boots. He sank down upon the frozen ground and kissed it. "Free soil!" he murmured. He turned to Silas, who was sitting quietly in the boat. "The saints bless you for your help."

" 'Tis little enough," Silas said. "I could not live with myself if I didn't strike a blow against this damnable traffic in human flesh. But you're far from free, Inch. You've still got to be cautious. 'Twould be far wiser to push on to Canada; but, since you insist, Boston will be safe enough. Our man Milliken will put you in touch with a law office where you can get work. The best of luck to you, young Inch!"

"Thank you. And to you and Madame, the blessings of God!"

A month later Inch climbed down from a railway car in the bleak city of Boston and started walking. He had not the faintest notion of where he was going. He had a strange desire to listen to the secret heart of this his chosen city. Here men were free, black men as well as white. It was a thought to be savored long and quietly.

AT HARROW, ON the day after the duel, Etienne Fox was feverishly packing his valise. Turning, he saw his father's lean frame draped against the door frame.

"So, lad, ye're planning to leave us? Where are ye going?"

"To the river—to follow in the footsteps of my esteemed father," he said. "I already have a place engaged on a packet. The captain is willing to have me—for a cut of my winnings."

"Ye're a fool," Stephen said. " 'Tis no life for the likes of ye."

"I play as well as you do!"

"Ye should, for I taught ye all I know. Suppose I make ye a sporting proposition?"

"What sort of proposition, Father?"

"Oh—just a friendly game of poker. For one half of the land now—against your giving up this tomfool idea."

Etienne gazed at Stephen and the matching sets of eyes held and locked. "Done!" he said.

Stephen smiled. "Come into the study, lad," he said softly.

The play went on all night, first one winning, then the other. As the first gray streaks of morning stole through the window, Stephen looked at his disheveled, red-eyed son. "Now to make an end," he said. "We're even, aren't we?"

"Yes," Etienne said. He had the oddest feeling that his father had been toying with him all night.

"Ye're agreed to stand by this hand?"

"Yes." Etienne's voice was muffled.

"My deal," Stephen said blandly. His hands, moving, made a whitish blur. After the third draw Stephen rested. Etienne looked at his father. He had three of a kind: the queens of diamonds, hearts and clubs. Such a hand was hard to beat. He spread it fanwise upon the table.

Stephen glanced down at the cards and smiled. Then he slowly revealed his hand. He held the ace, king, queen, jack and ten of spades.

"A royal flush!" Etienne said. "Such a hand wouldn't happen once in ten million years! You cheated, Father!"

Stephen continued to smile. "Perhaps. Or perhaps this is the ten millionth year. But ye lost, and I expect ye to abide by your wager like a gentleman."

"I won't!" Etienne stormed. "I won't!"

Stephen opened his mouth to say something, but stopped when he saw old Jean-Jacques standing in the doorway. "A lady to see the young master," he said. Then, leaning close to Etienne, his black face beaming, "It's Mademoiselle Ceclie!"

"Tell her I won't see her!" Etienne said.

"Don't be a fool, lad," Stephen said. "At least ye could hear her out."

Etienne stood up. "All right," he said. "Show her in, Jean-Jacques."

Ceclie looked small and lost in the vast expanse of the big hall.

Etienne hesitated in the study a moment, then walked firmly toward her.

"I've come to say good-by, 'Tienne," she said clearly, putting out one hand. "We're going back to Texas."

Etienne looked at her wordlessly. She came up very close to him and her brown eyes were tear bright. "You—you're glad I'm going, 'Tienne?"

"It seems to me," Etienne said dryly, "you should ask Paul."

"I should have expected that," she whispered, "but I didn't somehow. I guess it's because I love you so that I forget everyone else exists."

"You love me so much," Etienne mocked, "that you become Paul Dumaine's mistress! So much that you pose for obscene portraits—"

"My picture was beautiful!" Ceclie declared. "I wanted to give it to you . . . so that you'd hurt inside just a little the way you made me hurt!" She stopped and looked up at him. "Oh, 'Tienne, kiss me."

Etienne caught her up in his arms. Her mouth clung to his, hot and sweet, and then her fingers were digging into his flesh. "Never let me go, 'Tienne," she whispered. "Never!"

"Say it wasn't true about you and Paul," he said harshly. "Say it, Ceclie! Even if you lie!"

"All right," she whispered, "I'll say it, but now you'll never know. If you love me, it won't matter. I'm yours, I've always been yours, since the day I was born. If you doubt me, let me go quickly while I can still bear it."

"We'll be married today," Etienne said. "Then we'll both leave this accursed place. We'll go somewhere new—like Kansas."

He put his arm about her waist and the two of them walked through the open door into the study. "Father," Etienne began.

"So," Stephen said, "ye've made it up, have ye? Are you both sure ye aren't making a mistake?"

Ceclie's face flamed scarlet. "Is this one thing going to be held against me forever?"

"By me—no," Stephen said. "There was much that was wrong on both sides. But 'twill be a hellish marriage if both of ye are forever digging up the past to throw in the other's face."

"The past died five minutes ago, Father," Etienne declared. "I'll never resurrect it."

"Good," Stephen said, rising. "Now we'd all better ride out to Rosemont and see Phillippe. 'Tienne, go and ask Aurore to join me as soon as I am dressed for riding."

When Stephen came down the stairs, he found Aurore already waiting, dressed in her riding habit.

THEY FOUND PHILLIPPE having a frugal breakfast alone in the great dining hall of Rosemont.

"So, Fox," he said icily, "you find it necessary to bring your wife when you have difficult business."

"I came of my own free will, Phillippe," Aurore said, "and I came because I know what bad-tempered wretches both of you are. These wild, headstrong children of ours have decided to get married. So we are here to ask your consent. It seems to me to be the best thing. Nothing else will so effectively silence wagging tongues!"

Phillippe turned to Etienne. "So, lad," he said, "you want this girl of mine in spite of all she's done?"

"If she will have me," Etienne said, "in spite of all *I* have done."

Phillippe smiled mockingly. "The good God could have devised no more fitting punishment than to force you two to spend a lifetime together. You have my blessing. In fact, I'll come along to see the knot well tied."

"Oh, Father!" Ceclie said breathlessly.

Phillippe glared at her. "Don't thank me!" he said. "I'm heartily glad to be rid of you!"

Etienne's face darkened. "You're a beast!" he said.

"That I don't doubt. And so must your father be also, for the two of us to have had such children."

It took all of Stephen's powers to talk old Father DuGois into performing the ceremony, but at last it was done, and on the next afternoon at five o'clock Etienne and Ceclie boarded one of the boats bound upriver for Kansas. Etienne's pockets were well lined with money with which to purchase his new lands and, in addition, he had a blank draft, signed by Stephen against the latter's Philadelphia bank account.

In another of the packets that moved majestically from the quays that day, Paul Dumaine was sailing away from New Orleans forever.

CHAPTER NINETEEN

By early November of 1854 the cane crop was almost all in. The weather continued warm and the crushers in the sugar house were rolling and thumping.

On the morning of the last day of the harvest Julie was already mounted on the fat Shetland, awaiting her father when he came down the steps. Stephen smiled at the round, eager face. "You're so slow, Father!" Julie complained. "You're getting almost as lazy as that fat old Monsieur Le Blanc."

"Heaven forbid!" Stephen grinned as he swung into the saddle. They set out for their daily ride over the great plantation at a swinging trot. But suddenly a hired carriage turned in from the bayou road and moved toward them.

As they came abreast of the carriage, the driver pulled it up, and Stephen lifted his hat courteously. The man leaning out the window had a very narrow face with a large thin-lipped mouth that looked made for smiling. His voice, when he spoke, was deep. "Is this the plantation of Mr. Stephen Fox?" he asked.

"Aye," Stephen said, "and I am Stephen Fox. Whom do I have the honor of addressing?"

"My name is Thomas Meredith," the man said. "And this is my son and namesake. Tom, say hello to the gentleman."

A boy's head appeared at the window. His face was that of his father, but softened by youth. A heavy lock of dark brown hair curled damply over his high white forehead. Seventeen or so, Stephen decided. "Good morning, Mr. Fox," he said, and his voice had a Yankee crispness totally absent from the speech of his father. As he turned his enormous light gray eyes upon Julie, his wide mouth trembled a bit at the corners.

Julie's cheeks reddened, but she couldn't help smiling. "My name is Julie," she said clearly.

"Ye're welcome here," Stephen said. "Come up to the house."

"But you were about to leave," Thomas Meredith said.

"A routine inspection. It can wait." Stephen turned the palomino and Julie rode the pony to the other side of the carriage, and the little cavalcade moved slowly off in the direction of the house.

"You're wondering why we came?" Meredith asked.

"Frankly, yes."

"You have a son of mine buried upon your land. We came to arrange for the removal of the body to Boston."

Julie's eyes opened wide. "Oh, no!" she said.

"My sympathies, sir," Stephen said, "but I hope ye'll change your mind. The grave has become quite a shrine for Julie here. She tended the lad in his last hours, and he seems to have made a deep impression upon her."

"Dan was like that," Thomas Meredith murmured. "But you've made me feel better already . . . just knowing that he received such tender care."

When they reached the house, Aurore was waiting upon the upper gallery. Meredith and his son got down from the carriage and went up the broad stairs with Stephen and Julie.

"Aurore," Stephen said, "may I present the Thomas Merediths—father and son—of Boston. Gentlemen, Madame Fox."

Aurore smiled. "Come in. You're in time for late breakfast."

In the great hall young Tom Meredith stood open-mouthed. "It's—it's a palace," he whispered.

"Certainly there's nothing like it in Boston," his father declared. "Now you begin to understand our southern friends?"

Aurore ushered them into the dining salon and the Negroes appeared bearing café au lait and steaming mounds of *pain perdu*. Young Tom was staring curiously.

"Ye don't have many blacks in Boston," Stephen observed.

"Only a few," the boy said. "I can't get used to them."

"Your brother Dan said you were abolitionists," Julie blurted.

"Julie!" Aurore began, but Thomas Meredith was smiling.

"Dan was right," he said softly.

"But you're a southerner," Aurore said.

"Yes, madame. I was born in Alabama. When I was twenty, my father died and left me Pine Hill and three hundred slaves."

"And ye freed them all and sold the place. I remember that well," Stephen said. "It created quite a furor."

"Yes," Meredith said. "That was when I went to Boston."

"My husband has often expressed a desire to do exactly what you did," Aurore said. "But his friends and I have always held him back. I just don't see that slavery is morally wrong. We treat the Negroes kindly—much more so, in fact, than you treat your mechanics and hired laborers in the North."

Thomas Meredith smiled. "Two wrongs have never yet added up into a right. Besides, the way the blacks are brought to this country is unbelievably brutal. Oh, I know that the trade's been abolished, but it still flourishes illegally. Has Madame ever seen a slave ship—or smelled one?"

Aurore shook her head.

"Often as many as half the Negroes aboard die during the voyage. Even in the interstate trade the mortality is high. Would Madame sit down to dinner with a slave trader?"

"Heaven forbid!" Aurore said.

"You see? To make a living by dealing in black flesh is held despicable by the very people who buy slaves—good, kindly Christian people like Madame herself."

Aurore drew herself up very stiffly in her chair.

"But most of all I'm opposed to it because of the way slavery demoralizes the southern white. Eighty-five or ninety percent of the whites of this region don't own slaves. Slavery is profitable— for you. But it keeps millions of whites scratching for food in the rocky earth of the mountains and existing listlessly in the fetid, fever-ridden swamp bottoms. The point is that no section ever grew to greatness on a system that benefited only the few. . . . Then there are other things—not perhaps fit for the ears of ladies."

Stephen looked at Julie. "Suppose ye show young Tom about the place." Meredith nodded and they went out.

"Before my wife," Stephen said, "ye can speak freely."

"What I meant—if Madame Fox will forgive me—is the wide-spread practice of concubinage with slave women. Why, here in Louisiana, these mulattoes, quadroons and octoroons constitute a real danger. They're much more inclined to revolt than the blacks. Besides, this debauching of our best young men doesn't make for good physical health or mental stability."

Aurore looked at Stephen. "In that I agree," she said. "Most heartily!"

"Ye're right, of course," Stephen declared. "But I don't see a solution. Suppose I were to free my Negroes? Who would care for them? Ye've seen how freedmen fare. Your own Negroes, for instance—how did they make out when they were set free?"

"Some—a few—splendidly. They emigrated to Boston and New York and started small businesses: laundries, carpenter shops, bootblack stands. Some of them became paid house ser-

vants for wealthy New Yorkers. The vast bulk of them got along—
a sort of hand-to-mouth existence. But the rest . . ."

"Aye," Stephen said, "what about the rest?"

"They got into trouble. Petty thievery, mostly. The fact is, they
weren't ready for freedom. But that's what we've got to do now—
make them ready. For they're going to be freed. Either soon and
violently—or, God willing, in the future, gradually, of our own
free wills. That's the way I'd like to see it. . . . But we've talked
enough about this, don't you think? I'd like to see the spot where
Dannie lies, if you'll be so good . . ."

Stephen rose. "Come," he said, "I'll show ye."

YOUNG TOM MEREDITH sat uneasily on the gentle old nag that had
been saddled for him and looked over the vast acres. "I'd like to
see the slave quarters," he said suddenly.

"Well—all right," Julie said. "But they're nothing much to
see," she added.

A few minutes later young Tom sat upon the nag looking down
the long rows of neat whitewashed brick cabins. Negro children
played on the steps, and old grandmothers came out to wave at
Julie, their black faces shining with pleasure.

The boy's thin, sensitive face was intent and frowning.
"Where's the whipping post?" he demanded.

"You've been reading that horrible book by Mrs. Stowe," Julie
said angrily. "We don't beat our Negroes. You Yankees are so silly!"

"I—I'm sorry," young Tom managed. "I didn't mean to make
you mad."

"It's all right," Julie said. "You know, my father's going to let
me go north to school—when I'm sixteen."

"He is! Then please come to Boston. We have some dandy
schools for girls . . . and then I could see you."

At thirteen Julie was already a lady—and a Louisiana lady at
that. Her eyelids fluttered slowly, and just a hint of warm huskiness crept into her voice. "You—you'd like that, Tom?" she
murmured.

"Would I," Tom began, "would I!" Then he stopped, his face
covered with blushes and confusion.

Before he returned to the house, young Tom saw the chapel,
the infirmary, which was mostly occupied by Negro babies busily
sucking on bottles of herb tea or eating mush while their mothers

worked in the fields, the steamboat landing, the still unremoved wreckage of the *Creole Belle*, and the grave of his brother.

He stood silently before the little mound of earth, gazing upon the marble headstone that Stephen had caused to be erected. "My brother," he said, the corners of his mouth trembling a little. "I don't know a soul who disliked him. If somebody had to die, why did God have to take the best . . . ? Me, now . . . nobody would have missed me."

"Oh, don't say that, Tom! I'd have missed you—very much."

Tom looked at her, his gray eyes wide. "But you wouldn't even have known me," he said.

"That would have been worse," Julie murmured.

"We . . . I guess we'd better be getting back to the house."

The tiniest smile played about the corners of Julie's mouth. "All right, Tom," she said. Then she dug her heels into the pony's fat sides and started off at a brisk trot.

THE MEREDITHS lingered on at Harrow for two weeks. The day they took their leave was one of those rare winter days when the sun plays hide-and-seek with mountains of fleecy purple-and-white clouds. Where Dan Meredith lay in his long sleep, the light seemed to glow over the headstone.

Tom stood with his father beside the grave. A little farther off, Stephen and Julie watched them silently.

"Dad," young Tom said in a low voice, "let's leave him here. It—it's a kind of heaven in itself. Why, here, almost the whole year round he can have flowers. Julie will bring them; she promised me."

Thomas Meredith smiled gently at his son. "Yes, we'll leave him here," he said. "And now we'd better say our good-bys. The Foxes are a grand family. Our abolitionist friends rather oversimplify things; you see that now, son."

They turned and walked toward Stephen and Julie. Stephen put out his hand and Thomas Meredith took it firmly. "This has meant more to us than ever I can tell you," Meredith said. "We'll write—often. The country has need of men of goodwill in both sections. And if ever you visit Boston—"

"We'll call upon ye. That may be sooner than ye think."

Young Tom was holding Julie's plump white hand in his own slender fingers. "Good-by, Julie," he said simply.

"No," she said. "Not good-by—*au revoir*, Tom. You may kiss my hand; it's customary, you know."

The boy bent awkwardly over her hand, his face fiercely hot. Then he was gone, running toward the waiting carriage, without even a backward glance.

Thomas Meredith raised his hat toward the belvedere upon which Aurore stood, and made her a sweeping bow. Then father and son climbed into the carriage. The Negro clucked over the reins and the horses moved off slowly.

Stephen turned to his daughter. The tears in her eyes were flowing faster than she could blink them away. "Never weep over a lad, Julie. There is none of them worth it."

"Oh, but he is, Father, he is!"

"Perhaps. He does seem a good lad—that I'll grant ye."

As they turned toward the house, Julie caught him by the arm. "The post rider, Father! A letter from 'Tienne—I know it is!"

Stephen took the bulky envelopes from the rider. "Aye, ye're right," he said. "Here's one from 'Tienne. But this one is for him. We'll have to send it on. 'Tis from young McGarth. He's up in Boston these days, studying law at Harvard."

Stephen broke the seals on the letter from Etienne. " 'Dear Mother, Father and Julie,' " he read. " 'We finally arrived at the town of Lawrence after a horrible journey. I must confess that Ceclie stood it much better than I. She is becoming a most enchanting wife—very steady and capable. Kansas, and particularly Lawrence, is a hotbed of abolitionists, who openly boast of their intention to make the territory into a free state. Therefore I am removing immediately across the border into Missouri, where I am confident of obtaining lands suitable for my purposes. My mail will reach me at the general post office of Lawrence until I furnish you with a more exact address. Until such time, I remain, your devoted, obedient son and brother, Etienne.' "

"He isn't coming home," Julie pouted.

"Of course not, Julie. Ye shouldn't have expected that. Come along now, we must let your mother see this letter."

A FEW WEEKS later Etienne Fox rode into the office of the sheriff at Lawrence. The sheriff was violently proslave, and between these two, who had nothing else in common, this fact had made a bond. The proslavers were too much outnumbered in Kansas.

"Mornin', Mr. Fox," he drawled. "What can I do for you?"

Without answering, Etienne laid down the letter from Walter McGarth that Stephen had forwarded to him. The sheriff read it. "I take it that this black he's talkin' about ran away from you? Well, rest easy, Mr. Fox. I'll send a deputy after him this very day."

"Thank you," Etienne said.

The sheriff got up and walked to the door with Etienne. "How's your place acomin'?" he asked.

"Great. I've got most of it cleared already."

"That's good. I'll be aridin' past there one of these days."

"You do that," Etienne murmured politely.

"A cold fish," the sheriff muttered to himself as Etienne went out the door. "But he's a real gentleman—no mistake about that!"

Inch walked rapidly along the snow-covered sidewalk of State Street in Boston. With him was the venerable white-bearded Frederick Douglass, living proof that a Negro could be a scholar, a statesman, a valiant champion of his oppressed people—and a gentleman. And he, Little Inch—a black slave lacking even a last name, unless he chose to call himself Fox—had been elevated to the company of such a giant. The thought made him glow.

It had all come about when the Millikens discovered how well educated Inch was. He swept and cleaned their law offices during the day and read Blackstone at night. So the Millikens introduced Inch to the abolitionists Wendell Phillips, Theodore Parker and Thomas Wentworth Higginson. Here, they could tell their audiences, is an example of the intellectual heights to which a black man can rise. Here is proof positive that Dr. Douglass is not an exception. In short, Inch was being lionized by the abolitionists.

"When we are all free," Inch said now to Douglass, "we'll elect our own representatives to the Congress, and then—"

He never finished the sentence. For the long, lean white man who had been following them with deadly deliberation touched him on the shoulder. "Your name is Inch?" he drawled quietly.

"Yes," Inch said. "What do you want?"

"You're under arrest. You better come along quiet."

"Now, see here," Inch began.

"Go along with him, young Inch," Douglass said. "You'll be taken care of—depend upon that."

INCH WAS CONFINED, under heavy guard, in the courthouse. He wondered that it should take fifteen-odd policemen to keep one slim black in custody.

What he did not know was that at that very moment Faneuil Hall was seething with an excited crowd of antislavery men and women. Wendell Phillips was pouring forth his most impassioned oratory, deliberately inciting the crowd to riot. But it was a curiously Boston style of rioting that finally ensued: coolly, carefully planned, with lieutenants to direct it.

Phillips' comrade Higginson and a few others were to proceed directly to the courthouse and wait until Phillips arrived with the crowd from Faneuil Hall. Then, with seeming spontaneity, an outbreak was to occur. During the confusion Inch was to be rescued and spirited away to Canada.

The hours passed and Inch walked back and forth in the little anteroom that served as a cell. Outside, the Reverend Mr. Higginson squinted into the driving sleet. Why the deuce didn't Phillips come? At any moment some policeman might emerge from the building and discover the plotters.

Two short blocks away Wendell Phillips and Theodore Parker were standing on the glazed ice of the street looking at the wreckage of their carriage. The two men set out on foot for the courthouse. But, long before they reached it, the mob attack was under way. Confused, leaderless, the men hurled themselves through the snowdrifts at the side entrance in Court Square, but one of the policemen had already locked the door. Twelve of the strongest men lifted a joist and, pointing it at the side door, started forward at a dead run. The door gave way at last with a splintered crash. With a howl the mob poured through the doorway.

But the police were ready. As the mob rushed in, they brought clubs down with all their force upon the heads of the abolitionists. It was over within a few short minutes. Inch stood there watching as the men were hurled back out into the blinding sleet.

Afterward it was very quiet.

The trial, which took place on the following Monday, lasted less than half an hour. Richard Henry Dana pleaded for Inch with all his skill and brilliance, but there was no denying the fact that Inch was the person described in the articles presented.

At last Commissioner Loring read aloud: " 'The prisoner, one

Inch, a black of twenty-four years, is said to have escaped from the plantation Harrow, near New Orleans, Louisiana.' " He put down the paper and glared at Inch. "I have no alternative," he said at last, "but to return this man to his lawful owner, one Etienne Fox, now residing in the state of Missouri."

The following day Inch was led from his cell into the bright sunshine. Both sides of State Street were lined with men and women. Inch looked about him in awe. Every four feet along the entire length of the street a soldier stood with fixed bayonet to keep the crowd back.

Inch walked slowly at first, his head sunk upon his chest. But out of the corner of his eye he saw shop after shop draped in black. Even the flags were at half mast. As the little procession passed the Old State House, Inch could see a huge coffin swinging in the air, bearing the inscription: *The Funeral of Liberty!*

On the sidewalks women wept and men hissed and booed the soldiers. Slowly Inch straightened. By the time he reached Long Wharf, where the revenue cutter was waiting to bear him away, he was walking fully erect, his slim back very stiff and proud.

CHAPTER TWENTY

STEPHEN FOX SAT looking out of the window of his study. Under his hand lay a blank sheet of paper on which he had written: *June 17, 1858*, and the words: *My dear Julie*. But his eyes strayed over Etienne's letters, which were among those spread out before him. On one the ink had faded, but he was able to make out the date: *May 1856*. The words in that angular, bewildering script kept tugging at him. *John Brown . . . a grim and terrible man . . . you'll hear more of him, mark me, Father . . . Pottawatomie Creek . . . five men murdered cold-bloodedly . . . all proslavery*. This and the cryptic announcements of the births of Stephen's grandchildren: Victor, 1856; Stephen II, 1857; Gail, the only granddaughter, 1858. A mention or two about the sad state of the new plantation, a word about Ceclie; but always the bitter smoke and bloodshed of the flaming Kansas border. Here slavery was being fought over and men were dying.

Stephen frowned, picking up his long clay pipe. The letter from Julie must be answered. He picked it up and read it again:

Miss Angelina Shephard's Female Academy
#30 Shirley Street, Boston
April 30, 1858

Dear Papa:
I am at last becoming accustomed to this accursed school. Miss Shephard is really very kind, and Boston is a wonderful city. But I'm so homesick I could just die!

I still haven't seen Tom Meredith. He and his father are abroad, but they will return soon. I wonder if he has changed. Does all this sound silly—for a young lady of seventeen? Please write me and tell me about everything, and I do mean everything!

Lovingly,
Julie

Stephen sighed and picked up his pen.

JULIE CAME BACK to Harrow in the middle of July. But she was a changed girl. No longer did she ride to the bottomlands with her beloved papa. Instead she sat in the salon, playing pensive airs upon the grand piano and answering her mother absently or not at all. At seventeen Julie was a true Arceneaux beauty, with the lightest touch of the diablerie of her father thrown in. Her plumpness had given way to a soft slimness that now, because of her haphazard methods of eating, was becoming actual thinness.

"What ails ye, girl?" Stephen demanded. "Ye know, Julie, I don't think I'll send ye back to that school. Boston doesn't seem to have agreed with ye."

"No, Papa! I've got to go back—don't you understand? I've got to!"

"So—the wind lies in that quarter, eh? I hope ye won't be too disappointed when ye see your Yankee lad again."

"*If* I see him again. Papa, why doesn't he write?"

"I don't know, light o' my heart. But if ye want that pale ice-water stripling, I'll dust off the family shotgun—"

"Now you're teasing me. I think you're being horrid!" Then she was gone, dashing up the stairs to her room.

"Well, she's a Fox, all right," Stephen murmured. "What she wants, she wants with all her heart." He went into his study, picked up his pen and drew a sheet of paper toward him. *Thomas*

Meredith, Esquire, he wrote, *Meredith & Son, Merchandisers, State Street, Boston . . . My dear sir . . .*

It was late September before a reply came. There were two letters, both postmarked Paris, France, one of them addressed to Julie. Her fingers trembled as she broke the seals.

> Dear Julie,
>   I've wanted so long to write to you, but I dared not. You were something I dreamed about—as one dreams of angels. Then your father's letter was forwarded to us here, saying that you spoke of me often, that you asked about me—Julie, Julie, I thought I'd die of happiness.
>   And you go to Miss Shephard's school! Then I shall see you, and soon! 'Tis Harvard for me, instead of the University of Paris as I'd planned. Father was amenable to the suggestion—for, in his own quiet way, he likes you almost as much as I. My pen falters. *Au revoir*, Julie.
>
> > Ever,
> > Tom

Now the whole of Harrow changed. Julie's eyes were bright. She ate well, and rode with Stephen again over the vast plantation. And between her and Aurore there were hours of whispered conversation.

Finally, on the last day of the month, Stephen and Aurore stood upon the wharf at New Orleans and watched the boat bearing Julie northward for her second term find its place in the five o'clock parade of upriver packets. It was an impressive sight, as boat after boat slipped away from its moorings and headed upstream, the black clouds of smoke from their high twin stacks mingling in a pall of blackness that shut out the afternoon sun.

TOM CAME BACK from France early in the term and wasted a full month in vain attempts to see Julie. Miss Shephard would brook no contact between the young ladies of her school and members of the opposite sex. But no one in history has ever successfully devised a method short of murder that could keep apart a young couple determined to be together.

Julie saw Tom: on Sundays on her way to early mass; at night from her window while he stood shivering in the snow-blanketed street below. And she would meet him on afternoon walks—accidentally, of course, but with amazing frequency.

For them both this was a kind of torture: the words whispered hurriedly, the awkward, hasty kisses. In the end Miss Shephard herself brought matters to a happy conclusion by walking into Julie's room at two o'clock in the morning, just as Tom was walking away from a spot below Julie's window. She stunned Julie into speechlessness by accusing her of allowing Tom into her room, and confined her to quarters until her father could be notified to come and get her.

Julie could think of only one answer to this. By eight o'clock of the same morning her note was already in Tom's hands.

Promptly at midnight Julie opened her window. There was a low, bumping sound as the ladder came to rest against her casement. A moment later Tom's face appeared. He was shaking with nervousness, but a broad grin split his face.

They were married by a justice of the peace, and then took a train for New York. They went to the best hotel, for Tom was well supplied with money for the honeymoon, since the elder Meredith was in on the secret; but Julie lay in her new husband's arms and cried and cried, thinking about Harrow. Tom held her close to him and brushed the long golden hair with his hands.

AURORE STOOD ON the gallery and watched Stephen pounding up the alley of oaks at a hard gallop, waving something in his hand. He shouldn't ride like that at nearly sixty, she thought.

"Stephen! Be careful for God's sake!"

But Stephen was down from the horse and running up the stairs. "They're coming!" he cried. "Julie! Day after tomorrow!"

"I take it that her impetuous Yankee is with her?"

"Aye," Stephen growled. "But what's done is done . . . and we really shouldn't have expected cool heads of our children. Still, this accusation that Miss Shephard makes against them . . . "

"I don't believe a word of it!" Aurore said. "And, Stephen, if Julie doesn't volunteer an explanation, don't assume that her silence is a confession of guilt. There are some things in the heart of a woman that are not to be shared—not even with parents as tolerant as we try to be. Promise me, Stephen."

"All right," he said, "I promise, but just the same, I hope Julie will tell us the whole story."

Stephen went into his study and opened his other letters. One of them was from Etienne. His son had proved a steady correspondent. This fact pleased Stephen as much as it surprised him. Time and again, Stephen's advice was asked on all sorts of matters: running the plantation, dealing with the Negroes—even, to his amazement, the management of a much-too-spirited wife.

> We manage to eke out a living here. Ceclie currently suspects me—not without some justification—of carrying on an affair with one of the ladies of the town. Her tantrums of jealousy are something to behold! Inch continues surly and unreliable. I have a feeling he is preaching emancipation to my Negroes. I made the surprising discovery that a large number of them could read simple sentences and even write their names. Inch made no attempt to deny that it was he who had been teaching them, so I had him whipped. I have grown a beard. It adds enormously to my dignity, and even to my control over my household. . . .

Early the next morning Stephen and Aurore met Julie and her husband at the wharf in New Orleans. They had come down from New York by coastal steamer, around the tip of Florida and upriver from the Gulf. The trip had taken more than a month. As they stepped ashore, Aurore burst into sudden tears.

"Mother," Julie began, "what on earth . . . ?"

Stephen smiled at her gently, his blue eyes alight. " 'Tis the shock of seeing that ye're no longer a child," he said. "Ye've changed, Julie. In carriage and air and everything." He put out his hand to his new son-in-law. "Welcome home, Tom," he said.

Tom gulped two or three times before answering. Then he took Stephen's hand in an iron grip. "Thank you, sir. I'm awfully glad . . . I hadn't expected . . . "

"What's done is done," Stephen said. "Though I think that Julie rather cheated her mother. Aurore had entertained the idea of a wedding in the cathedral."

"I'm sorry, Mother," Julie said, her arms around Aurore's waist. "But then, you see, we had to get married rather suddenly."

Stephen's brows made white thundercaps. "Papa!" Julie said, stamping her small foot. "If you think what I think you're thinking, I'll never speak to you again!"

"Wait, Julie," Tom said. "Your father knows you too well for that. And I hope that I'll be able to prove to him that Northerners can be gentlemen."

"That ye've done already. Come, children. Now to Harrow."

As soon as they reached the plantation, Aurore sent invitations to the Damerons, the McGarths, the Le Blancs, the Lascals and the Sompayracs to dine with them that evening. This was the best excuse to entertain she had had in years.

By seven all the guests were there, and the great salon rang with laughter and toasts. The ladies made veiled hints for information about the affluence and social position of young Tom, which the lad answered with simple directness. "My father owns one of the largest mercantile establishments in Boston. I hope that you will forgive me for that, but really, neither cane nor cotton will grow in Massachusetts!"

"You know, young man," André Le Blanc said with heavy joviality, "you robbed me of a daughter-in-law. I had been planning on having Julie for my son's wife."

"I'm sorry, sir. I didn't know about that, but I would have fought every man in Louisiana for Julie."

"I don't blame you. Julie is a lovely creature—like her mother. May I propose a toast, gentlemen?" André got to his feet, lifting his glass. "To Madame and Monsieur Meredith," he said. "May their felicity herald a renewal of cordial relationships between the two great sections of our homeland that they represent."

"Papa! Don't drink that toast!" They all turned at once. Young Victor Le Blanc was standing in the doorway, his clothing dusty and his young face red and streaked.

Slowly André lowered the glass. "You had better explain that," he said. "And fast."

"I come from the newspaper offices," the boy said flatly. "While you sit here eating with a damned Yankee, southern soil is being outraged! Not four hours ago a Yankee abolitionist named John Brown attacked Harper's Ferry in Virginia. The fighting is still going on."

Stephen looked at Aurore.

"He's arming the slaves for insurrection!" the boy went on, his voice hoarse with passion. "At this very hour he holds the Federal Arsenal and is seizing the railroad."

"Ye're mistaken, lad," Stephen said quietly.

"I only wish I were, sir," Victor said, almost weeping with rage. "I was there when the first wire came in. And they're still coming in—every hour brings worse news." He turned to his father. "So, Papa, if you drink that toast, I say before this whole company—including the ladies—God damn your soul to hell!"

André put down his glass. "I have not drunk it, son," he said quietly.

Stephen looked around the table. Every glass stood full and untouched—every glass except one. Julie held her glass in her hand; then, with every eye upon her, she stood up and very slowly tilted back her head until the last drop was gone. Instantly Tom Meredith was upon his feet, his face very white. In one gulp he too drained his glass and stood beside his wife.

The chairs scraped back from the table. Stephen nodded to the servants. In a moment they were back with the hats and cloaks.

"I am very sorry," Stephen said. "Perhaps after we've all had time to think—"

"Think!" André snorted. "What is there now to think about, Stephen?"

CHAPTER TWENTY-ONE

WAKING SOMETIME IN the night of January 23, 1861, Stephen Fox lay very quietly by the slim form of his wife, a woman now in her fifties and thrice a grandmother. It was raining, a hard, pitiless downpour, and on the horizon there was the sound of distant thunder. Like guns, he thought. And he had a premonition that the end was near. The end of the brave new world of which men everywhere had had hope. Abe Lincoln striding out of Illinois like a prairie wind. Abe Lincoln, who might never have gained the White House had not his enemies split and quarreled among themselves, so that although he received a minority of the popular vote cast, he had won a majority in the electoral college. *If Lincoln is elected, we will secede.* Well, Lincoln had been elected and they had seceded: first South Carolina, then Mississippi, then Florida and Alabama, then Georgia. And now in Louisiana time was running out. Dear little Julie in bleak Boston and Etienne in Missouri with the grandchildren he had never seen, and time was running out. How would it be to kill men like the Merediths, sighting them over the heavy revolver barrel and pulling the trigger? How would it be . . . how?

But now he heard a thunderous knocking at the door below. He drew on his robe and started downstairs. Where the deuce were the Negroes? He threw back the bolts on the great doors. A tall man was standing there in the darkness, rain dripping from his huge western-style hat. His great black beard was rain-wet too. "Well, Father," he said. "Don't you recognize me?"

" 'Tienne! How on earth . . . ? Come in, lad!"

Etienne entered the long hall, looking about like a stranger, half amazed at the vastness and the grandeur of Harrow. "I guess I've become too accustomed to a log house on a Missouri prairie," he said. "How's Mother?"

"Very well—I'll have her called. But first, some dry clothing for ye," said Stephen, pulling the bell cord, arousing the servants. "Where are the children, lad, and Ceclie? Ye're not in trouble, are ye, 'Tienne? If it's money that ye need . . . "

"No, thank you, Father. I don't need anything. This last year the place showed a profit. So I cleared off all my debts, sold my Negroes—all but Inch, he's with Ceclie and the children in New Orleans. They'll be safer here, Father . . . if you don't mind having them."

"Mind? Are ye daft, lad? 'Twill be the greatest pleasure of my life. But were they in danger?"

"Yes. This secession business . . . it means war, Father. And already in Missouri there have been barns burnt and a few houses. I wanted Ceclie and the children out of it."

Georges was coming through the hall with the dry clothing. His woolly thatch was white now. His children, offspring of his marriage with Suzette, were now house servants at Harrow.

"Light a fire in the study, Georges," Stephen said. "Then go up and call Madame. Come, 'Tienne, 'tis best that ye change."

Afterward the three of them sat beside the fireplace. "I had a letter from Julie," Etienne said. "That husband of hers has enlisted in the Federal Navy. I suggested that she join us all here—I don't like the idea of her alone among those Yankees."

"Nor I," Aurore said. "If something should happen . . . "

"Something *will* happen," Stephen declared. "Ye may depend upon that, Aurore."

" 'Twill be soon over," Etienne said. "Why, we'd be in Washington within three weeks after it started—but I'm not sure those Yankees have any stomach for a fight."

"They fought well enough in Kansas, didn't they? Kansas came in free. And what do ye propose we use for ammunition? Cotton bales? Where are our foundries to cast cannon? I'll tell ye, 'Tienne, 'twill be long and frightful if it comes to war, and we will lose. That's why I'm going to do my utmost to keep Louisiana out of it. Perhaps then the other states will think twice."

"You paint a dismal picture, Father."

"But a true one. Still, that's not my chief reason for the stand I take. Ye see, I was a man grown when I came to this country, and soon I knew that there was nothing like it in all the earth. I don't believe any longer in aristocracy—even self-made aristocracy such as the South has. Ye can't have a land like America unless all the people have a hand in its shaping. Unless ye give the people their freedom, they will take it, and ye and yours will perish in the whirlwind."

"Even the blacks?"

"Aye. There is only so much work ye can get out of an owned thing, no matter how much ye beat him. 'Twould be cheaper in the long run to pay them a wage. But enough of this. I'll ride into New Orleans and bring in Ceclie and the children while ye rest."

"Yes," Aurore said, slipping her arms around her stepson's waist. "And I'll have Georges up as soon as you're awake—to shave off those horrible whiskers!"

"You'll have to indulge me in that," Etienne said, laughing. "I've grown quite attached to them."

STEPHEN CAME BACK from New Orleans in the yellow coach, holding his two-year-old granddaughter, Gail, in his arms, while the two boys—Victor, named after André's son, and little Stephen—crawled all over him, peering out the windows, anxious to be home. At Harrow he found a delegation waiting for him. He excused himself and conducted Ceclie and the children upstairs, then returned to the grand salon to talk with his guests. They were all working men, ill at ease amid the magnificence of Harrow.

Stephen called a slave and ordered wine and cigars. "Well, gentlemen," he said, "what can I do for ye?"

The big-muscled man sitting near the front got to his feet. "We are representatives of all the city trade guilds and unions and we need a spokesman when secession comes up for the voting. We've heard tell that ye've been on our side many a time. That's true, isn't it?"

"Yes. But first I'd better find out how ye want your votes cast."

"We be agin it—this secession business. And ye?"

"I'm your man," Stephen said. "To secede from the Union is a wicked folly. Ye men who came here from other lands know well what this country means. If slavery becomes too powerful, what chance has a free working man?"

"None. But this be queer coming from ye, Mr. Fox—seeing as how ye hold as many slaves as any man in the state."

"Aye. But 'tis written in my will that upon my death they're to be freed. When I came to this land, 'twas in my mind to rise in life and everybody else could go hang. But 'tis an old man I am now, and I know that we've all got to rise together or else we will all fall separately. Gentlemen, 'twill be a pleasure to serve ye."

Two days later he was notified in writing that he had been elected delegate-at-large to the special secession convention. The family watched him leave in silence, for not one of them there approved of his views in the matter. Stephen wished that he had Julie there to say an encouraging word, but she had not yet arrived.

He made the journey upriver to Baton Rouge by packet, and the next day he took his seat with the other delegates. He listened quietly to the debates, and when his turn came, he rose and recited figures on the extent of Louisiana's trade with the North and the amount of Louisiana capital held in northern banks. He pointed out that the idea that the South was economically self-sufficient was a suicidal fallacy. "And," he concluded, "can you name me one military article of any sort that is manufactured south of the Mason-Dixon line? With what will ye fight them? Your bare hands?"

In the end he was howled down, for he offered nothing but facts. The South has always preferred oratory.

The final vote was counted and the chairman read: "For Union delegates: 17,296; for secession delegates: 20,488." A difference, Stephen calculated, of merely 3192 votes in a by-no-means-unquestionable tally. Louisiana was out of the Union.

The next day, back in New Orleans, Stephen Fox offered his services to the Confederate Army of America.

EARLY IN FEBRUARY 1861, when Julie finally reached Harrow, she found that Etienne was already gone, swallowed up in the vast wilderness to the north. Her father was in command of a regiment of cavalry under General Mansfield Lovell, whose troops were assigned to the defense of New Orleans.

Nothing had changed—except that there were no men at Harrow other than the Negroes. Ceclie's temper grew daily more waspish as no word came from Etienne, but the children were a delight. Someday, when this silly war was over, Julie decided, there must be other children.

Stephen was able to visit Harrow often. His tall, rapier-lean figure was exceedingly handsome in the tailored gray uniform of a Confederate major; but he spoke little, and his eyes were troubled. Julie alone knew how much his decision had cost him.

The weeks drifted on and nothing happened. It was a curious comic-opera sort of war, and life had never been so gay in New Orleans. There were parties and dances without number, the colorful uniforms adding glamour to the occasions. While mail still came through from the North, Julie knew of the progress that Tom was making in his training and even a little of the blundering that was to mark the first year of federal operations.

Then on April 12, the picture changed. At 4:30 a.m. Confederate guns fired on Fort Sumter in the Charleston, South Carolina, harbor. Thirty-four hours later Major Anderson marched out of Sumter to the salute of fifty guns, and took ship aboard the relief vessels that President Lincoln had sent, sailing away to New York and glory even in defeat. And Pierre Gustave Toutant Beauregard, late of New Orleans, sent in a gray-clad garrison.

Now, indeed, it was war; but in New Orleans only a few women, like Julie and Ceclie, wept. Most of them waved their silken banners and cheered their men onward in blissful ignorance of the stench and mud and dysentery these men would face. Men would die holding pictures of sweetheart, mother or wife in their hands. But in New Orleans, they danced . . .

The entire Missouri border, where black-bearded Etienne Fox rode with the proslave irregulars, was flaming. Etienne lived in the saddle, riding out of Missouri into Arkansas, fighting at Pea Ridge, at Sugar Creek, Leesville, Elkhorn Tavern . . . seeing it all end in disaster for Confederate hopes. Missouri stayed in the Union.

That winter Ulysses S. Grant said, "No terms except an unconditional and immediate surrender can be accepted." And in New Orleans they continued to dance.

And young Lieutenant Thomas Meredith, Jr., United States Navy, stood aboard the gunboat and watched mortar shells loop into Fort Pulaski, off the coast of Georgia . . . saw the fort taken, and three hundred sixty prisoners with it.

Now, again, it was April. And at the Lascals plantation, below New Orleans, the flowers were as bright as they were at Harrow. Camille Lascals stopped halfway down the page of the letter she was writing to her brother, Henri, and walked out into the garden. She looked toward the river, which showed golden through the magnolia trees, and her brown eyes widened—for the river was no longer empty. A low schooner was butting its way upstream.

Camille ran back into the house for her pearl opera glasses. She leveled them at the schooner. She could see it clearly now—*S-a-c-h-e-m*, she spelled out. There—that was a Yankee flag! Ten minutes later she was pounding northward, toward New Orleans.

General Mansfield Lovell received her cordially and thanked her for her information. Camille rode homeward, escorted by six handsome cavalrymen, feeling quite the heroine. But when Major Stephen Fox suggested that one of his companies be sent to reconnoiter, the general said, "Humph! Arrant nonsense, Major Fox! I can't have my cavalry worn out because a silly girl thinks she's seen a Union sloop!"

TWENTY MILES BELOW the Confederate forts outside New Orleans, Admiral David Farragut had called a conference of his officers to hear the report of Captain Gerdes of the *Sachem*. Being second in command of the gunboat *Itasca*, Lieutenant Thomas Meredith was present. Captain Gerdes had done well. The artillery ranges had been calculated to the yard, and flags placed along the banks marked exactly the position that each vessel was to occupy. Admiral Farragut gave strict orders that once in position, the vessels were not to be moved a foot.

Tom could feel a hammer pulse at the base of his throat. He had schemed, begged, pleaded, to be transferred to Farragut's command. If he had to smash New Orleans into ashes, he'd get through to Harrow!

Tom returned to the *Itasca* and made a thorough examination. The guns were polished and ready and the shot piled up beside them. The fuses were cut and the canvas powder bags were at hand. Now the nineteen mortar schooners were moving upstream and the *Itasca* was taking its place among the six convoying gunboats. The shore slipped backward with agonizing slowness.

Just before morning the schooners anchored around a bend in the river, barely out of sight of the forts. Parties of men went ashore with axes, and when the sun came up, the masts of every vessel had been disguised with leafy boughs, so that from a distance it was impossible to say where the forest left off and the schooners began.

Tom could see feverish activity aboard the nearest mortar schooner. He saw the gunner jerk the lanyard, but, brace himself as he would, he was still shaken by the explosion. It rolled out over the river, awakening echoes, and Tom could see the black ball arching against the sky. Then another mortar spoke, and another, till the guns in the forts began to reply. At last it had begun.

ON APRIL 25, 1862, it rained. Standing upon the belvedere at Harrow, Aurore looked downriver toward New Orleans. No sound came from the city. Of course, she didn't really expect to hear the guns. They were at the forts ninety-odd miles below New Orleans. As long as the great chains that were stretched between Forts Jackson and Saint Philip held, no Yankee would be able to steam upriver. The good God would protect those chains and the forts, and her Stephen standing now behind his gunners on the ramparts of Fort Saint Philip.

Suddenly she heard the sound of hoofbeats and saw Ceclie pounding up the drive. She turned, closed the trapdoor behind her and went down the narrow stairway. The girl might have news.

Ceclie was standing facing Julie. Her face was grave and Julie swayed on her feet, her young face a chalky mask. "Oh, Mother," she wept, "Mother!"

Aurore slipped her arms around her daughter. But her eyes were fixed on Ceclie's face. "They broke the chains," Ceclie said harshly. "Like a piece of string. Then they ran the forts. Every ship we had on the river is either sunk or ablaze. New Orleans is burning. Warehouses, sugar, cotton, wharves, steamboats—everything."

Aurore wet her dry lips and her voice was a husky whisper. "The men in the forts," she got out. "Stephen . . . ?"

"Dead or captured," Ceclie said, and strode past them up the curving stairs.

FROM THE DECKS OF the gunboat *Pinola*, to which he had been transferred when the *Itasca* had been wrecked by a round shot through her boilers, Lieutenant Meredith looked out over the city. A pall of smoke hung over the waterfront. The levee was black with howling humanity hurling curses at the Yankees, shaking their fists and brandishing weapons. How much longer would he have to wait before he saw Julie? Had she changed? Perhaps now, after so much blood had stained the southern earth, she no longer wanted to see him. He felt sick and miserable and completely empty of triumph.

Up at Harrow, Julie, too, was waiting. The plantation was an island, shut off from all contact with the outside world. No word from Tom or Stephen or Etienne. All of them dead perhaps. Or maimed. Or blinded. Or taken prisoner. Pray God it was the last!

It was a bright day, and Julie sat with her mother on the upper gallery and gazed at the river. Aurore's face was drawn. Julie stretched out her hand to pat her mother reassuringly, when suddenly she saw the troop of Confederate horsemen burst from the trees and come racing up the drive straight toward Harrow. Without a word the two women went down the stairway.

The men were running up the stairs into the house. They were all thin, bearded, unkempt. Julie walked out upon the lower gallery and lifted her hand. "Gentlemen," she called, "I must ask you to explain . . ."

A tall man stopped before her. His black beard was matted with dirt and twigs, and his big, loose-lipped mouth split into a grin. " 'Tend to you later, filly, when I ain't so busy with the Yankees!" He whirled her around and slapped her smartly across the behind.

"Why, you . . . " Julie gasped, but the tall man was already past her and running up the stairs.

Julie turned toward the river. There, just opposite the landing, a gunboat drifted lazily. From its masthead the Stars and Stripes flapped listlessly. Julie could see the crew working feverishly, elevating the muzzle of the squat black mortar. She turned, wide-eyed, to Aurore, but at that instant the whole north wing of Harrow blazed with musket fire. They could hear the shrill whistle of the minié balls whining toward the gunboat.

Then the mortar aboard the *Cayuga* spoke bass thunder, shaking the sky and the river. The two women froze and watched the great black ball climb swiftly to the top of its arc, hang there lazily for agonizing seconds, then hurl down to smash into the central floor of the north wing. The walls of the second floor bulged out slowly, and the flames leaped skyward, past the roof. Afterward all the guns were silent.

"Oh, my God!" Julie whispered. "Oh, my God!"

But now the *Cayuga* was butting in to the landing, and a detachment of marines was springing ashore, coming forward on the double. The young lieutenant at their head came to a stop before Julie and Aurore and saluted smartly. "Buckets," he said. "Where've you got them?"

"The Negroes will show you," Aurore said with great dignity. Then she disappeared into the smoke-filled interior. In ten minutes a long line of marines and Negroes was passing buckets hand over hand. It took them four hours to put the fire out, during which the water and the bayonets the marines used to rip down draperies in the path of the flames ruined almost half of Harrow. Julie stood at her mother's side, her face tear-wet, and Ceclie held her two youngest children and stared at the fire with an expression of terrible rage.

When at last it was over, the young lieutenant drew out a small notebook and a pencil. "Your names, please?"

"Madame Stephen Fox," Aurore said. "And this is my daughter, Madame Thomas Meredith."

"Meredith?" the lieutenant said. "We've got a Lieutenant Tom Meredith aboard the *Pinola*—no relation, of course?"

Julie was clinging to Aurore, her face ablaze with joy.

"Her husband," Aurore said dryly. "You'll let him know?"

"Of course! And if you will permit me, madame, I'd like to say that Lieutenant Meredith is a very lucky man."

He saluted them and took his leave. They stood on the gallery and watched the marines moving off, bearing on improvised stretchers the blanket-wrapped bundles that had been men. Julie and Aurore wept, but Ceclie's face was clear and still. "Damn them," she said, "damn them to hell!"

The next day young Tom Meredith rode up to Harrow. He flew up the stairs three at a time, but when the great doors swung open, it was Ceclie who met him. "Please," he began, "is Julie . . . "

And Ceclie went up on tiptoe and spat full into his face. Then she marched back into the house. He was standing there, blinking foolishly and wiping his cheek, when Aurore crossed the vast hall and greeted him. "I'll send Julie to you," she said calmly, "if she wishes to come. But I cannot invite you in—not in that uniform."

Slowly Tom turned and went back through the door. He started down the stairs, his head sunk upon his chest. Then he heard the clatter of small slippers and Julie's breathless voice: "Tom! Oh, Tom!" He turned and stretched out his arms.

CHAPTER TWENTY-TWO

In the summer the sky above the prisoner-of-war camp at Fort Jackson was naked and cloudless. Inside the fort the heat shimmered. Shoveling sand into the canvas bags to be used as bulwarks if ever the Confederate forces swept southward was killing work, even for a young man. And Stephen Fox was sixty-two years old.

Sometimes Aurore was allowed to come out to the fort. But they talked little. Steel herself as she would, the sight of her Stephen, dirty, half starved, the raw sun sores visible under his long white hair, was too much for her. And, indeed, there was nothing to be said.

No, we haven't heard from 'Tienne. Yes, the children are well. The heat is terrible for Julie in her condition. And the diet isn't any too good. Ceclie—no, never tell him about Ceclie! Ceclie riding into town in a *new* riding dress, when all the other women were in rags, and disappearing for days. Silk stockings, too—silk! The officers riding up to Harrow—Yankee officers! She who had spat into Tom's face, and who had sworn venomously to her hatred of them. And 'Tienne dead perhaps, or maimed or blind . . . or mad.

There were other things she did not tell him as the days dragged into months. How she and Julie dug up the floors of the smokehouses and washed the dirt to obtain the precious salt. And the coffee that you drink here, my darling, bad as it is, is at least not sweet potato squares, dried in the sun and parched, ground up and boiled.

By the time Julie's son was born, a thin, listless infant of less than six pounds, New Orleans had settled down under the command of Union General Benjamin F. Butler. General Butler was the best administrator the city had ever had. He ordered the streets cleaned and the gutters flushed; the poor were fed for the first time in history; and under him New Orleans prospered.

But at Harrow things grew steadily worse. Julie, because of her meager diet, had no milk in her breasts, and the baby was dying slowly of starvation. Then, one day, Ceclie strode into the room with a Yankee haversack. In it were jugs of milk and rich foodstuffs that Harrow had not seen since the war began. Mutely, Julie shook her head.

"You're a fool," Ceclie said calmly. "You'll let your baby die because of your silly pride? Here, take these things. There are more where they came from." Then she was gone, her new, expensive boots making a rich clatter on the stair.

Aurore came into Julie's bedchamber to find the little fellow sucking rich whole milk lustily through a clean rag stuffed into the neck of a bottle. But Julie was crying like a whipped child, her whole body shaken with sobs. "I can't let him die, Mother," she sobbed. "Tom hasn't even seen him! But you know how Ceclie gets these things. Oh, Mother!"

"Hush, child," Aurore whispered. "It's time I had a talk with Ceclie. This can't be permitted any longer."

She opened the door to Ceclie's room without knocking. Ceclie was seated before the mirror, combing out her hair. Even in the dim light Aurore could see the scarlet lip salve on her mouth and the blaze of rouge showing through the rice powder. "Ceclie," she said firmly, "these men . . . Yankee officers . . ."

Without answering her, Ceclie got up and opened a drawer in her bureau and drew from it a letter. As she took it, Aurore could see that it was tear-stained, the ink lines blotted and fading. It was dated Pittsburg Landing, April 9, 1862.

> Dear Madame Fox,
> It is with a heavy heart that I communicate the following melancholy intelligence to you. Your husband, Lieutenant Colonel Etienne Fox, is missing in the action at Shiloh Church and must be presumed dead. He was last seen leading his cavalrymen in a charge upon the Union lines. I have been informed that the entire group was cut down by a concentration of musket fire and grapeshot. Colonel Fox was one of my bravest and most able officers. With deepest sympathy, I remain, your most obedient servant,
>
> Brigadier General N. Bedford Forrest
> Commanding

Aurore raised her eyes to her daughter-in-law. "And you kept this from me all these months?"

"Yes. You and Julie had enough to bear. So what does it matter what I do? And they are Yankee *medical* officers, my dear mother-in-law. Don't tell me you hadn't noticed that?"

"No. And I don't see what difference . . ."

Again Ceclie turned to the bureau. From the bottom drawer she dragged forth a wooden box filled with little white vials. "Quinine," Ceclie said. "I was hoping to get much more. But now there is no time. I am going across Lake Pontchartrain with it tonight. I've got a boat—old and leaky as the devil. So if I don't come back . . ."

Aurore's eyes softened. She looked at the girl, a long slow look.

"Yes, yes, I did everything you think to get them. But there are boys in the hospitals dying of the fever for lack of medicines. Boys Julie played with. Friends of 'Tienne. You'll take care of the children for me? Teach them what a man their father was. Say nothing of me . . . they'll forget quickly enough."

Aurore put her hand on Ceclie's shoulder. "I'm going with you," she said.

"No, I can't let you. What would Julie and the children do if—"

"They'll have to take the chance. I'm going, and we're both coming back. This thing must be done."

IT WAS PITCH-BLACK and the rains cried against the earth. They saddled their own horses, and when they reached the lake, hours later, the wind had freshened the water into whitecaps. Ceclie uncovered the boat from among the reeds near the shore. She picked up a tin pail and handed it to Aurore. "Get in," she snapped, "and start bailing."

It was morning before they reached the other side of the lake. The gale had died, but they were skin-soaked and aching when at last the prow of the pirogue crunched into the weeds. Aurore was so weak she could hardly stand. Ceclie, half dragging, half supporting her mother-in-law, stumbled up the sandy beach.

The surgeon general of the Confederate Armies himself welcomed them. When he saw the contents of the chest, the tears ran down into his beard. "God in His mercy bless you," he croaked.

Afterward they walked down the long rows of the bare frame hospital. The stench of gangrene was heavy on the air. As they

turned to enter one room, the surgeon general stopped them, but
not before they had heard the last grating scrape of the bonesaw.
They stood there, frozen for an instant, then they heard the sizzle
of the hot iron searing the torn flesh. A burning smell came
through the door, and with it the last mortal shriek of the poor
wretch within.

When Aurore and Ceclie got ready to go back, they found that
their boat had been caulked so that it no longer leaked. When
they reached the southern shore of Lake Pontchartrain, by nightfall of the next day, they found Yankee sentries waiting for them.

"My son was in that hospital . . . dying," Aurore lied with great
dignity. "I had to go to him—pass or no pass."

The young Yankee officer looked at her white hair and sighed.
His mother was like this . . . only not half so beautiful.

"You may go, ladies," he said wearily. "But please don't try a
trick like that again."

IT WAS LOST finally. And no man could say exactly the day or the
hour, for there were dozens of days, thousands of hours. Of
course there was Palm Sunday, April 9, 1865, at the McLean
house on the edge of Appomattox village in Virginia. But that was
merely the ceremonial burial of what had been a long time dying.

Lieutenant Colonel Etienne Fox sat on the deck of a steamboat
late in April of 1865 looking out over the Mississippi. In a little
while he would pass Harrow, but he did not intend to stop there.
First, New Orleans, and a night of rest and thinking.

Already the cane was high and the cotton was up and greening.
Nothing had changed—everything had changed. He had the curious feeling that he was an intruder-ghost in the land of the living. A
strange bewhiskered ghost with guts rotted by dysentery, a minié
ball aching dully in his shoulder, another in his thigh, three fingers
of his right hand left behind him at Chickamauga.

Now, until he was finally dead (for he had not died at Shiloh—a
ball had merely creased his tough skull and he had lain covered
by the maimed and dying wounded), he would awaken in the
night remembering how it was. How it was at Murfreesboro—
stepping beside the bodies of two young lads, one of them blond,
the other dark, and recognizing the Le Blanc brothers, Victor and
Armand. . . . How it was at Shiloh—waking under the hot, steaming
mound of dead and near-dead, smelling the blood-stench and

burned cloth and cold death-sweat; he had lain quietly and waited for a death that did not come. The Yankees had dug him out at last and taken him aboard the steamboat to Camp Douglass, the prisoner-of-war camp in Chicago. . . .

Now the packet was rounding the bend and the great white house appeared. Etienne's pale blue eyes widened at the sight of the ruined and smoke-blackened north wing. On the gallery three women stood and waved at the steamboat, and his breath came out in a great sigh. . . Aurore, Julie, Ceclie. They at least were all right. He would not alter his plans, however.

Ceclie . . . Ceclie. He remembered the tone of her letters, which had at last caught up with him, after Mississippi, in Tennessee. She seems almost sorry I'm alive, he had thought bitterly. The letters were stunned and mute. The children are well. Julie has a son. Your mother, too, is getting along splendidly. Never a note of gladness—the breath-gone "I love you, love you, love you, oh, my darling!" hot-whispered into his ear on many nights—of this, there was nothing in her letters; it was as though it had never been.

The rest of his life would have to be lived out in memories. In nightmare screaming. In forever backward-looking. In never forgetting. And this was the life that stretched out not for him alone, but for the whole South.

The first person Etienne saw when he stepped off the boat in New Orleans was Walter McGarth. He came rushing forward, putting out the one hand he had left and crying, " 'Tienne! So I'm not the only one! Thank God for that!"

"The only one?" Etienne demanded.

"That came back. All the old crowd, Pierre Aucoin, Henri Lascals, Jean Sompayrac, Bob Norton, Jim Duckett . . . they all got it. Have you come to fetch your father, 'Tienne?"

"My father? Where is he? I didn't know . . ."

"He's in the hospital. They moved him and some of the other sick prisoners up from Fort Jackson. They're being released to relatives when they're well enough to go home. Go to the commissioner of police, at the Saint Louis Hotel."

Etienne was off at once, tossing a muttered thanks over his shoulder. Everywhere in the streets of New Orleans were Union soldiers, swaggering, laughing, drunken. Finally Etienne reached the Saint Louis.

Inside the lobby he was stopped by a Negro policeman who demanded to know his business. When Etienne told him, he disappeared behind the doors of an office. Etienne looked at the legend on the door. *Cyrus R. Inchcliff*, it read, *Commissioner of Police*. In an incredibly short time the policeman was back, holding a folded paper.

"Here's your pass." He grinned. "The commissioner says you're an old friend of his. He told me to tell you to come back by here when you get your daddy."

At the hospital Etienne was conducted to a broad inner gallery where many patients sat enjoying the sun. He edged his way between them until at last he came to the tall man with white hair and snowy, neatly trimmed mustache and goatee, sitting quietly in a chair.

"Father," Etienne ventured. "Father . . ." But it was not until the man turned that he was sure. The great scar was there, and the fierce old falcon eyes.

" 'Tienne!" Stephen whispered. " 'Tienne!"

Etienne took a step forward, then with a strangled cry he swept the thin, frail old man into his arms.

Stephen pushed him back and looked at him, seeing the unabashed tears standing in his son's eyes. "Easy, lad." He grinned. "I'm all right. They've been good to me here. All the nurses are in love with me."

"I don't doubt it, Father," Etienne said, relief flooding his voice. "But come on, let's get out of here." Then he added, "Before we go home, there's one thing we might do. This police commissioner claims to be an old friend. He practically ordered us to return to his office."

"Then we'd better go. Things have changed, 'Tienne."

Half an hour later they emerged into the brilliant spring sunlight. They walked very slowly, for Etienne soon saw that his father was incapable of a faster pace. On the banquette outside the Saint Louis they paused until Stephen got his breath back. Then they climbed the steps into the lobby.

Without hesitation the black policeman ushered them into the commissioner's office. There the both of them stood transfixed. "Inch!" they said upon the same breath.

" 'Tienne!" Inch said. "And Monsieur Stephen! How glad I am to see you!" The mustache was new, black even against that coal-black face. That and the dressing gown of finest silk and the faintest suggestion of heaviness about the man. "Come into my study, gentlemen," he said politely.

They followed him. Stephen's eyes were gleaming with amusement, but Etienne was walking very stiffly.

"And now, 'Tienne," Inch began.

"You've forgotten your manners," Etienne said harshly.

"There have been changes," Inch murmured smoothly.

"None that I recognize!"

"Too bad," Inch said. "But let's not quarrel. You'll have dinner with your father and me, won't you?"

Etienne nodded grimly.

"Good," Inch said.

Etienne felt the short hairs on the back of his neck rising in fury, but he controlled himself and ate the excellent dinner that a servant brought in answer to Inch's ring.

"Brandy?" Inch said when they had finished, pushing forward the decanter. "It's from Harrow. I have many treasures from our former home."

"Our!" Etienne choked.

"I am sorry," Inch said softly. "I didn't mean to offend you."

Etienne stood up. "We'll be going now, Inch," he said.

"Wait . . . I want you to meet my son." There was the sound of footsteps upon the stair. "One word of caution, gentlemen," he whispered. "The lad was with Colonel Shaw at Fort Wagner. Sometimes he is . . . well, odd. The terrific artillery fire, you understand."

"I've seen many such cases," Stephen said.

The door crashed open abruptly, and instead of the child they had expected, a young man of perhaps twenty-five years stood in the doorway . . . a young man with white skin and red hair and freckles that dusted his high forehead. The little hairs on the backs of his hands were golden, and his eyes were a hard, pale blue, the brows white-gold, almost invisible against his fair skin. "Good morning, Father," he said simply, like a small boy. "Good morning, gentlemen."

Etienne stared at the young man. It's Father all over again, he thought.

"How do you like young Cyrus?" Inch asked. "Cyrus, this is Monsieur Stephen Fox and Monsieur Etienne, his son."

"Fox?" Cyrus echoed blankly. "Fox?"

Etienne was studying the young man. "Cyrus, hell," he declared. "That's—"

Inch smiled broadly. "You're mistaken, 'Tienne, in what you think. It was perhaps the virus of Harrow in my veins that gave him that shape and color. Or perhaps some prenatal influence upon his mother. . . . Still, he is very like a Fox, is he not?"

"Cyrus!" A voice floated down the stairway like the lower notes of a soft golden gong. Stephen's face was bleak. First the boy . . . so like, so like . . . and now this!

"Fox?" Young Cyrus puzzled. "Fox?"

Then the footsteps were coming down the stairs quickly. She looked almost the same despite her forty-three years. She had grown heavier, but her skin was still tawny and in her hair the golden fires still flickered. Her sea-green eyes looked from one to the other of them.

"Good morning, gentlemen," she said. "It is good to see you again."

"Fox!" Cyrus said triumphantly. "Now I've got it! Madame Ceclie Fox, the great beauty that Colonel Shane of the Medical Corps was always raving about. She used to come to the hospital when I was there. She was Dr. Shane's mistress—"

"Cyrus!" Inch roared.

"Let him go on," Etienne murmured. "You wasted your time at that law school, Inch. You should have studied at the Comédie Française. This is beautifully staged." He turned to the young man, whose face now held a look of blank amazement. "Tell me more about Madame Fox, lad. I'm most interested."

"I used to worship her from afar," Cyrus said. "But she wouldn't let anybody near her except Colonel Shane and that artist—Dumaine, his name was—that used to draw battle pictures for the newspapers. He and the colonel quarreled over her . . . and some say there was a duel, but I don't know about that."

"Come, Father!" Etienne roared. We're going—now!"

Inch made a gesture, touching his forehead with his finger. "Don't regard the boy's words too seriously, 'Tienne," he whispered. "Gun-shock victims have strange fantasies at times."

Stephen got to his feet slowly. When he spoke, his voice was very deep. "I don't know whether or not this is your way of taking vengeance for your years of bondage, Inch," he said. "But if it is, ye're being unwise. 'Tis a delicate course ye must steer."

"Yes," Inch said, a little sadly, "I know it. This came too soon. We weren't ready. White men will rule the South again." He paused, his eyes resting blankly upon Désirée as though she were not there. "You'll find a carriage outside waiting to take you to Harrow. And if there is ever anything that I can do . . ."

"Thank ye," Stephen said. "Good day to ye . . . and to ye, madame."

On the ride to Harrow Etienne was silent. The carriage swayed up the Bayou Road and the river was golden in the sunlight.

"I think the lad lied, 'Tienne," Stephen began. "Inch has a dangerously subtle mind."

Etienne looked at his father, his black beard bristling. "No, Father," he said quietly. "The boy didn't lie."

"Ye have no proof."

"No. Only a feeling . . . something about the tone of Ceclie's letters after she discovered I was alive."

Stephen turned his pale eyes upon his son's face. "Send her away if ye must, but ye'll do her no violence. Promise me that, 'Tienne."

Etienne looked past his father out over the face of the river. "I shan't touch her, Father," he said. The silence between them was thick and heavy.

Now Stephen looked out over the cypress grove, and the oak alley, which had come into sight. Beyond them, through the trailing streamers of Spanish moss, the house gleamed white—all except the blackened ruin of the north wing. "We must rebuild it," he said.

"No, Father," Etienne said. "We must never rebuild it. We'll build a new house—out on the old Waguespack place—but let Harrow stand as a reminder of what we suffered and what we will never forget or forgive!"

"For a little while," Stephen said, "we lived like gods. I'm not sure that it was good for us."

"Come, Father," Etienne said, "the women will be waiting."

Before they reached the stairs, Julie came flying down to them, and behind her was Aurore, her white hair gleaming in the sunlight. Ceclie came more slowly, the children clustered about her skirts.

"Oh, Papa!" Julie cried out. " 'Tienne! I'm so glad . . . so glad!"

Stephen kissed them and, after him, Etienne embraced the two women; then he strode up the stairway to Ceclie. He stood very quietly looking at her, his eyes bleak and fierce. "So," she whispered, "you've been told . . ."

"Yes," he said.

" 'Tienne, 'Tienne," she whispered, "I thought you were dead."

"No explanations, Ceclie!" He turned and rejoined the others. In the salon the talk was loose and disjointed. So many years had been lost, and never could the threads be rewoven or the pieces put back together again. While they talked, at a nod from Etienne, Ceclie rose and went up the stairs.

A few minutes later Etienne left the salon and went into the study. He opened his father's drawer and took out the little double-barreled derringer. Carefully he cleaned and oiled the richly ornamented weapon. Then he loaded it, slipping shells into both barrels, put it into his pocket and went up the stairs.

Ceclie was waiting for him, her eyes very wide and dark. Without saying anything, he took out the pistol, balancing it loosely in the palm of his hand. Ceclie inclined her head briefly toward the derringer. "For me?" she said.

"Yes."

She looked at him, a smile of pure amusement lighting her eyes so that they flamed suddenly, feline and joyous. Then she put one white arm upon the mantel and let her small body relax. Her eyes caught and held his as she came erect slowly. "Well," she said, "what are you waiting for?"

It will make a hole, he thought, a small but dreadful hole, black-ringed against her white flesh, and her life will pump through. He looked down suddenly at her hands. They would move no more through his hair. Never again the sweet, hot, fierce, desire-taloned ferocity. . . . A gasp caught in his throat and became a burn.

She took a step forward, and her hand came out and closed over the barrels of the derringer. Then gently she pulled it away from him, ever so slowly, his cold, nerveless fingers slipping down over the rich silver-mounted butt.

She stood there, holding the pistol; then, suddenly, she began to laugh. She laughed all over in great windy gusts of sound, metal-hard and ringing. "So, 'Tienne," she said, "you don't like playing the cuckold? Why? The role fits you so well. You were designed by nature to wear horns."

"Ceclie!"

"You coward! Your honor must be avenged—and with ceremony, too! I must die for doing exactly what I wanted to, when I wanted to, and with whom. No, 'Tienne, I'm afraid I must decline the honor of dying. You just aren't worth it."

She walked around him, still holding the pistol. In the doorway she turned. "I'm leaving you, 'Tienne," she said. "I'm going back to Texas." She looked at the elegant weapon, then, abruptly, she broke it open and stared at the chambers. Her eyes widened enormously, dark in her white face. "Two bullets," she whispered. "One for me, and one for—"

"Yes," he said, "yes!"

She looked at the pistol again, then she tossed it lightly upon the bed. She started back toward Etienne, walking slowly, her brown eyes burning like great dark coals, never leaving his face. Then she was close to him, and he could feel the warmth of her, hear the rustle of her breathing.

"I'm flattered," she said, and there was no laughter in her voice. "But don't you see—it's no good? This thing between us is a kind of poison. It's a sickness in the blood. All I do is torment you and make you wretched, and love you and hate you at the same time. Oh, 'Tienne, let me go! Keep me now and I'll leave you tomorrow or betray you. . . . There's nothing—"

But Etienne's big hands came down upon her shoulders and the fingers dug in until the flesh purpled beneath them. Then he pulled her against him hard and found her mouth.

She tore free at last, her lips poppy red and swollen. "I'll leave you," she warned. "I'll betray you! And there is still nothing . . ."

But he held her to him, breath-stopped, saying, "There is now, Ceclie. There is now!"

"Yes," she said, and her eyes were enormous, diamond-bright, tear-jeweled. "Yes, 'Tienne! There is now."

THE KING'S GENERAL

THE
KING'S GENERAL

A CONDENSATION OF THE NOVEL BY

Daphne du Maurier

ILLUSTRATED BY GINO D'ACHILLE

In the mid-1600s, when civil war raged
throughout England, Richard Grenvile was made
commander of His Majesty's Army in Cornwall.
Many years had passed since Richard's
scandalous whirlwind romance with the beautiful
and spirited Honor Harris. Now, as battling
armies draw near, the two are reunited
at the great stone manor house known as Menabilly.
And in this house of dark secrets Richard and
Honor rekindle their love as the forces of
Oliver Cromwell close in upon them.

Daphne du Maurier, who lived at Menabilly
for many years, loved the old mansion and the
rugged Cornish coast on which it stands.
She used both as the setting for some of
her best known stories, including the
now-classic novel *Rebecca*.

CHAPTER ONE

SEPTEMBER 1653. The last of summer. The first chill winds of autumn. The sun no longer strikes my eastern window as I wake, but, turning laggard, does not top the hill before eight o'clock. A white mist hides the bay sometimes until noon and hangs about the marshes, too. Because of this the long grass in the meadow never dries, but long past midday shimmers and glistens in the sun. The tides seem to make a pattern to the day. When the water drains from the marshes and the yellow sands appear, rippling and hard and firm, it seems to my foolish fancy lying here that I, too, go seaward with the tide, and my old hidden dreams that I thought buried for all time lie bare and naked to the day, just as the shells and the stones do on the sands.

It is a strange, joyous feeling, this streak back to the past. Nothing is regretted, and I am happy and proud. The mist and cloud have gone, and the sun, high now and full of warmth, holds revel with my ebb tide. Then, half consciously, I become aware of a shadow, of a sudden droop of the spirit. The first clouds of evening are gathering. And the surge of the sea comes louder now, creeping toward the sands. The tide has turned. The sands are covered. My dreams are buried. . . . Then Matty will come in to light the candles and to stir the fire, making a bustle with her presence, and if I am short with her or do not answer, she looks at me with a shake of her head and reminds me that the fall of the year was always my bad time. My autumn melancholy. Even in the distant days, when I was young, Matty, like a fierce clucking hen, would chase away the casual visitor. "Miss Honor can see nobody today."

My family soon learned to understand and left me in peace. Though *peace* is an ill word to describe the moods of black despair that used to grip me. Ah well . . . they're over now. Those moods at least. Rebellion of the spirit against the chafing flesh. Those were the battles of youth. But I am a rebel no longer.

A cynic when I was young, I am in danger of becoming a worse one now I am old. So Robin says. Poor Robin. My brother . . . Looking at him as he sits beside me, I note his graying locks, the pouches beneath his eyes, and the way his hands tremble when he lights his pipe. Can it be that he was ever light of heart and passionate of mind? Was this the man I saw once, in the moonlight, fighting his rival for a faithless woman?

Yes, the agony of the war has left its mark on both of us. The war—and the Grenviles. Maybe Robin is bound to Gartred still, even as I am to Richard. We never speak of these things. Ours is the dull, drab life of day by day.

Oh, God confound and damn these Grenviles for harming everything they touch. Why were they made thus, Richard and Gartred, so that cruelty for its own sake was almost a vice to be indulged in, affording a sensuous delight? Their brother, Bevil, had been so different. The flower of the flock, with his grave courtesy, his thoughtfulness, his rigid code of morality. And his boys take after him. There is no vice in Jack or Bunny that I have ever seen. But Gartred . . . Those serpent's eyes beneath the red-gold hair, that hard, voluptuous mouth; how incredible it seemed to me even in the early days when she was married to my brother Kit that anyone could be deceived by her. Still, her power to charm was devastating. Poor Kit was lost from the beginning, like Robin later. But I was never won, not for a moment.

Well, her beauty is marred now. But rumor has it that she can still find lovers, and she is said to be at least twenty years older than her latest conquest. The idea brings a flash of color into a gray world. And what a world! So many gone, so many penniless, and everywhere the people miserable. The happy aftermath of civil war. Spies of the Lord Protector, Cromwell, in every town and village, and if a breath of protest against the state is heard, the murmurer is borne straight away to jail. Manners are rough, courtesy a forgotten quality; we are each one of us suspicious of our neighbor. O brave new world!

The docile English may endure it for a while, but not we Cornish. We'll have another rising, there'll be more blood spilled and more hearts broken. But we shall still lack our leader. . . . Ah, Richard—my Richard—what evil spirit in you urged you to quarrel with all men, so that even the King is now your enemy? I picture you sitting lonely and bitter at your window, gazing out across the dull, flat lands of Holland. Resentful and proud to the end.

The King's General in the West. The only man I love . . .

It was after the Scillies fell to the Parliament that Jack and Bunny, having visited Holland and France, came down to Tywardreath to pay their respects to me. We talked of Richard, and immediately Jack said, "My uncle is greatly altered; you would hardly know him. He sits for hours in silence, looking out of the window of his dismal lodging, and he has no wish for company."

"The King will never make use of him again, and he knows it," said Bunny.

My heart was aching for Richard, and the boys perceived it. Presently Bunny said in a low tone, "My uncle doesn't speak of young Dick. I suppose we shall never know now what wretched misfortune overtook the boy."

I felt myself grow cold and the old sick horror grip me. "No," I said slowly. "No, we shall never know."

"If," pursued Bunny, as though arguing with himself, "Dick had fallen into enemy hands, why was the fact concealed? That is what puzzles me. The son of Richard Grenvile was a prize indeed."

I did not answer. I felt Jack move restlessly beside me, aware of my distress. "There is little use," he said, "in going over the past. We are making Honor tired."

Soon after, they kissed my hands and left. I watched them gallop away, young and free, and untouched by the years that had gone, the future theirs to seize. One day the King would come back to his waiting country, and Jack and Bunny, who had fought so valiantly for him, would be rewarded. The civil war would be forgotten, and forgotten, too, the generation preceding them, my generation.

It was then that the idea came to me that by writing down the events of those years I would rid myself of a burden. I would tell of the war and how it changed and hopelessly intermingled our lives, how we were all caught up in it and broken by it. Gartred and Robin, Richard and I, the whole Rashleigh family, pent up together in Menabilly, that house of secrets where the drama was played.

There is so much to say and so little time in which to say it. I will say for Richard what he never said for himself, and I will show how, despite his bitter faults and failings, it was possible for a woman to love him with all her heart and mind and body, and I that woman.

THE FIRST TIME I saw Gartred was when my eldest brother, Kit, brought her home to Lanrest as his bride. She was twenty-two and I, the baby of the family except for Percy, a child of ten.

We were a happy, sprawling family, very intimate and free, and my father, John Harris, cared nothing for the affairs of the world, but lived for his horses, his dogs, and the peaceful concerns of his small estate, Lanrest.

The wedding had taken place at Stowe, Gartred's home. Percy and I, because of some childish ailment, had not been present, which created a resentment in me from the first. I can remember sitting upright in bed, my eyes bright with fever, remonstrating with my mother.

"When Cecilia was married, Percy and I carried the train," I said. (Cecilia was my eldest sister.) "And we all of us went to Maddercombe, and the Pollexefens welcomed us."

My mother replied that Stowe was quite another place to Maddercombe, the Grenviles were not the Pollexefens, and she would never forgive herself if we took the fever to Gartred.

Everything was Gartred. Nobody else mattered. There had been a great commotion, too, about preparing the spare chamber for the bride and bridegroom. The servants were made to sweep and dust, the whole place was put into a bustle.

"It's on account of his being heir to his uncle, Sir Christopher at Radford, that she's marrying our young master," was the sentence I overheard amid the clatter in the kitchen. "It's not like a Grenvile to match with a plain Harris of Lanrest."

The words angered and confused me. Why should a Harris of Lanrest be a poor bargain for a Grenvile? For the first time I realized that marriage was not the romantic fairy legend I had imagined, but a bargain between important families, a tying up of property. With my father riding over to Stowe continually, and holding long conferences with lawyers and wearing a worried frown, Kit's marriage was becoming like some frightening affair of state.

Eavesdropping again, I heard the lawyer say, "It is not Sir Bernard Grenvile who is holding out about the settlement, but the daughter herself."

I pondered this awhile, then repeated it to my sister Mary. "Is it usual," I asked, "for a bride to argue thus about her portion?"

Although Mary was twenty, life had barely brushed her as yet, and I doubt if she knew more than I did. But I could see that she was shocked. "Gartred is the only daughter," she said after a moment. "It is perhaps necessary for her to discuss the settlement."

"I wonder if Kit knows of it," I said.

Mary then bade me hold my tongue. I was not to be discouraged, though, and while I refrained from mentioning the marriage settlement to the others, I went to plague Robin—my favorite brother even in those days—to tell me something of the Grenviles. He had just ridden in from hawking and stood in the stable yard, his dear handsome face flushed and happy, the falcon on his wrist.

"Have you reached the ripe age of ten, Honor," he inquired, "without knowing that in Cornwall there are only two families who count for anything—the Grenviles and the Arundells?" The bird watched me from beneath its great hooded lids, and Robin smiled and reached out his other hand to touch my curls. Then he said, "If I had been the eldest son, I would have been the bridegroom at this wedding." His smile had gone.

"Why? Did she like you best?" I asked.

He placed the hood over his bird and gave her to the keeper. When he picked me up in his arms he was smiling again. "Come and pick cherries," he said, "and never mind my brother's bride."

More than that I could not drag from him.

The next week they were all gone to Stowe for the wedding. Upon their return, as I had feared, my mother pleaded fatigue, as did the rest of them, and only my third sister, Bridget, unbent to me at all.

"This place is like a steward's lodge compared to Stowe," she told me. "You could put Lanrest in one pocket of the grounds there, and it would not be noticed."

"But Gartred, what of Gartred?" I said with impatience.

"I think Father was a little lost," she whispered. "All the men were so richly attired, somehow he seemed drab beside them."

"Never mind Father," I said. "I want to hear of Gartred."

Bridget smiled, superior in her knowledge. "I like Bevil the best," she said, "and so does everyone. They are all auburn-haired, you know. If we saw anyone with auburn hair, it was sure to be a Grenvile. I did not care for the one they called Richard."

"Why not? Was he so ugly?" I asked.

"No," she answered, "he was more handsome than Bevil. But he looked at us all in a mocking, contemptuous way. They told me at Stowe he was a soldier."

"But you still have not described Gartred," I said.

"Oh, I am too weary to tell you more until morning," she said. "But Mary and Cecilia and I are agreed upon one thing, that we would sooner resemble Gartred than any other woman."

So in the end I had to form my own judgment with my own eyes. We were all gathered in the hall to receive them—they had gone first from Stowe to my uncle's estate at Radford, the other side of Plymouth. The dogs ran out into the courtyard as they heard the horses. We were a large party because the Pollexefens were with us. Cecilia had her baby, Joan, in her arms—my first godchild, and I was proud of the honor—and we were all one happy, laughing family. Kit swung himself down from the saddle—he looked very debonair and gay—and I saw Gartred. She murmured something to Kit, who laughed and colored and held out his arms to help her dismount, and in a flash of intuition I knew Kit was not ours anymore, but belonged to her.

I hung back, reluctant to be introduced, and suddenly she was beside me, her cool hand under my chin.

"So you are Honor?" she said. Her inflection suggested that I was disappointing in some special way. She passed on to the big parlor, the remainder of the family following like fascinated moths. Percy, being a boy and goggle-eyed at beauty, went to her at once, and she put a sweetmeat in his mouth. She has them ready, I thought, to bribe us children as one bribes strange dogs.

"Would Honor like one, too?" She seemed to know instinctively that this treating of me as a baby was what I hated most.

I could not take my eyes from her face. She reminded me of something, and suddenly I knew. I was a tiny child again at Radford, my uncle's great barracks of a place, and he was walking me through the greenhouses in the gardens. There was one flower, an orchid, that grew alone; it was the loveliest flower I had ever seen. I stretched out my hand to stroke the soft velvet sheen, but my uncle pulled me back. "Don't touch it, child. The stem is poisonous."

Gartred was like that orchid. When she offered me the sweetmeat, I turned away, shaking my head, and my father said sharply, "Honor, where are your manners?"

Gartred laughed and shrugged her shoulders. Everyone turned reproving eyes upon me; even Robin frowned. That was how Gartred came to Lanrest. . . .

The marriage lasted for three years. They were more often at Radford and Stowe than at Lanrest, but when Gartred came home, I swear she cast a blight upon the place.

There were no children of the marriage. My sister Cecilia came to us regularly for her lying-in, but there was never a rumor of Gartred. She rode and went hawking as we did, never keeping to her room or complaining of fatigue. Once my mother had the hardihood to say, "When I was first wed, Gartred, I neither rode nor hunted, for fear I should miscarrry," and Gartred said, "I have nothing within me to lose, madam, and for that you had better blame your son." Her voice was low and full of venom, and my mother, bewildered, rose and left the room in distress. Soon afterward Kit came in and said to Gartred in a tone loaded with reproach, "Have you accused me to my mother?"

From that moment Kit's nature seemed to change. He wore a harassed air, wretchedly unlike himself, and his abject humility before Gartred made him despicable to my intolerant eyes.

We did not see them much, but when they did come to Lanrest, there was continual strain, and once a heated quarrel between Kit and Robin on a night when my parents were from home. It was midsummer, very stifling and warm, and I, playing truant from my nursery, crept down to the garden in my nightgown. The casement of the guest chamber was open wide, and I heard Kit's voice lifted in argument.

"Wherever we go," he said, "you make a fool of me before all men. I cannot endure it longer."

I heard Gartred laugh and I saw Kit's shadow reflected on the ceiling by the quivering candlelight.

"You think I remark nothing," he said. "You think I have sunk so low that to keep you near me, and to be allowed to touch you sometimes, I will shut my eyes to everyone. Do you think it was pleasant for me at Stowe to see how you looked upon Antony Denys? And this evening I saw you smiling across the table at my own brother."

I heard a step on the paving, and there was Robin standing beside me in the darkness. "Go away," he whispered to me, "go away at once."

Suddenly Kit's voice cried out, loud and horrible, "If that happens, I shall kill you. I swear to God I shall kill you."

Then Robin, swift as an arrow, stooped, took a stone in his hand, and flung it against the casement, shivering the glass to fragments. "Damn you for a coward, then," he shouted. "Come and kill me instead."

I looked up and saw Kit's face, white and tortured, and behind him Gartred with her hair loose on her shoulders. It was a picture to be imprinted always on my mind, those two there at the window, and Robin suddenly different from the brother I had always known and loved, breathing defiance and contempt. I was filled with hatred for Gartred, who had brought the storm to pass and remained untouched by it.

The next year smallpox swept through Cornwall like a scourge, and few families were spared. In June my father was stricken, dying within a few days, and we had scarcely recovered from the blow before messages came to us from my uncle at Radford to say that Kit had been seized with the same dread disease, and there was no hope of his recovery.

Father and son thus died within a few weeks of each other, and my second brother, Jo, the scholar, became the head of the family. When the two wills came to be read, both Kit's and my father's, we learned that although Lanrest, with Radford later, passed to Jo, the rich pasturelands of Lametton and the Mill were to remain in Gartred's keeping for her lifetime.

She came down with her brother Bevil for the reading, and even Cecilia, the gentlest of my sisters, remarked afterward upon the niggardly manner with which she saw to the measuring of every acre down at Lametton. The morning before she left, some impulse prompted me to hesitate before her chamber, the door of which was open. She had claimed that the contents of the room belonged to Kit, and so to her, and the servants, the day before, had taken down the hangings and removed the pieces of furniture she most desired. At this last moment she was alone, turning out a little secretaire that stood in one corner, and I saw the mask off her lovely face at last. Eyes narrow, lips protruding, she wrenched open a small drawer with such force that the hinge came loose. There were some trinkets at the back of the drawer— none, I think, of great value, but she had remembered them. Suddenly she saw my face reflected in the mirror.

"If you leave to us the bare walls, we shall be well content," I said as her eyes met mine.

"You always played the spy, from the first," she said softly.

"I was born with eyes in my head."

Slowly she put the jewels in a little pouch she wore hanging from her waist. "Take comfort and be thankful you are quit of me now," she said. "We are not likely to see each other again."

"I hope not," I told her.

Suddenly she laughed. "It were a pity," she said, "that your brother did not have a little of your spirit."

"Which brother?" I asked.

She paused, uncertain what I knew. Then, smiling, she tapped my cheek with her long slim finger. "All of them," she said.

She left Lanrest at noon, in a litter, with a great train of horses and servants from Stowe to carry her belongings.

"That's over," I said to myself. "That's the last of them. We have done with the Grenviles."

But fate willed otherwise.

CHAPTER TWO

M Y EIGHTEENTH BIRTHDAY. A bright December day in the year 1628. My spirits soaring like a bird, I looked out across the dazzling sea and watched His Majesty's fleet, returning from France, sail into Plymouth Sound. What a sight they were, some eighty ships or more, white sails bellying in the west wind, each carrying on her mainmast the standard of the officer in command. As the vessels drew opposite the fort at Mount Batten, they would be greeted with a salvo from the great guns and would dip their colors in a return salute. The people gathered on the cliffs waved and shouted, drums beat, bugles sounded, and the ships were seen to be thronged with soldiers pressing against the high bulwarks, clinging to the stout rigging.

The leading ship, a great three-masted vessel, carried the commander of the expedition, the Duke of Buckingham. She dropped anchor, swinging to the wind, and the other ships followed her, the sun gleaming upon their ornamental carvings.

Suddenly there was silence, and on the flagship commanded by the duke someone snapped an order. The soldiers who had crowded the bulwarks moved as one man, forming into line amidships. There came another order and the single tattoo of a drum; in one movement, it seemed, the landing boats were manned and lowered into the water. The maneuver had taken perhaps three minutes; and the perfect discipline of the whole proceeding drew from the crowd about us the biggest cheer yet.

"I thought as much," said a fellow below me. "Only one man in the West could turn an unruly rabble into soldiers fit for His Majesty's Bodyguard. There go the Grenvile coat of arms, hoisted beneath the duke's standards." Even as he spoke, I saw the scarlet pennant run up to the masthead, and as it streamed into the wind, the sun shone upon three gold rests.

"A fine finish to your birthday," said my brother Jo with a smile when we had returned to Radford. "We are all bidden to a banquet tonight at Plymouth Castle, at the command of the Duke of Buckingham."

Jo stood on the steps of the house to greet us, having ridden back from the fortress at Mount Batten. He had succeeded to the estate at Radford, my uncle Christopher having died a few years back, and much of our time now was spent between Plymouth and Lanrest. Jo had become a person of some importance, in Devon especially, and besides being undersheriff for the county, he had married an heiress into the bargain, Elizabeth Champernowne.

That night we embarked below the fortress and took a boat across the Cattwater to the castle. All Plymouth seemed to be upon the water or on the battlements. When we landed, we found the townsfolk pressing about the castle entrance and soldiers everywhere, laughing and talking with girls, who had decked them with flowers and ribbons for festivity.

In a moment we were in the great banquet hall with voices sounding hollow and strange beneath the vaulted roof. Now and again would ring out the clear voice of a gentleman-at-arms, "Way for the Duke of Buckingham," and a passage would be cleared for the commander as he passed among the guests, holding court even as His Majesty himself might do. The scene was colorful, exciting, and to my youthful fancy, it seemed that all this glittering display was somehow a tribute to my eighteenth birthday.

"How lovely it is. Are you not glad we came?" I said to Mary, who was my only unwed sister, now that Bridget, too, had married into a Devon family. I pressed forward, devouring everything with my eyes, when suddenly the crowd parted, a way was cleared and the duke's retinue was upon us, with the duke himself not half a yard away.

Mary, always reserved amid strangers, was gone, and I was left alone to bar his path. I stood an instant, and then, losing my composure, I curtsied low, as though to King Charles himself. Laughter floated above my head. Raising my eyes, I saw my brother Jo, his face a strange mixture of amusement and dismay, leaning toward me to help me to my feet, for I had curtsied so low that I was hard upon my heels and could not rise.

"May I present my sister Honor, Your Grace," I heard him say. "This is, in point of fact, her eighteenth birthday, and her first venture into society."

The Duke of Buckingham bowed gravely and, lifting my hand to his lips, wished me good fortune. "It may be your sister's first venture, my dear Harris," he said graciously, "but with beauty such as she possesses, you must see to it that it is not the last." He continued on in a wave of perfume and velvet, with my brother beside him, and as I swore under my breath, or possibly not under my breath but indiscreetly, someone behind me said, "If you care to come out onto the battlements, I will show you how to do that as it should be done." I whipped around, indignant. Looking down upon me from six feet or more, with a sardonic smile upon his face, was an officer still clad in breastplate of silver, worn over a blue tunic, with a blue-and-silver sash. His eyes were golden brown, his hair dark auburn, and his ears were pierced with small gold rings, like a Turkish bandit.

"Do you mean you would show me how to curtsy or how to swear?" I said to him in fury.

"Why, both, if you wish it," he answered. "Your performance at the first was lamentable, and at the second merely amateur."

His rudeness rendered me speechless. I turned and pushed through the crowd, making for the entrance. Then I heard the mocking voice behind me once again: "Way for Mistress Honor Harris of Lanrest." People looked at me astonished, falling back in spite of themselves, and so I walked on with flaming cheeks, scarce knowing what I was doing, and found myself in the cold air upon the battlements that looked out onto Plymouth Sound. My odious companion was with me still.

"So you are the little maid my sister so detested," he said.

"Who are you?" I said to him.

"Sir Richard Grenvile," he replied, "a colonel in His Majesty's Army, and knighted for extreme gallantry in the field."

"A pity," I said, "that your manners do not match your courage."

"And that your deportment does not equal your looks."

This stung me to fresh fury, and I let fly a string of oaths that I had once heard Jo or Robin, under great provocation, loose upon the stablemen. But if I had hoped to make Richard Grenvile blanch, I was wasting my breath.

"The English tongue is not fit for the occasion," he said. "Spanish is more graceful and far more satisfying to the temper. Listen to this." And he began to swear in Spanish, a stream of lovely-sounding oaths. "You must admit," he said, breaking off, "that I have you beaten." His smile, no longer sardonic but disarming, had me beaten, too, and my anger died within me. "Come look at the fleet," he said. "A ship at anchor is a lovely thing."

We went to the battlements and stared out across the sound. The ships, motionless upon the water, stood out in the moonlight, carved and clear.

"Were your losses very great at La Rochelle?" I asked him.

"No more than I expected in an expedition that was bound to be abortive," he answered, shrugging. "The only fellows who distinguished themselves were those in the regiment I have the honor to command, but as no other officer but myself insists on discipline, it was small wonder the attack proved a failure."

His self-assurance was as astounding as his former rudeness.

"Do you talk thus to your superiors?" I asked.

"Invariably," he answered. "That is why, although I am not yet twenty-nine, I am already the most detested officer in His Majesty's

Army." He turned away from the battlement. "Come now," he said, "let us see if you can curtsy better to me than you did to the duke. Take your gown in your hands, thus. Bend your right knee, thus. And allow your somewhat insignificant posterior to sink upon your left leg, thus."

I obeyed him, shaking with laughter; it seemed ridiculous that a colonel in His Majesty's Army should be teaching me deportment upon the battlements of Plymouth Castle.

"It is no laughing matter," he said gravely. "A clumsy woman looks so damnably ill-bred. There now, that is excellent. Once again. . . . Perfection." With appalling coolness he straightened my gown and rearranged the lace around my shoulders. "I object to dining with untidy women," he murmured.

"I have no intention of sitting down with you to dine," I replied with spirit.

"No one else will ask you, I can vouch for that." He marched me back into the castle. We were conspicuous as we entered, for the guests were already seated at the long tables in the banquet hall. My usual composure fled from me. "Let us go back," I pleaded, tugging at his arm. "See, the seats are all filled."

"Go back? Not on your life. I want my dinner." He pushed his way past the servants, nearly lifting me from my feet, as hundreds of faces stared at us. I could do nothing but hurry forward, tripping over my gown, borne on the relentless arm of Richard Grenvile to the far end of the hall where the Duke of Buckingham, and the nobility of Cornwall and Devon, such as they were, feasted with decorum, above the common herd.

"You are taking me to the high table," I protested.

"I'm damned if I'm going to dine anywhere else," he said. "Way there, please, for Sir Richard Grenvile." Chairs were pulled forward, people squeezed aside, and somehow we were seated at the table a hand's stretch from the duke himself.

I prayed for death, but it did not come. Instead I took the roast swan that was heaped upon my platter. The Duke of Buckingham turned to me, glass in hand. "I wish you many, many happy returns of the day," he said. I murmured my thanks and shook my curls to hide my flaming cheeks.

Richard ate with evident enjoyment, but I tasted nothing of what I ate or drank. At length the ordeal was over, and I felt myself pulled to my feet by my companion. The wine, which I had swallowed as though it were water, had made jelly of my legs, and I was obliged to lean upon him for support. I have scant memory indeed of what followed next. I have a shaming recollection of being assisted to some inner apartment of the castle, suitably darkened and discreet, where nature took her toll of me and the roast swan knew me no more. I opened my eyes and found myself upon a couch, with Richard Grenvile holding my hand and dabbing my forehead with his kerchief.

"You must learn to carry your wine," he said severely.

I felt very ill and very shamed, and tears were near the surface. "I have n-never eaten roast swan b-before," I stammered.

"It was not so much the swan as the Burgundy," he murmured. "Lie still now, you will be easier by and by." In truth, my head was still reeling, and I was grateful for his strong hand.

"Lean against my shoulder so," he said. "Poor little one, what an ending to an eighteenth birthday." He laughed, and yet his voice and hands were strangely tender.

"You are like your brother, Bevil, after all," I said.

"Not I," he answered. "Bevil is a gentleman, and I a scoundrel. I have always been the black sheep of the family."

"What of Gartred?" I asked.

"Gartred is a law unto herself," he replied. "You must have learned that when she was wedded to your brother."

"I hated her with all my heart," I told him.

"Small blame to you for that," he answered me.

"And is she content, now that she is wed again?" I asked him.

"Gartred will never be content," he said. "She was born greedy. She had an eye to Antony Denys, her husband now, long before your brother died."

I sat up and rearranged my curls, while he helped me with my gown. "You have been kind to me," I said, grown suddenly prim. "Perhaps, now, you had better take me to my brothers."

"Perhaps I had," he said.

I stumbled out of the little dark chamber to the lighted corridor. He looked down at me, smiling. "I will tell you one thing," he said. "I have never sat with a woman before while she vomited."

"Nor I so disgraced myself before a man," I said with dignity.

Then he bent suddenly and lifted me in his arms like a child. "Nor have I ever lay hidden in a darkened room with anyone so fair as you, Honor, and not made love to her," he told me. He held me for a moment against his heart, then set me on my feet again. "And now, if you permit it, I will take you home."

That is, I think, a very clear and truthful account of my first meeting with Richard Grenvile.

WITHIN A WEEK of the encounter just recorded I was sent back to my mother at Lanrest, supposedly in disgrace for my ill behavior. Such conduct would, my mother said severely, condemn me possibly for all time in the eyes of the world, and had my father been alive, he would more than likely have packed me off to the nuns for two or three years. As it was, she was left lamenting that, since both my married sisters, Cecilia and Bridget, were expecting to lie in again and could not receive me, I must stay at home. And home seemed to me very dull, since Robin had remained at Radford and my young brother, Percy, was still at Oxford.

I remember it was some weeks after I returned, a day in early spring when I had gone out to sulk in the apple tree, a favorite hiding place of childhood, that I observed a horseman riding up the valley. I scrambled down from the tree and caught a glimpse of a tall figure passing into the house. I followed, ready to eavesdrop at the parlor door, but encountered my mother on the stairs.

"You will please to go to your chamber, Honor, and remain there until my visitor has gone," she said gravely.

Afire with curiosity, I went silently upstairs. Once there, I rang for Matty, the maid who had served me and my sisters for some years now and had become my special ally. Her ears were nearly as long as mine, and she guessed at once why I wanted her. "I'll bide in the hallway when he comes out and get his name for you," she said. "A tall, big gentleman he was, a fine man, wearing a blue cloak slashed with silver."

Blue and silver. Grenvile colors. "Was his hair red, Matty?"

"You could warm your hands at it," she answered.

I sent Matty below, and paced up and down my chamber in great impatience. Very soon I heard the door of the parlor open and his footsteps pass through the hallway to the courtyard. It seemed eternity before Matty reappeared, her eyes bright with information. She brought forth a screwed-up piece of paper from beneath her apron, and with it a silver piece. "He told me to give you the note and keep the crown."

I unfolded the note, furtive as a criminal, and read:

Dear Sister, Although Gartred has exchanged a Harris for a Denys, I count myself still your brother, and reserve for myself the right of calling upon you. Your good mother, it seems, thinks otherwise. It is not my custom to ride some ten miles to no purpose; therefore, you will direct your maid forthwith to conduct me to some part of your domain where we can converse together unobserved. Your brother and servant, Richard Grenvile.

My first thought was to send no answer, but curiosity and a beating heart got the better of my pride. I bade Matty show the visitor the orchard. No sooner had she gone than I heard my mother's footsteps on the stairs.

"Sir Richard Grenvile, with whom you conducted yourself in so unseemly a fashion in Plymouth, has just departed," she said. "It seems he has left the Army for a while and intends to reside near to us at Killigarth."

I did not answer.

"I have never heard any good of him," said my mother. "He has always caused his family concern, being constantly in debt. He will hardly make us a pleasant neighbor."

"He is, at least, a very gallant soldier," I said warmly.

"That may be," she answered, "but I have no wish for him to ride over here, demanding to see you, when your brothers are from home. It shows great want of delicacy on his part."

With that she left me. In a few moments I was tiptoeing down the stairs into the garden. I then flew to the orchard and was soon safe in the apple tree. Presently I heard someone moving about below, and parting the blossoms in my hiding place, I saw Richard Grenvile stooping under the low branches. I broke off a twig and threw it at him, hitting him upon the nose. "Damn it—" he began, when, looking up, he saw me laughing at him from the apple tree. In a moment he had swung himself up beside me and with one arm around my waist had me pinned against the trunk. The branch cracked ominously.

"Descend at once. The branch will not hold us both," I said.

"It will if you keep still," he told me. To remain still meant that I must continue to lie crushed against his chest, with his arm around me and his face not six inches away from mine.

"We cannot possibly converse in such a fashion," I protested.

"Why not? I find it very pleasant," he answered. "Now, what

have you to tell me?" he said, for all the world as though it were I who had demanded the interview and not he.

I then recounted my disgrace, and how it seemed as if I must now be treated as a prisoner in my own home. "And it is no use your coming here again," I added, "for my mother will never let me see you. It seems you are a person of ill repute."

"How so?" he demanded.

"You are constantly in debt; those were her words."

"The Grenviles are never not in debt. It is the great failing of the family. What else did your mother say?"

"That it showed want of delicacy to come here asking to see me when my brothers are from home."

"She is wrong. It showed great cunning, born of long experience." He loosened his hold upon the branch and flicked at the collar of my gown. "You have an earwig running down your bosom," he said.

I drew back, disconcerted. "I believe my mother to be right," I said stiffly. "I think little is to be gained from our further acquaintance, and it would be best to put an end to it now."

"You cannot descend unless I let you," he said, and in truth I was locked there, with his legs across the branch. Then he laughed, and taking my face in his hands, he kissed me very suddenly, which, being a novelty to me and strangely pleasant, rendered me for a few moments incapable of speech or action.

"You can go now if you desire it," he said.

I did not desire it but had too much pride to tell him so. He swung himself to the ground and lifted me down beside him. Then he said, "If you bid your gardener trim that upper branch, we would do better another time."

"I am not certain," I answered, "that I wish for another time."

"Ah, but you do," he said, "and so do I. Besides, my horse needs exercise." He turned through the trees, making for the gate where he had left his horse, and I followed him silently through the long grass. He reached for the bridle and climbed into the saddle. "I will come again on Tuesday," he said. "Remember those instructions to the gardener." He waved his gauntlet at me and was gone.

I stood staring after him, telling myself that he was quite as detestable as Gartred and that I would never see him more; but for all my resolutions, I was there again on Tuesday. . . .

There followed then as strange and, to my mind, as sweet a wooing as ever maiden of my generation had. Once a week, and sometimes twice, he would ride over to Lanrest from Killigarth, and there, cradled in the apple tree—with the offending branch lopped as he had demanded—he tutored me in love, and I responded. He was but twenty-eight, and I eighteen. Looking back, it seems odd that our hiding place was not discovered. Maybe in his lavish fashion he showered gold pieces on the servants; certainly my mother passed her days in placid ignorance.

And then, one day in early April, my brothers Jo and Robin, and Jo's wife, Elizabeth, rode from Radford, bringing with them Edward Champernowne, a younger brother of Elizabeth's. I was happy to see my family but in no mood to exchange courtesies with a stranger—besides, his teeth protruded. After we had dined, Jo and Robin and my mother, with Edward Champernowne, withdrew to the book room that had been my father's, and I was left alone to entertain Elizabeth. She proceeded to praise her brother, who, she told me, had but recently left Oxford.

Later in the evening I was summoned to my mother's room. Jo was with her, and Robin, too, but Edward Champernowne had gone to join his sister. All three of them wore an air of well-being.

My mother kissed me fondly and said at once that great happiness was in store for me. Edward had asked for my hand in marriage, she and my brothers had accepted, and nothing remained now but to determine the date. I broke out wildly in a torrent of protestation, declaring that I would not wed him, that I would wed no man who was not of my own choice. In vain my mother argued with me; in vain Jo enthused upon the virtues of young Champernowne, and said my conduct had been such that it was amazing he should have asked for my hand at all.

"I tell you I will not marry him," I said.

Robin had not taken part in the conversation; now he rose and stood beside me, saying, "I told you, Jo, it would be little use to drive Honor if she had not the inclination. Give her time to accustom herself to the project, and she will think better of it."

"Champernowne might think better of it, too," replied Jo.

"It were best to settle it now while he is here," said my mother.

I looked at their worried, indecisive faces—for they all loved me well and were distressed at my obduracy—but "No," I told them, "I would sooner die." I flounced from the room, went to my chamber and thrust the bolt through the door. I waited till the whole brood of them were abed, and then, after changing my gown and wrapping a cloak about me, I stole from the house. For I was bent upon a harebrained scheme, which was no less than walking through the night to Killigarth, and so to Richard. I set off with beating heart down the roadway to the river, which I forded a mile or so below Lanrest. Then I struck westward, but the way was rough and crossed with intersecting lanes, and without star lore I had no knowledge of direction. I was ill used to walking any distance, and my shoes were thin. The night seemed endless and the road interminable, and dawn found me stranded by another stream.

About six o'clock I met a plowman tramping along the highway who pointed out the lane that led to Killigarth. I saw the tall chimneys of the house, and my heart misgave me for the sorry figure I should make before Richard. I came to the house like a thief and stood before the windows, uncertain what to do. I heard a clatter in the kitchens, the sound of laughter, men talking, and I wished with all my heart that I were back in my bedchamber in Lanrest. But there was no returning. I pulled the bell and heard the clanging echo through the house. Then I drew back as a servant came into the hall. "What do you want?" he asked of me.

"I wish to see Sir Richard," I said.

"Sir Richard and the rest of the gentlemen are at breakfast. Away with you now, he won't be troubled with you."

"I must see Sir Richard," I insisted, desperate now and near to tears, and then, as the fellow was about to thrust me from the door, Richard himself came out into the hall.

"Richard," I called, "it is I, Honor."

He came forward, amazement on his face. "What the devil—" he began; then, cursing his servant to be gone, he drew me into a little anteroom.

"What is it, what is the matter?" he said swiftly, and I, weak and utterly worn out, fell into his arms and wept. "Softly now, my love, be easy," he murmured, stroking my hair until I was calm enough to speak.

"They want to marry me to Edward Champernowne," I stammered, "and I have told them I will not do so, and I have wandered all night on the roads to tell you of it."

I felt him shake with laughter.

"Is that all?" he asked. "And did you tramp ten miles or more to tell me that? Oh, Honor, my little love, my dear."

I looked up at him, bewildered that he found so serious a matter food for laughter. "What am I to do, then?" I said.

"Why, tell them to go to the devil," he answered, "and if you dare not say it, then I will say it for you. Come in to breakfast."

I tugged at his hand in consternation, for God only knew what his friends would say to me. But, ignoring my protests, he dragged me into the dining room where the gentlemen were breakfasting.

"This is Honor Harris of Lanrest," he said. "You gentlemen are possibly acquainted with her." They all stood up and bowed, astonishment and embarrassment written plain upon their faces. "She has run away from home," said Richard. Somehow they all made their excuses and got themselves from the room, and we were alone.

"I was a fool to come," I said. "Now I have disgraced you before all your friends."

"I was disgraced long since," he said, "but it was well you came after breakfast rather than before."

"Why so?" I asked.

"I have sold Killigarth, and the lands I hold in Tywardreath," he answered. "Jonathan Rashleigh gave me a fair price. Had you blundered in sooner, he might have stayed his hand."

"Will the money pay your debts?" I said.

He laughed derisively. "A drop in the ocean," he said. "But it will suffice for a week or so, until we can borrow elsewhere."

"Why we?" I inquired.

"Well, we shall be together," he answered. "You do not think I am going to permit this ridiculous match with Edward Champernowne?" He held out his arms to me and I went to him.

"Dear love," I said, feeling suddenly very old and very wise, "you have told me often that you must marry an heiress or you cannot live."

"I should have no wish to live if you were wedded to another."

"We shall be penniless," I protested, thinking of the deeds, the lawyers and the documents that went with marriage. "I am the youngest daughter, Richard. My portion will be very small."

At this he shouted with laughter and lifted me in his arms. "It's your person I have designs upon," he said. "Damn your portion."

O WILD BETROTHAL, startling and swift, decided on in an instant, and all objections swept aside like a forest in a fire! My mother helpless before the onslaught, my brothers powerless to obstruct. The Champernownes, offended, withdrew to Radford, and Jo, washing his hands of me, went with them.

Richard was for taking horse to London and giving me refuge with the Duke of Buckingham, who would, he declared, eat out of his hand and give me a dowry into the bargain, but at this moment of folly Bevil came riding to Lanrest, and with his usual courtesy insisted that I go to Stowe and be married from the Grenvile home. Bevil's approval lent some smacking of decency to the whole proceeding, and within a few days my mother and I were housed at Stowe, where Kit had gone as a bridegroom nearly eight years before. I swam through the grandeur of Stowe aglow with confidence, bowing to the Grenvile kinsmen, listening while old Sir Bernard discoursed upon the troubles brewing between His Majesty and Parliament. And I remember standing for hours in the chambers of Lady Grace, Bevil's wife, while her woman pinned and gathered and tucked my wedding gown.

Richard was not much with me. I belonged to the women, he said, during these last days; we would have enough of each other by and by. *These last days*—what words of prophecy.

Nothing, then, remains out of the fog of recollection but that final afternoon in May. I can see now the guests assembled on the lawns, and how we all proceeded to the falconry for an afternoon of sport that was to precede a banquet in the evening.

There were the goshawks on their perches, preening their feathers, and farther removed, solitary upon their blocks in the sand, their larger brethren, the wild-eyed peregrines. The falconers came to leash and jess the hawks, and hood them for the chase. The stablemen brought the horses for us, and the dogs that were to flush the game yelped and pranced about their heels.

As Richard mounted me upon the little chestnut mare that was to be mine hereafter, a conclave of horsemen gathered about the gate to welcome a new arrival. "What now?" said Richard, and his falconer, shading his eyes from the sun, turned with a smile and said, "It's Mrs. Denys, from Orley Court. Now you can match your red hawk with her tiercel."

They were riding down the path toward us, and I wondered how she would seem to me, my childhood enemy.

"Greetings, sister," called Richard. "So you have come to dance at my wedding after all."

"Perhaps," Gartred answered, riding abreast of me, that slow smile that I remembered on her face. "How are you, Honor?"

"Well enough," I answered.

"I never thought to see you become a Grenvile. How strange the ways of Providence. . . . You have not met my husband."

I bowed to the stranger at her side, a big, bluff, hearty man a good deal older than herself. So this was the Antony Denys who had caused poor Kit so much anguish before he died.

"Where do we ride?" she asked, turning from me to Richard.

"In the open country, toward the shore," he answered.

She glanced at the falcon on his wrist. "A red hawk?" she said.

"I propose to put her to a heron today if we can flush one."

Gartred smiled. "A red hawk at a heron," she mocked. "You will see her check at a magpie and nothing larger."

"Will you match her with your tiercel?"

"My tiercel will destroy her, and the heron afterward."

They watched each other like duelists about to strike, and I had my first shadow of misgiving that the day would turn in some way to disaster.

We rode out to the open country. At first nothing larger than a woodcock was flushed, and to this were flown the goshawks. "Come," said Gartred scornfully, "can we find no better quarry and so let fly the falcons?"

Richard shaded his eyes from the sun and looked toward the west. A long strip of moorland lay before us, rough and uneven, and at the far end of it a narrow soggy marsh, where at all seasons of the year, so Richard told me, the seabirds came, curlews and gulls and herons. The marsh was still two miles away.

"I'll match my horse to yours, and my red hawk to your tiercel," said Richard suddenly, and even as he spoke, he let fly the hood of his falcon and slipped her, and put spurs to his horse. Within ten seconds Gartred had followed suit. Her gray-winged peregrine soared into the sun, and she and Richard were galloping across the moors toward the marsh. My mare, excited by the clattering hooves of her companions, took charge of me and raced like a mad thing in pursuit of the horses ahead of us, the yelping of the dogs and the cries of the falconers whipping her speed. My last ride . . . I could see Richard and Gartred racing neck to neck, flinging insults at each other as they rode, and in the sky the male and female falcons pitched and hovered, when suddenly away from the marsh ahead of us rose a heron, his great gray wings unfolding, his legs trailing. In an instant it seemed the hawks had seen their quarry, for they both began to circle above the heron, climbing higher and still higher, swinging out in rings until they were like black dots against the sun.

I tried to rein in my mare but could not stop her. Gartred and Richard had turned eastward, following the course of the heron, and now we were galloping three abreast, the ground ever rising toward a circle of stones in the midst of the moor.

"Beware the chasm," shouted Richard in my ear, pointing with his whip, but he was past me like the wind.

I tried to swerve, but the mare had the mastery, and I shouted to Gartred as she passed me, "Which way the chasm?" but she did not answer me. On we flew toward the circle of stone, the sun blinding my eyes, and out of the darkening sky fell the dying heron and the blood-bespattered tiercel, straight into the yawning crevice that opened out before me. I heard Richard shout and a thousand voices singing in my ears as I fell.

It was thus, then, that I, Honor Harris of Lanrest, became a cripple, losing all power in my legs from that day forward until this day on which I write, so that for some twenty-five years now I have been upon my back, or upright in a chair, never walking more or feeling the ground beneath my feet.

CHAPTER THREE

IT IS NOT MY purpose to survey here the suffering I underwent during those early months when my life seemed finished. It is enough to say that they feared at first for my brain, and I lived for many weeks in a state of darkness. As little by little clarity returned and I was able to understand the full significance of my physical state, I asked for Richard; I learned that after having waited in vain for some sign from me, some thread of hope from the doctors that I might recover, he had been persuaded by Bevil to rejoin his regiment. This was for the best. It was impossible for him to remain inactive. By the time he returned, I was home again at Lanrest and had sufficient strength of will to make my decision for the future. This was never to see Richard again. I wrote him first a letter, which he disregarded, riding down from London expressly to see me. I would not see him. He endeavored to force his way into my room, but my brothers barred the way. It was only when the doctors told him that his presence could but injure me further that he realized the finality of all bonds between us. He rode away without a word. I received from him one last letter, wild, bitter, reproachful—then silence.

In November of that year he married Lady Howard of Fitzford, a rich widow, three times wed already, and four years older than himself. I only hoped that her experience would make him happy, and her wealth ensure him some security.

Meanwhile I had to school myself to a new way of living and a day-by-day immobility. My family were all most good and tender. Percy returned from Oxford about this time; with his aid and his books I set myself the task of learning Latin and Greek. My sisters and their children, stung with pity at first, became easy in my presence. And Matty, my little maid, became my untiring bondswoman. After three years my back had so far strengthened that I was able to sit upright and move my upper body. I was helpless, though, in my legs, and during the autumn and the winter months I would feel the damp in my bones, which caused me great pain at times. Then Matty would stand like a sentinel at the door and bar the way to all intruders.

It was my dear, good Robin, my constant companion, who first thought to make a chair to propel me from room to room. He took some months designing it, and when it was built and I was carried to it and could sit up straight and move the rolling wheels without assistance, his joy, I think, was even greater than my own.

In 'thirty-two we had another wedding in the family. My sister Mary accepted the offer of Jonathan Rashleigh of Menabilly, who had lost his first wife in childbed the year before and was left with a growing family. It was a most suitable match. She was married from Lanrest, and with their father to the wedding came his children, Alice and John.

To the wedding also came Bevil Grenvile, close friend to Jonathan as he was to all of us, and I had a chance to speak with him alone. I asked him, not without some trepidation, how Richard did.

"I had not wished to speak of it," Bevil said at length. "All has gone very ill with him, Honor, ever since his marriage."

"How so?" I asked. "Has he not a son?"

For I had heard that a boy had been born to them a year or so before, on May 16 to be exact, the very date on which I had been crippled. I remember crying all night upon my pillow when I was told of it, thinking of the boy who, but for the workings of destiny, might have been mine.

"Yes," he answered, "he has a son, and a daughter, too, but whether Richard sees them or not I cannot say. He has quarreled with his wife, even laid violent hands upon her, so she says, and she is now petitioning for a divorce against him."

"How was Richard violent?" I asked. "Irresponsible and wild, perhaps, but nothing worse. His wife must have provoked him."

"As to that, I know nothing. She is a woman of some malice and of doubtful morals. But the truth is that Richard married Mary Howard for her money, then found he had no control over her purse or her property, the whole being in the power of trustees."

"Then he is no whit better off than he was before?" I asked.

"Rather worse, if anything," replied Bevil.

It was a sorry picture. That Richard should ill-use his wife was an ugly fact to face, but, having some inkling of his worse self, I guessed this to be true. He had married her without love and in bitterness of heart, and she, suspecting his motive, had taken care to disappoint him. What a rock of mutual trust on which to build a lasting union! I held to my resolve, though, and sent him no word of sympathy or understanding. Such a course was wisest, for he must lead his own life, in which I had no further part.

In the autumn of the following year we heard that Richard had left England for the Continent. There he saw service with the King of Sweden.

How much I thought of him and yearned for him during those intervening years does not matter to this story. Time heals all wounds, say the complacent, but I think it is not so much time as determination of the spirit. Five, ten, fifteen years—a large slice out of a woman's life. I had been a maid, and a rebellious, disorderly one at that, when I was first crippled; but in the year of 1642, when the war that was to alter all our lives broke forth, I was a woman of some two and thirty years, and a figure of some importance to the family at large. I came to be, after my mother died, the one who made decisions, whose authority was asked on all occasions, and it seemed that a legendary quality was woven about my personality, as though my physical helplessness must give me greater wisdom.

I accepted the homage with my tongue in my cheek but was careful not to destroy the fond illusion. The young people liked me, I think, because they knew me to be a rebel still, and when there was strife within the family, I was sure to take their part. Mary's stepchildren, the Rashleighs, were my constant visitors, and I found myself acting go-between in their love affairs. Jonathan, my brother-in-law, was a good, just man, but stern; a firm believer in the settled marriage as against the impulsive prompting of the heart. No doubt he was right, but when Alice, his daughter, turned thin and pale for languishing after that young rake Peter Courtney, I had them both to Lanrest and bade them be happy while the chance was theirs, and no one was a whit the wiser. They married in due course, and although it ended in separation, at least they had some early happiness together.

My godchild, Joan, the child of my sister Cecilia, was another of my victims. When young John Rashleigh, Mary's stepson, came down from Oxford to visit us, he found Joan at my bedside, and I soon guessed which way the wind was blowing. I had half a thought to send them to the apple tree but suggested the bluebell wood instead. They were betrothed within a week and married before the bluebells had faded.

But the war years were now upon us, and we all had more pressing problems. Trouble had been brewing for a long while, and we in Cornwall were much divided in opinion, some holding that His Majesty was justified in passing what laws he pleased, and others holding that Parliament was right in opposing the King's despotism. Civil war was talked of openly, and each gentleman, including Jack Trelawney and other of our neighbors, began to look to his weapons, his servants and his horses, so as to be ready. The women, too—like Cecilia at Maddercombe—busied themselves tearing strips of bed linen into bandages and packing their storerooms with preserves for fear of siege.

At the first open rupture in 'forty-two, my brothers Jo and Robin and most of our friends, including Jonathan Rashleigh, his son-in-law, Peter Courtney, and of course Bevil Grenvile, declared for the King. Robin and Peter Courtney joined His Majesty's Army, and both were given a company command immediately. Peter, after showing much dash and courage in his first action, was knighted on the field. Jonathan became collector for the royal cause in our district, and went about raising money—no easy matter, Cornwall being a poor county. But many families with little ready money to spare gave plate to be melted down into silver.

In spite of the successes of the first year, I could not believe that the Parliament would give way so easily. All the rich merchants of London were strongly in their favor, and I had an uneasy suspicion that their army was incomparably the better of the two. Our leaders wanted nothing in courage, but they lacked experience; equipment, too, was poor, and discipline nonexistent in the ranks. By autumn the war was getting rather too close for comfort. I had an uneasy Christmas, and at breakfast one morning in the third week of January word came that enemy troops had crossed the Tamar River into Cornwall and were even now on the road to nearby Liskeard.

I and Matty, with two elderly menservants and three lads, all that were left to us at Lanrest, were alone, unarmed and unprepared. There was nothing to do but secure the cattle and the sheep in the farmstead, and likewise bolt and bar ourselves within the house and wait. Once or twice we thought we heard cannon shot, sounding strangely distant in the cold clear air of January. But before nightfall we knew the King's men had won a victory, for Robin himself came riding home to cheer us, bringing several companions with him. They were all laughing and triumphant, for the two Parliament divisions had fled in dire disorder.

Bevil Grenvile had been the hero of the day in this, his first engagement. They described how he had led the Cornish infantry down one hill and up another. "It's in his blood," said one of the men. "Here's Bevil, a country squire all his life; put a weapon in his hand and he turns tiger. The Grenviles are all alike at heart."

"I wish to heaven," said another, "that Richard Grenvile would return from Ireland and join his brother."

There was a moment's awkward silence, for some of them remembered the past and recollected my presence in the room. Then Robin rose to his feet and said they must be riding back to Liskeard. Thus, in southeast Cornwall, war touched us briefly in 'forty-three and departed, and many boasted that summer would see the rebels in Parliament laying down their arms forever.

Alas, such optimism was ill judged. Victories we had indeed, but we lost, in that first summer, the flower of our Cornish manhood. The worst tragedy of the year, or so it seemed to us, was when Bevil Grenvile was slain at Lansdowne, struck down by a poleax just as he and his men had won the day. So, outwardly triumphant and inwardly bleeding, we Royalists watched the year draw to its close, and 1644 opened with His Majesty master of the West, but the Parliament elsewhere still unbeaten.

In the spring of the year a soldier of fortune returning from Ireland rode to London to receive payment for his services. He gave the gentlemen in Parliament to understand that in return for this he would join forces with them, and they gave him six hundred pounds and told him their plans for the spring campaign. He bowed and smiled—a dangerous sign had they but known it—and straightway set forth in a coach and six, with a host of troopers. At Bagshot Heath he descended from his coach and, calling his troopers about him, calmly suggested that they all now proceed to Oxford and fight for His Majesty, not against him.

The troopers, nothing loath, accepted, and the train proceeded to Royalist headquarters at Oxford, bearing with it a quantity of money, arms and silver plate, bequeathed by Parliament, and all the minutes of the secret council that had just been held in London.

The name of this soldier of fortune who had hoodwinked the Parliament in so scurrilous a fashion was Richard Grenvile.

ONE DAY TOWARD the end of April 1644 Robin came over from Radford to urge me to leave Lanrest and take up residence, for a time at any rate, with our sister Mary Rashleigh at Menabilly. Robin himself was taking part in the long-drawn-out siege of Plymouth, which alone among the cities of the West still held out for Parliament.

"It is impossible for Jo and Percy and me to do our duty," said Robin, "remembering all the while that you live here alone. Deserters and stragglers are constantly abroad, robbing on the highway, and the thought of you here, with a few old men and Matty, is a constant disturbance to our peace of mind."

Menabilly was already packed with Rashleigh relatives who had taken refuge there with Jonathan, and I said I had no wish to add to their number. Besides, I was set now in my ways, my days were my own, I followed a personal routine.

"You can live at Menabilly exactly as you do here at Lanrest," protested Robin. "Matty will attend you; you will have your own apartment and your meals brought to you, if you do not wish to mix with the company."

Seeing his anxiety, I said no more; and within a week I was being carried in a litter to Menabilly.

How strange to be on the road again. I felt oddly nervous and ill at ease, as if I had been suddenly transplanted to a foreign land. My spirits rose as John Rashleigh, my sister Mary's stepchild, came riding along the highway to meet me, a broad smile on his thin, colorless face. He was just twenty-three, and the tragedy of his life was that he had not the health or strength to join the Army, being cursed from babyhood with a malignant form of ague. He was a dear, lovable fellow, and his wife—my goddaughter, Joan—with her merry nature, made him a good foil.

"All is prepared for you, Honor," said John with a smile as he rode beside my litter. "There are over twenty of us in the house at present. My stepmother has put you in the gatehouse, for she says you like much light and air. The chamber there has windows looking both ways, over the outer courtyard to the west, and onto the inner court that surrounds the house. Thus you will see all that goes on about the place."

As we turned into the park, I saw the great stone mansion, flanked by high walls and outbuildings. After passing under the low archway of the gatehouse—my future dwelling—we drew up within the inner court. The house was foursquare, built around the court, with a big clock tower or belfry at the northern end, and the entrance to the south. On the steps stood Mary now to greet me, and Alice Courtney, her stepdaughter, and Joan, my godchild, both of them with their babies tugging at their skirts.

"Welcome, dearest Honor, to Menabilly," said Mary.

Alice, whose sweet face and temper endeared her to all, smiled and said, "The place is full of children, Honor; you must not mind." Since her marriage to Peter Courtney, Alice had produced a baby every year.

They carried me into the dark-paneled hall and, ignoring the long gallery that ran the whole of the house, bore me up the broad staircase to the western wing. I was immediately delighted with my apartment. There was a small room to the right for Matty, and nothing had been forgotten for my comfort.

"You will be bothered by no one," said Mary. "The apartments beyond the dressing room belong to the Sawles—cousins of

Jonathan's—who are sober and retiring and will not worry you. The chamber adjoining yours on the left is never occupied."

I passed the first few days becoming accustomed to my new surroundings and settling down, like an old hound to a change of kennel. By the fifth day I was sufficiently at home and mistress of my nerves to leave my chamber and take to my chair, in which, with John propelling it and Joan and Alice on either side and the children running before, I made a tour of the domain. The gardens to the east were extensive and surrounded by high walls. To the south lay pastureland and farm buildings and another pleasure garden, also walled, which had above it a high causeway leading to a summerhouse, fashioned like a tower with long leaded windows, commanding a fine view of the sea.

"This," said Alice, "is my father's sanctum. Here he does his writing and accounts and, watching from the windows, can observe every ship that passes, bound for Fowey." She tried the door of the summerhouse, but it was locked. "We must ask him for the key when he returns. It would be just the place for Honor and her chair, when the wind is too fresh upon the causeway."

But John did not answer. Perhaps it had occurred to him, as it had to me, that his father might not wish me for a companion. We made a circle of the grounds, returning to the outer court. I looked up at the gatehouse and noticed for the first time the barred window of the apartment next to mine and the great buttress that jutted out beside it.

"Why is that apartment never used?" I asked idly.

John waited for a moment or two before replying. "My father goes to it at times," he said. "He has furniture and valuables shut away."

"It was my uncle's room," said Alice, hesitating. "He died very suddenly, you know, when we were children."

Their manner was diffident, and I did not press the question, remembering all at once Jonathan's elder brother, who had died within eight days of his old father, supposedly of smallpox.

I was now ready for an introduction to the Rashleigh cousins of the Sawle and Sparke families, who were also inmates of the house. They were all assembled in the long gallery. There were fireplaces at either end, with the Sawles seated before the first and the Sparkes circled around the other, while in the center of the gallery my sister Mary with her stepchildren's families held the balance.

There were but two Sawles to three Sparkes. Old Nick Sawle was doubled up with rheumatism and almost as great a cripple as I was myself, while Temperance, his wife, came of Puritan stock and apparently was never without a prayer book in her hand. The Sparkes—two sisters and a brother—were engaged in a harmless game of cribbage. Will Sparke was one of those unfortunate high-voiced old fellows with a woman's mincing ways. Deborah made up in masculinity what her brother lacked, being heavily mustached and speaking from her shoes, while Gillian, the younger sister, was all coy prettiness in spite of her forty years.

After a short while in the gallery I was thankful enough to retire to my own chamber and blissful solitude. Matty brought me my dinner and was full of gossip about the servants and the house. I asked her what she knew of the apartment adjoining mine.

"It is a lumber room, they tell me," she answered. "Mr. Rashleigh has the key and has valuables shut away."

My curiosity was piqued, though, and I bade her search for a crack in the door. She put her face to the keyhole, but saw nothing. I gave her a pair of scissors, both of us giggling like children, and she worked away at the paneling for ten minutes or so until she had scraped a wide enough crack at which to place one eye. She knelt before it, then turned to me in disappointment. "There's nothing there," she said. "It is a plain chamber, much the same as this, with a bed, a table, and tapestry hangings on the wall."

I felt quite aggrieved, having hoped—in my idiot romantic fashion—for a heap of treasure. I bade her hang a picture over the crack and turned to my dinner. But later, when Joan came to sit with me, she said with a shiver, "You know, Honor, I slept once in this room when John had the ague, and I did not care for it."

"Why so?" I asked, drinking my wine.

"I heard soft footsteps in the chamber next door, like someone who walks with slippered soles for fear he shall be heard."

"A servant, perhaps," I suggested.

"No one has a key but my father-in-law, and he was from home then." She waited a moment. "I believe it was a ghost."

"Why should a ghost walk at Menabilly?" I answered. "The house has not been built fifty years."

"People have died here, though," she said. She watched me with bright eyes. "I think it was the ghost of the elder brother whom they call Uncle John. He was mad—a hopeless idiot. They used to keep him shut up in the chamber there."

This I had not heard before. "Are you certain?" I said.

"Oh, yes," she replied. "They say the chamber there was set aside for him, built in a special way—I don't exactly know how. And then he died, you see, very suddenly of the smallpox."

After a while she went away. But that night my thoughts kept returning to the idiot Uncle John, shut up in the chamber, year after year, from the first building of the house, a prisoner of the mind, as I was of the body.

THE NEXT DAY a messenger arrived bearing letters, and all the family gathered in the gallery to discuss the latest information about the war. Alice was reading aloud an epistle from her Peter.

"Sir John Digby has been wounded," she said, "and the Plymouth siege is now to be conducted by a new commander—Sir Richard Grenvile."

Mary was not in the gallery at the time, and she being the only person at Menabilly to know of the romance long finished and forgotten, I was able to hear his name without embarrassment. "And what," I heard myself saying, "does Peter think of his new commander?"

"As a soldier he admires him," Alice answered, "but I think he has not such a great opinion of him as a man."

"I have heard," said John, "that he hasn't a scruple, and once an injury is done to him, he will never forget it or forgive."

Will Sparke looked up from a letter in his hand. "So Richard Grenvile is commanding now at Plymouth. My heaven—what a scoundrel."

I began to burn silently, my old love and loyalty rising in me.

"You heard of his first action on coming to the West, I suppose?" said Will, warming to malicious gossip. "Grenvile rode straight to Fitzford, his wife's property, seized the contents and took all the money owed by the tenants to his wife for his own use."

"I thought," said Alice, "that he had been divorced."

"So he is. But that is Richard Grenvile for you."

"I wonder," I said calmly, "what has happened to his children."

"The daughter," said Will, "is with the mother in London, but the lad was at Fitzford with his tutor when Grenvile seized the place, and by all accounts is with him now. They say the poor boy is in fear and trembling of his father, and small blame to him."

I soon bade John carry me upstairs to my apartment, and I took to my bed, telling Matty I would see no visitors the rest of the day. For fifteen years the Honor that had been lay dead and buried, and here she was struggling beneath the surface once again at the mere mention of a name best forgotten. Richard on the Continent, Richard in Ireland, was too remote a person to swim into my daily thoughts. But now he was some thirty miles away only, and there would be constant talk of him, criticism and discussion; I would be forced to hear his name bandied and besmirched. Oh, yes, there was much reason for me to lie moody on my bed, with the memory of a young man smiling at me from the branches of an apple tree. Fifteen years . . . Richard would be forty-four now, ten years older than myself.

I was wondering, too, about his little son, who must be a lad now of thirteen or fourteen. Could it be true that the boy went in fear of his father? Supposing we had wedded, Richard and I, and this had been our son? As a child, would he have come running laughing to me? Would he be auburn-haired like Richard? Would we all three have ridden to the chase?

I must have fallen asleep because I was muzzy with a dream when I heard the movement in the next chamber. The night was pitch-black, for it was only quarter moon, and no glimmer came to me from either casement. I raised my head from the pillow, thinking the sound might be Matty in the dressing room, but it came from the other side. I held my breath and waited. Yes, there it was again. A stealthy footstep padding to and fro. I remembered Joan's tale of the mad Rashleigh uncle confined in there for years. Was it his ghost, in truth, that stole there in the shadows? The clock in the belfry struck one, and I became aware of a cold current of air coming into my apartment.

I remembered then that the closed-up door into the empty chamber beyond did not meet the floor but was raised two inches or so. It was from beneath this door that the current of air blew now—and to my certain knowledge there had never been a draft from there before. The muffled tread continued, stealthy, soft, and I thought of the ghost stories my brothers had recounted to me as a child, of how an earthbound spirit would haunt the place he hated, bringing with him a whisper of chill dank air. . . . One of the dogs barked from the stables, and this homely sound brought me to my senses. Was it not more likely that a living person was responsible for the cold current that swept beneath the door, and that the cause of it was the opening of the room's barred window?

I reached my hand out to the flint beside my bed and lit my candle. I pulled my chair close to me and, with the usual labor that years of practice had never mitigated, lowered myself into it. Softly I wheeled myself across the room and came abreast of the door. The picture that Matty had hung over the crack was on a level with my eye. I blew my candle. Then, very softly, holding my breath, I lifted the picture from the nail and peered with one eye into the slit. The chamber was in half-darkness, lit by a single candle on a bare table. I could not see to right or left—the crack was not large enough—but the table was in a direct line with my eye. A man was sitting there, his back turned to me. He was booted and spurred and wore a dark crimson riding cloak about his shoulders. He had a pen in his hand and was writing on a long white slip of paper. Here was flesh and blood indeed. With his back turned to me and his hat upon his head, I could make little of him. He then moved out of my line of view, taking the candle, and softly walked to the far corner of the room. I heard nothing after that and no further footsteps, and I became aware suddenly that the draft was no longer blowing beneath the door. Yet I had heard no sound of a closing window. The intruder, therefore, had, by some action unperceived by me, cut off the draft, making his exit at the same time. He had left the chamber, as he had entered it, by some entrance other than the door that led into the corridor. I replaced the picture on its nail and blundered back across my room, knocking into a table on the way and waking Matty.

"Have you lost your senses," she scolded, "circling round your chamber in the pitch black?" And she lifted me like a child and dumped me on my bed.

"I had a nightmare," I lied, "and thought I heard footsteps. Is there anyone moving in the courtyard, Matty?"

She drew aside the curtain. "Not a soul," she grumbled.

"You will think me foolish," I said, "but venture into the passage and try the door of the locked apartment next to this."

In a moment Matty was back again. "The door is locked like it always is," she said, "and, judging by the dust upon the latch, it has not been opened for months or more."

"No," I mused, "that is just what I supposed."

She stared at me and shook her head and, after grumbling a moment or two, went back to her own room. But my mind was far too lively to find sleep for several hours. I kept trying to remember the formation of the house, seen from without, and what it was that had struck me as peculiar the day before, when John had wheeled me in my chair toward the gatehouse. It was past four in the morning when the answer came to me. Menabilly was built foursquare around the courtyard, with clean straight lines and no protruding wings. But at the northwest corner of the house, jutting from the wall outside the fastened chamber, was a buttress, running tall and straight from the roof down to the cobbles.

Why would the first John Rashleigh have built such a buttress? And had it some connection with his idiot elder son?

Some lunatics were harmless; some were not. But even the worst were given air and exercise at certain periods of the day, and could hardly be paraded through the corridors of the house itself for that purpose. I smiled to myself in the darkness, for I had guessed how the intruder had crept into the apartment next to mine. He had come, as poor Uncle John had doubtless done nearly half a century before, by a hidden stairway in the buttress.

But why he had come, and what was his business, I had yet to discover.

CHAPTER FOUR

THE NEXT MORNING, wrapping my cloak about me, I announced to Matty my intention of going abroad. Joan came with me, and I persuaded her to wheel me first to the outer court, where I made a pretense of looking up to admire my quarters in the gatehouse. In reality I was observing the formation of the buttress, which ran the whole depth of the house on the northwest corner, immediately behind it being the barred chamber. The buttress was a little over four feet wide, and, if hollow, it could easily contain a stair. There was, however, no outlet to the court; this was certain. So any stairway within the buttress must lead underground, far beneath the foundations of the house, and into a passage running some distance to an outlet in the grounds.

We left the outer court and came by the path outside the steward's lodge. Mrs. Langdon, the steward's wife, was standing in the entrance; she insisted that we come in and have a glass of milk. While she was absent, we glanced about the neat room.

Joan pointed to a bunch of keys that hung on a nail beside the door. "As a rule old Langdon is never parted from his keys," she whispered.

"Has he been steward long?" I asked.

"Oh, yes," said Joan. "He came here when the house was built. There is no corner of Menabilly that he does not know." Curious, she examined the labels on the keys. "'Summerhouse,'" she read. With a mischievous smile she slipped it from the bunch and dangled it before my eyes. "You expressed a wish to peep into the tower on the causeway, did you not?" she teased.

At this moment Mrs. Langdon returned with the milk and Joan, like a guilty child, reddened and concealed the key within her gown. We chatted for a few moments, I drinking my milk in haste, and then we bade the good woman farewell.

"Now you have done for yourself," I said to Joan. "How in the world will you return the key?"

"I'll devise some tale or other to satisfy old Langdon," she said, laughing. "But since we have the key, Honor, it were a pity not to use it." She was an accomplice after my own heart.

We crossed the gardens and Joan propelled me through the gate onto the causeway. It was only when mounted thus some ten feet from the ground that a fine view of the sea could be obtained. Menabilly, though built on a hill, lay in a saucer, and I commented on the fact to Joan as she wheeled me toward the towered summerhouse at the far end of the causeway.

"Yes," she said, "the house was so built that no glimpse of it should be sighted from the sea. Old Mr. Rashleigh lived in great fear of pirates. But if the truth be told, he was not above piracy himself, and in the old days there were bales of silk and bars of silver concealed somewhere within the house, stolen from the French and brought hither by his own ships."

In which case, I thought privately, a passage known to no one but himself and his steward would prove of great advantage.

When we reached the summerhouse, Joan produced her key and turned it in the lock. "I must tell you," she confessed, "that there is nothing great to see. I have been here once or twice with my father-in-law, and it is naught but a rather musty room."

She wheeled me inside, and I glanced about. The walls were

lined with books, save for the windows, which commanded the whole stretch of the bay, and to the east showed the steep coast road that led to Fowey. Anyone, on horse or on foot, approaching Menabilly from the east would be observed by a watcher at the window; likewise a vessel sailing close inshore.

The stone floor was carpeted, save in one corner by my brother-in-law's writing table, where a strip of heavy matting served for his feet. Joan left me in my chair to browse up at the books, while she herself kept watch out on the causeway. There was nothing much to tempt my interest. Books of law, books of accountancy, and many volumes docketed as *County Affairs*.

I turned my chair from the desk, and as I did so, the right wheel stuck on some obstruction beneath the heavy matting. I bent down from my chair to free the wheel, turning up the edge of the mat as I did so. I saw then that the obstruction was a ring in the flagstone, which, though flat to the ground, had been enough to obstruct the smooth running of my chair. Seizing the ring with my two hands, I succeeded in lifting the stone some three inches from the ground before the weight of it caused me to drop it once again. But not before I had caught a glimpse of the sharp corner of a step descending into the darkness. . . . I replaced the mat just as my godchild came into the summerhouse.

"Well, Honor," she said, "have you seen all you have a mind to?"

"I rather think so," I answered, and in a few moments we were bowling back along the causeway, my mind full of my latest discovery. It seemed fairly certain there was a hidden pit tunnel underneath the flagstone in the summerhouse. I looked over my shoulder down the pathway to the beach, and thought how easy it would be for an incoming vessel to send a boat ashore with some half dozen men, and they to climb up the path, and for a watcher at the window of the summerhouse to relieve the men of any burden they should bear upon their backs. Was this what old John Rashleigh had foreseen when he built his tower? It seemed probable, but did the step beneath the flagstone have any connection with the buttress? One thing was certain. There was a secret way of entrance to Menabilly, through the chamber next to mine, and someone had passed that way only the night before, for I had seen him with my own eyes. . . .

We came to the end of the causeway and were about to turn into the walled gardens when Joan's little son, a child of three, came running to greet us. "Uncle Peter is come," he cried, "and another gentleman, and many soldiers. We have been stroking the horses."

To avoid running the gauntlet of the long windows in the gallery, where the company would be assembled, I bade Joan wheel me to the entrance in front of the house. As we passed through the door, we heard laughter and talk coming from the gallery, and, the wide arched door to the inner courtyard being open, we could see some troopers with their horses watering at the well beneath the belfry. I noticed that each fellow wore on his shoulder a scarlet shield with three gold rests upon it. . . .

For a moment I thought my heart would stop beating. "Find one of the servants quickly," I said to Joan. "I wish to be carried straightway to my room."

It was too late. Peter Courtney came out into the hall, his arm about his Alice, in company with several brother officers.

"Why, Honor," he cried, "this is a joy indeed. Knowing your habits, I feared to find you hiding in your apartment. Gentlemen, I present to you Mistress Honor Harris." Then his friends were bowing and exchanging introductions, and Peter, still laughing and talking, was pushing my chair into the gallery, which seemed full of people all chatting at the top of their voices. At the far end by the window I caught sight of Mary in conversation with someone whose tall back and broad shoulders were painfully, almost terrifyingly, familiar.

Peter, impervious to any doubtful atmosphere, propelled me slowly toward the window, while my sister Mary, overcome by cowardice, murmured a hasty excuse to her companion about summoning the servants to bring further refreshment, and fled. Richard turned and saw me. And as he looked at me it was as if my whole heart moved over in my body and was mine no longer.

"Sir," said Peter, "I am pleased to present to you my dearly loved kinswoman, Mistress Honor Harris of Lanrest."

"My kinswoman also," said Richard, and then he bent forward and kissed my hand.

"Oh?" said Peter vaguely, looking from one to the other of us. "I suppose all we Cornish families are in some way related. Let me fill your glass, sir. Honor, will you drink with us?"

At that moment a glass of wine seemed to me my only salvation. While Peter filled the glasses I had my first long look at Richard.

He had grown much broader, not only in the body, but also about the neck and shoulders. There was a brown weather-beaten air about him, and I saw one white streak in his auburn hair, high above the temple. It was, after all, fifteen years. . . .

And then he turned to give me my glass. The eyes that looked at me were quite unchanged. "Your health and fortune," he said quietly. I saw the little telltale pulse beating in his right temple, and I knew then that the encounter was as startling and moving to him as it was to me.

"I did not know," he said, "that you were at Menabilly."

"I came here a few days since from Lanrest," I answered, my voice perhaps as oddly flat as his. "My brothers said I must not live alone, not while the war continues."

At this moment Peter's small daughters came running to his knees, shrieking with joy to see their father. Peter, laughing an apology, was swept away into family life, and Richard and I were left alone beside the window. In a low voice, clipped and hard, he said, "If I am silent, you must forgive me. I had not thought, after fifteen years, to find you so damnably unchanged."

This streak back to the intimate past was curiously exciting. "Why damnably?" I said, watching him over the rim of my glass.

"Over a long period I have pictured you as an invalid, wan and pale, hedged about with doctors and attendants. Instead I find— this." He looked at me then with a directness that I remembered well.

"I am sorry," I answered, "to disappoint you."

"I am not disappointed, merely speechless. I shall recover shortly. Where can we talk? Have you not your own apartment?"

"I have," I replied with some small attempt at dignity, "but it would be considered somewhat odd if we retired there."

"You did not quibble at similar suggestions in the past."

"I would have you remember," I said with lameness, "that we have been strangers to each other for fifteen years."

"Do you think," he said, "that I forget it for a moment?" He turned then and beckoned to young John Rashleigh, just in from his day's ride and hovering at the entrance to the gallery, somewhat mud-stained and splashed, bewildered by the unexpected company.

"Hi, you," called Richard, "will you summon one of your fellow servants and carry Mistress Harris' chair to her apartment? She has had enough of the company downstairs."

"That is John Rashleigh, sir," I whispered to him, "the son of the house, and your host in his father's absence."

"Ha! My apologies," said Richard, walking forward with a smile. "Your dress being somewhat in disorder, I mistook you for a menial. How is your father?"

"Well, sir, I believe," stammered John in great nervousness.

"Delighted to hear it," said Richard. "When you see him, tell him that now I am come into the West, I propose to visit here frequently."

"Yes, sir."

"You have accommodation for my officers, I suppose?"

"Yes indeed, sir."

"Excellent. And now I propose to dine upstairs with my kinswoman, Mistress Harris. What is the usual method with her chair?"

"We carry it, sir. It is quite a simple matter."

John gave a nod to Peter, who came forward, and the pair of them each seized an arm of my chair.

"It were an easier matter," said Richard, "if the occupant were bodily removed and carried separately." And before I could protest, he had lifted me from the chair. "Lead on, gentlemen," he commanded.

The strange procession proceeded up the stairs—John and Peter ahead with the chair, and I with my head on Richard's shoulder and my arms tight about him for fear of falling.

"I was in error just now," said Richard in my ear. "You have changed after all."

"In what way?" I asked.

"You are two stone heavier," he answered.

And so we came to my chamber in the gatehouse.

I CAN RECOLLECT that supper as if it were yesterday. It might have been a day since we had parted instead of fifteen years. When Matty came into the room bearing the platters, her mouth pursed and disapproving, Richard burst out laughing, calling her "Old Go-between," which had been his nickname for her in those distant days. He asked her how many hearts she had broken since he saw her last, and soon had her blushing from head to toe.

Matty went off, guessing, no doubt, that for the first time in fifteen years I had no need of her services. Richard fell to eating right away, while I—still weak with the shock of seeing him—

toyed with the wishbone of a chicken. He started walking about the chamber before he had finished, a habit I remembered well, talking all the while about the defenses at Plymouth.

"My first two tasks were simple," he said. "I threw up a new earthwork at Mount Batten, and the guns I have placed there so damage the shipping that the garrison is hard put for supplies. Secondly, I have cut off their water power, and the mills within the city can no longer grind flour. Give me a month or two to play with, and I'll have 'em starved."

"And the blockade by land, is that effective now?"

"It will be when I've had time to organize it," he answered. "I found that most officers in my command are worse than useless— I've sacked more than half of them already. But when the rebels tried a sortie a week or two ago, we sent them flying back to Plymouth. And last week we sprang a little surprise ourselves, attacking one of their outposts. We beat them out of their position and took a hundred prisoners."

"Prisoners must be a problem," I said, "it being hard enough to find forage in the country for your own men. You are obliged to feed them, I suppose?"

"Feed them be damned," he answered. "They are hanged without trial for high treason."

"But, Richard," I said, hesitating, "that is hardly justice, is it?"

"I don't give a fig for justice," he replied. "The method is effective, and that's the only thing that matters."

"I am told the Parliament has put a price upon your head."

"What would you have them do?" He smiled and sat down beside me on the bed. "The rebels call me the Red Fox behind my back, and women use the name to threaten their misbehaving children, saying, 'Grenvile is coming; the Red Fox will have you.'" He laughed.

"It was not thus," I said softly, "that your brother Bevil's reputation spread throughout the West."

"No, and I have not a wife like Bevil had, nor a home I love, nor a great brood of happy children." His voice was suddenly bitter.

"Do you have your son with you?" I asked quietly.

"My spawn?" he said. "Yes, he is somewhere about my headquarters at Buckland Abbey with his tutor."

"What is he like?"

"Dick? Oh, he's a little handful of a chap with mournful eyes.

No sign of Grenvile in him—he's the spit of his damned mother."

There was a long silence. We had entered upon dangerous ground.

"Did you never try," I asked, "to make some life of happiness?"

"Happiness went with you," he said. "When you refused to see me that last time, I knew that nothing mattered anymore but bare existence. You have heard the story of my marriage with much embellishment, no doubt, but the bones of it are true."

"Had you no affection for her?"

"None whatever. I wanted her money. I have it now. And her property and her son. The girl is with her mother up in London. I shall get her, too, one day when she can be of use to me."

"You are very altered, Richard, from the man I loved."

"If I am so, you know the reason why."

The sun was gone now; the chamber seemed bleak. Every bit of those fifteen years was now between us. Suddenly he took my hand and held it against his lips. "Has no one told you," he said, "that you are more lovely now than you were then?"

"I think you flatter me," I answered, "or maybe I have more time now. I lie idle to play with paint and powder."

"There is no part of you that I do not now remember. You had a mole in the small of your back which gave you much distress. You thought it ugly—but I liked it well."

"Is it not time that you went downstairs to join your officers? I heard one of them say you were to leave tonight."

"You lie there so smug and complacent on your bed, very certain of yourself now you are thirty-four. I tell you, Honor, I care not two straws for your civility." He knelt then and put his arms about me, and the fifteen years went whistling down the wind.

"Are you still queasy when you eat roast swan?" he whispered.

He wiped away the silly tears that pricked my eyes and he smoothed my hair. "Beloved half-wit, with your damned pride," he said, "do you understand now that you blighted both our lives?"

"Had I not done so, you would soon have hated me, as you hated Mary Howard."

"That is a lie, Honor."

"Perhaps. What does it matter? The past is over."

"There I agree with you. But we have the future. My marriage is annulled; I am free to wed again."

"Then do so, to another heiress. There are many you might choose from, all agog for husbands."

"In all probability. But I want only yourself."

I put my hands on his shoulders and stared straight at him: the auburn hair, the hazel eyes, the little pulse that beat in his right temple. "No, Richard. I will not have you wedded to a cripple."

"And if I carry you by force to Buckland?"

"Do so, if you will; I can't prevent you. But I shall still be a cripple." I leaned back on my pillows, faint suddenly, and exhausted. Very gently he released me and smoothed my blankets. It was nearly dark; the clock in the belfry had already struck eight. I could hear the jingling of harness from the courtyard and the scraping sound of horses as the troopers prepared for their journey.

"I understand," he said, "what you have tried so hard to tell me. There can never be between us what there was once. I knew that all along, but it would make no difference."

"It would," I said, "after a little while."

"I shall always love you," said Richard, "and you will love me, too. We cannot lose each other now, not since I have found you again. May I come and see you often, that we may be together?"

"Whenever you wish," I answered.

"Do you have as much pain now as when you were first hurt?"

"Sometimes," I answered, "when the air is damp."

"Is there nothing can be done for it?"

"Matty rubs my legs and my back with lotion that the doctors gave her, but it is of little use. You see, the bones were all smashed and twisted; they cannot knit together."

"Will you show me, Honor?"

"It is not a pretty sight, Richard."

"I have seen worse in battle."

I pulled aside my blanket and let him look upon the crumpled limbs he had once known whole and clean. He was thus the only person in the world to see me so, except Matty and the doctors. I put my hands over my eyes, for I did not care to see his face.

"No need for that," he said. "Whatever you suffer you shall share with me from this day forward." He bent and kissed my ugly twisted legs, then covered me again with the blanket. "Will you promise never to send me from you again?"

"I promise."

"Farewell, then, sweetheart, and sleep sound this night."

He stood for a moment, his figure carved clear against the light from the windows opposite. Then he turned and left.

THAT RICHARD GRENVILE should suddenly become part of my life again was a mental shock. It was all too late. There could never be a life for us together, only the doubtful pleasure of brief meetings that the hazards of war at any time might render quite impracticable. What then? For me a lifetime of lying on my back, waiting for a chance encounter, and for him, after a space, a nagging irritation that I existed in the background of his life, expecting visits or messages that he found difficult to send—in short, a friendship that would become as wearisome to him as it would be painful to me.

I felt torn between two courses, lying there on my bed in the gatehouse. One was to see him no more, never, at any time. And the other was to spurn my own weak body that would be tortured incessantly by his physical presence, and give to him without reservation all the small wisdom I had learned, all the love, all the understanding that might yet bring to him some measure of peace. This second course seemed the more positive, for if I renounced him now, as I had done before, it would be through cowardice, a sneaking fear of being hurt even more intolerably than I had been fifteen years ago.

Strange how all arguments in solitude shrivel to nothing when the subject of them is close. So it was when Richard returned to Menabilly. He found me in my chair looking out toward the bay, and bending to me, he kissed my hand with all the old fire and love and ardor. I knew that I could not send him from me.

"I cannot stay long," he said. "I have word that those damned rebels have taken the fort at Inceworth. The sentries were asleep, of course, and if the enemy hasn't shot them, I will do so. I'll have my army purged before I'm finished."

"And no one left to fight for you, Richard."

"I'd sooner have hired mercenaries from Germany or France than these soft-bellied fools," he answered. And he was gone in a flash, leaving me half happy, half bewildered, with an ache in my heart that I knew now was to be forever part of my existence.

That evening Jonathan Rashleigh returned to Menabilly, having been some while in Exeter on the King's affairs, and in Fowey, at his town house on the quay, attending to his shipping business. A feeling of constraint came upon the place at his return, of which even I, secure in my gatehouse, could not but be aware. The servants were more prompt about their business, but less willing. The grandchildren, who had run about the passages in his absence, were closeted in their quarters. Voices in the gallery were more subdued. Alice and John and Joan found their way more often to the gatehouse, as if it had become a sort of sanctuary.

Presently Jonathan himself came up to pay his respects to me. He hoped I was comfortable, that I had everything I needed and did not find the place too noisy after the quiet of Lanrest. "And you sleep well, I trust, and are not disturbed at all?" His manner, when he asked this, was somewhat odd, a trifle evasive.

"I am not a heavy sleeper," I told him. "A creaking board or a hooting owl is enough to waken me."

"I feared so," he said abruptly. "It was foolish of Mary to put you in this room, facing as it does a court on either side. You would have been better in the south front." I noticed that he stared hard at the picture on the door, hiding the crack, and seemed about to ask a question. But after chatting a bit longer, he took his leave of me.

That night, between twelve and one, being wakeful, I sat up in bed to drink a glass of water and became aware of a cold draft of air blowing beneath the door of the empty room. That same chill draft I had noticed once before. And then, faint and hesitating, came a little scratching sound upon the panel of the door where I had hung the picture. Someone was in the empty room. . . .

The sound continued for five minutes, then ceased as suddenly as it had started. Once again the telltale draft of air was cut and all was as before.

In the morning when I was dressed and in my chair I wheeled myself to the door and lifted the picture from the nail. It was as I thought. The crack had been filled in. . . . Suspecting my prying eyes, Jonathan Rashleigh had given orders for my peephole to be covered. I pondered then upon the possibility that Jonathan's elder brother had not died of the smallpox some twenty years before but was still alive, living in animal fashion in a lair beneath the buttress, and that the only persons to know of this were my brother-in-law and his steward, Langdon, and someone else—a keeper, possibly—clad in a crimson cloak. Now I, a stranger, had stumbled upon this secret, a secret too sinister, too horrible, to live with day by day.

Fortunately the problem was solved for me two days after my brother-in-law's return. It was only then that my godchild, Joan, remembered how she had mischievously borrowed the steward's key to the summerhouse. She came to me that evening in great perturbation, for she had not the courage to take the key back to Langdon's house and confess the foolery. What was she to do?

"You are so clever, Honor," she pleaded, "and I so ignorant. Let me leave this key with you and so forget it."

"Very well, then," I answered, "we will see what can be done."

After she had gone, I dangled the key between my fingers. It was of medium size, like the one in my own door. A sudden thought struck me, and wheeling my chair into the passage, I listened for a moment to discover who stirred about the house.

It was a little before nine o'clock; the servants were still at supper. The moment seemed well chosen for a daring gamble. I turned down the passage and halted outside the door of the locked chamber. I listened again, then stealthily I pushed the key into the rusty lock. It fitted. It turned. And the door creaked open. . . . A link between this chamber and the summerhouse now seemed definite, and the chance to examine the room might never come again.

I edged my chair within the room, kindled my candle and looked about. The chamber was simple enough. Two windows, north and west, both with iron bars across them. A bed in the far corner, and the table and chair I had already seen through the crack. The walls were hung with heavy arras, tapestries, which were rather old and worn in many parts. I laid the candle on the table and wheeled myself to the corner that gave upon the buttress. This, too, had an arras hanging from the ceiling, which I lifted—and found nothing but bare stone behind it. I ran my hands over the surface but could find no join. But it was murky and I could not see, so I returned to the table to fetch my candle, first listening at the door to make certain no one was about.

It was while I waited there that I felt a sudden breath of cold air on the back of my head. I looked swiftly over my shoulder and noticed that the arras on the wall beside the buttress was blowing to and fro; and even as I watched, I saw, to my great horror, a hand appear from behind a slit in the arras and lift it to one side.

Someone wearing a crimson cloak stood with the arras pushed aside and a great black hole in the wall behind him. "Close the door gently, Honor," he said. "Since you are here, it is best that we should have an explanation and no further mischief." He let the arras drop behind him, and I saw then that the man was my brother-in-law, Jonathan Rashleigh.

I FELT LIKE a child caught in some misdemeanor and was hot with shame. "Forgive me," I said, "I have acted very ill."

He laid aside his cloak and drew a chair up to the table. "It was you," he said, "who made a crack in the panel? It was not there before you came to Menabilly."

I confessed that I was indeed the culprit. "I know I had no right to tamper with your walls," I said. "But there was some talk of ghosts, and one night last week I heard footsteps."

He looked closely at me. "How did you come upon that key?"

There was nothing for it but to tell him the whole story, putting the blame heavily upon myself and saying little of Joan. I said that I had looked about the summerhouse and admired the view, but as to my finding the flagstone—nay, he would have to put me on the rack before I confessed to that.

"And what do you make of it now you know that the nightly intruder is none other than myself?" he questioned.

"I cannot tell, Jonathan," I answered, "except that your family knows nothing of it."

At this he was silent. After a long pause he said, "John has some knowledge of the subject, but no one else, except my steward, Langdon. Indeed, the success of the royal cause we have at heart would gravely suffer should the truth become known."

This last surprised me, but I said nothing.

"Since you already know something of the truth," he said, "I will acquaint you further, if you will guard all knowledge of it."

I promised after a moment's hesitation, uncertain what dire secret I might now be asked to share.

"You know," he said, "that at the beginning of hostilities I was appointed by His Majesty's Council to collect the silver plate given to the royal cause in Cornwall and arrange for it to be taken to the mint at Truro?"

"I knew you were collector, Jonathan, no more than that."

"If some rebel could lay hands upon this treasure, the Parliament would be ten times richer. So it is necessary to have depots throughout the county where the plate can be stored until the necessary transport can be arranged. And to ensure secrecy, the

houses or buildings that serve as depots should contain hiding places known only to their owners."

How far from what I—with excess imagination—had supposed.

"The buttress against the far corner of this room," he continued, "is hollow in the center. A flight of narrow steps leads to a small room beneath the courtyard, where a man can stand and sit, though it is but five feet square. This room is connected with a tunnel that runs under the house and so beneath the causeway to an outlet in the summerhouse. It is in this small buttress room that I have been accustomed, during the past year, to hide the plate, working by night with my steward. No one knows that but myself and Langdon, and now you, Honor, who really have no right to share the secret."

I said nothing, for there was no possible defense.

"John knows the plate has been concealed in the house but has never inquired where and is, as yet, ignorant of the room beneath the buttress and the tunnel. You wonder, no doubt, why the house should have been so constructed?"

I confessed to some small wonder on the subject.

"My father," he said, "had certain—how shall I put it?—shipping transactions which necessitated privacy. So the tunnel was useful in many ways."

Your father, dear Jonathan, I said to myself, was nothing more or less than a pirate of the first order.

"It happened also," he said, "that my unfortunate elder brother was not in full possession of his faculties. This was his chamber. At times he was violent, hence the reason for the little cell beneath the buttress, where lack of air and close confinement soon rendered him unconscious and easy to handle."

The picture his words conjured turned me sick. I saw the wretched, shivering maniac choking for air in the dark room beneath the buttress, with the four walls closing in upon him.

Jonathan must have seen my change of face, for he looked kindly at me and rose from his chair. There were sounds of servants moving from the kitchens. "You will return now to your apartment," he said, "and I will go back the way I came. You may give me Langdon's key. If in future you hear me in this apartment, you will understand. I keep accounts of my collections here. Good night, Honor. And not a word of what has passed between us must be spoken to any other person."

THE PROGRESS OF the war caused us no small concern. The Earl of Essex was gathering a rebel army in numbers, and we felt it was but a matter of weeks before he passed into Devon, with nothing but the Tamar River then between him and Cornwall. The only one who viewed the approaching struggle with relish was Richard. "If we can but draw the beggar into Cornwall," he said at dinner one night, "and then come up in the rear and cut off all retreat, we will have Essex surrounded and destroyed."

The idea did not much appeal to Jonathan. "If we have fighting in Cornwall, the country will be devastated," he said. "The land is too poor to feed an army. We look to you, Grenvile, to engage the enemy in Devon and keep us from invasion."

"Our aim," said Richard, "is to destroy the enemy. In Devon there is no hope of encirclement. My only fear is that he will *not* cross the Tamar, in which case we shall have lost one of our greatest chances."

"You are prepared, then," said Jonathan, "to see Cornwall laid waste, and people homeless?"

"If you are not prepared to suffer for the King's cause," said Richard, "we may as well treat with the enemy forthwith."

There was some atmosphere of strain in the dining chamber after that. When my brother-in-law gave the host's signal for dispersal, it still being light, Richard took a turn with me upon the causeway, making himself attendant to my chair. "If Essex draws near to Tavistock," he said, "and I am forced to retreat, can I send the whelp to you?"

I was puzzled for a moment, thinking he alluded to his dog. "What whelp?" I asked. "I did not know you possessed one."

"My spawn, my son and heir. Will you have him here under your wing and put some sense into his frightened head?"

"Why, yes, indeed, if you think he would be happy with me."

"He would be happier with you than with anyone in the world. But I wonder what you will make of Dick. He is a scrubby object."

"I will love him, Richard, because he is your son."

"I doubt that sometimes when I look at him. He cries for a finger scratch. I would exchange him any day for young Joe

Grenvile, a kinsman whom I have as aide-de-camp at Buckland. He is up to any daring scheme, that lad."

"Dick is barely turned fourteen," I said. "Give him a year or two to learn confidence."

And so it was arranged, with Jonathan's permission, that Dick Grenvile and his tutor, Herbert Ashley, should add to the numbers at Menabilly. I was strangely happy and excited the day they were expected. I took pains with my toilet, wearing the blue gown that was my favorite and bidding Matty brush my hair for half the morning. And all the while feeling foolish to waste such time and trouble for a little lad who would not look at me. . . .

I was seated in the walled garden when the gate opened and a young boy came walking across the lawn toward me. He was taller than I had imagined, with the flaming Grenvile locks, an impudent snub nose and a swagger that reminded me instantly of Richard. And then as he spoke, I realized my mistake.

"My name is Joe Grenvile," he said. "They sent me from the house to bring you back. There was a slight mishap. Poor Dick tumbled from his horse as we drew rein in the courtyard—the stones were slippery—and he has cut his head. They took him to your chamber, and your maid is washing the blood."

"Is Sir Richard come with you?" I asked as he wheeled me down the path.

"Yes," said young Joe, "and greatly irritated, cursing poor Dick for incompetence, which made the little fellow worse. We have to leave again within the hour. Essex has reached Tiverton, you know, and Taunton Castle is also in the rebels' hands. Ours are the only troops left outside Plymouth."

"And you find all this greatly stirring, do you, Joe?" I asked.

"Yes, madam. I can hardly wait to have a crack at the enemy."

We found Richard pacing the hall. "You would scarcely believe it possible," he said, "that the whelp could tumble from his horse right on the very doorstep." Then he clapped Joe on the shoulder, and the boy looked up at him with pride and devotion. "We shall make a soldier of this chap anyway," he said. "Go draw me some ale, Joe, and a tankard for yourself."

"What of Dick?" I asked. "Shall I not go to him?"

"Leave him to the women and his useless tutor," said Richard. "You'll soon have enough of him. I have one hour to spend at Menabilly and I want you to myself."

We went to the little anteroom beyond the gallery, and there he sat with me while he drank his ale.

"Shall we see fighting in this district?" I asked.

"Impossible to answer. It depends on where Essex strikes." He put his tankard on the table and, first closing the door, knelt beside my chair. "Look after the little whelp, and teach him manners. If the worst should happen and there be fighting in the neighborhood, hide him under your bed—Essex would take any son of mine as hostage. Do you love me still?"

"I love you always."

"Then kiss me as though you meant it."

It was easy for him, no doubt, to hold me close for five minutes and have me in a turmoil with his lovemaking, and then ride away, his mind aflame with other matters. But for me, left with my hair and gown in disarray and long hours stretching before me to think about it all, it was rather more disturbing. I had chosen the course, though, and I must put up with the fever he engendered in me.

I patted my curls and smoothed my lace collar, then pulled the bell rope for a servant, who, with the aid of another, bore me in my chair to my apartment. I met Matty coming forth with a basin of water and strips of bandage on her arm.

"Is he much hurt?" I asked.

"More frightened than anything else," she said.

The servants set me down in the room and withdrew. Dick was sitting hunched up in a chair beside the hearth, a white shrimp of a boy with great dark eyes and tight black locks, his pallor worsened by the bandage on his head.

"Are you better?" I said gently.

He stared at me, nervously biting his nails all the while, and then said with a queer jerk of his head, "Has my father gone?"

"Yes, he has ridden away with your cousin. You are to stay here for the present. Did he not tell you who I am?"

"I think you must be Honor. He said I was to be with a lady who was beautiful. Why do you sit in that chair?"

"Because I cannot walk. I am a cripple."

"Does it hurt?"

"No, I am used to it. Does your head hurt you?"

He touched the bandage warily. "It bled," he said. "There is blood under the bandage."

"Never mind, it will soon heal." I took a piece of tapestry and began to work on it so he should not think I watched him.

"My mother used to work at tapestry," he said after a pause. "She had many friends, but I did not hear her speak of you."

"I do not know your mother, Dick. I only know your father."

"Do you like him?" The question was suspicious, sharply put.

"Why do you ask?" I said, evading it.

"Because I don't. I hate him. I wish he would be killed in battle." The tone was savage, venomous. "He is a devil. He tried to steal my mother's house and money and then kill her."

"Why do you think that?"

"My mother told me. She is in London now with my sister."

"Perhaps," I said, "when the war is finished, you will go back to her."

"I would run away to London now, but I might get caught in the fighting. Last week I saw a wounded man upon a stretcher. There was blood on him." His shrinking manner puzzled me.

"Why," I asked, "are you so much afraid of blood?"

"I did not say I was afraid," he said after a moment, "but I cannot bear to see it spilled. I have always been thus since a little child. It is not my fault."

"Perhaps you were frightened as a baby."

"That's what my mother told me. Once when she had me in her arms my father quarreled violently with her and struck her on the face and she bled. The blood ran onto my hands."

I began to feel very sick at heart. "We won't talk about it, Dick. What shall we discuss instead?"

"Tell me what you did when you were my age. Had you brothers and sisters?"

And so I wove him a tale about my past, thus making him forget his own. Afterward I read to him for a while. He came and curled up on the floor beside my chair, like a small dog that would make friends in a strange house, and when I closed the book, he looked up at me and smiled—and the smile for the first time was Richard's smile and not his mother's.

FROM THAT DAY forward Dick became my shadow. Seldom speaking, always watchful, he hovered continually about me, arriving early with my breakfast, walking beside my chair on the causeway, sitting beside me in the dining chamber.

Meanwhile, the news worsened. Word came that Essex had reached Tavistock, and the siege of Plymouth had been raised. A council was held among the gentry, and one and all decided to muster what men and arms and ammunition they could and ride to Launceston to help defend the county.

The following morning saw the preparations for departure. All on the estate who were fit to carry arms paraded before my brother-in-law with their horses and their kits packed on the saddles. Mary went from one to the other, handing them cake and fruit to cheer them on their way, and John was left with many long instructions. Then we watched them set off across the park—Jonathan Rashleigh, Langdon and this strange, pathetic little band full of ignorance and high courage, the tenants wielding their muskets as though they were hay forks.

At Menabilly we made a pretense of continuing as though all were as usual, but we were tense and watchful—our ears pricked for the rumble of cannon or the sound of horses. We were a quiet, subdued party who sat in the long gallery that evening.

The next day, shortly before noon, when some of us were assembled in the dining chamber to take cold meat, Mary cried, "There is a horseman riding across the park toward the house."

The rider clattered into the inner court, covered from head to foot with dust. "I have a message for Mistress Harris," he said, flinging himself from his horse. It was young Joe Grenvile.

"But how goes the battle?" "What of the rebels?" "What has happened?" Questions on all sides were put to him, and he had to push his way through to me with the letter.

"Essex will be in Bodmin by nightfall," he said. "We have just had a brush with Lord Robartes and his brigade, and we are in hot retreat to Truro, where Sir Richard plans to raise more troops."

A cry of alarm went up from all the company, but I was busy tearing open Richard's letter. I read:

My sweet love, The hook is nicely baited, and the poor misguided fish gapes at it with his mouth wide open. Essex will most probably be in Fowey tomorrow. His chief adviser is that crass idiot Jack Robartes, whose mansion at Lanhydrock I have just had infinite pleasure in pillaging. They will swallow the bait, hook, line and sinker. We shall come up on them from Truro, and the King, his nephew, Prince Maurice, and Ralph Hopton from the east, so the fish will be most prettily landed.

*Your immediate future at Menabilly being somewhat unpleas-
ant, it will be best if you return the whelp to me, with his tutor.
I have given Joe instructions on the matter. Keep to your
chamber, my dear love, and have no fear. We will come to your
succor soon. Your devoted servant, Richard Grenville.*

I turned to Joe and motioned that I should like to speak with
him apart. We withdrew to the sun parlor. "What is the plan for
Dick?" I asked.

"The boy and Mr. Ashley will embark by fishing boat for Saint
Mawes as soon as possible. I shall go with them to the beach, then
rejoin Sir Richard before the rebel cavalry reaches the district."

"There is, then, no time to lose," I answered. "I will ask Mr.
John Rashleigh to go with you; he will know the fishermen who
are most likely to be trusted."

I called John to come to me and hurriedly explained the plan.
He set forth straightway with Joe Grenville, while I sent word to
Herbert Ashley that I wished to speak to him. The tutor was a
young man with a sallow complexion and retreating chin, and he
looked much relieved when I told him that he and Dick were to
depart upon the instant. He went immediately to pack their
things. The task then fell upon me to break the news to my
shadow, who was standing by the side door, looking out at the
garden. I beckoned him to my side and explained that Menabilly
would be seized and we had arranged, therefore, for him and his
tutor to go by boat to Saint Mawes, where he would be safe.

"Are you coming, too?" he asked.

"No, Dick. I will remain at Menabilly."

"Then so will I."

"No, Dick. It is best for you to go."

He said nothing but looked queerly sulky and strange, and after
a moment or two went up to join his tutor.

The clock in the belfry had just struck three when they came
down ready for departure. Dick was still sulky, but with a cheerful voice I wished him a speedy journey. Then he and Herbert
Ashley set off to the beach to fall in with John Rashleigh and Joe
Grenville, who must by this time have matters well arranged.

Anxiety and strain had brought an aching back upon me. I sent
for Matty, and she, with help, carried me upstairs. I lay upon my
bed, wishing with all my heart that I could ride with Joe Grenville
instead of lying there, a woman and a cripple, waiting for the

relentless tramp of enemy feet. I had been abed but an hour when I heard once more the sound of a horse galloping across the park. Matty went to the casement. "It's Mr. John," she said, "in great distress by his expression. Something has gone amiss."

My heart sank at her words. In a moment or two I heard John's footstep on the stairs and he flung into my room. "We have lost Dick," he said. "He has vanished."

"What do you mean? What has happened?"

"We were all assembled on the beach," he said, his breath coming quickly, "and the boat was launched. There was a little cuddy below deck, and I saw Dick descend to it with my own eyes. Just before the men drew anchor some lads came running down in great alarm to tell us that the rebels had cut the road and that Polmear Hill, not two miles away, was already blocked with troops. At this, young Joe Grenvile turned to me with a wink and said, 'It looks as if I must go by water, too.' Before I could answer, he had urged his horse into the sea and was making for the sand flats half a mile away to the westward. It was half low tide, but he finally reached them and turned in his saddle to wave to us."

"But Dick?" I said. "You say you have lost Dick?"

"He was in the boat," John said stubbornly, "I swear he was. But we turned to watch young Joe put his horse to the water and swim for it. By heaven, Honor, it was the boldest thing I have ever seen a youngster do. And then Ashley, the tutor, called for Dick but could not find him. We searched the vessel from stem to stern, but he wasn't there. He was not on the beach. He was not anywhere. For God's sake, Honor, what are we to do?"

"Where is the boat now?" I asked.

"Lying offshore, waiting for a signal."

"Search the cliffs in all directions," I said, "and the grounds, and park and pasture. Was anything said to Dick upon the way?"

"I think not. I only heard Ashley tell him that by nightfall he would be with his father."

So that was it. A moment's indiscretion but enough to turn Dick from his journey. I bade John set forth, saying no word to anyone of what had happened. And, calling to Matty, I asked her to take me to the causeway. Once on the high ground I had a good view of the surrounding country, and I saw John Rashleigh strike out across the fields, but no sign of any other living soul.

Presently I sent Matty withindoors for a cloak, and on her

return she told me that stragglers were already pouring into the park from the roads, begging for shelter, for the route was cut to Truro and the rebels everywhere. Many were already kindling fires down in the warren and making rough shelter for the night. "And as I came out just now," she said, "there was a litter come to rest in the courtyard, and a lady within demanding harborage for herself and her young daughters."

"Go back, Matty," I said, "and see if my sister needs help."

She had not been gone more than ten minutes when I saw two figures coming across the fields toward me. It was John Rashleigh, and he had Dick with him.

When they reached me I saw the boy was dripping wet and scratched about the face and hands by brambles. He stared at me defiantly. "I will not go," he said. "You cannot make me go."

John Rashleigh shrugged in resignation. "It's no use, Honor," he said. "We shall have to keep him. The beaches are awash and I've signaled to the boat to make sail and take the tutor across the bay. As for this lad—I found him halfway up the cliff, a mile away, having been waist-deep in water for the past two hours. God only knows what Sir Richard will say to this bungle."

"Never mind Sir Richard, I will take care of him," I said. At this moment I turned my head toward the coast road and I saw, silhouetted on the skyline above the valley, a single horseman. In a moment he was joined by others who, following their leader, plunged down the narrow roadway to the cove. John saw them, too. Our eyes met.

"Have you your father's keys?" He nodded. "On your person?" Another nod. "Open, then, the door of the summerhouse."

He obeyed me without question and the door was flung open.

"Lift the mat from beneath the desk there," I said, "and raise the flagstone."

He looked at me in wonder but did as I had bidden.

"Don't ask me any questions, John," I said. "There is no time. A passage runs underground from those steps to the house. Take Dick with you now, first replacing the flagstone above your heads, and crawl with him along the passage to the farther end. You will come then to a small room like a cell, and another flight of steps. At the top of the steps is a door that opens, I believe, from the passage end. But do not try to open it until I give you warning from the house. Give me the keys. Go quickly."

There was no trouble now with Dick. He had gathered from my manner that danger was deadly near and bolted down into the hole like a frightened rabbit. John, descending after him, lowered the stone above his head and disappeared.

The summerhouse was as it had been. I turned the key in the lock and then put the keys inside my gown. I looked out to the eastward and saw that the skyline was empty. The troopers would be at Menabilly within ten minutes.

At that moment my godchild, Joan, came hurrying along the causeway to fetch me. "They are coming," she said. "We have seen them from the windows. Scores of them, on horseback, riding now across the park." Her breath caught in a sob, and she began running with me along the causeway. "I have searched everywhere for John," she faltered, "but I cannot find him. Oh, Honor—the children—what will become of us?"

I could hear shouting from the park, and from out beyond the gates came the sound of horses trotting. By the windows of the gallery they were waiting for us—Alice and Mary, the Sawles, the Sparkes, and two other faces that I did not know, the startled faces of strange children. I remembered then the unknown lady who had flung herself upon my sister's mercy, and as we turned into the hall, slamming the door behind us, I saw the horses that had drawn the litter still standing untended in the courtyard. Then I heard her voice, cold and clear, rising above the others in the gallery: "If only it is Lord Robartes, I can assure you all no harm will come to us. I have known him well these many years and am quite prepared to speak on your behalf."

"I forgot to tell you," whispered Joan. "She came with her two daughters an hour ago. It is Mrs. Denys of Orley Court."

Her eyes swung around to me. Those same eyes, narrow, heavy-lidded, and her golden hair, more golden than it had been in the past, for art had taken counsel with nature and outstripped it. She stared at the sight of me, then smiled her slow, false, well-remembered smile. "Why, Honor, this is indeed a pleasure. Mary did not tell me that you were at Menabilly."

I ignored the proffered hand, and as I stared back at her with foreboding in my heart, we heard the horses ride into the courtyard and the bugles blow.

And there being no brandy in the room, I poured myself some water from a jug and raised my glass to Gartred.

Through the windows of Menabilly we saw the troopers dismount, staring about with confident hard faces beneath their close-fitting skull helmets. There were more of them in the gardens, their horses' hooves trampling the green lawns and the little yew trees. And all the while the thin high note of the bugle, like a huntsman summoning his hounds to slaughter. In a moment we heard heavy footsteps clomping up the stairs, and into the gallery came three officers, the first a big burly man with a long nose and heavy jaw. I recognized him at once as Lord Robartes, the owner of Lanhydrock, who in former days had gone riding and hawking with my brother Kit.

"Where is the owner of the house?" he asked.

"My husband is from home," said Mary, coming forward, "and my stepson somewhere on the grounds."

"Is everyone else living in the place assembled here?"

"All except the servants."

"You have no malignants in hiding?"

"None."

Lord Robartes turned to the staff officer at his side. "Make a thorough search," he said. "Break down any locked door and test the paneling for places of concealment. Give orders to round up all livestock. We will take over this gallery and the ground floor for our personal use. Troops to bivouac in the park."

"Very good, sir." The officer stood to attention, then departed.

Lord Robartes drew up a chair to the table, and the remaining officer gave him paper and a quill. He then asked for the name and occupation of each member of the household, and documented us one by one, looking at each victim keenly. Only when he came to Gartred did his manner relax somewhat. "A foolish time to journey, Mrs. Denys," he said.

"There are so many soldiery abroad of little discipline and small respect," said Gartred languidly, "it is not very pleasant for a widow with young daughters to live alone, as I do. I hoped by traveling south to escape the fighting."

"You thought wrong," he answered.

Gartred bowed and did not answer. Lord Robartes rose and

turned to Mary and the rest of us. "When the apartments above have been searched, you may go to them. I must request you to remain there until further orders. Exercise once a day will be permitted in the garden. We shall take command of the kitchens, and certain stores will be allotted to you. Your keys, madam."

Slowly, reluctantly, Mary unfastened the string from her girdle.

"What about milk for the children?" said Joan, her cheeks very flushed, her head high.

"I have some five hundred men to quarter here, and their needs come first. If the children need more nourishment than the daily allotments provide, you must do without yourselves. Now you may go to your apartments."

This was the moment I had waited for. Catching Joan's eye, I summoned her to my side. "You must give up your apartment to Mrs. Denys," I murmured, "and come to me in the gatehouse. I shall move my bed into the adjoining chamber."

Her lips framed a question, but I shook my head. She nodded and, for all her agitation, went at once to Mary with the proposition.

We went out of the farther door, where the servants were huddled like a flock of startled sheep, and Matty and two others seized the arms of my chair. Already the troopers were in the kitchens, in full command, while down the stairs came two fellows and a noncommissioned officer bearing great piles of blankets and rich embroidered covers from Mary's linen room. I hated them upon the instant. Upstairs their muddied boots had trampled the floors and they had thrust their pikes into the paneling and stripped the hangings from the walls. In Alice's apartment one clumsy oaf had trodden upon the children's favorite doll, smashing its head to pieces, and at the sight of this, the little girls had burst into torrents of crying. I knew then the idiot rage that surges within a man in wartime and compels him to commit murder.

My room had suffered like disturbance. They had saved me the trouble of unlocking the barred chamber, for the door was broken. But upon entering, I saw that the arras that hung before the buttress was undisturbed. I looked out into the courtyard. Soldiers were gathered below, line upon line, their horses tethered and their tents already in process of erection, and all the while that damned bugle blowing, high-pitched and insistent. I turned from the window and told Matty that Joan and her children would now be coming to the gatehouse and I would remain here in the chamber that had been barred.

When the two rooms were in order and the servants had helped Matty to repair the door, thus giving me my privacy, I sent them from me. Cautiously I drew near the northeast corner of my new apartment and lifted the arras. I ran my hands over the stone wall as I had done before, and again I could find no division in the stone. Entry must be from without only, but I had warned John not to attempt to enter the chamber before I signaled, being confident at the time that I would be able to find the entrance from inside. He and Dick, meantime, were waiting in the cell below the buttress, and the sound of my voice would never carry through the implacable stone.

Another fear nagged at me with the recollection of my brother-in-law's words: "Lack of air and close confinement soon rendered him unconscious and easy to handle." Uncle John gasping for breath in the little cell beneath the buttress . . . How much air, then, came through to the cell from the tunnel beyond? *Enough for how many hours?*

I felt defeated, with no course to take. A little bustle from the adjoining room and a child's cry told me that Joan and her babies had come to my old apartment, and in a moment she appeared at the door, still worrying about John's absence. The hours wore on then with horrid dragging tedium, and the sun began to sink behind the trees. The air was thick with smoke from fires lit by the troopers. The children were restless, turning continually in their cots, calling for their mother, and when Joan was not hushing them, she was gazing from my window, reporting with indignation the slaughter of livestock and other actions of destruction.

For our evening meal Matty brought us two small portions of a pie upon one plate with a carafe of water. "These are for you," she said. "Mrs. Rashleigh and Mrs. Courtney fare no better."

Joan ate my piece of pie as well as hers, for I had no appetite. I could think only of how her husband and Richard's son had lain hidden in the buttress for hours now. Matty brought candles, and presently Joan went to the children next door, while Matty—all oblivious of my own hidden fears—helped me undress for bed. As she grimly brushed my hair, she said, "I've discovered that Mrs. Denys hasn't lost her taste for gentlemen." I said nothing, waiting for what would follow. "You and the others had pie for your suppers," she said, "but there was roast beef and Burgundy taken up to Mrs. Denys and places set for two upon the tray."

"And who was the fortunate who dined with Mrs. Denys?"

"Lord Robartes himself," said Matty with sour triumph.

I had suspected it was not mere chance that had brought Gartred to Menabilly. She was here for a purpose.

When Matty had blown out the candles and was gone, I lay back in my bed, my nerves tense and strained. I heard the clock in the belfry strike ten, then eleven, and then midnight. All was still and silent. Then I suddenly felt upon my cheek a current of cold chill air. I sat up in bed and waited. The draft continued, blowing straight from the arras on the wall.

"John," I whispered. I heard a movement from behind the arras. It was lifted aside and a figure stepped out, dropped on all fours and crept to my bed. "It is I, Honor," he said, and the dark figure, icy cold, climbed onto my bed and lay trembling beside me. It was Dick, the clothes still dank and chill upon him. He began to weep, and I held him close, warming him as best I could. When he was still, I whispered, "Where is John?"

"In the little room," he said, "below the steps. We waited there for hours, and you did not come. He has fainted. I got hold of the long rope that hangs above the steps and pulled. The hinged stone gave way and I came up into this room. I could not stay there longer, Honor. It's black as pitch and closer than a grave."

I wondered what to do, whether to summon Joan and thus betray the secret to another, or wait until Dick was calmer and then send him back with a candle to John's aid. And as I lay there, my heart thumping, my arms wrapped close about the sleeping boy, the belfry clock struck one, then two, then three. . . .

THE FIRST GRAY chinks of light were coming through the casement when I roused Dick and bade him light the candle and creep back to the cell. In a few moments he returned, his little ghost's face looking more pallid than ever.

"He is awake," he said, "but very ill and shaking all over."

At least John was alive, and a wave of thankfulness swept over me. But the ague, his legacy from birth, must have attacked him again with its usual ferocity, and small wonder after more than ten hours crouching beneath the buttress. Swiftly I bade Dick bring the chair beside my bed and with his assistance I lowered myself into it. Then I went to the door and gently called for Matty. In a moment or two she came from the little dressing room, her round plain face yawning beneath her nightcap, her eyes widening with wonder when she saw Dick.

"You love me, Matty, I believe," I said to her. "Now I ask you to prove that love as never before." She nodded, saying nothing. "Dick and Mr. John have been hiding since last evening," I said. "Mr. John is ill. I want you to go to him and bring him here. Dick will show you the way."

He pulled aside the arras, and now for the first time I saw how the entrance was effected. A large block of stone worked on a hinge, moved by a lever and a rope if pulled from beneath the narrow stair. This gave an opening smaller than a door, but wide enough for a man to pass through. There was something weird and fearful in the scene with the gray light of morning coming through the casement, and Matty, a fantastic figure in her night-clothes and cap, making her way through the gap in the buttress. As she disappeared down the dark little stairway with Dick, I heard the first high call of the bugle from the park. The soldiers would soon be astir; we had little time.

It was some fifteen minutes before they were all three within the chamber. Daylight had now filled the room and the troopers were moving in the courtyard down below.

John was quite conscious, thank God, and his mind lucid, but he was trembling all over and in a high fever. We held rapid consultation and agreed that no further person should be told how he had come into the house or that Dick was with us still.

John's story was to be that he had seen the troopers and hid until nightfall. But, his fever coming upon him, he had decided to return and had climbed up into the house by the lead piping that ran outside his father's window. For corroboration of this John must go at once to his father's room, where his stepmother was sleeping, and waken her and win her acceptance of the story. And this immediately, before the household was awake. When Matty returned and reported John was safely in his father's rooms, the first stage of the proceeding was completed.

Next I had to tell Dick that though he could remain in my apartment, he must be prepared to stay, perhaps for long hours at a time, in the secret cell beneath the buttress. He fell to crying at once, beseeching me not to make him stay alone in the dark cell.

I was well-nigh desperate. "Very well, then," I said. "Open the door, Matty. Call the troopers. Tell them that Richard Grenvile's son wishes to surrender himself. They have sharp swords and the pain will soon be over." God forgive me that I could find it in my heart to so terrify the lad, but it was his only salvation.

The mention of swords brought the thought of blood, as I knew it would. He turned to me, his dark eyes despairing. "Very well," he said, "I will do as you ask."

I bade Matty take the mattress from my bed and the stool beside the window and some blankets and bundle them through the open gap into the stair. "When it is safe for you to come, I will let you know," I said.

"But how can you," said Dick, "when the gap is closed?"

The old dilemma again. I looked at Matty in despair.

"If you do not quite close the gap," she said, "but let it stay open to three inches, Master Dick, with his ear put close to it, would hear your voice."

We tried it, and although I was not happy with the plan, it seemed the one solution.

For the next four weeks the rebels were our masters. When I look back now to the intolerable strain and anguish of that age-long August of 'forty-four, I wonder how I endured it. For I had to be on guard not only against the rebels but against my friends, too. It was Matty, acting sentinel as always, who kept them from the door when Dick was with me. My crippled state, and the fact that I often had "bad days," now became my only safeguards.

John's story had been accepted as full truth, and since he was quite obviously ill and in high fever, he was allowed to remain in his father's rooms with Joan to care for him instead of being removed to closer custody under guard.

Day in, day out, came the jingle of harness, the clatter of hooves, the march of tramping feet, the grinding sound of wagon wheels, and ever insistent above the shouting of orders, the bugle call hammering its single note. Once a day we were allowed within the garden for some thirty minutes. Up and down the muddied paths we went, stared at by the sentries at the gate. Never once did we see Gartred when we took our exercise.

"I see her from my window, walking with Lord Robartes," whispered Alice. "She is supposed to be a prisoner, too, but she is not treated so."

"She has turned the wartime stress to her advantage," I said.

"You mean she is for the Parliament?" asked Alice.

"Neither for the Parliament nor for the King, but for Gartred Denys," I answered. "She will smile on Lord Robartes and sleep with him, too, as long as it suits her. He would let her leave tomorrow if she asked him."

"Why, then," said Alice, "does she not do so and return in safety to Orley Court?"

"That is what I would give a great deal to find out."

It was some days before I had my answer.

On Sunday, August 11, the sun shone watery in a mackerel sky and a bank of clouds gathered in the southwest. There had been much coming and going all day, with troopers bringing many carts of wounded, who were carried to the farm buildings before the house. For the first time we were given soup only for our dinner. No reason was offered, but Matty, with her ears pricked, had gleaned some gossip from the courtyard.

"There was a battle yesterday on Braddock Down," she said. "They've lost a lot of men."

I poured half my soup into Dick's bowl and watched him drink it greedily, running his tongue around the rim like a hungry dog.

"The King and Prince Maurice have joined forces to the east," she said, "and Sir Richard with nigh a thousand men is coming up from the west. 'Your fellows are trying to squeeze us dry,' said the trooper in the kitchen, 'like a bloody orange.'"

If Matty's tale was true, then the Earl of Essex and ten thousand men were pent up in a narrow strip of land, with provisions getting low, only the bare land to live on, three armies in pursuit and no way of escape except the sea. The rain began to fall. And as I listened to it, remembering Richard's words, I heard the rustle of a gown and a tap upon my door.

Dick was gone in a flash to his hiding place and Matty cleared away his bowl and platter. I sat still in my chair with my back to the arras and bade them enter who knocked upon the door.

It was Gartred. She stood a moment within the doorway, a half-smile on her face. "Am I disturbing you, Honor?" she said. "You go early, no doubt, to bed?" Veiled contempt, mockery, the suggestion that because I was crippled I must be tucked in by half past nine, all these were in her voice and in her eyes.

"My going to bed depends upon my mood. And my company."

"You must find the hours horribly tedious, but no doubt you are used to it by now." She was looking about the room curiously. "You have heard the news, I suppose?" she said.

"That a skirmish was fought yesterday in which the rebels got the worst of it? Yes, I have heard that," I answered.

The last of the fruit picked before the rebels came stood in a platter on the table. Gartred took a fig and began to eat it, still looking about the room. Matty gave a snort of indignation that passed unnoticed and, taking her tray, left the chamber.

"If this business continues long," said Gartred, "we none of us here will find it very pleasant. Word came today that Richard is at Lanhydrock. It is ironic that we have the owner of Lanhydrock in possession here. Richard will leave little of it for him by the time this campaign is settled. Jack Robartes is black as thunder."

"It is his own fault," I said, "for advising the Earl of Essex to come into Cornwall and run ten thousand men into a trap."

"So it is a trap," she said.

I did not answer. I had said too much already, and Gartred was in quest of information. "Well, we shall see," she said, eating another fig with relish, "but I shudder to think what Jack Robartes would do to Richard if he could get hold of him."

"The reverse equally holds good," I told her.

She laughed and squeezed the last drop of juice into her mouth. "Your tongue hasn't blunted with the years," she said, "nor tribulation softened you. Tell me, do you still care for Richard?"

"That is my affair," I said.

"He is detested by his brother officers; I suppose you know that." She yawned and strolled over to the window. "His treatment of Dick is really most distressing. What did you think of the lad when he was here?"

"He was young and sensitive, like many other children."

"It was a wonder to me he was ever born at all," said Gartred. "And I am glad, for his sake, that Jack Robartes did not find him here." Once more she looked up at the walls and then again into the courtyard. "This is the room, isn't it," she said, "where they used to keep the idiot?"

"I have no idea."

"There is something odd about the formation of the house," she said carelessly. "Some cupboard, I believe, where they used to shut him up when he grew violent. . . . I am so sorry that my coming here forced you to give your room to Joan Rashleigh. I could so easily have made do with this one."

"It was much simpler," I said, "to place you and your daughters in a larger room, where you can entertain visitors to dinner."

"You always did like servants' gossip," she answered. "The hobby of all old maids." She paused, looking down at me. "My being here has at least spared you all, so far, from worse unpleasantness. I have known Jack Robartes for many years."

"Keep him busy, then, and have him mellow by morning. That's all we ask of you." I was beginning to enjoy myself at last.

She turned toward the door, her eyes sweeping the wall hangings. "I cannot guarantee," she said, "that his good temper will continue. He was in a filthy mood tonight. If they lose the campaign, they will lose their tempers, too. Jack Robartes will give orders to sack Menabilly and destroy inside and without."

"Yes," I said, "we are all aware of that."

"He must be a curious man, Jonathan Rashleigh, to desert his home, knowing full well what must happen to it in the end."

I shrugged my shoulders. And then she gave herself away. "Does he still act as collector for the mint?" she said.

For the first time I smiled. I now had my answer to the problem of her presence. "I cannot tell you," I said. "I have no idea. But if you wait until the house is ransacked, you may come upon the plate you think he has concealed. Good night, Gartred."

She stared at me a moment, then departed. At last I knew her business, and had I been less preoccupied with my own problem of concealing Dick, I might have guessed it sooner. It did not matter much to Gartred who won or lost the campaign in the West; she intended to have a footing on the winning side. I had heard since she was widowed for the second time that Orley Court was much burdened with debt and must be settled between her daughters when they came of age. The silver plate of Cornwall would be a prize indeed, could Gartred lay hands on it.

This, then, was her motive, with suspicion already centered on my room. She was playing her own game, and if she found she could not get what she wanted by playing a lone hand, she would lay her cards upon the table and damn the consequences.

This was what we had to fear, and no one in the house knew of it but myself. So Sunday, August 11, came and went, and we woke next morning to another problematical week, with three Royalist

armies squeezing the rebels tighter hour by hour, while a steady sweeping rain turned all the roads to mud.

Whether Gartred moved about the house or not I do not know. Alice said she thought she kept to her own chamber. I saw little of Joan, for poor John's ague was still unabated, but Mary came to visit me, her face each day more drawn as she learned of further devastation to Menabilly. There was, in fact, scarce anything left of the great estate. The gardens were spoiled, the orchards ruined, the timber felled, the livestock eaten. Whichever way the war in the West should go, Jonathan Rashleigh would be a bankrupt man.

Our feeding was already a sore problem. The children had their milk, but no more than two cupfuls for the day, and already I noticed a stary look about them. The old people suffered, too, and it was solely with Matty's aid that I could feed Dick at all. She had made an ally of the scullion, and was able to smuggle soup to my chamber beneath her apron. This same scullion fed us with rumors, too, most of them disastrous to his own side, which made me wonder if a bribe would make him a deserter.

Then we heard that Richard had seized Restormel Castle. It could not last much longer. Either Essex and the rebels must be relieved by another force marching to them from the east, or they must stand and make a fight of it.

Another Sunday came, and with it a whisper of alarm among the rebels that the country people were stealing forth at night and doing murder. Sentries were found strangled at their posts; other men were found with cut throats. The Cornish were rising. . . .

By Tuesday, the twenty-seventh, there was no soup for our midday dinner, only half a dozen loaves among the twenty of us. On Wednesday only one jugful of milk for the children, and that much watered. On Thursday Alice, Joan, Mary and I divided our bread among the children and made for ourselves a brew of herb tea with scalding water. We were not hungry. Desire for food left us when we saw the children tear at the stale bread and ask for more, which we could not give them.

And all the while the southwest wind tore and blustered in the teeming sky.

On Friday, the thirtieth of August, I lay all day on my bed. I let Dick come and lie upon his mattress next to me while he gnawed a bone that Matty had scavenged for him. His eyes looked larger than ever in his pale face. I slipped from one tearing dream to another. Hoofbeats woke me shortly after two. Matty opened the window and peered down into the outer court as they passed under the gatehouse to the courtyard; some dozen officers, she said, with an escort of troopers, and Lord Robartes there to receive the leader, on a great black horse, wearing a dark gray cloak. Even my tired brain seized that this was a council meeting and the Earl of Essex come to it in person. "Go find your scullion," I said to Matty. "Do what you will to him, but make him talk."

She nodded, tightening her lips. Before she went, she got Dick to his cell beneath the buttress.

Three, four, five o'clock, and I heard the horses pass beneath the archway once again and out across the park. At half past five Matty returned and told me the scullion was without and wished to speak to me. I bade her fetch my purse, which she did, and then, going to the door, she beckoned him within.

He stood blinking in the dim light, a sheepish grin on his face, but that face was lean and hungry. I gave him a gold piece, which he pocketed at once. "What news have you?" I asked.

He looked at Matty, and she nodded. " 'Tis only rumor," he said, "but it's what they're saying in the courtyard. The retreat begins tonight. They'll come this way, down to the beaches. The boats will take them off when the wind eases."

"Horses can't embark in small boats," I said. "What will your generals do with their two thousand horses?"

"There's talk of the cavalry breaking through Royalist lines tonight when the infantry retreat."

"What will happen to you and the other cooks?" I asked.

"We'll go by sea, same as the rest," he said.

"Not likely," I said. "Listen to the wind." It was soughing through the trees, and the rain spattered against my casement. "I can tell you what will happen," I said. "Morning will come and there won't be any boats. You will huddle there, in the driving rain, and the country people will come down on you from the cliffs with pitchforks in their hands."

The man was silent.

"Why don't you desert?" I said. "Go off tonight before worse can happen to you. I can give you a note to a Royalist leader." I offered him another gold piece and said, "If you break through to the King's Army and tell them what you have just told me—about the cavalry trying to run for it before morning—they'll give you plenty more of these."

He scratched his head, greedy but doubtful, and looked again at Matty.

"Even if you're held prisoner," I told him, "it would be better than having the bowels torn out of you by Cornishmen."

These last words settled him. "I'll go," he said, "if you'll write a note for me."

I scribbled a few words to Richard, which like as not would never reach his hands, but it was a venture worth trying. When the fellow had gone, with Matty to speed him on his way, I lay back listening to the rain and heard in the far distance the tramp of marching feet, with the bugle crying thin and clear above the moaning wind. When the morning broke, they were still marching upon the highroad, bedraggled, damp, dirty, hundred upon hundred making for the beaches.

Order was gone by midday Saturday; we heard the first sounds of gunfire as Richard's army broke upon them from the rear. Down from the fields came little running figures, first a score, then fifty, then a hundred, then a hundred more, to join a hopeless tangle of men and horses and wagons, all jammed and bogged together now in the sea of mud that had once been the park.

At five o'clock word went around the house that we were all to descend to the gallery. Even John from his sickbed must obey the order. Before I left my chamber I saw that Dick was safe within his cell, and this time, in spite of protestations, I closed the stone that formed the entrance. . . .

A strange band we were, huddled together in the gallery with wan faces. It was the first time I had seen John all month, and he looked most wretchedly ill, shaking still in every limb, his skin a dull yellow. No one saw the questioning look he gave me, or my answering nod, save Gartred. She sat a little apart from us, near the center window, with her daughters. They, too, were thinner and paler than before, but compared to the poor Rashleigh and Courtney babies, they were not ill nourished.

Gartred took no notice of us. Seated beside a little table, she played solitaire, turning the cards with faces uppermost. This, I thought, is the moment she has been waiting for.

Suddenly into the gallery came Lord Robartes, his boots splashed with mud, the rain running from his coat. His staff officers stood beside him wearing grim, purposeful faces as he confronted my sister Mary and her stepson, John.

"It has come to my knowledge," he said, "that your malignant husband, madam, and your father, sir, has concealed upon his premises large quantities of silver which by right belong to Parliament. I ask you to tell me where the silver is concealed."

Mary, God bless her ignorance, turned a bewildered face to him. "I know nothing of any silver," she said.

He turned from her to John. "And you, sir? No doubt your father told you all his affairs?"

"No," said John firmly, "I know nothing. My father's only confidant is his steward, who is with him at present."

Lord Robartes stared at John. Then he called to his officers. "Sack the house. Leave nothing of Menabilly but the bare walls."

At this poor John struggled to his feet. "You cannot do this," he said.

And my sister Mary threw herself upon her knees. "My lord Robartes," she said, "I swear by all I hold dear that nothing is concealed here. I implore you to show mercy to my home."

Lord Robartes stared down at her, his eyes hard. "Why should I show your house mercy when none was shown to mine? Be thankful that I spare your lives." And with that he turned on his heel and went from us.

We heard the major he had left in charge snap forth an order to his men—and straightway they started tearing at the paneling in the dining chamber and smashing the mullioned windows and hacking the great dining table to pieces. We heard them climb the stairs and break into the south rooms. As they tore down the door of Mary's chamber, she began to weep, long and silently, and Alice took her in her arms and hushed her like a child. Then Gartred looked toward me from her window.

"You and I, Honor, being the only members of the company without a drop of Rashleigh blood, must pass the time somehow. Tell me, do you play piquet?"

"I haven't played it since your brother taught me sixteen years ago," I answered.

"The odds are in my favor, then," she said. "Will you risk a *partie*?" As she spoke, she smiled, shuffling her cards, and I guessed the double meaning she would bring to it.

"Perhaps more is at stake than a few pieces of silver," I said.

"You are afraid to match your cards against mine?"

"No," I said. "No, I am not afraid." I pushed my chair over and sat opposite her at the table. Then started the strangest game of piquet I have ever played, for while Gartred risked a fortune, I wagered for Richard's son, and no one knew it but myself.

She led with the ace of hearts, to which I played the ten. As she took the trick, we noticed a dull, smoldering smell, and a wisp of smoke blew past the windows of the gallery.

"They are setting fire," said John quietly, "to the stables and the farm buildings before the house."

"The rain will surely quench the flames," whispered Joan.

The smoke of the burning buildings was bitter in the steady rain, and we could hear the sound of the axes overhead breaking to pieces the great four-poster bed where Alice had borne her babies. The glass mirror was thrown out onto the terrace, where it splintered into a thousand fragments.

"Fifteen," said Gartred, leading the king of diamonds, and "Eighteen," I answered, trumping it with my ace.

The tramping ceased from overhead as we started upon the third hand of the game, and all the while I knew that the rebels were now come to the last room of the house and were tearing down the arras before the buttress.

Mary raised a grief-stricken face. "If you would but say one word to the officer," she said to Gartred, "he might prevent the men from causing further damage."

"I could do much," said Gartred, "if I were permitted. But Honor tells me it is better for the house to fall about our ears."

"Honor," said Mary, "you know that it will break Jonathan's heart to see his home laid desolate. If Gartred can in some way save us and you are trying to prevent her, I can never forgive you."

"Gartred can save no one, unless she likes to save herself."

We were in our last game, each winning two apiece, when we heard them crashing down the stairs, the major in the lead. In the gallery he clicked his heels and bowed derisively to John. "The orders given me by Lord Robartes have been carried out," he announced. "Nothing is left within Menabilly house but yourselves, ladies and gentlemen, and the bare walls."

"And you found no silver hidden?" asked Mary.

"None, madam, but your own—now happily in our hands."

"Then this wicked destruction has been for nothing?"

."A brave blow has been struck for Parliament, madam, and that is all that we, her soldiers and her servants, need consider."

He bowed and left us, and in a moment we heard him ride away even as Lord Robartes had done an hour before. The flames licked the rubble in the courtyard, and save for their dull hissing and the patter of the rain, there was suddenly no other sound. A strange silence had fallen upon the place. Even the sentries stood no longer by the door.

I looked up at Gartred, and this time it was I who smiled and I who spread my cards upon the table. "Discard for *carte blanche*," I said softly. I led her for the first time and with my next hand drew three aces to her one and won the game.

She rose then and, after one mock curtsy to me, called her daughters and went upstairs.

I sat alone, shuffling the cards as she had done, while out into the hall faltered the poor weak members of our company, stricken at the sight of panels ripped, floors torn open, windows shattered. And all the while the driving rain that had neither doors nor windows now to bar it blew in upon their faces, soft and silent.

Then I heard a new note, sharp, quick, triumphant, coming ever nearer. It was the brisk tattoo of Royalist drums.

CHAPTER EIGHT

THE REBEL ARMY capitulated to the King in the early hours of Sunday morning. There was no escape by sea for the hundreds of men herded on the beaches. Only one fishing boat put forth for Plymouth, and she carried the Earl of Essex and Lord Robartes. We learned later that Matty's scullion had indeed proved faithful to his promise and borne his message to the Royalists at Bodinnick, but by the time the outposts upon the road were warned, the Parliament cavalry had successfully broken through Royalist lines and made good their escape to Saltash. The only one of our commanders who had hastened to pursue them was Richard Grenvile, leaving others to come to our succor at Menabilly.

First a soldier, last a lover, my Richard had no time to waste over a starving household and a crippled woman who had let a whole house be laid waste about her for the sake of the son he did not love. So it was not the father but poor sick John Rashleigh who crawled through the tunnel beneath the summerhouse to the buttress cell, found Dick unconscious, tugged at the rope to open the hinged stone and carried the fainting lad into my chamber. That was on Saturday night, after the house had been abandoned by the rebels. On Sunday morning, when a regiment of Royalist infantry arrived bringing food from their own wagons, we were all too weak to do little more than smile at them.

The first necessity was milk for the children and bread for ourselves. When we had regained a little measure of our strength and had kindled a fire in the gallery—the only room left livable— we heard once more the sound of horses, this time our own men coming home.

The scenes of joy and reunion then were not for me. Alice had her Peter, Mary had her Jonathan, and there was kissing and crying and kissing again. My brother-in-law praised me for my courage, but I did not want my brother-in-law; I wanted Richard. And Richard had gone to Saltash, chasing rebels.

Then, too, this sudden wild thanksgiving for deliverance and for victory seemed premature to me. The war was not over, for all the triumphs in the West. Only Essex and his men had been defeated. There were many thousands in the North and East of England who had yet to show their heels. And with our enemy Lord Robartes in command now at Plymouth, still stubbornly defended, there was something narrow and parochial in thinking the war over because Cornwall was free.

On the second day of our release I heard the sound of wheels in the outer court creaking over the cobbles and disappearing through the park. I asked Matty who had found transport to go away from Menabilly in so confident a fashion.

"Who else could it be but Mrs. Denys?" sniffed Matty. "Mr. Ambrose Manaton, a gentleman she knew in the Royalist party that rode here with Mr. Rashleigh, provided her escort."

So Gartred, like a true gambler, had thought it best to cut her losses. I smiled in spite of myself. "Did she see Dick before she left?"

"Aye," said Matty. "She stared at him, amazed, and asked him, 'Did you come in the morning with the infantry?' He grinned like a little imp and answered, 'I have been here all the time.'"

"Imprudent lad," I said. "What did she say to him?"

"She smiled—you know her way—and said, 'I might have

known it. Tell your jailer you are now worth one bar of silver.' "

That first week while we recovered our strength my brother-in-law and his steward set to work to find out how long it would take and what it would cost to make good the damage wrought upon the estate. The figure was colossal, beyond his means, and while the war lasted, no redress would be forthcoming. After the war, so he was told, the crown would see that he was not the loser.

The decision was now made among us to divide. The Sawles went to their brother at Penrice, the Sparkes to other relatives at Tavistock. The Rashleighs themselves, with the children, split up among near neighbors until a wing of Menabilly could be repaired. I was for returning to Lanrest until I learned, with a sick heart, that the whole house was wrecked beyond hope of restoration. There was nothing for it but to take shelter, for the time being, with my brother Jo at Radford. I might have gone to my sister Cecilia at Maddercombe, or my sister Bridget at Holbeton, but I chose Radford for the very reason that it was close to Plymouth—and Richard was once more commander of the siege.

"Why cannot you come with me to Buckland?" pleaded Dick, for the tutor, Herbert Ashley, had been sent to fetch him. "I would be content at Buckland and not mind my father if you would come and stand between us."

I smiled and ran my hand through his dark curls. "You shall visit me at Radford," I said, "and tell me of your lessons."

"It will not be the same," he said, "as living with you in the house. Shall I tell you something? I like you best of all the people that I know—next to my own mother."

The next day he rode away in company with his tutor, turning back to wave at me all the way across the park. I shed a useless sentimental tear for what might have been—the baby I had never borne, the husband I would never hold. Sickly figures in an old maid's dream, Gartred would have said. But sixteen years ago I had had my moment, and I swear I was happier with my one lover than Gartred ever had been with her twenty.

So I set forth upon the road again and turned my back on Menabilly. Jonathan escorted me as far as Saltash, where my brother Robin came to meet me. I was much shaken by the sights I witnessed on the road. The aftermath of war was not a pleasant sight. The country was laid waste, and that the fault of the enemy. In return the Cornish people had taken toll upon the rebel prisoners. Many were still lying in ditches, covered with dust and flies, stripped of their clothing and left for the hungry dogs to lick. I knew then as I peered forth from the curtains of my litter that war can make beasts of every one of us.

Robin looked well and bronzed. He was not under Richard's command but was colonel of the infantry under Sir John Berkeley, in the army of Prince Maurice. The King, he said, had decided to leave Grenvile to subdue Plymouth by slow starvation, while he and Prince Maurice marched east to join with his other nephew, Prince Rupert, and engage the Parliament forces hitherto unsubdued. I knew Richard would reckon this bad strategy, for Plymouth was one of the finest harbors in all England, and for His Majesty to have command of the sea was of great importance. Slow starvation had not conquered Plymouth before; why, then, should it do so now? What Richard needed for assault was guns and men.

As we traveled toward Radford, I noticed with secret pride that the only men who carried themselves like soldiers were those who wore the Grenvile shield on their shoulders. Some of Lord Goring's men were lolling about one village, drinking with the inhabitants, and from a nearby inn came a group of officers, laughing and very flushed. But the next post we passed was held by Grenvile men. There were perhaps a score of them standing by the postern, cleaning their equipment; they looked lean and tough, and I would have known them on the instant, even without the scarlet pennant with the three golden rests.

We came at length to Radford. My brother Jo was now a widower, Elizabeth Champernowne having died a few years before the war in childbed, and my youngest brother, Percy, with his wife, Phillippa, had come to live with him and look after Jo's son, a child of seven, they themselves being childless. The fighting did not touch them at Radford, for all its proximity to Plymouth, and the talk was all of the discomfort they had to bear by living within military control. I, straight from a sacked house and starvation, wondered that they should think themselves illused, with plenty of food upon the table, but no sooner had we sat down to dinner than Jo began to hold forth, with great heat, upon the dictatorial manners of the Army.

"His Majesty has conferred upon Richard Grenvile the designation of General in the West," he said. "Very good. I have no word to say against the appointment. But when Grenvile trades upon the title to commandeer all our cattle to feed his army, it is time we county gentry protested."

"The trouble with Grenvile," said Robin, "is that he insists that his fellows be paid. His men are like hired mercenaries. No free quarter, no looting, no foraging."

"Do you know," continued Jo, "that the commissioners of Devon are obliged to allot him one thousand pounds a week for the maintenance of his troops? I tell you, it hits us very hard."

"It would hit you harder if your house was burnt down by the Parliament," I said, and young Phillippa looked at me in wonder for my boldness. Woman's talk was not encouraged at Radford.

"That, my dear Honor," said Jo coldly, "is not likely to happen." Then he harped on about this new-styled "General in the West" requisitioning their horses and muskets for his siege of Plymouth.

"The fellow is without scruples," said Percy, "but in fairness, I must say that the country people tell me they would rather have Grenvile men in their villages than Goring and his cavalry. Goring's men are quite out of control, drunk from dawn to dusk."

"Oh, come." Jo frowned. "A certain amount of license must be permitted to keep the men in heart. We shall never win the war otherwise."

"You are more likely to lose it," I said, "by letting them loll about the villages with their tunics all undone."

It was upon this instant that a servant entered the room and announced Sir Richard Grenvile. He strode in, his boots ringing on the flagstone, and after a cool nod to Jo, the master of the house, he came at once to me and kissed my hand.

"Why the devil," he said, "did you come here and not to Buckland?" That he at once put me at a disadvantage among my relatives did not worry him. "The whelp is asking for you all day long. I have him outside with Joseph. Hi, spawn!" He turned on his heels, bawling for his son.

I never knew of any man save Richard who could in so brief a moment fill a room with his presence and become, as it were, the master of a house that was in no way his. Jo, Robin and Percy were like dumb servants waiting on the occasion, while Richard took command. Dick crept in cautiously, timid and scared as ever, his dark eyes lighting at the sight of me. Behind him strode young

Joseph Grenvile, Richard's kinsman and aide-de-camp, his features and coloring so like his general's as to make me wonder, not for the first time, whether he was not as much his son as Dick was.

"Have you all dined?" said Richard, reaching for a plum. "These lads and I could eat another dinner."

Jo, with heightened color, called the servants to bring back the mutton. Dick squeezed himself beside me, like a small dog regaining his lost mistress, and while they ate, Richard complained about the King having marched east without first seeing to it that Plymouth was subdued.

"The King should ask advice of soldiers," said Richard. "It's that damned lawyer who's to blame, that upstart Hyde, who is now chancellor of the exchequer. His Majesty won't move a finger without asking his advice. Fellows like this will lose the war for us."

"I have met Sir Edward Hyde," said my eldest brother. "He seemed to me a very able man."

"Able hell," said Richard. "Anyone who juggles with the treasury must be double-faced to start with. I've never met a lawyer yet who didn't line his own pockets before he fleeced his clients." After laying his hand a moment on Joseph's shoulder, he rose from the table. "Go on, lads, and see to your horses. Honor, I will take you to your apartment. Good evening, gentlemen."

I felt that whatever reputation I might have had for dignity in the eyes of my family was gone forever when he swept me off to my room. He laid me on my bed and sat beside me.

"You had far better," he said, "return with me to Buckland. Your brothers are all asses. And as for the Champernownes, I have a couple of them on my staff. You remember Edward, the one they wanted you to marry? Dead from the neck upwards."

"And what would I do at Buckland?" I said.

"You could look after the whelp," he said, "and minister to me in the evening. I get very tired of soldiers' company."

"There are plenty of women who could give you satisfaction."

"My God," he said, "if you think I want to bounce about with some fat female after a hard day's work sweating my guts out before the walls of Plymouth, you flatter my powers of resilience. Keep still, can't you, while I kiss you."

"I did not come to Radford," I said weakly, "to behave like this. You have placed me in a most embarrassing position."

"Don't worry, sweetheart," he said. "I did that to you sixteen years ago." I had half a mind to throw my pillow at him.

Below the window, waiting for him in the drive, Joe and Dick paced the horses up and down. "You and your double-faced attorneys," I said. "What about your own two faces? That boy out there—your precious Joseph—you told me he was your kinsman."

"So he is." He grinned, standing with his hand upon the door.

"Who is his mother?"

"A dairymaid at Killigarth. A most obliging soul. Married now to a farmer and mother of his twelve sturdy children."

"When did you discover Joseph?"

"A year or so ago. The likeness was unmistakable. I took some cheeses and a bowl of cream off his mother, and she recalled the incident, laughing with me in her kitchen. She bore no malice. The least I could do was to take him off her hands."

"You lived at Killigarth when you were courting me."

"Damn it," he said, "I didn't ride to see you every day."

In a moment I heard them all laughing beneath my window as they mounted their horses. And I thought how the blossom of my apple tree, so long dazzling and fragrant white, had a little lost its sheen and was become, after all, a common apple tree.

The following morning I heard the familiar sound of tramping feet; Matty, from the window, told me that a company of infantry was marching up the drive and they wore the Grenvile shield.

I bade the servants carry me downstairs to the hall. Here I discovered my brother Jo in heated argument with a young officer who declared coolly that his general wished to commandeer certain rooms of the house for himself as a temporary headquarters. Mr. Harris would be put to no inconvenience, as the general would be bringing his own servants, cooks and provisions.

"I protest this highly irregular proceeding," my brother said.

"The general has a warrant from His Majesty authorizing him to take over any place of residence in Devon or Cornwall that should please him. May I see the rooms, sir?"

My brother stared at the young officer for a moment, then turned on his heel and escorted him up the stairs.

I was alone when Jo came down again. "Well," he said grimly, "I suppose I have you to thank for this invasion."

"I know nothing about it," I answered, avoiding his eye.

"Nonsense, you planned it together last night, closeted there with him in your chamber." He looked down at me, his lips pursed. "You were always shameless as a girl," he said. "And now at thirty-four to behave like a dairymaid." He could not have chosen an epithet, to my mind, more unfortunate.

"My behavior last night," I said, "was very different from that of a dairymaid." But after that I felt brazen and unrepentant all the day, and when Richard appeared that evening in tearing spirits, commanding dinner for two in the apartment his soldiers had prepared for him, I had a glow of wicked satisfaction that my relatives sat below in gloomy silence while I ate roast duck with the general overhead.

"Since you would not come to Buckland," he said, "I had perforce to come to you."

"It is always a mistake," I said, "to fall out with a woman's brothers."

"Your brother Robin has ridden off with Berkeley's cavalry to Tavistock," he answered, "and Percy I'm sending on a delegation to the King. That leaves only Jo to be disposed of."

"And how long," I asked, "before Plymouth falls?"

He looked dubious. "They have the whole place strengthened. I'll never take it by direct assault unless I can increase my force by another thousand. I'm already recruiting hard up and down the county. But the fellows must be paid."

Richard had risen and was looking through the window toward the distant flickering lights of Plymouth. "Tonight," he said quietly, "I've made a gambler's throw. If it succeeds, Plymouth can be ours by daybreak."

"What do you mean?"

"I am in touch with the second-in-command in the garrison, a certain Colonel Searle. There is a possibility that for the sum of three thousand pounds he will surrender the city. Before wasting further lives I thought it worth my while to essay bribery."

I was silent. The prospect was hazardous and somehow smelled unclean. "How have you set about it?" I asked at length.

"Young Joe slipped through the lines tonight at sunset," he answered. "He bears upon him my message to the colonel."

"I don't like it. Supposing," I said slowly, "that they catch your Joseph?"

Richard smiled. "That lad is quite capable of looking after himself." But I thought of Lord Robartes as I had seen him last, sour and surly in defeat, and I knew how he detested the name of Grenvile.

"I shall be rising early," said Richard, "before you are awake. If by midday you hear a salvo from every gun inside the garrison, you will know that I have entered Plymouth."

He took my face in his hands and kissed it and then bade me good night. But I found it hard to sleep. I knew, with all the intuition in my body, that he had gambled wrong.

When I awoke, it was past ten o'clock. I heard the noises of the house and the coming and going of the soldiers in their wing, and at twelve o'clock I raised myself upon my elbow and looked out toward the river. Five past twelve. A quarter past. Half past twelve. There was no salvo from the guns.

The day dragged on, dull, interminable. At five o'clock, when Matty brought me my dinner on a tray, I asked if she had heard any news. She knew of none. But later, when she came to draw my curtains, her face was troubled.

"What is the matter?" I asked.

"Some trouble today in Plymouth," she answered. "One of their best young officers taken prisoner by Lord Robartes and condemned to death by council of war. Sir Richard has been endeavoring all day to ransom him but has not succeeded."

"Who is it?"

"The soldier did not say."

Later I heard horses coming up the drive and the sentries standing at attention. Footsteps climbed the stairs, slowly, heavily, and I heard him walk along the passage. Then his hand fumbled on the latch of my door. The candles were blown, and it was darkness. The household slept. He came to my side and knelt beside the bed. I put my hand on his head and held him close to me.

"They hanged him," he said, "above the gates of the town where we could see him. They hanged him before my eyes."

This was Richard's battle. I could not fight it for him. I could only hold him in the darkness.

"That rat Searle," he said, his voice broken, strangely unlike my Richard, "betrayed the scheme, and so they caught the lad. I went myself beneath the walls of the garrison to parley with Robartes. He gave no answer. And while I stood there waiting, they strung him up above the gate."

"Tomorrow," I said, "it might have been the same. A bullet

through his head. A thrust from a pike. This happens every day. An act of war. Joe died in your service, as he would wish."

"No," he said, his voice muffled. "It was my fault. On me the blame, now, tonight, for all eternity."

"Joe would forgive you. Joe would understand."

"I can't forgive myself. That's where the torture lies."

I thought then of all the things I wanted to lay before him. That this stroke of fate was but a grim reminder that cruelty begat cruelty; betrayal gave birth to treachery. In that moment when I held Richard in my arms I thought, We have come now to a crisis in his life. The dividing of the ways. Either to learn from this tragedy of a boy's death that the qualities he had fostered in himself these past years were now recoiled upon him; or to learn nothing, to continue through the years deaf to all counsel, unscrupulous, embittered.

"Richard," I whispered, "Richard, my dear and only love . . ." But he rose to his feet; he went slowly to the window, pulled aside the curtains and stood there with his face in shadow.

"I shall avenge him," he said, "with every life I take. No quarter anymore. No pardons. Not one of them shall be spared. His Majesty made me General in the West, and, by God, I swear that the whole world shall know it."

I knew then that his worse self possessed him, soul and body, and that nothing I could say or do would help him.

CHAPTER NINE

ALTHOUGH HIS MAIN headquarters was at Buckland, Richard was constantly at Radford during the six months that followed. I could have thrown my cap over the mills and gone to live with him at Buckland, but this I refused to do. Always, at the back of my mind, was the fear that with too great intimacy I would become a burden to him and the lovely freedom between us would exist no more. The knowledge of my crippled state, the sense of helplessness, so happily glossed over and indeed forgotten when he came to me at Radford, would have nagged me, a perpetual reproach, had I lived beneath his roof at Buckland. And even when he was most gentle and most tender I should have thought—with some devil flash of intuition—This is not what he is wanting. Sixteen years of discipline had taught me to accept my crippled state, but I was too proud to share its stigma with Richard. Oh, God, what I would have given to walk and ride with him, to move and turn before him with liveliness and grace.

And so the autumn passed and a new year came upon us once again. The whole of the West Country was held firmly for the King, save Plymouth, Lyme and Taunton, three garrisons that stubbornly defied all attempts at subjugation. In January Richard became sheriff of Devon, and with this additional authority he could raise fresh troops and levies. But he rode roughshod over the feelings of the commissioners of the county when he demanded men and money as a right. For the smallest pretext he would have a gentleman arrested and clapped into jail until a ransom was paid.

I think he became more hated every day by the merchants and the gentry, but by the common people more respected. His troops won such credit for high discipline that their fame spread far abroad, and this, I believe, sowed the first seeds of jealousy in the hearts of his brother commanders. None of them were professionals like himself but men of estate and fortune. Though many were gallant and courageous, warfare to them consisted of a furious charge upon blood horses, dangerous and exciting, and when the fray was over, back to their quarters to eat, drink and play cards, while the men they had led fended for themselves. But it was irritating, I imagine, to hear praise for Grenvile's men and to learn how they were paid and fed and clothed. Sir John Berkeley, for one, was glad enough to report to Prince Maurice that even if Grenvile's men were disciplined, the commissioners of Devon had no good to say of Grenvile himself, that in spite of all the fire-eating and hanging of rebel prisoners, Plymouth was still not taken.

Richard's blockade of Plymouth was complete by land, but the rebels having command of the sound, provisions and relief could be brought to them by sea, and this was the real secret of their success. All that he as commander of the siege could hope to do was to so wear out the defenders by constant surprise attacks that in time they would, from very weariness, surrender.

It was shortly after Christmas that Richard decided to send Dick to Normandy with his tutor. "Ever since Joe went," he said, "I've had a guard watch Dick day and night, and the thought of him so close to the enemy has become a constant anxiety."

So Dick and the timid, unconvincing Herbert Ashley set sail for

Normandy the last day of December. And while they rocked upon the Channel between Falmouth and Saint-Malo, Richard launched an attack upon Plymouth that this time, so he promised, would not fail.

"There are four forts to the north, in line abreast," he said. "I propose to seize them all. My main strength will fall upon the Maudlyn fort, the others being more in the nature of a feint to draw their fire." He was in tearing spirits, as always before a big engagement, and suddenly he said to me, "You have never seen my fellows, have you, in their full war paint prior to a battle? Would you like to?"

"Do you propose to make me your aide-de-camp?"

"No. I am going to take you around the posts."

It was three o'clock on a cold fine afternoon in January. One of the wagons was fitted as a litter for my person, and with Richard riding at my side, we set forth to view his army. It was a sight that even now, when all is over and done with, I can call before me with wonder and with pride.

The first signal that the general had come in person was a springing to attention of the guards before the camp, and within moments the air rang with a tattoo as the drums of every company sounded the alert. Swiftly my chair was lifted from the wagon, and with a stalwart young corporal to propel me, we proceeded around the camp. It was a strange review, me in my chair, a hooded cloak about my shoulders, and Richard walking by my side.

I can smell now the wood smoke from the fires, and I can see the men kneeling before the cooking pots, straightening themselves with a jerk as we approached and standing at attention like steel rods. We inspected the infantry first, then the cavalry drawn up on the farther field. We watched the horses being groomed and watered for the night, fine sleek animals—many seized from rebel estates.

The sun was setting fiery red, throwing a last dull, sullen glow upon the forts of Plymouth to the south of us, and I wondered how many of the Grenvile men about me would next day make themselves a sacrifice to the spitting thunder of the rebel guns. As evening fell, we visited the forward posts. Here the men were silent, motionless, and we talked in whispers, for we were scarce two hundred yards from the enemy defenses.

At the last post we visited, the men were not so prompt to

challenge us as hitherto, and I heard Richard administer a sharp reproof to the young officer in charge. The colonel in command of the post came forth to excuse himself, and I saw that it was my old suitor of the past, Jo's brother-in-law, Edward Champernowne. He bowed to me somewhat stiffly, and then, turning to Richard, he stammered several attempts at explanation. The two withdrew to a little distance. On his return Richard was silent, and we straightway turned back toward my wagon and the escort.

"You must return alone to Radford," he said. "I will send the escort with you. There will be no danger."

"And the coming battle?" I asked. "Are you confident?"

He paused a moment before replying. "Yes, I am hopeful. The plan is sound, and there is nothing wanting in the men. If only my seconds were more dependable." He jerked his head toward the post from which we had just lately come. "Your old lover, Edward Champernowne," he said, "I sometimes think he would do better to command a squad of ducks."

"Can you not replace him with some other?" I questioned.

"Not at this juncture," he said. "I have to risk him now." He kissed my hand and smiled, and I jogged back in the wagon to my brother's house, my spirits sinking.

Shortly before daybreak next morning the attack began. By midday we had the news that three of the forts had been seized by the Royalist troops, and the most formidable of them, the Maudlyn, had been stormed by the commanding general in person.

At three o'clock the news was not so good. The rebels had counterattacked, and two of the forts had been recaptured. We dined in the hall at half past five. We ate in silence, none of us having much heart for conversation while the battle only a few miles away hung in the balance. We were nearly finished when my brother Percy, who had ridden down to Plymstock to get news, came bursting in upon us.

"The rebels have gained the day," he said grimly, "and driven off Grenvile with the loss of three hundred men. It seems that Grenvile's covering troops, who should have come to his support, failed to reach him. A tremendous blunder on the part of someone."

"No doubt the fault of the general himself," said Jo dryly.

"They say in Plymstock that the officer responsible has been shot by Grenvile for contravention of orders," said Percy.

Just then a young secretary employed by my eldest brother

came into the room, much agitated. "What is the matter?" said Jo.

"Colonel Champernowne lies at Egg Buckland mortally wounded," said the secretary. "He was not hurt in battle but pistoled by the general himself on returning to headquarters."

There was a moment of great silence. Jo rose slowly from his chair, very white and tense, and turned to look at me, as did my brother Percy. I knew what they were thinking. Edward Champernowne had been my suitor seventeen years before, and they both saw in this sudden terrible dispute after the heat of battle no military cause but some private jealous wrangle, the settling of a feud. "This," said my eldest brother slowly, "is the beginning of the end for Richard Grenvile."

His words fell upon my ear cold as steel. Calling softly to a servant, I bade him take me to my room.

The next day I left for Maddercombe, to stay with my sister Cecilia, for to remain under my brother's roof one moment longer would have been impossible. The vendetta had begun. . . .

SNOWED IN AT Maddercombe with the Pollexefens, I knew little of what was happening. The thaw burst at the end of March, and we had the first tidings of the outside world for many weeks.

The Parliament, so we heard, was forming a new model army, likely to sweep all before it. The young Prince of Wales was now to bear the title of supreme commander of all the forces in the West, but being a lad of only fifteen years or so, the real authority would be vested in his advisory council, at the head of which was Hyde, the chancellor of the exchequer.

John Pollexefen shook his head as he heard the news. "There will be nothing but wrangles now between the prince's council and the generals," he said. "Lawyers and soldiers never agree. And while they wrangle, the King's cause will suffer."

"What is happening at Plymouth?" asked my sister.

"Stalemate," said her husband. "A token force of less than a thousand men left to blockade the garrison, and Grenvile with the remainder gone to join Goring and lay siege to Taunton. The spring campaign has started."

March turned to April; the golden gorse was in full bloom. And on Easter Day a horseman came riding down the valley, wearing the Grenvile badge. He asked at once for Mistress Harris and, after saluting gravely, handed me a letter.

"What has happened?" I asked before I broke the seal.

"The general has been gravely wounded," replied the soldier.

I tore open the letter and read Richard's shaky scrawl:

Dear heart, This is the very devil. I am like to lose my leg, if not my life, with a great gaping hole in my thigh below the groin. I know now what you suffer. Come teach me patience. I love you.

I folded the letter and, turning to the messenger, asked him where the general lay.

"They were bringing him from Taunton down to Exeter when I left," he answered. "He was very weak and bade me ride without delay to bring you this."

I looked at Cecilia, standing by the window. "Would you summon Matty to pack my clothes," I said, "and ask John if he would arrange for a litter and for horses? I am going to Exeter."

WE TOOK THE southern route, and at every halt upon the journey I thought to hear the news of Richard's death. When after six days I reached the capital of Devon it seemed to me I had been weeks upon the road.

Richard still lived. I repaired at once to the hostelry in the cathedral square, which he had taken for his personal use, and gave the sentry my name. A young officer immediately appeared from within, and something ruddy about his coloring and familiar in his courteous bearing made me pause a moment before addressing him correctly. "You are Jack Grenvile, Bevil's boy," I said.

"Yes. And my uncle will be most heartily glad to see you," he said. "He has talked of little else since writing to you."

"And how is he?" I asked as I was lifted from my litter and set down within the parlor of the great inn.

"Better than hitherto," Jack replied. "At first we thought to lose him. Directly he was wounded, I applied to the Prince of Wales to wait on him and attended him here from Taunton."

"Your uncle," I said, "likes to have a Grenvile by his side."

At this moment Richard's servant came down the stairs, saying the general wished to see Mistress Harris upon this instant. I went first to my room, where Matty washed me and changed my gown, and then with Jack Grenvile to escort me I went along the corridor in my wheeled chair to Richard's room.

It looked out upon the cobbled square, and as we entered, the great bell from the cathedral chimed four o'clock.

"God confound that blasted bell," said a familiar voice, sounding stronger than I had dared hope, from the dark-curtained bed in the far corner. "A dozen times I have asked the mayor of this damned city to have it silenced, and nothing has been done. And these pillows behind my head. Where the devil is Jack? Jack knows how I like them placed."

"Here I am, Uncle," said his nephew, "but you will not need me now. I have brought you someone with gentler hands than I." He pushed my chair toward the bed, smiling.

Richard pulled back the curtains. "Ah!" he said, sighing deeply. "You have come at last."

He was deathly white. His auburn locks were clipped short, giving him a strangely youthful look. For the first time I noticed in him a resemblance to Dick. I took his hand and held it. "I did not wait," I said, "once I had read your letter."

He turned to Jack at the foot of the bed. "Get out," he said.

"Sir," his nephew replied, clicking his heels, and I could swear that as he left the room young Jack Grenvile winked.

Richard lifted my hand to his lips and then cradled it beside his cheek. "This is a good jest," he said, "on the part of the Almighty. You and I both smitten in the thigh."

"Does it pain you much?" I asked.

"Pain me? My God, of course it pains me."

"Who has seen the wound?"

"Every surgeon in the Army, and each one makes more mess of it than his fellow."

I called for Matty, who was waiting outside the door, and she came in at once with a basin of warm water and bandages.

"Good day to you, Mutton-face," said Richard. "How many corporals have you bedded with en route?"

"No time to bed with anyone," snapped Matty, "carried at the rate we were. Now we've come here to be insulted."

"I'll not insult you, unless you tie my bandages too tight."

"Let's see what they have done, then." She unfolded the bandages and exposed the wound. With every probe of her fingers he groaned, calling her every name under the sun. "It's clean, that's one thing," she said. "I fully expected to find it gangrenous. But you'll have some of those splinters to the end of your days."

She washed the wound and dressed it once again, and all the while he held my hand as Dick might do. Then she finished, and he thumbed his finger to his nose as she left the room.

"Over three months," he said, "since I have seen you. Are the Pollexefens as unpleasant as the rest of your family?"

"My family were not unpleasant till you made them so."

"They always disliked me. Now they pursue their dislike across the county. You know the commissioners of Devon are in Exeter at this moment with a list of complaints a mile long to launch at me? It's all a plot hatched by your brother to have me shifted from my command and for Berkeley to take my place."

"Would you mind so very much? The blockade of Plymouth has not brought you much satisfaction."

"Berkeley is welcome to Plymouth. But I'm not going to lie down and accept some secondary command dished out by the prince's council while I hold authority from the King himself."

"His Majesty," I said, "appears by all accounts to have his own troubles. Who is this General Cromwell we hear so much about?"

"Another damned Puritan with a mission," said Richard. "He's a good soldier, though. His new model army will make mincemeat of our disorganized rabble."

"And knowing this, you choose to quarrel with your friends?"

"They are not my friends. They are a set of low, backbiting blackguards. And I have told them all so to their faces."

No man was ever a worse patient than Richard Grenvile, and no nurse more impervious to threats, groans and curses than Matty. He kept to his bed for five weeks, but by the end of May was sufficiently recovered to walk his chamber with a stick and at the same time curse his harassed staff for idleness.

"It is a splendid sign," Jack Grenvile said to me privately, "when my uncle gives vent to frowns and curses. It mostly means he is well pleased."

Meanwhile the prince's council had come to Exeter to have discussions with the Devon commissioners and to hear the complaints they had to make against Sir Richard Grenvile. It was unfortunate, I felt, that the head of the prince's council was that same Sir Edward Hyde whom Richard had once described to me as an upstart. I thought his manner very cold and formal, and I could see that he, in turn, bore little cordiality toward Richard.

What, in truth, transpired behind those closed doors I never discovered. It ended, so Richard told me afterward, when he scornfully declared to the three members of the prince's council, "Let Berkeley take over Plymouth if he desires. Give me power to raise men in Cornwall and in Devon, without fear of obstruction, and I will place an army at the disposal of the Prince of Wales that will be a match for Cromwell's Puritans." Whereupon he formally handed over his resignation as commander of the siege of Plymouth and sent the lords of the council packing off to Bristol to receive the prince's authority sanctioning him to a new command.

We waited ten days or more for the royal warrant confirming him in the appointment to raise troops, but it did not come. At last Richard declared that he would not cool his heels waiting for a piece of paper that few people would take the trouble to read; he intended to proceed at once to raise recruits for the new army.

"I cannot stand this hopeless mess an instant longer," he said. "I shall ride to Bristol to see the prince. Unless I can get satisfaction out of His Highness, I shall chuck the whole affair."

"You are not well enough to ride," I said.

"I can't help that. I won't stay here and have that hopeless nincompoop Berkeley obstruct every move I make. He is hand in glove with your blasted brother, that's the trouble."

"You began the trouble by making an enemy of my brother. All this has come about because you shot Edward Champernowne."

"What would you have had me do, promote the idiot?" he stormed. "A weak-bellied rat who caused the death of three hundred of my finest troops because he was too lily-livered to face the rebel guns and come to my support. A hundred years ago he would have been drawn and quartered."

I was thankful that when he left Exeter the next day he took his nephew Jack as aide-de-camp. He had three men to hoist him in the saddle and he still looked most unwell. He smiled up at me as I leaned from my window in the hostelry, and saluted with his sword.

"Have no fear," he said, "I'll return within a fortnight."

But he did not. . . .

On the eighteenth of June the King and Prince Rupert were heavily defeated by General Cromwell at Naseby. I had a message from Richard saying that he had been commissioned field marshal and ordered by the Prince of Wales to besiege Lyme, and that the rebel army was marching once again toward the West.

This news was hardly pleasant, and I thought of the relentless marching feet that I had heard a year ago at Menabilly. Was the whole horror of invasion to be endured once again?

I stayed on at Exeter. I had no home; one roof was as good to me now as another, and Richard had said he would send for me. I was nothing more nor less, by this time, than a camp follower. A pursuivant of the drum.

On the last day of June, when Jack Grenvile came for me with a troop of cavalry to bear my litter, Matty and I were packed and ready. "Where are we bound," I said gaily, "for Lyme or London?"

"For neither," he said grimly. "For a tumbledown residence in Ottery Saint Mary. The general has thrown up his commission." He could tell me little of what had happened, except that the bulk of forces that had been assigned to Richard's new command had suddenly been withdrawn by order of the prince's council, without a word of explanation to the general.

We came to Ottery Saint Mary, a sleepy Devon village where the inhabitants stared at the strange equipage that drew before the manor house as though they thought the world had suddenly grown crazy. Richard himself was seated in the dining chamber of his headquarters, his wounded leg propped up on a chair before him.

"Greetings," he said maliciously, "from one cripple to another."

"Would you care to tell me what you are doing here?" I asked.

"I am a free man," he answered, smiling, "beholden to no one. Let them fight the new model army in their own fashion."

"I thought," I said, "that you had become field marshal."

"An empty honor," he said, "signifying nothing. I have returned the commission to the Prince of Wales. Let him do with it as he pleases. What shall we drink for supper, Rhine wine or Burgundy?"

THAT WAS, I think, the most fantastic fortnight I have ever known. Richard, with no command and no commission, lived like a royal prince in the humble village of Ottery Saint Mary, his headquarters being the home of an unfortunate squire with vague Parliamentary tendencies and a well-stocked cellar and larder.

"We may as well be merry," he said, "while the money lasts."

"What will you do," I asked, "if the council sends for you?"

"Exactly nothing," he answered, "unless I have a letter, in his own handwriting, from the Prince of Wales himself."

Then at breakfast one morning a messenger came riding with the news that Bridgwater had been captured by rebel forces, and the Prince of Wales bade Sir Richard Grenvile come to him in Cornwall upon the instant with what troops he had.

"Is the message a request or a command?" asked my general.

"A command, sir," replied the officer, handing him a document, "not from the council, but from the prince himself."

Once again the drums were sounded for the march, and the long line of troops wound their way through the village and onto the highway. In a day or two we followed, Matty and I, to Werrington House, near Launceston, which was yet another property that Richard had seized without a scruple. We arrived to find Richard in fair spirits, restored to the prince's favor after a very awkward three hours before the council, during which it had been decided he should endeavor to raise a force of some three thousand men in Cornwall.

"They cannot afford to do without me," said Richard. "Men will rally to a Grenvile, but none other. I don't give a fig for the council or that snake Hyde. I am doing this only to oblige the prince, a lad after my own heart."

While Matty and I remained at Werrington, Richard traveled the length and breadth of Cornwall recruiting troops. It was no easy business. In the north, near Stowe, men did rally to his call, but farther south he met rebuffs. The last invasion had been enough for many Cornishmen, who wished only to be left alone to tend their land and business. Richard, during that summer and early autumn of 1645, made as many enemies among the Cornish landowners as he had among the Devon gentry. There was constant faultfinding, too, by the prince's council in Launceston, and scarcely a day would pass without some interfering measure from the chancellor, Edward Hyde.

The fall of Bristol to the Parliament came like the crack of doom in September. Chard, Crediton, Lyme, and finally Tiverton fell before the rebels in October, and Lord Goring had done nothing to stop them. Many of his men deserted and came flocking to join Richard's army, having greater faith in him as a commander. Then suddenly, without warning, Lord Goring threw up his command and went to France, giving as reason that his health had cracked.

"The rats," said Richard slowly, "are beginning, one by one, to desert the sinking ship."

The command in Devon was given to Lord Wentworth, an officer with little experience. He immediately went into winter quarters and declared that nothing could be done against the enemy until the spring. It was at this moment, I think, that the prince's council realized they were fighting a losing cause. . . .

Preparations were made to move from Launceston and go farther west to Truro. This, Richard told me grimly, could mean but one thing. They wanted to be near Falmouth, so that when the crisis came, the Prince of Wales and the leaders of the council could flee by ship to France.

"And the King?" I asked.

Richard did not answer for a moment. He had grown more worn and lined during the past few months, the result of his endless anxieties, and the silver streak that ran through his auburn locks had broadened. The raw November weather nipped his wounded leg, and I guessed, from my experience, what he must suffer.

"There is no hope for the King," he said at length, "unless he can come to some agreement with the Scots and raise an army from them. If he fails, his cause is doomed."

I knew only too well. For more than three years men had fought and suffered and died for King Charles, that proud, stiff little man with his rigid principles.

"Richard," I said, "would you, too, leave the sinking ship?"

"Not," he said, "if there is any chance of holding Cornwall for the prince."

"But if the prince should sail for France," I persisted, "and the whole of Cornwall be overrun—what then?"

"I would follow him," he answered, "and raise a French army of fifty thousand men and land again in Cornwall."

He knelt beside me, and I held his face between my hands.

"We have been happy in our strange way, you and I," I said.

"My camp follower"—he smiled—"my trailer of the drum."

"You know that I am given up as lost to all perdition by good persons," I said. "Even my dear Robin is ashamed of his sister. I had a letter from him this very morning. He implores me to leave you and return to the Rashleighs at Menabilly."

"You would be safer in Menabilly than in Launceston."

"That was said last time, and you know what happened then."

"Yes, you suffered," he said, "and the experience made a woman of you. When the crisis comes, I will send you and Matty to Menabilly. If we win the day, so far so good. If the cause is lost, then I will come riding to you at your Rashleighs', and we will get a fishing boat and sail across the Channel and find Dick."

"Do you promise?"

"Yes, sweetheart, I promise."

The next day the prince's council summoned Richard to Truro and asked what advice he could give them for the defense of Cornwall and how the safety of the Prince of Wales could best be assured. He composed a letter to the secretary of war and gave full details of his plan, much of which filled me with misgiving because the kernel of it was so likely to be misconstrued. He proposed, in short, to make a treaty with the Parliament, by which Cornwall would become a duchy separate from the rest of England and be ruled by the Prince of Wales, as duke. Thus gaining a respite, the people of Cornwall, and especially the western army, would become strong enough in a year or more to give effective aid to the King. (This last, it may be realized, was not to be one of the clauses in the treaty.)

Failing an agreement with Parliament, Richard advised creating a first line of defense that would make the whole of Cornwall into a virtual island by digging ditches from Barnstaple, on the north coast, south to the Tamar River, which empties into the English Channel. Any attempt at invasion could then be immediately repulsed by destroying all bridges along the riverbank. This line, he averred, could be held for an indefinite period.

When he had finished his report Richard returned to Werrington. A week passed, and no reply. Then at last a cold message came from the secretary of war saying that his plan had not found approval. The prince's council would consider other measures and acquaint Sir Richard Grenvile when his services would be required.

"So," said Richard, throwing the letter onto my lap, "the council prefer to lose the war in their own fashion. Let them do so. Time is getting short, and it would be wise, my Honor, if you sent word to Mary Rashleigh that you would spend Christmas with her."

"And you?" I said with that old sick twist of foreboding.

"I will come later," he said, "and we will see the new year in together in that room above the gatehouse."

And so on the third morning of December I set forth again, after fifteen months, for my brother-in-law's house of Menabilly.

CHAPTER TEN

M Y SECOND COMING to Menabilly was very different from my
first. As we turned in at the park gates and climbed the hill
toward the house, I saw at once that the walls had not been
repaired. Only a few lean cattle grazed within the park, and even
now, after a full year and more, I noticed great bare patches of
grassland where the rebel tents had stood, and the blackened
roots of the trees they had felled for firewood. I wondered, with a
strange feeling of sadness and regret, whether I would be as
welcome now as I had been fifteen months before. Glancing up at
my old apartment in the gatehouse, I saw that it was shuttered
and untenanted, even as the barred room beside it, and that the
whole west wing wore the same forlorn appearance. Then came
my sister Mary out upon the steps, and I noticed with a shock that
her hair had gone quite white. Yet she greeted me with her same
grave smile and gentle kiss. I was taken straightway to the gallery, where I found my dear Alice strung about as always with her
mob of babies, the newest of the brood, just turned twelve
months, clutching at her knee in her first steps. This was now all
our party. My goddaughter, Joan, was living with John and the
children in the Rashleigh town house at Fowey. My brother-in-
law, it seemed, was somewhere about the grounds. At once I had
to hear all the news of the past year, of how Jonathan had not yet
received one penny from the crown to help him in the restoration
of his property; whatever had been done he had done himself,
with the aid of his servants and tenants.

"Cornwall is become totally impoverished," said my sister
sadly. "Unless the war ends swiftly, we shall all be ruined."

"It may end swiftly," I said, "but not as you would wish."

"But they say His Majesty will soon send an army to the West."

"His Majesty is too preoccupied with keeping his own troops
together in the Midlands," I answered, "to concern himself about
the West."

"You do not think," said Alice anxiously, "that Cornwall is
likely to suffer invasion once again?"

"I do not see how we can avoid it."

"But—we have plenty of troops, have we not?" said Mary. "I
know we have been taxed hard enough to provide for them."

"Troops without boots or stockings make poor fighters," I said, "especially if they have no powder for their muskets."

"Jonathan says everything has been mismanaged," said Mary. "The prince's council says one thing—the commanders another."

Their expressions told me that Sir Richard Grenvile was being blamed at Menabilly as elsewhere for his high-handed ways. "Perhaps," I said, "having dwelt with Richard Grenvile for the past eight months, ever since he was wounded, I am prejudiced in his favor. I know his faults far better than you. But he is the best soldier in His Majesty's Army, and the prince's council would do well to listen to his advice." But I wondered, with a heavy heart, how many friends were now left to my Richard.

The weather was cold and dreary, and I spent much of my time within my chamber, the same pleasant room that Gartred had been given fifteen months before. It had suffered little in the general damage, for which, I suppose, thanks had to be rendered to her. I was content enough, yet strangely empty, for it comes hard to be alone again after eight months in company with the man you love. When I was with him the days were momentous and full; now they had all the chill drabness of December.

At Christmas came John and Joan from Fowey, and Peter Courtney, given a few days' grace from the watch on Plymouth. We all made merry for the children's sake, and maybe for our own as well. Cromwell and the rebels were forgotten as we roasted chestnuts before the two fires in the gallery. I remember, too, an old blind harpist who was given shelter for the night on Christmas Eve and came and played to us in the soft candlelight. I asked Jonathan if he was not afraid of thieves in these difficult times when so many homeless wandered the roads. Shaking his head, he gestured grimly to the few faded tapestries and worn chairs.

"I have nothing left of value," he said, and then, with a half-smile and a lowered voice, "Even the secret chamber and the tunnel contain nothing now but rats and cobwebs."

Next morning we woke to a white world, strangely still, and a sunless sky teeming with further snow to come, while clear and compelling through the silence came the Christmas bells from the church at Tywardreath. I thought of Richard at Werrington, and I feared that he would never keep his promise to come to me now, with snowdrifts deep upon the moors.

But he did come, at midday on the ninth of January, when a

thaw had made slush of the frozen snow, and the road was just passable to an intrepid horseman. He brought Jack Grenvile with him and Jack's younger brother, Bunny, a youngster of about the age of Dick who had spent Christmas with his uncle and now never left his side, vowing he would join the Army and kill rebels. As I watched Richard laugh and jest with him, I felt a pang of sorrow for Dick, lonely and unloved across the sea in Normandy. Why should Richard always show himself so considerate and kind to other lads, and remain a stranger to his own son?

My brother-in-law, who had known Bevil well, bade welcome to Bevil's boys, and after a fleeting moment of constraint, he welcomed Richard, too, with courtesy. Richard looked better, I thought, and after five minutes his was the only voice we heard in the long gallery, a sort of hush coming upon the Rashleigh family. None of them were natural anymore because of the general, and glancing at my sister Mary, I saw the well-known frown upon her face as she wondered which apartment could be given to him.

"You are on the way to Truro, I suppose?" she said to him, thinking he would be gone by morning.

"No," he answered, "I thought, while the hard weather lasted, I might bide with you a week at Menabilly and shoot duck instead of rebels."

I saw her dart a look of consternation at Jonathan. There was a silence, which Richard found not at all unusual, as he was unused to other voices but his own. If this continued, the atmosphere of Menabilly would be far from easy, but Jack Grenvile, with a discretion born of long practice, tapped his uncle on the shoulder. "Look, sir," he said, "there are your duck." And pointing to the sky above the garden, he showed the teal in flight.

Richard was at once a boy again, laughing, jesting. In a moment the men of the household fell under the spell of his change of mood, and John and Peter, and even my brother-in-law, were making for the shore. We wrapped ourselves in cloaks and went out to watch the sport, and it seemed to me that the years had rolled away when I saw Richard, with Peter's goshawk on his wrist, turn to laugh at me. For a brief moment the sun came from the white sky and shone upon us, and the world was dazzling.

This, I thought, is an interlude, lasting a single second. I have my Richard, Alice has her Peter, Joan her John. Nothing can touch us for today. There is no war. The enemy are not in Devon, waiting for the word to march. Surely Richard was mistaken. They could not come again.

There was a shouting from the valley, and up from the marshes rose the duck, with the hawks above them, circling, and I shivered of a sudden for no reason. Then the sun went blank, and a cat's-paw rippled the sea, while a great shadow passed across a nearby hill. Something fell upon my cheek, soft and clammy white. It was snowing once again. . . .

I SLEPT UNEASILY that night, and at one moment I thought I heard the sound of horses' hooves riding across the park, but I told myself it was only fancy and the wind stirring in the snow-laden trees. But when Matty came to me with breakfast she bore a note from Richard, and I learned that he and the two Grenviles and Peter Courtney had all ridden from the house shortly after daybreak. A messenger had come with the news that Cromwell had made a night attack on Lord Wentworth and, finding the Royalist army asleep, had captured four hundred of the cavalry while the infantry who had not been captured had fled in complete disorder.

Wentworth has been caught napping, Richard had scribbled on a torn sheet of paper, *which is exactly what I feared. I am riding forthwith to the prince's council and offering my services. Unless they appoint a supreme commander to take over Wentworth's rabble, we shall have the rebels across the Tamar.*

I rose that morning with a heavy heart. Upon going downstairs to the gallery, I found Alice in tears, for she knew that Peter would be foremost in the fighting when the moment came. My brother-in-law departed at midday to discover what help might be needed from the landowners and gentry in the possibility of invasion, and John set forth to warn the tenants on the estate that once again their services might be needed. The day was wretchedly reminiscent of that other day in August, nearly eighteen months before. But now there were no strong Cornish forces to lure the rebels to a trap, with another Royalist army marching in the rear.

In the afternoon one of the servants reported that the rumor ran in Fowey that the siege of Plymouth had been raised, and that Sir John Digby's troops, along with Wentworth's, were now retreating fast to the Tamar bridges.

We sat before the moldering fire in the gallery, a little group of wretched women. "The King will surely march west now," Alice

was saying. "He could not leave Cornwall in the lurch. When the thaw breaks . . ."

"Our defenses will withstand the rebels," Joan said. "They say we have a new musket—with a longer barrel—I do not know exactly, but the rebels will not face it, so John says. . . ."

"The rebels have no money," said Mary. "In London the people are starving. They have no bread. The Parliament is bound to seek terms from the King. When the spring comes . . ."

I wanted to put my fingers in my ears and muffle the sound of their voices. The rebels must give in. . . . They are worse off than we. . . . *When the snow melts, when the thaw breaks, when the spring comes . . .*

That evening, on going to my room, I looked out and saw the night was clear. I called Matty to me and told her I was resolved to follow Richard back to Werrington if transport could be found. I had, in my heart, a premonition that unless I did so I would never see him more. What I feared, I cannot tell. But it came to me that he might fall in battle and that by following him I would be with him at the last.

When I informed the Rashleigh family of my plan, they one and all begged me to remain, saying it was folly to travel the roads in such a season, but I was firm; and at length John Rashleigh arranged matters for me and accompanied me as far as Bodmin.

It was bitter cold upon the moors, and I had little stomach for my journey as, with Matty at my side, I left the Bodmin hostelry at daybreak. The long road to Launceston stretched before us, bleak and dreary, with great snowdrifts on either side. Although we were wrapped about with blankets, the nipping, nagging wind penetrated the carriage curtains, freezing our faces. Every now and then we would pass straggling figures making for the west, their apparel proclaiming that once they had been the King's men, but were now deserters. They wore a brazen, sullen look, and some of them shouted as we passed, "To hell with the war, we're going home," and shook their fists at my litter, jeering, "You're driving to the devil."

At last we came to Werrington, and when the startled sentry at the gates recognized me and let the horses pass through the park, I thought that even he, a Grenvile man, had lost his look of certainty and pride. We drew up into the cobbled court, and an officer came forth whose face was new to me. He told me that the general was in conference and could not be disturbed. I thought that Jack or Bunny might help me and asked, therefore, for Sir John Grenvile or his brother, Mr. Bernard.

"Sir John is no longer with the general," answered the officer. "The Prince of Wales recalled him to his entourage yesterday. And Bernard Grenvile has returned to Stowe. I am the general's aide-de-camp at present."

This was not hopeful, for he did not know me, and I thought how ill-timed and crazy was my visit. What could they do with me, a woman and a cripple, in this moment of stress and urgency?

I heard voices. "They are coming out now," said the officer. "The conference is over."

I caught sight of Colonel Roscarrick, whom I knew well, a loyal friend of Richard's, and I leaned from my litter and called to him. He came at once, in great astonishment, and gave orders for me to be carried into the house.

"Ask me no questions," I said. "I have come at a bad moment, I can guess that. Can I see him?"

Colonel Roscarrick hesitated for a fraction of a minute. "He will want to see you," he said. "But I must warn you, things are not going well for him." Then he went into the room that Richard used as his own and where we had sat together, night after night, for so long. He returned in a moment, took me to the room, then closed the door. Richard was standing by the table, his face set in hard, firm lines.

"What the devil," he said wearily, "are you doing here?"

"I am sorry," I said. "I could not rest once you were gone. If anything is going to happen—which I know it must—I want to share it with you. The danger, I mean. And the aftermath."

He laughed shortly and tossed a paper onto my lap. "There'll be no danger," he said, "not for you or me."

"What do you mean?"

"That letter, you can read it," he said. "It is a copy of a message I have just sent to the prince's council, resigning from His Majesty's Army. They will have it in an hour's time." He went to the fire and stood with his hands behind his back. "I went to them as soon as I returned from Menabilly and said if they wished to save Cornwall and the prince, they must appoint a supreme commander. They thanked me. They said they would consider the matter. I rode next morning down on Tamar-side to inspect the defenses.

There I commanded a certain colonel of the infantry to blow a bridge when need arose. He disputed my authority, saying his orders were to the contrary. Would you like to know his name?"

I said nothing. Some inner sense had told me.

"It was your brother, Robin Harris. 'I cannot take orders from a man,' he said, 'who has ruined the life and reputation of my sister. Sir John Digby is my commander, and Sir John has bidden me to leave this bridge intact.'"

I could see Robin, very red about the neck, with beating heart and swelling anger, thinking, dear damned idiot, that by defying his commander he was somehow defending me.

"What then?" I asked. "Did you see Digby?"

"No. He would have defied me, as your brother did. I returned here to take my commission from the council as supreme commander, and thus show my powers to the whole Army."

"And have you the commission?"

He leaned toward the table, seized a small piece of parchment and began to read with deadly emphasis and scorn. "'The council of the prince appoints Lord Hopton in supreme command of His Majesty's forces in the West and desires that Sir Richard Grenvile should serve under him as lieutenant general of the cavalry.'"

He tore the document to tiny shreds and threw the pieces in the fire. "This is my answer to them," he said. "Tomorrow, you and I will return to Menabilly."

"You can't do this," I said. "You must do as they tell you."

"Must?" he said. "There is no must. Do you think that I shall truckle to that confounded lawyer Hyde? I can see him, with his bland attorney's manner, talking to the council. 'This man Grenvile is dangerous,' he says to them. 'If we give him the supreme command, he will take matters into his own hands. We will give Hopton the command; Hopton will not dare to disobey. And when the enemy crosses the Tamar, Hopton will withstand them just long enough for us to slip across to Guernsey with the prince.' The traitor, the disloyal coward!"

I persisted. "Don't you understand, my love, it is you they will call disloyal if you refuse to serve under another man, with the enemy in Devon? It is you who will be reviled, not Hyde."

He would not listen; he brushed me away with his hand. And just then the new aide-de-camp knocked upon the door, bearing a letter in his hand. Richard took it, read the message, then with a laugh threw it in the fire.

"A summons from the council," he said, "to appear before them at ten tomorrow in the Castle Court at Launceston."

"Will you go?" I asked.

"I shall," he said. "And then proceed with you to Menabilly."

"You will not swallow your pride and do as they demand?"

"No," he said slowly, "this is a question of honor, not pride."

I went to bed, to my old room next to his. It was snowing when I woke, and dull and gray. I bade Matty dress me in great haste and sent word to Richard, asking if he would see me.

He came instead to my room and with great tenderness told me to stay abed. "I will be gone an hour," he said, "two at the utmost. I shall but stay to tell the council what I think of them and then come back to breakfast with you. My anger is all spent."

He kissed my two hands and then went away. I heard the sound of his horse trotting across the park. I went and sat in my chair beside the window, with a rug over my knees. It was snowing steadily. At midday Matty brought me meat, but I did not fancy it. I went on sitting at the window, gazing out across the park.

At a quarter to four a servant knocked on my door and asked in a hushed tone if Colonel Roscarrick could wait on Mistress Harris. I said certainly, and sat there filled with apprehension. Then the colonel stood before me, disaster written plainly on his face.

"They have arrested him," he said slowly, "on a charge of disloyalty to his prince and to His Majesty."

"Where have they imprisoned him?"

"There in Launceston Castle. They were waiting for us. I rode to his side and begged him to give fight. The whole Army, I told him, would stand by him. But he refused. 'The prince,' he said, 'must be obeyed.' Then he handed his sword to the governor, and before they took him away, he bade me see you safely to your sister."

I sat quite still, my heart numb, all passion spent.

"This is the end," said Colonel Roscarrick. "There is no other man in the Army fit to lead us but Richard Grenvile."

Yes, I thought, this is the end. Many had fought and died and all in vain. The bridges would not be blown now; the roads would not be guarded, nor the defenses held. The rebel troops would cross the Tamar, never to depart. The end of liberty in Cornwall, perhaps for generations. And Richard Grenvile, who might have saved his country, was now a prisoner of his own side.

"If we only had time," Colonel Roscarrick was saying, "we could send messengers to His Majesty imploring pardon."

If we only had time, when the thaw broke, when the spring came . . . But it was the nineteenth of January, and the snow was falling still.

THE NEXT DAY, the twentieth, just before noon, Colonel Roscarrick called on me with the news that Sir Richard Grenvile had been cashiered from every regiment he had commanded and dismissed from His Majesty's Army—and all without a court-martial.

"It cannot be done," he said with vehemence. "It is against every military code and tradition. We are to hold a meeting of protest today, and I will let you know at once what is decided."

Matty, too, fed me with tales of optimism. "There is no other talk about the town," she said, "but Sir Richard's imprisonment. Those who grumbled at his severity before are now clamoring for his release. This afternoon a thousand people went before the castle and shouted for the governor."

How typical it was, I thought with bitterness, that now, in his adversity, my Richard should become so popular. Fear was the whip that drove the people on. They had no faith in Lord Hopton or any other commander. Only a Grenvile, they believed, could keep the enemy from crossing the Tamar.

When Colonel Roscarrick came at last to see me I could tell from his weary countenance that nothing much had been accomplished. "The general has sent word," he said, "that he will be no party to release by force. He asked for a court-martial and a chance to defend himself before the prince, and he bids us serve under Lord Hopton."

"What orders have you," I asked wearily, "from your new commander?"

"None as yet. He is in the process of taking over and assembling his command. We expect to hear nothing for a day or two. Therefore, I am at your disposal."

"Perhaps," I said, "if I saw the governor myself?"

The governor, he said, was not the type of man to melt before a woman. "But I will go again," he assured me, "tomorrow morning, and ascertain at least that the general's health is good." And with that he left me to pass another lonely night.

I had just finished breakfast the next morning when a runner brought me a hurried message, full of apology, from Colonel Roscarrick, saying that he had received orders to march north to Torrington at once with Lord Hopton, and that if I had any friend or relative in the district, it would be best for me to go to them immediately. I had no friends or relatives, nor would I seek them if I had. I summoned Matty and told her to have me carried to Launceston Castle, for I wished to see the governor. I set forth, well wrapped against the weather, with Matty walking by my side and four fellows bearing my litter. When I came to the castle gate I demanded to see the captain of the guard.

"I would be grateful," I said to him when he came forth, "if you would give a message from me to the governor."

"The governor sees no one without a written appointment," the captain said, but he looked not unkindly, and I took a chance.

"I have come," I said, "to inquire after Sir Richard Grenvile."

"I regret, madam," he said, "but you have come on a useless errand. Sir Richard is no longer here." Panic seized me as I pictured a sudden, secret execution. But he went on to say, "He left this morning under escort for Saint Michael's Mount. After yesterday's demonstrations the governor judged it best to remove him from Launceston."

Saint Michael's Mount . . . some seventy miles away, in the western toe of Cornwall. How in the world was I to reach him there? I returned to my room with only one thought in my head now, and that to get from Launceston as soon as possible. But as I entered the door I was surprised to find my brother Robin.

"Thank God," he said, "I have sight of you at last. As soon as I had news of Sir Richard's arrest, Sir John Digby gave me leave of absence to ride here."

I was not sure whether I was glad to see him. It seemed to me at this moment that no man was my friend unless he was friend to Richard also. "Why have you come?" I said coolly.

"To take you back to Mary," he said. "The entire Army is in the process of reorganizing, and you cannot remain in Launceston without protection. I have orders to join Sir John at Truro, where he has gone with a force to protect the prince in the event of invasion. My idea is to leave you at Menabilly on my way thither."

I thought rapidly. Truro was the headquarters of the prince's council. There was a chance, faint yet not impossible, that if I went there, I could have an audience with the prince himself.

"Very well," I said. "I will come with you, but on one condition: that you let me journey with you all the way to Truro."

"What is to be gained by that?" Robin asked.

"Nothing gained nor lost," I answered. "Only for old time's sake, do what I demand."

He took my hand. "Honor," he said, his blue eyes full upon my face, "I want you to believe me when I say that no action of mine had any bearing on his arrest. Sir John himself has written to the council appealing for his swift release. He is needed at this moment more than any other man in Cornwall."

"Why," I said bitterly, "did you not think of it before? Why did you refuse to obey his orders about the bridge?"

"I lost my temper," he admitted. "You don't understand, Honor, what it has meant to me and Jo and all your family to have your name a byword in the county. Ever since you went to Exeter last spring people have whispered the foulest things."

"Is it so foul to love a man and go to him when he lies wounded?"

"Why are you not married to him, then?" said Robin.

"If I am not Lady Grenvile, it is because I do not choose to be."

"You have no pride, then, no feeling for your name?"

"My name is Honor, and I do not hold it tarnished."

"This is the finish, you know that?" he said after a moment's pause. "In spite of a petition signed with all our names, I hardly think the council will agree to his release."

"And what will be the outcome?"

"Imprisonment at His Majesty's pleasure, with a pardon, possibly, at the end of the war."

"And what if the rebels gain Cornwall?" Robin hesitated, so I gave the answer for him. "Sir Richard Grenvile is handed over, a prisoner, and sentenced to death as a criminal of war."

I pleaded fatigue then and went to my room, where I slept easily for no other reason but that I was bound for Truro, which was some thirty miles distant from Saint Michael's Mount. . . .

The snow of the preceding days had wrought havoc on the road, and it was well over a week before we came to Truro, only to discover that the council was now removed to Pendennis

Castle, and Sir John Digby and his forces were now also within the garrison. Robin found me and Matty a lodging at Penryn and went at once to wait on his commander, bearing a letter from me to Jack Grenvile, whom I believed to be in close attendance on the prince.

The following day Jack rode to see me—and I felt as though years had passed since I had last set eyes upon a Grenvile. I nearly wept when he came into the room.

"Have no fear," he said at once, "my uncle is in good heart and sturdy health. He bade me write you not to be anxious for him. It is rather he who is likely to be anxious on your part, for he believes you with your sister, Mrs. Rashleigh."

I determined to take young Jack into my confidence. "What is the opinion on the war?" I said.

He shrugged. "You see we are at Pendennis," he said quietly. "That in itself is ominous. There is a frigate at anchor in the roads with orders to set sail for the Scillies when the word is given. The prince himself is all for fighting to the end, but Sir Edward Hyde will have the last word, not the Prince of Wales."

"And your uncle?"

"He will remain, I fear, at the Mount."

"Jack," I said, "would you do something for me, for your uncle's sake?"

"Anything in the world," he answered, "for the pair of you."

"Get me an audience with the Prince of Wales."

He whistled and scratched his cheek, a very Grenvile gesture. "I'll do my best, but he is so hemmed about by the council that he dares do nothing but what he is told to do by Sir Edward Hyde."

"Make up some story," I urged. "You are his age and a close companion. You know what would move him."

He smiled—his father's smile. "As to that," he said, "he has only to hear you followed my uncle to Exeter. Nothing pleases him better than a love affair."

He left me with an earnest promise to do all he could. Then came a period of waiting that seemed like centuries, but was, in reality, little longer than a fortnight. On the fourteenth of February, the feast of Saint Valentine, I had a message from Jack Grenvile. The wording was vague and purposely omitted names. *The snake is gone to Truro. My friend and I will be able to receive you for a brief space this afternoon. I will send an escort for you.*

I went alone, without Matty, deeming in a matter of such delicacy it was better to have no confidante. True to his word, the escort came, and Jack himself awaited me at the entrance to the castle. A swift word to the sentry, and we were through the arch and within the precincts of the garrison before a single soul, save the sentry, was a whit the wiser. Two servants in the prince's livery came to carry me, and after passing up some stairs, I was brought to a small room within a tower and placed upon a couch. There were wine and fruit at my elbow, and a posy of fresh flowers. I would have relished the experience were not the matter upon which I sought an audience so deadly serious.

I was left for a few moments, and then the door opened again and Jack stood aside to let a youngster of about his own age pass before him. He was far from handsome, more like a gypsy than a prince, with his black locks and swarthy skin, but the instant he smiled, I loved him better than all the famous portraits of his father that my generation had known for thirty years.

"Have my servants looked after you?" he said at once. "Given you all you want?" And as he spoke, I felt his bold eyes look me up and down in cool, appraising fashion. "Come, Jack," he said, "present me to your kinswoman."

We ate and drank, and all the while he talked he stared. I wondered what story Jack had spun, and if the prince's boyish imagination was running riot on the thought of his notorious and rebellious general making love to me, a cripple.

"I have no claim to trespass upon your time, sir," I said at length, "but Sir Richard, Jack's uncle, has been my dear friend over a span of years. His faults are many, but his loyalty to yourself has never, I believe, been in question."

"I don't doubt it," said the prince. "But you know how it was. He got up against the council, and Sir Edward in particular. There was no choice but to sign the warrant for his arrest."

"Sir Richard did very wrong not to serve under Lord Hopton," I said. "Given reflection, he would have acted otherwise."

The prince rose to his feet and paced up and down the room. "It's a wretched affair all around," he said. "There's Grenvile at the Mount, the one fellow who might have saved Cornwall, while Hopton fights a hopeless battle up in Torrington. I can't do anything about it, you know. That's the devil of it. I shall be whisked away myself before I know what is happening."

"There is one thing you can do, sir," I said.

"What, then?"

"Send word to the Mount that when you and the council sail for the Scillies Sir Richard Grenvile shall be permitted to escape at the same time and commandeer a fishing boat for France."

The Prince of Wales stared at me for a moment, and then that smile again lit his face. "Sir Richard Grenvile is most fortunate," he said, "to have so *fidèle* an ally as yourself. If I am ever in his shoes and find myself a fugitive, I hope I can rely on half so good a friend." He glanced across at Jack. "You can arrange that, can't you?" he said. "I will write a letter to Sir Arthur Bassett at the Mount, and you can take it there and see your uncle at the same time. I don't suggest we ask for his company in the frigate when we sail, because I hardly think the ship would bear his weight alongside Sir Edward Hyde's."

The two lads laughed, for all the world like a pair of schoolboys caught in mischief. Then the prince turned, came to the couch, bent low and kissed my hand. "Have no fear," he said, "I will arrange it. Sir Richard shall be free the instant we sail for the Scillies. And when I return—for I shall return, you know, one day—I shall hope to see you, and him also, at Whitehall."

He bowed and went, forgetting me, I daresay, forevermore, but leaving with me an impression of black eyes and gypsy features that I remember to this day. . . .

I returned to Penryn, utterly exhausted now that my mission was fulfilled. Two days later Lord Hopton was defeated outside Torrington and the whole western army was in full retreat across the Tamar. On the twenty-fifth of February the rebels had taken Launceston, and on the second of March they crossed the moors to Bodmin. That night the Prince of Wales, with his council, set sail in the frigate *Phoenix*—and the war in the West was over.

The day Lord Hopton signed the treaty in Truro my brother-in-law, Jonathan Rashleigh, by permission of the Parliament, came down to Penryn to fetch me. The streets were lined with soldiers, not ours, but theirs. I sat with stony face, looking out of the curtains of my litter, while Jonathan Rashleigh rode by my side, his shoulders bowed, his face set in deep grim lines.

I was returning to Menabilly to be no longer a camp follower, but plain Honor Harris, a cripple on her back. And I did not care.

For Richard Grenvile had escaped to France.

CHAPTER ELEVEN

IN THE YEAR 1646 we were new to defeat, still learning its lessons. I think the loss of freedom was what hit the Cornish hardest. Our orders came from Whitehall, and a Cornish County Committee, way up in London, sat in judgment upon us. We could no longer pass our own measures and decide locally what was suited to each town and village. The County Committee's first action was to demand a weekly payment from the people of Cornwall to the revenue, an assessment so high that it was impossible to find the money. Then it sequestered the estate of every landlord who had fought for the King; the owners were allowed to dwell there only if they paid to the committee, month by month, the full and total value of the property. This crippling injunction was made the harder because most of the estates were fallen into ruin through the fighting, and it would take generations before the land gave a return once more.

A host of petty officials came down from Whitehall to collect the sums due to the County Committee; no man could buy even a loaf of bread without going cap in hand to one of these fellows and signing his name to a piece of paper. Whosoever wished to travel from one village to another must first have a pass, and then his motives were questioned, his family history gone into, and he might find himself arrested for delinquency at the end of it.

My brother-in-law, Jonathan Rashleigh, like other Royalist landlords, had his lands sequestered and was told that he must pay a fine of some one thousand and eighty pounds to redeem them. In July, broken and dispirited, he took the National Covenant, by which he vowed never again to take up arms against the Parliament. This bitter blow to his pride, self-inflicted though it was, did not satisfy the County Committee, for he was summoned to London in September and ordered to remain there until his full fine was paid. It remained for Mary, my poor sister, and John, his son, to so husband his estate that the debt could month by month be paid, but we well knew that it might take years, even the remainder of his life. His last words to me before he went to London were kind and generous. "Menabilly is your home," he said, "for as long as you desire. We all are sufferers in this mis-

336

fortune. Guard your sister, share her troubles. And help John. You have a wiser head than all I leave behind."

A wiser head . . . I doubted it. It needed a pettifogging mind and every low lawyer's trick to break even with the County Committee and the paid agents of Parliament. And every hand was needed if the land was to yield a full return. Even our womenfolk went out to work in the fields side by side with the tenants at harvesting, Mary herself, and Alice, while the children, thinking it fine sport, helped to carry the corn. There was none to help us. My brother Robin had gone to Radford to my brother Jo, who was in much the same straits as ourselves, while Peter Courtney, like many other young Royalists, had gone abroad to join the Prince of Wales—living was good at the French court. Alice never spoke a word of blame, but I think her heart broke when we heard that he had gone.

The Parliament agents were forever coming to spy upon us, to question us, to count the sheep and cattle, to reckon, it almost seemed, each ear of corn. The Parliament . . . From day to day the word rang in our ears. The Parliament decrees that produce shall be brought to market only upon a Tuesday. . . . The Parliament has ordered that all fairs shall be discontinued. . . . The Parliament warns that no one shall walk abroad one hour after sunset. . . . The Parliament warns that every dwelling will be searched each week for concealed firearms, weapons and ammunition. . . .

But that first year of defeat was, in some queer fashion, quiet and peaceful to me who bore no burden on my shoulders. Danger was no more. Armies were disbanded. The man I loved was safe across the sea in the company of his son, and now and then I would have word from him, in some foreign city. He was in good heart and spirits, and missing me, it would seem, not at all. He talked of going to fight the Turks with great enthusiasm, as if he had not had enough of fighting after three hard years of civil war. *Doubtless*, he wrote, *you find your days monotonous in Cornwall*. Doubtless I did. To women who have known close siege and stern privation, monotony can be a pleasant thing. . . .

A wanderer for so long, I found it restful to have a home at last and to share it with people whom I loved, even if we were all companions in defeat. God bless the Rashleighs, who permitted me those months at Menabilly. The Parliament could strip the place of its possessions, take the sheep and cattle, glean the harvest, but they could not take from me, nor from the Rashleighs, the beauty that we looked on every day. The devastation of the gardens was forgotten when the primrose came in spring, and the young green-budded trees. We, the defeated, could still listen to the birds on a May morning and watch the clumsy cuckoo wing his way to the little wood beside the hill. And I watched from my chair upon the causeway, in every mood from winter to summer. . . .

Quietest of all are the evenings of late summer, when the moon has not yet risen. Dusk comes slowly, the woods turn black, and suddenly, with stealthy pad, a fox creeps from the thistle park and stands watching me, his ears pricked. Then his brush twitches and he is gone, for here is Matty tapping along the causeway to bring me home; and another day is over. Yes, Richard, there is comfort in monotony. . . .

All at Menabilly have gone to bed. Matty carries me upstairs, and as she brushes my hair and ties the curling rags, I am almost happy. A year has come and gone, and though we are defeated, we live, we still survive. And as I think thus, I see Matty's round face looking at me from the mirror opposite.

"There were strange rumors in Fowey today," she says quietly.

"What rumors, Matty? There are always rumors."

"Our men are creeping back," she murmurs, "first one, then two, then three. Those who fled to France a year ago."

"Why should they return? They can do nothing."

"Not alone, but if they band together, in secret . . ."

I sit still, my hands in my lap, and suddenly I remember a phrase in the last letter that came to me from Italy. *You may hear from me*, he had said, *before the summer closes. . . .*

"Do they mention names?" For the first time in many months a little seed of anxiety and fear springs to my heart.

"They talk of a great leader," she says, "landing in secret at Plymouth from the Continent. He wears a dark wig, they say, to disguise his coloring. But they do not mention names. . . ."

SO THE WHISPERS started that early autumn of 'forty-seven, handed from one to the other. The Royalists were arming. Gentlemen were meeting in one another's houses. The laborers were conversing together in the field. A fellow on a street corner would beckon to another, for the purpose, it would seem, of discussing market prices; a question, a swift answer, and then the two would separate, but information had been passed, and another link forged. Let a fellow climb to repair his cottage roof against the rains of winter, and he would pause an instant, glancing over his shoulder, and, thrusting his hand under the thatch, feel for the sharp edge of a sword. . . . These were Matty's tales.

Names that had not been spoken for two years were now whispered by cautious tongues. Trelawney . . . Trevannion . . . Arundell . . . Bassett . . . Grenvile . . . Yes, above all, Grenvile. He had been seen at Stowe, said one. The Isle of Wight, said another. In Ireland . . . Sir Richard Grenvile was in Cornwall. . . .

John Rashleigh kept silent on these matters. His father had bidden him not to meddle, but to work night and day so that the groaning debt to Parliament might be paid. But I could guess his thoughts. If there were in truth a rising and Cornwall freed once more, there would be no debt to pay, and was it not something like cowardice for a Rashleigh not to join the company? Poor John. He was restless and sharp-tempered often, and Joan was not with us to encourage him, for her twin boys, born the year before, were sickly, and she was with them and the elder children at Maddercombe in Devon. Then, in the spring, Jonathan fell ill up in London, and Mary went to him. Alice was the next to leave. Peter wrote to her from France, desiring that she should take the children to Trethurfe, his home, which was—so he had heard—in a sad state of repair; would she see what could be done?

It became, of a sudden, strangely quiet at Menabilly. There was no one but John now for company, and I wondered what we should make of it together, he and I, through the long evenings.

"I've half a mind," he said on the third day we sat together, "to leave Menabilly in your care and go to Maddercombe. It is over six months now since I have seen Joan and the children, and not a word comes to us here of what is passing in the country. Only that the war has broken out again. Fighting in places as far apart as Wales and the eastern counties."

"Get yourself permission," I said, "and go to Maddercombe."

The sheriff of Cornwall at this time was a neighbor who, though firm for Parliament, was a just man; he granted John Rashleigh permission to visit his wife in Maddercombe in Devon. So it happened, in that fateful spring of 'forty-eight, I was, of all our party, the only one remaining at Menabilly. Even the steward's house was desolate, now that old Langdon had been gathered to his fathers. His keys, once so important and mysterious, were now in my keeping, and the summerhouse was my routine shelter on a windy afternoon. Most of the books were gone, stored in the house or packed and sent after my brother-in-law to London. The desk was bare and empty. Cobwebs hung from the walls. But the torn matting on the floor still hid the flagstone with the iron ring. . . .

I looked out toward the sea one day in March and watched the shadows darken. The clock in the belfry struck four. Matty was gone to Fowey and should be back by now. I heard a footstep on the path beneath the causeway and called, thinking it one of the farm laborers. The footsteps ceased, but no answer came.

I waited a moment, and then a shadow falling suddenly upon my right shoulder told me there was someone at the door. I whipped my chair around in an instant and saw the figure of a man, small and slight, clad in plain dark clothes like a London clerk, with a hat pulled low over his face. Something in his manner struck a chord. . . . Then he took his hat from his close black curls, and I saw him smile, tremulous, uncertain, until he saw my eyes, and my arms outstretched toward him.

"Dick," I whispered and he came and knelt by me, covering my hands with kisses. And then as he raised his head I saw he was a boy no longer, but a young man, with hair upon his lip. His voice, low and soft, was a man's voice.

"Have you grown thus in four small years?" I said.

"I shall be eighteen in two months' time," he answered, smiling. "Have you forgotten?"

I could not take my eyes from him, he was so grown, so altered. Yet the dark eyes, wary and suspicious, were the same. "Tell me quickly," I said, "before they come to fetch me from the house, what you are doing here and why."

He looked at me doubtfully. "I am the first to come, then?" he asked. "My father is not here?"

My heart leaped, but whether in excitement or in fear, I could not tell. "No one is here," I answered, "but yourself. Even the Rashleighs are from home."

"Yes," he said, "that is why Menabilly has been chosen."

"Chosen for what?"

He was slow to answer. "They will tell you," he said, "when they come."

"Who are they?" I asked.

"My father," he answered, "and Peter Courtney. Ambrose Manaton of Trecarrel, your own brother Robin, and of course my aunt Gartred."

Gartred . . .

"I think it best," I said slowly, "if you tell me what has happened since you came to England."

He rose then from his knees and swept dust from a place upon the windowsill to sit. "We left Italy last autumn," he said, "and came to London, my father disguised as a Dutch merchant, I as his secretary. Since then we have traveled England from south to north secretly as agents for the prince. At Christmas we went to Stowe. No one was there but the steward and my cousin Bunny. From Stowe it is but a step to Bideford and Orley Court. There we found my aunt Gartred, who, having fallen out with her Parliamentary friends, was hot to join us, and your brother Robin also."

Truly the world and its gossip had passed us by at Menabilly. "I did not know that Robin lived at Bideford."

"He and my aunt are very thick," he answered. "I understand that your brother has made himself her bailiff. She owns land, does she not, that belonged to your eldest brother who is dead?"

Yes, they could have met again that way. Why should I blame Robin, grown weary and idle in defeat? "And so?" I asked.

"And so the plans matured, the clans gathered. The Trelawneys, the Trevannions, the Bassetts. They are all in it, the length and breadth of Cornwall. Now the time draws near. Muskets are being loaded, swords sharpened. You will have a front seat at the slaughter." His voice held a strange note of bitterness.

"And you?" I asked. "Are you not excited at the prospect? Are you not happy to be one of them?"

"I tell you," he said passionately, "I would give all I possess, which is precious little, to be out of it! I begged him to let me stay in Italy, where I was content, after my fashion. I found that I could paint, Honor. I wished to make painting my trade. I had friends, too, fellows of my age, for whom I felt affection. But no. Painting was womanish, a pastime fit for foreigners. My friends were womanish, too, and would degrade me. If I hoped to have a penny to my name, I must follow him, do his bidding, grow like my Grenvile cousins. God in heaven, how I have come to loathe the very name of Grenvile."

Eighteen, but he had not changed. This was the little boy who had sobbed his hatred of his father.

"Perhaps," I said, "when—when this present business is concluded, you will be free to return to Italy. I will speak for you."

He picked at the fringe of his coat with his long slim hands. "There will be fighting," he said slowly, "men killing one another for no purpose, save to spill blood. Always to spill blood. . . ."

The fear in his eyes found an echo in my heart, and the old anxiety was with me once again. "When did you leave Bideford?" I asked.

"Two days ago," he answered. "Those were my orders. We were to proceed separately, each by a different route. Lady Courtney has gone to Trethurfe, I presume?"

"She went at the beginning of the month."

"So Peter intended. It was part of the ruse, you see, for emptying the house. Mrs. Rashleigh was inveigled up to London for the same purpose. And the last scheme of all, to rid the house of John, was quite in keeping with my father's character."

"John went of his own accord, to see his wife at Maddercombe."

"Aye, but he had a message first," said Dick. "A scrap of paper, passed to him in Fowey, saying his wife was overfond of a neighbor living in her father's house. I know, because I saw my father pen the letter, laughing with Aunt Gartred as he did so."

Damn them both, I thought, for cruelty. "Did your father," I said after a moment, "send any word to me? Did he know that I was here?"

"Of course. That is why he picked Menabilly rather than Carhayes. There was no woman at Carhayes to give him comfort."

I saw Richard, in my mind's eye, pen in hand, with a map of Cornwall spread on a table before him. And dotted upon the map were the houses by the coast that offered sanctuary. Trelawne— too deeply wooded. Penrice—not close enough to the sea. Carhayes—yes, good landing ground for troops, but not a single young woman. Menabilly—with a beach and a hiding place and an old love into the bargain. . . . And the pen would make a circle around the name of Menabilly.

So I had become a cynic in defeat. But all my anger was but a piece of bluff. I wanted nothing in the world so much as to play hostess once more to Richard, by candlelight, in secret, and to live again that life of strain and folly, anguish and enchantment.

IT FELL ON ME to warn the servants. I summoned each one to my chamber in turn. "We are entering upon dangerous days," I said. "Things will pass here at Menabilly which you do not see and do not hear. Visitors will come and go. Ask no questions. One incautious word, and your master up in London will lose his life, and probably we will also. I believe you are one and all faithful subjects of His Majesty?"

It was on Matty's advice that I took them thus into my confidence. "Each one can be trusted," she had said, "but a word of faith from you will bind them together, and not all the agents in the West Country will make them blab."

Peter Courtney was the first to come. No secrecy for him. He flaunted his pretended return from France, announcing loudly his desire to see his children. Gone to Trethurfe? Alice had misunderstood his letter. . . .

Poor Alice. "You might," I said to him, "have sent her a whisper of your safe return. She would have kept it secret."

But he shrugged a careless shoulder. "A wife can be a cursed appendage in times like these," he said. "To tell the truth, Honor, I am so plagued with debts that one glimpse of her reproachful eyes would drive me crazy."

"I doubt if your conscience worries you unduly."

He winked, and I thought how the looks that I had once admired were coarsened now with license and good living. Too much French wine, too little exercise.

"And what are your plans when Parliament is overthrown?"

Again he shrugged. "I shall never settle at Trethurfe," he said. "War has made me restless."

He whistled under his breath and strolled toward the window. One more marriage in the melting pot. . . .

The next to come was Bunny Grenvile. Bunny, at seventeen, already head and shoulders taller than his cousin Dick. Bunny with eager questing eyes and a map of the coast under his arm.

"Where are the beaches? The landing places? No, I want no refreshment. I want to see the ground." And he was off, a hound to scent, another budding soldier like his brother, Jack.

Our third arrival was Mr. Ambrose Manaton. He was, I suppose, a few years older than Peter Courtney, some four and thirty years. Sleek and suave, with a certain latent charm. He wore his own fair hair, curling to his shoulders. What exactly, I wondered, was his part in this campaign? I had not heard of him ever as a soldier. Money? Property? A Royalist rising cannot be conducted without funds. Did Ambrose Manaton, then, hold the purse? I wondered what had induced him to risk his life and fortune. He gave me the clue a moment after his arrival.

"Mrs. Denys has not yet arrived?"

"Not yet. You know her well?"

"We count ourselves near neighbors in north Cornwall and north Devon."

The tone was easy, the smile confident. Oh, Richard, my love of little scruple. So Gartred was the bait to catch the tiger. What had been going on all these long winter months at Bideford?

"My brother, Robin Harris, acts as bailiff to Mrs. Denys, so I understand?"

"Why, yes, something of the sort," said Ambrose Manaton. He studied the toe of his boot. His voice was a shade overcasual.

Robin and Gartred came together shortly before dark. I was alone in the gallery to receive them. The rule of Parliament had fallen lightly on Gartred. She was a little fuller in the bosom, but it became her well. And her hair was no longer gleaming gold, but streaked with silver white, making her look more lovely and more frail. She tossed her cloak to Robin as she came into the room, proclaiming in that first careless gesture all that I cared to know of their relationship. The years slipped backward in a flash, and there was she, a bride of twenty-two, already tired of Kit. It might have been Kit standing there in the gallery at Menabilly, with a dog's look of adoration in his eyes. But there was not only adoration in Robin's eyes. There was strain, too, and doubt. And the heavy jowls and puffy cheeks betrayed the easy drinker. Defeat and Gartred had taken their toll of my brother.

"We seem fated, you and I, to come together at moments of great crisis," I said to Gartred. "Do you still play piquet?"

Gartred smiled, drawing off her lace gloves. "Piquet is out of fashion. Dice is a later craze, but must be done in secret, all games of chance being frowned upon by Parliament."

"I shall not join you, then. You will have to play with Robin or with Ambrose Manaton."

Her glance at me was swift, but I let it pass over my head. "I have the consolation," she said, "of knowing that we shall not now play in opposition. We are all partners on a winning side."

"Are we?"

"If you doubt my loyalty," said Gartred, "you must tell Richard when he comes." She smiled again, and as I looked at her, I felt like a knight of old saluting his opponent before combat.

"I have put you," I said, "in the long chamber overhead. Robin is on your left, and Ambrose Manaton on your right, at the small bedroom at the stair's head. With two strong men to guard you, I think it hardly likely you'll be nervous."

Turning to Robin, she gave him some commands about her baggage. He went at once to obey her, like a servant.

"It has been fortunate for you," I said, "that the menfolk of my breed have proved accommodating."

"It would be more fortunate still," she answered, "if they could be at the same time less possessive." I saw her cat's eyes watching Robin's shadow in the hall. "My daughters are grown up," she said. "Orley Court becomes a burden. Perhaps I would like a third husband and security."

Which my brother could not give her, I thought, but which a man some fifteen years younger than herself, with lands and fortune, might be pleased to do. Mrs. Harris . . . Mrs. Denys . . . Mrs. Manaton?

"You broke one man in my family," I said. "Take care that you do not seek to break another."

"You think you can prevent me?"

"Not I. You may do as you please. I only give you warning. You will never play fast and loose with Robin, as you did with Kit. Robin would be capable of murder."

We made a strange company for dinner. Gartred, her silver hair bejeweled, at the head of the table, and those two men on either side of her, my brother Robin with ever-reaching hand to the decanter, his eyes feasting on her face, and Ambrose Manaton, cool and self-possessed, keeping up a flow of conversation about the corrupt practices of Parliament. I suspected he must have a share in it, from knowing so much detail.

On my left sat Peter Courtney, who from time to time caught Gartred's eye and smiled in knowing fashion, but as he did the same to the serving maid, I guessed it to be habit rather than conspiracy.

Dick, in the center, glowered, throwing black looks toward Bunny opposite, who rattled on about the letters he had received from his brother, Jack, who was grown so high in favor with the Prince of Wales in France that they were never parted.

As I looked at each in turn, I thought that, had Richard sought his hardest, he could not have found six people in the county more likely to fall out and disagree than those who sat around the table now. Were these to be the leaders of the rising?

Then the door opened of a sudden and he stood there, watching us. Gone was the auburn hair I loved; the curled wig that fell below his ears gave him a dark satanic look that matched his smile. "What a bunch of prizes," he said, "for the sheriff of the duchy if he chose to call. Each one of you a traitor."

He tossed his hat and cloak to a waiting servant and came to the empty chair at my right. "Have you been waiting long?" he said.

"Two years and three months," I answered him.

He filled the glass from the decanter at my side. "In January of 'forty-six," he said, "I broke a promise to our hostess here. I left her one morning at Werrington, saying I would be back again to breakfast with her. Unfortunately the Prince of Wales willed otherwise."

He lifted his glass and drained it in one measure, then put his hand on mine and held it on the table.

"Thank God," he said, "for a woman who does not give a damn for punctuality."

IT WAS LIKE Werrington once more. The old routine. The old haphazard sharing of our days and nights. He would burst into my chamber as I breakfasted, my toilet yet undone, my hair in curl rags, and pace about the room, talking incessantly, cursing all the while at some delay in the plans he was proposing.

Like Werrington once more. A log fire in the dining chamber. A large map in the center of the table. Richard seated with Bunny, instead of Jack, at his elbow. Robin standing by the door where Colonel Roscarrick would have stood. And Peter Courtney, riding into the courtyard, bearing messages from Trelawne.

The big conferences were held at night. It was easier then to move about the roads. The Trelawneys, Sir Charles Trevannion from Carhayes, the Arundells, Sir Arthur Bassett. I would lie in my chamber overhead and hear the drone of voices from the dining room below, and always that clear tone of Richard's would overtop them all. Would the French play? This was the universal doubt, expressed by the whole assembly, that Richard always brushed impatiently aside.

"Damn the French! We can do without them. Never a Frenchman yet but was not a liability to his own side."

"But," murmured Sir Charles Trevannion, "if they at least sent a token force to assist the prince in landing, the moral effect upon Parliament would be as valuable as ten divisions."

"The French hate fighting on any soil but their own. We won't need them once we hold the Scillies and the Cornish forts."

And so it would continue. Midnight, one, two, three o'clock . . . what hour they went and what hour he came to bed, I would not know, for exhaustion would lay claim to me long before.

Robin was given much responsibility. The bridge episode had been forgotten. Or had it? I would wonder sometimes when I watched Richard's eyes upon him. "Come, Robin," Richard would say after supper, "we must burn the midnight candle again. If I can do with four hours' sleep, so can the rest of you."

Richard, Robin, Peter and Bunny would crowd around the table, deciphering the messages Peter had brought. Dick would stand sentinel at the door, watching them wearily, resentfully. Ambrose Manaton would stand by the fire, consulting a great sheaf of figures.

"I shan't need your assistance, Ambrose," Richard would say. "Go and talk high finance to the women in the gallery."

And Ambrose Manaton, smiling, bowing his thanks, would walk from the room with a shade too great confidence.

"Will you be late?" I would say to Richard.

"H'm . . . h'm," he would answer absently. "Fetch me that file of papers, Bunny." Then of a sudden, looking up at Dick, "Stand straight, can't you? Don't slop over your feet." Dick's black eyes would blink, his slim hands would clutch at his coat. He would open the door for me to pass through, and all I could do to give him confidence would be to smile and touch his hand. No gallery for me. Three makes poor company. But upstairs to my chamber, knowing that the voices underneath would drone on for hours more. An hour, perhaps, would pass, and then I would hear the swish of a skirt upon the landing as Gartred passed into her room. Silence. Then that telltale creaking stair. The soft closing of a door.

One evening, when the conference broke early and Richard sat with me awhile before retiring, I told him bluntly what I had heard. He laughed, trimming his fingernails by the open window.

"Have you turned prude, sweetheart, in your middle years?"

"Prudery be damned, but my brother hopes to marry her."

"Then hope will fail him," replied Richard. "Gartred will never throw herself away upon a penniless colonel. She has other fish to fry, and small blame to her. Ambrose has a pretty inheritance. Gartred would be a fool if she let him slip from her."

How calmly the Grenviles seized fortunes for themselves.

"What exactly does he contribute to your present business?"

He cocked an eye at me and grinned. "We'd have difficulty in paying for this affair without him."

"So I thought," I answered.

"Taking me all around," he said, "I'm a pretty cunning fellow."

"If you call it cunning," I said, "to play one member of your staff against another. For my part, I would call it knavery."

"Ah, well," he said, "if the maneuver serves my purpose . . ."

Little by little the plans fell into line. The final message came from the prince in France. The French fleet had been put at his disposal; an army, under the command of Lord Hopton, would land in force in Cornwall, while the prince with Richard's nephew, Sir John Grenvile, seized the Scillies. All was to coincide with the insurrection of the Royalists under Sir Richard Grenvile.

Saturday, the thirteenth of May, was the date chosen for the Cornish rising. . . . The planning was over. Now the waiting began. A week of nerves, sitting with eyes upon the clock, at Menabilly. Richard, in high spirits as always before battle, played bowls with Bunny in the little walled green beside the steward's empty lodge. Peter, with sudden realization of his flabby stomach muscles, rode furiously up and down the beaches to reduce his weight. Robin was silent, his eyes strangely watchful, like a dog listening for a stranger's footstep. Gartred, usually so cool and indifferent when having the whip hand in a love affair, showed herself, for the first time, less sure. Whether it was because Ambrose Manaton was fifteen years her junior and the possibility of marriage with him hung upon a thread, I do not know, but a new carelessness had come upon her that was, to my mind, the symbol of a losing touch. She smiled too openly at Ambrose Manaton. She put her hand in his at the dining table. She watched him over the rim of her glass with that same greed I had noticed years before, when, peeping through her chamber door, I had seen her stuff the trinkets in her pouch. And Ambrose Manaton, flattered, confident, raised his glass to her in return.

"Send her away," I said to Richard. "God knows she has caused ill feeling enough already."

"If Gartred went, Ambrose would follow her," he answered. "I can't afford to lose my treasurer."

"Then send Robin packing. He will be no use to you anyway if he continues drinking in this manner."

"Nonsense. Drink in his case is stimulation. The only way to ginger him. When the day comes, I'll ply him so full of brandy that he will take Saint Mawes Castle single-handed."

"I don't enjoy watching my brother go to pieces."

"He isn't here for your enjoyment. He is here because he is of use to me, and one of the few officers that I know who doesn't lose his head in battle. The more rattled he becomes here at Menabilly, the better he will fight outside it."

"My God," I said, "have you no pity at all?"

"None," he said, "where military matters are concerned."

And leaning from the window in the gallery, he whistled Bunny to a game of bowls. I watched them jesting with each other like a pair of schoolboys without a care.

"Damn the Grenviles one and all," I said aloud, thinking myself alone.

But a boy's voice whispered in my ear, "That's what my mother said eighteen years ago."

And there was Dick behind me, his black eyes gazing out across the lawn toward his father and young Bunny.

CHAPTER TWELVE

Thursday, the eleventh of May. Eight and forty hours to go before the torch of war was lit once more in Cornwall. . . . Even Richard was on edge that morning when a message came saying the Parliamentary guards had been doubled at the chief towns throughout the duchy.

"One false move now," he said quietly, "and all our plans will have been made in vain."

We were gathered in the dining room, save only Gartred, who was in her chamber, and I can see now the drawn, anxious faces of the men as they gazed in silence at their leader. He stood by the window, his hands behind his back. We were all, I believe, a little sick with apprehension.

"If anything should go wrong," Ambrose Manaton ventured, hesitating, "what arrangements can be made for our own security?"

Richard threw him a contemptuous glance. "None," he said briefly. He returned to the table and gathered up his papers. "These are useless to us once the battle starts." He began to throw the maps and documents into the fire, while the others still stared at him, uncertain. "You look like a flock of crows before a funeral," said Richard. "On Saturday we make a bid for freedom. If any man is afraid, let him say so now, and I'll put a halter around his neck for treason to the Prince of Wales."

Not one made answer. Richard turned to Robin. "I want you to ride to Trelawne," he said, "and tell Trelawney and his son that the rendezvous for the thirteenth is changed. They and Sir Arthur Bassett must join Sir Charles Trevannion at Carhayes. Tell them to go tonight, skirting the highroads, and accompany them there."

"Sir," said Robin slowly, rising to his feet, and I saw the flicker of his glance at Ambrose Manaton.

"Bunny," said his uncle, "we shall rendezvous also at Carhayes at daybreak on the thirteenth. You have the boat standing by at Pridmouth. Tomorrow you can sail to Gorran and give my last directions about the beacon. A few hours on salt water will be good practice for your stomach."

He smiled at the lad, who answered it with boyish adoration. I saw Dick lower his head and trace imaginary lines upon the table with a hesitating hand.

"Peter?" said Richard.

Alice's husband leaped to his feet. "My orders, sir?"

"Go to Carhayes and warn Trevannion that the plans are changed. Tell him the Trelawneys and Bassett will be joining him there. Then return here to Menabilly in the morning."

Peter and Robin left the room together, followed by Bunny and by Ambrose Manaton. Richard yawned and stretched.

"Have you no commands for me?" said Dick slowly.

"Why, yes," said Richard. "Alice Courtney's daughters must have left some dolls behind them. Go search in the attics and fashion them new dresses."

Dick went paler than before, turned on his heel and left.

"Someday," I said, "you will provoke him once too often."

"That is my intention," answered Richard. "I hope to see him stand up to me at last, not take it lying down, like a coward."

"No other father in the world would act as harshly to his son as you do to your Dick."

"I do so only to purge his mother's blood from his veins."

"You will more likely kindle it."

He shrugged, and we fell silent a moment. "I saw my daughter up in London, when I lay concealed there," said Richard suddenly. "Studious, quiet, dependable. 'Bess,' I said, 'will you look after me in my declining years?' 'Yes,' she answered, 'if you send for me.' I think she cares as little for her mother as I do."

"Daughters," I said, "are never favorites with their mothers. Especially when they come to be of age. How old is she?"

"Near seventeen," he said, "with all that natural bloom upon her that young people have. . . ." He stared absently before him, and I thought, This moment is in a sense our moment of farewell, our parting of the ways, but he does not know it. Now that his daughter is old enough to take care of him, he will not need me.

That evening we all went early to our beds. And with Peter and Robin gone, Ambrose Manaton and Gartred were free to indulge their separate talents for invention until the morning, should the spirit move them. Thank God, I thought with cynicism, I can grow old with some complacency. I do not have to struggle for a third husband, not having had a first.

Near midnight I woke from a light sleep with a fancy that I had heard someone moving in the dining room below. I raised myself in my bed and listened. All was silent. I put my hand out and dragged my chair to me, then listened once again. Suddenly, unmistakably, came the stealthy tread of a footstep on the creaking telltale stair. Some intuition warned me of disaster. I lowered myself into my chair, and without waiting to light my candle—nor was there need with the full moon casting a white beam on the carpet—I propelled myself across the room and turned the handle of my door.

"Who is there?" I whispered.

No answer. Coming to the landing, I saw a dark figure crouching upon the stair, his back against the wall, the moonlight gleaming on the naked sword in his hand. He stood barefoot, my brother Robin, with murder in his eyes.

He said nothing, only waited to see what I would do.

"Two years ago," I said softly, "you disobeyed an order given you by your commander because of a private quarrel. That was in January of 'forty-six. Do you seek to do the same in May of 'forty-eight?"

"I have disobeyed no one," he said. "I gave my message. I parted with the Trelawneys at the top of Polmear Hill."

"Richard bade you accompany them to Carhayes."

"No need to do so, Trelawney told me. Two horsemen pass more easily than three. Let me by, Honor."

"No, Robin. Not yet. Give me first your sword."

He stood staring at me, looking, with his tumbled hair and troubled eyes, so like the ghost of our dead brother Kit that I trembled, even as his hands did on his sword. "You cannot fool me," he said, "you nor Richard Grenvile. This business was but a pretext to send me from the house so *they* could be together."

"Come sit with me in my chamber, Robin. Let us talk awhile."

"No, this is my moment. They will be together now. If you try to prevent me, I shall hurt you also." He brushed past my chair, tiptoeing, furtive, in his bare feet.

"For God's sake, Robin," I said, "do not go into that room."

For answer he turned the door handle, a smile upon his lips both horrible and strange. I wheeled then, sobbing, and went back to my room and hammered loudly on the dressing rooms where Dick and Bunny slept. "Call Richard," I said, "and bid him come quickly. And you, too, both of you."

A startled voice—Bunny's, I believe—made answer. I turned again toward the landing, where all was silent, undisturbed. Nothing but the moonlight shining into the windows.

Then, piercing the silence with its shrillness, came the sound for which I waited. The shocking horror of a woman's scream.

ACROSS THE LANDING to Gartred's chamber. The wheels of my chair turning slow, for all my labor, and all the while calling, "Richard! Richard!" in a voice I did not recognize.

Oh, God, that fight there in the moonlight, the cold white light pouring through the unshuttered windows, and Gartred with a crimson gash upon her face clinging to the hangings of the bed. Ambrose Manaton, his silk nightshirt stained with blood, warding off with his bare hands the blows that Robin aimed at him, until, with a despairing cry, he reached the sword that lay among his heap of clothes upon a chair. Their bare feet padding on the boards, they seemed like phantom figures, lunging, thrusting, now in moonlight, now in shadow, with no word uttered. "Richard!" I called again, for this was murder, here before my eyes.

He came at last, half clad, carrying his sword, with Dick and Bunny at his heels bearing candles. "An end to this, you idiots!" he shouted, forcing himself between them, his own sword shivering their blades, and there was Robin, his right wrist hanging limp, with Richard holding him, and Ambrose Manaton back against the farther wall, with Bunny by his side.

They stared at each other, Robin and Ambrose Manaton, like animals in battle. Robin, seeing Gartred's face, opened his mouth to speak, but no words came.

"Call Matty," said Richard to me swiftly. "Get water and bandages."

And I was once more turning to the landing and there was Matty, staunch, dependable, seizing the situation in a glance and fetching bowls of water, strips of clean linen. The room was lit now by some half dozen candles. The phantom scene was done; the grim reality was with us still.

Those tumbled clothes upon the floor, Gartred's and Manaton's. Manaton leaning upon Bunny's arm, stanching the cuts he had received, his fair curls lank and damp with sweat. Robin upon a chair, his head buried in his hands, all passion spent. Richard standing by his side, grim and purposeful. And one and all we looked at Gartred on the bed with that great gash upon her face from her right eyebrow to her chin, her blood staining the clean white linen and trickling onto Matty's hands.

Then, for the first time, I noticed Dick. His face was ashen, his eyes transfixed in horror. Suddenly he reeled and fell.

Richard made no move. He said to Bunny, between clenched teeth, "Carry the spawn to his bed and leave him." And as I watched Bunny stagger from the room, his cousin in his arms, I thought with deadly weariness, This is the end. This is finality.

"I shall hold no inquest," said Richard slowly. "What has been, has been. We are on the eve of deadly matters, with the future of a kingdom at stake. This is no time to seek private vengeance."

Not one of them made answer.

"We will snatch," said Richard, "what sleep we can now. I will remain with Ambrose in his room and, Bunny, you shall stay with Robin. In the morning you will go together to Carhayes, where I shall join you. I ask you, Matty, to remain here with Mrs. Denys. How is her pulse? Has she lost much blood?"

"She is well enough now, Sir Richard. The cut was jagged, but not deep. The only damage done is to her beauty."

Ambrose Manaton did not look toward the bed. This is their finish too, I thought. Gartred will never become Mrs. Manaton.

I felt Richard's hands upon my chair. "You," he said quietly, "have had enough to contend with for one night." He took me to my room and laid me down upon my bed. "Rest easy," he said. "A few hours more, it will be over. War makes a good substitute for private quarrels."

He left then and went back to Ambrose Manaton, not, I reflected, to offer comfort, but to make sure his treasurer did not slip from him in the few hours till daylight. Bunny had gone with Robin to his room, and this also, I surmised, was a precaution. Remorse and brandy have driven stronger men than Robin to their suicide.

The hours slipped by, and of a sudden I remembered Dick, who slept in the dressing room next door to me, alone. Poor lad, was he now lying wakeful like me, with shame upon his conscience? I thought I heard him stir and I wondered if he wished for company. "Dick," I called softly, but there was no answer. Later a little breeze rising from the sea made a draft in my room from the open window and, playing with the latch upon the door, shook it free, so that it swung to and fro, banging every instant like a loosened shutter. He must sleep deep, then, if it did not waken him. I climbed to my chair to shut it, and as my hand fastened on the latch, I saw through the crack of the door that Dick's bed was empty.

Next morning when I woke to find the broad sun streaming into my room, the scenes of the hours before held a nightmare quality. But when Matty bore me in my breakfast I knew them to be true.

"Yes, Mrs. Denys had some sleep," she answered to my query, "and will, to my mind, be little worse for her adventure until she lifts her bandage."

"Will the gash not heal, in time?" I asked.

"It will heal," she said, "but she'll bear the scar for her lifetime. She'll find it hard to trade her beauty now." She spoke with a certain relish. "Mrs. Denys has got what she deserved."

Had she? I knew only that since I had seen the gash on Gartred's face I hated her no longer.

"Were all the gentlemen to breakfast?" I said suddenly.

"I believe so."

"And Master Dick as well?"

"Yes. He came somewhat later than the others, but I saw him in the dining room an hour ago."

A wave of relief washed over me, for no reason except that he was safely in the house. "Help me to dress," I said to Matty.

Friday, the twelfth of May. . . . I found Robin in the gallery, standing with moody face beside the window, his right arm hanging in a sling.

"I thought you had departed with Bunny to Carhayes," I said.

"We wait for Peter Courtney," he answered dully.

"Does your wrist pain you?" I asked gently.

He shook his head and went on staring from the window.

"When the shouting is over and the turmoil done," I said, "we will keep house together, you and I, as we did once at Lanrest."

Still he did not answer, but I saw the tears start in his eyes.

"We have loved the Grenviles long enough," I said. "The time has come when they must learn to live without us."

"They have done that," he said, his voice low, "for nearly thirty years. It is we who are dependent upon them."

The door opened, and Richard came into the gallery, Bunny at his shoulder.

"I cannot understand it," he said, pacing the floor in irritation. "Here it is nearly noon. If Peter left Carhayes at daybreak, he should have been here long since."

"If you permit me," Robin said humbly, "I can ride in search of him. He may have stayed to breakfast."

"He is more likely behind a haystack with a wench," said Richard. "Go, then, if you like, but keep a watch upon the roads. I have heard reports of troops riding through Saint Blazey. The rumor may be false, and yet . . ."

Presently we heard Robin mount his horse and ride away. The hours wore on. At half past one there was a footfall on the stairs, slow and labored. Ambrose Manaton glanced subconsciously to the chamber overhead, then drew back against the window.

The handle of the door was turned, and Gartred stood before us like a specter. She was dressed for travel, one side of her face shrouded with a veil. "I wish," she said at length, "to return to Orley Court."

"You ask for the impossible," said Richard shortly. "In a few hours the roads will be impassable."

"I'll take my chance of that," she said. "I have done what you asked me to do. My part is played." Her eyes were upon Richard all the while and never once on Ambrose Manaton.

"I am sorry," said Richard briefly, "I cannot help you. You must stay here until arrangements can be made. We have more serious matters on our hands than the transport of a sick widow."

Bunny was the first to catch the sound of the horse's hooves galloping across the park. We waited, tense, expectant. The sound came closer, and suddenly the rider and his horse came through the arch beneath the gatehouse, and there was Peter Courtney, dust-covered and disheveled. He flung the reins to a startled waiting groom and came straightway to the gallery.

"For God's sake, save yourselves, we are betrayed," he said.

My heart went cold and dead within me.

"They have all been seized," Peter said. "Trelawney, his son, Charles Trevannion, Arthur Bassett and the rest. At ten this morning they came riding to the house, the sheriff with a whole company of soldiers. He said that a messenger had left a note at his house early before dawn, warning him that the whole party, Sir Richard Grenvile included, would be gathered at Carhayes. We made a fight for it, but there were more than thirty of them. I leaped from an upper window. I got the first horse to hand and put spurs to him without mercy. There are soldiers everywhere."

He looked around the gallery as though in search of someone.

"Robin gone?" he asked. "I thought so. It was he, then, I saw, when I was skirting the sands, engaged in fighting with five of the enemy or more. I dared not go to his assistance. My first duty was to you. What now, then? Can we save ourselves?"

We all turned to our commander. He stood before us, calm and cool. "Did you see their colors?" he asked swiftly.

"Some were from Bodmin, sir," said Peter, "the rest advance guards, line upon line of them. This is no chance encounter. The enemy are in strength."

Richard nodded and turned quickly to Bunny. "Go to Pridmouth," he said. "Make sail instantly. Set a course due south until you come in contact with the first outlying vessel of the

French fleet. Ask for Lord Hopton's ship. Give him this message." He scribbled rapidly upon a piece of paper.

"Do you bid them come?" said Ambrose Manaton. "Can they get to us in time?" He was white to the lips.

"Why, no," said Richard, folding his scrap of paper. "I bid them alter course and sail for France again. There will be no rising. The Prince of Wales does not land this month in Cornwall."

He gave the paper to his nephew. "Good chance, my Bunny," he said, smiling. "Give greetings to your brother, Jack, and with a spice of luck you will find the Scillies fall to you like a plum a little later in the summer."

"And you, Uncle?" said Bunny. "Will you not come with me? It is madness to delay if the house is likely to be surrounded."

"I'll join you in my own time," said Richard.

Bunny stared at him an instant, then turned and went.

"But what are we to do?" said Ambrose Manaton. "Oh, God, what a fool I have been to let myself be led into this business." He turned to Peter. "Who is the traitor? That is what I want to know. None but ourselves knew the change in rendezvous."

"Does it matter?" said Richard gently. "The deed is done."

"Matter?" said Ambrose Manaton. "Good God, here are we, ruined men, likely to be arrested within the hour, and you stand there like a fox and smile at me."

"My enemies call me fox, but not my friends," said Richard softly. He turned to Peter. "Tell the fellows to saddle a horse for Mr. Manaton, and for you also. I guarantee no safe conduct, but at least you have a sporting chance."

"You will not come with us, sir? It will go ill with you if they should find you."

"I am well aware of that."

"The sheriff suspects your presence here in Cornwall. Some wretch has seen you, sir, and with devil intuition has guessed your plans."

"Some wretch indeed," said Richard, smiling.

Soon their horses were galloping from the courtyard. The clock in the belfry struck two. Gartred lay back against the couch, the smile on her lips a strange contrast to the gash upon her face. Richard stood by the window, his hands behind his back. And Dick, who had never moved once in all the past half hour, waited, like a dumb thing, in his corner.

When the sound of the horses' galloping had died away, it was strangely hushed within the house. Then Richard began to speak, his back still turned to us, his voice soft and low.

"My grandfather," he said, "was named Richard also. He came of a long line of Grenviles who sought to serve their country and their kings. He died in battle nine years before my birth, but I remember, as a lad, asking for tales of him. He fell, mortally wounded, on the decks of his own ship, called the *Revenge*. He had fought alone with the Spanish fleet about him, and when asked to surrender, he went on fighting still. Masts gone—sails gone—the decks torn beneath his feet, but the Grenvile of that day had courage and preferred to have his vessel blown to pieces than sell his life for silver to the pirate hordes of Spain." He fell silent a moment, watching the pigeons on the lawn, then continued. "My uncle John," he said, "explored the Indies with Sir Francis Drake. He was killed there, and my father, who loved him well, built a shrine to him at Stowe."

There was no sound from any of us in the gallery, I in my chair, Gartred on the couch and Dick standing motionless in his dark corner.

"There was a saying born about this time," continued Richard, "that no Grenvile was ever wanting in loyalty to his king. My brother, Bevil, was not bred to war. He desired, in his brief life, nothing so much as to rear his children with his wife's care and live at peace among his neighbors. When war came, he knew what it would mean. But because he bore the name of Grenvile, he knew, in 'forty-two, where his duty lay. He wrote a letter at that time to our friend and neighbor John Trelawney, who has this day been arrested, and because I believe that letter to be the finest thing my brother ever penned, I asked Trelawney for a copy of it. I have it with me now. Shall I read it to you?"

He felt in his pocket slowly for a paper and read aloud:

" 'I cannot contain myself within my doors when the King of England's standard waves in the field for a cause so just as to make all those who die in it little inferior to martyrs. For mine own part I desire to acquire an honest name or an honorable grave. I never loved my life or ease so much as to shun such an occasion which, if I should, I were unworthy to succeed those ancestors of mine who have, so many of them, in several ages, sacrificed their lives for their country.' "

Richard folded the letter and put it once more into his pocket. "Bevil died at Lansdowne," he said, "leading his men to battle, and his young son Jack, a lad of but fifteen, straightway mounted his father's horse and charged the enemy. That youngster who has just left us, Bunny, ran from his tutor last autumn, playing truant, so that he might place himself at my disposal. I have no brief for myself. I am a soldier. My faults are many and my virtues few. But no quarrel, no dispute, no petty act of vengeance has ever turned me, or will turn me now, from loyalty to my country and my King. In the long and often bloody history of the Grenviles, not one of them until this day has proved a traitor."

His voice had sunk now, deadly quiet.

"One proud day," said Richard, "we may hope that His Majesty will be restored to his throne, or if not he, then the Prince of Wales. And the name of Grenvile will be held in honor in all England. Jack and Bunny can tell their sons in the years to come, 'We Grenviles fought to bring about the restoration of our King,' and their names will rank beside that of my grandfather, Richard, who fought on the *Revenge*." He paused a moment. "I care not if my name be written in smaller characters. 'He was a soldier,' they may say, 'the King's General in the West.' Let that be my epitaph. But there will be no other Richard in that book at Stowe. For the King's general died without a son."

A long silence followed his last words. Soon now it would come, I thought, the outburst, the angry frightened words or the torrent of wild weeping. For eighteen years the storm had been pent up, and the full tide of emotion could wait no longer.

But the cry was never uttered. Nor did the tears fall. Instead, Dick came from his corner and stood alone in the center of the room. The fear was gone now from the dark eyes, and the slim hands did not tremble. He looked older, older and more wise. Yet when he spoke, his voice was a boy's voice.

"Will you do it for me," he said, "or must I kill myself?"

It was Gartred who moved first. Gartred, my lifelong foe. She rose from her couch, pulled the veil about her face, came to my chair, and, with no word spoken, wheeled me from the room. We went out into the garden under the sun, our backs turned to the house. And neither she nor I nor any man or woman, alive or dead, will ever know what was said there in the long gallery at Menabilly by Richard Grenvile to his only son.

Tᴴᴱᴿᴱ ʜᴀᴅ ʙᴇᴇɴ no way to warn the Royalists that their leaders had been arrested, and the prospective rising, the rebellion of 'forty-eight, was now doomed to failure. They struck at the appointed hour and found themselves faced, not with the startled troops they had expected, but with the strong forces, fully prepared and armed, that came riding posthaste into Cornwall for the purpose. What was to have been the torch to light all England was no more than a sudden quivering flame, sputtering for a single moment in the damp Cornish air.

It was a servant, much agitated, who brought us the news that first evening that troopers were gathered at the top of Polmear Hill, and some were going down to the beaches while the rest were making for the park gates. I can see Richard now, his arms folded, seated in the dining chamber, deaf to all my pleading.

"When they come," he said, "they shall take me as I am. Mine is the blame. I am the man for whom my friends now suffer. Very well, then. Let them do their worst upon me, and by surrendering my person, I may yet save Cornwall from destruction!"

Gartred, her cool composure back again, shrugged in disdain. "Is it not a little late in the day to play the martyr?" she suggested. "You flatter yourself, poor Richard, if you think the mere holding of a Grenvile will spare the rest from imprisonment and death."

She did not look toward Dick. Nor did I. But he sat there, silent as ever, at his father's side.

"We will make fine figures on the scaffold, Dick and I," said Richard. "My neck is somewhat thicker, I know, than his, and may need two blows from the axe instead of one."

"You may not have the pleasure, nor the parade, of a martyr's execution," said Gartred, yawning, "but instead a knotted rope in a dank dungeon. Not the usual finish for a Grenvile."

"It were better," said Richard quietly, "if these two Grenviles did die in obscurity."

Dick spoke then, for the first time since that unforgettable moment in the gallery. "How about the Rashleighs?" he said. "If my father and I are found here by the enemy, will it be possible to prove to them that the Rashleighs are innocent in the matter?"

I seized upon his words like a drowning woman. "You have not thought of that," I said to Richard. "Who will ever believe that Jonathan Rashleigh and John, too, were not party to your plan? They will be dragged into the matter, and my sister Mary also. Poor Alice, Joan, a legion of young children. They will all of them, from Jonathan in London to the baby on Joan's knee, suffer imprisonment, maybe death, if you are taken here."

Richard rose to his feet and looked at me. "So you fear for your Rashleighs? And because of them you have no wish to throw me to the wolves? Very well, then. Where is the famous hiding place that four years ago proved so beneficial to us all?"

I saw Dick flinch and look away from me toward his father.

"Dick knows," I answered. "Would you share it with him?"

"A hunted rat," said Richard, "has no choice. He must take the companion that is thrust upon him."

The place might still be rank with cobwebs and mold, but it would give concealment when the troopers came. And no one, not even Gartred, knew the secret.

"Do you remember," I said to Dick, "where the passage led? I warn you, no one has been there for four years." He nodded, deathly pale. And I wondered what bug of fear had seized him now, when but a short while ago he had offered himself, like a little lamb, for slaughter. "Go, then," I said, "and take your father."

"The rope," he said, "the rope upon the hinge. What if it has frayed now, with disuse, and the hinge rusted?"

"It will not matter," I said. "You will not need to use it now. I shall not be waiting for you in the chamber overhead."

He stared at me, lost for a moment, dull, uncomprehending.

"Well?" Richard said. "If it must be done, this is the moment. There is no other method of escape."

There came into Dick's eyes then a strange look I had not seen before. "Yes," he said slowly, "if it must be done, this is the moment." He turned to his father, opening first the door of the dining room. "Will you follow me, sir?"

Richard paused on the threshold. "When the hounds are in full cry," he said, "and the coverts guarded, the Red Fox goes to earth." He smiled, holding my eyes for a single second, and was gone, after Dick, onto the causeway. . . .

Gartred watched them disappear, then shrugged her shoulders.

"I thought," she said, "the hiding place was in the house. Near your old apartment in the gatehouse. I wasted hours, four years ago, searching in the passage, tiptoeing outside your door."

There was a mirror hanging on the wall beside the window. She went to it and, pulling her veil aside, stared at the jagged crimson gash that ran from her eyebrow to her chin. She saw me watching her through the misty glass of the mirror.

"I could have stopped you," she said, "from falling with your horse into the ravine. You knew that, didn't you?"

"Yes," I said.

"You called to me, asking for the way, and I did not answer."

"You did not," I said.

"It has taken a long time to call it quits," she said to me. She came away from the mirror, took from her sack the little pack of cards I well remembered, and sat down by the table, close to my wheeled chair.

"We will play cards, you and I, until the troopers come," said Gartred Grenvile.

I DOUBT IF Colonel Robert Bennett and his company of soldiers had searched all Cornwall, they could have found a quieter couple than the two women playing cards in the dining hall at Menabilly.

Yes, there had been guests with us until today, we admitted. Sir Peter Courtney, and my brother, Robin Harris. No, we knew nothing of their movements. Why was I left alone at Menabilly by the Rashleighs? From necessity, not from choice. My home at Lanrest was burned down four years ago. And why was Mrs. Denys from Orley Court near Bideford a guest of mine at the present season? Well, she was once my sister-in-law and we had long been friends. . . . Yes, it was true my name had been connected with Sir Richard Grenvile's in the past. No, Mrs. Denys had never been very friendly with her brother. No, we had no knowledge of his movements. Yes, search the house, from the cellar to the attics; search the grounds. Here are the keys. Do what you will. We have no power to stop you.

"Well, you appear to speak the truth, Mistress Harris," Colonel Bennett said on the conclusion of his visit, "but the fact that your brother and Sir Peter Courtney are implicated in the rising that is now breaking out renders this house suspect. I shall leave a guard behind me, and I rather think, when the Parliamentary commander in the West, Sir Hardress Waller, comes into the district, he will make a more thorough search of the premises than I have had time to do today. Meanwhile—" He broke off abruptly, his eyes drifting, as if in curiosity, back to Gartred. "Pardon my indelicacy, madam, but that cut is recent?"

"An accident," said Gartred, shrugging. "A clumsy movement and some broken glass."

"It has more the appearance of a sword cut, forgive my rudeness. Were you a man, I would say you had been hurt fighting a duel."

"I am not a man, Colonel Bennett. If you doubt me, why not come upstairs to my chamber and let me prove it to you?"

Robert Bennett was a Puritan. He stepped back a pace, coloring to his ears. "I thank you, madam," he said stiffly. "My eyes are sufficient evidence."

She began to shuffle the cards, but Colonel Bennett made a motion with his hands. "I regret," he said shortly, "but whether you are Mrs. Denys or Mrs. Harris these days, your maiden name is Grenvile."

"And so?" said Gartred, still shuffling her cards.

"And so I must ask you to come with me down to Truro. There you will be held, pending investigation, and when the roads are quieter, you will have leave to depart to Orley Court."

Gartred rose. "As you will," she said, shrugging. "You have some conveyance, I presume? I have no dress for riding."

"You will have every comfort, madam." He turned then to me. "You are permitted to remain here until I receive further orders from Sir Hardress Waller. Meanwhile, I will leave a guard with instructions that you are not to leave the house, and he is to shoot on sight, should his suspicions be in any way aroused. Good evening. You are ready, Mrs. Denys?"

"Yes, I am ready." Gartred touched me lightly on the shoulder. "I am sorry," she said, "to cut my visit short. Remember me to the Rashleighs when you see them. And tell Jonathan what I said about the gardens. If he wishes to plant flowering shrubs, he must first rid himself of foxes. . . ."

"Not so easy," I answered. "They are hard to catch."

"Smoke them out," she said. "It is the only way. Do it by night; they leave less scent behind them. . . . Good-by, Honor."

"Good-by, Gartred."

She went, throwing her veil back from her face to show the vivid scar, and I have not seen her from that day to this.

I heard the troopers ride away across the park. Before the two entrance doors stood sentries, with muskets at their sides. And a sentry stood also at the outer gate and by the steps leading to the causeway. I sat watching them, then pulled the bell rope by the hearth for Matty. "Take me upstairs, Matty," I said slowly. "To my old room beyond the gatehouse."

I had not been there in all the past two years of my stay at Menabilly. The room had neither bed nor chair nor table. It had a dead, musty smell, and in the far corner lay the bleached bones of a rat.

"Go to the stone," I whispered. "Put your hands against it."

Kneeling, Matty did so, pressing against the large stone by the buttress. But it did not move. "No good," she murmured. "Have you forgotten that it only opens from the other side?"

Had I forgotten? It was the one thing that I remembered. "Smoke them out," Gartred had said. "It is the only way." Yes, but she did not understand. She thought them hidden somewhere in the woods. Not behind stone walls three feet thick.

"Fetch wood and paper," I said to Matty. "Kindle a fire. Here against the wall." There was a chance, a faint one, that the smoke would penetrate the cracks in the stone and make a signal. They might not be in the buttress cell, though. They might be crouching in the tunnel at the farther end, beneath the summerhouse. . . .

How slow she was, good Matty, faithful Matty, fetching dried grass and twigs. How carefully she blew the fire, how methodically she added twig to twig. "Hurry," I said. "More wood."

"Patience," she whispered. "It will go in its own time."

In its own time. Not my time. Not Richard's time. . . . The room was filled with smoke. It seeped into our eyes, our hair; it clung about the windows. But whether it seeped into the stones we could not tell. Matty went to the window and opened it a crack.

"There are four horsemen riding across the park," she said suddenly. "Troopers, like those who left just now."

I think I was nearer panic at that moment than any other in my eight and thirty years. "Oh God," I whispered, "what are we to do?"

Matty stamped upon the embers of the fire. "Come back to your chamber," she said. "Later tonight I will try here once again. But we must not be found here now."

She carried me in her broad arms from the dark musty room down to my chamber. We heard the troopers ride into the court-yard, and then the sound of footsteps below. Matty brushed the soot from my hair and changed my gown, and when she had finished, there came a tap at the door. A servant with frightened face whispered that Mistress Harris was wanted below. They put me in my chair and carried me downstairs. There had been four troopers, Matty said, riding across the park, but only three stood here, in the side hall. They cast a curious glance upon me as Matty and the servant put me down inside the door of the dining hall. The fourth man stood across the room by the fireplace, leaning upon a stick. And it was not another trooper like them-selves, but my brother-in-law, Jonathan Rashleigh.

For a moment I was too stunned to move, then I wheeled my chair to where he stood. He took my hand and held it, saying nothing. I looked up at him and saw what the years had done. His hair was white, his shoulders shrunk and drooping. His very eyes seemed sunk deep in his skull.

"What has happened?" I asked. "Why have you come back?"

"The debt is paid," he said, and even his voice was an old man's voice. "I am free to come to Cornwall once again."

"You have chosen an ill moment to return," I answered.

"So they warned me." He looked at me, and I knew then that he, a prisoner in London, had been a party to the plans.

"You came by road?" I asked.

"Nay, by ship," he answered, "my own ship, the *Frances*, which plies between Fowey and the Continent. Her merchandise has helped me pay my debt. She fetched me from Gravesend a week ago. We came to harbor but a few hours since."

"Is Mary with you?"

"No. She went ashore at Plymouth to see Joan at Madder-combe. We heard a rising was expected in Cornwall, and I hurried here, fearing for your safety."

"You knew John was not here? You knew I was—alone?"

"I knew you were—alone."

We both fell silent, our eyes upon the door. "They have arrested Robin," I said softly, "and Peter also, I fear."

"Yes," he said, "so my guards tell me." Then slowly, from his pocket, he drew a folded paper, a poster such as they stick upon the walls for wanted men. He read it to me.

" 'Anyone who has harbored at any time, or seeks to harbor in the future, the malignant known as Richard Grenvile shall, upon discovery, be arrested for high treason, his lands sequestered finally and forever, and his family imprisoned.' "

He refolded the paper. "This," he said, "is posted upon every wall in every town in Cornwall."

For a moment I did not speak. Then I said, "They have searched this house already. They found nothing."

"They will come again tomorrow," he said, leaning more heavily on his stick. "My ship the *Frances* anchors in Fowey only for the night. Tomorrow she sails for Holland. She carries a light cargo. The master of the vessel is an honest man, faithful to any trust that I might lay upon him. Already in his charge is a young woman, whom I thought fit to call my kinswoman. She will proceed to Holland also, in the *Frances*."

"I don't see what this young woman has to do with me. Let her go to Holland, by all means."

"She would be easier in mind," said Jonathan Rashleigh, "if she had her father with her."

I was still too blind to understand his meaning, until he felt in his breast pocket for a note, which he handed to me.

I opened it and read the few words scribbled in an unformed youthful hand. *If you still need a daughter in your declining years*, ran the message, *she waits for you on board the good ship* Frances. *Holland, they say, is healthier than England. Will you try the climate with me? My mother christened me Elizabeth, but I prefer to sign myself your daughter, Bess.*

I said nothing for a little while, but held the note there in my hands. I could have asked a hundred questions, but none of them mattered or were appropriate to the moment.

"You have given me this note," I said to Jonathan, "in the hope that I can pass it to her father?"

"Yes," he answered. "The *Frances* leaves Fowey on the early tide. A boat will put off to Pridmouth, as they go from harbor, to lift lobster pots dropped offshore. It would be a simple matter to pick up a passenger in the half-light of morning." He guessed then that Richard was concealed within the buttress.

"The sentries," I said, "keep watch upon the causeway."

"At this end only," he said softly, "not at the other."

"The risk is very great, even by night."

"But I think the person of whom we speak will dare that risk," he answered. "If you should deliver the note, you could give him this as well." In silence he handed me the folded poster. I took it and placed it in my gown.

"One other thing I would have you do," he said. "Destroy all trace of what has been. The men who will come tomorrow have keener noses than the local troops who came today."

"They can find nothing from within," I answered.

"But from without," he said, "the secret is less sure. I give you leave to finish the work begun by the Parliament in 'forty-four. I shall not seek to use the summerhouse again." I guessed his meaning as he stood there watching me. "Timber burns fiercely in dry weather," he said.

"Why do you not stay and do this work yourself?"

But even as I spoke, the door of the dining hall was opened, and the leader of the three troopers waiting in the hall entered.

"I am sorry, sir," he said, "but you have already had fifteen minutes of the ten allotted to you. Will you please make your farewell now and return with me to Fowey?"

"I thought Mr. Rashleigh was a free agent once again?"

"The times being troublesome, my dear Honor," said Jonathan quietly, "the gentlemen in authority deem it best that I should remain at present under surveillance. I am to spend the night, therefore, in my town house at Fowey." He turned to the trooper. "I am grateful to you," he said, "for allowing me this interview with my sister-in-law. She suffers from poor health, and we have all been anxious for her."

Without another word he went from me and I was left there with the lives, not only of Richard and his son, but also of the whole Rashleigh family, depending upon my wits and sagacity.

I waited for Matty, but she did not come to me, and, impatient at last, I rang the bell beside the hearth. The startled servant who came running told me that Matty was not to be found.

"No matter," I said, and made a pretense of taking up a book and turning the pages, wondering with an anxious, heavy heart what had become of her.

It was close to nine o'clock when I heard the door open. Turning in my chair, I saw Matty standing there, her gown stained green and brown with earth. She put her finger to her lips and came across the room and closed the shutters. As she folded the last one into place she spoke softly over her shoulder. "He is not ill-looking, the sentry on the causeway."

"No?"

She fastened the shutter, drew the heavy curtains, and came and stood beside my chair. "It was somewhat damp in the thistle park," she said. "But he found a sheltered place beneath a bush, where we could talk. . . . While he was looking for it, I waited in the summerhouse. I lifted the flagstone and left a letter on the steps. I said, if the rope be still in place upon the hinge, would they open the stone entrance in the buttress tonight at twelve o'clock? We would be waiting for them."

I felt her strong comforting hand and held it in mine.

"I pray they find it," she said slowly. "There must have been a fall of earth since the tunnel last was used. The place smelled of a tomb. . . ."

We clung to each other in the darkness, and I could hear the steady thumping of her heart.

I LAY UPON my bed upstairs from half past nine until a quarter before twelve. When Matty came to rouse me, the house was deadly still. I could hear one of the sentries pacing the walk beneath my window. The treacherous moon, never an ally to a fugitive, rose slowly above the trees in the thistle park. We lit no candles. Matty lifted me in her arms, and we trod the long twisting corridor to the empty gatehouse.

Inside the room that was our destination the smoke from our poor fire still hung in clouds about the ceiling. We sat down in the far corner and waited. . . . It was uncannily still, the quietude of a long-forgotten prison where no sunlight ever penetrates, where all seasons seem alike.

I felt Matty touch me on the shoulder, and as she did so, the stone behind me moved. . . . There came, upon my back, the current of cold air I well remembered, and I could hear the creaking of the rope upon its rusty hinge. Now Matty lit her candle, and I saw Richard standing there, earth upon his face, his hands, his shoulders, giving him, in that weird, unnatural, ghostly light, the features of a corpse new-risen from his grave.

"I feared," he said, "you would not come. A few hours more and it would have been too late."

"What do you mean?" I asked.

"No air," he said. "There is only room here from the tunnel for a dog to crawl."

I leaned forward, peering down the steps, and there was Dick, huddled at the bottom, his face as ghostly as his father's.

"It was not thus," I said, "four years ago."

"Come," said Richard, "I will show you. A jailer should have some knowledge of the cell where she puts her prisoners."

He took me in his arms and, stepping sideways, dragged me through the stone entrance and down the steps. Then I saw it for the first time, and the last, that secret room beneath the buttress. Six feet high, four square, it was no larger than a closet, and the stone walls, clammy with years, felt icy to my touch. There was a little stool in the corner, and by its side an empty trencher with a wooden spoon. Cobwebs and mold were thick upon them. Above the stool hung the rope, near frayed, upon its rusty hinge, and beyond this the opening to the tunnel, a round black hole, about eighteen inches high, through which a man must crawl and wriggle if he wished to reach the farther end.

"There has been a fall of earth and stones," said Richard, "from the foundations of the house. It blocks the tunnel but for a small space through which we burrowed. My enemies can find me a new name. Henceforth I will be badger, and not fox."

I saw Dick's white face watching me. What is he telling me, I wondered, with his dark eyes? What is he trying to say?

"Take me back," I said to Richard. "I have to talk to you."

He carried me to the room above, where the bare boards and smoky ceiling seemed paradise compared to the black hole from which we had come. We sat there, by the light of a single candle, Richard and Dick and I, while Matty kept a watch upon the door.

"Jonathan Rashleigh has returned," I said. "The County Committee has allowed him to come home. He will be able to live in Cornwall henceforth, a free man, unencumbered, if he does nothing more to rouse the suspicions of the Parliament."

"That is well for him," said Richard.

"He has endured two years of suffering and privation, and has earned repose. He has but one desire, to live among his family, in his own house, without anxiety."

"The desire," said Richard, "of almost every man."

"His desire will not be granted," I said, "if it should be proved he was a party to the rising."

"The Parliament would find it difficult to lay that upon him," Richard said. "Rashleigh has been two years in London."

For answer I took the folded poster from my gown, spread it on the floor, put the candlestick upon it, and read it aloud, as my brother-in-law had read it to me that afternoon. "They will come in the morning, Jonathan said, to search again."

A blob of grease from the candle fell upon the paper, and the edges curled. Richard placed it to the flame, and the paper caught and burned, wisping to nothing in his hands.

"You see?" said Richard to his son. "Life is like that. A flicker and a spark, and then it's over. No trace remains. Ah, well," he sighed, "there's nothing for it but to run our necks into cold steel. Are you ready, Dick? Yours was the master hand that brought us to this pass. I trust you profit by it now." He rose to his feet. "At least," he said, "they keep a sharp axe in Whitehall. I have watched the executioner do justice before now. He only takes a single stroke." He paused a moment, thoughtful. "But," he said slowly, "the blood makes a pretty mess upon the straw."

I saw Dick grip his ankle with his hand, and I turned like a fury on the man I loved. "Will you be silent?" I said. "Hasn't he suffered enough these eighteen years?" Then I threw him the note I was clutching in my hand. "There is no need for your fox head to lie upon the block. Read that and change your tune."

He bent low to the candle, and I saw his eyes change in a strange manner as he read, from black malevolence to wonder. "I've bred a Grenvile after all," he said softly.

"The *Frances* leaves Fowey on the morning tide," I said. "The master can be trusted. The voyage will be swift."

"And how," asked Richard, "do the passengers go aboard?"

"A boat, in quest of lobsters and not foxes, will call at Pridmouth as the vessel sails from harbor. The passengers will be waiting for it. I suggest they conceal themselves for the remainder of the night on the beach, near the hill."

"It would seem," said Richard, "that nothing could be more easy." His eyes were traveling beyond my head to plans and schemes in which I played no part. "From Holland to France," he murmured, "and once there, to see the prince. A new plan of campaign better than this last." His eyes fell back upon the note in his hand. " 'My mother christened me Elizabeth,' " he read, " 'but I prefer to sign myself your daughter, Bess.' "

He tossed it to Dick. "Well? Shall I like your sister?"

"I think," said Dick slowly, "you will like her very well."

"It took courage, did it not," pursued his father, "to leave her home, find herself a ship, and be prepared to land alone in Holland, without friends or fortune?"

"Yes," I said, "it took courage, and something else. Faith in the man she is proud to call her father. Confidence that he will not desert her should she prove unworthy."

They stared at each other, Richard and his son, brooding, watchful, as though between them was some dark secret understanding. Then Richard turned to the entrance in the buttress.

"Do we go the same way by which we came?"

"The house is guarded," I said. "It is your only chance."

"And when the watchdogs come tomorrow," he said, "and seek to sniff our tracks, how will you deal with them?"

"As Jonathan Rashleigh suggested," I replied. "Timber in dry weather burns easily and fast. I think the family of Rashleigh will not use their summerhouse again."

"And the entrance here?"

We peered, all three of us, into the murky depths. Suddenly Dick reached out to pull upon the rope, and the hinge also. He gave three tugs, and then they broke, useless forevermore.

"There," he said, smiling oddly. "No one will ever force the stone again, once you have closed it from this side."

"One day," said Richard, "a Rashleigh will come and pull the buttress down. What shall we leave for a legacy?" His eyes wandered to the bones in the corner. "The skeleton of a rat," he said, and with a smile he threw it down the stair.

"Go first, Dick," he said. "I will follow you."

Dick put out his hand to me, and I held it for a moment.

"Be brave," I said. "The journey will be swift. Once safe in Holland, you will make good friends."

He did not answer. He gazed at me with his great dark eyes, then turned to the little stair.

I was alone with Richard. We had had several partings, he and I. Each time I told myself it was the last.

"How long this time?" I said.

"Two years," he said. "Perhaps eternity." He kissed me long. "When I come back," he said, "we'll build a house at Stowe. You shall sink your pride at last and become a Grenvile."

I smiled and shook my head. "Be happy with your daughter," I said.

He climbed through the entrance and knelt upon the stair, where Dick waited. "I'll do your destruction for you. Watch from your chamber, and you will see the Rashleigh summerhouse make its last bow to Cornwall, and the Grenviles also."

"Beware the sentry," I said. "He stands below the causeway."

"Do you love me still, Honor?"

"For my sins, Richard."

"Are they many?"

"You know them all."

And as he waited there, his hand upon the stone, I made my last request. "You know why Dick betrayed you to the enemy?"

"I think so."

"Not from resentment, not from revenge. But because he saw the blood on Gartred's cheek. . . . Forgive him, for my sake, if not for your own."

"I have forgiven him," he said, "but the Grenviles are strangely fashioned. I think you will find he cannot forgive himself."

They stood, father and son, upon the stair, with the little cell below. Then Richard pushed the stone flush against the buttress wall. It was closed forever.

I waited a moment, then I called for Matty. "It's all over," I said. "Finished. No one will ever hide in the buttress cell again." I put my hand to my cheek. It was wet. I did not know I had been crying. "Take me to my room," I said to Matty.

I sat there, by the far window, looking out across the gardens. Hours long, it seemed, I waited, staring to the east, with Matty crouching at my side. At length I saw a little spurt of flame rise above the trees in the thistle park. Now, I said to myself, it will burn steadily till morning, and when daylight comes, they will say poachers lit a bonfire in the night that spread, unwittingly, catching the summerhouse alight. Now, I said also, two figures wend their way across the beach and wait there, in the shelter of the cliff. They are safe; they are together. I can go to bed and sleep and so forget them. And yet I went on sitting there, beside my bedroom window, and I did not see the moon, nor the trees, nor the thin column of smoke rising into the air, but all the while Dick's eyes looking up at me, for the last time, as Richard closed the stone in the buttress wall.

AT NINE IN THE morning came a line of troopers riding through the park. The officer in charge, a colonel, sent word to me that I must dress and descend immediately and be ready to accompany him to Fowey. When the servants carried me downstairs, I saw the troopers he had brought prizing the paneling in the long gallery.

"This house was sacked once already," I said to the officer.

"I am sorry," said the officer, "but the Parliament can afford to take no chances with a man like Richard Grenvile."

"You think to find him here?"

"There are a score of houses in Cornwall where he might be hidden," he replied. "Menabilly is but one of them."

I looked about me, at the place that had been my home now for two years. I had seen it sacked before. I had no wish to witness the sight again. "I am ready," I said to the officer.

I was placed in the litter, with Matty at my side, and as we set off, I heard the well-remembered sound of axes tearing the floorboards, of swords ripping the wood. This, I thought, is my farewell to Menabilly. I shall not live here again. I looked up from the path beneath the causeway. The summerhouse that had stood there yesterday was now charred rubble.

"By whose orders," called the officer, "was that fire kindled?"

I heard him take counsel of his men, and they climbed to the causeway to investigate, while Matty and I waited in the litter. In a few moments the officer returned. "What building stood there?" he asked me. "I can make nothing of it from the mess."

"A summerhouse," I said. "My sister, Mrs. Rashleigh, loved it well. Colonel Bennett, when he came yesterday, gave orders, I believe, for its destruction."

"Colonel Bennett," said the officer, frowning, "had no authority without permission of the sheriff."

I shrugged. "He is a member of the County Committee, and therefore can do much as he pleases."

"The County Committee takes too much upon itself," said the officer. "One day they will have trouble with the Army."

He mounted his horse in high ill temper and shouted an order to his men. A civil war within a civil war. Let them quarrel. It would help our cause in the long run. And I thought of the words that had been whispered two years ago in 'forty-six: *When the snow melts, when the thaw breaks, when the spring comes . . .*

We climbed the farther hill and so down to my brother-in-law's town house on Fowey quay. The first thing I looked for was a ship at anchor in the Rashleigh roads, but none was there.

Jonathan was waiting for me in the parlor. The room was dark-paneled, like the dining hall at Menabilly, with great windows looking out upon the quay.

"I regret," said the officer, "that until the trouble in the West has quieted down, we must keep a watch upon this house."

"I understand," said Jonathan. "I have been so long accustomed to surveillance that a few more days of it will not hurt me."

The officer withdrew, and I saw a sentry take up his position outside the window.

"I have news of Robin," said my brother-in-law. "He has been detained in Plymouth, but I think they can fasten little upon him. When this matter has blown over, he will be released."

"And then?" I said.

"Why, then he can become his own master and settle down to peace and quietude. I have a little house in Tywardreath that would suit him well, and you too, Honor, if you should wish to share it with him. That is—if you have no other plan."

"No," I said. "No, I have no other plan."

He walked slowly to the window, looking out upon the quay, white-haired and bent, leaning heavily upon his stick. "The *Frances* sailed at five this morning," he said slowly. "The fishing lad who went to lift his pots pulled first into Pridmouth and found his passenger waiting on the beach, as expected. He looked tired and wan, the lad said, but otherwise little the worse for his ordeal."

"One passenger?" I said.

"Why, yes, there was but one," said Jonathan, staring at me. "Is anything the matter?"

"There is nothing the matter," I said.

He went to his desk in the far corner, opened a drawer and took out a length of rope with a rusted hinge upon it. "As the passenger was about to board the vessel he gave the fisher lad this piece of rope and bade him hand it, on his return, to Mr. Rashleigh. A piece of paper wrapped about it had these words written on the face: 'Tell Honor that the least of the Grenviles chose his own method of escape.'" He handed me the little scrap of paper. "What does it mean? Do you understand it?"

"Yes, Jonathan," I said, "I understand." I sat there with the paper in my hands, and I saw once more the ashes of the summerhouse blocking forevermore the secret tunnel, and I saw, too, the silent cell, like a dark tomb, in the thick buttress wall.

He looked at me a moment and then went to the table and put the rope and hinge back in the drawer. "It's over now," he said, "the danger and the strain. There is nothing more we can do."

"No," I answered, "nothing more that we can do."

He fetched two glasses from the sideboard, filled them with wine from the decanter and handed one to me. "Drink this," he said kindly. "You have been through great anxiety." Then he lifted his glass. "To the *Frances*, and to the King's General in the West. May he find sanctuary and happiness in Holland."

I drank the toast in silence, then put the glass back upon the table. "You have not finished it," he said. "That spells ill luck to him whom we have toasted."

I took the glass again, and this time I held it up against the light so the wine shone clear and red. "Did you ever hear," I said, "those words that Bevil Grenvile wrote to John Trelawney?"

"What words were those?"

" 'For mine own part,' " I quoted slowly, " 'I desire to acquire an honest name or an honorable grave. I never loved my life or ease so much as to shun such an occasion which, if I should, I were unworthy to succeed those ancestors of mine who have, so many of them, in several ages, sacrificed their lives for their country.' "

I drank my wine then to the dregs.

"Great words," said my brother-in-law, "and the Grenviles were all great men. But Bevil was the finest of them. He showed great courage at the last."

"The least of them," I said, "showed great courage also."

"Which one was that?" he asked.

"Only a boy," I said, "whose grave will never now be found."

"You are crying," said Jonathan slowly. "This time has been hard and long for you. There is a bed prepared for you above. Let Matty take you to it. Come now, take heart. The worst is over. The best is yet to be. One day the King will come into his own again. One day your Richard will return."

I looked out across the masts to the blue harbor water. The fishing boats were making sail, and the gulls flew above them, crying, white wings against the sky.

"One day," I said, "when the snow melts, when the thaw breaks, when the spring comes . . ."

IN THE YEAR 1824 Mr. William Rashleigh of Menabilly had certain alterations made to his house. The architect summoned to do the work noticed that the buttress against the northeast corner of the house served no useful purpose, and he told the masons to demolish it. On knocking away several of the stones, they came upon a stair, leading to a small room at the base of the buttress. Here they found the skeleton of a young man seated on a stool, a trencher at his feet; the skeleton was dressed in the clothes of a cavalier, as worn during the period of the civil war. Mr. William Rashleigh gave orders for the remains to be buried with great reverence in the churchyard at Tywardreath, and he ordered the masons to so brick up the secret room that no one in the household should come upon it in the future. The exact whereabouts of the cell remained forevermore a secret held by Mr. Rashleigh and his architect.

On consulting family records, Mr. Rashleigh learned that certain members of the Grenvile family had hidden at Menabilly before the rising of 1648, and he surmised that one of them had taken refuge in the secret room and been forgotten. This tradition has been handed down to the present day.

DAPHNE DU MAURIER

WHAT HAPPENED TO THE PEOPLE IN THE STORY

Sir Richard Grenvile: The King's general never returned to England again. He bought a house in Holland, where he lived with his daughter, Elizabeth, until his death in 1659, just a year before the Restoration. He offered his services to the Prince of Wales in exile (afterward Charles II), but they were not accepted, owing to the ill feeling between himself and Sir Edward Hyde. He is said to have died in Ghent, lonely and embittered, with these words only for his epitaph: *Sir Richard Grenvile, the King's General in the West.*

Sir John Grenvile (Jack) and Bernard Grenvile (Bunny): These two brothers were largely instrumental in bringing about the restoration of Charles II in 1660. Both married, lived happily, and were in high favor with the King. John was created Earl of Bath.

Gartred Denys: She never married again, but, leaving Orley Court, went to live with one of her married daughters, Lady Hampson, at Taplow, where she died at the age of eighty-five.

Jonathan Rashleigh: He suffered further imprisonment for debt at the hands of the Parliament, but lived to see the Restoration. He died in 1675, a year after his wife, Mary.

John Rashleigh: He died in 1651, aged only thirty, in Devon, while on the road home to Menabilly, after a visit to London about his father's business. His widow, Joan, lived in Fowey until her death in 1668, aged forty-eight. Her son, Jonathan, succeeded to his grandfather's estate at Menabilly.

Sir Peter Courtney: He deserted his wife, ran hopelessly into debt, married a second time and died in 1670.

Alice Courtney: She lived the remainder of her life at Menabilly and died there, in 1659, aged forty.

Ambrose Manaton: Little is known about him, except that his estate, Trecarrel, fell into decay.

Robin and Honor Harris: The brother and sister lived in quiet retirement at Tywardreath, in a house provided for them by Jonathan Rashleigh. Honor died on the seventeenth day of November 1653, and Robin in June 1655. Thus they did not live to see the Restoration.

DÉSIRÉE

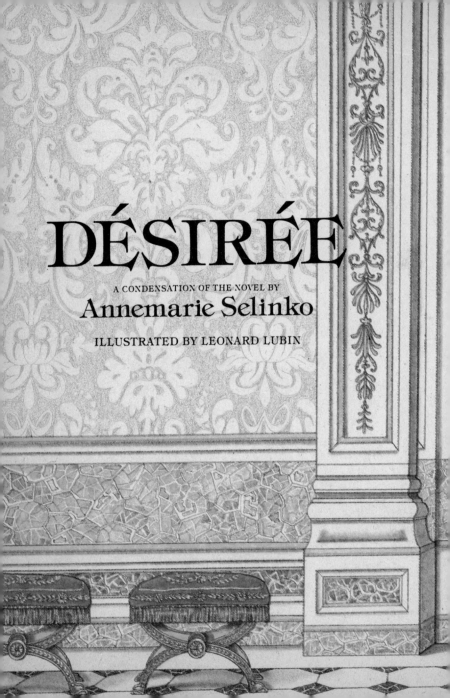

DÉSIRÉE

A CONDENSATION OF THE NOVEL BY

Annemarie Selinko

ILLUSTRATED BY LEONARD LUBIN

They were young and in love. She was the
daughter of a silk merchant of Marseilles;
he a Corsican by birth, a poor army officer with
little future. Soon after they met, he told her,
"I am my destiny. . . . I am one of the men
who will make world history."
Her name was Désirée; his, Napoleon
Bonaparte. And circumstances were to entwine
their lives for more than twenty years — even
after he had become Emperor of the French and
she the wife of one of his greatest enemies.

Annemarie Selinko was born in Vienna,
Austria. She had published three successful
novels before writing *Désirée*, which was an
immediate best-seller in both Europe
and the United States.

PART ONE

The Daughter of a Silk Merchant of Marseilles

Marseilles, end of March, 1794

LAST NOVEMBER I was fourteen, and Papa gave me this lovely diary for my birthday. There's a little lock at the side, so even my sister, Julie, won't know what I put in it. It was my last present from dear Papa, the silk merchant François Clary of Marseilles; he died two months ago of congestion of the lungs.

"What shall I write in that book?" I asked when I saw it among my presents. Papa smiled and kissed me on the forehead. "The story of Citizeness Bernardine Eugénie Désirée Clary," he said.

I am starting my story tonight, because I'm so excited I can't get to sleep. I only hope Julie won't be awakened by the flickering of the candle. She is only four years older, but she wants to mother me all the time.

Tomorrow I'm going with my sister-in-law, Suzanne, to see Deputy Albitte and ask him to release my brother, Etienne. Two days ago the police suddenly came to arrest Etienne. Such things do happen; it's only five years since the great Revolution, and they say it's not over yet. Lots of people are guillotined every day in the town hall square, and it's not safe to be related to aristocrats. Fortunately, we haven't any fine folk among our relatives. Papa made his own way, and he built up Grandpa's little business into one of the biggest silk firms in Marseilles. Papa was very glad about the Revolution, and almost cried when he read to us the first broadside giving the Rights of Man.

Etienne has been running the business since Papa died. When Etienne was arrested, Marie, our cook, who used to be my nurse, said to me, "Eugénie, I hear that Albitte is coming to town. Your sister-in-law must see him and try to get Citizen Etienne Clary set free." Marie always knows what's going on in town.

At supper we were all very dismal. Two places at the table were empty—Papa's and Etienne's. Mama won't let anyone use Papa's chair. I said, "Albitte is in town."

Mama said, "Who is Albitte, Eugénie?"

"Albitte," I said, proud of my knowledge, "is the Jacobin deputy for Marseilles. And tomorrow Suzanne must go to the town hall to see him. She must ask why her husband has been arrested, and insist it is a misunderstanding."

"But," Suzanne cried, looking at me, "he wouldn't receive me!"

"I think it might be better," said Mama doubtfully, "for Suzanne to ask our lawyer to see Albitte."

"We must see Albitte ourselves," I said. "If you're scared, Suzanne, I'll go and ask Albitte to release my big brother."

"Don't you dare!" said Mama. "I do not wish to discuss the matter further."

After supper I went upstairs to see whether Persson had got back. You see, in the evening I give Persson French lessons. He's tall and thin, with the sweetest old horseface, and he's the only fair-haired man I know. That's because he is a Swede. Sweden is somewhere up by the North Pole, I think. Persson's papa has a silk business in Stockholm, and Persson came to Marseilles for a year to be an assistant in Papa's business.

Persson had come in; we sat down in the parlor as usual, and he read to me from the newspapers, while I corrected his pronunciation. Then I got out the broadside about the Rights of Man that Papa had brought home, and Persson and I listened to each other reciting it, as we often do, because we want to learn it all by heart. Persson says he envies me because I belong to the nation that presented these great thoughts to the world. "Liberty, Equality and the Sovereignty of the People," he declaimed.

Suddenly Julie came into the room. "Would you come for a moment, Eugénie?" she said, and took me to Suzanne's room. Suzanne was hunched up on the sofa, and Mama was sitting next to her, trying not to look frail and helpless. "We have decided," said Mama, "that tomorrow Suzanne will try to see Deputy

Albitte. And," Mama added, "you are to go with her, Eugénie. It will be a comfort to her."

"Of course you must keep your mouth shut and let Suzanne do the talking," Julie hastened to add.

I was glad that Suzanne was going to see Albitte. But they were treating me, as usual, like a child, so I said nothing.

"Tomorrow will be a very trying day for us all," said Mama, getting up. "So we must go to bed soon."

I ran into the parlor and told Persson that I had to go to bed. He picked up the newspapers and bowed. I was at the door when he suddenly murmured, "I only wanted to say, mademoiselle, that I shall soon be going home. I've been here for a year and more, and they want me in the business in Stockholm. When Monsieur Etienne Clary comes back, I will return to Stockholm."

It was the longest speech I had ever heard Persson make. I couldn't quite understand why he told me before the others, but I wanted us to go on talking. "Is Stockholm a beautiful city?" I asked politely.

"To me it is the most beautiful city in the world," he answered. "Green ice floes sail about in the Mälaren, and in winter the sky is as white as a sheet." This description didn't make me think Stockholm particularly beautiful.

"Our business," he went on, "is in the Västra Långgatan, the most modern business center in Stockholm. It is just by the Royal Palace," he added proudly.

But I was not really listening. I was thinking about tomorrow, and how I must look as pretty as I can, so that for my sake they will release Etienne. . . .

"I should like so much to ask you a favor," I heard Persson saying. "Could I keep the broadside about the Rights of Man?"

"So you've become a Republican, monsieur?" I teased him.

"I am a Swede, mademoiselle," he replied, "and Sweden is a monarchy. But I will always treasure and revere it."

"You may keep the broadside, monsieur," I said, "and show it to your friends in Sweden."

At that moment I heard Julie's voice. "When are you coming to bed, Eugénie?" What Julie needs, I decided, is a husband; if she had one, my life would be easier.

I tried to sleep, but I could not stop thinking about tomorrow's visit to the town hall. And I kept thinking, too, of the guillotine. I see it so often when I am trying to get to sleep, and then I dig my head into the pillow to drive away the memory of the severed head I saw two years ago when Marie took me secretly to the square before the town hall. A red cart brought up twenty gentlemen and ladies in fine clothes, their hands bound behind their backs, and when the first person, a young man, was jerked onto the scaffold by the executioner, his lips were moving. I think he was praying. He knelt, and I shut my eyes; I heard the guillotine fall.

When I looked up, the executioner was holding a head in his hand. The mouth was wide open, as though about to scream. There was no end to that silent scream. I was horribly sick, and Marie took me out of the crowd.

When we got home I cried and cried. Papa put his arms around me and said, "The people of France have suffered for hundreds of years. And two flames rose from the suffering of the oppressed—the flame of justice, and the flame of hatred. The flame of hatred will burn down, but the other can never again be completely extinguished. Whenever and wherever in days to come men rob their brethren of their rights of liberty and equality, no one can say for them, 'Father, forgive them, for they know not what they do,' because, little daughter, after the Declaration of the Rights of Man they will know perfectly well what they are doing!"

The longer the time that has passed since that talk with Papa, the better I have understood what he meant. I feel very close to him tonight. Good night, Papa! You see I have begun to write down my story.

Twenty-four hours later

So much has happened. First of all, Etienne has been released and is sitting downstairs in the dining room with Mama, Suzanne and Julie, eating away. Second, I have met a young man with an interesting face and an unpronounceable name—Boonopat or Bonapart or something like that. Third, downstairs they are celebrating Etienne's return, and even though it was my idea to see Deputy Albitte, I am being punished; they call me a disgrace to the family, and they have packed me off to bed.

There's no one I can talk to. But my dear good papa must have foreseen how lonely you can be if you are always misunderstood. That is why he gave me this diary.

Today began with one row after another. First Julie told me Mama had decided I was to wear my horrid gray frock and a lace fichu tight around my neck. I fought against the fichu, but Julie shrieked, "Do you think we shall let you go to a government office in a low-necked dress like a—like a girl from the port?"

Julie and I share a bedroom. As soon as Julie had gone, I quickly borrowed her little pot of rouge. I dabbed it on carefully, and thought how difficult it must have been for the great ladies in Versailles, who used thirteen different shades, one on top of another, to get the right effect.

"My rouge!" said Julie crossly as she came back into the bedroom. "And without asking permission!" I quickly powdered my face; then I began to take the paper curlers out of my hair. I have such stubborn natural curls it's a terrible business to coax them into smooth ringlets hanging down to my shoulders.

We heard Mama's voice outside. "Isn't that child ready yet, Julie? She and Suzanne are to be at the town hall by two o'clock."

I tried to hurry, but I simply could not get my hair right. "Julie, can't you help me?" Julie has the light touch and finished doing my hair in five minutes.

I pulled open one drawer after another looking for my Revolutionary cockade. At the beginning of the Revolution everyone wore a cockade, but now the blue-white-red rosettes of the Republic are worn only by Jacobins, or by people like us who are going to see someone in a government office. At first I loved these rosettes showing the national colors of France. But now I think it's undignified to pin one's convictions onto one's frock or coat lapel. Naturally I found my cockade in the last drawer I opened. Then I ran downstairs with Julie.

Mama got out the cut-glass decanter of port wine, poured out two glasses and gave Suzanne one and me one. "Drink it slowly," she told me. "Port wine is strengthening."

I took a big gulp; it tasted sticky and sweet. It made me cheerful, too. I smiled at Julie, and then I saw there were tears in her eyes. "Eugénie," she whispered, "take care of yourself."

The wine was making me very lively. "Perhaps you're afraid Deputy Albitte might seduce me!"

"Can't you ever be serious?" Julie was plainly shocked. "It's not just a game going to the town hall—" She stopped short.

I looked straight at her. "I know what you mean, Julie. Usually the close relatives of arrested men are arrested, too. But nothing will happen to us," I said. "Even if it did, I'd know you were looking after Mama, and that you'd try to get me out. We two must always stick together, mustn't we, Julie?"

Suzanne did not speak on our way into the center of town. When we reached the large square in front of the town hall, I tried not to see the guillotine as we began to push our way through the great crowd that hung about the entrance.

In the narrow waiting room so many people were sitting and standing that one could hardly move. At the far end of the room there was another door, at which a young man in the uniform of the Jacobin Club stood guard. I caught hold of Suzanne's hand and we pressed on through to him. "We want to see Citizen Deputy Albitte, please," Suzanne murmured.

"Everyone in this room wants to see him," he said. "Write your name and business. There on the window ledge the citizeness will find paper and a quill." He might have been an archangel at the gates of Paradise.

We pushed through to the window ledge. Suzanne quickly filled out a form. Names? Citizeness Suzanne Clary and Citizeness Bernardine Eugénie Désirée Clary. Purpose of visit? Suzanne moaned as she wrote: *Concerns arrest of Citizen Etienne Clary*.

We struggled back to our Jacobin archangel. He glanced casually at the paper, then disappeared for what seemed to me an eternity. At last he came back. "You may wait. The citizen deputy will receive you. Your name will be called out."

Soon afterward we found two empty places on a bench by the wall and I began to look about. I noticed our shoemaker, old Simon, and I remembered his son, young Simon with the bowlegs, and how gallantly those bowlegs had marched in that procession eighteen months ago.

That was the beginning of it all, I thought, and I shall never forget it. Our country was being attacked on all sides by enemy armies of countries that would not tolerate our proclamation of the Republic. It was said our armies could not hold out much longer. But one morning I was awakened by singing under our windows. I jumped out of bed, and saw marching past the *volontaires* of Marseilles.

I knew many of the marchers. There were the apothecary's two nephews, and shoemaker Simon's bowlegged son, outdoing himself to keep pace with the others! There was Léon, the assistant from our own shop. And behind Léon I saw banker Levi's three sons. The Rights of Man had given them the same civil liberties as all other Frenchmen. Now they had put on their Sunday best to go to war for France. "*Au revoir*, Monsieur Levi," I shouted, and all three of them looked up and waved. The Levis were followed by our butcher's sons, and then came workmen from the docks in their blue linen tunics. They were all singing "*Allons, enfants de la patrie*," the new song, which was to become famous overnight, and I sang with them. Suddenly Julie was standing next to me. We gathered roses from the ramblers growing around the balcony and threw them down. Below, Franchon, the tailor, caught two of the roses and looked up, laughing. They still looked like ordinary citizens, whether in their dark coats or blue linen tunics.

In Paris they beat back the enemy—the Simons and Léons and Franchons and Levis. And now the song they sang as they marched to Paris is being played and sung all over France. It is called the "Marseillaise" because it was carried through the land by the men of our city. . . .

We waited for many hours to see Albitte. Sometimes I closed my eyes and leaned against Suzanne. Every time I opened them there were fewer people in the room. The archangel was calling out new names more often. But plenty of people who had been there before us were still waiting.

"I must find a husband for Julie," I said to Suzanne, hoping conversation would help me stay awake. "In the novels she reads the heroines fall in love when they are eighteen at the latest."

"Don't bother me now," Suzanne said. "I want to concentrate on what I must say in there." She glanced at the door.

I fell silent, and grew sleepier still. Port wine makes you gay, then sad, and finally tired. But it is certainly not strengthening.

"Don't yawn. It's very rude," Suzanne was saying.

"Oh, but we are living in a free republic," I murmured sleepily.

At last I slept—so soundly that I thought I was in bed at home. Suddenly a voice said, "Wake up, citizeness." Someone shook me by the shoulder. "You can't go on sleeping here!"

Startled, I pushed the strange hand from my shoulder. I was in some dark room, and a man with a lantern was bending over me.

"Don't be alarmed, citizeness," the man said. His voice was

soft and pleasant, but he spoke with a foreign accent. Now I could see his features more clearly. He was really handsome, with kind dark eyes, a very smooth face and a charming smile. He was wearing a dark suit and coat.

"I'm sorry to disturb you," the young man said politely. "My name is Citizen Joseph Buonaparte, secretary to the Committee of Public Safety in Paris, seconded to Deputy Albitte as his secretary during his journey to Marseilles. Our office hours were over a long time ago. I must lock up, and it's against the law for anyone to spend the night in the town hall."

Town hall, Albitte! Now I knew where I was. "Where is Suzanne?" I asked the friendly young man.

His smile broadened into a laugh. "I have not had the privilege of meeting Suzanne," he said. "I am the only person in the office. And I am going home now."

"But I must wait here until Suzanne comes back," I insisted. "You must excuse me, Citizen Boo—na—"

"Joseph Buonaparte," he said politely, helping me out. Then he sighed. "You're awfully persistent," he said. "What is this Suzanne's surname, and why did she want to see Albitte?"

"Her name is Suzanne Clary, and she is my brother Etienne's wife," I told him. "Etienne was arrested, and Suzanne and I came to ask for his release."

"Just a moment," he said. He took the lantern and disappeared through a door. I followed him. He bent over a large desk and began looking through some files of papers. "If Albitte received your sister-in-law," he explained, "your brother's file must be here. The deputy always asks for files before talking to the relatives of men."

I murmured, "The deputy is a very just and kind man."

He glanced up at me mockingly. "That's why Citizen Robespierre of the Committee of Public Safety commissioned me to assist him."

Heavens, I thought, here was someone who knew Deputy Robespierre, who will arrest his best friends to serve the Republic!

"Ah! 'Etienne Clary,' " the young man exclaimed in satisfaction. " 'Silk merchant of Marseilles.' Is that right?"

I nodded eagerly. "His arrest was a misunderstanding." Then I thought of something. "Listen, if you know Citizen Robespierre, perhaps you can tell him that Etienne's arrest was a mistake and—"

My heart stood still. For the young man shook his head slowly. "I can do nothing. There is nothing more to be done." He picked up a document. " 'The matter has been fully explained,' " he read, " 'and he has been set free.' "

I was trembling all over. "Does that mean that Etienne—?"

"Of course! Your brother is a free man. He probably went home with his Suzanne long ago."

I began to weep helplessly. I couldn't stop, the tears ran down my cheeks. "I am so glad, monsieur," I sobbed, "so glad!"

The young man was uncomfortable. He put down the file and busied himself with things on the desk as he said, "And now I'll take you home. It's not pleasant for a young lady to walk through the city alone at this time of night."

"Oh, but I cannot accept—"

He laughed. "Robespierre's friends permit no contradiction."

It's true that young ladies cannot be out alone in the evening without being molested. Besides, I did like him. So I accepted. "I am so ashamed of having cried," I said as we were leaving.

He pressed my arm reassuringly. "I understand. I have brothers and sisters, too. Sisters of about your age. And I love them."

After that I no longer felt in the least shy. "Marseilles isn't your home, is it?" I asked him.

"Yes, it is now. I am a Corsican," he said, "a Corsican refugee. We all came to France a little over a year ago—my mother, my brothers and sisters, and I. We had to leave everything we owned in Corsica, and escaped with our bare lives."

It sounded wildly romantic. "Why?" I asked.

"Because we are patriots," he said. "For twenty-five years Corsica has belonged to France. We were brought up as patriotic French citizens! Then a year ago English warships suddenly appeared off our coast."

"And have you friends in Marseilles?"

"My brother helps us. He was able to get Mama a small government pension. My brother was educated in France, in the Cadet College. He is a general."

"Oh," I said, speechless with admiration.

"You are a daughter of the late silk merchant François Clary, aren't you?"

I was startled. "How did you know that?"

He laughed. "You needn't be surprised. You said you were

Etienne Clary's sister, and I learned from the documents that Etienne is the son of François Clary. By the way, mademoiselle, you were right. Your brother's arrest was indeed a misunderstanding. The arrest warrant was actually made out in your father's name."

"But Papa is no longer alive!"

"Quite so, and that explains the misunderstanding. Recently an examination of certain pre-Revolution documents revealed that the silk merchant François Clary had petitioned to be granted a patent of nobility."

I was astonished. "I don't understand. Papa never had any liking for the aristocracy. Why should he have done that?"

"For business reasons," he explained. "I suppose he wanted to be appointed a purveyor to the court."

"Yes. Papa's silks were famous for their excellent quality," I added proudly.

"His petition was regarded as—well, unsuited to the times. A warrant for his arrest was issued, and when our people went to his address, they found only the silk merchant Etienne Clary, so they arrested him. I assume that your sister-in-law, Suzanne, convinced Deputy Albitte of her husband's innocence. Your brother was released. Your sister-in-law must have hurried to the prison at once to get him. But all that is over and done with. What interests me," he continued, and his voice was soft, almost tender, "what interests me is not your family but yourself, little citizeness. What is your name?"

"My name is Bernardine Eugénie Désirée. They call me Eugénie. But I should much prefer Désirée."

"All your names are beautiful," he said. I felt myself blushing. I had a feeling that the conversation was taking a turn that Mama would not have approved. "Are you allowed to take a walk with a young man?" he inquired.

"So far, I've never known any young men," I said without thinking. I had completely forgotten Persson.

He pressed my arm and laughed. "But now you know one."

"Will you call on us, Citizen Boonapat?" I asked.

"Shall I come soon?" he rejoined, teasing.

But I did not answer at once. I was full of an idea that had just occurred to me—Julie! Julie, who needs to find a husband. Julie, who so loves reading novels. She would adore this young man with the strange foreign accent.

"Come tomorrow," I said, "tomorrow after the shop has been closed for the day. If it is warm enough, we can sit in the summerhouse—it's Julie's favorite spot in the garden." I considered that I had been extremely diplomatic.

"Julie? Who is Julie?"

We had already reached our road, and I had to talk quickly. "Julie is my older sister," I said. "She is eighteen. And very pretty," I assured him eagerly, but then I wondered whether Julie would really be considered pretty. "She has lovely brown eyes," I declared, and so she has.

"Your mother would welcome me?" he asked. He did not seem at all certain, and, quite frankly, I wasn't sure either.

"I am sure she would," I insisted, determined to give Julie her chance. Besides, there was something I wanted myself.

"Do you think you could bring your brother, the general?" I asked. "I've never seen a real general close up."

"Then you shall see one tomorrow. True, at the moment he has no command; he is working out some scheme or other. Still, he is a real general. And, as we have so few acquaintances in Marseilles, he would be delighted to come."

"There must be a great difference in age between you and your brother," I said, for this man seemed very young.

"No, not much difference. My brother is a year younger. Twenty-four. But he is aggressive, and full of astonishing ideas. Well, you'll see him tomorrow yourself."

Our house was now in sight. Lights shone from the ground-floor windows. "That is where I live."

Suddenly the young man's manner changed. When he saw the attractive white villa, he quickly said, "I mustn't keep you, Mademoiselle Eugénie. I'm sure your family is anxious about you. It was a great pleasure to escort you, and I shall call tomorrow in the late afternoon, with my younger brother. That is, if your mother does not object."

At that moment the house door opened and Julie's voice pierced the darkness. "Eugénie, is that you, Eugénie?"

"*Au revoir, mademoiselle,*" he said.

Five minutes later I was informed that I was a disgrace to the family.

Mama, Suzanne and Etienne were at the dining table when Julie brought me in in triumph.

"Thank God," Mama said. "Where were you, my child? We sent Marie to the town hall, but the building was closed. Great heavens, Eugénie, to think that you walked through the town alone at this late hour!"

"But I did not walk alone," I said. "Albitte's secretary accompanied me. He is a very nice young man who knows Robespierre personally. At least he says he does. By the way, I have—"

Etienne, who had not been able to shave during his three days in prison but otherwise was quite unchanged, interrupted me. "What is his name?"

"Boonopat or something like that. A Corsican. By the way, I have—"

Again they would not let me finish.

"And you walked about the town alone with this strange Jacobin in the evening?" Etienne shouted at me.

"He is not a complete stranger; he introduced himself to me. His family lives in Marseilles. They are refugees."

"Refugees from Corsica?" said Etienne contemptuously. "Probably nothing but adventurers!"

I defended my new friend. "I think he has a very respectable family. His brother is a general, and I have been trying to say that I have invited them both here tomorrow." Then I started quickly on the soup Marie had brought me.

"You will have to cancel that invitation," said Etienne, banging the table. "Times are too unsettled to offer hospitality to two escaped Corsican adventurers."

"And it's not proper for you to invite a gentleman you met by chance in a government office." This from Mama.

"Eugénie, I am ashamed of you," said Julie in tones of deep sorrow.

"But these Corsican refugees have so few friends in town," I ventured. I hoped to appeal to Mama's soft heart.

"People whose origins we know nothing about? Out of the question. Don't you ever consider your good name?" Etienne's experience during the last few days had destroyed his self-control. "You are a disgrace to the family!" he shouted.

"Etienne, she is only a child and does not know what she has done," said Mama.

At that, unfortunately, I, too, lost my temper. I was burning with rage. "Once and for all, I am neither a child nor a disgrace!"

For a moment there was silence. Then Mama commanded, "Go to your room at once, Eugénie!"

Marie brought my supper to my room, then sat down on Julie's bed. "What happened? What's wrong?"

When we are alone, Marie always speaks informally: she is my friend, not a servant, and I believe she loves me as much as her own natural child, Pierre, who is being brought up by foster parents somewhere in the country.

I shrugged my shoulders. "It's all because I've invited two young men here tomorrow."

Marie nodded thoughtfully. "Very clever of you, Eugénie. It's time Mademoiselle Julie met some young men."

Marie and I always understand each other.

Marseilles, the lovely month of May is almost over

His name is Napoleone Buonaparte.

When I wake up in the morning and think of him, my heart feels heavy with the weight of my love. I never knew you really *feel* love.

I had better tell it all just as it happened, beginning two months ago. As I had arranged with Joseph Buonaparte, the two brothers came to see us the afternoon after my unfortunate call on Deputy Albitte. Etienne had closed the shop and was waiting in the parlor with Mama, so that the young men should see at once that our home is not without manly protection.

Nobody had spoken more than a few words to me during the day. They were still vexed with my improper behavior. After dinner Julie disappeared into the kitchen; she had decided to make a cake. When I saw her taking it out of the oven, her forehead was damp with perspiration and her hair was a mess.

"You're going about things the wrong way, Julie," I blurted. "Go powder your nose. That's much more important than baking cakes."

"Will you listen to the child, Marie!" cried Julie, irritated.

"If you ask me, Mademoiselle Julie, I think the child is quite right," said Marie as she took the cake tin from her.

In our room Julie did her hair and carefully put on some rouge, while I looked out the window.

"Aren't you changing?" Julie asked in surprise.

I really didn't see any point in it. I quite liked Monsieur Joseph, but in my mind I had already betrothed him to Julie. As for his brother, the general, I couldn't imagine him taking any notice of me. I was interested only in his uniform. While I was looking out of the window I saw them coming. And was I disappointed! He was such a small man, smaller than Monsieur Joseph, who is only middle-sized. And nothing glittered on him, not a single star or ribbon. Only when they reached the gate did I see narrow gold epaulets on his dark green uniform. His boots weren't polished, and I couldn't see his face because it was hidden by an enormous hat, with nothing on it but the cockade of the Republic. "He looks very poor," I murmured.

Julie had joined me at the window. "He looks very handsome," she said.

"Oh, you mean Monsieur Joseph! Yes, he looks quite elegant. But look at his little brother, the general!" I shook my head and sighed. "Such a letdown!"

WHEN JULIE AND I went down to the parlor, Joseph and Napoleone both jumped up and bowed almost too politely. Then we all sat, stiff and strained, around the oval mahogany table.

"I have just been thanking Citizen Joseph Buonaparte," said Mama, "for his kindness in seeing you home, Eugénie."

At that moment Marie came in with liqueur and Julie's cake. While Mama filled the glasses and cut the cake, Etienne said, "Is it indiscreet, Citizen General, to inquire whether you are in our city on official business?"

"You may ask anything you like, Citizen Clary," the general replied. "I make no secret of my plans. In my opinion the Republic is wasting its resources in endless defensive warfare on our frontiers. We must go on the offense. It will help replenish our treasury, and will show Europe that the people's army has not been defeated."

I paid attention—but not to the words. Napoleone's face was no longer concealed by his hat, and though it was not a handsome face, it was stronger, more compelling, more wonderful than any face I had ever seen.

"The offense?" Etienne was looking at him openmouthed. "When our army has such limited equipment . . ."

The general waved his hand and laughed. "Limited? *That's* not the word! Our army is a beggars' army. Our soldiers at the frontiers are in rags; they march into battle in wooden shoes."

I leaned forward and looked hard at him. I wanted to see him laugh again. When he laughs, his face becomes very boyish.

Etienne, too, was engrossed. "And on what front could an offensive operation be successfully carried out?" he asked.

"On the Italian front, naturally. We will drive the Austrians out of Italy. A very cheap campaign. Our troops can easily take care of themselves in Italy. So rich and fertile a country!"

"And the Italian people? They are still loyal to the Austrians."

"We will liberate the Italian people. In all the provinces we shall proclaim the Rights of Man. I've practically completed the plans. At present I am on a tour of inspection, looking at our fortifications here in the south. Citizen Robespierre personally entrusted me with this duty."

Etienne clicked his tongue, a sign that he was impressed. "A great plan"—he nodded—"a bold plan. If only it succeeds!"

The general smiled at Etienne. "Have no fear, Citizen Clary, it will succeed," he said, getting up. "And which of the two young ladies will be so kind as to show me the garden?"

Julie and I both jumped to our feet. And Julie smiled at Joseph. I don't know just how it happened, but two minutes later we four found ourselves—without Mama and without Etienne—in the garden. Because the gravel path to the summerhouse is very narrow, we had to go two by two. Julie and Joseph went ahead, and I walked with Napoleone, racking my brains for something to say to make a good impression on him.

"When do you think my brother and your sister will be married?" he said all of a sudden.

I thought at first that I couldn't have heard him properly. "They have only just met," I stammered.

"They are made for each other," he declared. "You know that, too. You yourself were thinking yesterday evening that it would be a good thing for them to marry. After all, at her age young ladies are usually betrothed."

I felt I'd surely sink through the earth. But I was angry, too. "I thought nothing of the sort, Citizen General!" I felt that in some way I had compromised Julie.

He stopped and looked me in the face. He was only half a head taller than I, and though it was getting dark, his face was so close to mine that I could see his eyes sparkling. I was also surprised to find that men can have long eyelashes.

"You must never have any secrets from me, Mademoiselle Eugénie. I can see deep into the hearts of young ladies. Besides, Joseph told me last night that you had promised to introduce him to your elder sister. You also told him that she was very pretty. That's not true—and you must have had good reason for your little white lie."

"We must hurry," I said to that. "The others must be in the summerhouse already."

"Hadn't we better give them a chance to get better acquainted before they become betrothed? Joseph will very soon be asking for her hand."

"How do you know that?" I asked, puzzled.

"We talked about it last night," he replied.

"But last night your brother had never met my sister," I retorted, outraged.

Then he very gently took my arm, and he spoke so tenderly and trustingly that we might have been friends for years. "Joseph also told me that your family are well-to-do. Your father is no longer living, but I assume that he left a considerable dowry for you and your sister. Our people are very poor. I have three young sisters and three young brothers, and Joseph and I have to provide for Mama and all of them. You have no idea, Mademoiselle Eugénie, how expensive life is now in France."

"So your brother only wants to marry my sister for her dowry?" My voice shook with indignation.

"How can you say that! Your sister is a lovely girl—so friendly, so modest, with such pretty eyes. Joseph finds her charming. They will be very happy together."

"I'm going to tell Julie everything you've said," I warned him.

"Of course. That's why I've explained it so carefully. Tell Julie, so that she'll know that Joseph will soon be asking for her hand. You must realize that before I take over as commander in chief in Italy, I want to see my family well settled. After my first Italian victories, I will of course look after my whole family." He paused. "And—believe me, mademoiselle—I shall look after them well!"

We had come to the summerhouse and could see that Julie and Joseph had completely forgotten us. They were sitting close together on a little bench, holding hands.

We all four went back then to the house, and the brothers Buonaparte said they must be going. But Etienne spoke up. "My mother and I would be honored if the citizen general and Citizen Joseph Buonaparte would stay to supper with us. It's been a long time since I've had an opportunity to participate in such interesting conversation."

Julie and I hurried to our room to do something about our hair. "Thank goodness," she said, "they both made a good impression on Mama and Etienne."

"I must tell you," I said, "that Joseph Buonaparte will soon ask for your hand. And mostly because"—I stopped, my heart was beating so—"because of the dowry!"

"How can you say such a thing!" Julie's face was flaming.

"Has he told you already that he wants to marry you?" I asked.

"Whatever put that idea into your head? Why, we just discussed things in general, and how poor his family is, and how he has to help his mother and the younger children. I think that's very fine of him. . . . Eugénie," she exclaimed, "I won't have you constantly using my rouge!"

On our way down to the dining room Julie suddenly put her arm around my shoulders. "I don't know why," she whispered, and she kissed me, "but I'm so happy!"

I suppose that's love. For myself, I had a queer heaviness around my heart. Napoleone—a queer name.

THAT WAS ALL two months ago.

And yesterday I was kissed for the first time and Julie was betrothed. The two events belong together somehow.

Since that first visit the two brothers have been to see us almost every day. Etienne—who could have believed it?—invited them. He never gets enough of his talks with the young general. Ever since Joseph showed us the clipping from a December *Moniteur* that tells how his brother succeeded in driving the English and the Royalists out of Toulon and was made a brigadier general, Etienne has been fascinated with Napoleone and talks to him of practically nothing but the Italian plans.

"It is our sacred duty," says Napoleone, "to instill into all the European peoples the idea of Liberty, Equality and Fraternity. And if necessary—with the help of cannon!"

I always listen to these talks just to be near Napoleone, though they weary me terribly. But when we are alone, Napoleone never talks about cannon. And we are often alone. After supper Julie always says, "Don't you think we ought to take our guests into the garden for a bit, Mama?"

"Go along, children!" Mama says, and we four, Joseph and Napoleone and Julie and I, disappear in the direction of the summerhouse. Before we get there, Napoleone generally says, "Eugénie, what do you say to a race? Let's see which of us can get to the hedge first!" Then I lift up my skirt and Julie cries, "Ready—set—go!" and Napoleone and I run for the hedge, while Joseph and Julie disappear into the summerhouse.

Sometimes Napoleone wins the race, and sometimes I do; but if I get there first, I know that Napoleone has purposely let me win. The hedge is just chest high. Usually we lean close together against the foliage, look up at the stars and have long talks. But the less we talk, the nearer together we seem. Now and then a bird somewhere sings a melancholy song. The moon hangs in the sky like a golden lantern, and I think, Dear Lord, let this evening last forever, let me go on forever close to him.

Yesterday Napoleone unexpectedly asked, "Are you never afraid of your destiny, Eugénie?"

"Why should one be afraid of what one doesn't know?"

"Most people say they don't know their destiny," he said, his face very pale in the moonlight. "I am my destiny. I know my fate. I am one of the men who make world history."

I stared at him, dumbfounded. It had never occurred to me that anyone could think such things. Suddenly I laughed.

At that he drew back. "You laugh, Eugénie?"

"Please forgive me," I said. "It was only because—I was afraid of your face, so white in the moonlight, so strange."

"I don't want to shock you, Eugénie," he said. His voice was tender. "I can understand your being frightened. Frightened— of my great destiny. Do you believe in me, Eugénie?"

His face was so near that I trembled and involuntarily closed my eyes. Then I felt his mouth hard on my lips. . . .

That night I couldn't get to sleep. Julie's voice came out of the dark. "I've something I must tell you," she whispered. "A tremendous secret. Tomorrow afternoon Joseph is coming to speak to Mama, to ask for my hand!"

I sat up in bed, wildly excited. "Julie! You are betrothed!"

"Sh! Not so loud! Tomorrow afternoon I shall be betrothed. If Mama makes no objection."

I leaped out of bed and ran over to her. "Now you are a fiancée, nearly a bride. Has he kissed you yet?"

"A young lady allows herself to be kissed only after her mother approves the betrothal," Julie explained severely. "But you are still too young to understand such things."

I THINK I'M TIPSY, just a little tipsy, and it's very pleasant. Julie just became betrothed to Joseph, and Mama sent Etienne down to the cellar for the champagne Papa bought years ago, to be saved for such an occasion. They are all still sitting on the terrace, discussing where Julie and Joseph will live. Napoleone has gone to tell his mother. And I came up to my room to write it all down.

I don't know how it happened, but in the last few days I had quite forgotten that our Swede, Monsieur Persson, was going away today, leaving by the mail coach at nine in the morning. Luckily I remembered his departure the moment I woke up this morning. I jumped out of bed, put on my dress, and ran down to the dining room, where Persson was having his farewell breakfast. Mama and Etienne were urging him to eat as much as possible. The poor man has a frightfully long trip ahead of him. Marie had given him a picnic basket with two bottles of wine, a roast chicken, hard-boiled eggs and preserved cherries.

Finally Etienne and I marched him to the mail coach. Etienne carried one of the traveling bags and Persson struggled with a big parcel, the other bag, and the picnic basket. I begged him to let me carry something, and at last he reluctantly gave me the parcel, saying that it contained something very precious. "The most beautiful silk brocade," he confided to me, "that I have ever seen. A silk your dear papa himself bought and at that time intended for the Queen at Versailles. But events prevented the Queen . . ."

"Yes," said Etienne, "and in all these years I have never offered that brocade to anyone. Papa always said such royal silk was only suitable for a court dress."

"But the ladies in Paris are still elegantly dressed," I objected.

Etienne sniffed contemptuously. "The ladies in Paris are no longer ladies! On the contrary, they prefer transparent muslins. Heavy brocade is no longer worn in France today. But in Monsieur Persson's country there is a royal court, and Her Majesty the Queen of Sweden will need a new robe and will appoint Monsieur Persson a purveyor to the court."

"You mustn't keep brocade too long, it goes to pieces," I informed Persson—from head to toe the daughter of a silk merchant.

"This material won't rot," declared Etienne. "There are too many gold threads woven in."

The parcel was quite heavy, and I held it in my two arms, clasped to my breast. When at last we reached the mail coach, the other passengers had already taken their seats. Persson got into an excited discussion with the postilion, who placed his luggage on the roof of the coach. Persson told him that he would not let the big parcel out of his sight but would hold it on his knees. The postilion objected, but in the end Persson got awkwardly into the coach with his parcel of brocade and the picnic basket. The door was shut but Persson opened it again. "I shall always hold it in honor, Mademoiselle Eugénie," he shouted.

Etienne, with a shrug of his shoulders, asked, "Whatever does he mean?"

"He means the Rights of Man," I replied, surprised at myself because my eyes were wet. "The broadside." As I said it, I thought that a fine man was vanishing forever from my life.

Etienne went back to the shop and I went with him. I feel quite at home in the Clary silk shop. Papa always said it was in my blood because I am a true silk merchant's daughter. But I think it is because as a little girl, I so often went there with Papa and he always told me where the different bolts of silk came from. And I watched Papa and Etienne take a piece of material between their fingers to see whether it would crush easily, whether it was new or old material, and I had learned to do the same.

I busied myself in the shop for a while, then finally went home. There I found Mama in an awful state, for Julie had announced that Joseph was coming that afternoon to speak to her. Julie, too, was almost ill from excitement. I took the distracted girl into the garden and sat with her in the summerhouse.

At five o'clock there arrived a gigantic bouquet, with Joseph hidden behind it. The bouquet and Joseph were escorted into the parlor by Marie; then Mama was informed and the door of the parlor closed behind them both. I pressed my ear to the keyhole, while Julie leaned against the door.

Someone laughed behind us. "Well, are we to congratulate you?" Napoleone! He'd just arrived. "May I, as a future brother-in-law, share the intolerable suspense?"

Julie's patience collapsed. "Do what you like, but leave me in peace!" she sobbed.

At that Napoleone and I went on tiptoe to the sofa. Suddenly Mama came to the door and said in a shaky voice, "Julie, please come in."

Julie dashed into the parlor like a mad thing, the door closed, and I—yes, I threw my arms around Napoleone's neck and laughed and laughed. Then I realized he was wearing the same threadbare green uniform as always. "You might have worn your gala uniform, respected General."

"I have none, Eugénie," he confessed. "I have never had enough money to buy myself one, and all we get from the state is the field uniform I have on."

"Children, I have a great, a very great surprise for you!" Mama stood before us, laughing and crying at the same time. "Julie and Joseph—" Her voice quavered. Then she pulled herself together. "Eugénie, call Suzanne! And see if Etienne is home yet." Then we all drank champagne. . . .

My nice little tipsiness is gone. I'm only tired and a bit sad. For I'll soon be alone in our white room and I'll never be able to use Julie's rouge again. I want to think about something cheerful. When is Napoleone's birthday? Perhaps the allowance I've saved will be enough for a gala uniform. But where do you buy a gala uniform for a general?

Marseilles, beginning of August

Napoleone has been arrested.

I have been living in a bad dream since last evening. Except for me, the whole town is wild with joy. People are dancing in front of the town hall, bands march by one after another and the mayor is planning a ball. Last week Robespierre and his brother were arrested, and the next morning hauled off to the guillotine. Everyone who had anything whatsoever to do with them is now afraid. Joseph has already lost the post he got through Napoleone's friendship with Robespierre's brother. So far, more than ninety Jacobins have been executed in Paris. Etienne says he will never forgive me for bringing the Buonapartes to our home. Mama insists that Julie and I attend the mayor's ball. But I can hardly laugh and dance when I don't know where they've taken Napoleone.

Until last week Julie and I were very happy. Julie was working eagerly on her trousseau and embroidering the letter *B* on pillowcases, tablecloths, towels and handkerchiefs. Joseph came to see us every evening, often with his mother and his brothers and sisters. If Napoleone wasn't inspecting some fortification or other, he appeared too, and there was interminable talk about politics. It seems that lots of deputies have got rich on bribes. Deputies Tallien and Barras are rumored to be millionaires. Robespierre unexpectedly arrested the beautiful Marquise de Fontenay, whom Deputy Tallien had previously rescued from the guillotine and released from prison and who, since then, has been his mistress. Many believe Robespierre arrested her only to annoy Tallien. Others believe that Tallien and Barras were afraid of being arrested themselves. In any event, they organized a great conspiracy with a certain Fouché.

At first we could hardly believe these rumors. But when the first newspapers arrived from Paris telling of the downfall of Robespierre, the whole town changed with a bang. Flags were hung from windows, shops were closed and the mayor released all political prisoners. Fanatical members of the Jacobin Club, however, were quietly arrested. Napoleone and Joseph were very worried. Napoleone sat for hours in our summerhouse and told me that he would have to take up a new profession. "You don't really think," he said, "that an officer in whom Robespierre was interested will be kept on in the Army?"

Then last evening Napoleone was having supper with us. Suddenly we heard marching feet, voices, a loud knock on our door. We all sat there petrified. Then the door flew open and a soldier burst into the room. "Is General Napoleone Buonaparte in your house?"

Napoleone quietly stepped over to him. The soldier clicked his heels together and saluted. "Warrant for the arrest of Citizen General Buonaparte!" He handed Napoleone a piece of paper.

Napoleone read it, then let the paper drop and considered the soldier carefully. "Even on a warm summer evening the uniform of a sergeant in the Republican Army should be buttoned according to regulations!" While the embarrassed soldier fumbled with his uniform, Napoleone turned to Marie. "Marie, my sword is in the hall. Please hand it to the sergeant!" And with a bow to Mama: "Excuse the interruption, Citizeness Clary."

Later I crept out by the back door. Though Mama had frequently invited the Buonaparte family to our home, Madame Letizia had never returned the invitation. The family lived in the poorest quarter of the town, behind the fish market, and I imagine Madame Letizia was ashamed to ask us there. But now I was on my way to tell her and Joseph what had happened.

When I reached the fish market, I asked a man where the Buonapartes lived. He pointed—third house on the left. I saw a narrow staircase, stumbled down the stairs, pushed open a door and found myself in Madame Buonaparte's kitchen. It was a large room lit by only one miserable candle, standing in a cracked teacup. The smell was frightful. Joseph, wearing a crumpled shirt, sat at the table reading a newspaper by the candlelight. Nineteen-year-old Lucien, opposite him, was writing. In the dark recess of the kitchen someone was washing clothes. It was so hot that I almost suffocated.

"Joseph," I said, startling him.

"Has someone come in?" Napoleone's mother stepped into the circle of candlelight, drying her hands on her large apron.

"It's I, Eugénie Clary," I said. "They've arrested Napoleone."

There was deathly silence. Then Madame Buonaparte groaned, "Holy Mary, Mother of God." Joseph cried, "I've seen it coming!" Lucien managed a broken, "How awful!"

They asked me to sit down on a wobbly chair and tell them about it. Brother Louis—sixteen years old and very fat—came out of the adjoining room and listened. I was interrupted when little Jérôme, Napoleone's ten-year-old brother, rushed into the kitchen, followed by twelve-year-old Caroline. When Caroline noticed me, she said, "Oh, la, la—one of the rich Clarys!"

A horrible family, I decided, but I was ashamed of thinking so.

Joseph was saying, "If they were soldiers, not police, who arrested Napoleone, then he is not in prison but under some sort of military arrest. The military authorities would never execute a general without a trial; he'll come before a court-martial."

"But why have they arrested him?" Madame Buonaparte asked.

"Napoleone knew Robespierre," Joseph muttered, "and submitted his crazy plans to the minister of war through Robespierre. What madness!"

"Politics!" Madame Buonaparte moaned. "Signorina, politics are my family's misfortune. The father of my children—God rest his soul—devoted his life to politics, lost his clients' cases and left us nothing but debts. And my sons . . . Where does it lead? To being arrested!"

"But your son Napoleone is a genius, madame," I said softly.

"Yes—unfortunately," she answered, staring into the flickering light of the candle.

"We must find out where they have taken Napoleone and try to help him," I said, looking at Joseph.

"The military commandant of Marseilles must know where they have imprisoned Napoleone," Lucien said. By his family, Lucien is considered a budding poet and a dreamer; nevertheless, he made the first practical suggestion.

"Colonel Lefabre is the military commandant," Joseph said, "and he can't bear Napoleone. Only a little while ago Napoleone told the old man what terrible condition the local fortifications are in."

"I'll go to see him tomorrow," I suddenly heard myself saying. "Madame Buonaparte, will you pack up a nice parcel of linen and perhaps a little food, and send it to me tomorrow morning? I'll take it to this colonel and ask him to give it to Napoleone."

"*Grazie tanto, signorina,*" Madame Buonaparte said, and while Joseph went to get his coat to take me home, she assured me, "I'll send Paulette to you tomorrow morning with the parcel." She thought of something else. "Now, where is Paulette? She said that she and Elisa were going to see a friend across the road and be back in half an hour. And here they're out again till all hours."

I remembered that Elisa, Napoleone's eldest sister, was only seventeen. And Paulette? Paulette is exactly as old as I.

Joseph and I walked in silence through the town. Then, as we approached our villa, Joseph said, "They simply can't send him to the guillotine—that's a military regulation. The worst they can do is to shoot him."

"Joseph!"

His features were sharply drawn in the moonlight. He does not love his brother, I realized with a shock. In fact, he hates him. Because Napoleone is younger and yet was able to get him a post, because Napoleone . . .

". . . But we belong together," Joseph was saying, "Napoleone and I and our brothers and sisters, and we must stick together."

At breakfast Etienne announced that Julie must postpone her wedding. A Jacobin brother-in-law would be a family disgrace, and bad for the business as well. Julie began to sob. Marie came into the dining room and beckoned to me, and I went out into the kitchen, where I found Paulette with the parcel.

Paulette's nose is narrow like Napoleone's; her dark blond hair is done up in a thousand tiny ringlets. She has plucked her eyebrows so that only a thin line remains. I think Paulette is very beautiful, but Mama doesn't wish me to be seen with her.

"Come," I said, "let's go quickly before anyone notices us."

Paulette came here only a year ago, but she knows her way about Marseilles far better than I do. She knew exactly where to find the military commandant, and never stopped talking as we walked there.

She kept coming excitedly back to the former Marquise de Fontenay, who was now Madame Tallien. "People in Paris are mad about her. Her hair is coal black, and so are her eyes; and the walls of her house are all lined with silk. Every afternoon she receives all the famous politicians there, and I've heard that if one wants a favor from the government, one need only tell her about it. . . . By the way, do you think that your brother, Etienne, would give me some material for a new dress? Rose might be nice, and—" She broke off. "There, over there is the military commandant's office. Do you want me to go in with you?"

I shook my head. "I think it's better for me to see him alone." She nodded seriously. I held the parcel close, walked briskly toward the military headquarters and asked the guard on duty to announce me to Colonel Lefabre.

I was conducted into a bare room and there, behind the huge desk, was the foursquare colonel, who had a square red face and wore an old-fashioned pigtail wig. I put the parcel on the desk, swallowed desperately and didn't know what to say.

"What is in that parcel, citizeness? And who are you?"

"A cake and undergarments, drawers, Citizen Colonel Lefabre, and my name is Clary."

His watery blue eyes studied me from head to toe. "Are you a daughter of the late silk merchant François Clary?" I nodded. "I used to play cards with your papa. A very honorable and respected man." He continued to stare at me. "What do I do with these drawers, Citizeness Clary?"

"The parcel is for General Napoleone Buonaparte. He has been arrested. We don't know where he is."

"And what has François Clary's daughter to do with this Jacobin Buonaparte?" the colonel asked me slowly.

I felt very hot. "His brother Joseph is engaged to my sister, Julie."

"And why hasn't his brother or your sister come?"

The watery eyes continued to gaze at me intently. "Joseph is afraid. Relatives of arrested men are always afraid, aren't they?" I spoke with difficulty. "And Julie is crying because Etienne—that's our older brother—has refused to allow her to marry Joseph. And we've had all this trouble because—all because you, Citizen Colonel, have arrested the general."

"Sit down," was all he said, and I sat down on the edge of a chair beside his desk. The colonel took a pinch of snuff, then said, "Your brother, Etienne, is quite right. I don't know this Joseph Buonaparte. He's not in the Army. But the other brother, this Napoleone Buonaparte—"

"*General* Napoleone Buonaparte!" I interrupted.

"As for this general, it was not I who had him arrested. I only carried out orders from Paris. Buonaparte has Jacobin sympathies, and all such officers—I mean all the extreme elements in the Army—have been arrested."

"And what will happen to him?"

"I've not been informed." The colonel indicated it was time for me to leave. I stood up. "The linen and the cake," I said, pointing to the parcel. "Perhaps you could give him these things?"

"Nonsense. Buonaparte isn't here any longer. He was taken to Fort Carré in Antibes."

I had not been prepared for this blow. The red face before me blurred; I wiped away my tears, but fresh tears came. "Can't you send him the parcel, Citizen Colonel?"

"My dear child, I have better things to do than look after the underclothing of an uncouth youngster who is allowed to call himself a general."

I sobbed loudly. He took another pinch of snuff; the scene obviously embarrassed him greatly. "Do stop crying," he said. "I can't stand tears. I'll send one of my soldiers to Fort Carré with the parcel. Are you satisfied now?"

I tried to smile, but I was at the door before I could whisper, "Thank you very much, Citizen Colonel."

He cleared his throat and said, "Listen, Citizeness Clary, I will tell you two things in confidence. First, this will not cost this Jacobin general his head. Second, a Buonaparte is not a suitable match for a daughter of François Clary. Good-by, citizeness."

When I reached home I learned that Julie had got her way. Her wedding is not to be postponed. I sat with her in the garden and helped her embroider her napkins with beautifully rounded *B*'s.

Marseilles, middle of September

Julie's wedding was to be a very quiet affair; only our family and the innumerable Buonapartes had been asked. Mama and Marie had been baking cakes for days, and the evening before the wedding Mama almost collapsed with worry that it wouldn't go well. It was decided that Julie was to take a bath before going to bed. We bathe oftener than other people—almost every month—because Papa had very modern ideas and installed a large wooden tub especially for this purpose in the laundry. Mama poured in some jasmine scent, and Julie felt like Madame Pompadour herself.

Neither Julie nor I could sleep, so we discussed Julie's new home. It's half an hour by carriage from our villa. Suddenly we stopped talking and listened. ". . . *Le jour de gloire est arrivé.*" Someone was whistling underneath our window. The second line of our Marseilles song. And also—Napoleone's signal. Whenever he comes to see us, he announces his approach to me from afar by this whistle. Could it be? I jumped out of bed, tore open the window and leaned out. A figure emerged from the darkness and stepped out onto the gravel path.

I forgot to close the window, I forgot to put on my bedroom slippers, I forgot that I was wearing only a nightgown, I forgot what's proper and what isn't—I ran down the stairs, opened the house door, felt the gravel under my bare feet and felt Napoleone's mouth on the tip of my nose. In the darkness one can't be sure where a kiss will land! Thunder sounded in the distance as he held me close and whispered, "Aren't you cold, *carissima?*" And I said, "Only my feet—I have no slippers on." He lifted me up and carried me to our doorstep. We sat there and he took off his coat and wrapped it around me. "When did you get back?" I asked.

"They released me because there is no evidence against me. But I am very unpopular with the gentlemen at the Ministry of War," he said, and added that he hadn't actually been home yet. I put my cheek against his shoulder and was very happy. "And many thanks for the parcel. Colonel Lefabre wrote that he was sending it only to please you." I could feel his lips on my hair.

Suddenly he said, "I asked to be tried by a court-martial. Then I would have had an opportunity to explain my plans to some senior officers. But they would not grant me even that. So now they will send me off to one of the dullest sectors of the front and—"

"It's raining," I interrupted. The first heavy drops of rain were falling on my face. We could hear thunder again, and above us a window rattled.

"Is anyone there?" Etienne called down. At the same time we could hear Suzanne's voice: "Shut the window, Etienne, and come to me—I'm frightened—" Etienne's again: "There is someone in the garden. I must go down and look."

Napoleone got up and stood under the window. "Monsieur Clary—it's me. General Buonaparte!" A flash of lightning illuminated the small slender figure in the tight-fitting uniform.

"But you are still in prison!" Etienne roared. "And anyway, what are you doing in the middle of the night, in this weather, in our garden?"

I jumped up, unmindful of my compromising situation, and stood next to Napoleone. "He's talking to me—Eugénie," I called.

"General, you owe me an explanation." Etienne's nightcap fairly quivered with rage.

"I have the honor to request the hand of your younger sister in marriage, Monsieur Clary," Napoleone called up to him. He had put his arm around my shoulder.

"Eugénie, come into the house at once," commanded Etienne.

"Good night, *carissima*. We'll meet tomorrow at the wedding party," Napoleone said, and kissed my cheek. His spurs clanked down the gravel path. I slipped into the house. At the open door of his bedroom stood Etienne in his nightgown, holding a lighted candle. "If Papa had lived to see this—" he snarled.

In our room Julie sat up in bed. "I heard everything," she said, then murmured thoughtfully, "Madame General Buonaparte."

JULIE WAS ALMOST too late at the registry office. We couldn't find her new gloves. When Mama was young, everyone was married in church, but since the Revolution, people must be married in a registry office. Mama had talked of her own white bridal veil, which she wanted Julie to wear, but Julie had a rose-colored dress with real Brussels lace. She wore roses to match, and had rose-colored gloves from Paris, which she had misplaced. The marriage was arranged for ten o'clock in the morning, and just five minutes before ten I found the gloves under Julie's bed. At last Julie hurried with Mama and Etienne off to the registry office, where Joseph and his two witnesses, Napoleone and Lucien, were waiting.

I hadn't really had time to dress. I had successfully begged Etienne for some sky-blue satin, and I think my new dress is very grand. But after all, I'm almost a bride, too, though so far Etienne acts as if my betrothal were merely a disturbance in our garden in the middle of last night.

The guests came before I was ready: Madame Letizia and all the other brothers and sisters. Then the wedding party arrived! Julie and Joseph ran over to us, and all the Clarys and all the Buonapartes formed such a confused cluster of people that Napoleone and I had a chance to kiss each other very thoroughly until someone cleared his throat indignantly—Etienne, of course.

At the bridal table Julie was so excited that her cheeks were pink and her eyes were shining, and for the first time in her life she was really pretty. We drank Julie's and Joseph's health, and had got to Marie's wonderful marzipan cake, when Napoleone rose quickly, without first politely tapping his glass, and thundered, "Quiet for a moment." We flinched like frightened recruits. Napoleone declared abruptly that he was glad to take part in this family celebration. Then he paused. So far, of course, the young couple had been the center of attention. But now Napoleone looked at me and I knew what was coming.

"And so I take this opportunity, while the Clary and Buonaparte families are together on this joyful occasion"— his voice softened— "to inform you that last night I asked for Mademoiselle Eugénie's hand in marriage and that Eugénie has consented."

A storm of good wishes burst from the Buonapartes and I found myself in Madame Letizia's arms. But I glanced over at Mama. Mama looked as though she'd been hit over the head. She turned toward Etienne. At that moment Napoleone, glass in hand, stepped over to him and smiled—and the power Napoleone has over people is astonishing. For Etienne touched Napoleone's glass with his. Paulette embraced me and called me sister, Madame Letizia murmured something happily in Italian and everyone was terribly excited.

Soon Julie and Joseph got into the carriage to drive to their new home. We all walked to the garden gate with them. I put my arm around Mama's shoulder and told her there was no reason to cry. Then more liqueur and cake were served. Finally all the Buonapartes except Napoleone left. Mama turned to him and placed both her hands pleadingly against his chest.

"General Buonaparte, promise me one thing—I am appealing to you. . . . Eugénie is still very young. Please wait for the wedding until she is sixteen, will you?"

Whereupon Napoleone kissed Mama's hand, and without another word I knew this was a promise.

The very next day Napoleone was ordered to report for duty in the Vendée, where he was to command an infantry brigade. I squatted on the grass in the warm September sun and watched him pace up and down, hands clasped behind his back, pale with fury, as he explained to me how disgracefully he was being treated. To the Vendée! To track down hidden Royalists! "I am an artillery expert and not a policeman," he shouted. "They begrudge me the triumph of a court-martial. They'd rather bury me in the Vendée—keep me away from the front, let me be forgotten—!"

"You can ask for your discharge," I ventured quietly. "With the money Papa left me I could buy a little country house, or perhaps you might join Etienne in the firm—"

"Eugénie, are you mad?" He stared at me. "Do you seriously believe that I would settle down to sell silk ribbons in your brother's little shop? Do you realize that I am the best general in

France?" With that he began pacing up and down again, this time in silence. Suddenly: "I leave tomorrow! I'll go to Paris, talk to the gentlemen in the Ministry of War."

"But isn't it a serious offense if an army officer disobeys orders?"

"Yes, it is. If one of my recruits disobeys, I have him shot. Perhaps I'll be shot, too, when I get to Paris. I'll take Junot and Marmont with me." Lieutenant Junot and Captain Marmont, Napoleone's adjutants since the action in Toulon, consider his destiny theirs.

"Can you lend me some money?" he went on. I nodded. "Junot and Marmont haven't enough to pay the bill for their room here in Marseilles. How much can you lend me?"

I had been saving up for his dress uniform. Ninety-eight francs were hidden under the nightgowns in my dresser. I ran up to my room and fetched the money. He counted it carefully and said, "I owe you ninety-eight francs." Then he grasped my shoulders and held me close. "You'll see, I'll convince everyone in Paris. They must give me the supreme command in Italy."

"When are you going?" I asked.

"As soon as I bail my adjutants out of their inn. And don't forget to write. Send your letters to the Ministry of War in Paris; they'll forward my mail to the front. And don't be sad—"

"I shall have a lot to do," I said. "I'll be embroidering the initials on the linen for my trousseau."

He nodded eagerly. "*B*'s for Madame General Buonaparte—" Then he untied his horse and rode off toward the town.

As he disappeared down the quiet street of villas, he looked small and very lonely.

Paris, twelve months later

Nothing is more unpleasant than running away from home. I've been sitting continuously in a traveling coach with very bad springs for days. And I've no money for my return journey. But I shan't need it; I'll never go back.

I arrived in Paris two hours ago. It was almost dusk and all the houses looked alike, one next to the other, with no front gardens. I had no idea Paris was so vast. I got a hackney carriage and showed the coachman the slip of paper on which I had written the address of Marie's sister. I gave him all the money I had, but he was rude because I had nothing left for a tip. Marie's relatives, the Clapains, live in the rear building—a wing, really—of a house not far from the Tuileries, I think. We drove past the palace, which I recognized from the pictures I've seen.

Marie's sister, Madame Clapain, was very kind to me. At first she was embarrassed because I am the daughter of Marie's "gentry." But when I told her that I'd come secretly to Paris, she asked if I was hungry and how long I wanted to stay. I said one night, perhaps two. I began to eat, and then Monsieur Clapain came home. He is a carpenter and told me that these rooms are in the rear building of an aristocratic mansion confiscated by the government and turned into apartments for families with many children.

Immediately after the meal Madame Clapain said she'd like to take a walk with her husband; she seldom has a chance to because there is no one to look after the children. But with me here, she could put the children to bed and go without worry.

After they left I felt terribly alone and strange in this huge city until I rummaged in my traveling bag and found my diary. With my fiancé away in Paris, nothing happened in my life, so I've not written in it for a whole year. But now I will try to explain why I ran away from home.

Etienne got me some damask for tablecloths and linen for sheets after Napoleone left, and I embroidered one rounded *B* after the other. I called alternately on Madame Letizia in her basement apartment and Julie and Joseph in their charming little villa. But Madame Letizia talked of nothing but money. Julie and Joseph, on the other hand, gazed at each other, giggled and seemed brazenly happy. Nevertheless, I went to see them often because Julie wanted to know what Napoleone had written to me, and I wanted to read his letters to Joseph.

Unfortunately, we all have the impression that my fiancé is having a bad time in Paris. There was a fearful row a year ago when he arrived at the Ministry of War, because he had disobeyed orders to go to the Vendée. Napoleone discussed his Italian plans again; and to get rid of him, the minister of war sent him to the Italian front—on an inspection tour. When he got there, he was rebuffed by the generals, and then came down with malaria. He returned to Paris. The minister of war was furious and

Napoleone was discharged from the Army without a pension. A terrible situation. . . . For money, he pawned his father's watch, and from time to time, he draws military maps. His old threadbare uniform was a great anxiety. He tried to mend the trousers himself, but the seams burst open. Naturally he sent in a request for a new uniform, but the state does not grant uniforms to unemployed generals. In his despair he went where they all go when they want to get something done—to the home of the beautiful Madame Tallien.

We now have a government called a "Directorate," administered by five directors. However, according to Joseph, only one of our directors has real authority, and that is Director Barras. He was a count by birth, but became a fanatical Jacobin at the right time. Then, with the help of Tallien and the deputy called Fouché, he brought about the fall of Robespierre and saved the Republic from the "tyrants." As Barras is unmarried, he has asked Madame Tallien to act as his hostess every afternoon and to receive "guests of the French Republic."

One of Etienne's business friends told us that champagne flows like water at Madame Tallien's and that her drawing rooms are crowded with amusing ladies who are her friends and with war profiteers who buy confiscated aristocratic homes at a low price from the state and sell them at a huge profit to the *nouveaux riches*. The two most beautiful women are Madame Tallien herself and Josephine de Beauharnais. Madame de Beauharnais is Barras' mistress, and she always wears a narrow red ribbon around her neck to show that she is related to "a victim of the guillotine." It is no longer a disgrace, but rather a distinction to claim such a relationship. (This Josephine is the widow of the General de Beauharnais who was beheaded, and therefore she is a former countess.) When Mama asked Etienne's friend if there were no virtuous women left in Paris, he said, "Well, yes, there are, but they are very expensive."

Napoleone called one afternoon on the ladies Tallien and Beauharnais and introduced himself. They both thought it perfectly horrid of the minister of war to refuse him a new pair of trousers and the supreme command in Italy. They both promised to get him at least a new pair of trousers. But, they said, he must change his Italian name. Napoleone at once wrote to Joseph: *I have decided to change my name and I advise you to do the same.*

No one in Paris can pronounce Buonaparte. From now on I am Bonaparte—and Napoleon instead of Napoleone. Please inform the whole family. We are French citizens, and I want my name to be French when it is written in the book of history. His trousers are in shreds, his father's watch is pawned, but still he thinks of making world history.

During the last few months I've had very few letters from Napoleon, though he writes to Joseph twice a week. His letters to me no longer say anything. They still begin *Mia Carissima*, and end by saying that he presses me to his heart. But not a word about when we'll be married. Not a word to show that he knows that in two months I'll be sixteen. To his brother Joseph he writes pages about the fashionable ladies he meets at Madame Tallien's. *I have learned to appreciate the role distinguished women can play in the life of a man,* Napoleon assures his brother enthusiastically, *women with understanding, women of the great world.* These letters to Joseph make me sick.

A week ago Julie decided to accompany Joseph on a business journey. Since it was the first time that one of her children was to be away for any length of time, Mama wept and wept, and to distract her, Etienne arranged to take her to a spa. That is why I was unexpectedly alone in the house with Marie.

My decision was made suddenly, on an early autumn afternoon when I was sitting in the summerhouse with Marie. "I must go to Paris," I said. "I know it's crazy but—I must go to Paris."

"Well," Marie said, "then go. But you promised your mama to postpone your wedding until you are sixteen. Why go now?"

"If I don't go now, there may not be any wedding." For the first time I put into words what I had dared only to think.

"What is her name?" Marie said.

"I'm not sure. Perhaps it's Madame Tallien, but it may be the other one, Barras' mistress. Her name is Josephine, she was once a countess. But I don't know anything definite—and, Marie, you mustn't think horrid things about him. When he sees me again . . ."

"Yes," Marie said, "you must go. My Pierre left me when he was called up for military service—and he never came back. After our little Pierre was born, I wrote to him that the child was with a foster mother and I'd taken service as a wet nurse with the Clarys because I had no money. But my Pierre never answered. I should have tried somehow to go to see him."

Marie has told the story of faithless Pierre and her unhappy love affair so often that it is as familiar as an old song. "You couldn't go to him, it was too far away," I said.

"You will go to Paris," Marie said. "You can spend the first few nights at my sister's. After that, you can decide what to do next."

In the evening I packed a traveling bag. I stuffed in the blue silk dress I'd got for Julie's wedding. My most beautiful dress. I'll wear it, I thought, when I go to Madame Tallien's house to see him again.

The next morning Marie took me to the coach station. I had just enough money for the journey to Paris. At the last moment she handed me a large gold medallion. "I haven't any money. I send all of my wages to little Pierre. So take the medallion. It is gold; your mama gave it to me. You can easily sell it so that you'll have money for the return journey." Then Marie turned away abruptly.

For four days I was shaken about in the coach along a dusty interminable road. And I was continuously imagining what it would be like to go to Madame Tallien's house. As Napoleone goes there every afternoon, it is the best place to meet him. And anyone can go, because Madame Tallien keeps open house. I'll ask for General Bonaparte—I must remember to call him Napoleon. He'll take my arm and introduce me to his grand new friends. Perhaps he has some friends with whom I can stay until we've written to Mama and got her consent to my marriage. And then we'll be married and . . .

I hear them coming home. Monsieur and Madame Clapain. And tomorrow—dear Lord, how happy I am about tomorrow!

Paris, twenty-four hours—no, an eternity—later

It is night and I am again sitting in Madame Clapain's kitchen. Perhaps I've not ever been away and today was only a bad dream—perhaps I'll wake up. But I can hear every word that was said, and the rain beats against the windows.

It has rained all day long. I got very wet on my way to Madame Tallien's. I wore the lovely blue silk dress. But I discovered that for Paris my dress with its tight sleeves is very unfashionable. Here the ladies wear dresses that look like chemises, with transparent shawls around their shoulders. And no one wears long sleeves anymore.

It was not difficult to find Madame Tallien's house; it took me only half an hour to get there. The house is not much larger than our villa at home and built in country style, but brocade curtains shimmer behind the windows. It was still early in the afternoon, but I wanted to be waiting in one of the drawing rooms when Napoleon arrived.

A number of people were hanging about the entrance, but I walked straight toward the doorway. I lifted the latch, the door opened, and there was a lackey in red livery with silver buttons. He looked me up and down and asked condescendingly, "Have you an invitation?"

"I thought—well, I thought everyone could go in."

He stared at me insolently. "Ladies like you must keep to the rue Honoré and the Palais Royal."

I blushed furiously and could hardly speak. "I must go in. There's someone in the house I must see."

"Madame Tallien's orders—citizenesses are not invited unless they have a gentleman escort." He slammed the door in my face.

I joined the crowd standing in the rain outside. "A month ago we all got in without any trouble," a heavily rouged girl with purple-painted lips remarked, and winked at me. "But some foreign paper published an article saying that Madame Tallien's house was run like a brothel."

"She herself doesn't care, but Barras makes her keep up appearances," another girl said. "You're new here, aren't you?" she asked, glancing pityingly at my old-fashioned dress.

"That Barras!" said the girl with the purple lips. "Two years ago he was paying Lucille twenty-five francs a night, and today he can afford to keep the Beauharnais! But I hear that the Beauharnais has taken up with a very young officer who likes squeezing a woman's hands and gazing into her eyes."

"I wonder why Barras stands for that," the other girl remarked.

"Barras wants to be on good terms with men in uniform. Besides, he's probably sick to death already of Josephine and her white frocks."

A young man leaned down and spoke to me. "You are from the provinces, citizeness?" He smelled horribly of wine and cheese, and touched my hand as though by chance. At that moment I knew: I can't stand this another moment.

Another hackney carriage rolled up. I rushed over to it like a madwoman and bumped into a terribly tall man wearing an officer's coat. "I beg your pardon, citizen," I said to him, "but I should like to belong to you."

"What do you want?" he asked, startled.

"For a few moments I'd like to belong to you. You see, ladies aren't allowed to go into Madame Tallien's house without an escort. And I must get in, I must—and I have no escort!"

The officer looked me up and down, and suddenly making up his mind, he offered me his arm. "Come along, citizeness."

The lackey, recognizing me at once, glanced at me indignantly, then bowed deeply to the officer and took his coat. I went over to a tall mirror, pushed the soaking strands of hair out of my face, and was taking out my powder puff when the officer said impatiently, "Well, are you ready, citizeness?"

I turned quickly. He was wearing a beautifully tailored uniform with heavy gold epaulets and was obviously regretting his decision to bring me in with him. He probably thought me one of the street girls, and I was quite hot with shame. "Please excuse me, I didn't know what else to do," I whispered.

"When we get inside, behave decently and don't disgrace me," he said severely, and offered me his arm. We found ourselves in a large room crowded with people. My companion turned to me brusquely. "Your name?"

No one must know that I am here, I thought quickly. "Désirée," I whispered.

"Désirée—and what next?" my escort asked irritably. I shook my head desperately. "Please—no other name."

Whereupon the lackey was instructed to announce, "Citizeness Désirée and General Jean-Baptiste Bernadotte." The people standing near us turned around. A black-haired woman in a yellow veillike gown left a group and glided toward us.

"What a pleasure, Citizen General," she twittered, holding out both hands to him.

"You are too kind, Madame Tallien," he said, bowing. "My first outing—as usual when a poor soldier from the front has some leave—is to find the magic circle of the beautiful Thérésa."

"The poor soldier from the front is flattering, as usual! And yet he has already found companionship in Paris—?" Her dark eyes studied me critically and then lost interest. "Come with me, Jean-Baptiste—you must speak to Barras."

I found myself suddenly left all alone in Madame Tallien's glittering salon. I couldn't see Napoleon anywhere. True, I saw a lot of uniforms, but none as shabby as my fiancé's. In one of the adjoining rooms someone was playing the violin, and lackeys in red livery, balancing huge trays, circled among the guests.

Two gentlemen came over and stood beside me chatting and taking no notice of me. They said that the people of Paris wouldn't tolerate the increasing living costs much longer and that social unrest was inevitable. "If I were Barras," said one, "I'd simply shoot down this rabble, my dear Fouché." The other replied, "He'd have to find a man willing to do the shooting!" Then the first man said he'd seen General Bernadotte among the guests. But the one called Fouché shook his head. "That man? Never on your life." Then he continued, "But what about that little wretch who is running after Josephine?"

At that moment someone clapped hands and I heard Madame Tallien's twittering voice. "Please, all come into the green drawing room—we have a surprise for our friends." I moved along into the next room with the others, but it was so crowded that I couldn't see what was happening. Glasses of champagne were passed around; I took one, and then we crowded together more closely still to make way for the hostess. Madame Tallien passed near me, and I could see that she had nothing on under the yellow veils—it was most indecent. "Please form a circle around the sofa," she called out, and we obediently placed ourselves around it. Then I saw Napoleon!

Sitting right there on the sofa. With a lady in white. He had beautifully pressed trousers and a new uniform tunic. His thin face was no longer tanned, but unhealthily pale. The lady next to him was leaning back, resting her arm on the back of the sofa. Her tiny head, with brushed-up curls, was thrown back. Her eyelids were painted silver, and she had a narrow red velvet ribbon around her neck. I knew she was the widow Beauharnais, Josephine.

"Have you all champagne?" That was Madame Tallien's voice again. The slender figure in white was now smiling at Napoleon, a very intimate smile. "Citizens and citizenesses, ladies and gentlemen, I have the great honor to make an announcement." Thérésa Tallien held up her glass. "Our beloved Josephine has decided once more to enter the holy state of matrimony." She stopped to heighten the effect of her words and glanced at Barras. He nodded. "Josephine has become engaged to Citizen General Napoleon Bonaparte."

"*No!*"

I heard the scream as distinctly as the others did. It pierced the room and hung loosely in the air. A deathly silence followed. Then I realized it was I who had screamed.

I was standing in front of the sofa; I saw Madame Tallien move away in terror, and the other woman—the one in white on the sofa—was staring at me. I looked at Napoleon—only at him. His eyes were like glass, translucent and without expression. A vein was throbbing at his right temple. Then I looked at the woman—shining silvery eyelids, tiny wrinkles around her eyes, lips rouged a dark red. How I hated her! I flung my champagne at her and it splashed over her dress; she screamed hysterically.

I don't know how I left the drawing room and got past the horrified guests, who shrank away from me. I know only that suddenly I was running along a rainy wet street, that my heart was pounding, and that I instinctively found my way to a quay and finally reached the bridge. The Seine, I thought—now everything will be all right. I walked slowly along the bridge, leaned over the parapet and saw many lights dancing in the water. I was more alone than I had ever been in all my life. I placed my hands on the parapet to pull myself up and . . .

At that very moment someone with an iron grip grabbed my shoulders. I tried to shake off the strange hands and shouted, "Leave me alone! Let me go!" But I was firmly dragged away from the parapet. It was so dark that I couldn't see who he was, but I heard a masculine voice, louder than the rain, say, "Calm yourself. Don't be foolish—here is my carriage."

I kept on struggling wildly, but the stranger pushed me into the carriage, sat down next to me and called to the coachman, "Drive on—it doesn't matter where, but drive on."

My teeth were chattering and my wet hair was pouring small streams of water over my face. A hand reached for mine, a large warm hand. I sobbed, "Let me get out!" Yet I clutched at this strange hand because it was the only bit of warmth in my life.

"You yourself asked me to be your escort at Madame Tallien's. And now we two are staying together until I've seen you home, Mademoiselle Désirée."

His voice was soft and quite attractive. "Are you General Bernadotte?" I asked. Then everything came back to me and I screamed, "Leave me alone! I can't bear generals."

"Well, there are generals—and generals," he said and laughed. I heard a rustle in the dark and a coat was laid across my shoulders. "Wrap yourself in this."

A memory flashed through my mind of another general's coat on another rainy night. The carriage rolled along and I sobbed into the strange coat.

"I felt responsible for you," he was saying, "and when you left the reception so precipitously, I followed you in a hired carriage. I wanted to leave you alone as long as possible."

"And why did you not leave me alone altogether?"

"It was no longer possible," he replied quietly.

"Forgive me for having disgraced you," I said.

"It's all right," he said. "I'm only sorry for your sake."

"I poured the champagne over her white dress on purpose," I murmured. Suddenly I began to cry again. "She is far more beautiful than I am—and a great lady—"

He pressed my face against his shoulder. "Just cry yourself out," he said. "Just cry."

I cried as I've never cried before. We drove through the streets for hours, it seemed, until I had no more tears left. After a while I asked, "Do you know General Bonaparte personally?"

"No. I saw him once, casually, in the waiting room of the Ministry of War. I don't like him."

"Why?"

"I don't know. One can't explain the attraction or antipathy one feels for people. You, for example, I find attractive."

We were silent again. The carriage rolled on through the rain. "I believed in him as I have never believed in any other human being," I heard myself saying. "We were to have been married in a few weeks. And now without a word he . . ."

"He would never have married you, little girl. He has been engaged for a long time to the daughter of a wealthy silk merchant in Marseilles. Madame Tallien told me about it this afternoon. 'Our little general is sacrificing a large dowry to marry Barras' discarded mistress,' is what she said. So you see, he would not have married you in any case. Forgive me, but it is better for you to face the facts about Bonaparte. First it was a wealthy merchant's daughter, now a faded countess with useful connections. You, on the other hand, little one, have no connections and no dowry."

"How do you know that?"

"One can tell by looking at you," he said. "You are only a little girl, a very good little girl. You don't know how great ladies behave or how social life is conducted in drawing rooms. And you obviously have no money or you would have slipped a note to the Tallien's lackey and he would have admitted you. Yes, you are an upright little thing and—" He paused. Suddenly he burst out, "And I should like to marry you."

"Let me get out! Don't make fun of me."

"Perhaps I did not express myself well—but I've never had an opportunity to meet young girls like you. And, Mademoiselle Désirée, I mean it—I'd like very much to marry you."

"In Madame Tallien's drawing room there were crowds of ladies who seem to have a preference for generals," I said. "I have not!"

"You don't think I would marry one of those cocottes—forgive the word, mademoiselle."

I was too tired to answer, much too tired to think. I could not understand what this Bernadotte, this tower of a man, wanted of me.

"We are simple people," he was saying. "Without a revolution, I wouldn't be a general; not even an officer, mademoiselle. Before the Revolution no bourgeois was ever promoted beyond the rank of captain. My father was a lawyer's clerk. I joined the Army when I was fifteen. For a long time I was a sergeant; and gradually—well, now I am a general commanding a division. But perhaps I am too old for you?"

"I don't know how old you are. And it doesn't matter, does it?"

"But it does. Perhaps I really am too old; I am thirty-one."

"I'll soon be sixteen," I said. "And I'm very tired. I'd like to go home now."

"Of course. Forgive me, I am very inconsiderate. You live—?"

I told him the address and he gave it to the coachman.

"Will you consider my proposal? In ten days I must return to the Rhineland. Perhaps you could give me an answer by then?" He spoke slowly. "My name is Jean-Baptiste Bernadotte. For years I have been saving part of my pay. I could buy a little house for you and the child."

"For what child?" I asked involuntarily.

"For our child, naturally," he said promptly. "I want so much to have a wife and a child. But I'm almost always at the front, and so I couldn't come visit your family and take walks with you and do whatever a man is supposed to do before he proposes marriage. I have to decide quickly—and I have decided."

"General Bernadotte," I said, "in the life of every woman there is only one great love."

"How do you know?" he asked quickly.

How *did* I know this? "It says so in all the novels and it must be true," I said.

At that moment the carriage creaked to a stop. We had arrived at the Clapains' house. He opened the carriage door and helped me out. A lantern hung over the house door and I could see his face. He had beautiful white teeth, a wise forehead and a huge nose. I said, "Good night and thank you."

But he didn't move. "When may I come for your answer?"

I shook my head. "It wouldn't do, General. It isn't that I'm too young for you, but you can see—I'm much too short for you!"

When I came into the Clapains' kitchen, I was utterly exhausted. I am sitting at the kitchen table writing and writing. The day after tomorrow this Bernadotte will come here to inquire after me. But I will certainly not be here. I don't know where I'll be.

Marseilles, three weeks later

I have been very ill. Cold in the head, sore throat, very high fever, and what the poets call a broken heart. In Paris I sold Marie's gold medallion for just enough to pay for my journey home. Marie put me right to bed, called the doctor, and sent a messenger to Mama, who returned at once to nurse me. So far, no one has discovered that I have been in Paris.

Now I am lying on the sofa on the terrace, covered with many blankets. Joseph and Julie returned from their journey yesterday and are coming to see us this evening. Marie has just run out to the terrace. She is flourishing an extra broadside and seems very excited.

General Napoleon Bonaparte has been appointed military governor of Paris. Hunger riots in the capital have been suppressed by the National Guard.

The broadside goes on to report that mobs of rioters stormed the Tuileries and that Barras entrusted General Napoleon Bonaparte, a former officer, with the command of the National Guard, whereupon this general demanded unrestricted powers and assembled some cannon. When the mob pressed forward, a single cannon shot was enough to drive the rabble back. Order has been reestablished and this man who has saved the Republic from further chaos is now military governor of Paris.

I remembered a conversation I overheard at Madame Tallien's: "If I were Barras, I'd shoot down the rabble, my dear Fouché." "But he would have to find someone willing to shoot."

WHILE I WAS THINKING about the broadside, I heard Joseph and Julie come into the parlor. The door to the terrace was not quite closed and I heard Julie tell Mama that Napoleon had written that he was engaged to General de Beauharnais' widow, and they were to tell me that he would always be my best friend. Mama wailed, "The poor, poor child!"

Later they came out to the terrace and sat down beside me. Julie stroked my hand. Joseph was obviously ill at ease. "I regret to say that I have something to tell you, Eugénie, and—both Julie and I are—very upset—"

I interrupted him. "Never mind, Joseph—I know. The door to the parlor was open and I heard everything you said."

Suddenly I realized that a part of my life was over. "From now on," I announced, "I no longer wish to be called Eugénie. My name is Bernardine Eugénie Désirée. I prefer Désirée."

In the Palazzo Corsini, home of His Excellency,
the Ambassador of the French Republic in Rome,
December 27, 1797

I have got out my diary and have begun to write in it again. My pen scratches, the only sound in this huge room.

I have not seen Napoleone—only his mother still calls him that; the whole world talks of Napoleon Bonaparte—since that moment in Paris. My family still knows nothing of that encounter. He married Josephine the following spring and left for Italy two days after the wedding; he was entrusted by the government with the supreme command! He won six battles within fourteen days. This delighted Etienne, who spent days telling everyone how years ago Napoleon had spoken to him of his Italian plans. And Etienne always says that he is not only Napoleon's brother-in-law but his best friend as well.

After the Austrians evacuated northern Italy Napoleon founded new states and selected Italians to govern them in the name of France. Overnight the words *Liberty, Equality, Fraternity* were inscribed on all public buildings. The people of Lombardy, the first of these states, were forced to surrender a large sum of money, three hundred carriage horses and their most beautiful art treasures. Napoleon sent everything to Paris. First, however, he deducted the pay for his troops from the Italian money. The directors in Paris didn't know what was happening to them: money in the national treasury, Italy's most beautiful horses drawing their carriages and valuable works of art in their drawing rooms.

Napoleon himself wrote and signed, quite independently, all the treaties with the various parts of Italy he had liberated. The government in Paris grumbled that this went beyond the powers of a supreme commander; this was foreign policy. But Napoleon ignored their objections. When it was suggested in Paris that embassies should be accredited to the new Italian states, he finally wrote to the government and listed several gentlemen to be chosen as ambassadors of the Republic. At the head of the list was his brother Joseph.

So Joseph and Julie went to Italy from Paris, where they had moved soon after Napoleon was appointed military governor. Whatever happens, Napoleon always finds a post for his brother Joseph. In Paris Napoleon had introduced him to Barras and other politicians speculating in houses. Joseph began to prosper and soon bought a small house for himself and Julie in the rue du Rocher. Joseph had become a very important man in Paris, as the brother of Bonaparte, whom the foreign press called "the strong man of France" and our own papers praised as "the liberator of the Italian people," so when the French government named him an ambassador, no one was surprised.

After Joseph and Julie moved into their Italian marble palace, Julie was very unhappy and wrote desperate letters asking me to come and stay with her. So Mama let me go. Since then, I have been living in horrible high rooms with black-and-white tile floors; I sit in pillared halls in which various weird bronze fountains spout water.

We are surrounded by the clanking of spurs and the rattling of swords because Joseph's embassy staff consists chiefly of officers.

Tomorrow evening Joseph is giving the largest ball yet arranged by the embassy. Although a small army of lackeys, cooks and chambermaids buzzes around us, Julie feels personally responsible for the whole circus and clings to me, moaning that things will "go badly." She inherited this unfortunate attitude from Mama.

In spite of battles and victories and peace treaties and newly formed states, Napoleon has also found time to take care of the rest of his family. From the beginning, couriers from Italy arrived in Marseilles with letters and money for Madame Letizia. She moved to a more respectable apartment. Caroline was sent to the same fashionable boarding school in Paris as Hortense de Beauharnais, Napoleon's stepdaughter. The Bonapartes have really risen in the world!

Napoleon was furious because his mother allowed Elisa to marry a certain Felix Bacciocchi, whom he described as a "worthless music student." Afraid that Paulette, too, might bring someone of whom he disapproved into the family, he arranged with lightning speed for her marriage to a General Leclerc, despite her complaint that "Leclerc is the only officer we know with whom I'm not the tiniest bit in love."

Unpleasant and incomprehensible as it may seem, and in spite of all the world history Napoleon has been making, he has not forgotten me. He is apparently determined to make amends, so with Julie's and Joseph's approval, he keeps sending me eligible bachelors.

The first was Junot, his personal adjutant in the Marseilles days, and now a general. He appeared one day, urged me to join him in the garden and declared that he had the honor to ask for my hand in marriage. I thanked him and refused. But these were Napoleon's orders, Junot remarked artlessly! I shook my head, and Junot rode back to Montebello.

The next candidate was Marmont, Napoleon's other handsome adjutant. Marmont is also a general now; he did not ask me directly, but with artful insinuations. By marrying Joseph's sister-in-law, he would become related to Napoleon, and at the same time acquire a considerable dowry. I countered Marmont's delicate approach with an equally tactful "No." Then I went to Joseph and said, "I am not an order or a decoration to be awarded to some deserving general. And if I'm not left in peace, I'll go back to Mama."

I hope this will convince him.

JULIE AND I sat in the courtyard this morning studying the names of the aristocratic Italian families who will be represented at tonight's embassy ball. Most Italians are enthusiastic about the ideas of the Republic, but many of them seem embittered by the heavy cost to them of our occupation and the fact that Napoleon selects all of their officials. Today there were loud and threatening shouts around the palace gate. Joseph explained why.

Last night a few Roman citizens were arrested as hostages because a French lieutenant had been killed in a tavern brawl. A deputation from the Roman City Council arrived at the palace; these men asked to speak to Joseph. And a crowd collected outside to see what was happening.

But Joseph would not receive the deputation. He declared that the whole matter had nothing to do with him. From the very beginning, it had been the responsibility of the military governor of Rome. Meantime the noise outside grew louder.

Later Julie stopped by my room. "Désirée, may I lie down on your bed? I'm afraid to be alone!"

I said, "But, of course. I'll be writing in my diary—"

"You don't still keep your diary! How funny." She smiled a tired smile.

"Why funny?"

"Because everything is so very different." She sighed and lay down, fully dressed, on my bed and began to cry. "I don't want to live in these strange palaces," she sobbed. "I want a home like everyone else. What are we doing in this foreign country where people hate us? We don't belong here. I want to go home."

She told me then that a letter had just come from Mama in Marseilles. Etienne and Suzanne had decided to move to Genoa, where he was opening a branch of the Clary firm. French businessmen have splendid opportunities in Genoa now, and Italy is the center of the silk trade. And as Mama does not wish to remain alone in Marseilles, she is moving to Genoa with Etienne and Suzanne. She assumes that for the present I shall be staying with Julie, and she prays to God that soon I shall find a dear, kind husband. Yes—and Etienne wants to sell our house in Marseilles.

Julie had stopped crying. We stared at each other, horrified. "That means that we have no home," she whispered.

At that moment there was a knock at the door and Joseph came in. The tears returned. "I want to go home," Julie cried.

"And so you shall," he said tenderly. "Tonight there is the big ball, and tomorrow we leave. Back to Paris. I, too, have had enough of Rome. I shall request the government to give me a new and perhaps more important post. And we can return to our home in the rue du Rocher."

"And Désirée comes with us," Julie sobbed.

"Where else could I go?" I said.

Julie raised a tearstained face. "We'll have a very good time in Paris, we three—you and Joseph and I. You have never been there, so you have no idea, Désirée, how wonderful Paris is. Such a huge city. Lovely parks—and so many lights . . ."

Julie and Joseph left to make arrangements for tomorrow's journey, and I sank down on my bed. Paris . . . so many lights . . . But when I closed my eyes, all I could see were the lights that dance at night on the ripples of the Seine.

Paris, April 1798

I have seen him again.

We were invited by him to a farewell reception; he is about to sail with his armies for Egypt. He told his mother that with the pyramids as a base, he intends to unite the East and the West, and to turn our Republic into a world empire. Madame Letizia later asked Joseph whether Napoleon ever suffered from feverish attacks of malaria, since her poor boy did not seem quite right in the head.

Napoleon and Josephine live in a small house in the rue de la Victoire that Josephine bought in her Barras days. At that time the street was called rue Chântereine. After Napoleon's Italian victories, the Paris Town Council changed the name to Victoire in his honor. It is unbelievable how many people crowded into the two tiny drawing rooms of this rather insignificant house yesterday.

During the morning Julie had made me sick with her affectionate anxiety. "Are you excited? Do you feel anything for him?" I didn't know, but I thought that he and Josephine would still be furious because of the scene I had made that day at the Tallien's.

I had a new gold dress with a rose petticoat, and the day before yesterday I had my hair cut. Josephine was the first Parisienne with short hair, but now other fashionable women are imitating her childish curls brushed up high on the head. My hair is so thick and heavy that it will take time to train properly. My new dress is cut very low in the neck, but I was certain that no matter what I wore, I'd look like a country bumpkin compared to Josephine. My nose is still turned up and will be, I suppose, until the end of my days. This is particularly unfortunate because since the conquest of Italy "classical profiles" are the rage.

We left at one o'clock to drive to the rue de la Victoire, where the small drawing room was already swarming with Bonapartes. Madame Letizia and her daughters now live in Paris. All the members of the family see one another constantly, and Caroline, and Josephine's daughter—the square, blond Hortense—had been allowed to leave their fancy boarding school for one day to wish their brother and stepfather a successful journey to the pyramids.

Among the Bonapartes I noticed a slender, blond and very young officer with an adjutant's sash. I asked Caroline who he was, and she whispered, "Napoleon's stepson!" He came over to me and presented himself shyly: "Eugène de Beauharnais," he said, "personal adjutant of General Bonaparte."

The only members of the family who had not appeared were our host and hostess. At last a door opened and Josephine came in. "How nice that the whole family is here," she said. Her white dress clung to her slender figure, and a shawl of red velvet edged in ermine was draped around her shoulders. She went over to Madame Letizia and said, "Your son Lucien has just written Napoleon that he is married."

"I know he has." Letizia's eyes narrowed. "Is my second eldest son by any chance dissatisfied with his brother's choice?"

Josephine shrugged. "It seems he is."

Then the door flew open and there was Napoleon, his thin face red with fury. "Mother, did you know that Lucien has married an innkeeper's daughter?"

Madame Letizia looked Napoleon up and down—from his impeccable uniform, made by the best military tailor in Paris, to his highly polished and elegant small boots. "What don't you like about your sister-in-law, Christine Boyer from Saint Maximin, Napoleone? As far as I know, she is a fine girl with an excellent reputation." Madame Letizia looked casually at Josephine's narrow white figure.

"Unfortunately," Joseph interjected, "we cannot all marry former countesses."

Napoleon whirled around and stared at him. The small vein hammered in his right temple. "I have the right to demand suitable marriages from my brothers," he said. "Mother, I want you to write to Lucien at once that he is to get a divorce."

At that moment he noticed me. This was it—this meeting so feared and so longed for. Quickly he came forward and took both my hands in his. "Eugénie! I'm so pleased you came." His eyes never left my face. "You have become very beautiful, Eugénie. And quite grown up."

I withdrew my hands. "After all, I'm almost nineteen." It sounded gawky and naive. "And we've not seen each other for a long time, General." That was better.

"Yes, a long time. The last time—where did we last meet?" He looked at me and laughed. Lights danced in his eyes as he remembered our last meeting and found it funny. "Josephine, you must meet Eugénie, Julie's sister!"

"But Julie tells me that Mademoiselle Eugénie prefers to be called Désirée." The slender figure in white came closer to Napoleon. Nothing in her mysterious smile showed she recognized me. "It is very good of you to have come, mademoiselle." Josephine took his arm. "We can dine now," she said.

At the table I sat between Paulette's husband, the boring General Leclerc, and Josephine's son, the shy Eugène de Beauharnais. Napoleon talked incessantly. In Marseilles he spoke in short, broken sentences. Now he spoke fluently, very sure of himself and not in the least interested in anyone else's ideas. When he started on "our archenemies, the British," Paulette groaned, "Not that again!"

While Napoleon was explaining that he intended not only to destroy England's colonial power but also to liberate Egypt, I happened to glance at Hortense. The child—no, at fourteen one is no longer a child—this squarely built young girl, who does not in the least resemble her charming mother, was listening to Napoleon enthralled. Small red patches had appeared on her cheeks. It can't be, I thought, but Hortense is in love with her stepfather. It wasn't funny, it was sad and awful.

"Please finish your dinner, Bonaparte; we are expecting guests," Josephine said. She called him Bonaparte, I noticed. Probably this use of the surname was customary in aristocratic families. Napoleon obediently began to shovel in his food.

"Mama wants to drink your health," Eugène de Beauharnais said, interrupting my thoughts. I reached for my glass. Josephine smiled at me very slowly; she raised her glass to her lips, and as she put it down again, she winked at me. So she remembered. . . . Then, with a "Coffee in the drawing room," she rose.

It seemed as though everyone had come to wish Napoleon a successful journey. Even Barras, a director of the French Republic, was there, dressed in gold-embroidered lilac. In the drawing room Napoleon sat down on the sofa beside him; and Eugène, who seemed to feel responsible for seating the many guests, moved up a gilded chair and asked Police Director Fouché to be seated. Fouché was a thin-faced, familiar-looking man, and I soon realized where I had seen him before—that day at Madame Tallien's. Now an elegant young man with a slight limp and hair powdered in the old-fashioned manner entered the room. Fouché jumped up quickly.

"Dear Talleyrand—do join us!"

The gentlemen were discussing our ambassador in Vienna, who, I gathered, had hoisted our French Republican flag on some Austrian national holiday. The Viennese had then stormed the embassy and tried to pull it down.

"We should not have appointed a general as ambassador in Vienna, but a professional diplomat," someone was saying.

Talleyrand, who seemed to be in charge of our foreign affairs, smiled. "Our Republic has not yet a sufficient number of professional diplomats. We must do the best we can."

"And besides"—this was Barras' nasal voice—"besides, this general is one of our most able men, don't you agree, General Bonaparte? When you were in urgent need of reinforcements in Italy during the worst part of the winter, this Bernadotte marched the best division in the Rhine Army across the Alps in ten hours."

Talleyrand studied his polished fingernails. "At any rate," he said, "it was right to raise the Republican flag in Vienna. After this offense against our embassy, Bernadotte left Vienna at once, but I think that an apology from the Austrian government will reach Paris before he does. We could not have found a better man."

An almost imperceptible smile passed over Barras' swarthy face. "A man of vision—with political foresight as well." The director looked at Napoleon. "A convinced Republican who is determined to destroy enemies of the Republic either inside France or abroad. As this man has justified the government's confidence, it would be only natural that his next appointment be—"

"Minister of war!" Police Director Fouché finished for him.

Napoleon's lips narrowed. But now Barras turned his attention to Thérésa Tallien, who had appeared before us. "Our beautiful Thérésa." He smiled and rose heavily.

Thérésa restrained him. "Do stay, Director. And here is our Italian hero. . . . A delightful afternoon, General Bonaparte. Josephine looks charming. May I present Ouvrard to you; he supplied your Italian Army with ten thousand pairs of boots. . . . Ouvrard, here he is in person—'the strong man of France'!" The round little man following in her wake bowed almost to the floor.

Napoleon's sister Elisa nudged me. "Her latest friend! Army contractor Ouvrard. She had been living with Barras again until recently. She gave him up for a time to Josephine, you know."

I suddenly felt that I could not stand another minute of this. I jumped up, walked quickly to the door and looked for a mirror in the hall where I could powder my nose. The hall was almost dark. Before I got as far as the candles flickering before the tall mirror, I jumped back in surprise. Two people pressed close together in a corner sprang apart. I saw a shimmering white dress.

"Oh—I beg your pardon." I spoke involuntarily.

The white figure stepped swiftly forward into the candlelight. Josephine casually tidied her childlike curls. "May I present to you Monsieur Hippolyte Charles. This is my brother-in-law Joseph's charming sister-in-law—we are both his sisters-in-law, so we are related, are we not, Mademoiselle Désirée?"

A very young man, no more than twenty-five, bowed gracefully before me. Josephine laughed softly. "Mademoiselle Désirée is one of my former rivals," she added.

"A victorious or defeated rival?" Monsieur Charles asked.

There wasn't time to answer; spurs jingled and Napoleon shouted, "Josephine, our guests are asking for you."

"I was just showing Mademoiselle Désirée and Monsieur Charles the Venetian mirror you presented to me in Montebello, Bonaparte." Josephine was unperturbed. "I want you to meet one of our young army contractors. . . . And now, Monsieur Charles, you shall have the wish of your heart. You may shake hands with Italy's liberator." Josephine's laugh was charming and quickly dissipated Napoleon's irritation. She put her hand on Charles's arm. "Come with me—I must look after my other guests."

Napoleon and I stood alone in the flickering candlelight. He had stepped over to the mirror and was staring at his reflection. In this light deep shadows ringed his eyes and his thin cheeks were hollow. "You heard what Barras said?" he asked abruptly.

"Yes, I heard him, but I don't understand politics."

He kept staring into the mirror. " 'Enemies of the Republic inside France.' Lovely expression. He meant me. For he is quite aware that today I could—" He stopped. "We generals saved the Republic, and we hold it together. We might suddenly wish to form our own government. Since they beheaded the King, the crown has been in disrepute, like something tossed in the gutter. One need only bend down and pick it up."

He spoke as in a dream. And again I felt as I had near the hedge in our garden: first frightened, and then with a childish desire to laugh away this fear. He turned abruptly; his voice was sharp: "But let the directors go on quarreling. I am going to Egypt, where I shall raise the flag of the Republic . . ."

I felt I had to say something to distract him. "Forgive me for interrupting, General," I said. "But why do you torment me?"

"How, little Désirée?" He moved closer and his voice was suddenly gentle, even pitying.

"With these offers of marriage! These generals you send. I've had enough of it; I want peace."

"Believe me, only in marriage can a woman find the real meaning of her life," Napoleon said unctuously.

"I—I should like to throw these candlesticks at your head," I burst out, digging my fingernails into my palms.

He smiled that irresistible smile that had once meant heaven and earth and hell to me. "We are friends, aren't we, Bernardine Eugénie Désirée?" he asked.

"Oh, there you are, Désirée—get ready, we must be going." It was Julie, who had come into the hall with Joseph.

They both stopped in surprise when they saw Napoleon and me standing stiffly opposite each other. Then suddenly and casually Napoleon lifted my hand to his lips.

Paris, four weeks later

The happiest day of my life began like all my other days in Paris. After breakfast I was watering the two palms that Julie had brought from Italy and keeps in the dining room. Julie sat across the table from Joseph, who was reading a letter. I only half listened as he said, "There, you see, Julie—he has accepted my invitation! I wasn't sure he'd come. He's been overwhelmed with invitations. Everyone wants to hear what actually happened in Vienna."

I left the room to refill the watering can. When I returned, Joseph was saying, ". . . wrote to him that my honored friend, Director Barras, and my brother Napoleon said such splendid things about him that I wished to welcome him in my own home for a modest meal. An intimate little family dinner party—that will be best! Then Lucien and I can talk to him undisturbed. So— Josephine, Lucien and Christine, you and I." He looked at me. "Yes, and of course the child. Make yourself beautiful tonight, Désirée."

How they bore me, these "intimate family dinner parties" that Joseph loves giving for some deputy, general or ambassador. He arranges them so that he can learn political secrets to pass on in long letters to Napoleon, who is on his way to Egypt.

And perhaps Lucien comes only so as not to hurt Julie's and Joseph's feelings. A few days ago, shortly after Napoleon's departure, Lucien and his Christine moved to Paris. Madame Letizia found them a place to live and they manage somehow. When he was told that Napoleon expected him to divorce the innkeeper's daughter, Lucien was convulsed. "My military brother seems to have gone mad! What doesn't he like about my Christine?"

"Her father's inn," Joseph tried to explain.

"Well, our mama's father has a peasant's farm on Corsica," Lucien said, laughing, "and it's a small farm at that." Then he suddenly frowned, stared at Joseph and said, "Napoleon has some very remarkable ideas for a Republican."

While I was putting on a yellow silk dress, Julie slipped into my room and sat down on my bed. I was in a bad humor, trying to sweep my curls up and keep them there with two combs. "These political dinners bore me beyond belief," I grumbled.

"Josephine didn't want to come at first," Julie said. "She

recently bought that country house, Malmaison, you know. Then Joseph explained how important it is for Napoleon to stand in well with this particular man."

We heard a carriage drive up to the door, and Julie hurried off. But I didn't go down to greet the guests until the babble of voices was very loud and I felt that Julie was probably waiting for me before having dinner announced. It occurred to me that I might go to bed and say I had a headache, but I was already at the drawing room door. The very next moment I would have given anything in the world if I actually had gone to bed with a headache.

He stood with his back to the door; nevertheless, I recognized him at once—a tower of a man in a dark blue uniform with vast gold epaulets and a sash in the Republican colors. The others—Joseph, Julie, Josephine, Lucien and his Christine—stood in a semicircle around him, toying with small glasses. I remained paralyzed at the door, staring horrified at that broad-shouldered back. The semicircle soon found my behavior peculiar. They stared at me over the guest's shoulder, and finally the tall man stopped talking and turned around.

His eyes went wide with astonishment. I could hardly breathe, my heart beat so hard. "Désirée, come along, we're waiting for you," Julie said. At the same time Joseph came over, took my arm and said, "And this is my wife's little sister, General Bernadotte; my sister-in-law, Mademoiselle Désirée Clary."

I couldn't look at him. I concentrated on one of his gold buttons as he kissed my hand, and I heard Joseph say, "We were interrupted, dear General. You were saying that . . ."

"I—I've quite forgotten. . . ." His was the voice of the rain-drenched bridge, the voice in the dark corner of the carriage.

"Please come to dinner," Julie said, but General Bernadotte didn't budge until Julie took his arm. Joseph and Josephine, Lucien, Christine and I followed.

At the table General Bernadotte seemed a trifle absentminded. He busied himself mechanically with some expensive trout, and Joseph had to raise his glass twice before the general noticed and realized that we were waiting to drink to our guest of honor. Hastily he raised his own glass and we drank. Then he turned to Julie abruptly: "Has your sister been living in Paris very long?" The question startled Julie; she didn't understand it. "You are both from Marseilles, I know that. But has your sister been in Paris long?" he persisted.

Julie pulled herself together. "No, she's been here only a few months. It's the first time she's ever been in Paris. And you like it here very much, don't you, Désirée?"

"Paris is a lovely city," I recited, stiff as a schoolgirl.

"Yes, when it's not raining," he said, and his eyes narrowed.

"Oh—even in the rain." Christine, the innkeeper's daughter, spoke eagerly. "Paris is a fairy-tale city, I think."

"You are right, madame. Fairy tales can happen even in the rain," he replied seriously.

Joseph was getting restless. "Yesterday I had a letter from my brother Napoleon," he said meaningfully. "His journey is progressing according to plan."

"Then your brother has good luck," Bernadotte said good-naturedly, and raised his glass to Joseph. "To the good health of General Bonaparte. I am greatly indebted to him." Joseph didn't know whether to be offended or pleased.

It happened while we were eating the spring chicken, and Josephine precipitated it. At Julie's, "It's the first time she's ever been in Paris," Josephine raised her thin plucked eyebrows, looked curiously at me, then glanced at Bernadotte with interest. It is possible, very possible, that she recalled seeing Bernadotte at Madame Tallien's that afternoon. So far, she hadn't said much, but now she bent her curly head to one side, twinkled at Bernadotte and asked, "It can't have been easy for you as an unmarried ambassador in Vienna, General Bernadotte. Did you often miss the presence of a lady at the embassy?"

Bernadotte firmly put down his knife and fork. "How right you are, dear Josephine—and may I call you Josephine, as I did in the old days at your friend Madame Tallien's? I cannot tell you how unhappy I've been not to be married. But"—he turned to the others at the table—"but I ask you, what am I to do?"

No one knew whether he was joking or in earnest. Julie finally said, "I suppose you haven't found the right lady yet, General."

"Yes, madame, I have found her. But she simply vanished, and now—" He shrugged his shoulders in a comic gesture of embarrassment and looked at me. His whole face was gay with laughter.

"And now you must look for her and ask her to marry you," cried Christine.

"You are quite right, madame," Bernadotte said seriously. "I shall!" With that he jumped up, pushed back his chair and turned to Joseph. "Monsieur Joseph Bonaparte, I have the honor to ask for the hand of your sister-in-law, Mademoiselle Désirée Clary."

Deathly silence. A clock ticked and I was sure they could also hear my heart pounding. I stared at the white tablecloth.

"I don't quite understand, General Bernadotte. . . . Are you serious?" I heard Joseph ask.

"Very serious."

"I—think you must give Désirée time to consider your honorable offer," Joseph said.

"I have given her time, Monsieur Bonaparte."

"But you've only met her for the first time!" Julie's voice trembled with excitement.

I raised my head. "I should be very happy to marry you, General Bernadotte." Was that my voice? All those astonished faces. I don't know how I got out of the dining room, but suddenly I was upstairs on my bed and weeping. Then Julie was there, trying to soothe me. "You don't have to marry him unless you want to, dear. Don't cry—"

"But I can't help crying," I sobbed, "I'm so terribly happy!"

Though I washed my face in cold water and powdered profusely, Bernadotte said, when I reappeared in the drawing room, "I see you have been crying again, Mademoiselle Désirée!"

Julie and I were embarrassed. Bernadotte, who was not in the least disconcerted, asked Julie politely, "Madame, would you object if I invited your sister for a little drive?"

Julie nodded understandingly. "Of course not, dear General. When? Tomorrow afternoon?"

"No, I thought—right now," Bernadotte said.

"But it's already dark!" Julie was horrified.

I rose firmly. "Only a short drive, Julie," I said.

We drove in his open carriage through the fragrance of lime blossoms and the dark blue spring evening, not saying a word. As we approached the Seine, Bernadotte called out to the coachman. The carriage stopped at a bridge.

"This is the bridge," Bernadotte said; and we walked close together to the center, where we leaned over the parapet and watched the lights of Paris dancing on the water. And I knew then what I should have known ever since that wretched moment in a dark carriage when Jean-Baptiste's hand embodied all the warmth in my life—I belonged to him.

"I called at the Clapains' several times and asked about you, but no one would give me any information," he said at last.

I nodded. "They knew that I had come to Paris secretly."

On the drive home he put his arm around my shoulder. My head reached just to his epaulets. "You said that you were too small for me," he said.

"Yes, perhaps it doesn't matter."

"I like you the way you are."

I pressed my cheek against his shoulder, but the gold wire epaulets scratched my face. "These horrible gold things bother me," I murmured.

He laughed softly. "I know you can't bear generals."

I pushed the thought aside and went on happily scratching my cheek on the epaulets of a general named Bernadotte.

When we returned to the drawing room, the other guests had already gone. Julie and Joseph greeted us.

"We have decided to be married very soon, if you approve," Bernadotte told Joseph—though actually we hadn't discussed the wedding at all. "Tomorrow I'll begin looking for a nice little house, and as soon as I find one, we'll be married."

Like a beloved far-off melody, the memory sang in my heart: "I have saved part of my pay for years; I can buy a little house for you and the child—"

"I'll write Mama tonight. Good night, General Bernadotte," I heard Julie saying. And Joseph: "Good night, dear brother-in-law! My brother Napoleon will be delighted with this news."

As soon as Joseph was alone with Julie and me he said, "Désirée, you are marrying one of the most distinguished men in the Republic—"

"The trousseau," Julie interrupted. "If Désirée really is to be married soon, we must begin to worry about the trousseau! Embroidering the monograms takes time."

"The trousseau is ready in Marseilles," I said. "We need only have the boxes sent. I finished the monograms ages ago."

"Yes, of course," Julie said, her eyes open wide with surprise. "The monograms are done. *B*—"

"*B, B*, and again *B*." I smiled.

I am so *completely* happy.

PART TWO

Marshal Bernadotte's Lady

Sceaux, near Paris, autumn of 1798

I MARRIED GENERAL Jean-Baptiste Bernadotte in 1798, the sixth
year of the Republic, at the registry office in the Parisian suburb
of Sceaux. After the ceremony we all drove to the rue du Rocher,
where Julie had prepared a banquet to which Joseph had invited
every last Bonaparte living in Paris or anywhere near. Mama
had hoped to come up from Genoa, but she has been sick and
decided the journey would be too strenuous. Jean-Baptiste hates
family gatherings, and since he has no relatives in Paris anyway,
he asked only an old comrade from the cavalry. To my surprise,
Joseph had even invited General Junot. Junot is attached to
Napoleon's staff in Egypt and was in Paris only to report to the
government on Napoleon's entry into Alexandria and Cairo and
on his victorious battle of the Pyramids.

Since it's now fashionable to be married in the evening, our
dinner party began very late. Julie had wanted me to stay in bed
all day to look as rested and pretty as possible. But I had to help
Marie arrange our new dishes in the kitchen cupboard, one of the
many things to be done in the little house that Jean-Baptiste
found for us in the rue de la Lune in Sceaux. The first time I saw
our little house I said to Jean-Baptiste, "I must write Etienne to
send you my dowry right away."

Jean-Baptiste's nostrils quivered in contempt. "What do you
take me for? Would I furnish my home with my bride's money?"

"But Joseph used Julie's dowry—" I began.

"Don't compare me to the Bonapartes," he said sharply. But
then he put his arm lovingly around me and laughed. "Little girl,
today Bernadotte can afford to buy you only a doll's house in
Sceaux! But if you crave a castle, well . . ."

We were standing under the big chestnut tree in our future
garden. I wanted to belong here, in this tiny house, not live in
some palace, as I had for those long months in Italy. I quickly
exclaimed, "Promise me that we'll never have to live in a castle!"'

"We belong together, Désirée," Jean-Baptiste said, no longer

442

smiling. "Tomorrow I could be at the front, camping in the open. The day after tomorrow my headquarters could be in a castle, and I would, of course, ask you to join me. Would you refuse?"

"I will never refuse," I said, "but I would not be happy."

Jean-Baptiste had the attic rebuilt into two small bedrooms for Marie and Fernand. Of course I brought my Marie and Jean-Baptiste his Fernand.

"How do you think your Marie and my Fernand will get on together?" Jean-Baptiste had asked.

Fernand comes from Pau, Jean-Baptiste's home town in Gascony, and they joined the Army at the same time. Jean-Baptiste got one promotion after another, but every time an attack was ordered, Fernand, who is small and fat, had a stomachache. Nevertheless, he wanted to remain a soldier to be near Jean-Baptiste, and he has a passion for polishing boots and getting grease spots off a uniform. So two years ago Fernand was honorably discharged from the Army and now devotes his full time to carrying out every last wish of Jean-Baptiste's. "I am my general's valet and former schoolmate," he said when he was presented to me.

As it turned out, Fernand and Marie immediately began to quarrel. Marie claimed that Fernand stole food from the pantry, while Fernand accused Marie of taking his shoe brushes—he has twenty-four of them—and the general's laundry, which she had decided to wash without asking him. But that, of course, was sometime after the dinner party the evening of my wedding day, at which I was so bored.

The conversation on that occasion was chiefly about Napoleon's Egyptian campaign. Joseph was determined to convince my poor Jean-Baptiste, who is already sick of the subject, that the conquest of Egypt is fresh proof of Napoleon's genius. And Lucien, who envisions his brother Napoleon proclaiming the Rights of Man all over the world, supported Joseph.

"I think it's impossible," Jean-Baptiste said, "for us to hold Egypt for long. The English also believe we can't."

"But Napoleon has already won the battle of the Pyramids. Enemy casualties were twenty thousand, ours less than fifty. Magnificent," Joseph declared.

Jean-Baptiste shrugged. "Magnificent? The glorious French Army, equipped with modern heavy artillery, killed twenty thousand half-naked Africans. I would call it a magnificent victory of cannon over spears and bows and arrows! The English, meanwhile, have no idea of fighting us on land. Why should they? Their fleet is far superior to ours. And as soon as they have destroyed the ships that carried Bonaparte's armies to Egypt—" Jean-Baptiste looked around the table. "Don't you see? Your brother and his victorious regiments will be cut off from the motherland, caught in the desert like mice in a trap. This Egyptian campaign is a wild gamble and the stake is too high for our Republic!"

I realized that Joseph and Junot would immediately write Napoleon that my husband had called him a gambler. What I didn't yet know, and what no one in Paris would have believed on the night of my wedding, was that Jean-Baptiste Bernadotte had predicted precisely what had already happened. Sixteen days earlier the English fleet, under the command of a certain Admiral Nelson, had practically destroyed the whole French fleet in the Bay of Abukir, and General Bonaparte was desperately trying to establish contact with France.

I yawned for the second time—it's not quite the thing for a bride to do, but I yawned. Jean-Baptiste got up and said quietly, "It's late, Désirée. We must go home." It sounded so intimate— "We must go home."

We drove to Sceaux in an open carriage through the hot, still summer night. When we reached our house, we saw no one. All was silent, but the dining room was lit up. Tall candles shone out from the silver candlesticks Josephine and Napoleon had given us for a wedding present. A gleaming white damask cloth, champagne glasses, a dish of grapes, peaches and marzipan cakes were on the table; and in the wine cooler, a bottle of champagne.

"Marie did it," I said delightedly.

But Jean-Baptiste said, "No, it was Fernand." He warily examined the champagne bottle. "If we drink any more tonight, we'll both have horrible headaches in the morning." I nodded and Jean-Baptiste blew out the tall candles.

Our bedroom was pitch-dark. I groped my way to the window, pulled the curtains aside and let in the moonlight. I heard Jean-Baptiste go into the next room and bustle about. To give me time to undress and go to bed, I thought gratefully. I quickly slipped off my dress. My nightgown lay on the silk coverlet of the big double bed. I put it on, slid under the blanket—and shrieked.

"For God's sake, Désirée—what's wrong?" Jean-Baptiste stood beside the bed.

"I don't know. Something stabbed me." I moved. "Ouch!"

Jean-Baptiste lit a candle. I sat up and threw back the blanket: *roses!* Roses and more roses—with sharp thorns!

"What idiot—?" exclaimed Jean-Baptiste, while we both gaped in astonishment at the bed of roses. I began to collect them. "Undoubtedly Fernand," I said. "He wanted to surprise us."

"You're unfair to the lad; it was your Marie, of course," Jean-Baptiste replied. "Roses—in a soldier's bed!"

The roses I had fished out of the soldier's bed were now strewn on the night table, and their fragrance filled the room. Suddenly I realized that Jean-Baptiste was looking at me and that I had only a nightgown on. I quickly sat down on the bed and closed my eyes tight. I didn't see him blow out the candle.

The next morning we discovered that Marie and Fernand had actually agreed about something: to decorating our bridal bed with roses, and they had both forgotten about the thorns.

JEAN-BAPTISTE HAD taken two months' leave so that he could spend the first weeks of our marriage with me undisturbed. But from the moment we heard about the destruction of our fleet at Abukir, he had to report every morning to the Luxembourg Palace and take part in consultations with the minister of war. He would return late every afternoon, and we would sit under the chestnut tree drinking coffee. I blinked contentedly at the sinking sun, knowing I was actually married to him for always—and not dreaming. . . .

One day Jean-Baptiste came home at noon. I was helping Marie preserve plums and ran out through the garden to meet him. "We're making so much plum jam you can have it every morning for breakfast all winter."

"But I won't be here to eat your jam," he said calmly and called toward the house. "Fernand! Get my field uniform ready, pack the saddlebags. I leave tomorrow morning at seven." A terrible fear lay like a cold hand on my heart. Then Jean-Baptiste spoke to me softly and tenderly, as to a child. "You've always known that I would go to war again, haven't you? You are married to an officer, you are a sensible young woman. You must pull yourself together and be courageous—"

"I don't want to be courageous," I said.

"Désirée, I go to cross the Rhine with a sham army, and I must throw back the enemy with it."

"There is nothing you can't do, Jean-Baptiste," I said, and I loved him so much that tears came to my eyes.

He shrugged his shoulders. "The government, unfortunately, seems to agree with you and will allow me only an inadequate complement of raw recruits to attack the Rhineland."

"The man I bought the plums from this morning was very put out with the Army and the government," I murmured. "He said, 'As long as General Bonaparte was in Italy, we had one victory after another. As soon as he left there and went off to the pyramids, things went from bad to worse.' "

"Yes, but it never occurred to the plum dealer that although Napoleon won many victories, he never permanently fortified the conquered territory. As a result, we are now obliged to defend the frontiers with ridiculously small forces while Bonaparte suns himself on the banks of the Nile. And this is 'the strong man.' "

It was a long, long night. I lay alone in our wide bed and counted the hours as the clock struck in our little church in Sceaux. My husband was downstairs in his study, poring over maps. Finally I must have dozed off, for I suddenly awoke in terror, certain that something terrible had happened. Jean-Baptiste was asleep beside me. But I had awakened him. "Is something wrong?" he murmured.

"I had a terrifying dream," I whispered, "that you were riding off—to war."

"I really am riding off to war tomorrow," he answered. He put his arm under my head and drew me closer. "Désirée, I don't want the days to seem long for you while I am away, so I think you should take some lessons."

"Lessons? But, Jean-Baptiste, I haven't learned anything since I was ten years old. I went to school when I was six, at the same time as Julie. The nuns taught us. But when I was ten, all the convents were dissolved."

"That's just it. I thought you might take lessons in music and deportment."

"Deportment? Do you mean dancing? I know how to dance. I danced at home, on the anniversary of every Bastille Day, in the square in front of the town hall."

"I don't mean only dancing," he explained. "How to curtsy, the gestures with which a lady invites her guests to move from one room to another. If I should be appointed military governor anywhere, you would be the first lady of the district and would have to receive innumerable dignitaries in your salon."

"Salon!" I was outraged. "Jean-Baptiste, are you talking about palaces again?"

"You can't imagine how eagerly the Austrian aristocrats and the foreign diplomats in Vienna waited for our ambassador to make a fool of himself. They positively prayed that I'd eat my fish with a knife. We owe our Republic impeccable manners, Désirée." After a while he added, "I want you to take piano lessons and study singing." I gathered that he didn't wish to be contradicted. "My friend, the violinist Rodolphe Kreutzer, accompanied me to Vienna when I went there, and he brought a Viennese composer to see me at the embassy. His name was Beethoven. They played together many evenings, and I was sorry I had not learned to play some instrument when I was a child. I asked Kreutzer yesterday to write down for me the name of a music teacher. Begin the lessons and write to me regularly about your progress."

Again a cold hand clutched at my heart. "Write to me regularly," he had said. Letters. Only letters would be left. I stared at the curtains, my eyes wide open. Jean-Baptiste had gone to sleep again.

A fist hammered on our door. "It's half past six, General," Fernand announced.

Half an hour later we were sitting at the breakfast table, Jean-Baptiste in his field uniform. I had no more than started my breakfast when the dreaded farewells began. Horses neighed; I heard men's voices; spurs clanked and Fernand rushed outside. "Sir, the gentlemen of your staff are here."

"I am ready." And to me Jean-Baptiste said, "Good-by, my darling one, write me regularly. The Ministry of War will send me your letters by special courier. Good-by, Marie, take care of Madame."

He was already out the door. Suddenly the room, gray in the morning light, spun around me; then everything went black.

When I came to, I was lying on my bed. The room reeked of vinegar. Marie's face floated above me. "You fainted, Eugénie."

I pushed the cloth with the vinegar smell off my forehead. "I wanted to kiss him again, Marie," I said wearily. "In farewell."

Bells ringing in the New Year woke me. From the street I can hear merry voices and laughter and drunken singing. Why is everyone so happy when a new year begins? I am unutterably sad. In the first place, I have quarreled with Jean-Baptiste by letter. Second, I am afraid of this new year.

The day after Jean-Baptiste left, I obediently drove to the music teacher's, the one Rodolphe Kreutzer recommended. He is a spindly little man with bad breath. I had to pay him in advance, then sit down at a piano and learn what the notes are called. As I drove home from my first lesson, I felt dizzy and was afraid I might faint again. Since then, I've rented a piano so I can practice at home. And I've also begun taking dancing and deportment lessons from Monsieur Montel, a perfumed ballet dancer recommended by someone to Jean-Baptiste. He teaches me how to curtsy to invisible dignitaries.

I'm always reading in the *Moniteur* of Jean-Baptiste's victorious progress in Germany. But he never mentions the war in his letters. Instead, he asks incessantly how my lessons are going, and sounds like an elderly uncle. I am a very bad correspondent; my letters to him are always too short and never say what I really want to tell him—that I am very unhappy without him and long for him terribly. I also never write about my lessons. Why should I, a confirmed Republican, the daughter of a respectable silk merchant in Marseilles, be trained to be a "great lady"? Jean-Baptiste is a general, of course, and probably one of the "coming men"; but he, too, comes of a simple family, and anyway, in the Republic all citizens are equal.

I got up and wrote him a long, long letter. In it I said that I had not married an old sermonizer but—I thought—a man who understood me. The little man with the bad breath who gives me finger exercises, and that perfumed cross between an archbishop and a ballerina, Monsieur Montel, could both go to the devil. I sealed the letter quickly without reading it over and had Marie take it to the Ministry of War for immediate forwarding to General Bernadotte's headquarters.

The next day I was terrified that Jean-Baptiste might be really angry, so I drove to Monsieur's to take my lesson, and afterward I sat for two hours at the piano practicing scales and feeling as gray and gloomy as our leafless chestnut tree. A whole week crept by and at last came Jean-Baptiste's answer.

My dear Désirée, I have no wish to treat you as a child, but as a loving and understanding wife . . . And then he began again to discuss the progress of my education.

I still have not answered his letter. And now something else has happened that makes further letter writing impossible.

Yesterday, when Marie brought me a cup of broth, I pushed it away. "That greasy soup is revolting," I said.

"You must make yourself eat, you know," Marie said. "You need nourishment now."

"Why?"

Marie smiled and put her arms around me. "You know quite well why, don't you?"

"No, I don't know . . . and it's not true, it can't be true!" I tore upstairs and flung myself down on my bed.

Of course I had known, but I had refused to believe it. I stared up at the ceiling for a long time, trying to imagine what it would be like. It's quite normal, I said to myself; all women want children. But children are a terrible responsibility, and I'm so ignorant. . . . A little boy with black curls like Jean-Baptiste . . . I laid my hands tentatively where he was. *My* little human being, I suddenly thought, part of myself.

Marie came upstairs with the soup.

"Marie," I said, "when you were expecting your little Pierre, were you very happy?"

She sat down beside me on the bed. "Naturally not. I wasn't married."

"I've heard that when—I mean if you don't want a child, you can—there are women who can help," I said hesitantly.

Marie looked at me speculatively. "Come," she said tenderly, "eat the soup. Then write to the general. Bernadotte will be delighted."

I shook my head. "I cannot write about things like that. I wish I could talk to him." I drank the soup, dressed, drove to Monsieur Montel's and learned to dance a new quadrille.

This morning I had a great surprise—Josephine came to see me! She's been here before, but only with Julie and Joseph.

Marie brought us hot chocolate, and I asked politely, "Do you hear regularly from General Bonaparte, madame?"

"Irregularly," said she. "The English are blockading his lines of communication. Now and then a small vessel gets through." I couldn't think of anything else to say. Josephine saw the piano. "Julie tells me you are taking piano lessons, madame," she remarked.

I nodded. "I am also taking dancing lessons. I don't want to disgrace my Bernadotte."

"It's not so simple being married to a general—I mean a general off at the front," Josephine said. "Misunderstandings can occur so easily."

They certainly can, I silently agreed. "You can't always write what you mean."

"That's true," Josephine agreed. "And other people meddle in matters that aren't any of their business and write malicious letters." She drank her chocolate. "Joseph, for instance. Our mutual brother-in-law intends to write Napoleon that yesterday he came to see me at Malmaison and found Monsieur Charles there. You remember, the charming young army contractor? And also that he was in his dressing gown. Imagine Joseph bothering Napoleon with such a trivial matter."

"Why ever was Monsieur Charles walking around in a dressing gown at Malmaison?"

"It was only nine o'clock in the morning, and Joseph arrived very unexpectedly." Josephine paused. "I can't bear to be alone so much; I've never been alone in my whole life." Her eyes filled with tears. "And since we generals' wives must stick together against our mutual brother-in-law, I thought you might ask Julie to persuade Joseph not to write to Bonaparte."

So that was what Josephine wanted from me. "Julie has no influence on Joseph's actions," I replied truthfully.

Josephine's eyes were those of a terrified child. "You won't help me?"

"Tonight I'm going to Joseph's for a small New Year's dinner, and I'll speak to Julie," I said. "But you mustn't expect too much, madame."

Josephine stood up, obviously relieved. "I knew you would understand my position."

I drove half an hour earlier than I'd planned to the rue du

Rocher. Julie fluttered excitedly around, rearranging the table decorations. "I've given you Louis Bonaparte as a dinner partner. The fat boy is such a bore, I can't very well inflict him on anyone else," she said.

"I'd like to ask you something," I said. "Can you ask Joseph not to write Napoleon anything about the dressing gown—I mean the dressing gown Monsieur Charles was wearing at Malmaison?"

"The letter to Napoleon has already gone off," said Joseph at that very moment. He had come into the dining room and was standing by the sideboard, pouring himself a brandy. "I'd like to bet Josephine came to you today and asked you to intercede for her. Didn't she, Désirée?"

I shrugged. "It's none of your business. And Napoleon, off in Egypt, can't undo what's done. It will only make him unhappy. Why trouble him?"

Joseph looked at me with interest. "Still in love with him? I thought you had forgotten him long ago."

"Forgotten?" I was astonished. "No one can ever forget a first love."

"And therefore you want to spare him this great disillusionment." Joseph seemed to enjoy this conversation. "But my letter is already on the way."

"So there's no point in discussing it further," I said.

Joseph filled two more glasses. "Come, Julie, Désirée, we three must wish one another Happy New Year before our guests arrive."

Dutifully, Julie and I each took a glass, and suddenly I felt wretched. I hastily put the glass back on the sideboard.

"Aren't you well, Désirée?" cried Julie.

I felt beads of sweat on my forehead, fell into a chair and shook my head. "It's nothing—it often happens."

"If she's ill, I must write to General Bernadotte right away," Joseph said.

"Don't you dare, Joseph. I want to surprise him!"

"What with?" asked Joseph and Julie simultaneously.

"With a son," I announced, suddenly proud. I stood up. "And now I'm going home. Don't be hurt, but I'd rather go to bed and sleep over the New Year."

Joseph had poured still more brandy, and he and Julie drank to me. Julie's eyes were wet.

"Long live the Bernadotte dynasty," Joseph said, laughing.

I enjoyed this jest. "Yes, a toast to the Bernadotte dynasty," I replied. Then I drove home.

Now at last the church bells are silent and I am facing this New Year all alone. No, not quite alone. . . . We'll face the future together, little unborn son, and hope for the best. For the Bernadotte dynasty!

Sceaux, July 4, 1799

Eight hours ago I had a son. He has dark silky down on his head and dark blue eyes. I'm so weak that they would be very upset if they knew that Marie gave in and secretly brought me my diary. The midwife is sure I am going to die, but the doctor thinks he can pull me through.

I hear Jean-Baptiste's voice out in the living room. Dear, dear Jean-Baptiste . . .

Sceaux, a week later

Now not even my pessimistic midwife thinks I'm going to die. I lie propped up with pillows while Marie brings me my favorite food, and the war minister of France sits on my bed and discusses the raising of children.

Jean-Baptiste came back very unexpectedly. After New Year's Day I had pulled myself together and written him again; but only short letters, and not at all affectionate, because I longed for him so terribly and at the same time I was angry with him. I read in the *Moniteur* that he had captured Mannheim and become governor of Hesse, and was ruling over the German inhabitants in accordance with the laws of our Republic. Then, one afternoon about two months ago, I was sitting at the piano, practicing, when the door behind me opened. "Marie, that's the Mozart minuet I've learned as a surprise for our general. Does it sound all right?"

"It sounds wonderful, Désirée, and it's an enormous surprise for your general!" Jean-Baptiste took me in his arms, and after two kisses it was as though we'd never been separated. Then my hero looked at me and asked, "Why didn't you write me, little girl, that we're expecting a son?" (The possibility of a daughter never occurred to him either.)

I frowned and tried to look furious. "Because I didn't want my old sermonizer to worry about interruptions in my education. But calm yourself, General; your son has already begun his lessons in correct deportment at Monsieur Montel's, tucked under his mother's heart."

Jean-Baptiste forbade me to go on with my lessons; he hardly wanted me to leave the house, so anxious was he about my health.

Meanwhile, all Paris talked of a domestic crisis and dreaded riots—some organized by Royalists, who are gaining strength again, and others organized by the extreme left, the austere Jacobins. It seems that Director Barras hoped to exploit this discontent. With the collaboration of Director Sieyès, an old Jacobin, he was planning to get rid of three of his fellow directors. But he was afraid such a coup d'état might result in more riots, so he asked Jean-Baptiste to stand by him as his military adviser. But Jean-Baptiste refused, saying Barras should obey the Constitution, and if it needed changing, he should ask the deputies.

Joseph thought my husband was crazy. "You could be the dictator of France tomorrow, with the support of your troops."

"Quite so," answered Jean-Baptiste quietly. "But you seem to forget, monsieur, that I am a confirmed Republican."

Then about three weeks ago Barras and Sieyès succeeded in forcing the three directors to resign without help from Jean-Baptiste, and began appointing new ministers. Since we're conducting a war on all fronts, and the Republic is still at risk, everything depended on the choice of a new minister of war.

Early in the morning of July 2 a messenger arrived with an urgent summons for Jean-Baptiste. He went right to town, and I sat under the chestnut tree all day, feeling uncomfortable. The evening before, I had eaten a whole pound of cherries, and they were rumbling around in my stomach. Suddenly pain stabbed through me like a knife. "Marie," I called. "Marie!"

Marie came, gave me one look and said, "Up to the bedroom. I'll send Fernand for the midwife." (Fernand had come back from Germany with Jean-Baptiste.)

"At last that fellow is good for something," Marie said when she came up to the bedroom.

"It's just the cherries," I insisted. At that moment the knife jabbed again; this time I screamed, and when the pain was over, I began to cry. "Julie—I want Julie," I moaned.

Fernand came back with the midwife and was sent off to fetch Julie.

The midwife! She had huge red arms and a broad red face with a real mustache, reminding me of a giantess in some gruesome fairy tale. She gazed at me observantly and, it seemed to me, with considerable contempt. "It's going to take you forever," she prophesied.

An endless afternoon turned into an endless evening; the evening into a long, long night; a dusky dawn dragged into a sticky hot morning. Then it was afternoon again, another evening, another night. By then, I could no longer tell one time of day from another. Occasionally I sensed Julie's nearness; someone kept wiping my forehead and cheeks. I could hear Marie's quiet voice. The giantess stood over me; candles flickered—was it already dark again? Then Jean-Baptiste was sitting on my bed, holding me in his arms. . . . Something whimpered in the room—high and squally. My lids were like lead, but after a while I opened my eyes. Julie held a small bundle of white cloth in her arms, and Jean-Baptiste stood beside her. He turned and came over to the bed. He knelt down and took my hand and laid it against his cheek, his completely unshaven cheek—and wet, too. Do generals also weep? "We have a fine son, but he's still very small," he reported.

"They're always small at the beginning," I whispered. Julie showed me the bundle. A crab-red little face with scrunched-up eyes peeped out of the wrappings.

"I must ask you all to leave the room. The wife of our minister of war needs rest," announced the doctor.

"The wife of our minister of war? Does he mean me, Jean-Baptiste?"

"I have been the French minister of war since the day before yesterday," Jean-Baptiste said.

"And I haven't yet congratulated you," I murmured.

"You were very busy." He smiled.

MY SON WILL have a Nordic name, Oscar. It was Napoleon's idea. When he learned, from one of Joseph's long-winded letters, that I was expecting a baby, he promptly wrote: *If it's a son, Eugénie must call him Oscar. And I want to be his godfather.* When we showed Jean-Baptiste this letter, he laughed. "We mustn't offend your old admirer, little girl. As far as I'm concerned, he can be the boy's godfather. And the name Oscar Bernadotte sounds distinguished." That settled the matter.

In two weeks we are moving to another house. A minister of war must live in Paris, and therefore Jean-Baptiste has bought a small villa in the rue Cisalpine, around the corner from Julie. We'll have a real nursery and a drawing room where Jean-Baptiste can receive the officials who often call on him in the evening.

I myself am doing marvelously. I'm not so weak anymore, although I have callers all day long and this makes me tired. Josephine came, and even Thérésa Tallien; and also that woman writer with the pug face, Madame de Staël, who is married to the Swedish ambassador. She told me that France had at last found the one man who can restore order, and that everyone considers my Jean-Baptiste the real head of the government.

But it is dreadful that my husband all alone has to save our Republic. He gets home from the Ministry of War at eight o'clock, has a small meal served at my bedside, and then goes down to his study to dictate to a secretary half the night. He leaves at six in the morning for the Ministry, and Fernand says that the camp bed Jean-Baptiste had put up in the study is often unused.

One evening, during our meal, Fernand announced that Joseph wished to see Jean-Baptiste.

"The last person I wanted to see today," grumbled Jean-Baptiste.

Joseph appeared. First he leaned over the cradle and declared that Oscar was the most beautiful child he had ever seen. Then he asked Jean-Baptiste to go down to the study with him. "Our conversation will bore Désirée," he ventured.

Jean-Baptiste shook his head. "I have so little opportunity to be with her, I would rather stay. Sit down."

They both sat beside my bed and Jean-Baptiste sought my hand. Peace and strength flowed from his nearness; I closed my eyes.

"What would you say if Napoleon decided to return to France?" Joseph asked.

"I would say that Napoleon cannot return unless the minister of war recalls him from Egypt."

"My dear brother-in-law, in Egypt a supreme commander of Napoleon's stature is now superfluous. The Egyptian campaign is more or less at a standstill and can therefore—"

"—be regarded as a fiasco, as I predicted it would be."

"I wouldn't express it so baldly. Still, my brother's talents could be used to greater advantage on another front. You realize that there are already conspiracies against the government?"

"As minister of war I could hardly be unaware of it. So you suggest that I recall your brother to put down these conspiracies?"

"Yes, I thought that—"

"It's up to the police to expose conspiracies. No more, no less."

"Of course. But I can confidentially advise you that influential circles are considering a consolidation of the powerful political forces. For example, if you yourself and Napoleon, the two most capable—" Joseph got no further.

"Stop that drivel. Come to the point: Certain people want a dictator. Your brother Napoleon wishes to be recalled from Egypt in order to compete for the position."

Joseph nervously cleared his throat. "I spoke to Talleyrand today. The ex-minister thinks there might be support for a change in the Constitution."

"I am familiar with Talleyrand's point of view. Also the aims of various Jacobins. I can inform you, too, that the Royalists are concentrating all their hopes on a dictator. But I have sworn loyalty to the Republic and under all circumstances will uphold our Constitution. Is this answer clear enough?"

"Supposing that my brother came to the conclusion that as a passionate patriot, he must return—what then?"

Jean-Baptiste's hand gripped mine like iron, but just for a moment. He relaxed, and I heard him say quietly, "A supreme commander's place is with his troops. He led these troops into the desert, and he must remain with them until a way is found to bring them back. Otherwise, as minister of war, I should be obliged to place your brother before a court-martial, and I assume that he would be condemned and shot as a deserter. Even a civilian like yourself must see this, Monsieur Bonaparte."

After Jean-Baptiste accompanied Joseph downstairs, I tried to sleep. But I kept remembering a young girl who had raced with a scrawny, insignificant-looking officer all the way to a hedge. The distorted face of the officer was frightening in the moonlight. "I am my destiny," the officer had said. The girl had laughed.

He will come back from Egypt. Come back and destroy the Republic if he has a chance. He cares nothing for the Republic, or for the rights of its citizens; nor can he understand a man like

Jean-Baptiste. . . . Then other words came back to me: "My little daughter, whenever and wherever in the future men may seek to deprive their brothers of liberty and equality, no one can say for them, 'Father, forgive them for they know not what they do.'" Jean-Baptiste and Papa would have understood each other.

Paris, November 9, 1799

He has come back.

And today he succeeded in his coup d'état; for the last few hours he has been head of state. Several deputies and generals have been arrested. Jean-Baptiste says that any moment we may expect the state police to search our house. It would be unspeakably awful if Police Director Fouché, and then Napoleon, got hold of my diary. So I am quickly, tonight, writing down what has happened. Then I shall lock the book and give it to Julie for safekeeping. Napoleon will never let the police rummage through the bureau drawers of his sister-in-law.

I'm sitting in the salon of our new home in the rue Cisalpine. Many people, in silent groups, are standing in front of our house. When I asked Fernand why they were there, he paused, then decided to tell me the truth. "They want to see what happens to our general. The rumor is that he will be arrested. General Moreau has been already."

I am ready for a long night. Jean-Baptiste paces up and down in the dining room next to the salon. And we wait.

Yes, Napoleon suddenly came back, as I was sure he would. Four weeks and two days ago, accompanied only by his secretary, he landed at the port of Fréjus in a small merchant vessel that had eluded the British. He hired a special coach, drove directly to his house on the rue de la Victoire in Paris, and confronted Josephine with accusations of infidelity, as had been reported to him by Joseph. He then announced he was divorcing her and locked her out of his study, where he spent several hours dictating letters to countless deputies and generals to advise them personally of his return. Josephine came and stood outside the locked study door, sobbing loudly for two whole hours. At last he opened it. The next morning Napoleon woke up in Josephine's bedroom.

I got all this straight from Julie. "And do you know what Napoleon said to me?" Julie added. "He said, 'Julie, if I divorce

Josephine, all Paris will know that she was unfaithful to me and laugh at me. But if I stay with her, everyone will be convinced that the stories about her were merely malicious gossip. I never, under any circumstances, want to be laughed at.'"

Meanwhile the news spread like wildfire through Paris: General Bonaparte had returned victorious from Egypt. Curious crowds gathered around his house, shouting, *"Vive Bonaparte!"* and Napoleon showed himself at the window and waved.

There certainly would never have been a coup today if Jean-Baptiste had still been minister of war when Napoleon returned. But shortly before, he had quarreled violently with Director Sieyès over the failure of the government to provide arms and uniforms for the thousands of army recruits he was having trained, and was so angry that he resigned. Since Sieyès supported Napoleon, it seems probable that he foresaw Napoleon's return and intentionally quarreled with Jean-Baptiste so as to force his resignation. Jean-Baptiste's successor dares not have Napoleon court-martialed because some of the generals and deputies rejoiced too much over Napoleon's return.

During those autumn days, Jean-Baptiste had many callers. General Moreau had come and declared that the Army must intervene if Napoleon dared a coup d'état. A troop of Jacobin city councillors from Paris asked if General Bernadotte would take command of the National Guard if there was trouble. Jean-Baptiste replied that he must first be authorized to do so by the government—that is, the minister of war—so the city councillors departed disappointed.

Then, one Sunday morning, when we were to drive to Villa Mortefontaine, Joseph and Julie's new country house, I suddenly heard a well-known voice in our drawing room: "Eugénie—I must see my godson!" I dashed downstairs. There he was, his face tanned, his hair shorn. "We wanted to surprise you and Bernadotte. Since we're invited to Mortefontaine too, Josephine and I thought we'd drive by and take you. I must meet your son, and I've not yet seen General Bernadotte since my return."

"You look wonderfully well, my dear," said Josephine, standing slender and graceful at the terrace door.

Jean-Baptiste brought Oscar down, and Napoleon bent over our son, trying to tickle his chin. Oscar cried shrilly until I rescued him.

While we drank Marie's bittersweet coffee, Josephine entangled me in a discussion of roses—she's laid out a magnificent garden at Malmaison—so I didn't hear all of the conversation between Jean-Baptiste and Napoleon. But Josephine and I were suddenly silent when Napoleon said, "I'm told that if you were still minister of war, Bernadotte, you would have me court-martialed and shot. What particularly have you against me?"

"I think you know our service regulations better than I do, General Bonaparte," Jean-Baptiste answered with a smile.

Napoleon leaned toward Jean-Baptiste, and the change in him was startlingly apparent. His shorter hair made his head seem rounder, his gaunt cheeks fuller, and his chin jutted out practically square. Even his smile was different. The smile I had once loved so much, which could fleetingly transform his whole stern face, was now fixed, compelling and—solicitous. Why this set smile, and for whom? Jean-Baptiste, of course. Jean-Baptiste was to be won over as a friend, a confidant, an enthusiastic ally.

"I have returned from Egypt to place myself at the disposal of our country, for I consider my Egyptian assignment completed. The few thousand men I left behind in Africa can mean nothing to the French Army, which you, as minister of war, expanded to one hundred and forty thousand men. While a man like me, in the Republic's present desperate situation, could—"

"The situation is not desperate," Jean-Baptiste said calmly.

"No?" Napoleon smiled. "People on all sides have told me that the government is no longer in control. The Royalists are active once more. The Army and its leaders must maintain civil peace and discipline, and set up a form of government worthy of the ideals of the Revolution. If men of all parties—I emphasize all parties—came to me and asked for a coalition of all the positive forces in the country, and wanted me to draft a new constitution to realize the ideals of the Revolution, would you stand by me, Bernadotte? Could France count on you?"

With a bang Jean-Baptiste set down his cup. "Listen to me, Bonaparte. If you are here to suggest I commit high treason, I must ask you to leave my house."

Away went the ingratiating look in Napoleon's eyes. The familiar little vein throbbed at his right temple.

Jean-Baptiste rose, strode to the terrace door and gazed out, as though reaching for words in the gray autumn sky. Then he turned abruptly, came over and dropped his hand heavily on

Napoleon's shoulder. "General Bonaparte, I have served under your command in Italy. I have seen how you plan a campaign. I assure you France boasts no better commander in chief. You can take an old sergeant's word for this. But what the politicians suggest is unworthy of a general of the Republican Army. Don't do it, Bonaparte!" Napoleon's face was expressionless. Jean-Baptiste let his hand slip from Napoleon's shoulder. "If you persist in this, I shall fight you and your followers by force of arms, provided . . ."

Napoleon glanced up. "Provided what?"

"Provided I am ordered by the recognized government to do so."

"How stubborn you are," Napoleon murmured. Whereupon Josephine suggested that we start for Mortefontaine.

In the days following, all Paris spoke of nothing but whether or not Napoleon would dare try a coup d'état. Then, yesterday evening, General Moreau, several other gentlemen from the War Ministry and the same city councillors who had been here earlier descended on us like an avalanche. They insisted that Jean-Baptiste take command of the National Guard to prevent Napoleon's entry into the Senate and the Council of Five Hundred.

Jean-Baptiste patiently explained again. "I cannot act under orders from the Paris Municipal Council. Nor from my comrade, dear Moreau. I must be empowered to act by the government itself. If the directors are no longer in office, my orders must come from the Council of Five Hundred." He paused, then added evenly, "But I think that tomorrow Napoleon will demand from the deputies command of the National Guard for himself."

Throughout the next day a continual stream of messengers arrived, officers of all ranks, and finally a young captain hurried into the room. "General Bernadotte, the Consular Government has been proclaimed. Bonaparte is the First Consul!"

It seems that during the morning Napoleon had gone first to the Senate, then to the Council of Five Hundred, where he asked to be heard. When he began to speak, there was a general uproar. The Bonaparte contingent forced their way to the rostrum. Their opponents—and these were members of all parties—jumped up, made their way to the exits and found them blocked by troops. Who ordered these troops into the chamber to "protect" the deputies has not been explained. However, General Leclerc, Paulette's husband, was seen at their head. The National Guard, normally responsible for the safety of the representatives, lined up with the troops.

In an impassioned speech Napoleon then talked some drivel about a conspiracy against the government, and asked that he be granted in this hour of national peril unrestricted powers to act.

Soon a voice shouted, *"Vive Bonaparte!"* Ten voices joined in, then thirty, then eighty. And the deputies, surrounded on all sides by muskets, cheered helplessly.

At this point Police Director Fouché arrived and discreetly requested those members who it was feared might disturb the new "peace and order" to follow him. Then the chamber, which now had great gaps, began deliberating on a new constitution and the formation of a new government, to be headed by three consuls. General Napoleon Bonaparte was unanimously elected First Consul, and at his request the Tuileries was placed at his disposal as his official residence.

This evening, while I sat in the bedroom with Oscar in my arms, Jean-Baptiste came up and sat beside me. "General Moreau has just been arrested," he told me.

Oscar was asleep, so we went downstairs and waited for the state police. I began to write in my diary.

There are nights that never end. . . .

Suddenly a carriage stopped in front of our house. Now they have come to take him away, I thought. I jumped up and ran into the salon. Jean-Baptiste, standing motionless, put his arm around me. Never in my life have I been so close to him.

Once, twice, three times—the door knocker banged. At the same time we heard voices. First a man's voice, and then a woman's laugh. I fell into the nearest chair and suddenly found myself crying. It was Julie. Dear Lord, only Julie. . . .

We were all in the salon. Joseph and Lucien and Julie had come directly from the Tuileries, where celebration and discussions had been going on all night. "We drank too much champagne, but after all, it's a big day. Napoleon will govern France, Lucien is minister of the interior, and Joseph is to be foreign minister—at least he's on the list—" Julie prattled on. "You must forgive us for waking you, but as we drove past your house, I said we could at least say good morning to Désirée and Jean-Baptiste . . ."

"You didn't wake us up; we haven't slept," I said.

461

". . . And the three consuls will be advised by a State Council consisting of real experts. You may be chosen for this council, Bernadotte," Joseph was saying.

"Josephine wants to do over the Tuileries," Julie continued. "Her bedroom will be decorated in white. . . . And imagine—he says she must have a regular court household, including a 'reader' to read aloud to her and three ladies-in-waiting."

"I insist on the release of General Moreau," I heard Jean-Baptiste say.

"Protective custody and nothing more, I assure you—to protect Moreau from the mob. No one knows what the people of Paris might do in their wild enthusiasm for Napoleon and the new Constitution." This from Lucien.

A clock struck six. "We must go." Julie embraced me. "It's so wonderful for Joseph," she whispered.

Jean-Baptiste showed our guests to their carriage. Suddenly out of the fog sprang several of those unknowns who with us had waited through the endless night. *"Vive Bernadotte!"* someone shouted. The voice quavered. *"Vive Bernadotte!"* There were only three or four voices; it was ridiculous for Joseph to cringe with terror.

A gray rainy day has begun. A National Guard officer has just left the following message: *Order from the First Consul—General Bernadotte is to report to him at eleven a.m. in the Tuileries.* I am closing and locking my diary. I shall take it to Julie.

Paris, March 21, 1804

It was mad of me to drive alone at night to the Tuileries to see him. I realized this from the start. Nevertheless, I climbed into Madame Letizia's carriage, still trying to decide what to say to him. I would walk through the long empty corridors of the Tuileries, slip into his study, stand in front of his desk and explain to him that . . . he cannot have the man shot!

Cannot? He can do anything.

As the carriage rolled along, I meditated on the past years. I have danced at weddings, curtsied to Napoleon as though to royalty, celebrated the victory of Marengo at Julie's—all minor events. The big ones have been Oscar's first tooth, Oscar's first "Mama," and Oscar, for the first time without my help, walking on chubby, unsteady little legs from the piano to the chest of drawers. I remembered these years and tried desperately to put off thinking of the moment when I intended to force my way into the presence of the First Consul.

Julie returned my diary just a few days ago. "I was tidying up my chest of drawers," she said, "and I found your book. You'll have a lot to catch up on." Julie laughed. "I don't suppose you've even mentioned that I have two daughters."

"No, I gave you the diary the night after the coup d'état. But now I'll write down that over two and a half years ago Zénaïde Charlotte Julie was born, and thirteen months later, Charlotte Napoleone."

I took the diary from her. I must, first of all, I thought, write that last summer Mama died in Genoa after a heart attack. On the sad day that Etienne's letter arrived with the news, Jean-Baptiste said to me, "A law of nature is that we do not outlive our children. It would be unnatural if we did." He wanted to comfort me, but it was not much comfort, I found.

And now I was driving through the night in Madame Letizia's carriage. On Napoleon's desk lay a sentence of death waiting for a stroke of his pen. What would I say to him?

One may no longer talk with him as with other people. One may not even sit down unless he suggests it. The morning after that endless night of waiting for Jean-Baptiste's arrest words flew between him and Napoleon.

"You have been elected, Bernadotte, to represent the Ministry of War in my State Council," the First Consul told him. "I am responsible for the Republic, and I cannot afford to lose one of her ablest men. Will you accept?"

Jean-Baptiste told me that there was a long pause. A pause in which he looked out of the window at the soldiers of the National Guard with their blue-white-red cockades. A pause in which he told himself that the directors had resigned and had recognized the Consular Government, that the Republic had delivered itself up to this man to avert civil war.

"You are right, the Republic needs each of her citizens, Consul Bonaparte. I therefore accept."

Early the next morning Moreau and all the arrested deputies were set free. Moreau, what's more, was given a command. Napoleon appointed Jean-Baptiste supreme commander of our

Army of the West, guarding the Channel coast against English attacks. Napoleon won the battle of Marengo, and Paris went mad celebrating. Today our troops are scattered all over Europe in the innumerable provinces the Republic now occupies. Napoleon has allowed the exiled aristocrats to come back, and the former great of Versailles move through the rooms of the Tuileries and curtsy before the leader of the Republic.

And the Bonapartes—how they have changed! A couple of weeks after the coup Minister of the Interior Lucien Bonaparte and First Consul Napoleon Bonaparte quarreled terribly: first about the censorship of the press that Napoleon had introduced, then about the banishing of writers. And constantly about Christine, the innkeeper's daughter, who had been forbidden to enter the Tuileries. Lucien didn't last long as minister of the interior. But when Christine took sick, began to cough blood, and then died, the most expensive wreath at her funeral was inscribed: *To my beloved sister-in-law Christine—N. Bonaparte.*

Napoleon then demanded that Lucien marry the daughter of one of the repatriated aristocrats. But Lucien turned up at the registry office with the red-haired widow Jouberthou, who had been married to some unknown bank clerk. Whereupon Napoleon signed an expulsion order against Citizen Lucien Bonaparte. The former minister of the interior of the French Republic left for Italy.

Jérôme Bonaparte, once such a dreadful child, is now a naval officer. On one of his voyages he landed at an American port and married a young lady from Baltimore. This naturally made Napoleon furious. Now Jérôme is on his way home, and, to please his distinguished brother, he has agreed to divorce his American wife. *But she is very rich,* was Jérôme's only written protest to Napoleon.

And it was about two years ago that Napoleon betrothed his stepdaughter, Hortense, to his brother Louis. Louis, a fat, flat-footed youth, preferred an actress at the Comédie Française, and Napoleon feared another mésalliance in the family. Hortense, however, sulked and screamed, and refused to talk to her mother. Finally they sent for Julie.

"Can I help you?" Julie asked. Hortense shook her head. "You love someone else, don't you?" Julie said. Hortense nodded almost imperceptibly. "I'll talk to your stepfather," Julie said.

Hortense shrugged her shoulders hopelessly. "Is this other man married?" Hortense's lips parted and she suddenly laughed. Laughed and laughed—like one gone mad. That finished my patient Julie. Without thinking, she slapped Hortense hard.

Hortense was struck dumb. She took a couple of deep breaths. "I love—*him*," she said softly.

Julie stood up and took Hortense's hand. "You'd better marry Louis. Louis is his favorite brother."

The nuptials were celebrated a few weeks later.

Finally, Paulette, Napoleon's favorite sister, is now a countess. After her General Leclerc was ordered to San Domingo, where he died of yellow fever, Napoleon practically shoved the aging Count Camillo Borghese at Paulette.

They're all so changed, I thought. But why do they think I'm the only one who can, perhaps, still talk to Napoleon?

The carriage was nearing the Tuileries and I thought over my project with some despair. This Bourbon, the Duke of Enghien, who was apparently in the pay of the English and was threatening to restore the Republic to the Bourbons, had been arrested in a small town called Ettenheim in Germany. Four days earlier, on Napoleon's orders, three hundred dragoons had crossed the Rhine, snatched the duke and dragged him to France. Now he was waiting in the fortress at Vincennes for his fate to be decided. A court-martial had condemned him to death for high treason and the death sentence had been sent to the First Consul. The old nobility, now frequent visitors at Josephine's, had naturally implored her to beg Napoleon for clemency. But when Josephine had tried to get a word in at lunch that day, Napoleon had shut her up with a "Please don't bother me."

At supper that night I noticed that Jean-Baptiste was unusually quiet. Suddenly he banged his fist on the table. "Do you realize what Bonaparte has done? With the help of three hundred dragoons he has seized a political enemy in a foreign country and brought him to France for a court-martial. And he's under oath to uphold the Rights of Man."

At that very minute we heard a carriage drive up. "It's after ten," I said. "Much too late for callers."

When Fernand announced, "Madame Letizia Bonaparte," I was astonished.

In recent years Madame Letizia hasn't aged, she seems younger. Her face, which used to be drawn and careworn, is fuller. But she still wears her hair peasant fashion, knotted at the back of her neck. And when she sat down in the drawing room and slowly drew off her light gray gloves, I couldn't help staring at her smooth hands and thinking of those red chapped hands that in the old days were always washing clothes.

"General Bernadotte, do you believe that my son will have this Duke of Enghien shot?" she asked immediately.

"It is not only possible, but very probable."

"General Bernadotte, do you understand the full meaning of this death sentence?" Madame Letizia's eyes were wide. "Murder! My son is about to commit murder. This man was dragged to France by force to be shot. With this shot France will be exposed to the world as a republic in which murder is condoned. I won't have Napoleone become a murderer, do you understand?"

"You should speak to him, madame," Jean-Baptiste suggested.

"No, no, signor—" Her voice shook. "That would do no good. Napoleone would say, 'Mama, you don't understand!' She must go, signor—she, Eugénie."

My heart stood still. I began to shake my head desperately.

"Signor General, you don't know it, but before, when my Napoleone was arrested and we were afraid that he'd be shot, she—Eugénie—rushed to the authorities and helped him. Now she must go to him. She must remind him, and ask him . . ."

"I don't believe it would impress the First Consul," said Jean-Baptiste.

But Madame Letizia didn't give up. "Eugénie—pardon, Signora Bernadotte—help me. If your son, your little Oscar, were about to sign this death sentence . . ."

"Désirée, get ready to drive to the Tuileries." Jean-Baptiste spoke calmly but very firmly.

I got up. "You'll come with me, won't you, Jean-Baptiste?"

"You know, little one, that that would deprive the duke of his last chance." Jean-Baptiste took me in his arms. "You must speak to Napoleon alone. I fear you won't have much success, but you must try, darling." His voice was full of pity.

I still objected. "It wouldn't look well. So many women go to the Tuileries alone at night." All Paris knows that Napoleon is unfaithful to Josephine, so I didn't care whether Madame Letizia heard me or not.

"Put on your hat, take a wrap and go," Jean-Baptiste said.

"Use my carriage, madame," Madame Letizia said. "And, if you don't mind, I'll wait here till you come back."

I nodded mechanically, then hurried to my room and with shaking fingers tied on my new hat with the pale pink roses.

SINCE HARDLY A month goes by that Police Chief Fouché doesn't foil some plot against the First Consul, no one can enter the Tuileries without being stopped every ten steps. Nevertheless, everything went so smoothly that I was painfully embarrassed. Each time I was challenged, I said, "I wish to speak to the First Consul," and was allowed to pass. No one asked me my name or the purpose of my visit. The soldiers merely smiled.

I finally reached the anteroom of the office of the First Consul. The two soldiers standing guard asked me nothing at all, so I opened the door and went in. A young man in civilian clothes sat at a desk writing. I cleared my throat twice before he looked up, startled. "What do you want, mademoiselle?"

"I want to speak to the First Consul."

"You've made a mistake, mademoiselle. These rooms are only offices."

"I wish to speak to the First Consul. Go in and ask him if he can be disturbed for a moment. And don't call me mademoiselle, but madame. I am Madame Jean-Baptiste Bernadotte."

"Mademoi—madame—your pardon—it was a mistake." He disappeared, and returned immediately. "Madame Jean-Baptiste Bernadotte, the First Consul will see you. May I ask Madame to follow me."

"This is the nicest surprise I've had for years." Napoleon was waiting for me at the door. He took my hands and kissed them, first my right hand, then my left. I withdrew my hands quickly, and didn't know what to say.

He urged me into the armchair beside his desk, where I noticed a single document with a blood-red seal. In the fireplace was a roaring fire. It was unbearably hot.

He snatched some printed sheets from a small cluttered table and held them under my nose. "Here are the first copies off the press. The *Code Civil* of the French Republic is completed. The laws for which we fought the Revolution—written down, ready to be enforced, valid forever." Year after year he'd shut himself up with our leading experts on civil law, compiling France's new civil codes. "I have given France the most humane laws in the world," he said. "Read this—this applies to children. The oldest son has no more rights than his brothers and sisters. And here: new marriage laws that make possible not only divorce but also separation."

"People already call it the *Code Napoléon*," I remarked. I wanted him to keep in good humor. He tossed the sheets of paper on the mantelpiece.

"But I'm boring you," he said, coming closer. "Take off your hat, madame. It doesn't suit you at all."

"It's a new hat. Jean-Baptiste says it looks very well on me."

He retreated quickly. "Of course, if the general says so . . ." He began to stride up and down. "May I ask to what I owe the honor of this late visit, madame?" His voice was sharp.

I've annoyed him, I thought miserably, and hastily untied the ribbons on my hat. Then I realized he was close behind me. I felt his hand touch my hair very lightly. "Eugénie," he murmured, "little Eugénie." His voice was as it had been on that rainy night in Marseilles when we became engaged.

"I wanted to ask you something." I heard my voice tremble.

"Naturally," he said cuttingly. "Most people who come to see me now have a favor to ask. What can I do for you, Madame Jean-Baptiste Bernadotte?"

His sneering superiority was more than I could bear. "Had you flattered yourself that I would call on you in the middle of the night unless I had an important reason to?"

My rage seemed to amuse him. "No—but perhaps I secretly hoped you might." I can't even make him take me seriously, I thought. My fingers plucked at the silk roses on my new hat, and a tear trickled down my cheek.

"You are ruining your new hat, madame." I didn't look up. "What can I do to help you, Eugénie?" There he was again—the Napoleon of the old days. Tender, sincere.

"I beg you to reprieve him."

Silence. The fire crackled. "You mean the Duke of Enghien?" I nodded and waited for his answer.

"Who sent you to me with this request, Eugénie?" I plucked at the roses on my hat, tearing off one petal after another. "I asked who sent you? Bernadotte?" I shook my head. "Madame, I am accustomed to having my questions answered."

I looked up. His head was thrust forward, his mouth distorted. "You needn't shout at me, I'm not afraid," I said. And I wasn't.

"I remember that you like to play the role of the courageous young lady. I remember that scene in the Tallien's salon." He hissed the last part.

"I am not at all courageous." I lifted my head and sought his eyes. "I'm actually a coward. But if there's a great deal at stake, I can pull myself together. Once, before that day in Madame Tallien's salon, I was very courageous. That was when my fiancé—you know I was once engaged, long before I met General Bernadotte—when my fiancé was arrested after the fall of Robespierre. We feared he might be shot. His brothers considered it very dangerous, but I went to the military commandant of Marseilles with a parcel of underclothes and a cake . . ."

"Yes. And that's precisely why I must know the person or the persons who sent you here tonight. They know me very well. They have found a possible way to save this Enghien's life—I said only a *possible* way. I am curious. Who knows me well enough and is smart enough to exploit it? And yet is obviously opposed to me politically. Well?"

I smiled. How he complicated, how politically involved everything appeared to him.

"Try, madame, to see the situation through my eyes. The Jacobins reproach me for allowing the *émigrés* to return, and say that I intend to turn over the Republic to the Bourbons. Our France—the France of the *Code Napoléon!* Doesn't that sound like madness?" He went over to the desk and picked up the document with the red seal. "If this Enghien is executed, I shall have proved to France and to the world that I condemn all the Bourbons as dangerous traitors." He was holding the document in one hand. The seal on it looked like a huge drop of blood.

"You asked me who sent me here tonight." I spoke loudly. "Before you make a final decision I will answer your question. It was your mother."

He lowered his hand slowly. "I didn't know my mother was interested in politics," he murmured.

"She doesn't consider this death sentence a political issue."

"But?"

"Murder."

"Eugénie—now you have gone too far!"

"Your mother fervently begged me to talk to you. It's not exactly a pleasure."

The shadow of a smile flitted over his face. He fumbled among a pile of documents on another small table. Finally he found what he wanted. He unrolled a large piece of drawing paper. "How do you like this? I haven't shown it to anyone yet."

In the top corner was a drawing of a large bee. In the center a square buzzing with little bees, spaced out at regular intervals. "Bees?" I asked, startled.

"Yes, bees. It's an emblem that I will use everywhere. On the carpets, curtains, liveries, court carriages, the coronation robes of the Emperor—" He looked at me. "Do you understand me—do you, Eugénie?" He was unrolling another sheet. Lions this time—lions crouching, lions leaping. Now a drawing of an eagle with outspread wings—enormous, menacing. "I've decided on this one for my coat of arms. The coat of arms of the Emperor of the French."

Napoleon stood at the desk again, staring at the document with the red seal. He leaned over, grabbed the pen, wrote a single word on the document and poured sand over it. Then he shook the bronze bell on his desk violently and the secretary hurried in. Napoleon carefully folded up the document. "Sealing wax!" The secretary brought over wax and a candlestick. Napoleon watched him with interest. "Drive to Vincennes immediately and deliver this in person to the commandant of the fortress." With his back to the door, bowing deeply, the secretary left the room.

"I would like to know what you have decided." My heart was pounding, my voice was hoarse.

Napoleon went down on his knees before me and began to gather up the silk rose petals. "You've ruined your hat, madame," he remarked, and gave me a handful of torn petals. "Don't worry about it," he added. "The hat wasn't really becoming to you."

Napoleon escorted me through the corridors of the Tuileries, past guards who saluted noisily, right to the carriage.

"Your mother's carriage. She's waiting for my return. What shall I tell her?"

He bowed. "Wish my mother a pleasant good night. And I thank you kindly for your visit, madame."

In our parlor I found Madame Letizia right where I had left her, in the armchair at the window. The sky was already light. "Did he send a message to Vincennes?" she asked.

I nodded. "Yes, he did, but he wouldn't tell me what he had decided. He told me to wish you a pleasant good night, madame."

"Thank you, my child," Madame Letizia answered and rose. At the door she turned. "In any event—thank you."

Jean-Baptiste took me in his arms and carried me up to the bedroom. "Did you know that Napoleon intends to be crowned Emperor?" I murmured. "He told me himself."

Jean-Baptiste stared at me, then left and went into the dressing room. I heard him pacing up and down in there for a long time. I couldn't get to sleep until finally I felt him next to me and I could bury my face in his shoulder.

I slept late. Marie brought me my breakfast in bed and a late edition of the *Moniteur*. On the first page I read that this morning at five o'clock in the fortress at Vincennes the Duke of Enghien had been shot.

A few hours later Madame Letizia left Paris to join her exiled son Lucien in Italy.

Paris, May 20, 1804

"Her Imperial Highness, Princess of the French—" Fernand announced this morning. And in swished my sister, Julie.

"*Madame la maréchale*, I trust you slept well," Julie said.

"Very well, thank you, Imperial Highness," I replied with the deep curtsy Monsieur Montel had taught me.

"I've come early," said my sister. "I'm so worried by this big move to the Luxembourg Palace."

Marie, who had brought us lemonade, remarked sarcastically, "The lovely villa in the rue du Rocher is no longer good enough for the Princess Julie."

"You're unjust, Marie," Julie said. "I hate palaces. But the heirs to the French throne always have lived in the Luxembourg."

Julie, wife of the heir apparent to the throne of France, looked uncomfortable. But Marie had no sympathy. "The late Monsieur Clary wouldn't have approved. Your papa was a real Republican."

"Leave us alone awhile, Marie," I begged. "We will sit and drink our lemonade."

The lemonade was just like the last few days: sweet—bittersweet. My Jean-Baptiste has been made a marshal of France, every soldier's dream. For my husband the dream's come true, only not at all in the way we'd imagined it.

After the execution of the Duke of Enghien I was worried about Jean-Baptiste. General Moreau and certain other officers were arrested and accused of conspiring with the Royalists. But Jean-Baptiste, just as before, was summoned to the Tuileries by the First Consul.

"The French nation has chosen me. You will not oppose the Republic?"

"I have never opposed the Republic," answered Jean-Baptiste quietly.

Then everything happened in rapid succession. Jean-Baptiste was instructed in strictest confidence to order a marshal's uniform from his tailor. General Moreau was found guilty of high treason, but not condemned to death, only exiled. He sailed for America, wearing his French general's uniform. The day before yesterday Consul General Napoleon Bonaparte allowed himself to be surprised by the decision of the Senate to elect him Emperor. Yes, Napoleon has been proclaimed Emperor of the French.

Yesterday, against the backdrop of an imposing military parade, "His Majesty" presented marshals' batons to the eighteen most famous generals in the French Army. After the presentation he advanced on Jean-Baptiste with that solicitous smile, seized his hand and urged him to consider him "not only your Emperor, but also your friend." Jean-Baptiste never moved a muscle.

I watched this ceremony from a platform erected for the wives of the eighteen new marshals, holding Oscar by the hand. Although he wasn't invited, I thought Oscar should see his papa made a marshal of France.

Julie was on the platform reserved for the imperial family. Since an emperor must have a distinguished family, Napoleon had designated his brothers—with the exception of Lucien, of course—imperial princes, and their wives imperial princesses. Joseph will be recognized as the successor to the throne until Napoleon has a son. Madame Letizia's title raised quite a problem. Napoleon finally decided to present her to the nation as *Madame Mère. Madame Mère*, incidentally, is still in Italy with Lucien. Hortense, the wife of the flat-footed Prince Louis, has now become a princess by marriage. Eugène de Beauharnais, son of Her Majesty, the Empress Josephine, will also be called prince. Napoleon's sisters had not been elevated to imperial princesses. But Caroline stood next to me during the ceremony, being, like me, a *madame la maréchale*. Just before the fall of the Directorate she had married Napoleon's friend General Murat, who had served with him in Egypt and now was made a marshal of France also.

Tonight the eighteen marshals and their wives dined with the imperial family in the Tuileries. The walls, carpets and curtains swarmed with gold embroidered bees. Many hundreds of sewing women must have worked day and night to finish these decorations in time.

"Where will it all end?" said I tactlessly to Julie.

"You're making a great mistake, Désirée, not taking Napoleon seriously," Julie said.

"You forget. I was the very first person under the sun who did take him seriously," I told her.

In our carriage on the way home I asked, "What are you thinking about, Jean-Baptiste?"

"About the collar of my marshal's uniform. It's too tight and makes me uncomfortable." He began to loosen his collar. I watched him. "The uniform is too small for you," I said.

"That's true, my little girl. The marshal's uniform *is* too small for Sergeant Bernadotte."

When we got out of the carriage at our house a group of young men in shabby clothes immediately descended on us. "*Vive Bernadotte!*" they shouted. "*Vive Bernadotte!*"

Jean-Baptiste hesitated a fraction of a second. "*Vive l'Empereur*," he finally answered.

But when we were alone together, he remarked, "You will be interested to hear that the Emperor has given the police minister confidential instructions to watch over not only the private lives but also the private correspondence of his marshals."

I thought this over, then said, "Julie told me that in the winter he will be crowned. He will have the Pope come to Paris for the occasion."

Jean-Baptiste shook his head. "But that is impossible, Désirée. The Pope never leaves the Vatican to crown anyone in a foreign country. Nothing like that has ever happened."

"Joseph says that Napoleon will force the Pope to come here."

Jean-Baptiste stared straight ahead. Suddenly he said, "I will ask Napoleon for some independent administrative post, preferably far away from Paris. Perhaps command of an entire province. Not only military command, do you understand? I believe I could make any province prosper. Then I will show them!"

"Whom will you show what?"

"How to run a country. I'll show the Emperor and all his generals."

"But then you'd have to go away again," I objected in despair.

"I will have to go away in any event. Bonaparte will never bring France lasting peace. And we marshals will be riding all over Europe with our armies until"—he paused—"we have killed ourselves with victories."

Paris, November 30, 1804

Who should arrive in Paris a few days ago with a retinue of six cardinals, four archbishops, six prelates and a whole army of personal physicians, secretaries, soldiers of the Swiss Guard and lackeys? Pius VII. The Pontiff has actually come to Paris to crown Napoleon and Josephine.

The coronation will be in two days. For months Paris has talked of nothing else. Members of the imperial family have been rehearsing for weeks. This afternoon we, too, the wives of the eighteen marshals, were ordered to the Tuileries to rehearse the Empress's coronation procession. When I got there I was shown into Josephine's white salon. Napoleon's three sisters were quarreling over His Majesty's expressed wish that they and his sisters-in-law carry Her Majesty's coronation robe train.

"Carry her train indeed. Don't make me laugh." This, indignantly, from Paulette.

"Even if he throws me out of France, like poor Lucien," yelped Elisa Bacciocchi, "I won't do it."

"But Julie and Hortense have to carry the train, too, and they aren't objecting, although they're both imperial highnesses," Joseph said, trying to calm his sisters.

"Imperial highnesses," hissed Caroline. "And why weren't we, the Emperor's own sisters, called highnesses?"

"Ladies, I implore you," moaned the master of ceremonies, Despréaux.

"Now—can we begin the rehearsal?" Josephine had entered by

a side door. To her shoulders were fastened two sheets sewn together to represent the enormous train of the coronation robe, which hadn't been finished. We all sank down in a court curtsy.

Despréaux sidled over to us. "The eighteen marshals' wives will unfortunately be seventeen," he announced. "For, as a sister of the Emperor, Madame Murat will help carry the train. Now," he mused, "I don't see how seventeen ladies can form pairs and go two by two to precede Her Majesty."

"May I help you work out this difficult strategic operation?" asked someone behind us. We turned, and sank again into a deep court curtsy. "I suggest that only sixteen marshals' wives lead Her Majesty's procession. Then will follow, as arranged, Marshal Sérurier with Her Majesty's ring, Murat with her crown, and finally one of the marshals' wives carrying—a cushion with Her Majesty's lace handkerchief. It will be a very poetic touch."

"A stroke of genius, Your Majesty," exclaimed Despréaux, bent double in one of his best bows.

"And this lady with the lace handkerchief . . ." Napoleon peered reflectively at us. I already knew but I didn't want to. "We will ask Madame Jean-Baptiste Bernadotte to assume this responsibility," the Emperor said, and turned to his sisters.

Paulette started right in. "Sire, we do not wish—"

"Madame, you forget yourself" came like the crack of a whip from Napoleon. No one may address the Emperor without his speaking first. He turned to Joseph. "More trouble?"

"Sire, the ladies Bacciocchi and Murat and the Countess Borghese don't want to carry the Empress's train," Joseph said.

"Then Their Imperial Highnesses, the Princesses Julie and Hortense Bonaparte, will carry the train alone," Napoleon decided.

"The train is much too heavy for two alone," said Josephine, gathering her sheets around her and going over to Napoleon.

"If we can't have the same privileges as Julie and Hortense, we won't take on the same duties," Elisa burst out.

"Quiet!" Napoleon shouted. "My sisters seem to forget that any distinctions they receive depend on my bounty."

In the deafening silence Josephine's voice rippled like a gentle melody. "Sire, I beg that in your graciousness you raise your sisters to imperial highnesses."

She needs allies, went through my head; she's afraid. Perhaps the rumors are true, perhaps he really is considering a divorce. . . .

Napoleon began to laugh. The scene had apparently amused him enormously. "All right," he said to his sisters, "if you promise to behave."

"Sire!" screamed Elisa and Caroline delightedly. Paulette relapsed into, *"Napoleone, molti grazie!"*

"I would like to see Her Majesty's coronation procession," Napoleon said abruptly. "Proceed!"

So we marched in order up and down the room several times, stopping only when Napoleon turned to leave. At that, of course, we curtsied again.

Then refreshments were served and Josephine sent a lady-in-waiting to ask me over to her sofa. She wanted me to know that she was pleased about my distinguished new duty. She sat between Julie and me and gulped champagne. Her eyes, under the silver lids, looked unnaturally large. But the curls, piled high on her head, looked, as always, young and carefree.

Suddenly Joseph stood before us. "His Majesty requests Your Majesty to come to his study at once. The Pope refuses to crown you."

Josephine's small rouged mouth smiled derisively. "And on what grounds does the Holy Father refuse?"

Joseph looked discreetly in every direction. "The Pope has learned that His Majesty and Your Majesty had only a civil ceremony, and were not married in a church. He has declared—pardon me, these are the words of the Holy Father—that he cannot crown the concubine of the Emperor of the French."

Josephine thoughtfully studied her empty glass. "And how has His Majesty decided to answer the Holy Father?"

"His Majesty will probably argue with the Pope."

"There's one very simple solution." Josephine smiled and rose. "We'll be married in a church. Then everything will be in order."

While Joseph dashed after Josephine so as not to miss her conversation with Napoleon, Julie said thoughtfully, "I wonder if she didn't tell the Pope herself. She's so afraid of a divorce, and it would be horrid of him to leave her now. Just because she can't have any more children."

"But after a church ceremony it won't be so easy for him to get a divorce."

"He does love her," Julie said. "He can't let her down."

"Believe me," I said. "Napoleon can . . ."

There was a rustle of gowns all through the room. Everyone curtsied. The Empress had returned. Josephine took a glass of champagne and came over to Julie and me. "Tonight a cardinal is going to marry us quietly in the palace chapel. Isn't that funny after almost nine years of marriage?"

At home Jean-Baptiste was waiting for me in the dining room. "What kept you so long in the Tuileries?" he demanded.

"I listened to the Bonapartes quarrel with one another. Then we rehearsed. And I've been given a special part—carrying a handkerchief for Josephine on a cushion. Isn't that an honor?"

"I don't want you to take a special part. I forbid it."

I sighed. "The Emperor wishes it."

I would never have believed that anything could so upset Jean-Baptiste. His voice was almost shrill. "And I can't endure it. My wife can't expose herself before the whole world."

"Why are you so angry?" I asked.

"They'll point at you. They'll say, Madame Jean-Baptiste Bernadotte, the Emperor's young love, whom he cannot forget. Now, as before, his little Eugénie. And I'll be the laughingstock of Paris."

I just gaped at Jean-Baptiste. No one knows as well as I how strained his relationship with Napoleon is. How he is tortured by the constant feeling that he has betrayed the Republican ideals of his youth. How impatiently he waits for approval of his request for an independent command far away from Paris. And Napoleon lets him wait, wait, wait. But I certainly never expected this jealous scene. I went to him. "There's no sense letting a whim of Napoleon's upset you, Jean-Baptiste."

He pushed me away. "He's in love with you. He wants to make you happy so that you—"

"Jean-Baptiste!"

He put his hand to his forehead. "Forgive me, it's not your fault," he murmured. At that moment Fernand appeared and set the soup tureen on the table. Silently we took our places. Jean-Baptiste's hand, raising the spoon to his mouth, shook.

"I won't take part in the coronation ceremonies," I said. "I'll stay in bed and be sick."

Jean-Baptiste didn't answer. After dinner he left the house.

Now, sitting at his desk writing, I'm trying to decide whether Napoleon really is in love with me again. That interminable night in his office, before the Duke of Enghien was shot, he spoke to me in his long-ago voice. I believe that night he remembered the hedge in our garden in Marseilles. How strange that in two days the little Bonaparte of the hedge will be crowned Emperor of the French.

The clock in the dining room struck midnight. Where is Jean-Baptiste? Tomorrow I'll stay in bed with a terrible cold, and the next day, too. I'll beg to be excused. . . .

LAST NIGHT—NO, it was already today—I fell asleep over my diary. I woke up only when someone took me in his arms and carried me to the bedroom. The gold braid on the epaulets scratched my cheeks as usual. "I love you very much, Jean-Baptiste," I muttered sleepily. "And I'm seriously ill with a cold in the head and a sore throat and can't take part in the coronation ceremony of the mighty Emperor of the French."

"I will convey Madame Bernadotte's regrets to the Emperor." And after a while: "You must never forget, little one, that I love you very much. Do you hear me, or are you already asleep?"

Paris, the night after Napoleon's coronation, December 2, 1804

Things didn't happen as I'd planned. The day before yesterday Jean-Baptiste explained to the master of ceremonies that a heavy cold and high fever would keep me from the coronation. I actually stayed in bed all that day. But by yesterday morning I was so bored, I dressed and went to the nursery, and Oscar and I killed a National Guardsman—I mean a toy one. We wanted to see what the head was stuffed with. It turned out to be sawdust, which spewed out all over the floor.

Suddenly the door opened. Fernand announced Napoleon's personal physician and showed Dr. Corvisart into the nursery, where he bowed to me politely and said, "His Majesty has asked me to inquire about Madame's health. I am glad I can inform him that Madame has recovered."

"Doctor, I still feel very weak," I said hopelessly.

Dr. Corvisart raised his eyebrows. "I believe I can reconcile with my conscience the opinion that Madame is strong enough to carry Her Majesty's lace handkerchief at the coronation. I urgently advise you to be there." Then he picked up his black bag and left.

In the afternoon my rose-colored coronation dress and the white ostrich feathers to wear in my hair were delivered from the couturier firm of Le Roy. Later snow began to fall, and at six o'clock a sudden cannon blast set our windows rattling. I ran to the kitchen and asked Fernand what was wrong. "Every hour, from now until midnight, salutes will be fired," he said, and went on polishing Jean-Baptiste's sword with fanatical zeal.

I went up to the nursery and sat by the window with Oscar on my lap. It was already dark, but I lighted no candles. Oscar and I watched the snowflakes dancing in the lantern light in front of our house. They reminded me of my Swedish friend, Persson.

"There is a city," I said, "where the snow falls every winter for many months. And the whole sky looks freshly washed."

"What city?" Oscar asked.

"Stockholm. And it's far, far away."

"Does Stockholm belong to the Emperor?"

"No, Oscar. Stockholm has its own king."

Again the cannon roared. Oscar flung his arms around me. "You mustn't be afraid," I said. "They're only cannon saluting the Emperor."

Oscar looked at me. "I'm not a bit afraid of cannon, Mama. And someday I'll be a marshal of France, like Papa. Or a sergeant. Fernand was a sergeant, too." He was excited. "Fernand says I can go to the coronation with him tomorrow."

"Oh, no, Oscar, children aren't allowed in the cathedral."

"But Fernand will take me to the door of the cathedral and we can see the whole procession. Please, Mama!"

"When you are bigger, you may see a coronation," I heard myself saying.

"But will the Emperor be crowned again later?" asked Oscar.

"No, but we will go, Oscar, both of us. Mama promises you. And it will be a much more beautiful coronation than the one tomorrow. . . ."

"Madame shouldn't tell the child such tales." Marie's voice came from the darkness behind us. She lit the nursery candles, and I left my place at the window. I couldn't see the dancing snowflakes anymore.

Later Jean-Baptiste came up to tell Oscar good night. Then, for the first time in ages, I prepared our evening meal myself. Marie, Fernand and the kitchen maid were all out. Free performances were being given at every theater. Yvette, my new lady's maid, had vanished at noon. Julie had explained to me that a marshal's wife can neither do her own hair nor sew on buttons, so I had finally hired this Yvette, who before the Revolution had powdered some duchess's hair and naturally considers herself far grander than I.

After supper we went to the kitchen. I washed the dishes and my marshal put on Marie's apron and dried them. "I always used to help my mother," he remarked. Then: "Joseph told me the Emperor's personal physician came to see you."

"In this city everyone knows everyone else's business." I sighed.

"No," said Jean-Baptiste, "not everyone, but the Emperor knows a great deal about a great many people. That's his system."

WHEN WE AWOKE in the morning it had stopped snowing, but it was colder. While Fernand was helping Jean-Baptiste into his uniform, Yvette arranged the white ostrich feathers in my hair. I sat at my dressing table and stared in horror at the mirror. With this headdress I looked like a circus horse.

Marie flung open the door. "This has just been delivered for you, Eugénie. It's from the imperial household."

Yvette took the little red leather box and laid it before me. Marie naturally didn't leave; Jean-Baptiste came and stood over me. I looked up and met his eyes in the dressing-table mirror. Napoleon has surely thought up something dreadful and Jean-Baptiste will be furious, I thought. My hands shook as I pressed the lock and the box flew open. Inside was a small jewel box of sparkling gold. On the lid hovered an imperial eagle with outstretched wings.

"Open it," Jean-Baptiste ordered.

I pulled off the lid. There, on red velvet, sparkled—gold pieces. I looked at Jean-Baptiste. His face was very pale. "They're gold francs," I murmured, and sifted the top coins through my fingers. Something rustled. I pulled out a piece of paper from among the gold pieces. Napoleon's handwriting— large uneven letters that danced before my eyes, then finally formed words.

*Madame la maréchale, In Marseilles you were kind enough
to lend me your secret savings so that I might travel to Paris.
This journey has brought me good fortune. It is an obligation
that I take pleasure in meeting today, and thank you. N.*

"Ninety-eight gold francs, Jean-Baptiste," I said, and then explained in a rush. "I had saved up my pocket money to buy the
Emperor a decent uniform, his old one was so shabby, but he
needed the money to pay his debts."

I was greatly relieved when Jean-Baptiste smiled.

We arrived at the archbishop's palace shortly before nine
o'clock and were shown into a large room on the upper floor,
where we greeted the other marshals and their wives. We all
crowded near the windows and looked down on the milling
throng at the portals of Notre-Dame. The prefect of police had
stopped all traffic, so the specially invited ladies and gentlemen
arrived at the cathedral on foot, shivering as they scurried
through the cold. A few carriages drove up anyway—foreign
princes invited as guests of honor.

I watched the arrival of a battalion of dragoons and the Swiss
Guard following. Then came the Pontiff's carriage, drawn by
eight gray horses, and we immediately recognized the Empress's
gala coach, which had been placed at the Pope's disposal. The
Pope came into the archbishop's palace, but we had no chance to
welcome him. He donned his vestments in a downstairs room,
left the palace at the head of the highest ecclesiastical dignitaries
and walked slowly toward Notre-Dame.

The crowd kept silent. Only a few women knelt as the Pope
passed, while most of the men didn't even take off their hats. The
Pope made the sign of the cross in the clear frosty air, then
disappeared through the portals. Like a red wave, the ranks of
cardinals closed in behind him.

"It's time right now for the Emperor's arrival," someone said.
But the Emperor kept the people of Paris, the marching regi-
ments, the distinguished guests and the head of the Holy Roman
Church waiting for him another whole hour.

At last a salvo of cannon proclaimed that the Emperor had left
the Tuileries. Suddenly we were all silent. The valets handed the
marshals their blue capes, which they flung over their shoulders.
Then, instinctively, we all lined up.

It sounded like a rumbling storm—first far away, then louder, and finally raging: *"Vive l'Empereur . . .Vive l'Empereur . . ."*

First, on horseback and in gold-laden uniform, came the governor of Paris. Behind him thundered the dragoons. Then mounted heralds in embroidered lilac velvet, carrying staffs embellished with gold bees. Such splendor dumbfounded me. And once, I thought, I saved my pocket money to buy him a new uniform. One gilded carriage after another discharged passengers—the Emperor's aides, then the ministers, and finally the imperial princesses, all in white, wearing coronets in their hair. Julie came over to me quickly and squeezed my hand. "Fix your coronet," I whispered. "It's crooked."

Like the sun suddenly emerging on this gray wintry day came the Emperor's carriage, gilded all over and decorated with golden palm leaves. On top gleamed four enormous bronze eagles, their claws clutching laurel branches and a large golden crown. The coach was lined with green velvet, the Corsican color. Eight horses with white feather plumes snorted to a stop.

In one corner of the carriage sat the Emperor, dressed in purplish-red velvet, and when he alighted, we saw he wore wide breeches and white silk stockings embroidered with jewels. He looked very strange, like an opera star with too-short legs.

The Empress, on the other hand, sitting at his left, looked more beautiful than ever. In her curls shone the largest diamond I had ever seen. And Josephine's smile—radiant and young—came from her heart. The Emperor had had a religious marriage ceremony performed, she had nothing more to worry about. . . .

In the palace Napoleon and Josephine quickly put on their coronation robes. For a second Josephine's mouth tightened with the strain of standing erect under the weight of her purple robe. But then Julie and Hortense, Elisa, Paulette and Caroline picked up the train. Napoleon laboriously pulled on a pair of gloves, the fingers stiff with gold embroidery. "Can we begin?" he said.

Despréaux had already distributed all our paraphernalia. Now we awaited his signal to take up our rehearsed positions. But Napoleon had turned away and was studying himself in a mirror. Not a muscle in his face moved. The ermine collar of his coronation robe reached nearly up to his ears, and I remembered how he had stared into another mirror just before he sailed for Egypt. "The crown of France lies in the gutter," he had said. "One need only bend down and pick it up." Well, Napoleon had bent down and fished the crown out of the gutter. The imperial crown.

Our embarrassed whispers and aimless standing about reminded me of a funeral. I looked at Jean-Baptiste, who was holding the velvet cushion with the Emperor's Chain of the Legion of Honor that he had to carry in the procession. Now, Papa, I thought, we carry the Republic to its grave, and your daughter Julie is a princess and wears a small gold crown. . . .

"What are we waiting for?" Napoleon sounded impatient. "We will go to the cathedral."

Fanfares blared forth. Slowly and solemnly we began moving toward the cathedral, passing the crowds held back by a cordon of soldiers. The air was icy cold. I held the cushion with Josephine's lace handkerchief like some sacrificial offering and stared straight ahead. As I entered Notre-Dame, music from the organ and the smell of incense wiped out all thought.

Not until we came to the choir did I see the altar and the two gold thrones on the right. On the throne at the left sat, still as a statue, a little old gentleman in white—Pius VII. I looked around and saw Josephine approaching the altar, smiling ecstatically. At the lowest step to the double throne at the right of the altar, she paused. I craned my neck to see Napoleon's entrance.

First came Marshal Kellermann with the large imperial crown. After him, other marshals with the scepter, the orb and Charlemagne's sword. Then Jean-Baptiste with the Chain of the Legion of Honor, next Eugène de Beauharnais with the Emperor's ring, and finally the lame foreign minister, Talleyrand, with a gold wire contraption into which the Emperor was to let fall his robe during the ceremony.

The exultant notes of the "Marseillaise" poured triumphantly from the organ. The song of Marseilles, song of my girlhood. Once I had stood in my nightgown on the balcony of our white villa and tossed roses down to our volunteers: to Franchon, the tailor, and to the shoemaker's bowlegged son, and the Levi brothers in their Sunday suits—citizens all, marching away to defend the young Republic against the whole world.

Napoleon walked slowly up to the altar, with his brothers Joseph and Louis carrying the train of his purple robe. Finally he stood beside Josephine. His brothers and the marshals lined up together behind him. The Pope rose and said the mass.

Then Marshal Kellermann stepped forward and held out the crown to the Pope. Napoleon let the purple robe slip from his shoulders to be caught by Talleyrand. Solemnly the Pope pronounced the blessing, then held high the heavy crown to set it on Napoleon's bowed head.

But Napoleon's hands in his gold-embroidered gloves reached up. He impetuously seized the crown, held it above his head for a short second, then put it on. Napoleon had violated all the rituals of coronation. He had crowned himself.

The organ swelled; the sword, the orb and the golden scepter were presented to the Emperor. Jean-Baptiste dropped the Chain of the Legion of Honor around his neck and Talleyrand put the purple robe back on his shoulders. The Emperor slowly ascended the steps to his throne. *"Vivat Imperator in aeternum,"* proclaimed the Pope.

Thereupon Pius VII made the sign of the cross before Josephine's face and kissed her on the cheek. At this point Murat was to have handed him Josephine's crown. But Napoleon had already covered the short distance from his throne and held out his hands. So Murat gave the crown not to the Pope but to Napoleon. For the first time that day the Emperor smiled, and he very carefully set the crown on Josephine's childish curls. Escorted by Napoleon, Josephine moved toward the throne, and the Pope and his entourage withdrew.

Napoleon, his face expressionless, sat next to Josephine on the double throne and stared straight ahead. I was standing in the front row below and couldn't take my eyes off him. What does a man think about when he has just crowned himself Emperor of the French? A muscle twitched near his mouth, he clamped his lips together firmly and suppressed a yawn.

"Does the Emperor wear his crown in bed at night?" Oscar asked as I put him to bed that evening.

"No, I don't think so," I said.

"Perhaps it's too heavy," Oscar decided.

I had to laugh. "Too heavy? No, darling, Napoleon doesn't find the crown the least bit heavy; quite the opposite."

Two hours later I danced the Viennese waltz for the first time in my life, at a really large reception given by Joseph for all the foreign princes and diplomats and also for all the marshals.

Although I'd practiced waltz steps at Monsieur Montel's, I didn't really know how to dance to these sweet three-quarter tunes. But Jean-Baptiste showed me. He held me very close and counted in his sergeant's voice, "One, two, three—one, two, three—" At first I felt like a recruit. But he gradually relaxed, and as we turned and whirled, the ballroom in the Luxembourg seemed a surging sea of lights, and I felt him kiss the top of my head.

Someone shouted, "A toast to the Emperor!" Glasses clinked.

"Let's go on dancing," I whispered, "on and on—"

Jean-Baptiste kissed my hair again. The crystal chandeliers sparkled in a thousand colors and the whole ballroom revolved around us. One, two, three—don't think back, but only of Jean-Baptiste's lips and dancing the waltz. . . .

In a stagecoach between Hanover, in Germany, and Paris,
September 1805

We were very happy in Hanover—Jean-Baptiste, Oscar and I. The valuable parquet floor in the royal palace was the only real bone of contention. "That Oscar thinks the ballroom floor was built for the son of the military governor to slide on doesn't surprise me. He is a six-year-old child. But that you—" Jean-Baptiste would shake his head but his eyes would smile. And every time I'd promise never again to take a running start and slide with a swish across the shining floor of the ballroom of the former kings of Hanover, now occupied by Monseigneur Jean-Baptiste, marshal of France, governor of the kingdom of Hanover. But the next day I couldn't resist the temptation, and away we'd go, sliding again, Oscar and I. It was really scandalous; for, after all, I was the first lady of Hanover, and even had a small court, consisting of a reader, a lady-in-waiting and the wives of my husband's officers. Unfortunately, I sometimes forgot.

Yes, we were happy in Hanover. And Hanover was happy with us. That sounds odd, for Hanover was conquered territory and Jean-Baptiste the commander of an army of occupation. But my husband had started planning how to govern the country justly and efficiently the moment Napoleon announced, two weeks after the coronation, that he had at last approved Jean-Baptiste's request for an independent command and that Marshal Bernadotte would become governor of Hanover.

Jean-Baptiste began his "rule" in this Germanic country by introducing the Rights of Man. Corporal punishment was forbidden; the ghettos were abolished. A former sergeant knows how to feed soldiers, so requisitions on the citizens of Hanover to maintain our troops weren't oppressive. Jean-Baptiste set the tax rate, and the citizens' earnings increased, for he also did away with customs barriers; Hanover is like an island in the middle of war-devastated Germany, trading in every direction. When the citizens of Hanover became really wealthy, Jean-Baptiste raised their taxes a little. With this extra revenue he bought grain and sent it to northern Germany, where there was a famine. The people of Hanover were puzzled that a marshal of France should do this for his poor conquered enemies, but no one can long resent anyone who treats him like a decent human being.

And Jean-Baptiste was happy working. From six o'clock in the morning until late at night he would pore over files of documents on his desk. Occasionally I'd also find him reading fat volumes. "How much an uneducated sergeant has to learn," he'd say. "But I'm learning, little girl. And I want to do my best. If only things stay quiet." We both knew what he meant.

After supper our officers and their ladies usually sat in my salon and we discussed the news from Paris. The Emperor was apparently still preparing his invasion of England. And Josephine was running up more debts, but this was only mentioned in whispers. Sometimes Jean-Baptiste invited professors from the university, who tried to explain their ideas to us in atrocious French. One of them read a play to us in German, by an author named Goethe. Another told us about a great physician in Göttingen who has restored many people's hearing. This particularly interested Jean-Baptiste. "I have a Viennese friend who must go to Göttingen and see this professor. I'll write him. He can also visit us, Désirée. He's a musician I met in Vienna when I was ambassador. A friend of Kreutzer—you remember him!"

Never will I forget the evening the Viennese musician, whose name is Beethoven, spent with us. Monsieur Beethoven is a middle-sized, thickset man with the wildest hair ever seen in our dining room. His round face has pockmarks and a flat nose. Since I knew the poor man was deaf, I shouted right at him how very pleased I was to have him with us. Jean-Baptiste asked, mostly out of politeness, for the latest news from Vienna. But the musician answered earnestly, "Vienna is prepared for war. It expects the Emperor's armies to attack Austria."

Jean-Baptiste wrinkled his brow. He hadn't wanted to be taken so literally. "How do the musicians in my orchestra play?" he put in quickly. Jean-Baptiste had given instructions that all the members of the former royal Hanover orchestra be placed at this Beethoven's disposal and rehearse with him three whole mornings in the great hall.

The stocky man merely shrugged his shoulders. Jean-Baptiste repeated the question as loudly as possible. The musician raised his heavy eyebrows, the eyes blinked mischievously. "I understood you perfectly, Marshal Bernadotte. The members of your orchestra play very badly."

After supper we all took our seats in the great ballroom. The members of the orchestra uneasily tuned their instruments and peered at us shyly. Herr van Beethoven walked among them, giving them final instructions in German. Then he turned and came over to us. "I had intended dedicating this symphony to General Bernadotte," he remarked thoughtfully. "It might be more correct now to dedicate it to the Emperor of the French. But"—he paused—"we shall see."

The awkward figure climbed up on the podium. He rapped on the music stand with his baton. It was dead still. He spread out his arms, swung them up and—it began. Music that rejoiced and shouted, enticed and promised. Like a prayer and like a cry of triumph. I leaned forward to look at Jean-Baptiste. His face was stony, but his eyes shone.

None of us had noticed that a courier had appeared at the door with a letter. An aide-de-camp got up quietly, looked fleetingly at the sealed message and then went immediately to Jean-Baptiste. My husband took the letter and began to read. Then he wrote a few words on the pad he always carries with him. The aide-de-camp disappeared with the message.

Jean-Baptiste was no longer erect, his eyes no longer shone with rapture. Only at the end—when once again the soaring music sang of freedom, equality and brotherhood—did Jean-Baptiste lift his head and listen. There was a storm of applause. Herr van Beethoven bowed awkwardly, obviously embarrassed, and indicated the musicians, of whom he had been so scornful. They rose and we applauded some more.

"Thank you, Beethoven," Jean-Baptiste said. "With all my heart, I thank you."

The pockmarked face shone happily. "Do you still remember, General, how one evening at your embassy in Vienna you played the 'Marseillaise' for me?"

"On the piano, with one finger. That's all I can do." Jean-Baptiste laughed.

"That was when I first heard it. The anthem of a free people—I often thought of that evening while I was writing this symphony. That's why I wanted to dedicate it to you, a young general of the French people."

I noted that three aides now stood behind Jean-Baptiste, their faces tense, but he waved them away.

"Then came a younger man who carried the message of your people beyond the French frontiers—beyond all frontiers." Again Beethoven paused. "So I thought I should dedicate the symphony to him. What do you think, General Bernadotte?"

"Monseigneur," one of the aides whispered.

Jean-Baptiste drew himself up and passed his hand across his face as though to wipe away a memory. "Herr van Beethoven, I thank you for your concert." He turned toward our guests. "I must bid you farewell. Tomorrow morning early I ride with my troops to the front." Jean-Baptiste bowed and smiled. "The Emperor's orders. Good night, ladies and gentlemen."

He offered me his arm.

WHEN JEAN-BAPTISTE took leave of me at dawn he said, "You and Oscar must return to Paris today, little girl. Give him a big kiss for me, and write often. The Ministry of War will—"

"—forward my letters. I know." I held his hand against my face. "Jean-Baptiste, will this never end? Will it always go on?"

"The Emperor's orders: Conquer and occupy Bavaria. You are married to a marshal of France; it shouldn't surprise you." His voice was expressionless.

"And when you've conquered Bavaria?"

A big shrug. "From Bavaria we march against Austria."

"And then? Why does Napoleon make the young men march into still more new wars, still more new victories? The frontiers of France have not needed to be defended for a long time. France has no more frontiers, France—"

"France is Europe," said Jean-Baptiste, "and France's officers march, my child. The Emperor's orders."

Later that morning, as I prepared to leave Hanover, Herr van Beethoven was announced. I already had my hat on my head and Oscar was beside me, proudly clasping his little traveling bag. Beethoven bowed clumsily.

"I'd be pleased," he said, "if you would tell General Bernadotte that I cannot, after all, dedicate the new symphony to the Emperor of the French. Him least of all." He paused. "I will call the symphony *Eroica*—in memory of a hope that was never fulfilled." He sighed. "General Bernadotte will understand."

"I'm sure he'll understand," I said, and held out my hand.

"Do you know, Mama, what I want to be?" asked Oscar as our coach rolled along the endless country roads. "I want to be a musician, a composer like this Herr van Beethoven. Or—a king!"

"Why a king?"

"Because a king can do good for a lot of people."

Paris, June 4, 1806

It's spring and Jean-Baptiste still hasn't come home. His letters are short and tell me nothing. He's governing in Ansbach, trying to introduce there the reforms he did in Hanover.

One day Julie took me unawares. There she was in the salon in a great state of excitement. "I have become a queen," she said, "Queen of Naples." She was very pale. "Oh, Désirée, it's terrible. We'll have to go to Italy again and live in one of those monstrous marble palaces. I'm so scared." Julie hid her face in her hands, and I went over to comfort her. "I'm just not equal to the task," she cried. "More receptions, more court balls, and in a foreign country. We'll have to leave Paris—"

Julie paused. Suddenly she smiled at me. "And it's all your fault. You brought Joseph to our house in the first place."

I smiled, too. "So, I take it congratulations are in order," I said. "Your daughters are princesses now, and everything will be for the best."

"The Emperor has decided to change the occupied territories into independent states that can be ruled by the imperial princes and princesses. We—Joseph and I—will rule Naples and Sicily. Elisa is Duchess of Lucca. And Louis and Hortense, King and

Queen of Holland. Murat, since he's married to Caroline, will be Duke of Kleve and Berg. Caroline would be offended if she didn't get the revenue from some country or other. And someone has to rule these places we've conquered," said Julie.

"Who conquered them?" I asked pointedly.

Julie didn't answer. "I have to go now. Le Roy is making my robes of state. And I must pack," she moaned. "Will you come with me?"

"No, I'm waiting for my husband. Sometime he has to come home."

I heard no more from the Queen of Naples until this morning, when a carriage drove up. My heart stopped, as it does every time an unexpected carriage draws up in front of my house. But it was not Jean-Baptiste.

Oscar ran to Julie. "Aunt Julie!" he exclaimed. Julie hugged him, then looked at me over his curly head. "Before you read it in the *Moniteur*—it will be announced tomorrow morning—Jean-Baptiste has been made Prince of Pontecorvo. Congratulations, Princess!" She smiled. "Congratulations, little Crown Prince of Pontecorvo!" She kissed Oscar.

"I don't understand. Jean-Baptiste is not a brother of the Emperor." It was the first thing I thought of.

"But he's governing Ansbach and Hanover so magnificently, the Emperor wants to honor him," exulted Julie. "Aren't you pleased, Highness?"

"I suppose. . . . But tell me, where is Pontecorvo?"

Julie looked blank. "The name sounds Italian, so maybe it's near Naples. Then you'd live close to me. But"—her face fell—"that's too good to be true. Your Jean-Baptiste is still a marshal; the Emperor needs him for his campaigns."

And when, I thought, will my Jean-Baptiste ever come home?

In a traveling coach somewhere in Europe, summer of 1807

Marienburg, my destination's called. A colonel, assigned to me by the Emperor, is sitting next to me with a map open on his knees. "Marienburg is not far from Danzig," the colonel says. Marie, sitting opposite, grumbles continually about the muddy roads. Madame la Flotte, who has become my companion during Jean-Baptiste's long absence at the front, says little.

"They were fighting on these roads just a few weeks ago," the colonel says. "But now, of course, we're at peace."

Yes, Napoleon has once again concluded a peace treaty. The *Moniteur* had told us all about how Jean-Baptiste had encircled and taken Lübeck by storm. Then followed the endless winter when I waited in Paris and had so little news from him. Berlin fell and the enemy troops were pursued across Poland. Again and again Jean-Baptiste's regiments threw back flank attacks against our Army. The Emperor won the battles of Jena and Eylau and Friedland, collected representatives of the European states at Tilsit and dictated his peace conditions to them. Then, quite unexpectedly, Napoleon returned to Paris. And his lackeys rode from house to house inviting people to attend a huge victory celebration at the Tuileries.

I took my new dress out of my wardrobe, Yvette arranged my unruly hair, and I wore the pearl-and-ruby tiara Jean-Baptiste had sent by special messenger last August on our wedding anniversary. It's so long since we've seen each other—such a terribly long time.

"Your Highness will have a wonderful time," Madame la Flotte said enviously. She was often right in her observations, but she could not possibly know what awaited me at the Tuileries. The last thing I expected was to have a good time.

We assembled in the great ballroom, of course, and waited until the "Marseillaise" trumpeted forth. At that, we curtsied low and the Emperor and the Empress entered. Napoleon and Josephine made the rounds slowly, engaging some guests in conversation and making others miserable by ignoring them. Napoleon stopped near me to speak to some Dutch dignitaries. I'd heard that the Dutch were very dissatisfied with French rule. I therefore rather expected the Emperor to scold the dignitaries, so I hardly listened to him. Instead I studied him. Napoleon had changed. The sharp face under the short hair had filled out, and his supercilious smile was disdainful. He looked as though he had been laced into his trim general's uniform. He was definitely getting fat.

"Gentlemen," he was saying, "I think our Army, now occupying the whole of the Continent, has given outstanding evidence of bravery. In Tilsit I was informed that one of the marshals of France had been wounded." A pause. My heart thudded in the silence. Then Napoleon said, "It is the Prince of Pontecorvo." And at that moment I knew Napoleon had already seen me. This was the way he wanted me to hear the news—in the presence of a thousand strangers. He wanted to punish me. For what?

"My dear Princess," he began as I dipped into a deep curtsy, "I deplore the necessity of imparting such sad news to you. The Prince of Pontecorvo, who has distinguished himself during the campaign, was slightly wounded in the throat at Spandau. I hear he is already much improved. I beg you not to worry."

"And I beg for the opportunity to go to my husband, sire," I said faintly.

"The prince has been transferred to Marienburg for better nursing care. I advise you, Princess, not to undertake this journey. There's been fighting in these provinces. It is not a sight for beautiful women. . . ." He spoke coolly, but he watched me all the time with interest. This is his revenge, I thought, because I went to him the night before the execution of the Duke of Enghien. Because I eluded him that night. Because I love Jean-Baptiste, a general he hadn't chosen for me.

"Sire, I beg you with all my heart for permission to go to my husband. I haven't seen him for nearly two years."

Napoleon's eyes never left my face. "Nearly two years. You see, gentlemen, how the marshals of France sacrifice themselves for their country." With an amused smile he turned to one of his aides. "A pass for the Princess of Pontecorvo and one woman companion." His eyes lighted on a tall grenadier. "Colonel Moulin! You will escort the princess and be responsible to me for her safety." And then to me: "When do you plan to leave?"

"Tomorrow morning, sire."

"Please convey my warm regards to the prince and tell him you bring a gift from me. In recognition of his services"—Napoleon's smile was almost a sneer—"I present him with the residence of the former General Moreau in the rue d'Anjou. I recently bought it from his wife. I'm told that the general has chosen America for his exile. It's a pity; a capable soldier, but unfortunately a traitor to France. A great pity . . ."

As I curtsied, I saw only his back. He had clasped his hands behind him, as he used to in moments of stress. General Moreau, I thought, who would not betray the Republic and was sentenced to exile for life. Now the Emperor has bought his house and is giving it to Moreau's best friend, Jean-Baptiste, whom he hates but cannot do without.

That's how I come to be traveling along country roads, through battlefields strewn with dead horses, past little mounds of earth on which are warped, hastily-put-together wooden crosses. It's raining, raining all the time.

I have left Oscar for the first time since he was born. In the early-morning hours before my departure, I drove with the child to Madame Letizia in Versailles. The Emperor's mother had returned from Italy not long after Napoleon's coronation, and now lives in the Trianon.

"Go without anxiety to your Bernadotte. I'll take good care of Oscar," she promised. "Remember, I've brought up five sons."

Brought up badly, I thought. But one doesn't say such things to the mother of Napoleon.

IT WAS LATE at night when our carriage finally drew up in front of Jean-Baptiste's headquarters. The Marienburg is no palace. It's a gray, hideous medieval fortress, dilapidated and unhomelike. Soldiers swarmed around the entrance. Such heel clicking and excitement when Colonel Moulin showed my pass. The marshal's wife in person.

"I want to surprise the prince; please don't announce me," I said as I alighted. Two officers led me through the gateway and along a cold, damp corridor. Finally we came to a little anteroom, and Fernand hurled himself at me. He was splendidly turned out in a wine-red lackey's uniform with huge gold buttons. "How elegant you've become, Fernand." I laughed.

"We are now the Prince of Pontecorvo," he explained, showing me the coat of arms on the buttons.

"How is my husband, Fernand?"

"We are now quite well again," Fernand informed me.

I put my finger on my mouth: "Ssh." Fernand understood and very quietly opened the door.

Jean-Baptiste didn't hear me. He was sitting at the desk, studying a huge volume. The collar of his dark blue uniform was open, and he was wearing a white scarf. Under his chin the scarf was loose, and I saw a white bandage. A huge map hung on the wall, and in the background I saw Jean-Baptiste's narrow camp cot, a table with his silver washbowl and bandage material. I went nearer. For the first time in days I felt warm and safe. I was tired, dreadfully tired, but I was at last at my destination. "Your Highness," I said. "Dear Prince of Pontecorvo . . ."

At the sound of my voice he jumped up. "My God—*Désirée!*" He was beside me in two rapid strides. His mouth was gentle. "Little girl, little girl," he said; and held me close.

The door suddenly opened and Marie and Fernand entered. "My Eugénie can't spend the night in this bug-infested fortress," cried Marie.

"Bugs? Not one," Fernand cried back. "These damp walls kill all animal life."

"Hearing those two quarrel takes me back to the rue Cisalpine." Jean-Baptiste laughed. With a shock I remembered the Emperor's gift. After supper I would tell him about Moreau's house.

"Fernand, you are to see that, within half an hour, a bedroom and a salon are ready for the princess," Jean-Baptiste ordered. "The aide on duty is to requisition furniture from the surrounding estates. Good furniture. And the princess and I wish to dine alone. Here in my room."

As Fernand set a small table, I said, "You've bought new silver with the initials of the Prince of Pontecorvo. At home I'm still using ours with the simple *B*."

"Have the *B* removed and the new coat of arms engraved on it, Désirée. You needn't economize, darling. We are very rich. I had a letter today in which the Emperor informs me he will present me with estates in Poland and Westphalia that will guarantee me an annual income of over three hundred thousand francs."

Fernand finally left us alone. I took a deep breath. "We are wealthier than you know," I began. "The Emperor has given us General Moreau's house. In the rue d'Anjou."

"Moreau's house," Jean-Baptiste murmured. "Moreau himself has gone into exile. To me, on the contrary, the Emperor gives fine presents. It's not easy to take the joy out of a man's reunion with his wife. But the Emperor of the French has done it."

"I'll get the new house all ready and comfortable. You have to come home. Oscar always asks for you," I said helplessly.

"Moreau's house will never be home to me, merely quarters, where I sometimes visit you and Oscar. . . ." He stared at the map on the wall, then said, "I shall write Moreau. From Lübeck one can write to Sweden. From Sweden letters are sent on to England and to America. And in Sweden I have friends."

My memory stirred, a memory half forgotten but suddenly very clear. Stockholm, the sky like a white sheet . . . Now Jean-Baptiste was speaking with animation.

"When I took Lübeck, I found Swedish troops in the town. The people of Sweden wanted to stay neutral, but a squadron of Swedish dragoons had been sent by their mad young King, Gustavus the Fourth, to fight against France. He's a religious maniac who thinks he's been chosen by God to destroy Napoleon. Sweden interests me, and to learn more about it, I invited the captured officers to supper. These officers explained that when Gustavus broke with us in this war, he counted on winning the Tsar's support. The Swedes are always afraid Russia might take Finland away from them."

"Finland? Where is Finland?" I asked, confused again.

"Come here, I'll show you the whole thing on the map," said Jean-Baptiste, and so I had to look at the map. "But now the Tsar has joined with the Emperor. And Napoleon is giving the Tsar a free hand in the Baltic States. So what do you think this Gustavus is up to? This madman has declared war on Russia also, because of Finland."

I was studying the map. I'd been traveling day and night to take care of my husband, and instead I had to have a geography lesson. "How could the Swedes ever hold Finland if the Tsar decides to occupy it?"

"You see, even an ignorant little girl like you asks this question. Naturally they couldn't hold Finland. If I were asked to advise the Swedes, I would suggest ceding Finland to Russia and working toward union with Norway, which is now ruled by the King of Denmark, whom the Norwegians don't like. Such a union would at the very least have a sound geographical basis."

"Did you explain this to the Swedish officers in Lübeck?"

"Very clearly. I said, 'Gentlemen, a Frenchman who studies the map, a marshal who knows something of strategy, tells you that Russia needs Finland to safeguard her frontiers. Your country will be ravaged if you don't give in to the Tsar on the question of Finland. As to your second enemy, the Emperor of France, if Gustavus continues to feel he's an instrument of God destined to destroy Napoleon, the Emperor will one day order the conquest and occupation of Sweden. Save your country by armed neutrality! And if you want a union of states, gentlemen, stand by Norway.'"

"You expressed it very well, Jean-Baptiste. How did the Swedes reply?"

"You can't imagine how nonplussed they were. Especially one of them named Mörner. 'You're betraying your secret plans, monseigneur,' he kept saying. 'How can you divulge your plans to us?' Do you know what I said?"

"No," I said, getting a little closer to the narrow camp cot. I was so tired I could hardly keep my eyes open. "What did you say, Jean-Baptiste?"

"'Don't look at me,' I said, 'but at the map.'" Jean-Baptiste paused. "The next morning I sent them home. Now I have friends in Sweden."

"Why do you need friends in Sweden?"

"Friends are useful everywhere and at all times. . . . Little girl, are you asleep?"

"Almost," I murmured. I was trying to make myself comfortable on the narrow camp cot. "I'm so tired," I said.

"I believe that the Swedish officers will speak to their ministers and give them no rest until the Swedish King abdicates. His uncle would succeed him—Charles the Thirteenth. This uncle has, unfortunately, no children. He's also said to be somewhat senile. . . . Why are you wearing three petticoats, darling?"

"Because it rained all the time during the journey. I was cold. . . . If I make myself as thin as possible and get way over to one side, there'll be room for both of us on the camp cot. We could try—"

"Yes, we could try, my darling."

Sometime during the night I woke up.

"Are you comfortable, little girl?"

"I'm marvelously comfortable. Why aren't you asleep, Jean-Baptiste?"

"I'm not tired. So many thoughts . . ."

"The Mälaren is in Stockholm, and on it float green ice floes," I said softly.

"How do you know that?"

"I knew a man named Persson. . . . Hold me closer, Jean-Baptiste, so I'm sure I'm really with you. Otherwise I'll think it's all a dream. . . ."

NOT UNTIL AUTUMN, when Jean-Baptiste and his officers went to Hamburg, did I return to Paris. I had good weather on my trip home. We saw no more dead horses. And only a few graves. One could forget that the route led across battlefields. One could forget that here thousands of men lie buried. But I did not forget.

In our new home on the rue d'Anjou in Paris, July 1809

The church bells woke me up very early. I thought perhaps it was the birthday of one of the many kings in the Bonaparte family. Napoleon continues to allow all his relatives to rule something. Now his youngest brother, Jérôme, reigns over several conquered German principalities—he is Jérôme the First, King of Westphalia. Joseph, incidentally, isn't King of Naples anymore, but of Spain, though the Spaniards want no part of him and are rebelling. Murat, however, is ruling peacefully in Naples with Caroline. That is, Caroline is ruling, since Murat is also a marshal and finds himself constantly at some front.

The church bells . . . Which Bonaparte could be having a birthday? Not King Louis of Holland, nor Eugène de Beauharnais, viceroy of Italy. Not Paulette—the only Bonaparte who doesn't care a fig for politics. She cares only for her amusement and her lovers. On Paulette's birthday no bells are rung. Nor on Lucien's. Lucien is still in exile. He tried to take his family to America, but en route his ship was captured by the English. Now Lucien lives as an "enemy alien" in England. Always watched, but still free. He recently wrote just that to his mother in a letter. No bells for Lucien. . . .

The door opened a crack. "I'll have your breakfast brought up," Marie said.

"Why are the bells ringing, Marie?"

"Why are they ever rung? The Emperor has won another great victory."

"Where? When? Is there anything in the paper?"

"I'll send your breakfast and the young lady who reads to you." Marie is always amused because, like the other court ladies, I must employ the daughter of an impoverished aristocratic family to read to me. The Emperor insists that we marshals' wives be waited on as if we were all eighty years old. I am twenty-nine.

Yvette brought my morning chocolate. She opened the windows and the fragrance of roses filled the room. The garden here is very small, the house is right in the city. I gave away most of Moreau's furniture and bought some new things—white-gold, luxurious. At first I didn't know what I ought to do with a bust of the former owner; our friend Moreau is unfortunately still in disgrace. I finally put it in the hall. In the salon opposite I had to hang a portrait of the Emperor, and I chose one showing Napoleon as First Consul. The face is thin and tense, the hair is long, the eyes have a faraway look, and the mouth is that of the youthful Napoleon who once leaned against a summer hedge and said that there were men destined to make world history.

The bells . . . "Yvette," I said, "send in Mademoiselle and Oscar."

The child and my reader came in at the same time. I arranged my pillows, and Oscar sat beside me. "Mademoiselle will read to us from the *Moniteur*. We've had another victory."

That's how we learned that a great battle had been fought at Wagram, near Vienna. An Austrian army of seventy thousand men was completely destroyed. The names of most of the victorious French marshals were given. Jean-Baptiste wasn't mentioned. And yet I knew he and his troops were in Austria. Napoleon had given him command of all the Saxon regiments in his army.

At that moment there was an urgent knock at the door and Madame la Flotte came in. "Princess, His Excellency Minister Fouché begs to be received!"

Police Minister Fouché had never before called on me. "Run along, Oscar. I must dress quickly. Yvette—Yvette!" Yvette was already beside me with the lilac-colored day dress. "Madame la Flotte, show His Excellency into the little salon. Mademoiselle, give him the *Moniteur* to read."

A smile flitted across Madame la Flotte's pretty face. "Princess, the minister of police reads the *Moniteur* before it goes to press. It's part of his job." She and the reader vanished.

I went reluctantly downstairs. Fouché—someone once called him the bad conscience of the nation. People fear him because he knows too much. But I have no guilty conscience, Monsieur Fouché! I'm just worried, terribly worried. The communiqué doesn't mention Jean-Baptiste, and I'm afraid I know what has happened.

When I came in, the minister of police jumped up. "I come to congratulate you, Princess—we've won a great victory, and I read that the Prince of Pontecorvo and his eight thousand Saxon troops were the first to storm Wagram, beating back forty thousand men to do so."

"Yes—but there was nothing about it in the paper," I stammered with relief, and sat down.

"No, it's not in the newspaper, but in an order of the day your husband addressed to his Saxon troops, praising them for their valor."

Fouché paused, selected a piece of candy from a Dresden china box on a little table between us. "I have also read the copy of a letter from His Majesty to the Prince of Pontecorvo, in which the Emperor says the prince's order of the day contains many things contrary to fact. For instance, His Majesty explains it was Oudinot, not your husband, who seized Wagram, and the Saxons under your husband's command did not fire a single shot. In conclusion, he informs the Prince of Pontecorvo that in this campaign he in no way distinguished himself. The Emperor enclosed a copy of this letter in his note to me. I have received an order to"—again that ominous pause—"to watch the movements of the Prince of Pontecorvo and censor his correspondence."

"That will be difficult, Your Excellency. My husband is still with his troops in Austria."

"You are mistaken, dear Princess. He is expected momentarily in Paris. After this exchange of letters with the Emperor, he resigned command of his troops and, because of his health, was granted leave for an indefinite period."

Why not play out the comedy? "May I think a moment?" I put my hand to my head. "I'm not very clever. You say that my husband's Saxon troops distinguished themselves fighting as allies of France—is that right?"

"So the prince wrote in his order of the day."

"And why does this annoy the Emperor?"

"In a secret circular letter to all his marshals the Emperor explained that he personally commands his troops, and it is his prerogative to praise any of them. Besides, our French Army is responsible for our victories, not foreign troops."

I stood up. "Excuse me, Your Excellency, I want to get things ready for Jean-Baptiste's return. Thank you so much for your call, though I don't quite know why you came."

"Can't you really guess, honored Princess?"

No, I was thinking, I can't. If the Emperor wants to exile us, he will exile us. If he wants to court-martial Jean-Baptiste, he will court-martial him. If he wants grounds for anything, his minister of police will provide them. . . . Then a thought came. I tried to keep my voice steady. "Your Excellency, if you thought I would help you spy on my husband, you made a great mistake."

"Most women have unpaid bills at their dressmaker's," Fouché ventured quietly.

I lost my temper. "Now you have gone too far, monsieur."

"Our revered Empress, for example, always has overdue bills at Le Roy. I am naturally at Her Majesty's service at all times."

Is he implying that he pays the Empress? For what services? It's unbelievable, I thought. And knew, of course, it was true. "Don't go to any trouble for me," I said in disgust. "And now you really must excuse me."

"Just a moment, honored Princess. Would you give the prince a message from me?"

"What about?"

"The Emperor is in Vienna. It is impossible to warn him that English troops are massed, ready to land on the Channel coast, at Dunkerque, and in Antwerp, and they plan to march directly to Paris. I have therefore, on my own reponsibility, decided to call up the National Guard. I want Marshal Bernadotte, as soon as he returns, to assume command of these forces and to defend France."

Fouché toyed with the Dresden china box. I said, "The Emperor distrusts him—yet you would give him command of the National Guard to defend our frontiers?"

Fouché shrugged. "To whom should I give the command, Princess? I am a former mathematics teacher and was never even a sergeant. Heaven has sent me a marshal, and heaven be praised. Will you deliver my message to the prince?"

I nodded. Suddenly I had a new idea. Perhaps it is a trap. "But I don't know whether my husband will consider this command if it's without the knowledge of His Majesty," I said.

Fouché stood all too close to me. "Don't worry, madame. If it involves the defense of France, Marshal Bernadotte will accept the command." And, very quietly: "As long as he is a marshal of France." Whereupon he kissed my hand and departed.

That same evening Jean-Baptiste's coach stopped before our house. He was accompanied only by Fernand. Two days later, away he went again. Headed for the Channel coast.

Villa la Grange, near Paris, autumn of 1809

I have little time to write in my diary. I spend the whole day with Jean-Baptiste and try to cheer him up.

Fouché didn't exaggerate the danger back in July. The English did land on the Channel coast. But within days Jean-Baptiste accomplished a miracle. He fortified Dunkerque and Antwerp so well that all the attacks were beaten off, and countless English soldiers and quantities of booty fell into his hands before the English got their ships out.

This news infuriated the Emperor. In his absence a minister had dared to call up the National Guard, and to name as supreme commander the very marshal who was under police supervision. At the same time Napoleon had to acknowledge publicly that without Fouché's mobilization of untrained peasant boys who were then made into an army by Jean-Baptiste, France would have been lost.

Fouché has been elevated to the aristocracy and is now Duke of Otranto. He is about as familiar with his romantic-sounding duchy as we are with Pontecorvo. The Emperor personally designed Fouché's coat of arms: a gold column with a snake coiled around it, which has caused great merriment, although no one mentions it. Napoleon is indebted to Fouché, but he's seized this opportunity to tell him what he thinks of him.

Everyone waited to see if Jean-Baptiste would be honored, but the Emperor didn't even write him a word of thanks.

We now live in la Grange, a big beautiful villa near Paris. Jean-Baptiste bought it because he hates the house in the rue d'Anjou, where he says shadows lurk in every corner. I enjoy each single day that Jean-Baptiste is out of favor and we can be together quietly in the country. From Julie, of course, I hear what's going on in the outside world. She and Joseph have returned. Our armies in Spain were practically annihilated by the Spanish patriots after Joseph, as King of Spain, assumed entire command and wouldn't listen to advice.

Julie tells me that Napoleon may soon leave Josephine. The

rumor is that he intends to divorce her because he hopes to found a dynasty with an Austrian archduchess, a daughter of the Emperor Franz. Poor Josephine. She's been unfaithful to him, but she would never desert him, even if things went badly for him.

Yesterday we had an unexpected visitor: Count Talleyrand, grand seigneur of the Empire. He is the most powerful man in the service of Napoleon, even though, in heated arguments with the Emperor, he has warned against further wars. It seems, however, that Napoleon cannot forgo his diplomatic services. I'm really fond of the lame "grand seigneur." He's witty and charming. I can hardly realize he was once a bishop—the first bishop to take the oath to the new Republic.

"Why haven't I seen you in Paris for so long a time, dear Prince?" he asked Jean-Baptiste.

"That shouldn't surprise Your Excellency. You may have heard that, because of my health, I am on leave."

Talleyrand nodded seriously, asked solicitously whether Jean-Baptiste was feeling any better, then inquired, "Have you had any interesting news from abroad?"

"Ask Fouché, he reads all my mail. Before I do," Jean-Baptiste added quietly. "However, I've heard nothing worth mentioning."

"Not even greetings from your Swedish friends?"

Jean-Baptiste looked at Talleyrand and nodded. "Yes, I've had greetings. The Swedes have deposed their mad King and proclaimed his uncle, the thirteenth Charles, King."

Talleyrand smiled. "I've been told this uncle is old and sickly."

"He has adopted a young relative to succeed him. Prince Christian Augustus von Holstein-Sonderburg-Augustenburg."

"How easily you speak these names," mused Talleyrand.

"I lived long enough in the North to accustom myself to them."

Talleyrand tapped his chin speculatively with the gold top of the cane he always carries. "I wonder . . . A year ago the Emperor left to your discretion the invasion of Sweden. You were satisfied to do nothing. Why was this?"

"You've said yourself that the Emperor left it up to me. He wanted to help the Tsar conquer Finland. Our help was not needed." Jean-Baptiste leaned forward in his chair. "I'm tired, Excellency. Tired of questions, tired of suspicion."

Talleyrand immediately stood up. "Then I shall make my request quickly and go."

Jean-Baptiste rose too. "A request? I can't imagine what a marshal fallen into disfavor could do for the foreign minister."

"It concerns Sweden. I learned yesterday that the Swedish Council of State has sent some gentlemen to Paris to discuss the resumption of diplomatic relations between their country and ours. These gentlemen asked after you in Paris at once. They say the young officers with whom you supped after the conquest of Lübeck speak of you often. You are considered a friend of—mm— of the Far North. And these gentlemen probably hope that you will say a good word for their country to the Emperor."

"As you see, people in Stockholm are ill-informed," Jean-Baptiste murmured.

"I should like to ask you to receive these gentlemen," said Talleyrand evenly. "I shouldn't like the Swedes to get the idea that the Emperor is not availing himself of the services of one of his most famous marshals. It would create the wrong impression abroad. You see, the reason for my request is very simple."

"Too simple," Jean-Baptiste said. "Far too simple for a diplomat like you. And—far too complicated for a sergeant like me. I don't understand you. I really don't, Excellency."

"It's only a question of duty," Talleyrand said. "I feel duty-bound to one continent—ours. To Europe as a whole. And naturally, especially to France. I kiss your hand, beautiful Princess. Good-by, dear friend—it was a very stimulating conversation!"

Jean-Baptiste spent all afternoon riding. In the evening he helped Oscar with his arithmetic until the poor child's eyes ached and I took my tired youngster off to bed. We didn't mention Talleyrand's visit again, because before we went to bed we had an argument over Fernand. Jean-Baptiste said, "Fernand complains that you are too generous with tips, that you give him money every few minutes."

"You yourself said we're rich now and I don't have to be so economical. If I want to give pleasure to your old school friend, why should he complain?"

"No more tips. Fernand gets a monthly salary from Fouché."

"What!" I was dumbfounded.

"Little girl, Fouché asked Fernand to keep an eye on me, and Fernand accepted because he thought it would be silly to lose the money. But he came right to me and suggested that I give him that much less. Fernand is the most decent fellow under the sun."

"And what does he tell the minister of police about you?"

"Every day there's something to report. Today, for instance, I helped Oscar with his arithmetic. Very interesting for the former mathematics master."

Paris, December 16, 1809

It was horrible. Yesterday the Emperor ordered his entire family, his government, his court and his marshals to assemble. In their presence he divorced Josephine.

Jean-Baptiste and I had been asked to be in the throne room of the Tuileries at eleven o'clock in the morning. At half past ten I was in bed, pretending to be asleep. I opened my eyes and looked at Jean-Baptiste imploringly. He nodded. "Stay in bed, little one. You have a bad cold. Take care of yourself."

I closed my eyes again and pulled the quilt up to my chin. I, too, shall grow older, I thought, with wrinkles around my eyes, and no longer able to bear children. . . .

Before the clock struck twelve, Jean-Baptiste was back, and Julie came with him. Jean-Baptiste promptly loosened his high embroidered collar and muttered, "The most painful scene I have ever witnessed." With that, he left my bedroom.

Julie told me what had happened. "We all had to stand in the throne room," she said, "each in an assigned place. The Emperor and Empress came in together, Josephine in white as usual. And she had powdered herself pale. Exactly right for a martyr . . ."

"Julie, don't be so unkind. It must have been terrible for her."

"Of course it was. It was deathly still. The Emperor began to read a document. Something about how hard this step was for him, but that no sacrifice was too great if made for the sake of France. . . . And that Josephine, for thirteen years, had made his life beautiful, and she was always to keep the title of an empress of the French. He read so fast it was difficult to follow. He wanted it over with as quickly as possible."

"And then what happened?"

"That's when it got so dreadful. Someone handed the Empress a document, and she began to read aloud in a voice so low no one could hear. Suddenly she burst into tears. It was awful. She handed the sheet to Count Regnaud, who was standing behind her, and he went on with it."

"What did the document say?"

"That, with the permission of her beloved husband, she hereby declared she could bear no more children. And, for the sake of France, the greatest sacrifice was being demanded of her that any woman could be asked to make. That she thanked Napoleon for his goodness, and is convinced this divorce is necessary so that France can someday be ruled by direct descendants of the Emperor. But the dissolution of her marriage could in no way change the dictates of her heart. . . . Regnaud read all this as passionately as he would read a prescription. And all the time she was sobbing her heart out. Afterward, in the Emperor's large study, Napoleon and the Empress signed the divorce decree and then we signed as witnesses. Hortense and Eugène led their weeping mother away. The Emperor said, 'I believe that a luncheon has been prepared for my family in the great hall. Excuse me.' Whereupon he disappeared and the others all rushed to the buffet. That's when I saw Jean-Baptiste leaving. He told me you were sick and I came home with him."

Julie powdered her nose and chattered on. "Tomorrow morning she leaves the Tuileries and goes to Malmaison. The Emperor has given her Malmaison and paid all her debts. Besides, she's to get an annual pension of three million francs; two million must be paid by the state, and one million by the Emperor."

"Will Hortense go with her to Malmaison?"

"She will probably drive with her there tomorrow. But Hortense is keeping her apartments in the Tuileries."

"And Josephine's son?"

"Eugène will continue as viceroy of Italy. He asked to resign, but the Emperor wouldn't let him go. After all, he adopted Josephine's children long ago. And Hortense was sure her oldest son would be heir to the throne. She's furious. The Hapsburg princess, whom the Emperor is marrying, is eighteen years old, and will have masses of princes. The Hapsburgs are so horribly prolific." Julie put on her crown. "I must go back to the Tuileries now, dear. The Bonapartes won't like it if I don't celebrate with them. *Au revoir*, Désirée. Get well soon."

I lay a long time with my eyes closed. How very much Julie has changed! Am I to blame? I brought the Bonapartes to our home. To the home of honest, simple Citizen Clary. Papa, I never knew, I never dreamed, it would be like this.

I WENT TO sleep very early. So I had quite a shock when Marie and Madame la Flotte suddenly appeared at my bedside. "Queen Hortense begs to be received."

"Now? What time is it?" I was utterly confused.

"Two o'clock in the morning. But the Queen of Holland won't be turned away. She is very upset and weeping." La Flotte wore an expensive dressing gown, the sleeves adorned with ermine. Perhaps Fouché pays her dressmaker's bills, I thought.

"Better get properly dressed. You're probably needed in the Tuileries," Marie said firmly, and brought me a plain blue dress.

Hortense's nose was red from crying. "Princess, my mother sent me to ask you to come to her at once."

"Me?" I was astonished. "In the middle of the night?"

"The Empress won't see anyone," Hortense moaned, "just you."

"All right," I sighed.

The Empress's apartments were only dimly lighted. But when Hortense opened the door to Her Majesty's bedroom, the light nearly blinded us. On every table, on the mantelpiece, even on the floor stood candlesticks. Wide-open half-packed trunks gaped at us. Everywhere lay clothes, hats, gloves, robes of state and negligees in wild disorder. A diamond tiara glittered under an armchair. The Empress lay with outstretched arms on the wide bed, sobbing into the pillow. We could hear hushed women's voices from the next room. Josephine, however, was all alone.

"Mama, I've brought the Princess Pontecorvo," said Hortense. Josephine just dug her fingernails deeper into the silk coverlet. "Mama," Hortense repeated.

With decisive steps I went to the bed and grabbed Josephine's shoulders. She stared at me with swollen eyes. She's become an old woman, I realized with a start. In this one night she's become an old woman. . . .

"Désirée—" her lips moved. Then fresh tears streamed down her unrouged cheeks. I sat on the edge of the bed and she twined her fingers around mine. She'd cried away her makeup. Her childlike curls were very loose and damp on her temples. Pitilessly the many candles bathed her face in uncompromising light. "I've been trying to pack," said Josephine, still weeping.

"Your Majesty needs sleep above everything," I said, and asked Hortense to blow out all but one of the candles.

"You must stay with me tonight, Désirée." Her lips trembled.

"You know he loves me as he loves no one else—doesn't he?"

So that's why she wanted to see me. Because I know better than anyone else how much he loves her. "Yes, only you, madame. When he met you, he forgot everyone else."

A small smile played around her mouth. "You threw a champagne glass at me—and I made you very unhappy, little Désirée. Forgive me, I didn't mean to." I stroked her hand and let her go on about earlier times. How old was she then? Not much older than I am today.

"Mama, you'll like it at Malmaison. You've always considered it your real home," came from Hortense.

Josephine winced. Who'd interrupted her memories?

"Hortense," I said to the Queen of Holland, "your mother must rest. Ask someone to bring a cup of hot tea. And didn't Dr. Corvisart leave a sleeping draft for Her Majesty?"

Hortense fumbled among the bottles and jars on the dressing table and finally handed me a small bottle. "Five drops, he said."

"Thank you. And good night, madame."

I took off Josephine's crumpled white dress, slipped the gold sandals from her tiny feet and covered her up. A maid brought in the tea and I sent her right away. Then I carefully dripped six drops from the bottle into the tea. Josephine sat up obediently and drank. "Like everything else in my life—very sweet, with a bitter aftertaste." She smiled, then fell back onto the cushions. "You weren't there this morning for the official ceremony," she said drowsily.

"No, I thought you'd prefer me not to be."

"I did." A brief pause. She breathed more regularly. "Don't desert him, Désirée!" The drops had apparently confused her. But they were calming her. I stroked her hand slowly.

"When he loses his power . . ." Her eyes closed. I let go of her hand. "Stay with me—I'm frightened."

"I'll sit down in the next room and wait until Your Majesty wakes up. Then I'll accompany Your Majesty to Malmaison."

"Yes, to Malmai—"

She was asleep. I blew out the candle, went into the next room, groped my way over to the window and pulled the heavy curtains apart. A gloomy winter morning had dawned. By its faint light I found a deep comfortable chair, tucked my legs under me and tried to sleep. All was quiet.

Suddenly I sat up. Someone was coming. Spurs jingled. I tried to look over the high back of my chair. Who had entered the bedroom of the Empress without knocking?

He. Naturally—he.

He stood in front of the mantelpiece, peering around the room. Involuntarily I stirred. He looked quickly toward my chair. "Is someone here?" He sounded angry.

"Only me, sire, the Princess of Pontecorvo," I stammered, trying to get my legs out from underneath me.

"The Princess of Pontecorvo?" Incredulously he came closer, as, finally, I stood up and sank down into a deep curtsy.

"Tell me, Princess, what are you doing here at this hour?" asked Napoleon. He took my hand as I rose.

"Her Majesty asked me to stay with her tonight. Her Majesty has at last gone to sleep," I whispered. Because he said nothing, I continued. "I'd better leave and not disturb Your Majesty here."

"You don't disturb me, Eugénie." He paused. "I wanted to bid farewell to this salon. Tomorrow—this morning the workmen come." I nodded, embarrassed to be here at this farewell. He stared at me intently. "You're exhausted, Eugénie. Sit down again." He led me back to my armchair. "But I still don't understand what you are doing here."

"The Empress wanted to see me because I reminded Her Majesty"—I swallowed—"I reminded Her Majesty of the afternoon on which she became engaged to General Bonaparte. It was a very happy time in the life of Her Majesty."

He sat down unceremoniously on the arm of my chair. "And in yours, Princess?"

"I was very unhappy, sire. But it's so long ago, and long since healed." He tried to put his arm around my shoulder, but I made myself stiff and leaned my head against the back of the chair.

"Look, there she is. Don't you think she is beautiful, Eugénie?" He held out a snuffbox on which a miniature was painted. I saw a young face with porcelain-blue eyes and very rosy cheeks.

"It's hard to judge these snuffbox miniatures," I said. "They all look alike to me."

"Marie Louise of Austria is very beautiful, I'm told. The Hapsburgs are one of the oldest ruling families in the world, did you know? An archduchess of Austria is worthy of the Emperor of the French."

I sat up straight because I wanted to see his face. Was he serious? That a Hapsburg princess is good enough for the son of the Corsican lawyer Buonaparte?

Again he stared off into space. Then suddenly he asked, "Can you waltz?" I nodded. "Can you show me? Everyone in Austria waltzes, I heard in Vienna, but I had no time to try. Show me how they waltz."

"Not now, not—here." Horrified, I pointed to the door of Josephine's bedroom. "Sire, you'll wake her."

His face was distorted. "Now. And here. Show me! This is a command, Princess."

I rose. "It's difficult without music," I said. Then I began to revolve slowly. "One, two, three, and one, two, three—that's how one waltzes, Your Majesty."

But he wasn't watching me. He still sat on the arm of the chair, staring into space. His heavy face looked gray and puffy in the early light. "I was so happy with her, Eugénie."

"Is it—necessary, Your Majesty?"

"I can't make war on three fronts. I must defend the Channel coast, and my friend the Russian Tsar is arming, but Austria . . . Austria will make peace if the Emperor's daughter is married to me. She will be my hostage, my sweet eighteen-year-old hostage." He took out the snuffbox again and gazed at the rosy portrait. Then he stood and surveyed the room as though to impress on his memory forever the tapestries on the wall and the shape of the lovely sofa. As he turned to leave, I curtsied low. He put his hand gently on my head and stroked my hair absentmindedly. "Can I do anything for you, dear Princess?"

"Yes, if Your Majesty would be kind enough to send up some breakfast. Strong coffee, if possible."

His laughter sounded young, awakening memories. Then he quickly left the salon, his spurs clanking.

At nine o'clock in the morning I escorted the Empress through the back door of the Tuileries and hurried her down the stairs. Hortense was already waiting in the carriage.

"I'd expected Bonaparte would bid me farewell," said Josephine softly as the carriage started up.

"The Emperor rode to Versailles very early this morning," Hortense said. "He's spending a few days with his mother."

All the way to Malmaison not another word was said.

She looks, unfortunately, just like a sausage.

The new Empress, that is. The wedding festivities are over, and the Emperor spent five million francs to decorate Marie Louise's apartments in the Tuileries. Yesterday, along with all the other marshals, ambassadors, dignitaries and princes, we were summoned to be presented to the new Empress.

It was exactly as it had been—last time. The great ballroom, the thousand candles, the crowd of uniforms and court gowns, the striking up of the "Marseillaise," the flinging open of the folding doors, the entrance of the Emperor and Empress.

Marie Louise had been squeezed into a tight-fitting pink satin gown, hung all over with diamonds. She is much taller than the Emperor, and, in spite of her youth, she has plenty of bosom. Her face is pink, too, and very full, and she uses almost no makeup. She smiles incessantly. But then, she's the daughter of a genuine Emperor and has probably been brought up to smile always. She watched her father's armies march off to fight against Napoleon and lived through the occupation of Vienna. She must have hated the Emperor from childhood, and then her father made her marry him. Still, she never stops smiling.

When the imperial couple had taken their places on their thrones, the orchestra played a Viennese waltz. A bittersweet sophisticated perfume drifted by—Paulette. She put her arm around my shoulder. "The Emperor has decided Marie Louise is pregnant." Paulette shook with laughter.

"Since when?"

"Since yesterday." The exotic perfume wafted away.

Jean-Baptiste was leaning against a window, watching the crowd indifferently. I went over to him. "Can we go home soon?" He nodded and took my arm.

"I've been looking for you, dear Prince." Suddenly Talleyrand barred our way. "These gentlemen have asked to be presented to you." Behind him stood several enormously tall officers in foreign uniforms. Dark blue, with blue-and-yellow sashes. "Count Brahe, a member of the Swedish embassy. Colonel Wrede, here for the wedding, brings the felicitations of His Majesty the King of Sweden. And Lieutenant Baron Karl Otto Mörner, who arrived here from Stockholm only this morning. He is, by the way, a cousin of the Mörner who was once your prisoner in Lübeck."

"We continue to correspond," said Jean-Baptiste quietly.

"I am here on a tragic mission, Prince," Mörner said in fluent French. "I bring news that the Swedish heir to the throne, Prince Christian Augustus, has been killed in an accident."

Jean-Baptiste's fingers dug suddenly into my arm, but only for a fraction of a second. "How terrible," he said calmly. "I extend my sincere sympathy."

"Has a successor to the late heir already been chosen?" Talleyrand asked. He sounded casual, polite, interested.

I happened to look at Mörner. How odd: he kept staring at Jean-Baptiste with a peculiar expression. So did Colonel Wrede. What can they possibly want of my husband? I thought.

Baron Mörner said, "On the twenty-first of August the Swedish Parliament will meet to decide on a successor to the throne."

"I beg of you again to express my sympathy to the King of Sweden and tell him how deeply I mourn with him and his people," Jean-Baptiste said.

"Is that the only message?" Mörner burst out.

Jean-Baptiste looked from one to another, and finally at young Count Brahe, who couldn't have been more than nineteen years old. "Count Brahe, I believe you belong to one of the most distinguished families in Sweden. And so I ask you to remind your friends and fellow officers that I was not always a prince, not always a marshal of France. In your aristocratic circles I would be called a former Jacobin general. And I began as a simple sergeant. I ask you to remember this"—he took a deep breath—"so that you will not reproach me later. Farewell, gentlemen."

PART THREE

Our Lady of Peace

Paris, September 1810

SOMEONE SHONE A light in my face. "Get up at once, Désirée, and dress quickly! The most beautiful dress you own." Jean-Baptiste stood with a candlestick by my bed, buttoning the tunic of his marshal's uniform.

"Have you gone mad, Jean-Baptiste? It's still night."

"I've had Oscar wakened, too. I want the child to be present."
Voices and footsteps sounded on the ground floor. Yvette shuffled in, wearing her maid's dress over her nightgown. "Hurry, please. Help the princess," Jean-Baptiste ordered her impatiently.

"Has something happened?" I demanded.

"Yes—and no. You'll hear it all yourself."

"Tell me, Jean-Baptiste—" But he had already left my room. I was angry. "Yvette, bring me the silk I wore at court the other day. And my jewel box. If no one will tell me what's going on, I'll wear everything I own."

Jean-Baptiste returned and took my arm. "Come on, Désirée! We can't keep them waiting any longer."

"What's it all about? Will you please tell me?"

"The greatest moment of my life, Désirée!"

At the door of the large hall Fernand and Marie shoved an excited Oscar at us. They'd arrayed the child in his best suit and flattened his stubborn hair with water.

The salon was brightly lit. Every candelabra we possess was aglow. Several gentlemen awaited us. Foreign uniforms, blue-and-yellow sashes. At our entrance, they all bowed most deferentially. Then a young man in a dusty tunic and mud-spattered boots stepped forward with a large sealed document. Under his eyes were deep shadows. The hand holding the document shook. "Forgive me, I've been in the saddle for days," he murmured.

"Gustaf Fredrik Mörner of the Upland Dragoons," said Jean-Baptiste, "I'm happy to see you again." So this was the Mörner who had been Jean-Baptiste's prisoner at Lübeck.

"Your Royal Highness—"

My heart missed a beat. Jean-Baptiste calmly took the document Mörner was holding out to him.

"Your Royal Highness—I have the honor to report that the Swedish Parliament has unanimously elected the Prince of Pontecorvo heir to the Swedish throne. His Majesty, King Charles the Thirteenth, wishes to adopt the Prince of Pontecorvo and to receive him in Sweden as his beloved son. May I present these gentlemen to the prince?"

Jean-Baptiste nodded. "Wrede and Count Brahe I have already met."

Mörner presented the other dignitaries, and Jean-Baptiste took a deep breath. "I accept the decision of the Swedish Parliament," he said. "I thank His Majesty, King Charles the Thirteenth, and the Swedish people for their trust in me. I swear to do everything in my power to justify this trust."

The Swedes all bowed low. And at this moment Oscar stepped forward and stood alongside the Swedes, bowing as respectfully as they to his papa and mama.

Jean-Baptiste reached for my hand. "The Crown Princess and I thank you for bringing this message directly to us."

Then many things happened fast. The members of our household were at the door. Madame la Flotte did a court curtsy. Yvette sobbed. Only Marie seemed normal. She had on her wool dressing gown over her old-fashioned linen nightshirt.

"Marie," I said in a whisper, "did you hear? The Swedish people offered us the crown. Marie—I'm frightened."

"Eugénie—" And then a tear rolled down her cheek, while she, my dear Marie, curtsied to me.

Jean-Baptiste studied the document Mörner had brought. "Before I send Prince Pontecorvo's answer to Stockholm," Mörner said, "I must draw your attention to one paragraph in that document. It concerns nationality. The adoption requires that the Prince of Pontecorvo be a Swedish subject."

Jean-Baptiste smiled. "Had you thought I would succeed to the throne of Sweden as a French citizen? Tomorrow I shall apply to the Emperor of France and ask His Majesty to allow me and my family to relinquish our French citizenship."

I'm dreaming, I thought. They had wakened me in the middle of the night to inform me that the Swedish King wants my husband to be his son. That makes my husband Crown Prince of Sweden. I'd always thought one could adopt only children. Sweden! Stockholm, the city over which the sky lies like a white sheet. Now Persson will read it all in the newspaper. And won't know that the wife of the new Crown Prince is the little Clary girl of long ago.

"Mama, the gentlemen say that my name is now Duke of Södermanland," said Oscar. His cheeks were flushed with excitement. "Will you enjoy Sweden, Mama?"

Silence all around me. They all wanted to hear my answer. Waiting for me—no, they can't expect that. This is my home, I am still a Frenchwoman. I . . . "I don't know Sweden yet, Oscar," I said. "But I'm looking forward to seeing it."

"The Swedish people can ask no more, Your Royal Highness," said Mörner gravely.

His harsh accent reminded me of Persson, and I wanted to say something friendly. "Someone I knew in my youth lives in Stockholm. His name is Persson and he's a silk merchant. Do you happen to know him?"

"I regret not, Your Royal Highness. There are many with the name Persson in Sweden."

Someone pulled back the curtains. The sun had long since risen. Jean-Baptiste's marshal's uniform sparkled as, bidding farewell, he said, "Good night—or rather, good morning, gentlemen."

Somehow I got up to my bedroom. Then Jean-Baptiste was there, beside my bed. "Try to pronounce 'Karl Johan,'" he urged. "That's what I'll be called. Karl after my adoptive father, the Swedish King, and Johan is the Swedish form of Jean." He rolled the words around on his tongue happily. "Karl Johan . . . Karl the Fourteenth Johan. And Crown Princess Desideria."

I sat up with a start. "That's too much! I won't be called Desideria."

"It is the wish of the Swedish Queen, your adoptive mother-in-law. Désirée is too French for her."

I fell back on my pillow. "Do you believe one can suddenly deny one's self? Go to Sweden—and play Crown Princess? Jean-Baptiste, I think I'm going to be very unhappy."

But he wasn't listening. "In Latin, little girl, Desideria means Désirée—'the desired one.' Could there be a more beautiful name for a crown princess whom the people themselves have chosen?"

"No, Jean-Baptiste, the Swedes didn't choose me. They need a strong man. But the daughter of a silk merchant, who knows only a Monsieur Persson—no, they could not want me."

"Désirée, I shall ask the Emperor that we be permitted to relinquish our French citizenship in order to become Swedish subjects. You agree, don't you?" I didn't answer. Didn't even move. "Désirée, I won't do this if you're against it."

I still gave no answer.

"Désirée, do you realize what's at stake?"

At that I looked at him. As though for the first time. The former sergeant with the wise forehead over which dark curly hair tumbled. The large bold nose, the deep-set eyes, searching yet confident. The small passionate mouth. "Yes, Jean-Baptiste," I said slowly, "I know what's at stake."

"And you will come with me and Oscar to Sweden?"

"If I'm really—desired. And"—at last I found his hand, held it to my cheek—"and if you'll swear never to call me Desideria!"

"I swear, my darling."

"Then the Crown Princess will continue her night's sleep. But first, I'd love to know how a crown prince kisses."

". . . And how does a crown prince kiss?"

"Marvelously well. Just like my old Jean-Baptiste."

I SLEPT LONG but restlessly. And woke up feeling that something terrible had happened. Two, said the clock on my night table. Two in the afternoon? I heard Oscar's voice in the garden, then a strange man's voice. Through the closed shutters daylight filtered in.

I got up and dressed, then, and stared into the mirror. Desideria, Crown Princess of Sweden. Desideria! A hideous name. But one preferred by my adoptive mother-in-law. I don't even know my adoptive mother-in-law's name. Nor exactly why the Swedes chose Jean-Baptiste to be their Crown Prince. . . . I opened the shutters and looked down into the garden.

"No, Your Royal Highness must catch the ball—here it comes!" cried young Count Brahe. Brahe threw hard. Oscar lurched as he caught the ball. But—he caught it. Then he looked up and saw me at my windows. Young Count Brahe bowed.

"I should like to talk to you, Count Brahe. Have you time?"

"We broke a windowpane in the dining room, Highness," he confessed.

"I hope the Swedish state will be responsible for the repairs." I found I was smiling.

Count Brahe clicked his heels together. "Sad to say, the Swedish state is practically bankrupt."

"So I thought." It just slipped out. "Wait, I'll come down to the garden."

I sat between the young count and Oscar on the little white bench in front of the arbor. I was seeking desperately for a way to begin, but finally burst out with, "Please tell me honestly, dear Count, just why Sweden has offered the crown to my husband."

"His Majesty, King Charles the Thirteenth, is childless, and we

have for years admired the great ability and administrative powers of His Royal Highness and—"

I interrupted. "I've been told that one king was deposed because people believed him mad. Is he really mad?"

Count Brahe crumpled a leaf between his fingers and said, "We
assume so."

"And where is he now, this—mad Gustavus?"

"In Switzerland, I believe."

"He has a son, hasn't he?"

"Yes, another Gustavus. He is Oscar's age—the age of the heir
apparent. But Parliament has deprived him, too, of all rights to
the Swedish crown. The people fear the bad blood in the Vasa
family. It is a very old dynasty, Highness, and there's been much
intermarriage. Besides, the House of Vasa will soon be too poor to
pay the palace gardeners. When the commoners were told that
the Prince of Pontecorvo is very rich, they voted for him."

I was thinking of what Jean-Baptiste had told me that first rainy
night when we drove through the streets of Paris. "For years I've
saved a part of my pay. I can buy a small house for you and the
child." A little house, Jean-Baptiste, not the Royal Palace in
Sweden. I buried my face in my hands and wept.

WE'D BEEN SUMMONED to wait on the Emperor at eleven o'clock in
the morning. Five minutes before eleven we were in the anteroom in which Napoleon keeps diplomats, generals, princes and
ministers—foreign and domestic—waiting for hours. At our entrance there was a sudden hush. Jean-Baptiste instructed one of
the Emperor's aides to announce the "Prince of Pontecorvo,
marshal of France, with his wife and son."

We might as well have been on an island. No one wanted to
recognize us, no one congratulated us. Everyone there knew
what had happened: a foreign people had offered Jean-Baptiste a
crown. And within, on the Emperor's desk, lay Jean-Baptiste's
request to resign from the Army and relinquish his French allegiance. Everyone knew that a terrible scene awaited us.

The clock struck eleven. The private secretary of the Emperor,
Monsieur Ménéval, appeared. "His Majesty will see the Prince of
Pontecorvo and his family."

At one end of the Emperor's study is a huge desk, and it seems
an endlessly long way from the door to this desk. The Emperor

usually meets his friends halfway, in the middle of the room. We, however, had to walk the entire length. Napoleon stood at the desk, motionless as a statue. Behind him stood Count Talleyrand.

The three of us lined up in front of the desk, Oscar in the middle. I sank into a curtsy. The Emperor never stirred, just kept staring at Jean-Baptiste. In his eyes flared an evil spark. "You've submitted a remarkable request, Prince. You say you are being adopted by the Swedish King, and ask permission to surrender your French citizenship. Almost incomprehensible, if one thinks back. But you're perhaps not thinking back."

Jean-Baptiste's lips were tightly closed.

"Don't you remember the time when a young recruit helped defend the frontiers of a new France? Or the day on which the Emperor of the French appointed you a marshal of France?"

Jean-Baptiste was silent.

"Perhaps you even saved France. I told you once that I cannot renounce the services of such a man as you. Bernadotte—I repeat, I cannot let you go." Napoleon sat down. He pushed aside the application. "But since the Swedish people have chosen you"— he shrugged, laughed lightly—"heir to their throne, as your Emperor and supreme military commander, I hereby give you permission to accept. And that's that."

"And I shall inform His Majesty, the King of Sweden, that I cannot accept. The Swedish people want a Swedish crown prince, sire," said Jean-Baptiste calmly.

Napoleon jumped up. "Nonsense, Bernadotte! Look at my brothers—Joseph, Louis, Jérôme. Did any of them give up their French citizenship? Or my stepson, Eugène, in Italy?"

Jean-Baptiste didn't answer. Napoleon came around from behind his desk and began to pace up and down the room. My eyes met Talleyrand's. The former bishop was leaning on his stick, tired from standing so long. What was he thinking?

Suddenly the Emperor stopped and confronted me. "Princess," he said softly, "do you realize that the Swedish royal house is mad? The present King is incapable of pronouncing one coherent sentence, and his nephew had to be deposed because he was crazy! Is your husband also crazy? Crazy enough to give up his French citizenship for the Swedish succession?"

"I must ask you not to insult His Majesty, Charles the Thirteenth, in my presence," said Jean-Baptiste sharply.

"And you, Princess, what do you say to this? Bernadotte also asks that you and the child be allowed to relinquish French citizenship."

"It's a matter of form, sire," I heard myself say. "Without this we cannot succeed to the Swedish throne." I looked at Jean-Baptiste. But he was staring right past me. Talleyrand, however, nodded almost imperceptibly.

"Point two: your resignation from the Army. That can't be done, Bernadotte, it really can't." The Emperor was back behind the desk again, reading the application. "I cannot consider doing without one of my marshals. If England doesn't surrender, I will need you, whether you are Crown Prince of Sweden or not. Your Swedish regiments will become a part of our great Army." Unexpectedly, he looked up and smiled. "I shall permit you to become a Swede if you remain a marshal of France."

"I request you to allow me to resign from the French Army."

Napoleon pounded the desk with his fist. It sounded like a clap of thunder.

"My feet hurt. May I sit down, sire?" I said. The Emperor looked at me. The glitter in his eyes dimmed, replaced by a faraway look. Was he, perhaps, seeing a girl in a garden, at dusk, a young girl racing to a hedge, and himself, to please her, letting her win?

"Please—sit down," he said quietly. "Let's all be seated."

So we gathered cozily around his desk. "You wish to leave the Army, Prince of Pontecorvo? To fight with our armies, not as a marshal of France, but as one of our allies? Do I understand you correctly?"

So that's what Napoleon wanted, had wanted all the time. An alliance with Sweden. "It was extremely sagacious of the Swedish people to prove their friendship with France by choosing one of my marshals. Now, I trust, Sweden will stop trading with England and stop secretly forwarding English goods to our other allies, Germany and Russia. You will clear this up in Sweden. And, if necessary, declare war on England."

"I shall serve the interests of Sweden with all the means at my disposal," Jean-Baptiste said. "And if Your Majesty's government is negotiating a treaty of friendship with Sweden, I believe I will be able to serve the interests of my former country as well."

"Of course, had I been asked," Napoleon said, "I should have

preferred that one of my brothers become Crown Prince of Sweden. But since I wasn't consulted but only confronted with the
surprising results of this election—I congratulate you, dear
Prince."

"Mama, he doesn't scare me a bit."

Talleyrand bit his lip to stifle his smile. Napoleon considered
Oscar thoughtfully. "Strange that I chose a Nordic name for this
particular godchild." He clapped Jean-Baptiste on the shoulder.
"Doesn't life play tricks, Bernadotte?" And to me: "No doubt
you've heard, Princess, that the Empress is pregnant. Her Majesty
is expecting a son who will be called King of Rome."

I nodded. "I rejoice with you, sire."

Napoleon looked again at Oscar. "I understand why you must
become Swedish, Bernadotte. Particularly for the child. I'm told
that the deposed mad King also has a son. You must never lose
sight of this exiled son, Bernadotte. Meanwhile, you are prince of
a small territory under French domination. I am forced to deprive
you of the principality of Pontecorvo and its very considerable
revenues."

Jean-Baptiste nodded. "In my request I specifically asked that
you do so, sire."

"I think you're right, Bernadotte," said Napoleon slowly, and
stood up. We also rose. The Emperor studied the application for
the last time. "And your properties in France? In Lithuania? In
Westphalia?" he asked absentmindedly.

"I'm selling them, sire."

"To pay the debts of the Vasa dynasty?"

"Yes, and to maintain the court of the Bernadotte dynasty."

Napoleon reached for his pen, and glanced once more at Jean-
Baptiste and me. "When I sign this document, Bernadotte, you,
your wife and your son will cease to be French citizens. This
signature also means that I have accepted your resignation from
the Army. Shall I sign it, Bernadotte?"

Jean-Baptiste nodded. I groped for his hand. The clock struck
twelve. A bugle call, a sentinel's signal, sounded in the courtyard,
drowning out the scratching of the pen.

On the way home Jean-Baptiste sat hunched in a corner of the
carriage. We didn't speak, but we understood each other perfectly.
When we were finally alone in our little salon, we sat side by side
on the sofa, as tired as though we'd come a great distance. After a

while Jean-Baptiste got up, went over to the piano and hit the keys with one finger. The "Marseillaise."

"Today," he said, "I saw Napoleon for the last time in my life."

Paris, September 30, 1810

This noon Jean-Baptiste left for Sweden; Oscar and I will join him later. He'd been so busy the last few days that we had no chance for a proper good-by. The French Foreign Ministry compiled a list of Swedes who are considered here to be particularly important. Baron Mörner, whom Jean-Baptiste appointed his aide-de-camp, and young Count Brahe briefed him on the names. Messengers from Stockholm arrived constantly with reports of the magnificent preparations for Jean-Baptiste's reception. Every morning the pastor of the Evangelical Community in Paris came to give Jean-Baptiste religious instruction. Before his arrival in Sweden Jean-Baptiste will renounce the Roman Catholic Church and become a Protestant. In Sweden Protestantism is the state religion.

"Must I become a Protestant, too, Jean-Baptiste?" I asked.

He thought this over. "I don't think that's necessary; do as you like. But Oscar must learn the Augsburg Confession of Faith by heart and, if possible, in Swedish. Count Brahe can help him."

This is just one of many duties young Count Brahe has assumed recently. A day or so after we had talked in our garden he astonished me by announcing that he had asked to be appointed, for the present, as my aide. "My request has been granted. I am at your service, Your Highness."

Very tall and boyishly slim, nineteen years old, dark eyes and curls like my Oscar's: Count Magnus Brahe, scion of one of the oldest and proudest families in Sweden, personal aide to the former Mademoiselle Clary, daughter of a silk merchant from Marseilles.

"I have also requested the honor of accompanying Your Royal Highness to Stockholm," he added softly.

I smiled, and for the first time, it seemed, my awful anxiety about the welcome that might await me in Sweden abated a little.

Jean-Baptiste has also suggested that Count Brahe help me learn by heart the names on the list of important Swedes.

"But I can't pronounce them," I complained to Jean-Baptiste.

"One can learn anything if one wants to," he said, and added, "You must get ready for the journey. I don't want you and Oscar to stay here any longer than necessary. As soon as I've prepared your apartments in the Royal Palace in Stockholm, you must set off. Promise me that?" He sounded very insistent. I nodded.

"By the way, I've been considering selling this house," he said thoughtfully.

"No, no—Jean-Baptiste, you mustn't do that to me," I pleaded. "It's my home! We will surely come back to Paris. Then we'll be glad to have our house."

It was late at night and we were sitting on Jean-Baptiste's bed, surrounded by his packed traveling bags. "If I ever return to Paris, it will be difficult and painful," he muttered, and stared into the candlelight. "But you are right, it would be best to have a place here. We'll keep the house, little one."

The Danish port of Elsinore, late on the night of December 21, 1810

I never realized that nights could be so long and so cold. Tomorrow Oscar and I embark on the warship that will carry us across the narrow strait to Sweden. We will land in Hälsingborg, where Sweden will welcome Crown Princess Desideria and her son, the heir apparent. My good little son.

Marie, who is asleep in my dressing room, put four hot-water bottles in my bed, but I'm shivering in spite of them. I'd like to get up, tiptoe into Oscar's room, sit beside his bed and hold his hand, as I have so often done on nights when I felt lonely. My son, I never guessed a time would come when I couldn't freely go to your bedside. But you no longer sleep alone in your room. Colonel Villatte—for many years your father's faithful aide—is escorting us. Your father gave orders that Villatte was to sleep in your room, and Count Brahe in the next, until we reach the Royal Palace in Stockholm. To protect you, darling.

We left our home in the rue d'Anjou the end of October. Oscar and I went to Julie's to spend the last few days with her. But young Brahe and the gentlemen from the Swedish embassy in Paris were impatient for us to leave France. I learned the reason for their impatience just yesterday.

We said good-by to Julie on the third of November, and set out for Sweden in three carriages. I was in the first carriage with Colonel Villatte and the doctor—Jean-Baptiste had engaged a personal physician for our journey—and Madame la Flotte. The second carriage followed with Oscar, Count Brahe, Marie and Yvette. In the third was our luggage. For the next six weeks we sat from early until late in our carriages. And every evening there's been a banquet or a reception in our honor. One day, near Nyborg, in Denmark, a courier from Napoleon overtook us. He dashed up carrying a large package and said, "Your Royal Highness, may I deliver this with highest regard from His Majesty? When His Majesty heard that Her Highness had left Paris, he murmured, 'Terrible time of year to go to Sweden,' and ordered me to ride after Your Highness and to deliver this gift. The Emperor said, 'Hurry, Her Highness will need this gift badly.'"

When we unpacked the Emperor's present, my heart stood still. A sable stole. The most magnificent sable I'd ever seen. "One of the three stoles the Tsar gave him," whispered la Flotte in awe. We'd all heard about these three sable stoles. Josephine had one, the second went to Paulette, the Emperor's favorite sister, and the third—yes, the third is now on my knees. Nevertheless, I'm still cold. In the old days a general's coat warmed me better: Napoleon's coat that stormy night in Marseilles; Jean-Baptiste's coat one rainy night in Paris.

My candles have burned low, and I must try to sleep. I did not hear until I got here that just before we began our travels, Napoleon had sent Sweden an ultimatum: Either declare war on the English, or be considered at war with France, Denmark and Russia. I was told that the State Council had been convened in Stockholm, and all eyes had focused on the new Crown Prince.

"Gentlemen," Jean-Baptiste had said, "I ask you to forget that I was born in France, and that the Emperor holds in his power what is dearer to me than anything on earth—my wife and son, who are still in France. I will not take part in this meeting of the State Council, as I do not wish, in any way, to influence your decision."

Now I understood why the gentlemen of the Swedish embassy in Paris had been anxious for Oscar and me to hasten our departure. The Swedish State Council decided to declare war against England on November 17. But Count Brahe told me, "His Royal Highness, the Crown Prince, sent a secret messenger to England asking that this declaration be considered a mere formality. Sweden wishes to continue trading with England, and suggests that from now on English ships entering Swedish harbors fly the American flag."

I have tried in vain to understand all these developments. Napoleon could have held Oscar and me as hostages. But he let us go, and even sent me the sable. Jean-Baptiste, on the other hand, requested the State Council to take no notice of his family. Sweden is more important to him. Sweden is to him the most important thing on earth.

In the Royal Palace, Stockholm, spring of 1811

At last the sky was like a fresh-washed sheet and ice floes swam in the roaring waters of the Mälaren! Spring doesn't come gently to this country, but tumultuously, passionately, fighting.

On one of these spring afternoons one of my new ladies-in-waiting appeared before me. "Her Majesty invites Your Royal Highness to have a cup of tea in Her Majesty's salon." That surprised me. Every evening Jean-Baptiste and I dine alone with Oscar, and then we spend at least an hour with the Queen. But I've never called on the Queen by myself.

I dashed to my dressing room, brushed my hair, put on the fur-lined shawl Jean-Baptiste had recently given me, and walked up the marble staircase to Her Majesty's salon.

They were seated around a little table—all three of them—bent over their needlework. Queen Hedwig Elisabeth Charlotte, my adoptive mother-in-law, who is just over fifty and very energetic and clever, and who should be fond of me, Jean-Baptiste told me. The former queen mother, Sophia Magdalena, who has every reason to hate me: her son is exiled, and her grandson, who is Oscar's age, has been deprived of all his rights to the throne. And Princess Sofia Albertina, an old maid of indeterminate age, with a faded face and a childish bow in her hair.

"Sit down, madame," the Queen said.

The three ladies continued to embroider until tea was served. The Queen motioned the lackeys out of the room. Not a single lady-in-waiting was present. "I want to talk to you, dear daughter," she said.

Princess Sofia Albertina bared her teeth in a malicious smile.

The former queen mother stared indifferently into her teacup.

"To ask, dear daughter, whether you yourself feel that you are fulfilling your duties as Crown Princess of Sweden?"

I felt myself blushing. "I don't know, madame," I said. "I can't judge, because it's the first time I've ever been a crown princess."

The Queen's voice was smooth as silk. "That is extremely unfortunate for the Swedish people and for him whom the Swedish people have chosen as heir to the throne. So I will tell you, my dear daughter, how a crown princess must behave." The Queen took a slow sip of tea. "A crown princess never takes a drive with one of her husband's aides without a lady-in-waiting."

Did she mean faithful Villatte? "I—Colonel Villatte and I—we like to talk about old times," I said finally.

"At court functions crown princesses should converse graciously with everyone. You act as though you were deaf and dumb."

"Madame, if one is not too clever or too well educated, and yet must conceal one's thoughts, one is forced—to be silent!" I folded my hands in my lap. Everything ends, and so would this tea party.

"From one of my lackeys I hear that your servant has inquired about the shop of a certain Persson. You are to make no purchases whatever at this shop."

I lifted my head. "Why not?"

"This Persson is not a purveyor to the court, and never will be. I myself have made inquiries, madame. This Persson is known to have lived in France at the time of the Revolution. Since his return, he has associated with students, writers and other muddle-headed creatures, discussing with them the very ideas that were the undoing of the French nation."

"I don't quite understand, madame. Persson once lived with us in Marseilles, he worked with Papa in the shop. I gave him French lessons, we learned the Rights of Man by heart—"

"Madame"—like a slap in the face—"I must insist you forget that. It is incredible that this Persson took lessons from you"—she was breathing hard—"or that he had anything to do with your father."

"Madame, Papa was a highly respected silk merchant, and the firm of Clary is today a very substantial one."

"And you, madame, are Crown Princess of Sweden."

A long silence followed. I looked down at my hands, trying to collect my thoughts. But my mind blurred.

"I'd like you to consider seriously what I have said and to act accordingly," the Queen said icily. "You should never for an instant forget the position of our dear son, the Crown Prince, madame." That finished me.

"Your Majesty reproaches me because I cannot forget who and what my papa was. You tell me not to forget my husband's position. I want you to know—I forget nothing and nobody."

Without waiting for the Queen's permission, I stood up. The three ladies sat up straighter than ever. "In my home in Marseilles, madame, the mimosa is now in bloom. When it's a little warmer, I will return to France."

That worked. All three jumped. "You would go—back?" the Queen asked haltingly. "When did you decide this?"

"This instant, Your Majesty."

"It's politically unwise. You must talk it over with the Crown Prince," she said rapidly.

"I do nothing without my husband's consent."

"And where will you live in Paris, madame? You have no palace there."

"I never have had a palace there. But we kept our home in the rue d'Anjou. An ordinary house, but so beautiful to me. I am not used to living in palaces. I—hate palaces, madame."

The Queen had regained her poise. "Your country house near Paris might perhaps be more suitable."

"La Grange? We sold la Grange and everything else to pay Sweden's debts abroad. Very large debts, madame."

She bit her lip. Then quickly: "No, that won't do—Crown Princess Desideria of Sweden in an ordinary Paris dwelling . . ."

"I shall discuss it with my husband. Anyway, I have no intention of traveling under the name of Desideria of Sweden." I felt my eyes fill with tears. I mustn't cry now. "Perhaps Your Majesty will put your mind to a suitable incognito for me. Now, may I go?"

And I slammed the door behind me so hard the sound echoed through the marble corridors.

I WENT DIRECTLY to Jean-Baptiste's study. In the anteroom an aide barred the way. "May I announce Your Royal Highness?"

"No, thank you. I am accustomed to entering my husband's apartments without being announced." Whereupon I went into Jean-Baptiste's study.

Jean-Baptiste sat at his desk, a pile of documents before him, while he listened to the chancellor and two other gentlemen. A green eyeshade cast a shadow over his face. Because here the days are so short, he has to read mostly by artificial light. Fernand has already told me how greatly his eyes trouble him, though Jean-Baptiste has tried to keep it from me. He took the eyeshade off in a hurry when I came in.

"Has something happened, Désirée?"

"No. I just want to talk to you. I'll sit quietly in a corner and wait until you're finished."

I pulled a chair up to the big round stove and warmed myself. When at last Jean-Baptiste wished the gentlemen good evening, they bowed to him and to me, and backed out of the room. "Now, what is it, little one?" he said.

"I'm leaving, Jean-Baptiste. When it's summer and the roads are better. I'm going home, dearest," I said softly.

"Have you gone mad? You are at home. Here in the Royal Palace in Stockholm."

"But I must leave, Jean-Baptiste," I insisted. And repeated to him word for word my conversation with the Queen. He listened without comment. Then he broke loose. Like a storm.

"And I have to listen to this nonsense. Her Majesty and Her Royal Highness cannot get along. I must say the Queen is right. You don't always behave like—what's expected. You'll learn, of course, you'll learn. But, God knows, I can't be bothered with this now. Have you any idea what's happening in the world? What's at stake? Our very existence—the existence of Europe."

His voice was hoarse with excitement. "Napoleon's system creaks in every joint. In the South there's been no peace for a long time. In Germany his enemies are secretly uniting. Napoleon can no longer depend on the Tsar, so he will attack Russia. And when finally there is a new coalition, under the leadership of England and Russia, then Sweden must decide. For or against Napoleon."

"Against him? That—that would mean that you would fight against France—"

"No, Napoleon and France are not the same. And have not been for a long time. So I can do no more than serve Sweden with all my strength. Not for a second can I consider myself or my past, but only the policies that will secure Sweden's independence. Right now, Napoleon is concentrating troops on the frontiers of

Swedish Pomerania. If he won a war against Russia, he would simply overrun Sweden."

"How can you keep talking about Sweden's destiny and not realize that's exactly why I must immediately return to Paris? Here I can only embarrass you, but in Paris I could do a lot."

"Don't be childish. Would you perhaps spy on the Emperor for me? I have my spies in Paris, never fear. I might tell you that our old friend Talleyrand not only corresponds secretly with the Bourbons, but with me. And Fouché, now fallen into disfavor . . ." Jean-Baptiste sighed. "Désirée, I cannot let you go. Here you are the Crown Princess. Enough. That settles it."

"But I am not the Desideria the Swedish nobles wanted. Let me go, Jean-Baptiste. In Paris I'll try to educate myself so that someday you won't have to be ashamed of me, you and Oscar. It will strengthen your position."

"But I can't have the Swedish Crown Princess in Paris as Napoleon's hostage. My own decisions would be influenced if you were in danger, and—"

"Once you urged the Swedish State Council not to concern itself with the fate of those you loved most. We were still in France then, Oscar and I. No, Jean-Baptiste, you can't consider me. If the Swedes are to be loyal to you, you must stand by them."

I took his hand, pulled him down on the arm of my chair. "Besides, do you seriously believe that Napoleon would ever let his brother Joseph's sister-in-law be arrested? And others need me, too, Jean-Baptiste. Perhaps there will come a day when my house will be the only place in which my sister and her children can take refuge. Let me go, Jean-Baptiste, I beg of you."

He shook his head. "No, no! Désirée, I cannot carry on if I don't know you're near me. And I don't know how things will work out. Perhaps you won't be able to get back for a long time. Europe will soon be one vast battlefield, and you and I . . ."

"Dearest, I couldn't go with you to the front in any case."

"Désirée, the child needs you."

Yes, the child. All the while I'd been trying to stifle this thought. The idea of being separated from Oscar was like a throbbing wound.

"Oscar is the heir apparent. Surrounded by three tutors and an aide-de-camp. Since our arrival in Stockholm, he has had very little time for me. Every minute is planned. At first he will miss me very much, but he'll soon realize that an heir apparent never considers his feelings. Only his duties. In this way our child will grow up like a born prince."

I leaned my head on Jean-Baptiste's shoulder and wept. He drew me to him, but said nothing. I pulled myself together and got up. "I think it's time for dinner." Jean-Baptiste remained, poised on the arm of the chair. I walked to the door. I waited for one word from him. For his decision. I would accept it as a final judgment. Whatever he decides, it will be the end of me, I felt.

"And how am I to explain your leaving to Their Majesties and to the court?" The decision was made.

"Say that my health demands that I spend the autumn and winter in Paris because I can't stand this cold climate." I left the room quickly.

Drottningholm Castle, June 1811

Midnight had long since passed and still it's not dark. Summer nights in the North stay light. These long twilights seem as unreal as a dream. And these last days before I leave are indeed a twilight interlude—the last words, the farewells. Tomorrow morning, traveling incognito as the Countess of Gotland, I start my return trip to France.

I turn over the pages of my diary. . . . "For years I have been saving part of my pay. I could buy a little house for you and the child," Jean-Baptiste had said, and I wrote it down. Jean-Baptiste bought the little house in Sceaux, very small and very comfortable, and we were happy there. . . .

Anyway, on the first of June the court moved to the summer residence, Drottningholm Castle. As far as the eye can see, there are beautifully aligned linden trees, perfectly clipped hedges and a maze of paths. I came with them to Drottningholm only because I wanted to see the famous Vasa palace in which Oscar will from now on spend his summers. Oscar, my child, when I see you again, you will no longer be a child—at least not my child—but a real prince, a royal highness, trained to the throne.

For weeks the court couldn't grasp the idea that I was actually going. People gossiped and glanced surreptitiously at me. Strangely, they are blaming the Queen. The rumor is that she wasn't a good mother-in-law to me and drove me away.

On the evening of our arrival a play was presented in the little theater of Drottningholm Castle. One of my ladies-in-waiting, Mariana von Koskull, sang a few arias. The King applauded enthusiastically, but Jean-Baptiste seemed indifferent. Odd, for a while during the long dark winter, I had thought . . . But now, since I've decided to leave, the great tall Koskull, the Valkyrie, seems to have lost all charm for Jean-Baptiste. Dearest, though I should be far away in Paris, I'd still be deeply hurt. Yet the words spoken in the twilight of this indescribably horrible last evening were so very clear. . . .

Their Majesties gave a farewell banquet in my honor, and after dinner there was dancing. The King and Queen sat on gilded chairs with high stiff backs. I danced with many, including Count Brahe, who is now on Jean-Baptiste's staff, his youngest secretary. Later we went into the garden, and I said, "I must thank you, Count Brahe. You have stood by me gallantly since I came here. Forgive me for disappointing you."

His dark head was bowed, and he gnawed on the little mustache he's cultivating. Suddenly he looked up desperately. "I beg Your Royal Highness not to leave—I implore you to stay. This is not the time for you to leave."

"Not the time? I don't understand you, Count Brahe."

He turned away. "A letter from the Tsar has come, Highness. More I dare not say."

"Then don't say it. You are one of the Crown Prince's secretaries. You should not discuss His Royal Highness's correspondence with me. I hope the letter was friendly."

"Too friendly," said Brahe earnestly. "The Tsar offered to make the Crown Prince a member of his family, if it would secure His Royal Highness's position in Sweden."

I was stupefied. "What does that mean? Does the Tsar also want to adopt us?"

"The Tsar means only His Royal Highness." Finally Brahe turned his tormented face toward me. "There are other ways of establishing a family relationship, Your Highness."

At last I understood. There are other ways. . . . Napoleon married off his stepson to a Bavarian princess. Napoleon himself is the son-in-law of the Austrian Emperor. A man need only marry a princess. It's that simple. An act of state, a document; like the one Josephine had to read out. . . .

"That would undoubtedly secure His Royal Highness's position," I heard myself say.

"Not in Sweden. The Tsar took Finland away from us; we can't forget so quickly. But in the rest of Europe . . ."

Josephine sobbing on her bed. It can be done quite easily.

". . . in the rest of Europe, His Royal Highness's prestige would doubtless be increased."

But Josephine had no son. I have a son.

" . . . So I would like to repeat that now is not the time for Your Highness to leave."

"Yes, Count Brahe. Right now." I held out my hand to him. "I ask you from my heart to stand by my husband loyally. Colonel Villatte, my husband's oldest and most faithful aide, is returning to Paris with me. I expect you to take his place. My husband will be very much alone. I'll see you in the morning, Count Brahe."

I did not return to the ballroom immediately, but wandered, bewildered, down to the park, past the clipped hedges. Tonight the park seemed infinite, haunted by ghosts. The summer wind sang softly through the leaves. Suddenly I saw a shadow—a figure dressed all in black, and it was moving toward me. I screamed, wanted to run away, but I couldn't.

"I'm sorry if I frightened you." Close beside me on the moonlit gravel walk stood the former queen mother, Sophia Magdalena. "I often take a walk on beautiful summer nights. I sleep very badly, madame. And this park holds many memories for me."

How could I reply? Her son and her grandson had been exiled. My husband and my son had been called in. "I'm saying good-by to these paths, which I don't really know," I said politely. "Tomorrow morning I go back to France."

We walked on, side by side. "I think often about your leaving. And I believe I'm the only one who knows why." She took my arm. This startled me so that I jumped back. "Are you afraid of me, child?" Her voice sounded deeply sad. "Afraid of a sick and lonely woman?"

I nodded. "Yes," I said slowly, "I am afraid of you, madame. Because, like the other ladies of your family, you are disturbed by me. I don't belong here." I paused, then continued. "But I also understand you, madame. Our aims are very similar." Tears welled in my eyes. "You stay in Sweden, madame, as a constant reminder to the people of your exiled son and your exiled grandson. As long as you are here, no one can forget the last of the Vasas." I lowered my voice and confided to her our common secret. "You are the mother of an exiled king, and your staying serves his interests. And I best serve the interests of the future king by leaving."

She didn't move—slender, very erect, a black shadow in the green twilight. "You are right," she said at last. Strains of a woman singing fluttered through the trees. It was the voice of Mademoiselle von Koskull.

"But are you also sure you're serving your own best interests, madame?" the old woman asked.

"Quite sure, madame. I'm thinking of a distant future, and King Oscar the First," I answered quietly. With which I bowed deeply to her and went alone back to the palace.

Two o'clock in the morning. . . . I have described my last evening, there's nothing further to add. I still can't escape my thoughts. Has the Tsar daughters? Or sisters?

Oh—I'm seeing ghosts again. My door is opening very softly. I feel like screaming, but perhaps I'm mistaken—no, the door is really opening. I pretend to be writing—

Jean-Baptiste. My beloved Jean-Bap—

Paris, January 1, 1812

At the very moment all the church bells of Paris rang in the New Year, we found ourselves alone together—Napoleon and I.

Julie had surprised me with the invitation. "The Emperor and the Empress are holding a reception. The family has been asked for ten o'clock, and you must definitely come with us."

That day Julie and I were sitting in the parlor in the rue d'Anjou. Julie was telling me about her children, her household worries, and about Joseph. He complains constantly about the French generals who were defeated in Spain and couldn't hold his throne for him. Julie, on the other hand, seems contented with her life. She frequents court circles, considers the Empress truly majestic and, like Napoleon, finds the little blond, blue-eyed King of Rome delightful.

Julie never understood why I did not announce my return at the Tuileries. But I live very quietly, and see only Julie and my closest friends. That's why this invitation came as such a surprise. There had to be some particular reason for it. But what?

I wore my white-gold dress for the occasion, and diamond earrings that had been given me by Sophia Magdalena. I put on the sable stole, though I wasn't cold. In Stockholm it's freezing now, at twenty to twenty-five degrees below zero. . . .

The whole family had already assembled in the Empress's salon, and they all rushed to welcome me. I had become a genuine crown princess. Madame Letizia admired my earrings, and wanted to know what they cost. I was glad to see *Madame Mère* again, with her Parisian ringlets and beautifully manicured nails. And Paulette, the Princess Borghese, looks more dainty, more delicate, more beautiful than ever.

"Do you remember the New Year's Eve when you were expecting Oscar?" Joseph asked me. I nodded. "We drank a toast to the Bernadotte dynasty." Joseph laughed. Not a pleasant laugh.

It was after eleven. The Emperor had not yet appeared. "His Majesty is working," Marie Louise explained. "At midnight he will welcome the New Year with the child in his arms."

"It's bad for the child's health to wake him up and show him off to so many guests," Madame Letizia scolded.

Ménéval, the Emperor's secretary, had come in. "His Majesty wishes to speak to Her Royal Highness, the Crown Princess of Sweden." Marie Louise showed no surprise at this summons. But the Bonapartes stopped talking as I made for the door.

The Emperor looked up fleetingly from his papers when Ménéval showed me into the study and then disappeared. "Please be seated, madame." That was all. I sat down and waited. He read on, and I had time to study him. His face has gotten fleshy, his hair very thin. This face, I realized, I had once dearly loved. I well remember my love. Only I had forgotten the face.

The clock on the mantlepiece ticked toward the New Year. "You don't need to intimidate me by keeping me waiting, sire," I said. "I am by nature timid, and I'm particularly afraid of you."

"Eugénie—" At last he looked up. "One waits until the Emperor speaks. Didn't Monsieur Montel teach you that at least?"

"Sire, did you send for me to lecture me on questions of etiquette?"

"Among other things. I wish to know, madame, what brought you back to France."

"The cold, sire."

He leaned back and crossed his arms on his chest. "And why have you not presented yourself at court? The wives of my marshals regularly pay their respects to Her Majesty."

"I am no longer the wife of one of your marshals, sire."

"Of course. I'd almost forgotten. We are now dealing with Her Royal Highness, Crown Princess Desideria of Sweden. But court courtesy demands that members of foreign royal houses request an audience when they visit my capital, madame."

"I'm not on a visit. This is my home."

"I see." He got up. "And do people in Sweden consider you clever enough to send you here as a spy?"

"No, quite the opposite. It's because I'm stupid that I had to come back."

He hadn't expected this answer. "What do you mean?"

"Remember the Eugénie of the old days? I didn't make a good impression on the Swedish court. And since it's important that we—Jean-Baptiste, Oscar and I—be liked in Sweden, I came home. It's all very simple really."

"So simple that I don't believe you." Like the crack of a whip. "Madame, the political situation has become so extremely critical that I must ask you to leave France."

I stared at him, utterly disconcerted. "But I have no home except the house in the rue d'Anjou."

"Tell me, madame, has Bernadotte gone mad?" Napoleon asked abruptly. He pawed through the papers on his desk and picked out a letter. I recognized Jean-Baptiste's handwriting. "I offer Bernadotte an alliance with France and he turns it down. The Tsar's empire will soon cease to exist. *The greatest army of all time will occupy Russia.*" The words intoxicated him. "At our side Sweden could again become a great power. I've promised Bernadotte Finland if he marches with us. But Bernadotte, a French marshal, is not participating in this campaign!"

I looked at the clock. "Sire, it's nearly midnight."

He didn't hear me. "Two hundred thousand Frenchmen, one hundred and fifty thousand Germans, eighty thousand Italians, sixty thousand Poles—not counting one hundred and ten thousand volunteers from other countries. The Grand Army of Napoleon the First." He turned, his face distorted by fury. "And Bernadotte thinks nothing of this army!"

I shook my head. "Sire, Jean-Baptiste Bernadotte is responsible for the well-being of Sweden. Whatever he does, he does solely to serve the interests of Sweden."

"Who is not for me is against me." Suddenly he stood and rang a bell on the desk. Ménéval shot into the room.

"Here—deliver this by special courier immediately." Napoleon turned to me. "That, madame, is an order to Marshal Davout. Davout and his troops will cross the frontier and occupy Swedish Pomerania. What do you say to that, madame? Will Bernadotte defend Swedish Pomerania? It would amuse me to see him and Davout fighting each other."

"Amuse you?" I thought of the battlefields. The pathetic mounds of earth, the wind-lashed crosses. And this amuses him . . .

"And now, madame, are you aware that if you don't leave France of your own free will, I can have you arrested as a hostage, and thus force the Swedish government into an alliance?"

I smiled. "My fate would not influence the decision of the Swedish government. But my arrest would prove to the Swedes that I am willing to suffer for my new country. Will you really make a martyr of me, sire?"

The Emperor was annoyed at the thought of making a Swedish national heroine out of Madame Bernadotte. He shrugged. "I expect you to urge your husband to try to win our friendship." His eyes gleamed. "In your own interests, madame."

At that moment the bells rang. The bells of Paris proclaiming the New Year. As though in a trance Napoleon stared into space and said, in a hushed voice, "A great year in the history of France has begun." Then, abruptly: "But we must hurry, Her Majesty is expecting us."

IN THE EMPRESS'S SALON I saw the little King of Rome for the first time. The Emperor held him in his arms, and the poor thing, seeing all the Bonapartes, the foreign diplomats in court uniform and the giggling ladies, screamed in terror. The Emperor, to quiet his shrieking son, tickled him tenderly. Marie Louise, beside the Emperor, looked at the baby with astonishment. She seemed unable to grasp the fact that she had borne Napoleon a child.

Napoleon came over to me with the yelling baby, beaming. "You must stop crying, sire; kings do not weep," he told the infant. Without thinking, I took the child and held him tight.

Under his lace finery he was very damp. When I caressed the blond hair at the nape of his neck, he stopped crying and peered around timidly. I held him close. Oscar, I thought. Oscar is at this moment drinking champagne in the Queen's salon. . . . He touches his glass politely with Their Majesties'. Mademoiselle von Koskull warbles an aria. In a few days Jean-Baptiste will know that Davout has marched into Swedish Pomerania. The Koskull warbles on . . .

I kissed the silky blond hair and handed the infant to his nurse. "He is very damp," I whispered to her. She then carried the child out. The Emperor and the Empress, in a pleasant mood, conversed graciously.

I was tired, I wanted to go home. But the Emperor again came up to me, the Empress on his arm. "And here's my beautiful little hostage," he said. The onlookers laughed. "Ladies and gentlemen, you don't yet know what I mean. You see that Her Highness is not laughing. Marshal Davout has unfortunately been forced to occupy part of the northern homeland of Her Highness."

How silent the room then became. Napoleon spoke directly to me. "I take it the Tsar has more than I to offer, madame. I am told he is even offering the hand of a grand duchess. Does this tempt our former marshal?"

"Marriage to a member of an ancient royal house is always tempting to men of simple middle-class origins," I said slowly. The bystanders were abashed.

"Undoubtedly." The Emperor smiled. "But such temptation endangers your own position, madame. As an old friend, I advise you to write to Bernadotte and urge him to conclude an alliance with France. For the sake of your own future, madame."

"My future is assured, sire. At least as queen mother."

He looked at me, quite startled. "Madame, until the Swedish-French alliance is concluded, I do not wish to see you at court," he said, and moved off with Marie Louise.

Marie was waiting up for me at home. I'd given Yvette, La Flotte and the others the evening off.

"Happy New Year, Marie. The Emperor has created the largest army of all time and I'm to write to Jean-Baptiste about an alliance. Can you tell me how I got involved in world history?"

"Eugénie," Marie said cautiously, "when are you returning to Stockholm?"

If I hurry, I thought desperately, I may be in time to celebrate my husband's engagement to a Russian grand duchess.

The year 1812 has begun. I think it will be terrible.

Paris, April 1812

Marie's son, Pierre, is here, quite unexpectedly. He volunteered for the Grand Army, and his regiment will leave for the front from Paris. Until now, I have regularly paid eight thousand francs a year to buy Pierre off from military service. (I've always had a guilty conscience about Pierre. After his birth Marie sent him to foster parents so that she could be my wet nurse and earn her living.) Pierre is now a tall, brawny fellow, tanned by the southern sun. He has Marie's dark eyes, but a jaunty look he must have inherited from his father. His uniform is spanking new; even his blue-white-red cockade gleams.

Marie, as always, practically lost her mind over him. Her bony hands stroked his arms shyly. "But why?" she asked again and again. "You were so happy in the estate manager's post Her Highness got for you."

Now Pierre showed his startlingly white teeth. "Mama, we must do it. Join the Grand Army, conquer Russia, occupy Moscow. The Emperor has called us to arms to unite Europe at last."

No, a man couldn't possibly toil in a vineyard near Marseilles when the Emperor was assembling the greatest army of all time. Day and night I see from my window the regiments on their way to Russia, their bands blaring forth. Their heavy tread shakes the houses. At the sound of drums, people rush to their windows to cheer them on.

PIERRE stood at attention and saluted.

"Come home safe, Pierre!" I said.

Marie went with him to the door.

Outside, a regiment passed by with beating drums and blaring trumpets. Colonel Villatte came in. Since the mobilization of the Grand Army, he's been terribly restless.

"Why do soldiers march into battle with music?" I asked.

"Because martial music is inspiring," Villatte said. "It helps the men keep in step. And prevents them from thinking too much."

At that moment Count Rosen, my newly appointed Swedish

aide, arrived. He had a dispatch in his hand. "I have important news for Your Highness. On April fifth Sweden concluded an alliance with Russia."

My heart skipped a beat. Jean-Baptiste had made his choice.

"Colonel Villatte—" Then my voice failed me. Villatte—Jean-Baptiste's comrade, his aide at all his battles, the true friend who had followed us to Sweden, our Villatte . . .

"Your Highness wishes?"

"We have just learned that Sweden and Russia have become allies." I couldn't look at him. "You are a French citizen, and a French officer, Colonel. I think this alliance with the enemies of France will make it uncomfortable for you to remain in my house. You once asked for leave of absence from your regiment to help us. Now I ask you to feel free of these obligations."

"Highness, I can't leave you alone now," Villatte said.

I looked at the young Count Rosen and said, "I am not alone. Count Rosen will protect the Crown Princess of Sweden if it should be necessary." I didn't mind if Villatte saw the tears streaming down my cheeks. "I know how you feel. You must either resign from the French Army, as Jean-Baptiste did, or"—I waved toward the window, toward those long lines of marching men—"or march on, Colonel Villatte."

"Not march, ride," protested Villatte, as a colonel of the cavalry.

I smiled at him. "Ride, then, Colonel. And come back to us, safe and sound."

Paris, middle of September, 1812

I am unspeakably alone in this large city of Paris. Julie asked me to spend the hot summer days at their country house, Villa Mortefontaine, but for the first time in my life I couldn't say even to her what I think. We once shared a young girls' room in Marseilles, but now she sleeps beside Joseph Bonaparte. And Marie? Marie is the mother of a soldier marching through Russia with Napoleon. That leaves—how comical—only my Swedish aide as my confidant. Count Rosen is Swedish with every beat of his heart. For centuries Sweden has been bled by wars against Russia, and blond Count Rosen doesn't understand why the new Crown Prince has made a pact with the archfiend.

Just a few hours ago Count Talleyrand, adviser to the Ministry of Foreign Affairs, and Fouché, Duke of Otranto and former minister of police, were here. They called on me separately.

Talleyrand came first. But before I could present Count Rosen to him, the Duke of Otranto was announced, and seemed unpleasantly surprised to find Talleyrand with me. "I'm glad Your Highness has company. I had been afraid Your Highness would be very lonely."

"I was very lonely until this instant," I said, sitting down on the sofa under the portrait of Napoleon. The two gentlemen sat opposite me. Yvette brought in tea.

"This gentleman is France's famous police minister who, because of his health, has retired to his estates," I explained to Count Rosen, who was busily passing teacups.

"Information seems to reach the Duke of Otranto's estates as readily as the Foreign Ministry in Paris," Talleyrand remarked.

"Some news travels fast," Fouché said, drinking his tea.

"What are you talking about?" I asked politely. "The French victories are no secret. The bells have scarcely stopped ringing out the capture of Smolensk."

"Yes, Smolensk." Talleyrand was considering Napoleon's youthful portrait with interest. "However, Your Highness, in half an hour the bells will ring again to report the victory at Borodino. This leaves the road to Moscow open."

Had he come to tell me this? Victories, victories, for many years nothing but victories. I must tell Marie that Pierre will soon be marching into Moscow. "Then the Russian campaign will soon be over? Have another little piece of marzipan, Excellency."

"Has Your Royal Highness heard anything from His Royal Highness, the Crown Prince, recently?" Fouché inquired.

I laughed. "That's right, you no longer read my mail. Your successor could tell you that Jean-Baptiste hasn't written me for two weeks."

"The Swedish Crown Prince has been away." Fouché never took his eyes off me. "The Tsar asked the Swedish Crown Prince to meet with him in Finland," he announced triumphantly, and then looked at Talleyrand.

"What does the Tsar want with Jean-Baptiste?" I whispered.

"Advice," said Talleyrand. "A former marshal, familiar with the Emperor's tactics, is the perfect adviser in a situation like this."

"And on the basis of this advice, the Tsar has sent no emissaries to the Emperor to ask for peace, but has let our armies press forward," Fouché said. "By the day after tomorrow, undoubtedly, the Emperor will be in the Kremlin."

"Won't the war end when the Emperor gets to Moscow?" I said.

Silence fell. Then Fouché said, "The French Army has marched into villages burned to the ground by the inhabitants, to find only charred granaries. The French Army is marching from victory to victory—starving. The Emperor had not reckoned on this. But he hopes to fatten up his troops in Moscow, where the Army will winter. Moscow is a wealthy city, and can supply our troops. So you see, everything depends on the entry into Moscow."

"And on the advice your husband has given the Tsar," Talleyrand said.

"But how can there be any doubt?" Count Rosen asked in surprise. "The Russians have a hundred and forty thousand men under arms, and Napoleon has . . ."

"Almost half a million"—Talleyrand nodded—"but a Russian winter without proper quarters could destroy even the biggest and best of armies, young man."

At last I understood. Without proper quarters . . . I understood, all right. And a great fear caught at my throat.

At that moment the bells started pealing. Madame la Flotte threw open the drawing room door and shouted, "A new victory! The battle of Borodino has been won."

We never moved. Waves of ringing bells surged over us. Napoleon wants to spend the winter in Moscow. What advice has Jean-Baptiste given the Tsar?

Fouché and Talleyrand have their spies in every camp; they'll always be on the winning side. Since they have come to see me today, they must believe that Napoleon will lose this war. While victory bells ring out in Paris, Jean-Baptiste has intervened and assured the freedom of a small country far up north. But Pierre will freeze, and Villatte will bleed to death.

Talleyrand was the first to leave. Fouché didn't leave until the bells were silent. As he bowed over my hand, he said, "The Swedish Crown Princess and I have the same goal—peace."

I went out to the garden and sat down on a bench. The roses were through blooming, the grass had withered. I suddenly feared my own house and all my memories. I went to my room and began to write. How long will I be so alone?

Paris, two weeks later

Julie and Joseph planned a large party to celebrate Napoleon's entry into Moscow. But I didn't want to go, and wrote to tell Julie. The very next day she came to see me.

"I'm terribly anxious to have you come," she declared. "I want to stop this malicious gossip about you and Jean-Baptiste. Naturally your husband should have joined Napoleon in his Russian campaign; then they couldn't say Jean-Baptiste has allied himself with the Tsar."

"Julie, Jean-Baptiste *has* allied himself with the Tsar."

"Do you mean that—that it's true, what people say?"

"I don't know what people say, Julie. Jean-Baptiste has met the Tsar and given him advice."

"Désirée, you truly are a disgrace to the family."

"Which family do you mean?"

"The Bonapartes, of course."

"I'm no Bonaparte, Julie. I'm a Bernadotte."

"You are a sister-in-law of the oldest brother of the Emperor," she declared. "And Joseph insists that you come. Don't make things hard for me, Désirée."

We hadn't seen each other for weeks. Julie's face is thinner; the lines at the corners of her mouth are deeply etched. A terrible tenderness overwhelmed me. Julie, my Julie, is a harassed, faded, profoundly disappointed woman. Perhaps she's heard about Joseph's love affairs, perhaps he treats her badly because he himself becomes more embittered every year. Why does she stay with him? For love? For duty? Or for sheer obstinacy?

"If it will help in any way, I'll come," I said.

"Yes, please come. Joseph wants all Paris to know that Sweden is still neutral." She stood up.

"I'll bring Count Rosen, my Swedish aide."

"Your—? Yes, of course, your aide. Do bring him, there'll be so few men. They're all away."

The high bronze candelabra in the Elysée Palace sparkled. I knew people were whispering behind my back, but my back was protected by the tall young Count Rosen. They struck up the "Marseillaise." The Empress entered, and I bowed a little less deeply than the other ladies, for I am a member of a ruling house.

Since the birth of the little King of Rome, Marie Louise has gained weight. She laces herself very tightly. I saw there were beads of sweat on her short nose, and I was suddenly sad. Since she was small, she must have heard that Napoleon was a parvenu, a tyrant and an enemy of her country. Now he is her husband. And her country, Austria, is said to be secretly negotiating with Napoleon's enemies, Russia and England.

Joseph went over to the Empress and raised his glass of champagne. "On September fifteenth," he said, loudly enough for all of us to hear, "at the head of the most glorious army of all time, the Emperor entered Moscow and took up his residence in the Kremlin, the palace of the tsars. Our victorious Army will spend the winter in the capital of our defeated enemy. *Vive l'Empereur!*"

As I drank, Talleyrand appeared beside me. "Was Your Highness forced to come?" he asked.

"Whether I'm here or not has no meaning, Excellency. I don't understand politics."

"How strange that fate should have chosen you to play such a decisive role, Your Highness." He paused. "Perhaps someday I'll come to you with a most important request—a request in the name of France."

"Do tell me—what on earth are you talking about?"

"I am very much in love, Your Highness. In love with France."

Before I could reply, there was a voice right behind us. "My brother should feel at home in the Kremlin by now," said Joseph. "Sheer genius that he could get through so quickly. Our troops will be able to winter peacefully in Moscow."

But Talleyrand shook his head. "Unfortunately, I can't agree with Your Majesty. A courier arrived half an hour ago. Moscow has been in flames for two weeks. Even the Kremlin is on fire."

From far away I heard the waltz tunes. The candles flickered, Joseph's face was like a mask, greenish white, the eyes wide open, the mouth gaping with horror. "How did the fires start?" he asked hoarsely.

"Incendiaries, undoubtedly."

"And our troops, Your Excellency?"

"Will be forced to withdraw."

"But the Emperor has told me many times that under no circumstances would he lead the troops across the Russian steppes during the winter," said Joseph.

"I'm only telling you what the courier reported: The Emperor cannot spend the winter in Moscow because Moscow is burning down." Talleyrand raised his glass to Joseph. "Don't let your face betray you, Your Majesty. The Emperor would not want the news known prematurely. *Vive l'Empereur!*"

"*Vive l'Empereur*," Joseph repeated mechanically.

"Your Highness?" Talleyrand raised his glass to me. But I was petrified. I saw the Empress waltzing with an old gentleman crippled with gout. One doesn't leave a ball before Her Majesty has retired, but I was tired and confused. No, no—not confused. I saw everything clearly, so terribly clearly.

"Good night, Joseph, my love to Julie. Good night, Your Excellency," I murmured.

Torchbearers ran alongside my carriage, as always when I drive out to an official function. Watching the flames, I said to the young man beside me, "Do you know Moscow, Count Rosen?"

"No, Your Highness. Why?"

"Because Moscow is burning, Count. Moscow has been burning for fourteen days."

"The advice of His Highness to the Tsar . . . ?"

We said no more.

Paris, December 16, 1812

In Josephine's white-and-gold salon at Malmaison ladies rolled bandages for the wounded in Russia, and in her boudoir Josephine herself, tweezers in hand, bent over me, plucking my heavy brows. It hurt, but the thin arched line made my eyes seem larger. I had come to the most fashionable woman in France for advice. If the Swedes must have a parvenu crown princess, she should at least be beautiful.

Josephine next took a small jar of silver makeup, rubbed a little of it on my eyelids and studied my face in the mirror. At that moment I noticed the morning edition of the *Moniteur* on her dressing table. It had a bulletin issued by the Emperor. Bulletin 29. I began to read.

"You must make up like this, Désirée," Josephine was saying. "A little green on the eyelids and, above all, the silver."

"Have you read this, madame?" With shaking hands, I held out the paper to her.

•Josephine gave it a fleeting glance. "Naturally. It confirms what we've feared for a long time. Bonaparte admits that the Grand Army is no more. He has lost the war with Russia. I take it he'll soon be back in Paris. . . . Have you ever thought of using henna when you wash your hair?"

I continued to read: *This army, the greatest in history, was completely demoralized. It had no cavalry, no artillery and no transport. The enemy, apprised of the disaster that had befallen us, exploited our weakness. Cossacks ambushed our columns. . . .*

In these words Napoleon informed the world how his Grand Army had foundered during its retreat through the snowy wasteland of Russia. He soberly enumerated the losses. Of the hundred thousand cavalrymen who had ridden off to Moscow, for example, only six hundred riders were left. Six hundred—Napoleon's cavalry! The words *exhaustion* and *starvation* appeared again and again. At first I could not take it in. I read on. Bulletin 29 closed with the words: *The health of His Majesty was never better.*

Suddenly I understood. The rumors were true. Terribly true. Ten thousand men, a hundred thousand men, stumbling through the snow, crying from pain like children, because their arms and legs are frozen. They suddenly fall and can't get up again. Ravenous wolves surround them. The men scream in horror. . . . But His Majesty's health has never been better.

When I looked up, a strange face confronted me in the mirror. Large, melancholy eyes under silvered lids. An upturned nose, delicately powdered. And curved lips, a deep cyclamen pink. So I, too, can look elegant. I lowered my new face over the newspaper again. "And what will happen now? What will happen to France?" I asked dully, despairingly.

A shrug. "Bonaparte isn't France." Josephine was polishing her shining fingernails. "Napoleon the First, by the grace of God, Emperor of the French. . . ." She looked at me strangely. "Why aren't you in Stockholm, Désirée?"

"In Stockholm there is already one queen, and one queen mother. Isn't that enough?"

"Are you afraid of your predecessors?"

My eyes filled with tears. I swallowed hard.

"Predecessors aren't dangerous," Josephine said softly. "Only successors. You see, I was afraid you were here for his sake. Because you still loved him—Bonaparte."

It has rained continuously since my visit to Malmaison. But people still stand on street corners and read Bulletin 29 aloud to one another. I know of no family that hasn't a close relative in Russia.

Yesterday evening I couldn't get to sleep. Finally I sat down at the desk in the little salon and tried to write to Oscar. Count Rosen was reading Danish newspapers. Marie sat in a corner working on a gray shawl she's been knitting for Pierre ever since she heard about the icy Russian steppes. We've had no news from him.

If Oscar were here, he'd be called up for military service in a few years. How do other mothers stand it? Marie knits, and the snow falls incessantly in Russia, white and soft, burying sons.

At that moment I heard a carriage stop in front of my house, then a thundering knock at the door. Marie put down her knitting. We heard voices in the hall. "I will speak to no one. I have already retired," I said quickly. Count Rosen left the salon. Very soon I heard him escorting someone into the adjoining large salon. Incredible to admit anyone at this late hour against my express wishes.

Then he came back into the little salon, his movements oddly stiff and formal. "His Majesty, the Emperor."

"The Emperor is still at the front," I declared.

"His Majesty has just returned." The young Swede was pale with excitement. "His Majesty, accompanied by one gentleman, insists on speaking to Your Highness immediately."

I didn't move. What does one say to an Emperor who leaves his army stranded in the Russian snow? No, not stranded, for there is no army anymore. He lost his army. He must know now that Jean-Baptiste is allied with the Tsar, and had advised him how to defend Russia. . . . And he comes first to me . . .

The large salon was very bright. Marie was putting candles in the last of the tall candelabra. The coachman had lit a fire in the big fireplace. On the sofa, under the portrait, sat General Caulaincourt, the Emperor's chief equerry. Caulaincourt wore a sheepskin coat and a woolen cap pulled down over his ears. His eyes were closed. The Emperor stood close to the fire, his arms on the mantelpiece. He seemed so tired that he had to lean against something to stay upright. Neither of them heard me come in.

"Sire," I said softly, and went over to the Emperor.

Caulaincourt awoke, snatched off his woolen cap and stood at attention. The Emperor slowly raised his head. I forgot to bow. I stared at his face aghast. For the first time in my life I saw Napoleon unshaven. His beard was reddish, his bloated cheeks slack and gray. His eyes looked at me, but did not focus.

"Count Rosen," I said sharply, "take His Majesty's coat."

"I am cold, I'll keep my coat on," Napoleon muttered.

"Marie, brandy and glasses." Marie had to play the part of a lady-in-waiting at this hour of the night. "Please sit down, sire," I said, and sat myself on the sofa. The Emperor didn't budge. Marie brought brandy and glasses. "Sire," I said, "a glass of brandy." The Emperor didn't hear me.

I looked at Caulaincourt questioningly. "We've driven without stopping for thirteen days and thirteen nights," he murmured. "No one in the Tuileries knows yet that we have returned. His Majesty wanted to talk with Your Highness first."

It was fantastic. The Emperor had traveled thirteen days and thirteen nights to cling like a drowning man to my mantelpiece. I got up and poured out a glass of brandy and took it to him. "Sire, drink this, you'll feel warmer."

At last he raised his head and looked at me. He swallowed the brandy in one gulp.

"Perhaps you'll sit down, sire?" I suggested.

"Thank you, I'd rather stand near the fire. But please don't let it disturb you, madame, gentlemen. Please be seated."

I sat down again on the sofa. "May I ask, sire—?" I began.

"No, you most certainly may not ask anything, Madame Jean-Baptiste Bernadotte," he roared.

"Sit down, Count Rosen," I entreated my young Swede. Rosen had jumped up, and already had his hand on his sword. "His Majesty is apparently too tired to be courteous, or to explain to what I owe the honor of this unexpected call."

The Emperor ignored us. He was staring at the portrait above my head. The portrait of the First Consul, the young Napoleon with the thin face, the shining eyes. In a monotone he began to speak. More to the portrait than to me. "Do you know where I've come from, madame? I've come from the steppes, where my soldiers lie buried. Where Murat's hussars stagger through the snow. I have come from a bridge that collapsed under Davout's grenadiers. The ice floes cracked their skulls, and the icy water turned red. I have—"

"How can I send him this shawl?" Marie leaped to her feet, rushed to the Emperor, fell on her knees and clutched his arm fiercely. "I am knitting a warm shawl for my Pierre. I've written down the number of his regiment. Your Majesty has couriers. Help a mother, Your Majesty. Send a courier . . ."

Napoleon tore himself loose. "Are you mad, woman? She asks me to send a shawl to Russia, a shawl—" He began to laugh, shook with laughter, groaned with laughter. "A shawl for my hundred thousand dead, a warm gray shawl for my Grand Army—" There were tears in Napoleon's eyes—from laughing.

I led Marie to the door. "Go to bed, dearest, go to bed."

Napoleon was silent. He walked to the nearest chair and sank down into it. "Forgive me, I am very tired."

The minutes ticked away, and none of us stirred. Then in a clear hard voice he said, "I have come to dictate to you a letter for Marshal Bernadotte, madame."

"Please have one of Your Majesty's secretaries write this letter."

"I wish *you* to write this letter, madame. To inform the Swedish Crown Prince that we have returned to Paris to prepare the final defeat of the enemies of France." The Emperor stood up and began pacing the room. "We wish to remind the Swedish Crown Prince of the young General Bernadotte who once rushed to the assistance of General Bonaparte. He led regiments from the Rhine Army across the Alps to become the decisive factor in the victorious Italian campaign. Do you remember this, madame?"

I nodded.

"Remind Bernadotte of those reinforcements he brought to me in Italy. Then write him that fourteen days ago I heard the regimental song of that Rhine Army in the Russian snow. Two grenadiers, who could go no farther, were digging themselves into the snow. And while they waited for the wolves, they sang this song. . . . They must have been former comrades of your husband's. Don't forget to mention this incident."

My fingernails dug into my palms.

"Marshal Bernadotte advised the Tsar to secure peace in Europe by taking me prisoner during the retreat. Tell your husband, since I am safe in your Paris salon, madame, that I myself will secure the peace of Europe. And to defeat the enemies of France—and the enemies of a permanent peace everywhere—I offer Sweden an alliance. You understand, madame?"

"Yes, sire, you offer Sweden an alliance."

"I want Bernadotte to march with me again. Write your husband exactly that, madame." His eyes were fastened on young Count Rosen's face. "After the peace Sweden will be given Pomerania, of course, and Finland."

The young man repeated the word carefully. "Finland?"

"Sweden is to have Finland, Pomerania and—northern Germany from Danzig to Mecklenburg. We'll reestablish Sweden as a great power." Napoleon smiled at Rosen, the engaging smile of the old days, then turned back to me.

"Madame, write tomorrow. I must know where I stand."

"You have not said, sire, what will happen if Sweden doesn't accept this alliance."

He didn't answer. Just looked again at his youthful portrait. "A good portrait. Did I really look like that? So—thin?"

I nodded. "Before, in Marseilles, you used to look desperately hungry."

"Before—in Marseilles?" He looked at me in surprise. Then he drew his hand across his forehead. "For a moment I had forgotten. I had to speak to the Crown Princess of Sweden. But you also are still Eugénie."

"Drive to the Tuileries, sire, and have a good sleep."

"I can't, my dear. Bernadotte has established the coalition: Russia-Sweden-England. Even the Austrian ambassador in Stockholm frequently dines with Bernadotte. I shall wipe Sweden off the map if Bernadotte will not march with me." He was shouting again. Then, unsteadily, he turned to go.

"You will bring your husband's answer to me personally, madame. If it should be a refusal, you part from me forever. It would no longer be possible for me to receive you at court."

I bowed. "Nor would I care to come, sire."

Count Rosen escorted the Emperor and Caulaincourt to the door. I went slowly from candelabra to candelabra, blowing out the candles.

Rosen returned. "Will Your Highness write to the Crown Prince tomorrow?"

"Yes, Count, and you will help me with the letter."

"Does Your Highness believe that the Crown Prince will answer the Emperor?"

"I am convinced of it. And it will be the last letter my husband will ever write to the Emperor." The fire in the fireplace had died down, leaving many ashes.

I spent the rest of the night at Marie's bedside, trying to comfort her. Today special editions of the newspapers announced that His Majesty had returned unexpectedly from Russia. The health of His Majesty was never better.

Paris, end of January, 1813

At last a courier has arrived with letters from Stockholm. Oscar wrote to me, and his handwriting is regular and quite mature. In six months he will be fourteen, a thin, awkward lad in a Swedish cadet uniform.

> On January 6 we saw a wonderful performance at the Theatre Gustavus III. Mademoiselle George, a famous actress from the Théâtre Français, appeared. After the play, Papa gave a supper party for her, and Papa and the actress talked on and on about Paris and the old days. The lady-in-waiting Mariana von Koskull was so jealous that she took to her bed a whole week with a cold in the head. Papa works sixteen hours every day, and looks awful; that theater party for Mademoiselle George was his first in many weeks. . . .

I laughed. And cried a little, too, and had a great desire to spend a week in bed with a cold like Mariana von Koskull.

From Jean-Baptiste I found only a few scribbled lines: *My dearest little girl, I am overwhelmed with work, and will write more next time. Thank you for your account of the Emperor's visit. I will answer the Emperor, but I need time. My answer will not be only to him but also to the French nation and to posterity. I'll send it through you, as he asks. But I regret that you may have another difficult interview. I embrace you. Your J.-B.*

A page of music fell out of the envelope. *Oscar's first composition. A Swedish folk dance*, was scrawled in the margin.

I sat right down at the piano and played it. "I want to be a composer—or a king," Oscar had said in the coach on our way from Hanover to Paris. I suddenly thought of Herr van Beethoven with the disheveled hair: "To the memory of a hope that was not fulfilled."

The courier had also brought letters for Count Rosen. "Good news from home, Count?" I asked him later.

"The letters are very discreet. But between the lines I read that the Allies—Russia, England and Sweden—have asked His Royal Highness to plan the coming campaign. And Austria is very kindly disposed toward these plans."

So it's true, I thought—Napoleon's father-in-law, the Austrian Emperor, will fight against him, too.

"The occupied German territories are prepared to revolt," Count Rosen continued. "And preparations for this campaign, the greatest in history, are being made secretly in Stockholm." Count Rosen's voice was hoarse with excitement. "Sweden will be a great power again. And Your Highness's son—"

"Oscar has sent me his first composition," I said. "It's a Swedish folk dance. Why are you looking at me so oddly?"

"I was surprised, Your Highness. I didn't know that the heir apparent was musical."

"You prefer to discuss military campaigns?"

"I was thinking of the empire that His Royal Highness, the Crown Prince, will one day bequeath his son. Sweden has chosen one of the greatest generals of all time to succeed to the throne. The Bernadotte dynasty will reestablish Sweden as a great power."

"The Bernadotte dynasty," I said in disgust. "Your Crown Prince will fight these battles for the people, for rights that we call Liberty, Equality and Fraternity. He's fought for them since he was fifteen—" I stopped because Count Rosen was looking at me uncomprehendingly. "A great musician, who understands nothing of politics, once spoke of a hope that was not fulfilled," I said softly. "Perhaps this hope may yet be fulfilled, at least in Sweden. And your little country will then really be a great power, Count. But different from what you are imagining. A great power, whose kings will make no more wars, but will have time to write poetry, to compose music. . . . Aren't you happy that Oscar composes?"

"Your Highness, you are the strangest woman I've ever met," exclaimed the young count.

The note was delivered to me at seven o'clock in the evening. I ordered the carriage immediately, and asked Count Rosen to accompany me to the Hôtel Dieu.

"The Hôtel Dieu is a hospital," I explained to him. "I've just received word from Colonel Villatte. Somehow he was able to get Marie's son to the Hôtel Dieu. I want to take Pierre home."

"And Colonel Villatte?" Rosen asked.

"He's suffering from a shoulder wound. But he's been assigned to the Rhineland to try to assemble the survivors of his regiment."

"An odd name—Hôtel Dieu," Rosen said thoughtfully.

"The Lord's House. A beautiful name for a hospital. The wounded used to be taken to military hospitals outside the city. But this time so few got back to Paris that military hospitals weren't needed."

The hospital gate was locked. Rosen pulled the bell cord and the door opened a crack. The porter had only one arm, and I saw by his medals that he'd been wounded in the Italian campaign. "No visitors allowed," he said.

"This is Her Royal Highness—"

"No visitors allowed."

I pushed past Count Rosen and said quickly, "I have a permit to visit the hospital."

The disabled soldier looked skeptical, but finally admitted us to a dark gateway lighted only by the candle in his hand. "Your pass, madame?"

"I haven't it with me. But I've come for a wounded man. I am King Joseph's sister-in-law."

He held the candle up so that the light fell on my face. "I recognize you, madame. I have often seen you at parades. You are Marshal Bernadotte's wife."

I smiled in relief. "Have you perhaps served under my husband?" His face didn't relax. He was silent. "Can someone show us the way to the wards?" I said.

He handed me the candle and stepped back. "Marshal Bernadotte's wife," he sneered. With that he spat loudly.

Count Rosen turned angrily toward the man. "Forget him," I said. "We must search for Pierre." But my hand was shaking.

Count Rosen took the candle from me, and we groped our way up the broad staircase and along a corridor with many doors. We heard moaning and sharp cries. I resolutely pushed open the first door. The moaning was right at my feet. I took the candle from Rosen and looked down. There were beds on both sides of the room, and in the middle a row of straw mattresses. On one of these lay a man with a bandaged head who kept whimpering, "Water, water." The other end of the room, where a nun sat at a table, seemed very far away.

"Sister—" But my voice could not be heard above the moaning. I raised my skirts so as not to brush against the poor man's wounded face and groped my way forward. "Sister—" At last the nun heard me and came over to us.

"Sister, I'm looking for a wounded man named Pierre Dubois."

"We can't help you. There are so many here we don't know their names." She spoke gently, but indifferently.

"Then how can I find him?"

"I don't know," said the nun. "Go from bed to bed." She turned and went back to her table.

I closed my eyes for a moment. Then Rosen and I began walking from straw sack to straw sack, directing our light on every face. Irresolutely I looked down on bandaged eyes and noses, bitten, bleeding lips. Perhaps . . . no, not that one. I saw a smile on a waxy yellow face and went on. It was the smile of a man who had just died. This search I am glad to spare you, Marie. It's more than a mother could bear. At last, the door. Pierre was not in this ward.

We went to the next, searching, searching. The light from my candle fell on an emaciated arm with a small round wound, covered with a crust. The crust moved—lice. Still no Pierre.

In the corridor Rosen leaned suddenly against the wall, swayed forward a few steps and was sick. I wanted to comfort him, but that would have embarrassed him. In front of the next door I said, "I'd better go in alone. Wait here for me."

My candle had already hovered over all the beds on the right side. At the end of the room sat an old nun reading a little black book. "I'm looking for a certain Pierre Dubois," I said, and realized myself how hopeless my voice sounded.

"Dubois? I believe we have a Dubois here. . . ." She led me to the left bank of beds. To the last bed. I raised my candle. The dark eyes were wide open, staring at me. The swollen lips had bloody cracks. "Pierre."

He continued to stare straight ahead.

"Pierre—don't you recognize me?"

"Of course," he murmured indifferently. "*Madame la maréchale.*"

I leaned over him. "I've come to take you home, Pierre. To your mother." His face showed no emotion.

I turned, perplexed, to the nun. "I want to take him home. His mother is waiting. I have a carriage. Perhaps someone will help me—"

"The porters have all gone home. You must wait until tomorrow, madame."

But I didn't want to leave Pierre there another minute. "Is he very badly wounded? My ai—gentleman waiting outside could help, if he can just manage the stairs . . ."

The nun lifted my hand, so that the candlelight fell on the blanket. Where Pierre's legs should have been, it was flat. Quite flat. "I have a coachman downstairs who can help me," I said quietly. "I'll be right back, Sister."

I sent Count Rosen to ask our coachman to come up, and to bring all the robes we had in the carriage. Together we wrapped Pierre up like a package.

That's how I brought Marie's son home to her.

Paris, beginning of April, 1813

In half an hour I shall speak to him for the last time. I studied myself in the mirror. So this was how he would remember me: a crown princess with silver eyelids, a violet velvet costume, a bouquet of pale violets in the low V neck. And a new hat with a rose-colored bow that ties under my chin.

Yesterday evening a courier from Stockholm brought me Jean-Baptiste's answer to Napoleon. The letter was sealed, but Count Brahe had enclosed an exact copy for me, and also informed me that a copy had been given to all the newspapers.

"The sufferings of the Continent make peace imperative," Jean-Baptiste had written. "Your Majesty cannot refuse this demand for peace without increasing tenfold the sum of the crimes you have already committed. What benefits has France derived that could possibly compensate her for her enormous sacrifices?

She has gained nothing but military glory and superficial fame, while misery exists everywhere within her borders. . . ."

And I'm to deliver this letter to Napoleon. I read on: "I was born in the beautiful country of France. Her honor and well-being can never be a matter of indifference to me. But I shall always, to the best of my ability, defend the nation that elected me Crown Prince. In this conflict between world tyranny and freedom, I shall say to the Swedes: I am fighting with you, and for you, and all freedom-loving peoples will bless our struggle. . . ." The letter ended on a personal note: "Whether you decide for peace or war, sire, I shall always retain for Your Majesty the regard of a former comrade-in-arms."

I put the copy back on the night table and picked up the sealed letter. I had been told to be at the Tuileries at five in the afternoon. In the next few days the Emperor and his new army leave for the front. Russia is on the move, Prussia has joined with Russia. Napoleon had made up his mind long ago.

Count Rosen and I drove in the open carriage. The air smelled of spring, and the blue dusk softened the outlines of everything around us. Count Rosen wore the dress uniform of the Swedish dragoons and his aide's sash. "You accompany me on difficult missions, Count," I said. Since that night at the hospital, there's been a strange comradeship between us.

We didn't have to wait. The Emperor received us in his large study. Caulaincourt and Méneval were there, as well as Count Talleyrand. Napoleon, with folded arms, stood in front of the desk, leaning back on it. I bowed, and without a word handed him the sealed letter.

The sealing wax cracked. The Emperor read it without betraying any emotion, then handed it to Méneval. "A copy for the archives of the Foreign Ministry, the original to be kept with my private papers." And to me: "You're all dressed up, Highness. Violet suits you. But what a peculiar hat." This was worse than the outburst of fury I had expected. It was ridicule. "Have you made yourself beautiful to bring me this"—he snorted—"this piece of treachery?"

I bowed. "May I ask leave to withdraw, sire?"

"You not only may withdraw, madame, you absolutely must withdraw," he roared. "Bernadotte is at war with me. He gives orders to fire on the regiments he himself has led in countless battles. And you, madame, dare come here—wearing violets . . ."

"Sire, the night of your return from Russia, you urged me to write to my husband and to bring you his answer myself. I'm sure you are seeing me for the last time. I wore violets because they suit me. Perhaps you'll have a pleasant memory of me. May I now—for always—withdraw?"

There was a painful pause. Count Rosen stood, stiff as a statue, behind me. Talleyrand eyed me with interest. Ménéval and Caulaincourt stared at the Emperor in astonishment. Napoleon was definitely disconcerted. "The gentlemen will wait here. I want to speak to Her Highness a moment alone," he said finally. "Ménéval, pour the gentlemen some brandy."

I followed Napoleon into the same small study where years before I had pleaded in vain for the life of the Duke of Enghien. "You wanted to say something to me, sire? I refuse to discuss His Royal Highness, the Crown Prince of Sweden."

"Who wants to talk about Bernadotte," he said irritably. "It wasn't that, Eugénie, it was only"—he was staring at my face, as if he wanted to impress each feature on his memory—"only when you said you hoped I would have pleasant memories of you . . ." He turned away. "People can't part like that when they've known each other so long, can they?"

I stood in front of the fireplace. It was growing dark. What did he want?

"In these last weeks I have organized a new army of two hundred thousand men. By the way, England has promised Sweden one million pounds to pay for the equipment of Bernadotte's troops. Did you know that, madame?"

I didn't answer. Besides, I hadn't known it. The darkness would soon lay like a wall between us.

"They say the Tsar has promised Bernadotte the crown of France," Napoleon said slowly. "If Bernadotte should even play with this thought, it would be the blackest treachery ever perpetrated by a Frenchman."

"Naturally. A traitor to his own convictions. May I withdraw now, sire?"

"If you should ever feel in personal danger in Paris, madame— I mean, if people should molest you—you must immediately seek refuge with your sister, Julie. Will you promise me that?"

"Yes, of course. And the other way around."

"What do you mean—'the other way around'?"

"That my house is always open to Julie."

"You, too, are reckoning on my defeat, Eugénie?" He came very close to me. "Your violets have a bewitching fragrance. . . ." He took my hand. "What a pity you're married to Bernadotte," he murmured. I groped toward the door. "Eugénie!"

But I already stood in the light of the large study. The gentlemen sat, drinking brandy. I bowed for the last time.

The Emperor escorted me out of the study and to the door. We didn't say another word to each other.

Paris, summer of 1813

The coachman has carried Pierre into the garden. I am sitting at the window watching Marie bring her son a glass of lemonade. Bees buzz around the rosebushes, and there's also the sound of marching feet as the regiments pass the house. In step, always in step. . . . The sons of France have perished in Russia. Now, they say, mere children are being recruited. The children of France are marching to war, singing the "Marseillaise."

Below, in my garden—yes, Pierre has finished his lemonade. Marie sits beside her son. Her arm supports his back. I have given him Oscar's room, and Marie also sleeps there. But I must find a room for Pierre on the ground floor; it's too difficult always carrying him up and down the stairs. And I must find something for him to do, a real occupation. That's most important. Perhaps I might entrust to him the management of my household affairs.

TALLEYRAND CALLED ON me this evening. Apparently only to inquire if I didn't feel lonely. I told him, "I am, unfortunately, used to having my husband at the front."

Talleyrand nodded. "And yet, under other circumstances, Your Highness would be alone, but not lonely."

I shrugged my shoulders. "If you see my sister, Your Excellency, give her my love. Julie can't come here anymore. King Joseph has forbidden her."

"I also miss your two faithful aides, Your Highness."

"Colonel Villatte has been on active duty for a long time in Russia. And Count Rosen told me a few days ago that, as a Swedish nobleman, he must fight at the side of his Crown Prince.

I told him to ride with God and come back safe and sound. Just as I told Villatte. . . . You're right, Excellency—I am very lonely."

We sat in the garden and drank chilled champagne. Talleyrand told me that Fouché had a new post—governor of Illyria, an Austrian state the Emperor set up especially for him. "The Emperor can no longer afford intrigues in Paris," Talleyrand declared. "And Fouché always intrigues."

"And you—isn't the Emperor afraid of you, Excellency?"

"Fouché intrigues to win power or to hold it. I, on the other hand, want nothing but the well-being of France."

I saw the first star twinkle in the blue velvet sky. It was still so hot one could hardly breathe.

"How quickly our allies drop away," Talleyrand remarked between sips of champagne. "First the Prussians, who, by the way, are under your husband's supreme command. Austria naturally doesn't want to be left out if France is defeated and the spoils are divided, so she's joining the Allies."

I had to swallow hard before I could speak. "The Austrian Emperor can't make war on his own daughter and his grandson."

"No? My dear Highness, he's already at war with them." Talleyrand smiled. "It's not yet appeared in the *Moniteur*."

I didn't stir. Talleyrand's amiable voice continued. "The Emperor has forced our reluctant allies, the Danes, to declare war on Sweden. Your husband therefore has the Danes at his back, Highness. Nevertheless, the Allies have eight hundred thousand men under arms, and the Emperor not even half that."

Talleyrand emptied his glass and stood up. "Remember, Highness," he said, "the day may come when I shall ask a favor of you."

I watched him limp away.

Paris, November 1813

Whenever I go to sleep at night, I have the same dream. Jean-Baptiste rides alone across a battlefield. Like the one I saw on my way to Marienburg. Mounds of loose earth, deep craters where cannonballs had fallen. Jean-Baptiste rides a white horse; he leans forward in the saddle. I cannot see his face, but I sense that he is sobbing.

At first I thought the horses I heard neighing were part of my dream. I sat up and listened. There came a cautious knock at the front door. According to my bedside clock, which was barely visible to me, it was four thirty in the morning.

I got up, put on my dressing gown and went downstairs. Again a knock—very light—so as not to frighten anyone. "Who's there?"

"Villatte," and at practically the same time, "Rosen."

I pushed back the heavy bolt. In the light of the big lantern that hangs above the door, I distinguished two figures. "We've come from Leipzig," Villatte said. "We've been riding day and night." His face was dirty and unshaven. "The decisive battle has been lost."

"Has been *won!*" Rosen declared passionately.

"And why aren't you with the fleeing French Army, Colonel?"

"I am a prisoner of war, Your Highness."

"Rosen's prisoner?"

A ghost of a smile flitted over Villatte's face. "His Highness didn't have me marched off to the prison barracks with the others, but ordered me to ride to Paris immediately to be with Your Highness until"—he gulped—"until the enemy troops enter Paris."

The three of us went to the kitchen and sat down. I heard the full story. "On the morning of October nineteenth Bernadotte stormed Leipzig," said Villatte quietly.

"Did you see Jean-Baptiste yourself, Villatte? Is he well?"

"Very well. I saw him with my own eyes in the midst of the worst fighting—at the gates of Leipzig. It was a terrible battle." Villatte stared into the pale light of the oil lamp on the kitchen table. "His hair has turned gray, madame."

I turned to Rosen. "Tell me everything you know, Count."

"So much has happened—I caught up with His Highness at Trachtenburg Castle. And I was there when His Highness explained his half-circle plan of attack for the Allied troops to the Tsar of Russia, the Emperor of Austria and the Allied general staff. Someone said to His Highness, 'The plan of a genius,' at which His Highness answered, 'Yes, but not original. It's based on Napoleon's tactics.'

"His Highness had, of course, known all along that the decisive battle would be at Leipzig," Rosen went on, "where the Allied armies were to meet. On Monday, October eighteenth, His Highness had our cannon placed in position, and the town of Schönefeld was assaulted. Schönefeld was defended by French and Saxon regiments under Marshal Ney's command."

Villatte smiled. "As you see, madame, the Emperor chose his best troops to oppose Bernadotte. The Emperor hadn't forgotten that Bernadotte had once praised the Saxons in an order of the day, saying they held like men of iron."

"If I hadn't seen it with my own eyes, Your Highness," Count Rosen added, "I wouldn't have believed it. For the first time during the entire campaign His Highness wore his parade uniform: violet velvet coat, conspicuous from afar, and white ostrich plumes on his three-cornered hat. He rode a white horse. He signaled the attack, spurred his white horse and galloped straight toward the enemy lines, that is, toward the Saxon regiments. And the regiments—"

"The regiments stood firm as iron." Villatte laughed. "Not a shot was fired."

"No, not a shot," repeated Rosen. "Right in front of the Saxons, His Highness reined in his horse. The Saxons presented arms. 'Vive Bernadotte!' one of them cried, and 'Vive Bernadotte!' rose in chorus. His Highness raised his baton, turned his white horse and rode back. Behind him marched the Saxons in parade step. Twelve thousand men and forty cannon came over to us."

"And what did Jean-Baptiste say?"

"His Highness gave a brief order telling his men where to place the cannon," Rosen said. "During the battle His Highness was offered a field glass, but refused it. 'I know what's happening, I know,' he said. 'Ney has very little ammunition left, his artillery are firing only every five minutes—now the guards are seeking cover in the city of Leipzig.'"

"And the next morning?"

"His Highness had suggested to the three other sovereigns that Leipzig be stormed by his troops. The Austrian Emperor, the Tsar of Russia and the King of Prussia, each on a separate hill, watched through their field glasses, and—by God, we did it."

Villatte took up the story. "Bernadotte, at the head of his troops and in full regalia again, stormed the Grimma Gate of Leipzig. Our French infantry hurled itself against the enemy. Madame, it was a battle such as I have never seen. Man against man, Bernadotte on his white horse, always in the middle of it all, with his white ostrich plumes, holding only his field marshal's baton in his hands."

"Finally the French were routed," Rosen said triumphantly.

"No, we were ordered to retreat," Villatte corrected him. "The Emperor—"

"Your Emperor fled through the West Gate when His Highness entered Leipzig," Rosen insisted.

Villatte shrugged his shoulders.

"And after that, Count Rosen?" I asked.

"His Highness rode to the market square in Leipzig and, by chance, the French prisoners were led past him. His Highness suddenly raised his baton and pointed at a colonel. 'Villatte, come here, Villatte.' "

"I stepped out of the ranks, madame," Villatte said, "and that's how we met again. 'Villatte, what are you doing here?' he asked. 'I'm defending France, Marshal,' I answered. 'Then I must tell you that you are defending France very badly, Villatte,' Bernadotte said. 'Moreover, I expected you to stay with my wife in Paris.'

" 'The marshal's wife herself sent me to the front,' I said, and he didn't answer. I thought he wanted me to leave. But as soon as I moved, he leaned down from his horse and grabbed my shoulder. 'Colonel Villatte, you are a prisoner of war. I order you to return to Paris without delay and to take up your residence in my wife's house. Give me your word of honor as a French officer that you will not desert my wife until I myself get there.' Those were his words."

I lowered my eyes. Then I heard Rosen's voice: "With that, His Highness turned to me. 'And here's the second faithful aide to Her Highness. Count Rosen, you will accompany Colonel Villatte to Paris!'

" 'In my Swedish uniform?' I asked in horror. 'The Allies have not yet officially marched into France.' His Highness looked at Villatte. 'Colonel, you will be responsible to me for Rosen's safe arrival in Paris, and for arranging with the proper civil authorities his right of asylum in my wife's home. And you, Rosen, are responsible for guarding our prisoner of war.' "

"And before we could say any more," Villatte added, "Bernadotte commanded, 'Forward march. Au revoir, Count. Au revoir, Villatte.' "

A clock struck half past six. "Go to your rooms, gentlemen," I said to my two heroes. "You'll find everything just as you left it."

Then I went up to Jean-Baptiste's room. When had it been dusted last? Jean-Baptiste had long ago sent all that meant anything to him to Stockholm. I opened the window to air out the room.

"Don't stand at the open window in your dressing gown, you'll catch cold," Marie said. "What are you doing here, anyway?"

"France has been defeated. The Allied troops are marching to Paris. Jean-Baptiste is coming home, Marie."

"He should be ashamed of himself," came from between clenched teeth.

My cavalier, I thought, my poor, lonely cavalier. . . .

Paris, last week in March, 1814

"I hear at the baker's shop that the Cossacks rape all women, old ones, too," Marie announced excitedly.

At that, for the first time, we heard the distant thunder. We stared at each other. "Cannon at the city gates," I whispered.

That was two days ago. Since then, the guns of Paris have never been silent. Are they our guns? Austrian, Prussian, Russian?

I don't know where Jean-Baptiste is. I only know that he will come. I've had no letters. Germany and France lie between us, and the intervening land is one huge battlefield. A smuggled note told how Jean-Baptiste, after the battle of Leipzig, refused to pursue the French troops across the Rhine. He dictated a letter to the Tsar demanding that the frontiers of France be respected. France was not Napoleon. It was Napoleon who had been defeated. Then Jean-Baptiste marched north with his Swedes toward Denmark. And now the Prussians, the Russians and the Austrians are marching into France.

The windowpanes are rattling; the guns are very close. I must not think about Jean-Baptiste . . . Jean-Baptiste is fighting his private war. From Kiel he sent the Danish King an ultimatum. It was only under great pressure from Napoleon that the Danes had declared war on Sweden. So when Jean-Baptiste demanded that Norway be ceded to Sweden, and offered a great deal of money as compensation, the Danes agreed, on condition that they retain Greenland, the Faroe Islands and Iceland. The Danish King, however, indignantly refused the money. The Norwegians were not for sale, he said. . . . So I am now Crown Princess of Sweden and Norway.

I don't know where Jean-Baptiste is. Some believe that Napoleon, in desperation, has secretly asked him for help. The Paris newspapers, in the meantime, allege that Jean-Baptiste is mentally ill—no, I can't go on.

I don't know where he is but I know he's coming home—coming home through the ruins. . . .

Paris, March 30, 1814

Today, at seven o'clock in the morning, Marie came into my room. "You are to go to the Tuileries immediately. King Joseph has sent a carriage. You are to go to Julie at once."

I dressed quickly. Julie and I, by Joseph's orders, haven't seen each other for months. And now suddenly this urgent message.

It was cold driving through the deserted streets. Street cleaners were sweeping away rumpled copies of a proclamation that had been secretly distributed urging the restoration of the Bourbons. At the entrance to the Tuileries I saw carriages, traveling coaches and wagons of every kind. Relays of lackeys loaded heavy iron boxes on the wagons. The crown jewels, I thought, the treasures of the imperial family.

I made my way to the door between the waiting carriages, and asked to be received by Joseph immediately. "Just tell him his sister-in-law is here," I explained to the officer on duty.

To my surprise, I was escorted to the private apartments of the Empress. As I entered the large salon, a heated discussion was in progress between Joseph and his brother, King Jérôme of Westphalia, whose kingdom had long since been taken away by the Allies. The Empress, wearing a traveling coat and hat, sat on a sofa, acting like a guest.

"Well?" asked Marie Louise calmly and indifferently. "What are we to do? Shall I leave with the King of Rome or stay here?"

"Madame"—Jérôme raced to her from behind the sofa—"if you leave the Tuileries now, you and your son may forfeit your claim to the imperial crown of France. Madame, trust the National Guard. You've heard the oath sworn by the officers: as long as the Empress and the King of Rome are in Paris, Paris will not fall—"

"Jérôme," Joseph interrupted. "Remember the letter from His Majesty. Napoleon said he would rather see his son in the Seine than—"

"But the Guard will make a superhuman effort, Joseph."

"A few hundred men . . . I realize the presence of the Empress would inspire not only the Guard but also the people of Paris to resist to the last. Her departure would be—"

"Flight," Jérôme shouted.

"All right—the flight of the Empress and the King of Rome would lower the morale of the people. But I can't take the responsibility alone . . ."

"I only want to do my duty, and not be reproached afterward," Marie Louise explained apathetically.

I was still near the door. "Excuse me, I won't disturb you, I only . . ." They all turned.

"The Crown Princess of Sweden in the salon of the Empress?" roared Jérôme.

"Jérôme, I myself asked Her Royal Highness here because Julie—" Joseph, utterly disconcerted, looked to my sister. I looked, too, and for the first time saw Julie. She sat on a sofa at the far end of the salon with her daughters. Tears streamed down her cheeks. I went to her quickly.

"Don't be upset. You and the children are coming home with me," I whispered.

"If the Empress and the child go to Rambouillet," Joseph said, "I must go, too."

"I thought you had orders as commandant of Paris to hold the city," said Julie in a low voice.

"But the Emperor wrote me that I shouldn't leave his son," Joseph said breathlessly. "The whole family will come with us. Julie, I ask you for the last time—"

Julie shook her head. "No—I'm afraid we'll be chased from palace to palace, and in the end the Cossacks will get us. Let me stay with Désirée, Joseph. Her house is safe. Isn't it, Désirée?"

Joseph and I looked at each other. "You can stay at my house, too, Joseph," I said at last.

He shook his head and managed a smile. "Perhaps Napoleon will come back and save Paris. Then in a few days I can be with Julie again. If not . . ." He kissed my hand.

At this moment a lackey announced Talleyrand. He came in wearing the uniform of a grand seigneur of the Empire, his face looking tired and strained. "Your Majesty," he said to the Empress, "the minister of war begs you to leave Paris immediately with the King of Rome. Marshal Marmont does not know how long he can hold the road to Rambouillet. I deeply regret being the bearer of this tragic news."

There was almost complete silence. Then Marie Louise asked, "Am I still to meet His Majesty in Rambouillet?"

"His Majesty is on his way to Fontainebleau, and from there will hurry here to the defense of Paris," Joseph said.

"But I mean His Majesty, the Emperor of Austria—my papa!"

Joseph went white to his lips. The vein in Jérôme's forehead swelled. Only Talleyrand smiled pityingly and showed no surprise. At the door Marie Louise turned around once more. "If only no one reproaches me later," she said, and left.

Now we could hear the child outside crying and screaming. Instinctively I went to the door. Two governesses were trying to get the little Napoleon downstairs to his mother's carriage. The child, with Marie Louise's blond curls and his father's stubborn chin, hung on to the banister and screamed.

Hortense took over. "I know how to deal with little boys," she said with a smile, and, using experienced pressure, sprung the child's small fingers loose. "There. Now go down like a good boy."

"Exit Napoleon the Second," murmured Talleyrand beside me. He looked at his watch. "And I must go, too, Your Highness. My carriage is waiting."

"Are you going with the Empress?"

"Of course. But I will, unfortunately, be taken prisoner by the Russians at the gates of Paris. Therefore, I must not be late; the Russian patrol is expecting me. *Au revoir*, dear Highness."

"Perhaps Marshal Marmont will free you. You deserve it," I said contemptuously.

"You think so? Then you'll be disappointed. Marshal Marmont is very busy at the moment negotiating for the surrender of Paris. But keep this news to yourself, Highness. We want to avoid unnecessary confusion and bloodshed."

Then at last I was in my carriage with Julie and her daughters, driving back to the rue d'Anjou. And there, for the first time since the day Julie became a queen, Marie spoke to her. She put a motherly arm around Julie's thin shoulders and led her upstairs. "Marie," I said, "Julie will sleep in Oscar's room, and the children can use Madame la Flotte's. We'll move La Flotte to the guest room."

"And General Clary, Monsieur Etienne's son?" Marie asked.

"He arrived an hour ago and wants to stay here." Etienne had sent his son, Marius, to the War Academy instead of training him for Papa's business. And Marius, with the help of God and Napoleon, had become a general.

"Count Rosen and Colonel Villatte can share a room. Then General Clary can sleep in Colonel Villatte's bed," I decided.

"And the Countess Tascher?" Marie asked, nodding toward the salon. There I found Etienne's daughter, Marcelline, who is married to a Count Tascher. "Aunt, I'm so frightened in my own house. The Cossacks may arrive at any moment," she sobbed.

"And your husband?"

"Somewhere at the front. Marius spent the night with me, and we decided to come here for the present."

I gave her the guest room. La Flotte would have to sleep on a divan in the dressing room.

About five o'clock in the afternoon the cannon stopped roaring. Villatte and Rosen returned from a walk and said that the Allies were demanding unconditional surrender.

"What about my children's governess?" Julie moaned. "If she hasn't a room of her own, she'll give notice. Who's sleeping in Jean-Baptiste's bed?"

Not your governess! I thought furiously, and fled. Fled to Jean-Baptiste's empty bedroom. I sat down on the wide empty bed, and listened to the night outside, listened. . . .

Paris, March 31, 1814

At two o'clock this morning the treaty of surrender was signed. When I looked out of my window the Swedish flag waved over my front door, where Count Rosen had hung it. A great crowd of people waited in front of our house. Their angry mutterings carried up to my window.

"What do these people want, Villatte?"

"The rumor is that His Highness will soon arrive."

"But what do these people want of Jean-Baptiste?"

Before Villatte could answer, a carriage drove up. Gendarmes held back the crowd. I saw Hortense climb out of the carriage with her boys, nine-year-old Napoleon Louis and six-year-old Charles Louis Napoleon. The babble of voices ceased as Hortense hastily herded the boys into the house.

La Flotte appeared. "Queen Hortense wants to know if the Emperor's nephews can, for the present, remain here. She herself will go to her mother at Malmaison."

"Tell Her Majesty I'll take good care of the children." I saw Hortense, below, get back into her carriage. *"Vive l'Empereur!"* the crowd shouted as she drove off.

Paris, April 1814

On March 31 the troops of the Allies marched into Paris. The Cossacks galloped down the Champs Elysées; the Prussians moved forward in serried ranks; the Austrians marched to the beat of drums. The Parisians, meanwhile, were lining up at the baker's or begging the grocer for a small sack of flour. The granaries outside Paris have been plundered and burned. The roads to the southern districts are barricaded. Paris is hungry.

On April 1 a provisional government was set up to negotiate with the Allies. At its head is Talleyrand. The Tsar was quartered in the Palais Talleyrand, where Talleyrand gave a great ball in his honor, attended by members of the old nobility whom Napoleon had allowed to return from exile. Champagne flowed, and the Tsar produced, as if by magic, flour, meat and caviar.

Napoleon is at Fontainebleau with five thousand guardsmen. Caulaincourt is negotiating in the name of the Emperor with the Allies, and on April 4 Napoleon signed an act of abdication in favor of his son. But two days later the Senate announced that a regency for Napoleon the Second was out of the question. Only the restoration of the Bourbons would guarantee a lasting peace. The police no longer wear blue-white-red cockades, but white cockades, the symbol of so much bloodshed during the Revolution.

Most of the Bonapartes have fled from Rambouillet with the Empress to Blois. The Empress, safe in the arms of His Majesty, her papa, has begged him to protect her and *her* child. Her child now, only hers. The Austrian Emperor calls his little grandson Francis. He doesn't like the name Napoleon.

From Blois Joseph has written Julie several letters, which were smuggled through the lines. Julie and her children are to stay with me until the new government and the Allies have decided the fate of the Bonaparte family.

Julie has asked me for money to pay her governess's salary. "Joseph took all our money and the securities with him," she said. "My jewelry, too." Pierre, now my manager, paid the governess. Then my nephew, Marius, also borrowed money. Marcelline used my carriage with the Swedish coat of arms to take a drive and came back with two new hats. She had the bill sent to me.

On the morning of April 11 Pierre asked to talk to me. I found him in the former porter's rooms on the ground floor. On his desk stood our money box—open and empty. Pierre handed me a piece of paper covered with long rows of figures, an account of payments since the first of April. "Last month," he said, "I sold Your Highness's French government securities, and we've been living on the proceeds. Unfortunately, there is nothing left. We haven't a sou. Can Your Highness count on money from Sweden anytime soon? Or from His Highness, the Crown Prince?"

"But I don't know where His Highness is."

"I can, of course, borrow. Any sum will be at your disposal if Your Highness will sign a promissory note."

"I can't borrow money as Crown Princess of Sweden. It would make a dreadful impression."

Marie had come in. "You can sell some silver dishes, or pawn them," she suggested.

"No, that won't do either. Everything is engraved. All Paris would know immediately that we have no money. And that would look bad for Sweden."

"How, then, will you feed all the people under your roof?" Marie demanded.

I stared at the empty box. A hush fell over the room. "Marie, in Papa's time the firm of Clary had a warehouse in Paris, didn't it?"

"Of course. In the Palais Royal. Monsieur Etienne visits it whenever he comes to Paris from Genoa. Hasn't he ever mentioned it?"

"No, there was no reason to."

Marie raised her eyebrows. "No? Who inherited the half of the firm that belonged to your mama?"

Pierre answered for me. "According to law, you, Queen Julie and your brother each inherited a third of this half. So a sixth of the firm of Clary belongs to Your Highness."

"Marie, please call a carriage for me at once."

THE HIRED CARRIAGE stopped before a roomy, very elegant basement shop in the Palais Royal. A small sign in dignified gold letters said: *François Clary, Silks, Wholesale and Retail.* I had the coachman wait, and entered an office beautifully furnished with delicate chairs and little tables. Only some large rolls of silk on the half-empty shelves along the walls showed what kind of business was transacted here. Behind a handsome mahogany desk sat an elderly man in a well-cut business suit, the white cockade of the Bourbons in his buttonhole. "What can I do for you, madame?"

"Are you the Paris manager of the Clary firm?"

The man bowed. "At your service, madame. White for the Restoration is in great demand."

"Business is good, Monsieur—?"

"Legrand, madame, Monsieur Legrand," he introduced himself. "Yes, Monsieur Clary shipped these white materials from Genoa months ago, right after the battle of Leipzig. Monsieur Clary, the head of the firm, is politically well informed." He cleared his throat impressively. "He is the brother-in-law of the victor of Leipzig, the Crown Prince of Sweden."

"And for weeks you have been selling white silk, roll after roll. While French troops fought to hold back the Allies, here you sat, coining money." I was suddenly very angry.

"Madame, I'm merely an employee," he said, hurt and on the defensive. "Besides, most of our accounts have not been paid. The ladies who bought the white material can't pay until the Bourbons return. Then their husbands will have important positions." He paused and eyed me suspiciously. "What can I do for you, madame?"

"I need money. How much have you here?"

"Madame, I—I don't understand . . ."

"A sixth of the firm of Clary belongs to me. I am a daughter of the late founder."

"But Monsieur Etienne has only two sisters, Madame Joseph Bonaparte and Her Royal Highness, the Crown Princess of Sweden."

"That's right, and I am the Crown Princess of Sweden. How much money have you in the shop, monsieur?"

Monsieur Legrand groped in his breast pocket, tremblingly drew forth his glasses, put them on and looked at me. Then he bowed. I held out my hand to him and he sniffled with emotion.

"I was an apprentice in your papa's business in Marseilles when Your Highness was still a child—a dear child, Your Highness, but naughty, very naughty!"

"I'm not naughty anymore," I said. "I am only trying to do my best in these troubled times. . . . A Clary must not go into debt. In all these years I've never taken my share of the firm's profits. So now I must take all you have on hand."

"I have very little, Your Highness. The day before he left Paris King Joseph asked for a large sum." My eyes widened in amazement, but he did not notice. "Twice a year King Joseph drew his wife's share of our profits. Here," said Legrand, and he gave me a bundle of bank notes. "This is all we have at the moment."

"It's something," I said, stuffing the money into my bag. "And, Monsieur Legrand, we must collect the outstanding accounts immediately. My carriage is outside. Take it, drive from customer to customer and collect. If anyone refuses to pay, make him return the goods."

"But I can't leave. Our apprentices were called up, and I'm expecting the buyer from Le Roy's any moment."

"While you settle the accounts, I'll attend to the customers here." With that, I took off my hat and coat.

Legrand stammered, "But—Highness . . ."

"Don't worry. As a girl, I often helped in the shop in Marseilles. Hurry, monsieur!" Doubtfully, Legrand made for the door. "Monsieur, a moment." He turned. "Please take off the white cockade when you call on behalf of the firm of Clary."

"Highness, most people are wearing—"

"Yes, but not former apprentices of my papa. *Au revoir.*"

When I was alone, I sat at the desk, my eyes smarting. A naughty child—I was a naughty and a carefree child. My papa had taken my hand and explained to me the Rights of Man. That time will never be again.

The bell over the shop door tinkled. I leaped up. A light blue frock coat with fancy embroidery and a white cockade. "You're the buyer from Le Roy's, aren't you? What may I show you?"

"I'd like to speak to Monsieur Legrand."

I told him I was sorry but Monsieur Legrand would be away for several hours.

"Have you any pale lilac muslin?" he asked. "The Empress Josephine needs a lilac gown to receive the Tsar."

571

"She's going to receive the Tsar?"

"Naturally. So she can discuss her financial situation with him. The financial affairs of the Bonapartes are already being negotiated. Have you any pale lilac muslin or not?"

I found a roll of the sheerest muslin and peeled off some of the transparent material for him to see. "The color of lilac blooms," I said. "Exactly right for Josephine at the moment. Becoming, and slightly melancholy. By the way, we're selling now strictly for cash."

"That's out of the question. Our customers don't pay us promptly. Naturally, as soon as the situation is clarified . . ."

"The situation *is* clarified," I said firmly. "The franc is falling. We're almost sold out. We sell only for cash." I carried the roll back to the half-empty shelves.

His eyes lingered hungrily on a few rolls of satin. "Marshal Ney's wife," he was murmuring to himself.

"Light blue satin?" I suggested. "Madame Ney is quite ruddy and wears light blue well."

He looked at me curiously. "You're well informed, and well versed in the silk trade, Mademoiselle—?"

"Désirée," I said amiably. "Take light blue satin for Madame Ney. At the prewar price." From the roll hung a label in Etienne's spidery handwriting. I named the sum. "Cash."

He slowly began counting out his money. I measured eight meters of satin, daringly made a tiny incision in the material with a large pair of scissors, and tore it across firmly—just as I'd seen Etienne and Papa rip off a length of silk. "And the lilac muslin?"

"The Empress never pays cash," he grumbled. I ignored him. "Seven meters of muslin," he sighed.

"Take nine meters. She'll want a shawl to go with the gown."

He unhappily counted out the money for Josephine's melancholy dress.

I served three more customers and finally Legrand returned. The shop happened to be empty. "Have you collected all the accounts, monsieur?"

"Not all, but several. Here." He handed me a leather pouch full of bank notes.

"I'll sign a receipt," I said. I thought a minute, and wrote: *Désirée, Crown Princess of Sweden, née Clary.* "From now on, I'll settle regularly with my brother, Etienne," I said. "And

Monsieur Legrand, stock lilac muslin—the newest thing, you'll soon see. *Au revoir.*"

My carriage was waiting. As I got in, the coachman wordlessly handed me a newspaper. On the way to the rue d'Anjou I read the special edition. The carriage rocked, the letters danced . . .

> The Allied powers having proclaimed that the Emperor Napoleon was the sole obstacle to the establishment of peace in Europe, the Emperor Napoleon, faithful to his oath, declares that he renounces for himself and his heirs the thrones of France and Italy and that there is no personal sacrifice, even of his life, which he is not prepared to make on behalf of France.

All that in a single sentence. . . . And already copies of this special edition lay discarded in the gutters.

With a jolt, the carriage stopped. A line of gendarmes barred the entrance to the rue d'Anjou. The coachman opened the carriage door. "We can't drive any farther; the rue d'Anjou is cordoned off. Official business."

"But I must go to the rue d'Anjou, I live there." I alighted, paid the coachman and began to walk toward my house. Gendarmes lined both sides of the road. I was almost home when I was stopped by a mounted police captain. "You may go no farther."

I looked up at him and recognized the man who for years had guarded our house on behalf of the minister of police.

"Let me through," I said. "You know where I live."

"His Majesty, the Tsar of Russia, is about to call on Her Royal Highness, the Crown Princess of Sweden. I have orders to let no one pass the house," he snarled without looking at me.

The Tsar was coming to see me. The Tsar. . . . "Then let me through quickly, I must change," I stormed. "You know perfectly well that I live in that house!"

"I had mistaken Your Highness for the wife of Marshal Bernadotte," he said, looking at me at last. His eyes gleamed wickedly. "I beg your pardon—a mistake." Then he shouted, "Clear the way for the Crown Princess of Sweden!"

At home they'd been waiting for me. The door flew open, Marie grabbed my arm. "Hurry, hurry. In half an hour the Tsar will be here."

Upstairs in my dressing room Marie ripped off my clothes and flung a dressing gown around me. Yvette began to brush my hair.

I rubbed the dust of the shop off my face with rose water, dabbed silver paint on my eyelids, rouge on my cheeks. Marie put on my silver sandals.

At that instant I saw Julie in the mirror. She had on a purple gown and was holding one of her small crowns. "Shall I wear a crown when you present me to the Tsar, Désirée?"

I looked at her uncomprehendingly. "Present you to the Tsar?"

"I mean—I thought—you will surely call me by my old title. I'll ask him to protect my interests and the children's . . ."

"You should be ashamed of yourself, Julie Clary. *Your* interests—" My mouth was dry. "Napoleon abdicated just a few hours ago. You got two crowns from him. Now you must wait to see what's decided about you. You aren't a queen anymore."

Something clattered to the floor. Her little crown. She slammed the door behind her. Yvette put the earrings of the queen mother of Sweden in my ears, and helped me into the same violet gown I had worn at my farewell audience with Napoleon.

"By the way, Eugénie, someone sent flowers for you," Marie said. "Violets. They're on the mantelpiece in the little salon. It's time you went down."

I floated down the stairs as in a dream. Below in the hall they were all assembled—Marius, Marcelline, Madame la Flotte, Hortense's sons, Julie's daughters—all dressed in their best attire, even the children. I beckoned to Count Rosen. "You will escort me to the small salon, Count."

"And we—?" Marcelline blurted out.

I was already at the door. "I wouldn't ask any Frenchman or Frenchwoman to be presented to the sovereign of an Allied power before peace has been concluded."

The little salon was spotless. On the table under the mirror were champagne glasses and sweetmeats. On the mantelpiece, a silver basket of violets—pathetically small and wilted—and a sealed envelope. Then the blare of trumpets and the sound of horses' hooves. A carriage stopped. I stood stiffly erect.

The door was flung open. A dazzling white uniform, sparkling gold epaulets, a giant with a round boyish face, blond curls and an unaffected smile. Right behind him—Talleyrand. Behind them both milled many foreign uniforms. I bowed, and held out my hand for the blond giant to kiss.

"Your Highness, I pay my respects to the wife of the man who has contributed so much to the liberation of Europe," said the Tsar. He sat down beside me on the small sofa. In the armchair opposite sat Monsieur Talleyrand. My two servants served champagne.

"I am exceedingly sorry that Your Highness's husband didn't enter Paris at my side." The blue eyes narrowed. "Perhaps Your Highness knows when I may expect the Crown Prince?"

I shook my head and drank champagne.

"The provisional government of France under the leadership of our friend here"—the Tsar raised his glass to Talleyrand—"informs us that France longs for the return of the Bourbons. Personally, this surprises me. What is Your Highness's opinion?"

"I don't understand politics, sire."

"In our various discussions your husband gave me the impression that the French people do not care very much for the Bourbon dynasty. I, therefore, suggested to His Highness that he urge the French people to choose their great marshal, Jean-Baptiste Bernadotte, Crown Prince of Sweden, as the new King of France." The Tsar held out his empty glass to an aide.

"And what did my husband answer, sire?"

"Oddly enough, Highness, nothing." The Tsar downed his freshly filled glass and looked at me mournfully. "The Emperor of Austria and the King of Prussia are in favor of the Bourbon restoration. Since the Swedish Crown Prince hasn't answered me, I shall follow the wishes of the French government"—his glance sought Talleyrand—"and of my allies. Too bad," he said, and then abruptly: "What a charming room this is, madame."

We stood up, and the Tsar looked out into the garden. "This is Moreau's former house," I said.

He closed his eyes suddenly as at a painful memory. "Moreau served on my general staff after he returned from America. He died early in September. A cannon shot shattered both his legs. Hadn't Your Highness heard?"

I leaned my head against the cool windowpane. "Moreau was an old friend of ours. In the days when my husband still hoped the Republic could be saved for the French people." We were alone by the window. Not even Talleyrand could hear us.

"And it's because of this Republic that your husband didn't accept my suggestion, madame?" I was silent. "No answer is also an answer." He smiled.

Suddenly I thought of something that made me indignant. "Sire, you offered my husband not only the crown of France but also a Russian grand duchess."

He laughed. "Do you know what your husband said to that? 'I'm already married.' And the subject was dropped." He bowed over my hand. "If I had had the honor of meeting you sooner, Highness, I would never have made that suggestion to the Crown Prince. The ladies of my family who might have been considered are, I regret, not pretty, while you . . ."

THE DOOR HAS long since closed behind my royal guest, but I am too tired to move. The servants had begun to clear away the empty champagne glasses when my glance fell on the wilted violets. "Count Rosen, where did those flowers come from?"

"Caulaincourt brought them. He came from Fontainebleau, and was on his way to Talleyrand to turn over the signed instrument of abdication."

I went over to the fireplace. The sealed envelope was not addressed. I tore it open: a piece of paper empty except for one scrawled initial: N. In the back of my mind some random misgiving stirred. Why?

"Your Highness—forgive me for—disturbing you," Rosen stuttered from behind me. "I'm sorry to trouble you. For some weeks now, His Highness has not managed to send me my pay."

"Pierre, as my steward, will pay you immediately."

"But only, Highness, if you'll not be inconvenienced. Your Highness has not received any revenue either for some time."

"Of course not. But today I worked to earn money for our household."

"Highness!" He was horrified.

"Don't be shocked. I sold silk. Nothing dishonorable, Count. You know that I'm the daughter of a silk merchant."

"Anyone would have lent Your Highness whatever money you needed."

"Certainly, Count Rosen. But my husband has finally finished paying the House of Vasa's debts with his personal savings. I don't want to accumulate new debts for the House of Bernadotte. And now, dear Count, good night."

Marie was waiting for me in my dressing room. I stumbled over something shiny and started to pick it up, but Marie said, "Leave it, it's only one of Julie's crowns." She undressed me as if I were a child and put me to bed.

I woke in the middle of the night. It was very dark and very still. My heart was pounding. I held my head, trying to remember. . . . What had awakened me—a thought, a dream? Something I'd had a vague presentiment about all evening. All at once, it came to me. The abdication and the violets. The violets—

I lit the candle and went into my dressing room. The newspaper lay on the table. Slowly, word for word, I read it through. *The Emperor Napoleon, faithful to his oath . . . renounces . . . there is no personal sacrifice, even of his life . . .*

Yes—no sacrifice, even of his life. . . . These words had awakened me. He means to take his own life, the violets prove it. When a man feels he's reached the end of his life, he undoubtedly thinks back to his youth. He remembers a young girl who leaned with him against a hedge. Not so long ago he saw the girl again, wearing violets. In the park at Fontainebleau many violets are now in bloom. He asks one of the soldiers of the guard to pick violets while he signs the instrument of abdication. Caulaincourt can take the violets when he delivers the documents in Paris, a last greeting from a man alone with his youth. . . . And his death?

AFTER BREAKFAST I sent for Colonel Villatte. "Please go to Talleyrand's office this morning," I asked him, "and inquire on my behalf about the health of the Emperor." Villatte looked puzzled, but I made no explanation.

By this afternoon the crowd outside our house was larger than ever before. In front of the door two Russian guardsmen marched solemnly up and down.

"A guard of honor," Count Rosen murmured. "They've probably heard a rumor that His Royal Highness is arriving sometime today. After all, tomorrow is the official entry of the victorious Allies into Paris. It's inconceivable that His Highness will not lead the Swedish troops in the victory parade."

Inconceivable, yes, inconceivable . . .

Before dinner Colonel Villatte returned and took me aside. "At first no one wanted to talk. But when I said that I asked on behalf of Your Highness, Talleyrand spoke to me in confidence." Villatte whispered then, telling me what I had already guessed. The attempt had been made. But Napoleon had failed.

It didn't occur to me until dessert that everyone was sitting in gloomy silence. Even the children.

"Is something wrong?" I asked.

"Désirée," Julie said miserably, "the children want so much to see the victory parade tomorrow, but no one dares ask you if you'll let us use the carriage with the Swedish coat of arms. In your carriage they'd be safe—the poor, pathetic Bonaparte children."

I looked at the children, delicate and shy. "Naturally, my carriage is available to anyone who wants to see the victorious troops. I won't need it tomorrow. I'm staying home all day."

Paris, middle of April, 1814

That night, the twelfth of April, I didn't blow out the candle on my night table. The curious crowd in front of the house had scattered. It was very quiet in the rue d'Anjou. Midnight: only the footsteps of the two Russian sentries echoed. The clock struck one. The day of the victory parade had dawned. Every muscle in my body was tense. I listened.

Rolling wheels shattered the silence. They rattled to a stop in front of my house. *Click-clack:* the sentries presenting arms. A hard knock on the door. Voices. Three, four—but not the voice for which I waited. I lay rigid, my eyes closed. Someone ran up the stairs, two steps at a time. Flung open my bedroom door, kissed my mouth, my cheeks, my eyes, my forehead.

Jean-Baptiste. My Jean-Baptiste. He knelt beside my bed, not moving now, his face on my hand. With my free hand I stroked his hair. How light it shone in the candlelight—it had gone gray, really entirely gray. "Jean-Baptiste, you're home, home again at last. You've had a long journey."

"A journey—yes, a horribly long journey," he said tonelessly.

I sat up. "Come, you must rest. Your room is ready, and—"

He slowly raised his head. Then he drew his fingers across his brow, as though he wanted to wipe away a memory. "But I haven't come alone. I've brought Brahe as aide-de-camp, Löwenhjelm as chamberlain, and Admiral Stedingk, and—"

"It's impossible, the house is already overcrowded. Julie and her children and the sons of Hortense and—"

He jumped up. "Do you mean to tell me you're harboring all

these Bonapartes and supporting them at the expense of the Swedish court?"

"No, only Julie and various children—children, Jean-Baptiste. My house is open to them. And to the Clarys. You sent me the two aides yourself. And the household expenses, as well as the salaries, I'm paying myself."

"What do you mean—yourself?"

"I'm selling silk. In a shop, you know." I was putting on my beautiful green velvet dressing gown with the sable collar. "The firm of Clary."

Then a miracle happened. He laughed. "My little girl, my priceless little girl." He held out his arms. "Crown Princess of Sweden and Norway—selling silk. Come, come here to me." I went to him. "Fourteen days ago I sent a courier to you with money."

"Unfortunately, he didn't get here."

Jean-Baptiste looked serious again. "The Swedish headquarters will be in a palace in the rue St. Honoré. It was requisitioned long ago. My staff can probably go right there." Then he opened the door between my bedroom and his.

I held up the candle. "Your bed is made," I said, "the bedspread has been turned back, everything's ready for you."

But he stared into his room as though he'd never seen it before. "I'll stay at the Swedish headquarters, too," he said without expression. And hastily: "I'll have to receive a great many people. And this wouldn't do—I can't receive them here."

"Five minutes ago you wanted to live here with your entire staff!" I exclaimed angrily.

He put his arm around my shoulder. "I've only come back to Paris for a few days. But I can't return to this room. Forgive me, Désirée, it was my mistake. There's no return from where I've been." He held me close. "There—and now, let's go down. My gentlemen hope that you will welcome them. And Fernand has probably prepared a meal." The thought of Fernand helped me back to reality. I put on rouge and powder.

"How is Oscar?" I asked. For months my child had lived alone among strangers in Stockholm. Jean-Baptiste extracted some letters from his breast pocket. "The heir apparent has composed a regimental march," he announced proudly. For a moment my heart beat happily.

Arm in arm, Jean-Baptiste and I walked into the dining room and I greeted our guests warmly. We sat in front of the fireplace in the large salon and drank Fernand's coffee. Jean-Baptiste peered at the portrait of the First Consul. Suddenly he turned to me and demanded cuttingly, "And him?"

"The Emperor is waiting in Fontainebleau for his fate to be decided. Last night he tried to commit suicide."

"What?" they all cried together—Brahe, Löwenhjelm, Admiral Stedingk, Count Rosen. Only Jean-Baptiste said nothing.

"Since the Russian campaign, the Emperor has always carried poison," I said. "Last night he swallowed some of it. His valet saw him and took action at once. That's all."

Jean-Baptiste was staring into the fire; his mind seemed far away. There was a painful silence. Brahe cleared his throat. "Your Highness, about the victory parade tomorrow . . . "

Jean-Baptiste's absentminded expression changed. "Victory! I came here only to clear up any possible misunderstanding between the Tsar and me. The Tsar will never understand why I didn't cross the Rhine with him, why I wouldn't fight on French soil, why I haven't responded to his letters. But Sweden can't afford a breach with the Tsar—can't you see?"

Löwenhjelm determinedly took a package of handwritten letters from a portfolio he was carrying. "Your Highness," he said loudly, "about the Tsar's proposal that—"

"Don't say it," Jean-Baptiste shouted. The eyes of the Swedes turned on me. I was their last hope.

I went over and knelt beside him and laid my head on his arm. "Jean-Baptiste, the Tsar suggested that you become King of France, didn't he?"

He stiffened, but I went right on. "You haven't answered the Tsar. And that's why Paris is now preparing for the return of the Bourbons. The Tsar has finally agreed to the proposals of the other Allies and Talleyrand's suggestions. But the Tsar is still proud to be your friend. And he understands perfectly why you couldn't accept the crown of France. I explained it all to him."

"You explained it all to him?" Jean-Baptiste looked me full in the face.

"Yes, he came to pay his respects to the wife of the victor of Leipzig." I stood up. "And now I'll wish you good night—or rather, good morning, gentlemen. I hope by now everything has

been made ready for you in the rue St. Honoré." I hurried out of the salon. I couldn't bear to watch Jean-Baptiste leave his own home to spend the night in a palace around the corner.

He caught up with me on the stairs. In my bedroom he let me undress him like a child. Finally I pulled the covers over us both and blew out the candle. Morning was already creeping in through the shutters, but still Jean-Baptiste could not sleep. He moaned and put his head on my shoulder. "Napoleon sent my oldest regiments against me."

"Forget, Jean-Baptiste, forget. Remember instead *why* you fought!"

"Why did I? For the restoration of the Bourbons, perhaps, Désirée? Exactly what did you say to the Tsar?"

"That in France you're a Republican, and in Sweden a crown prince. In somewhat different words. But he understood me."

His breathing was quieter. There was a long pause. "Did you tell the Tsar anything else, little girl?"

"Yes, that you didn't want the French crown, but longed with all your heart for a Russian grand duchess. So he wouldn't think you'd turn down all his suggestions!"

"Mmmm."

"The Tsar thinks you'd better stay with me. He says the grand duchesses he knows are not at all pretty."

"Mmmm."

At last he fell asleep.

WHEN THE BELLS started to peal, I went out to the garden. They would ring continuously all the while the victorious troops, led by the Tsar of Russia, the Emperor of Austria, the King of Prussia and the Crown Prince of Sweden, marched through Paris.

The children had driven off with Madame la Flotte and their governess in my carriage. Julie had stayed in bed.

That morning, just before Jean-Baptiste had left the house in his Swedish field marshal's dress uniform, he had looked around my room—a look of farewell, not of homecoming—then had pressed my hand to his lips and said, "Promise me you won't watch the parade. I don't want you to see me."

That's how I came to be sitting alone in the garden, and no one announced my unexpected caller.

"Highness," a voice shouted above the bells. Startled, I turned to see a familiar figure in a deep bow before me. So he's still around, I thought. Fouché, the former minister of police, wore an inconspicuous frock coat and an enormous white cockade.

"I've come with a message from Talleyrand for Madame Julie Bonaparte." He took something out of his breast pocket. "It concerns the future of the members of the Bonaparte family." He handed me a copy of a long legal document. "Our new government is truly generous, Your Highness."

"I'll give it to my sister," I said. "Can you tell me where the members of the family will live?"

"Abroad, Highness, never in France."

Julie, who always felt miserable away from home, was now an exile. And why? Because I once brought Joseph to our house. I must try to help her, I thought. I looked again at the document in my hand. "And General Bonaparte?"

"Very favorable conditions. The general may himself choose a residence anywhere outside France. A troop of four hundred men, whom he may choose himself, can accompany him. They're discussing Elba. A charming little island, reminiscent of the Emperor's birthplace. The same vegetation as Corsica, I hear."

"And the Empress?"

"Will become Duchess of Parma. That is, if she renounces her son's right of succession. But these details will be decided in Vienna at a large congress. It will mean the formation of a new Europe. The dynasties dispossessed by Napoleon will return to their thrones. . . . I gather that His Highness will also go to Vienna. To press his claim to the Swedish throne." Fouché cleared his throat mildly. "Unfortunately, there are some who question whether this claim is, as they say, 'legitimate.' I, of course, am at His Highness's service, to represent him in Vienna."

I could not stand the sight of him another minute. I stood up. "I don't understand what you mean. I'll give the document to my sister."

After Fouché bowed his way out, I went to have a talk with Julie about the document that disposed of her future in such a businesslike manner. Julie buried her face in the pillows and sobbed, "But I won't go, I won't. . . . Désirée, you must see that I stay—with the children."

I stroked her straggly hair. "But Joseph? What if Joseph can't get a permit to stay?"

"Joseph wrote me from Blois. He wants to go to Switzerland. I'm to follow with the children. But I won't." She sat up suddenly. "Désirée, you'll stand by me until it's all settled? You won't go to Sweden, but stay here and help me?"

"I'll stay with you, Julie."

Paris, early May, 1814

On the evening King Louis the Eighteenth gave his first court ball in the Tuileries, I had a cold. Not a real cold, of course, but I went to bed. Just as I had before Napoleon's coronation. Marie brought me milk and honey and I began to read the papers.

The *Moniteur* reported Napoleon's departure for Elba on April 20, giving almost no details. In the *Journal des Débats*, however, there was an interesting article. "The Crown Prince of Sweden," I read, "intends to divorce his wife, Désirée Clary, sister of Madame Julie Bonaparte. After the divorce the former Crown Princess of Sweden will continue to live in her home in the rue d'Anjou. The Crown Prince, on the other hand . . ." I took a swallow of hot milk and honey. "The Crown Prince, on the other hand, has a choice between a Russian and a Prussian princess. . . . An alliance between former Marshal J.-B. Bernadotte and one of the reigning dynasties," it was explained, "will secure his future in Sweden."

I didn't want to read any more newspapers. I thought about the Bourbons' court ball and wondered whether Jean-Baptiste had accepted the invitation. Since that first night, we've hardly been alone with each other.

I lay in bed imagining the guests—so many familiar faces!—assembled in the large ballroom in the Tuileries. . . . The folding doors are opened wide, the ladies' dresses rustle as they curtsy, but where is the "Marseillaise"? Forbidden, of course, forbidden. The eighteenth Louis leans heavily on his cane; he suffers from dropsy and can hardly walk. The tired old gentleman surveys the ballroom. Here the Parisians beat and kicked my brother, he must be thinking—

My thoughts were interrupted. Someone was coming up the stairs, hurrying, two steps at a time. That's odd, I thought, everyone was already asleep. "I hope I didn't wake you, little girl."

Jean-Baptiste! No gala uniform. Only the dark blue field uniform. "I'm sorry that you've gone to bed. I've come to say good-by. I'm leaving tomorrow morning."

Tomorrow, so soon . . .

"I've done my duty here, made my triumphal entry. Besides, my agreement with Denmark has been signed. The Great Powers have recognized the ceding of Norway to Sweden. But, imagine, Désirée, the Norwegians don't want it."

So this was to be our farewell—talking about Norway. "Why not?" I asked.

"They want to be independent."

"Then let them!" I sat up in bed. I was thinking, Jean-Baptiste, can this really be the end?

" 'Let them, let them.' How you simplify things. I promised Sweden this union. It would console them for the loss of Finland, and I can't afford to disappoint the Swedes."

"Afford? The Swedish Parliament elected you, once and for all, successor to their throne, Jean-Baptiste."

"And the Swedish Parliament can, once and for all, depose me and recall the Vasa prince. With the Bourbons back in power, my child—away with the Jacobin general, call the old dynasty back!"

My heart lay heavy and hard as a stone in my breast. "Even if you married a member of an old dynasty, Jean-Baptiste?" I said. "You came to say good-by and to suggest—" I kept my voice under control. "Tell me what you have to say to me. But say it quickly, or I'll go mad."

He looked at me in bewilderment. "It's not important. I had my carriage wait because I wanted to suggest that you drive with me once more through the streets of Paris."

I began to weep.

"What's the matter, Désirée?"

"I thought—you wanted—a divorce," I sobbed, and threw back the bedclothes. "And now I'll dress quickly and we'll drive through the streets, Jean-Baptiste, together."

The carriage rolled along beside the Seine. It was an open carriage. I put my head on Jean-Baptiste's shoulder, and felt his arm around me. The lights of Paris danced in the dark water. Jean-Baptiste had the carriage stop. We got out and strolled, arm in arm, to "our bridge," and leaned over the parapet. I spoke to the dancing lights. At first I stuttered, then it came more easily. "If you believe it would be better for you and Oscar to divorce me and marry a princess—then get a divorce. I make only one condition."

"And that?"

"That I become your mistress, Jean-Baptiste."

"Out of the question. I'm not going to start keeping mistresses at the Swedish court! Besides, I can't afford a mistress. You'll just have to remain my wife, Désirée, whatever happens!"

Our Seine rippled beneath us like music. "But perhaps you could do me a favor and refrain from selling silk personally," he remarked as we sauntered back to the carriage.

The stars were very near as we drove home. "When may I expect you in Stockholm, My Royal Highness?"

"Not yet." His epaulets scratched my cheek. "The next few years will be hard enough for you. And you know how ill suited I am to the Swedish court."

He looked at me intently. "You have no other reasons for staying here?"

"Yes, Jean-Baptiste. Here I'm needed. There I'm superfluous. I must help Julie."

"I defeated Napoleon at Leipzig. But even so, I can't get rid of the Bonapartes."

"I'm thinking of the Clarys," I said sorrowfully.

Paris, May 30, 1814

Yesterday evening a weeping ex-lady-in-waiting from Malmaison was announced. Josephine had died at noon. Recently she'd caught a heavy cold taking an evening walk with the Tsar in the park at Malmaison. "The evening was quite cool, but Her Majesty refused to wear a wrap. Instead, she wore a new muslin gown, very décolleté, with only a light transparent scarf."

I remember that muslin, Josephine; too light for a May evening. Lilac, wasn't it? Sweet, melancholy, and so becoming.

The ex-lady-in-waiting handed me a note. "Bring the children with you—my one comfort," Hortense had scrawled. Hortense and Eugène de Beauharnais had been living with their mother.

So this morning, with Julie and the two sons of the former Queen of Holland, I drove to Malmaison. There we found Hortense in deep black mourning. Solemnly she flung herself first into my arms and then into Julie's.

Eugène de Beauharnais sat at a lady's tiny desk riffling through some papers. This erstwhile shy young man whom Napoleon had appointed viceroy of Italy pointed to the pile of papers on the desk and sighed. "Unbelievable—stacks of unpaid bills. For hats, rosebushes, gowns from Le Roy's. Why would Mama, living in retirement, need twenty-six gowns?"

Hortense begged us to sit down. Stiff and silent, we sat on Josephine's white salon sofa. The folding doors to the garden were open, and the fragrance of Josephine's roses wafted in.

Hortense dabbed at her now-dry eyes with her handkerchief. "You know that I'm now divorced?"

We nodded politely as Hortense's lover, Count Flahaut, came in.

"Do you want to see her?" Hortense asked suddenly.

Julie shook her head firmly. "Yes," said I, without thinking.

"Count Flahaut, take Her Royal Highness upstairs."

We went up one flight. "The dear departed is still in her bedroom," he whispered.

The tall candles burned without flickering. The shutters were closed tight. Gradually my eyes became accustomed to the semi-darkness. At first I shrank from looking at the dead woman. But then I went closer. I recognized the velvet coronation robe that lay in gentle folds across the bed, and the ermine-lined cape around her shoulders. For the last time Josephine's maid had arranged the thinning hair of the fifty-one-year-old woman in childlike curls. Once more, silver paint on the eyelids and rouge on the cheeks. How sweetly Josephine smiled in her eternal sleep, sweetly and coquettishly . . .

"She's still charming," remarked a voice at my elbow. An old gentleman with bloated cheeks and silvery hair had emerged from the darkness of a corner. "My name is Barras," he announced, and raised his lorgnette to his eye. "Have I had the honor of meeting Madame?"

"Long ago," I said. "When you were a director of the Republic, Monsieur Barras."

"Was she close to you, madame?"

No, she only broke my heart, I thought, and I began to cry.

"A fool, that little Bonaparte, a fool," Barras whispered, smoothing out a crease in Josephine's purple robe. He turned to me. "Don't cry for Josephine, madame. Josephine died as she lived.

On the arm of a very powerful man who promised one May evening among the roses at Malmaison to pay all her debts." The old gentleman vanished again into the darkness of his corner.

When I got downstairs, I quickly walked out of the open door that led to the garden. On a stone bench sat a little girl watching a tiny artificial pool where baby ducklings swam awkwardly behind a fat mother duck. I sat down beside the child. She had brown hair that fell in curls to her shoulders and was wearing a white dress. When she looked up at me and smiled, my heart skipped a beat—very long eyelashes, a sweet heart-shaped face. I asked, "What's your name?"

"Josephine, madame."

She had blue eyes, her skin was very fair, and in her thick hair sparkled golden lights. Josephine—and yet not Josephine.

"Are you one of the ladies-in-waiting, madame?" she asked.

"No. Why did you think so?"

"Because Aunt Hortense said that the Crown Princess of Sweden was coming to call. Princesses always have ladies-in-waiting. If they're grown-up princesses."

"And little princesses?"

"They have governesses."

"Are you the daughter of Prince Eugène?"

"Yes. But Papa probably isn't a prince anymore. If we're lucky, the Allies will give him a duchy in Bavaria. My grandfather, my mama's papa, is the King of Bavaria."

"So you're a princess," I said. "Where's your governess?"

"I ran away from her," the child said, dabbling her hand in the water. "Are you perhaps a governess?"

"Perhaps I'm a princess, too."

"Impossible. You don't look like a princess." The eyelashes fluttered, she cocked her head slightly and smiled. "But I like you. Have you any children?"

"A son, but he's in Sweden."

The child sighed. "My governess." She grimaced like a street urchin. "She makes me sick! But don't tell anyone I said so, madame."

I walked back to the house reflectively, and something important occurred to me. Something I must never forget. If one must found a dynasty, I thought, why not found a charming one?

That evening, as we drove home through the gathering darkness, Julie suddenly cried, "Look, a shooting star—quick, make a wish."

So I made a wish, quickly, impulsively. "The Swedes will call her Josefina," I said out loud.

"What in the world are you talking about?" Julie demanded.

"About the shooting star that's just fallen from heaven."

Paris, late autumn, 1814

Oscar wrote to me from Norway. I've pasted his letter in my diary so I won't lose it. *My dear Mama*, he says. *My most affectionate congratulations—you have become Crown Princess of Norway! Norway and Sweden are now united, and the King of Sweden is also the King of Norway. In fact, we've completed a campaign in which we conquered Norway. And last evening I came here with Papa to Christiania, which is the capital of Norway.*

But I'd better tell you things in order. Papa's entry into Stockholm after the liberation of France was wonderful. The people in the streets through which Papa's open carriage drove were so excited and happy. His Majesty fell on Papa's neck and cried like a child for joy. But Papa was tired and sad. Do you know why, Mama?

Although the Danes had ceded Norway to us, the Norwegian Parliament declared that the country wanted to be independent, and would defend its independence. Our Swedish officers were enthusiastic about a possible war. But Papa said, "Oscar, these Norwegians are a brave people, risking this war with Sweden with only half as many troops as we and no ammunition to speak of." Papa was deeply moved. He then handed me a document and said, "Read that carefully, Oscar. I'm giving the Norwegians the most liberal constitution in Europe."

Nevertheless, the brave people insisted on fighting for their independence. A few days later our troops stormed the first Norwegian Islands. The whole campaign lasted only fourteen days. Then the Norwegians requested a cessation of hostilities. Their Parliament was to be convened on November 10 (today) and Papa was asked to appear personally in Christiania to confirm the union of Norway and Sweden. So here we are.

Last evening, when we entered Christiania in a gala coach

brought from Stockholm, the streets were dark and deserted. At the governor's palace, one-storied and very modest, the president of the Norwegian Parliament, with the members of the government, welcomed Papa. Papa plunged into a resounding speech about the union and about how Norway's new constitution defends the Rights of Man.

But the Norwegians weren't impressed.

Afterward, I went with Papa to his bedroom, where he ripped off his decorations. He looked tired and sad again. "Today I'm robbing a small freedom-loving people of their independence. Oscar, one grows old and outlives oneself."

Dear Mama, I feel terribly sorry for Papa, but one can't be a crown prince and a Republican at the same time. Please write him a gay, loving letter.

With hugs and kisses, your son, Oscar

P.S. Could you possibly get hold of Herr van Beethoven's Seventh Symphony in Paris and send it to me?

Paris, March 5, 1815

This afternoon began like many other afternoons. I've reorganized my household, keeping Pierre as my steward, but letting Madame la Flotte go, and making Marcelline Tascher my lady-in-waiting. And I've appointed my nephew, Marius Clary, my equerry, while Count Rosen remains my aide. Today, with Marius' help, I was drafting a request to the eighteenth Louis to extend Julie's permit to remain in France as my guest. Julie was writing a long letter, saying nothing, to Joseph in Switzerland. Then Count Rosen came in and announced a visitor.

Fouché entered. He was in a state of high excitement. "I hope I haven't interrupted Your Highness in some important business?" he said.

"My sister has just drafted a request to His Majesty, King Louis," Julie answered.

"This morning I might have had an opportunity to support your petition, madame." He peered at Julie with amusement. "His Majesty offered me a very influential post—minister of police. But I refused."

"If the King offered you the Ministry of Police," declared Marius, "he must feel insecure."

Fouché smiled. "In his place, I'd feel insecure, too. After all, he's gaining ground."

"Who's gaining ground? What are you talking about?" I asked.

"The Emperor, of course."

The whole room began to spin, shadows danced before my eyes. As from afar, Fouché's voice reached me: "Eleven days ago the Emperor with his troops embarked at Elba . . . landed at Golfe Juan with only four hundred men . . . will march in triumph to Paris. Other countries will undoubtedly . . ."

My nephew, Marius, was beaming. "Napoleon will have the entire Army behind him. We're on the march—on the march once more."

"Against all of Europe?" asked Marcelline dryly. Then, in a more subdued voice: "You don't seriously believe that the Emperor will succeed?"

"Yes." Marius was emphatic. "Yes, he will succeed."

Julie rose. "I'll write my husband all about it. It will interest him very much."

Fouché shrugged. "Don't bother. The King's secret police would get your letter immediately. And besides, it's practically taken for granted that the Emperor informed all his brothers of his plans from Elba."

"Please excuse me, I have a headache," I said. And I did. Painful, pounding. I left the salon, went upstairs, lay on my bed, and had nothing to say to anyone. Not even to myself. Especially not to myself. . . .

Soon after eight o'clock that evening Marie announced the former Queen of Holland. I pulled the covers over my head. Ten minutes later Julie leaned over my bed. "Désirée, don't be so cruel. Poor Hortense implores you to receive her."

I resigned myself to my fate. "Let her come up, but only for a minute."

Hortense shoved her two angular little boys in first. "Don't deny my poor children your protection. Take them until everything is over," she sobbed. "The King can have them arrested any moment and hold them as hostages against the Emperor. My children are still the heirs of the dynasty, madame."

"The heir to the dynasty is named Napoleon, like his father—and lives at present in Vienna," I said calmly.

"And if something happens to that child?" she hissed. "I

implore you—the King will not dare follow my children into the house of the Swedish Crown Princess. I implore you—"

"Of course the children can stay here." I hastily yanked the covers over my head.

But I wasn't destined to rest that evening. I had hardly got to sleep when candlelight and rattling woke me up again. Someone was rummaging in my chest of drawers. I sat up.

"Julie! Are you searching for something?"

"My little crown, Désirée. Do you know what's become of it? I want to try it on again."

Paris, March 20, 1815

Last night Louis the Eighteenth slunk out of the Tuileries, and now the Bourbons are back in their perennial exile. This morning the Tricolor was hoisted over the deserted Tuileries.

The lackeys and cleaning women in the Tuileries—always the same—are once again hanging dark green draperies. Hortense has taken charge. She's had all the gilded imperial eagles hauled out of the cellar, and has dusted them personally.

A courier from the Emperor has informed Julie that His Majesty will reach the Tuileries at nine o'clock this evening. She is so excited that she can't even fix her daughters' hair. "The rest of the family are still on the way. Hortense and I have to receive him alone. . . . Désirée, I'm so afraid of him!"

"Nonsense, Julie, he's your brother-in-law. What is there to be afraid of?"

"This triumphal procession—from Elba to Paris! Regiments falling on their knees before him . . ."

"Julie, the Army cheers, but all the other people are silent!"

Uncomprehendingly, she stared at me. Then she asked to borrow the diamond earrings given to me by the former queen mother of Sweden. I hope Joseph will bring back her jewels. . . .

Meantime, Marie filled my bathtub and scrubbed the Bonaparte boys. They will drive to the Tuileries later with Julie.

"Do you believe he's coming back, Aunt?" Louis Napoleon suddenly asked me.

"Of course, the Emperor's nearly in Paris."

"I mean his son, the little King of Rome," said Louis Napoleon hesitantly, avoiding my eyes.

That's when I got out my diary and began to write.

At eight o'clock that night a state carriage from the Tuileries arrived for Julie and the children. My house became very quiet.

"I'd give a lot to be there in front of the Tuileries," Count Rosen said. "To see the arrival."

"Put on a civilian suit, pin on a Tricolor badge!" I exclaimed. He looked dazed. "Hurry," I urged. With which I slipped into a coat and grabbed a hat.

We had trouble getting through the dense crowds around the Tuileries, and finally left our hired carriage. One could get farther on foot. Suddenly mounted guards rode full tilt into the crowd. "Clear the way!" In the distance a storm seemed to have broken loose. The storm roared nearer, was upon us. *"Vive l'Empereur! Vive l'Empereur!"* The carriage came in sight, the horses galloping wildly toward the Tuileries. Officers of all ranks galloped after it. Around us and over us reverberated one single shout.

On the open staircase lackeys stood with torches. The carriage door was flung open, and for a fraction of a second, I saw the figure of the Emperor. Then the crowd surged forward through the cordon of guards and lifted the Emperor to their shoulders. They carried him up the open staircase, back to the Tuileries. The torchlight flickered over his face; he was smiling, his eyes closed.

Again a carriage rolled up. Again all necks were craned. This time they murmured in disillusionment. Only Fouché, come to welcome the Emperor. Only Fouché, at his service. . . .

Paris, June 18, 1815

Marie had just brought me breakfast when the bells of Notre-Dame began to ring. We hadn't expected a victory, and yet the bells were proclaiming it. Just as in the old days.

Julie is living with Joseph again in the Elysée Palace. Madame Letizia and all the Bonaparte brothers have returned—even that self-exiled Republican, Lucien. In the Tuileries Hortense is hostess. She dines with Napoleon and arranges court balls to shorten his nights. For at night Napoleon wanders aimlessly through the empty apartments of the Empress and the deserted nursery of the little King of Rome. He's written one letter after another to Marie Louise, and says Her Majesty may arrive at any moment from Vienna. But Marie Louise and the child have not come.

Immediately after his return Napoleon announced the first free elections since the days of the Republic. So France elected a new National Assembly, and one of the new deputies is Lafayette. It can't be the same man, I thought, when I read the election returns. Not after all these years. But Marie said it was. The very same General Lafayette who first proclaimed the Rights of Man.

Papa often told us children about the Marquis de Lafayette, who, at nineteen, outfitted his own ship and sailed to America to fight as a volunteer for the independence of the United States. In appreciation, the Continental Congress made him a major general. . . . No, Papa, I haven't forgotten what you told me. And this young marquis returned to France and, in a frayed American general's uniform, mounted the rostrum in the National Assembly in Paris and read the Declaration of the Rights of Man. You brought home the newspaper that day, Papa, and read the declaration to your small daughter. Word for word, so I'd never forget it. . . . Then Lafayette founded France's National Guard to defend our new Republic. But what happened to him after that?

Jean-Baptiste could tell me. But Jean-Baptiste is in Stockholm. His ambassador has left Paris; all the foreign diplomats have gone. Foreign countries are refusing to reestablish diplomatic relations with Napoleon.

In the end it was Lucien Bonaparte who, when he called on me one day, answered my question.

"Lafayette's been busy with his vegetable garden," he told me, "on a small, very modest estate. When the mob stormed the Tuileries and carried the heads of the aristocrats around on pikes, Deputy Lafayette protested. An order for his arrest was issued. Lafayette fled but was captured at Liège and was in prison for many years. Not until the days of the Consulate was he released."

"And then, Lucien?"

"Then he cultivated his vegetables. The man had fought all his life for the Rights of Man—do you suppose he wanted anything to do with the First Consul? Or with the Emperor Napoleon?"

Napoleon has disillusioned the Army. The state treasury is empty, their pay hasn't been raised. Day and night gendarmes ride through villages routing out peasant lads to turn into soldiers. But the peasants go into hiding. The officers who once rode with Napoleon from victory to victory now produce doctors' certificates. And the marshals? The marshals have country estates to which they have retired. Napoleon quickly appointed new marshals, however, and then he marched at the head of his last army across the frontier to intercept the Allies.

That was three days ago. His order of the day was published everywhere: *For every courageous Frenchman the time has come to conquer or die.* After this direful proclamation people hoarded foodstuffs, the theaters emptied, the restaurants went dark. Paris awaited the *coup de grâce.*

And then, this morning, the miracle: victory bells rang out.

I dressed and went into the garden. A bee buzzed. At first I wandered aimlessly. Then I stopped and listened. It was deathly still again. No bells. No cannon. Only the bee.

At that moment Lucien Bonaparte arrived. We sat down together on a bench and Lucien gazed dreamily at the garden. "How beautiful a little piece of turf can be," he said. "So quiet, so wonderfully quiet."

"Yes. The victory bells just stopped ringing."

"They were a mistake, Désirée. Napoleon has won only a skirmish—the overture to a great battle. The decision rests with Waterloo. . . ."

Paris, June 23, 1815

The first intelligible words Julie was able to utter when she burst into my dressing room were, "He has abdicated." The rest of the story came out between sobs. "He came back—in the middle of the night—in an old post chaise. His own carriage fell into the hands of the Prussian general Blücher—and the Prussians may be in Paris any moment. He drove right to us in the Elysée. He said that he must call up a hundred thousand men at once—for a new army—and he urged poor Lucien to go before the National Assembly in his name."

"And did Lucien go?"

Julie nodded. "Yes, and he came back barely twenty minutes later. When Lucien mounted the rostrum, the deputies shouted, 'A bas Bonaparte!' and bombarded him with inkwells. Lucien tried to say the nation had deserted his brother. But Lafayette jumped up. 'Two million men have fallen. In Africa, in Russia, all over Europe, the bones of your sons and brothers whiten. . . . It is enough!' Without a word, Lucien left the rostrum.

"Joseph and Lucien talked with Napoleon all night. Until dawn—I had to keep serving coffee and brandy—the Emperor paced up and down, pounded on the table, screamed . . ." Julie covered her face with her thin hands.

"Then this morning Lafayette declared in the National Assembly, 'If General Bonaparte does not abdicate within the hour, I will demand his deposition.' Fouché came to us with this threat. Finally the Emperor signed—Fouché stood beside him. The new government is called a Directorate. They're negotiating now with the Allies, and Fouché is one of the five directors. I'm so afraid of them." She began to weep helplessly again. "And in the streets they screamed at me, 'A bas les Bonapartes!' "

Again the door of my dressing room burst open—Joseph. His face was gray. "Julie, you must pack. The Emperor is leaving immediately for Malmaison. The whole family is to go. Come, Julie, hurry."

With a wild cry, Julie dug her fingers into my shoulders. "Julie—you must go with your husband," I said, and pulled her to her feet. Joseph, avoiding my eyes, led Julie to the door.

It's just a year since Josephine died. All the roses are blooming now at Malmaison.

Paris, during the night of June 29–30, 1815

His sword lies on my night table; his destiny has come full circle, and I was the instrument. They say I fulfilled a patriotic mission. But my heart is heavy. . . . Perhaps this night will be over sooner if I write in my diary.

I had lain awake for hours this morning, listening to cannon rumble by, to be set up in front of the city gates. Then, at dawn, Count Rosen asked to speak to me right away. "Respectfully reporting, Your Highness," he said, as he finished buttoning the tunic of his parade uniform. "Representatives of the nation wish to speak to Your Highness as soon as possible. It is of the utmost importance, the courier assures me."

Representatives of the nation? What did they want of me? I slipped into a thin white muslin dress and white sandals, then hurried downstairs to the large salon. On the sofa, under the portrait of the First Consul, sat three gentlemen. They rose as I entered.

Two of the nation's representatives were Their Excellencies Fouché, one of the five directors at present governing France, and Talleyrand, who just yesterday returned from the Congress of Vienna, where he had all along represented the France of the Bourbons. But I didn't recognize the old man between them. Short and very thin, he wore an old-fashioned white peruke and a faded foreign uniform. His eyes shone with a curious brilliance.

"Your Highness, may we present General Lafayette?" said Talleyrand.

My heart skipped a beat. I curtsied, awkwardly as a schoolgirl. And Lafayette smiled so simply, so sincerely, that I gathered courage to say, "I never thought I'd have the honor of meeting Lafayette in person, and in my own salon." I stopped in embarrassment. Then I went on. "Can I do something for you, gentlemen?"

Talleyrand answered very softly, very rapidly. "Perhaps Your Highness remembers I once intimated that I might someday ask a very great favor of you in the name of France?" I nodded. "Today the French nation has a favor to ask of the Crown Princess of Sweden."

Then Fouché said, "Allied troops are at the gates of Paris, Your Highness, and Talleyrand, as minister of foreign affairs, has communicated with the commanders in chief, Wellington and Blücher. To forestall an attack, we are offering unconditional surrender."

"But the Allies have informed us," Talleyrand explained, "that they will consider our proposals only if General Bonaparte leaves France without delay."

"When we informed General Bonaparte that his departure is the wish of the French government," Fouché said, his voice cracking, "the reply was so incredible as to leave the impression that Malmaison harbors a madman. Yesterday General Bonaparte demanded that he be given supreme command of what remains of the Army in order to beat back the enemy from the gates. Not until such a defensive action is taken will General Bonaparte agree to go abroad. In other words—a bloodbath for Paris!"

My mouth was very dry. What did they expect me to do?

Talleyrand appealed to me. "The Allied troops have reached Versailles. We cannot capitulate or protect Paris from destruction while General Bonaparte is in France. He must leave Malmaison by this evening, and be on his way to Rochefort."

"Why Rochefort?"

"When General Bonaparte abdicated, he insisted that two frigates of the French Navy be placed at his disposal. The frigates are waiting for him in Rochefort harbor."

Fouché consulted his watch.

I asked softly, "What have I to do with this?"

"You, dear Crown Princess, as a member of the Swedish royal house, are in a position to talk to General Bonaparte in the name of the Allies." Talleyrand smiled, clearly amused.

"Your Highness can also convey to General Bonaparte the French government's answer to his impudent suggestion." Fouché extracted a sealed letter from his breast pocket.

Slowly I shook my head. "You are mistaken, gentlemen. I'm only a private person here."

"My child, you haven't been told the whole truth."

I jumped. For the first time, I heard Lafayette's deep, serene and kindly voice. "General Bonaparte has assembled a few battalions in Malmaison—young men, ready for anything. The general might reach a decision that wouldn't affect the ultimate outcome, but would cost the lives of several hundred men. Several hundred human lives mean a great deal, my child. General Bonaparte's wars have already cost Europe millions of human lives," the quiet voice continued relentlessly.

I looked up and saw, over their shoulders, the portrait of the young Napoleon. And I heard my own voice. "I'll try, gentlemen."

COUNT ROSEN, WEARING Sweden's blue-and-yellow sash over his parade uniform, accompanied me on the drive to Malmaison. Close behind us galloped a lone rider, General Becker, the commissary assigned by the Directorate to watch over the former Emperor of the French. Near Malmaison the road was barricaded, the National Guardsmen stood watch. When they recognized General Becker, they quickly pushed the barricade aside. My carriage was allowed to pass. I tried to pretend that things were as they used to be. A visit to Malmaison . . .

The carriage stopped, and Count Rosen helped me out. Ménéval appeared on the open staircase. And then I was surrounded by familiar faces. Hortense ran to me—and Julie. Beside Joseph and

Jérôme was Lucien. Madame Letizia waved to me from the open window of the white-and-gold salon. How glad they all were to see me.

"Joseph," I gulped, "please, I must speak to your brother."

"How kind of you, Désirée. But the Emperor is expecting an important communication from the government in Paris, and is not to be disturbed until it comes."

"Joseph, it is that message I am bringing to your brother."

"And—?" they all asked in one breath.

"I have to give it first to General Bonaparte."

Joseph's face went pale when I said "General Bonaparte."

"His Majesty," he said, "is on the bench in the maze."

"Wait here, Count Rosen," I whispered.

In the intricacies of the maze, so charmingly devised by Josephine, one turns again and again, then comes suddenly and surprisingly to the little white bench on which only two can sit, very close together. It was there I found Napoleon.

He wore the green chasseur uniform, and his thin hair was carefully brushed back. Unseeingly, he stared at the flowering hedge before him. Then he turned his head a little and saw my white dress. "Josephine," he murmured. "Josephine."

When no answer came, he looked up. He was surprised and very pleased. "Eugénie— It's been many long years since you and I looked at a flowering hedge together." He moved over to one side of the little bench for two. "I'm waiting for an extremely important message from the government." He frowned.

"You need wait no longer, General Bonaparte. I bring the government's answer." I pulled Fouché's letter out of my handbag. He hastily broke the seal. I didn't watch while he read.

"Why do you, a casual guest, a lady making a friendly call, bring me this letter, madame? Did the government not consider it sufficiently important to send me their answer by a minister?"

"I'm not a casual visitor, General Bonaparte. Nor a lady making a friendly call." I took a deep breath. "I am the Crown Princess of Sweden. The French government has asked me to inform you that the Allies will consider the surrender of Paris only after you have left France. To save Paris from destruction, it is imperative that you leave today."

"I make an offer to repulse the enemy at the gates of Paris, and they reject it," he roared.

"The first Allied troops have reached Versailles," I said quietly. "Do you want to be taken prisoner here at Malmaison?"

"Don't worry, madame, I know how to defend myself."

"That's just it. Unnecessary bloodshed must be avoided."

His eyes narrowed. "And what of the honor of a nation?"

I could mention the millions, I thought, who have already died for the honor of this nation. But he knew these figures better than I. I clenched my teeth and kept silent.

"You say the French government wishes me to leave. And—the Allies?" His face was contorted.

"The Allies insist on taking you prisoner, General."

He looked at me steadily. "This scrap of paper from the so-called French government refers to frigates in Rochefort. I'm to embark for whatever destination I choose. . . . Madame, why doesn't the government hand me over to the Allies?"

"I think . . . it would embarrass the gentlemen."

"I must merely board one of the waiting frigates, name my destination, and . . ."

"The harbor of Rochefort, like all French ports, is patrolled by the English Navy. You wouldn't get far, General."

We were sitting so close together that I could hear every breath he drew. "When I saw you awhile ago, recognized your face, I felt for a moment that my youth had come back. I was wrong, Your Royal Highness."

It was hot and still and the hedge smelled sweet. I spoke as in a dream, the words came of themselves. "I remember perfectly the evening you told me you knew your destiny. That was the first time I was afraid of you."

"And that was the first time I kissed you, Eugénie."

I smiled. "You were thinking about my dowry, General."

"No, Eugénie—not entirely."

I sensed he was watching me sideways, that something had occurred to him. "And if I don't let myself be taken prisoner, but give myself up voluntarily as a prisoner of war—what then? Another island? Perhaps that rock in the ocean called Saint Helena they suggested at the Congress of Vienna? They say the climate there is very unhealthy." Naked fear showed in his eyes. "Is it—Saint Helena?"

"I honestly don't know. Where is Saint Helena?"

"Beyond the Cape of Good Hope. Far beyond, Eugénie!"

"Nevertheless, General, I wouldn't let myself be taken prisoner. I'd much rather go voluntarily." I stood up. He didn't move.

"I'm going now," I said. "But you have until—this evening."

Suddenly he stood up and began to roar with laughter. "Shall I keep them from taking me prisoner?" He felt for his sword. "Shall we cheat Blücher and Wellington of their sport?" He ripped the sword from its scabbard and held it out to me. Steel glinted in the sunlight. "Take it, Eugénie, take the sword of Waterloo!"

Hesitantly I stretched out my hand. "At this moment I surrender myself to the Allies. I consider myself a prisoner of war. I have handed over my sword to the Crown Princess of Sweden, because"—his words tumbled over one another—"because we've reached the hedge, Eugénie. And you have won."

"I can hardly explain the hedge to the French government." I stared in dismay at the sword I clutched awkwardly by the hilt.

He grimaced. "Eugénie, don't hold the sword like an umbrella."

"And your answer to the government, General?"

"Show them my sword and say that in an hour—no, in two—I leave for Rochefort. My fate after that depends on the Allies." Napoleon paused. "The frigates are, under all circumstances, to wait in Rochefort."

"They're lying at anchor beside the English cruiser *Bellerophon*," I said. Then I turned to leave.

He was staring ahead. "After my first abdication I tried to commit suicide. In Fontainebleau . . : but my life was saved. I have not yet fulfilled my destiny. You've probably never been suspended between life and death, madame?"

"The evening you became engaged to Josephine, I tried to drown myself in the Seine."

His eyes bored through me. "You tried to . . . And how were you rescued, Eugénie?"

"Bernadotte pulled me back."

He shook his head, baffled. "How strange. Bernadotte pulled you back. You will be Queen of Sweden. I hand you the sword of Waterloo. . . . Do you believe in predestination?"

"No, only in curious coincidences." I held out my hand to him.

"Tell my brothers to prepare everything for my departure. But first I wish to be alone here for a while. And, Eugénie, our engagement—long ago—it wasn't only the dowry. . . . Now, go—go very quickly. Before I repent."

By the time we 'reached the outskirts of the city, darkness had fallen. In front of every house whispering groups had gathered. I was thinking, Now Napoleon has put on his civilian clothes, he is driving to the coast. He has started on his long journey. Paris is saved. . . .

Near the rue d'Anjou we came upon a crowd of people surging forward. Someone called, "The Crown Princess of Sweden!" Others took up the cry. In front of my house torches burned high. As I alighted from the carriage, I reached for the sword. Then I started into the house. The hall was brightly lighted. I blinked in the sudden brightness. At many strangers.

"I thank you in the name of France, citizeness." Lafayette came forward to meet me. His hand lay protectingly under my arm as he led me into the room.

"Who are all these people?" I whispered, dumbfounded.

Talleyrand had joined us. Behind him stood Fouché with a white cockade on his coat lapel. Everyone was bowing.

"The people of Paris have been waiting for hours for the return of Your Highness," said Fouché rapidly.

"Tell them that the Em—that General Bonaparte has surrendered to the Allies and has departed. Then they will go."

"They want to see you, citizeness," Lafayette said.

"Me? See me?"

Lafayette nodded. "You bring us peace. Capitulation without civil war. You have saved many lives. Show yourself to the people, citizeness." Helplessly, I let him lead me to a window overlooking the rue d'Anjou. Shouts rose from the darkness. Lafayette flung wide his arms. The shouting ebbed away. The old man's voice rang like a trumpet: "Citizens and citizenesses, peace is assured. General Bonaparte has given himself up as a prisoner of war, and to a woman, to a citizeness chosen by a freedom-loving people in the Far North as their Crown Princess—Napoleon has surrendered his sword. The sword of Waterloo!"

Again shouts rose from the darkness. I stepped to the window and with both hands I held out the sword. Torches glowed, the darkness below me seethed. Then I made out the words they kept shouting to me. Exultantly, again and again: *"Nôtre dame de la paix! Nôtre dame de la paix!"*

Our Lady of Peace! Tears streamed down my cheeks.

PART FOUR

The Queen of Sweden

Paris, February 1818

I'VE KNOWN FOR years that one day it would happen. Now it has. I am Queen of Sweden. And nothing can undo it. The moment the Swedish ambassador entered the room, I understood. He remained at the door and didn't move. Then he bowed. We were both most uneasy. His bow was so deep, so—solemn. Then I saw the mourning band on his arm.

"Your Majesty, I come with sad news. King Charles passed away on the fifth of February. His Majesty has delegated me to inform Your Majesty of all the circumstances, and to give you this letter."

I reached out a trembling hand and took the letter. "Sit down, Baron," I murmured, and sank into the nearest chair. My hands shook as I broke the heavy seal. On a large sheet of paper Jean-Baptiste had scribbled: *Dearest, You are now Queen of Sweden. Please behave accordingly. In great haste, Your J.-B.* And below, a postscript: *Don't forget to destroy this letter at once.*

I let the letter fall and saw that the ambassador with his band of mourning was watching me. I quickly tried to assume a sad and dignified expression. "My husband writes me that I'm now Queen of Sweden."

At that the ambassador began to smile. "On February sixth His Majesty was proclaimed by the royal heralds King Karl the Fourteenth Johan of Sweden and Norway, and the wife of His Majesty was proclaimed Queen Desideria."

"And the—circumstances?" I asked.

"The old gentleman passed away peacefully. He had a stroke on the first of February, and we knew the end was near. On the evening of February the fifth His Majesty and His Highness, the Crown Prince, were in the sickroom."

The Crown Prince. Oscar—Crown Prince Oscar . . .

"At a quarter to eleven it was all over."

I bowed my head. "And then?"

The ambassador went on quickly. "At midnight His Majesty

received members of the government, who swore the oath of allegiance to him, a ceremony required by the Constitution. Early in the morning His Majesty was proclaimed by the royal heralds King of Sweden and Norway and after that attended the service of mourning. Meanwhile, the citizens of Stockholm had gathered at the palace gates to do homage to their sovereign. The next day His Majesty, for the first time, ascended his throne in Parliament, and took the royal oath. . . . The coronation ceremony will be held the eleventh of May, a date specifically requested by His Majesty for some reason."

"On the eleventh of May, just twenty-five years ago, the soldier Jean-Baptiste Bernadotte became a sergeant in the Army of the French Republic. It was a great day in my husband's life, Your Excellency."

I rang for tea. Marcelline came in to help me serve it. As I offered the ambassador his tea, he said, "You're very kind, Your Majesty."

Poor Marcelline was so shocked she dropped a cup, with a crash. Soon afterward the ambassador took his leave. But Marcelline was still staring at me in awe. "Her Majesty, Queen of Sweden and Norway!" She rolled out the words impressively. "You'll go to Stockholm, of course. That means we can't go see Aunt Julie in Brussels. She counted so much on your visit—"

"I must order some mourning outfits tomorrow," I said, interrupting her. Then I hurried up to my bedroom. I simply threw myself on the bed and stared into the darkness.

Julie Bonaparte—exiled from France, like all the others with the name Bonaparte. They allowed her to stay in my house for only one week after Napoleon's departure. But then I had to pack her boxes and take her and the children across the Belgian frontier.

Since then I've written innumerable requests to the eighteenth Louis asking him to authorize her return. And after every refusal I've gone to Brussels to comfort the always-ailing Julie. Brother-in-law Joseph didn't stay around long. He sailed to America and bought a farm in New York State. His letters sound contented. But Julie drags herself from sofa to bed, from bed to sofa. How can he have imagined that she'd ever be well enough to follow him to America?

How many faraway faces seem to haunt me from the darkness.

Hortense in Switzerland, Julie in Brussels, Joseph in America. The other Bonapartes in Italy. In the end King Louis even sent his minister of police, Joseph Fouché, into exile. But I was still here. And King Louis was going to call on me.

Marie came in and lighted the candles. She'll scold me for lying on the silk bedspread with my shoes on, I thought. But Marie didn't scold me at all. She looked at me respectfully, just like Marcelline. "Your niece told me about it," Marie said.

"I know what you're thinking. That my papa wouldn't have approved. I know it myself. You don't have to tell me."

"Eugénie, let me take off your dress."

I raised my arms. She slipped off my dress. "There. Now, sit up straight and lift your head. If you're a queen, then at least be a good one. When do we leave for Stockholm?"

I picked up the letter and reread Jean-Baptiste's casual scrawl. Written in such haste, so full of anxiety that I might be unworthy of him. At that instant I made my decision. I reached for a candle and held the letter to the flame.

"We'll leave in three days. Then I won't have time to receive King Louis. By the way, we're going to Brussels, Marie. Julie needs me. In Stockholm I'm superfluous."

"But they can't have a coronation without us!" Marie protested.

"Apparently they can. Or they would have invited us to it."

Paris, June 1821

The letter lay among many others on my breakfast table. At first I thought I must be dreaming. The dark green seal showed clearly the crest of the Emperor, a coat of arms forbidden all over the world. The letter was addressed to Her Majesty, Queen Desideria of Sweden and Norway. I finally opened it.

> *Madame, I have been informed that my son, the Emperor of the French, died on May the fifth of this year on the island of Saint Helena. His earthly remains will be buried with military honors. The English government has forbidden the erection of a tombstone with the name* Napoleon. *Only the inscription* General N. Bonaparte *has been allowed. Therefore I have decided that the grave will remain unmarked.*
>
> *I am dictating these lines to my son Lucien, who frequently stays with me in Rome. Unfortunately I am now blind. Lucien*

has begun to read aloud to me my son's memoirs, dictated on Saint Helena. They contain the sentence: Désirée Clary was Napoleon's first love. *Since the manuscript is soon to be printed, please let me know whether this sentence should be omitted. We understand you must consider your exalted position, and will gladly comply with your wishes. I send you my son Lucien's kind regard, and remain as always your devoted . . .*

The blind old woman's signature was barely legible and in Italian: *Laetizia, madre di Napoleone.*

Later in the day I asked my nephew, Marius, how the letter with the green coat of arms had come to my house.

"An attaché to the Swedish embassy brought it. The letter was delivered to the Swedish chargé d'affaires in Rome. Was it an important letter?"

"The last I shall ever receive with the Emperor's crest. I want you to send some money to the English ambassador asking that in my name a wreath be laid on the grave at Saint Helena. On the nameless grave, you'd better add."

"Aunt, your wish cannot be granted. There are no flowers on Saint Helena. The terrible climate of the island kills all plant life."

I sat down at my desk and began my reply to his mother.

After a few minutes Marius interrupted my writing.

"Aunt Julie once intimated that you—" he stammered. "Or rather, that he once—I mean that . . ."

"You can read about it in his memoirs." I sealed my letter. "Nothing will be left out."

In a hotel room in Aix-la-Chapelle, June 1822

That I could once again experience all the sweetness, the anxiety, the impatience of a first meeting, I thought this morning as I put on my rouge. Not too much, I told myself. I'm forty-two years old; the boy must not think I'm trying to seem younger. But I want him to find me attractive. . . .

"And when will I see him?" I asked for about the hundredth time.

"He's arriving in Aix this morning. The appointment's at half past twelve, Aunt. In your salon," Marcelline answered patiently.

"And will he dine with me?"

"Of course. Accompanied by his chamberlain, Karl Gustaf Löwenhjelm."

"My Löwenhjelm's uncle." My Löwenhjelm is Gustaf, too, recently sent from Stockholm to replace Count Rosen, who went back home. But he's so pompous and distant I hardly dare speak to him.

"Otherwise, Aunt, only Marius and I will be there. So you'll be able to talk to him freely."

My Löwenhjelm, his Löwenhjelm, Marcelline and Marius. No, I made up my mind. "Marcelline, be sweet and send me my Count Löwenhjelm."

Oscar had never been in Aix, I thought. After the long drive he'll want exercise. The hotel is near the cathedral. Like any tourist, he'll want to see the cathedral. . . .

Löwenhjelm listened carefully. "And be sure your uncle agrees to leave as soon as he sees me," I said.

My Löwenhjelm was horrified at this breach of ceremonial protocol, but I refused to give in. "As Your Majesty commands," he sighed.

So I put on my hat with the traveling veil that came down over my cheeks. Besides, I thought, it's dark in the cathedral.

I sat on a choir bench and folded my hands. Eleven years is a long time, I thought. He has grown up. A young man sent abroad to find a bride in the courts of Europe.

That morning countless tourists visited the cathedral. They surged around the tomb of Charlemagne. I followed every one with my eyes. Him? asked my heart. Could that one be my unknown son?

I recognized him immediately by his walk, the slight turn of his head. He wore a dark civilian suit, and he is almost as big as his father. Only slender, yes, much, much slenderer. I stood and walked over to the tomb of Charlemagne, where he was leaning a little forward to read the inscription. Löwenhjelm looked up, and silently moved away.

"Is that Charlemagne's tomb?" I heard myself ask in French. It was the silliest question in the world; it said so on the tomb.

"As you see, madame," he replied, without looking up.

"I know that my behavior is unseemly, but—but I'd like very much to meet Your Highness."

He turned to me. "You know who I am, madame?"

The dark fearless eyes of his childhood. And the same thick hair. My hair . . . But a strange little mustache.

"Your Highness is the Crown Prince of Sweden. And I—I'm a sort of compatriot. My husband lives in Stockholm . . ." I hesitated. He looked at me steadily. "I wanted to ask Your Highness something, but it will take a little time."

He looked around. "Perhaps we could stroll while we talk."

I nodded. There was a lump in my throat. I pulled my veil over my face and we left the cathedral, crossed a wide road and entered a narrow street. He stopped at a small café. "May I offer my charming compatriot a glass of wine?" It wouldn't be proper, I thought. "It's not very grand here," he went on amiably, "but we can at least talk undisturbed, madame." Then, to my horror, he asked, "Waiter, have you any champagne?"

"Not so early in the morning!" I objected.

"Why not? Anytime, if there's something to celebrate. I want to celebrate knowing you, madame."

The waiter brought champagne and filled our glasses. "*Skäl*, unknown countrywoman! French and Swedish both, aren't you?"

"Like Your Highness," I said.

"No, madame, I'm only Swedish now," he said quickly, "and Norwegian. This champagne tastes awful, doesn't it?"

"Too sweet, Your Highness."

"We seem to have the same tastes, madame. I'm glad. Most women prefer sugary-sweet wine. Our Koskull, for instance."

I caught my breath sharply. "What do you mean—'our Koskull'?"

"The lady-in-waiting Mariana von Koskull. First, the late King's ray of sunshine. Then Papa's favorite. When Papa accepted the etiquette of the Swedish court, he didn't want to upset or change anything. He took over the Koskull, too. What surprises you, madame?"

"That you—tell all this to a stranger," I said.

"A countrywoman, madame. You must realize that my father is the loneliest man I know. My mother hasn't come to see him for years. Papa works sixteen hours a day, and spends the late evening hours with a few close friends like Count Brahe, if this name means anything to you. Mademoiselle von Koskull often joins them. With a guitar. She sings Swedish drinking songs for Papa."

"But the court balls, the receptions? One can't have a court without them."

"Papa can. Don't forget, madame, we have no queen at our court. And my father has become very odd. A king beset by a neurotic fear of being deposed. He now absolutely forbids newspapers to publish any article personally displeasing to him, although the Swedish Constitution guarantees freedom of the press. Madame, the King himself violates the Constitution. Do you realize what that means?"

Oscar's face went pale with misery. I asked tonelessly, "Your Highness, you're not set against your father?"

"No. Or it wouldn't upset me so. . . . Madame, Sweden has him to thank for her independence. Yet today he opposes every liberal tendency in Parliament. Things have gone so far that some people—individuals, madame, not any party—talk of forcing the King to abdicate in my favor."

"You mustn't even think of that, Highness," I whispered.

His thin shoulders slumped forward. "I know, madame. But how can I make my father realize that the French Revolution also brought about changes in Sweden? Papa should receive commoners instead of having only the old nobility at court functions. Papa must refrain from talking in every speech about his military achievements, and about the private fortune he has sacrificed for Sweden. Papa must—"

I couldn't bear it any longer. I had to interrupt him. "And this Koskull?"

"I don't think she's ever done more than sing songs for him. Though, of course, Papa was a man in the prime of life when his loneliness began. He locks himself in his study, and is out of touch with reality. He needs—" He broke off. There were deep furrows in his forehead as he filled the glasses again. The champagne tasted flat. "When I was a child, madame, I wanted to see Napoleon's coronation. I wasn't allowed to. I can't remember why, but I remember my mother saying, 'We'll go to another coronation, Oscar. You and I. Mama promises. Yes, madame, I went to another coronation. But my mother didn't come. . . . Why are you crying?"

"Your mother's name is Desideria—the desired one. Perhaps her presence was not desired."

"Not desired? My father had her proclaimed Queen in two marvelous countries, and she—she never came to either. Do you think a man like my father would beg her to?"

"Perhaps your mother isn't suited to be a queen, Highness."

"The people of Paris shouted '*Nôtre dame de la paix*' up at my mother's window because she prevented a civil war. My mother wrested Napoleon's sword from him."

"No, he gave it to her."

"Madame, my mother is a wonderful woman. But she is at least as stubborn as my father. I assure you that the Queen's presence in Sweden is not only desirable, but necessary."

"If that is so," I said softly, "the Queen will come."

"Mama. Thank God, Mama! And now take off the veil so I can see you, really see you. . . . Yes, you haven't changed. You're even more beautiful."

"When did you recognize me, Oscar?"

"Recognize? I only stationed myself at Charlemagne's tomb to wait for you. From the beginning, I meant to see you again without witnesses, and had racked my brain to arrange it. Then Count Löwenhjelm tipped me off that you had beaten me to it."

"Oscar, is everything you told me about Papa true?"

He took my hand and pressed it to his cheek. "Of course. I only exaggerated a little to speed your homecoming. When are you coming?"

Homecoming—homecoming to a foreign land. "Oscar, you don't know how deeply they hurt me in Stockholm."

"Mama, who could hurt you now? You're the Queen." Suddenly he thought of something. "Mama, back there in the cathedral you said you wanted to ask me something. Did you say that only to start a conversation?"

"No, I do want to ask you something. It's about my daughter-in-law."

"There's no such person. Papa has compiled a long list of princesses I'm to see. One more hideous than the other."

"I'd so much like to have you marry for love, Oscar."

"Believe me, I'd rather, too. But you forget who I am."

"Listen, Oscar, it has been arranged that from here you travel with me to Brussels for a wedding. Aunt Julie's daughter Zénaïde is marrying a son of Lucien Bonaparte's. Joseph Bonaparte is returning from America for the occasion. From Brussels I'm going to Switzerland to visit Hortense, the daughter of the beautiful Josephine. I want you to go with me. I want you to meet Hortense's niece, the little Shooting Star."

"The little what?"

"Her father is Eugène, the former viceroy of Italy. Now he's called the Duke of Leuchtenberg. The child is the most beautiful little Josephine you could ever imagine."

"No matter how beautiful she is, I still couldn't marry her. An obscure little Leuchtenberg isn't a suitable match for the Crown Prince of Sweden—for a Bernadotte, Mama!"

"Let me tell you something, Oscar. Her paternal grandfather was Vicomte de Beauharnais, a general in the French Army. And her grandmother was the most beautiful woman of her time, who, by her second marriage, became Empress of the French. Your paternal grandfather was a lawyer's clerk, and I know nothing at all about your papa's mother."

"But Mama—"

"Let me finish! Her maternal grandfather is the King of Bavaria, and a member of one the oldest royal families in Europe. Your maternal grandfather, on the other hand, was the silk merchant François Clary from Marseilles."

He beat his brow. "The granddaughter of a courtesan!"

"Yes—and an enchanting one at that. I've seen little Josephine only once, as a child, but—the same smile, the same charm as the older Josephine."

Oscar sighed. "Mama, Papa will never consent."

"I'll talk to Papa. All you have to do is see the Shooting Star."

"Waiter, the bill."

Arm in arm we walked to our hotel. My heart beat fast from happiness and too much bad champagne.

"How old is she, Mama?"

"Just fifteen. But I'd already been kissed at that age."

"You were a precocious child, Mama. Why do you call her a shooting star?"

I wanted to explain it to him. But the hotel was in sight, and he turned suddenly serious. "Mama, promise me you'll come with my bride-to-be on her journey to Stockholm."

"Yes, I promise."

"And that you'll stay?"

I hesitated. "Only if I succeed in being a good queen."

"All you need is practice, Mama."

"I'll carry out several reforms at the Swedish court," I whispered in his ear.

He smiled. "Let's let the evening sun go down before the Shooting Star falls from heaven."

I nodded. "Let's retire Mademoiselle Koskull to a well-earned rest," I suggested.

"Mama, we're both a little drunk," Oscar declared. Then we began to laugh and couldn't stop.

On the way to the Royal Palace, Stockholm, spring of 1823

"How beautiful our country is," whispered my daughter-in-law, Crown Princess Josefina of Sweden, her eyes shining as we stood side by side at the railing of an imposing cruiser that was taking us past the many small islands around Stockholm. The official wedding celebration was to begin after we reached Stockholm, even though Oscar and Josefina had already been married in Munich. But Oscar hadn't been there. The Catholic Shooting Star naturally had wanted to be married in a Catholic Church, and Oscar is a Protestant. He, therefore, had been married by proxy in Munich.

"We are nearing Vaxholm, one of our strongest fortifications, Your Majesty," Chamberlain Count Gustaf Löwenhjelm told me, and handed me a field glass.

"Our country," the Shooting Star, the granddaughter of Josephine had said—our country? But I've brought with me little bits of France. Marie and Pierre, of course. Marcelline as chief stewardess of my household, and Marius to administer my finances and become a Swedish court official. And Yvette, of course, the one person except Julie who can cope with my unruly hair.

Julie . . . How strong are the weak. How tenaciously she had clung to me, and for how many years she had implored me, "Don't leave me, Désirée, write another petition to the King of France. I want to live in Paris. Stay with me, help me." My petitions were of no avail, but I'd always stayed near her. Until, at her daughter's wedding, she had said, "Zénaïde and her husband will live in Florence. Italy reminds me of Marseilles. I'll move to Florence with the young couple." And Joseph had announced he would eventually join her there. "So everything will be for the best," Julie had said indifferently. She'd entirely forgotten about me. . . .

"I'm so happy, Mama," Josefina, beside me, whispered. "From

the very first moment, at Aunt Hortense's, Oscar and I felt we were made for each other—"

Then the fortress of Vaxholm was welcoming us. A salute of guns boomed out and a small boat steered toward us. "Josefina, powder your nose quickly. Oscar is coming on board."

I hardly heard the roar of cannon. The coast was black with waiting people, the wind carried their cheers through the blue air and more and more little boats, with garlands of flowers, danced around our ship. Oscar and Josefina stood close together and waved.

"Your Majesty, we'll soon land," announced Löwenhjelm.

Yvette rushed up and held a mirror in front of my face. Powder, rouge, a little silver on my eyelids. Marie's work-worn hands put the heavy sable stole over my shoulders. Silver-gray velvet and sables seemed suitable for a mother-in-law. Then the cannon were silent and music resounded, an exultant fanfare. Löwenhjelm again handed me the field glass.

A violet velvet cape. White plumes on the hat.

Suddenly everyone whisked away. All alone I stood on the ship's bridge. The Swedish national anthem burst forth. Two gentlemen strode together up to the bridge to escort me to land. Count Brahe smiled and Count Rosen went pale with excitement. But a hand in a white glove motioned them both aside. The violet velvet cape came forward, and on my arm I felt Jean-Baptiste's strong, very familiar hand. I felt him look at me, yet I dared not meet his eyes. Because I had made a dreadful discovery! I'm in love with him still.

The crowd yelled, the cannon thundered, the orchestra rejoiced, as Oscar escorted his Crown Princess ashore. A little girl in a white dress, practically invisible behind a huge bouquet, recited a poem, then, obviously relieved, thrust the flowers at me. No one expected me to thank her. But when I opened my mouth there was a sudden hush.

"*Jag har varit länge borte*—" I was stiff with fear, but my voice was loud and calm.

They held their breaths. Swedish—the Queen speaks Swedish. I'd composed my own little speech and Count Löwenhjelm had translated it. Then I had learned it by heart. Word for word. It was hard to do. My eyes filled as I concluded with the words: "*Länge leve Sverige!*"

During my first visit to Drottningholm I had cried through the light summer nights. Now—twelve years later—I have to dance through them. Oscar and the Shooting Star, of course, whirl from one party to another. And I'm forcing Jean-Baptiste to go, too. Naturally, he makes a hundred excuses. Work and more work. Even his age is dragged in. Jean-Baptiste is sixty years old, it's true, but he couldn't be healthier. I've even transformed the lonely bachelor quarters in the Stockholm Royal Palace and here in Drottningholm into fine court households.

Yesterday I went to bed early, but I couldn't sleep. The clock struck midnight. The sixteenth of August, I thought. The sixteenth of August is dawning and I want to go to Jean-Baptiste. I began to wander through the unearthly night quiet of the palace, and finally groped my way to his dressing room. Someone shouted in French, "Who's there?"

"A ghost, Fernand!" I laughed. "Only a ghost."

"Your Majesty frightened me," declared Fernand. Then he got up from his camp cot, which barred the way to Jean-Baptiste's bedroom, and bowed. He wore a long nightshirt and held a pistol in his hand.

"Do you always sleep in front of His Majesty's door?"

"Always," Fernand assured me. "Because the marshal fears a coup d'état."

At that, the door was flung open. I dipped into a court curtsy. "Your Majesty, a ghost requests an audience."

And then, for the first time since my arrival in Drottningholm, I entered Jean-Baptiste's bedroom. On the desk documents were piled high. On the floor lay leather volumes in confusion. Jean-Baptiste stretched wearily. His voice was tender. "And why does the ghost walk tonight?"

I sat down comfortably in an armchair. "It's the ghost of a young girl who once married a general and lay on a bridal bed full of roses and thorns." Jean-Baptiste sat on the arm of my chair and put his arm around me. "That happened twenty-five years ago," I said softly.

"My God," he shouted, "it's our silver wedding anniversary!"

I crept closer to him. "Yes, and in the whole kingdom of

Sweden no one but us will remember it. No cannons, no school-children reciting poems. How lovely, Jean-Baptiste."

"We have both come a long way," he murmured. He closed his eyes and held me tighter.

"You have reached your goal, Jean-Baptiste," I whispered. "And nevertheless, you're afraid—of ghosts." He felt heavy against me. He seemed tired, very tired. "What are the ghosts you fear?"

"Vasa," he groaned. "At the Congress of Vienna the last Vasa king—the exiled one—presented his claim to the throne."

"That was eight years ago. The Allies ignored his claim. Besides, the Swedes deposed him. You were proclaimed and crowned King."

"But the Liberal opposition in Parliament . . ."

"Do they speak of the Vasas?"

"No, never. But the opposition newspapers always harp on the fact that I wasn't born here."

I straightened up. "Jean-Baptiste, it's simply the truth."

"From opposition to revolution is a short step," he muttered stubbornly. "And I can be murdered or deposed to make room for the last of the Vasas. He's an officer in the Austrian Army."

At that, I decided to lay the ghost of the Vasas to rest once and for all. "Jean-Baptiste, in Sweden the Bernadotte dynasty rules, and you are the only one who seems not to realize it." He shrugged. "But, unfortunately, there are people who feel that, in your fear of the opposition, you disregard the Constitution." I didn't look at him. "The Swedes put great stock in the freedom of their press, dearest. And every time you suppress a newspaper, someone or other suggests you should be forced to abdicate."

He recoiled as though I'd hit him. "The Vasa prince . . ."

"Jean-Baptiste, no one has mentioned the Vasa prince."

"Who, then? They must want someone as my successor?"

"Oscar, of course. The Crown Prince."

A deep sigh of relief. "Is that true?" he whispered. "Look me in the eye—is that really true?"

"The Bernadotte dynasty is established, Jean-Baptiste, established. And why should I run into Fernand outside your door, wearing his nightshirt and waving a pistol, when I want to visit you late at night?"

The candles had burned low. "My darling, you shouldn't visit

615

me late at night. Queens don't creep around palaces in their dressing gowns. You're supposed to wait in your apartments with true feminine restraint until I come to you."

Later—much later—we drew back the curtains from the windows. The Drottningholm park was bathed in golden sunlight. I stood close to Jean-Baptiste. "As for Oscar—" I began.

He laughed. "No, I'm not afraid of our young rascal." Then, very gently, he kissed me on the top of my head.

I took his arm. "Come with me. We'll have breakfast together just as we did twenty-five years ago."

In my dressing room we found a great surprise. On the breakfast table, set for two, was a huge bouquet of fragrant roses. Propped against the vase was a note.

"To Their Majesties, our Marshal J.-B. Bernadotte and his wife, with best wishes—Marie and Fernand."

Jean-Baptiste began to laugh—and I to cry. We're so very different, and yet . . . and yet.

The Royal Palace, February 1829

I really feel sorry for the old Princess Sofia Albertina. The last Vasa in Sweden lies dying, with a silk merchant's daughter holding her hand. This morning she unexpectedly sent one of her ancient ladies-in-waiting: it was the last wish of Her Highness, Princess Sofia Albertina, to speak to me—alone!

She lay on a sofa, her skin stretched taut over her sunken cheeks. The old face forced a smile. "I'm very grateful to Your Majesty for coming. I hear Your Majesty is very busy."

"Yes, we are. Jean-Baptiste with affairs of state and Oscar—"

She nodded. "I know. Oscar often calls on me." A pause. Somewhere a clock ticked. . . .

"Your Majesty visits many hospitals?" she asked.

"That's part of my job. Besides, I want to improve them."

The clock ticked. . . .

"I'm told you speak some Swedish, madame," she said next.

"I try, Highness."

"Our aristocrats speak excellent French."

"But commoners, too, study foreign languages. They must expect the same of us. That's why I speak Swedish when I receive deputations of citizens—as well as I can, Highness."

She seemed to have fallen asleep, and her wrinkled face was as white as her powdered hair. I began to feel terribly sorry for the dying princess. No member of her family at her side, her brother dead, her nephew declared insane and banished.

"You're a good queen," she said unexpectedly. "And you're a very clever woman." A shadow of a smile flitted over her face. "Once, when Hedwig Elisabeth reproached you for being only a silk merchant's daughter, you flounced out of the room, and shortly afterward left Sweden. People here never forgave Hedwig Elisabeth for that. A court without a young crown princess—" There was a long silence. "Oscar has brought the children to see me—little Charles, and the new baby."

"The new baby is called Oscar, too," I said proudly.

There was another silence. Then, to my great surprise, she said, "I wanted to talk to you about the crown, madame."

She's delirious, I thought. "Which crown?" I asked out of politeness.

"The crown of the Queen of Sweden." Her eyes were wide open, her voice was calm and clear. "Perhaps you don't even know that we also have a crown for our queens. I am the last Vasa in Sweden, and I ask the first Bernadotte to accept the ancient crown. Madame, promise me you will be crowned?" Her fingers reached out for my hand. "I no longer have time to plead with you. . . ."

I laid my hand in hers.

"I've had them read aloud to me the memoirs of this Napoleon Bonaparte. How strange"—she examined me critically—"the two outstanding men of our time have been in love with you."

The Royal Palace, May 1829

"Your Majesty," said Oscar, "may I ask where we go from here?" We were tramping through the narrow alleys behind the palace.

"To a silk shop. It belongs to a man named Persson. I've never been there."

At that, Oscar lost his patience. "Mama! I canceled two appointments and postponed an audience to accompany you on an errand. Are you taking me to a silk shop? Why don't you have the court purveyors come to you?"

"Persson is not a court purveyor. I want to see his shop, and I want you to meet him."

For a moment Oscar was speechless. Then he said, "A silk merchant, Mama?"

My spirits sank. Perhaps it was a bad idea to bring Oscar with me. Sometimes I forget my son is a crown prince. I was very simply dressed, and was wearing a mourning veil. But all the passersby recognized His Royal Highness and bowed and stared. And he continually smiled and saluted.

"Persson was an apprentice to your grandfather Clary in Marseilles." I swallowed desperately. "He's the one person in Stockholm who knew my papa and my home."

At that Oscar tenderly took my arm.

It was a relatively small shop, but displayed in the window I saw fine-quality silk and velvet. Oscar pushed open the door. The crowd of customers in front of the counter, mostly middle-class women in good dark street dresses, were fingering the various materials with such concentration that they didn't even notice Oscar's uniform. We were elbowed this way and that until finally our turn came and a blond horsefaced young man asked me, "May I serve you?"

"I'd like to see your silk," said I in my broken Swedish. At first he didn't understand me, and I repeated it in French.

"I'd better call my father, who speaks very good French," he said eagerly, and disappeared through a side door. I had pushed back my veil to see the material better. Suddenly, all the other customers were gaping at us.

At that moment the side door opened. Our Persson hadn't changed very much, though his blond hair had gone gray and his blue eyes weren't shy anymore. They were calm and self-sufficient. "Madame wishes to see some silk?" he asked in French.

"Your French, if possible, is worse than ever, Monsieur Persson," I declared. "And I once took so much trouble with your accent."

He opened his mouth to say something, but he couldn't get out a word. There was dead silence in the shop. I tried to help him. "Monsieur Persson, I want to see your silk," I said clearly.

Confused, he mumbled something about "Mademoiselle Clary" in his atrocious French.

That was too much for Oscar. The crowded shop, the eavesdropping ladies, and Persson stuttering in French . . . "Perhaps you'd be good enough to take Her Majesty and me to your office and show us the silk there," he said in Swedish.

I felt completely at home in the small office, with the firm's books open on the high desk and swatches of silk everywhere. Over the desk hung a framed broadside, yellowed but immediately recognizable. "Well, here I am, Persson," I murmured. "I'd like to present my son. Oscar, Monsieur Persson was apprenticed to your grandfather in Marseilles."

"Then it surprises me, Monsieur Persson, that you were not long ago appointed purveyor to the court," Oscar remarked amiably.

"I never applied for it," said Persson slowly. "Besides, I've had rather a bad name in certain circles since my return from France." He took down the framed broadside. "Because of that," he said, handing it to Oscar.

"That's the first printing of the Rights of Man," I said. "Papa—your grandfather—brought it home. And Monsieur Persson and I learned it together by heart. Before his return to Sweden, he asked me for this broadside as a remembrance."

Oscar took the broadside to the window and began to read it. Persson and I looked at each other. He'd stopped trembling, his eyes were wet. "To think you remember all that, mademoi—I mean, Your Majesty," said Persson hoarsely.

"Naturally. That's why—that's why it took me so long to come to see you. I was afraid you might take offense, that—"

"Take offense at you?" Persson asked in dismay.

"That I'm now Queen. You and I were always Republicans."

At that Persson lost his shyness completely and whispered, "That was in France, Mademoiselle Clary. But in Sweden we're both monarchists." He glanced at Oscar, still engrossed in the Rights of Man, and added, "Provided, of course—that—"

I nodded. "Yes, provided that— But you have a son yourself. It all ultimately depends on the training of the children."

"Of course. And His Royal Highness is, after all, a grandson of François Clary," he reassured me.

· We were silent for a moment. Then I said, "I need a new dress, Persson."

He was now very dignified. "An evening dress, Your Majesty?"

"An evening dress, which I must wear by day. Have you any material that's suitable for a coronation gown?"

"Of course." Persson nodded. He opened the door. "François," he called, "bring me the white brocade from Marseilles." And to me: "I've taken the liberty of calling my son François in memory of your papa."

I held the heavy roll of brocade on my knees. Oscar laid aside the framed broadside and examined the material. "Wonderful, Mama, the real thing." I stroked the stiff silk, felt the woven threads of genuine gold.

"Why have you never offered this to anyone at the court?" I asked. "The late Queen would have loved it."

"I've kept the brocade in memory of your papa and the firm of Clary, Your Majesty. Besides, I am not a court purveyor. The brocade is not for sale."

"Not even today?" Oscar asked.

"Not even today, Your Highness." And, bowing before me: "May I have the honor of presenting it to Your Majesty?"

My head dropped, I couldn't speak.

"I'll send the material to the palace immediately, Your Majesty," Persson said, and I stood up. "If Your Majesty will wait just a moment . . ." Persson was rummaging in the wastebasket. He found a discarded newspaper and wrapped it around the framed broadside. "May I ask Your Majesty to accept this, too. I've wrapped it so Your Majesty won't be embarrassed carrying it. I myself have had several unpleasant experiences because of it."

Then, arm in arm, Oscar and I were walking back to the palace. I searched for the right words. "Oscar, perhaps you feel you've wasted an afternoon." The first sentries presented arms and I felt how impatient Oscar was. But I had to stop on the bridge. The Mälaren frothed beneath us.

"Are you going to discuss this broadside Persson gave us? Mama, for me the Rights of Man are no longer a revelation. Here every educated person has heard of them."

"I still want to tell you that . . ." I stared into the shimmering water. A childhood memory cropped up—a severed head rolling in bloody sawdust. "It's true, Oscar, that the Rights of Man have long since been proclaimed. But you must only and always defend them, and teach your children to."

Oscar was silent. He was silent for a long time. Then he took the package, took off the newspaper wrappings and let them flutter into the Mälaren.

"Désirée, I implore you, don't be late for your own coronation!" Jean-Baptiste had been repeating this all morning, while pacing up and down. On my bed lay the white-gold dress made of the brocade Papa had once held in his hand. Beside it was the purple robe of the queens of Sweden, and the small ancient crown, freshly polished. I had not dared try it on.

"Mama, it's high time." Josefina had come into the dressing room from my salon, where the entire court had assembled.

"Aunt, you haven't much time," Marcelline said. My Marie— old, bent, but determined—was as busy as all the rest, trying to hurry me.

"Leave me alone," I begged. "Please, all of you, leave me alone a moment."

If a woman is vain and studies her face every day in the mirror, it's no shock to find it older. It happens so gradually. I am fortynine years old, and I've laughed so much and wept so much that I have many little wrinkles around my eyes. The two lines down to the corners of my mouth date from the time when Jean-Baptiste was fighting the battle of Leipzig. Most women don't have to look young when they are forty-nine. Their children are grown or their husbands have arrived. They belong to themselves again. Not me. I'm only beginning. I powdered my nose as thickly as possible. When the organ plays, I'll weep. And my nose will turn red. If only, once in my life—if only today—I could look like a queen. But I wasn't born to be a queen. I am so frightened. . . .

"How young you are, Désirée—not a single gray hair!" Jean-Baptiste stood behind me. He kissed my hair.

I had to laugh. "Lots of gray hairs, Jean-Baptiste, but dyed for the first time."

I looked around. Jean-Baptiste had donned the crown of the kings of Sweden. He seemed suddenly very strange and very large—no longer my Jean-Baptiste, but Karl the Fourteenth Johan, the King.

The King sat down beside my dressing table. "May I stay here?" I nodded and called Yvette, who brought the curling iron and began to roll up the little side curls.

"Don't forget Her Majesty's hair must lie flat on top or the crown won't sit right," Jean-Baptiste warned. He took out his notes for the coronation ceremony.

"Remember, Désirée, the coronation procession opens with pages and heralds. After them come members of the government, then the deputies. Finally a delegation from Norway. You will, of course, be crowned also as Queen of Norway. Perhaps you ought to have another coronation there."

"No," I said. "Not in Norway. Never forget that you forced Norway into this union. In a hundred years we'll both be sitting on a comfortable cloud in heaven looking down at an independent Norway, and we can discuss it again. . . . Call Marie, she must help me put on my coronation dress."

Marcelline and Marie rushed in at the same time. I put on the dress and took a deep breath. It was the most beautiful thing I had ever seen.

"What happens next, Jean-Baptiste? Who will march behind the Norwegian delegation?"

"Your two counts with the royal insignia that should have been carried by the highest officials of the state," Jean-Baptiste said, "but you insisted—"

"Yes, I insisted that Count Brahe and Count Rosen carry them. When other Swedes had not yet become accustomed to a silk merchant's daughter, they were her knights."

"Behind them will come the crown, carried on a red cushion by the lady you selected for this honor."

"Mademoiselle Mariana von Koskull, the former lady-in-waiting." I winked at Jean-Baptiste. "In appreciation of her services to the royal houses of Vasa and Bernadotte."

Marie was about to adjust my purple robe, but Jean-Baptiste took it from her and laid it tenderly over my shoulders. We stood side by side in front of the big mirror.

"It's like a fairy tale," I whispered. "Once upon a time there was a tall king and a tiny queen." I turned quickly. "Jean-Baptiste—the broadside!"

He understood. He took the frame from the wall. And stood before me, holding out the broadside. I bowed to kiss the glass over the faded text of the Rights of Man. When I looked up, Jean-Baptiste's face was white with emotion.

The folding doors to the salon were flung open. And what happened next was like a dream. . . . Descending the marble staircase of the palace . . . catching a glimpse of Count Brahe and Count Rosen . . . Josefina and Oscar climbing into an open carriage. And at last came the gilded coach for Their Majesties. Then cheers from all sides . . . Jean-Baptiste smiling and waving, and I wanting to smile and wave myself. But I was numb. For they were shouting to me alone, "Long live the Queen," and I was going to cry. I couldn't help myself.

At the church Jean-Baptiste himself arranged the folds of my purple robe and escorted me to the portals. . . . "Blessed be they who come in the name of the Lord," the archbishop said. Then the organ music rose triumphantly . . . the archbishop placed the crown on my head. . . .

It is late night, and everyone thinks I've gone to bed to rest up for the festivities tomorrow in honor of Queen Desideria of Sweden and Norway. But I wanted to write this last page in my diary. Once the pages were all empty and white. I was fourteen years old and asked what I should write in it. And Papa answered, "The story of Citizeness Bernardine Eugénie Désirée Clary."

Papa, I've written the whole story and have nothing more to add. For the story of this citizeness is finished, and that of the Queen begins. I'll never comprehend how this all came about. But I promise you, Papa, to do all I can so as not to disgrace you, and never to forget that, all your life long, you were a highly respected silk merchant.

ACKNOWLEDGMENTS

The condensations in this volume have been created by
The Reader's Digest Association, Inc., and are used by
permission of and special arrangement with the publishers
and the holders of the respective copyrights.

The Foxes of Harrow, copyright 1946, renewed © 1973 by
Frank Yerby, is used by permission of The Dial Press, New York,
and Laurence Pollinger Ltd., London.
The King's General, copyright 1946, renewed © 1973 by
Daphne du Maurier Browning, is used by permission of
Doubleday & Company, Inc., New York, and Victor Gollancz Ltd., London.
Désirée, by Annemarie Selinko, copyright © 1953, renewed © 1981 by
William Morrow & Co., Inc., is used by permission of
William Morrow & Co., Inc., New York, and William Heinemann Ltd., London.
The publishers wish to acknowledge the special assistance
of Joy Gary in the preparation of the final American version
of this novel. Translated from the German.